The
MX Book
of
New
Sherlock
Holmes
Stories

Part XXIII – Some More
Untold Cases
(1888-1894)

THE MX BOOK OF NEW
SHERLOCK HOLMES
STORIES

PART XXIII: SOME MORE
UNTOLD CASES
1888-1894

SOUTHAMPTON
STREET

359

EDITED
By
David
Marcum

OFFICES

TRADITIONAL HOLMES
ADVENTURES
COMPILED FOR THE
BENEFIT OF THE
RESTORATION OF
UNDERSHAW

ISBN Hardback 978-1-78705-660-2
ISBN Paperback 978-1-78705-661-9
AUK ePub ISBN 978-1-78705-662-6
AUK PDF ISBN 978-1-78705-663-3

Published in the UK by
MX Publishing
335 Princess Park Manor, Royal Drive,
London, N11 3GX
www.mxpublishing.co.uk

David Marcum can be reached at:
thepapersofsherlockholmes@gmail.com

Cover design by Brian Belanger
www.belangerbooks.com and *www.redbubble.com/people/zhahadun*

CONTENTS

Forewords

Adventures

(Continued on the next page . . . .)

(Continued on the next page . . . .)

(Continued on the next page . . . .)

(Continued on the next page . . . .)

(Continued on the next page . . . .)

PART V – Christmas Adventures

(Continued on the next page . . . .)

PART VI – 2017 Annual

(Continued on the next page . . . .)

PART VII – Eliminate the Impossible: 1880-1891

PART VIII – Eliminate the Impossible: 1892-1905

(Continued on the next page . . . .)

Part IX – 2018 Annual (1879-1895)

(Continued on the next page . . . .)

Part X – 2018 Annual (1896-1916)

Part XI: Some Untold Cases (1880-1891)

(Continued on the next page . . . .)

(Continued on the next page . . . .)

PART XIV: 2019 Annual (1891 -1897)

(Continued on the next page . . . .)

(Continued on the next page . . . .)

Part XVII – (1891-1898)

Part XVIII – (1899-1925)

(Continued on the next page . . . .)

The Tollington Ghost – Roger Silverwood
You Only Live Thrice – Robert Stapleton
The Adventure of the Fair Lad – Craig Janacek
The Adventure of the Voodoo Curse – Gareth Tilley
The Cassandra of Providence Place – Paul Hiscock
The Adventure of the House Abandoned – Arthur Hall
The Winterbourne Phantom – M.J. Elliott
The Murderous Mercedes – Harry DeMaio
The Solitary Violinist – Tom Turley
The Cunning Man – Kelvin I. Jones
The Adventure of Khamaat's Curse – Tracy J. Revels
The Adventure of the Weeping Mary – Matthew White
The Unnerved Estate Agent – David Marcum
Death in The House of the Black Madonna – Nick Cardillo
The Case of the Ivy-Covered Tomb – S.F. Bennett

Part XIX: 2020 Annual (1892-1890)

Foreword – John Lescroart
Foreword – Roger Johnson
Foreword – Lizzy Butler
Foreword – Steve Emecz
Foreword – David Marcum
Holmes's Prayer (A Poem) – Christopher James
A Case of Paternity – Matthew White
The Raspberry Tart – Roger Riccard
The Mystery of the Elusive Bard – Kevin P. Thornton
The Man in the Maroon Suit – Chris Chan
The Scholar of Silchester Court – Nick Cardillo
The Adventure of the Changed Man – MJH. Simmonds
The Adventure of the Tea-Stained Diamonds – Craig Stephen Copland
The Indigo Impossibility – Will Murray
The Case of the Emerald Knife-Throwers – Ian Ableson
A Game of Skittles – Thomas A. Turley
The Gordon Square Discovery – David Marcum
The Tattooed Rose – Dick Gillman
The Problem at Pentonville Prison – David Friend
The Nautch Night Case – Brenda Seabrooke
The Disappearing Prisoner – Arthur Hall
The Case of the Missing Pipe – James Moffett
The Whitehaven Ransom – Robert Stapleton
The Enlightenment of Newton – Dick Gillman
The Impaled Man – Andrew Bryant
The Mystery of the Elusive Li Shen – Will Murray
The Mahmudabad Result – Andrew Bryant

(Continued on the next page . . . .)

The Adventure of the Matched Set – Peter Coe Verbica
When the Prince First Dined at the Diogenes Club – Sean M. Wright
The Sweetenbury Safe Affair – Tim Gambrell

Part XX: 2020 Annual (1891-1897)
Foreword – John Lescroart
Foreword – Roger Johnson
Foreword – Lizzy Butler
Foreword – Steve Emecz
Foreword – David Marcum
The Sibling (A Poem) – Jacquelynn Morris
Blood and Gunpowder – Thomas A. Burns, Jr.
The Atelier of Death – Harry DeMaio
The Adventure of the Beauty Trap – Tracy Revels
A Case of Unfinished Business – Steven Philip Jones
The Case of the S.S. Bokhara – Mark Mower
The Adventure of the American Opera Singer – Deanna Baran
The Keadby Cross – David Marcum
The Adventure at Dead Man's Hole – Stephen Herczeg
The Elusive Mr. Chester – Arthur Hall
The Adventure of Old Black Duffel – Will Murray
The Blood-Spattered Bridge – Gayle Lange Puhl
The Tomorrow Man – S.F. Bennett
The Sweet Science of Bruising – Kevin P. Thornton
The Mystery of Sherlock Holmes – Christopher Todd
The Elusive Mr. Phillimore – Matthew J. Elliott
The Murders in the Maharajah's Railway Carriage – Charles Veley and Anna Elliott
The Ransomed Miracle – I.A. Watson
The Adventure of the Unkind Turn – Robert Perret
The Perplexing X'ing – Sonia Fetherston
The Case of the Short-Sighted Clown – Susan Knight

Part XXI: 2020 Annual (1898-1923)
Foreword – John Lescroart
Foreword – Roger Johnson
Foreword – Lizzy Butler
Foreword – Steve Emecz
Foreword – David Marcum
The Case of the Missing Rhyme (A Poem) – Joseph W. Svec III
The Problem of the St. Francis Parish Robbery – R.K. Radek
The Adventure of the Grand Vizier – Arthur Hall
The Mummy's Curse – DJ Tyrer
The Fractured Freemason of Fitzrovia – David L. Leal
The Bleeding Heart – Paula Hammond
The Secret Admirer – Jayantika Ganguly

(Continued on the next page . . . .)

The following contributions appear in the companion volumes:
The MX Book of New Sherlock Holmes Stories
Part XXII – Some More Untold Cases (1877-1887)
Part XXIV – Some More Untold Cases (1895-1903)

Editor's Note:
Duplicate Untold Cases

In some instances, there are multiple versions of certain Untold Cases contained within this volume. Each of these are very different stories and do not contradict one another, in spite of their common jumping-off place. As explained in the Editor's Foreword, no traditional and Canonical versions of the Untold Cases are the definitive versions to the exclusion of the others. They simply require a bit of additional pondering and rationalization to consider what was going on in Watson's thinking, and why he chose to present them in this way.

In this volume, the reader will encounter several versions of "The Manor House Case", "Some of the Skirmishes with John Clay", and "The Tired Captain" – *Enjoy!*

Editor's Foreword:
Watson's Obfuscations
by David Marcum

<u>Obfuscate:</u>

Merriam-Webster –

1 – a: to throw into shadow, darken;
b: to make obscure
2 – Confuse

Dictionary.com –

The act or an instance of making something obscure, dark, or difficult to understand

Watson obfuscated. Without a doubt. To pretend that he did otherwise would be rather naïve.

We have obvious evidence or this, and also that which is much more indirect and must be inferred.

That isn't to say that Watson is an actual *liar*, with the habitual and intentional regular misrepresentations that this word implies. A true liar cannot help him or herself. Such a person chooses falsehoods over truth with the same lack of thought as when taking a breath. Some liars do so occasionally, while others do it dozens of times per day in the very visible public eye, regardless of the damage that they cause.

When Watson obfuscated, it was for a reason.

Consider: Watson wanted to record his Sherlock Holmes's various investigations so that the public would be aware of his friend's abilities, and so that credit for the solution of his investigations would be properly pointed in Holmes's direction. At the end of their first shared adventure, after Holmes explains how he followed the scarlet thread of murder through the tangled skein to a correct solution, Watson cries: *"It is wonderful! Your merits should be publicly recognized. You should publish an account of the case. If you won't, I will for you."*

Holmes replies, *"You may do what you like, Doctor."* – likely little realizing just what he had let himself in for.

A moment later, Watson added, *"I have all the facts in my journal, and the public shall know them."* And so they would – but it would be nearly seven years before that occurred. Watson made that promise in

1

early March 1881, but *A Study in Scarlet* wouldn't be published until late November 1887, in *Beeton's Christmas Annual.*

In the meantime, Holmes continued to investigate, and Watson continued to assist him – more and more as his health improved following his grievous mid-1880 war injury, and also as Holmes's practice continued to grow and thrive. We view those cases now as something from a long-ago time, stirring within us longings for those mysterious gaslit streets and foggy nights. Sometimes we tend to forget that when Watson first began publishing in 1887, those stories were essentially contemporary. Adventures might occur in streets or locations that no longer exist, but they certainly existed then. Our Heroes made their way across London in hansom cabs and growlers, and while those are long gone, that was the norm then. And when Watson was writing about Holmes's cases, they weren't recountings of events that had occurred decades before – some had happened only a few months before they were published.

Consider "The Red-Headed League", which took place in October 1890. (There is a bit of confusing contradiction within the story regarding this date, but that will be addressed in a moment.) Watson, then married for a couple of years and living in nearby Paddington, relates how he'd stopped by to visit Holmes and found him in consultation with Mr. Jabez Wilson concerning the rather comical pawnbroker's recent connections to the mysterious aforementioned League, and his subsequent grievances against them – for they had been paying him steadily for months to spend his mornings copying the *Encyclopaedia Britannica*, and just that morning he'd found that this unusual post had been terminated without any previous warning.

As expected, the matter resolved satisfactorily, and Watson recognized that this was a tale that should be shared. He probably wrote up his notes to a certain degree within a matter of days, and added them to an ever growing stack of narratives. Then, just a few months later – specifically on May 4th, 1891 – Holmes was presumed to have died at the Reichenbach Falls, which gave Watson even more motivation to recall the promise that he'd made on March 6th, 1881, at the end of *A Study in Scarlet*: "*Your merits should be publicly recognized. You should publish an account of the case. If you won't, I will for you.*"

As of the spring of 1891, Watson had only published two accounts of Holmes's cases, *A Study in Scarlet* (in late 1887, in the aforementioned *Beeton's*), and *The Sign of the Four* (in February 1890, appearing first in *Lippincott's Monthly Magazine*). With the idea of paying tribute to his fallen friend, Watson, assisted by his friend and literary agent, Dr. – and later Sir – Arthur Conan Doyle, approached the publisher of the recently formed *Strand* magazine – itself only in business since January 1891 – and arranged for some short sketches of Holmes's cases to be published, beginning with "A Scandal in Bohemia" on June 25th, 1891. The world was electrified – and soon after the obfuscations began to creep in – sometimes from carelessness or accidentally, and sometimes because Watson had no choice.

For example, from the distance of so many years, it's difficult to know exactly which names within The Canon are accurate, and which have been *adjusted* due to Watson's effort to protect the players. It's entirely possible that Jabez Wilson's identity was true as presented – for there is some argument that his modest pawn shop could only have benefitted by being associated with such an interesting story – Wilson could have dined out for the rest of his life on his version of it, were he able to overcome the personal embarrassment at his own gullibility. But as those initial two-dozen stories were published in *The Strand* between June 1891 and December 1893 (when "The Final Problem" appeared to a stunned and dismayed public), it's obvious that some facts must have been changed to protect those involved.

For instance, "The Boscombe Valley Mystery", which occurred in June 1889, was published in October 1891, just a little over two years later. It ends with a dying murderer's confession that is to be kept secret – and yet, here is Watson publishing it to great interest in a widely read magazine when the events were still somewhat fresh in the public mind. But some delicate obfuscation was occurring here. Try finding Boscombe Valley on a map. And if the location was disguised, then it's likely that the names were as well. What other information was smudged and altered to hide the specifics while providing the gist of the cases, while also making sure to highlight Holmes's brilliance?

Of course, if locations and the names of involved parties could be changed, then dates could be altered as well. There are a number of chronological inconsistencies within The Canon that can be blamed on all sorts of reasons – a misreading of Watson's handwriting by a careless typesetter is always likely. Certainly similar carelessness by Watson's Literary Agent was another reason, as he failed to pay enough attention to the preparation of Watson's works for publication while he was instead distracted by his own lesser-known efforts. And of course, Watson certainly made some intentional changes for reasons of discretion.

As early as the publication of *The Sign of the Four* in 1890, there are unexplained discrepancies. We know that the case occurs in 1888, because it says that 1882 was six years earlier. But then a letter, supposedly sent that first day of the investigation, is postmarked "*July*", while just a couple of chapters later, Watson comments that it's a "*September evening*". The internal evidence seems to set this case in September 1888, and the reference to July is likely a printer's error – Watson's short-hand notes probably said *"9"* when referring to the month that the letter was postmarked, but the printer read it as a *"7"*.

Other dating errors can be found elsewhere in The Canon – simply examine "The Red-Headed League", where Watson says that he had called upon Holmes *"one day in the autumn of last year"*. Since this adventure was published in *The Strand* in August 1891, most chronologicists place it in 1890. (This year is later confirmed in the story.) But then it gets tricky. Watson said it was *"in the autumn"*. And yet, in regard to publication of the first advertisement for the League, Watson writes: *"It is* The Morning Chronicle *of April 27, 1890. Just two months ago."* April is *not* two months ago from the autumn – and in just a few lines *"autumn"* is narrowed down to *"October"*. The hapless client, Jabez Wilson, then reports that eight weeks have passed from his initial interview and hire by the curious League to that very same morning, when he decides to visit Holmes, after discovering this notice pinned at the office where he has been laboring:

The Red-Headed League
is
Dissolved
Oct. 9, 1890

For a Sherlockian chronologicist, this ought to be pure gold: An actual firm date as a jumping-off place. The day that Jabez Wilson visited Holmes was October 9th, 1890. But . . .

. . . the events of the story clearly take place on a *Saturday* – in fact, they *have* to occur on a *Saturday* to make any sense – and October 9, 1890 was a *Thursday*! So our solid date, the one fixed point we can grab when trying to date this case, is ephemeral.

And that throws the whole thing open to interpretation or adjustment. All of the major chronologicists still agree that "The Red-Headed League" occurs in October, and most – but not all – still put it in 1890. But in October 1890, some favor October 4th, or 11th, or the 18th – all Saturdays, but *not* October 9th. Gavin Brend will only say October 1890 without picking a specific day. Others choose entirely different years – Baring-Gould 1887 and Ernest Bloomfield Zeisler 1889 – and even then, they don't set it on October 9th, instead picking October 29th or October 19th respectively, because both are Saturdays.

And what to do about that pesky April reference when Jabez Wilson was initially hired, eight weeks before his visit to Holmes? It can't have been *April* as listed, but it could have been *August*. That fits, and the realization that someone – again, the typesetter at The Strand? The Literary Agent? – mis-read Watson's notes, perhaps taking the abbreviation *Au* for *Ap*, becomes the most likely explanation for this inconsistency.

So is this tempest in a chronological teapot due to careless errors, or did Watson have some reason for deliberately confusing the facts? Sidney Paget's original *Strand* illustration had the October date, which serves as a confirmation, seemingly showing *Oct. 9, 1890*:

with a little square of cardboard hammered on to the middle of the panel with a tack. Here it is, and you can read for yourself."

He held up a piece of white cardboard, about the size of a sheet of notepaper. It read in this fashion :—

"THE RED-HEADED LEAGUE IS DISSOLVED. Oct. 9, 1890."

Sherlock Holmes and I surveyed this curt announcement and the rueful face behind it, until the comical side of the affair so completely overtopped every other consideration that we both burst out into a

"Well,' said I, 'the gentleman at No. 4.'
"'What, the red-headed man?'
"'Yes.'
"'Oh,' said he, 'his name was William Morris. He was a solicitor, and was using my room as a temporary convenience until his new premises were ready. He moved out yesterday.'
"'Where could I find him?'
"Oh, at his new offices. He did tell me the address. Yes, 17, King Edward-street, near St. Paul's.'"
"I started off, Mr. Holmes, but when I got to that address it was a manufactory of artificial knee-caps, and no one in it had ever

"THE DOOR WAS SHUT AND LOCKED."

But a closer look (see next page) even brings that into question, as it isn't clear if the month is *Oct.* or something that maybe starts with an "*A*", or if the date is a *9* or a *4*. (As the image isn't reproduced brilliantly here, an independent investigation by the reader is strongly encouraged.)

And the date isn't the only possible obfuscation in this story. Jabez Wilson is initially interviewed by "the League" and subsequently employed for eight weeks at *7 Pope's Court, Fleet Street*. No such location can be found. (A much more likely candidate is Mitre Court, leading from Fleet Street to King's Bench Walk.) Strangely, while this address is changed, as is the location of Wilson's pawnshop in "Saxe-Coburg Square" (probably Charterhouse Square), another address listed in the narrative, 17 King Edward Street, is accurate and can be visited today – although the buildings look nothing like what was there in 1890.

In some cases, such as "The Second Stain", Watson avoided giving a year at all, being careful to avoid any hints as to when this sensitive matter occurred. (Sharp Sherlockian chronologicists, however, have mostly settled the question anyway.) In other cases, Watson provides specific dates that must be disregarded.

For instance, there's "Wisteria Lodge", which begins with Watson's statement that, "*I find it recorded in my notebook that it was a bleak and windy day towards the end of March in the year 1892 . . . .*" – which is clearly impossible, as at that point in 1892, Holmes had been presumed dead for ten months and was somewhere in the area of Tibet. This, too, is likely a misreading of Watson's notes, seeing the "*5*" in *1895* as a "*2*".

In *The Hound of the Baskervilles*, the inscription on Dr. Mortimer's walking stick indicates that it was presented in *1884*, and a little bit later, Holmes refers to this date as "*five years ago*". Easy enough to do a little math and come up with a time-frame for *The Hound*: Autumn *1889*. And yet . . . .

If Watson met Mary Morstan in *The Sign of the Four* in September 1888, and certainly married her not long after (as well as purchasing a medical practice which would consume some of his time – although not all of it!), then how is it that he's still living in Baker Street in Autumn 1889, eating breakfast and with plenty of time to leave both Mary and his practice to go away for weeks, journeying indefinitely to Dartmoor in Sir Henry Baskerville's company?

And then there's "A Scandal in Bohemia", in which Watson states that he hadn't seen much of Holmes since his marriage, and he says that he's stopped by to visit "*on the twentieth of March, 1888*". So if he didn't meet Mary Morstan until *September 1888*, who exactly had he recently married several months before that?

And then there's "The Noble Bachelor", in which Lord St. Simon – Was that his real name, or was it obfuscated? – is listed as having a birth-date of 1846, and Holmes says that he's forty-one years old. A little basic math then tells us that this adventure occurs in 1887 – but at the start of the narrative, Watson explains that "*It was a few weeks before my own marriage, during the days when I was still sharing rooms with Holmes in Baker Street . . . .*" So we know that Watson met Mary Morstan in September 1888, but Autumn 1887 was just a short time before his marriage (NOBL), and he was already married in March 1888 (SCAN), and he was able to go away for weeks in Autumn 1889 (HOUN). Clearly there is conflicting information.

As a Sherlockian Chronologicist, I've long been satisfied with the obvious solution that Watson had a *first* wife before Mary Morstan. This first wife's existence somewhat clears up some of these chronological problems. It was William S. Baring-Gould who initially posited this first-wife's existence in *Sherlock Holmes of Baker Street* (1962), his brilliant biography of Holmes, naming her Constance Watson *née* Adams. Baring-Gould speculated that Watson, at the time of publication, adjusted the dates of those stories that occurred while Constance was alive, or didn't mention her by name, in order to protect the feelings of his second wife, Mary. Without knowing what was in Watson's heart, this explanation is as good as any – and goes to show that the Good Doctor was willing to obfuscate when necessary.

And now, turning this lumbering ship of an essay toward the theme of this current set of books, another obfuscation was used when discussing what has come to be known as *The Untold Cases*.

In "The Problem of Thor Bridge", Watson tells us that:

7

Somewhere in the vaults of the bank of Cox and Co., at Charing Cross, there is a travel-worn and battered tin dispatch box with my name, John H. Watson, M.D., Late Indian Army, painted upon the lid. It is crammed with papers, nearly all of which are records of cases to illustrate the curious problems which Mr. Sherlock Holmes had at various times to examine. Some, and not the least interesting, were complete failures, and as such will hardly bear narrating, since no final explanation is forthcoming. A problem without a solution may interest the student, but can hardly fail to annoy the casual reader . . . Apart from these unfathomed cases, there are some which involve the secrets of private families to an extent which would mean consternation in many exalted quarters if it were thought possible that they might find their way into print. I need not say that such a breach of confidence is unthinkable, and that these records will be separated and destroyed now that my friend has time to turn his energies to the matter. There remain a considerable residue of cases of greater or less interest which I might have edited before had I not feared to give the public a surfeit which might react upon the reputation of the man whom above all others I revere. In some I was myself concerned and can speak as an eye-witness, while in others I was either not present or played so small a part that they could only be told as by a third person.

Thank heavens Watson maintained this amazing tin dispatch box, wherein can be found so many more incredible Sherlockian adventures beyond the pitifully few sixty of them that came to us by way of a detour across the First Literary Agent's desk. By some counts, there are over one-hundred-and-forty additional *Untold Cases* referenced in The Canon – the number goes up or down based on the interpretation of what was truly one of Holmes's cases, or if he was just referring to some affair in which he wasn't associated, or even if a missing comma means one case or two, (as in "*the repulsive story of the red leech and the terrible death of Crosby the banker*", which may be one case or two, and the same for "*the Addleton tragedy and the singular contents of the ancient British barrow*").

Over the decades, as lost Watsonian manuscripts have been discovered all around the world, some confusion has occurred when multiple versions of an Untold Case appear, leading some Sherlockians to wonder which is the actual *true* version, and which is a clever *fake*? As I explained in the foreword to *The MX Book of New Sherlock Holmes Stories: Some Untold Cases* (Parts XI and XII, 2018), there are over two-dozen legitimate versions of that most famous Untold Case *The Giant Rat of Sumatra* (as mentioned in "The Sussex Vampire"), and more have been added since then (listed here, in no certain order, except for the first):

- *The Giant Rat of Sumatra* – Rick Boyer (1976) *(Possibly the greatest pastiche of all time)*
- "*Matilda Briggs* and the Giant Rat of Sumatra", *The Elementary Cases of Sherlock Holmes* – Ian Charnock (1999)
- *Mrs. Hudson and the Spirit's Curse* – Martin Davies (2004)
- "The Giant Rat of Sumatra" – Leslie Charteris and Denis Green. [Originally broadcast on radio on July 31, 1944 as part of the *Sherlock Holmes* radio show, script reprinted in *The MX Book of New Sherlock Holmes Stories: XI – Some Untold Cases (1880-1891)* (2018)]
- *Sherlock Holmes' Lost Adventure: The True Story of the Giant Rats of Sumatra* – Laurel Steinhauer (2004)
- *The Giant Rat of Sumatra* – Paul D. Gilbert (2010)
- "The Giant Rat of Sumatra", *The Lost Stories of Sherlock Holmes* – Tony Reynolds (2010)
- *The Giant Rat of Sumatra* – Jake and Luke Thoene (1995)
- "The Adventure of the Giant Rat of Sumatra", *Mary Higgins Clark Mystery Magazine* – John Lescroart, (December 1988)
- "The Case of the Sumatran Rat", *The Secret Chronicles of Sherlock Holmes* – June Thomson (1992)
- "Sherlock Holmes and the Giant Rat of Sumatra", *More From the Deed Box of John H. Watson MD* – Hugh Ashton (2012)
- "The Case of the Giant Rat of Sumatra", *The Secret Notebooks of Sherlock Holmes* – Liz Hedgecock (2016)
- "The World is Now Prepared" – "slogging ruffian" (Fan Fiction) (Date unverified)
- "The Giant Rat of Sumatra", *Sherlock Holmes: The Lost Cases* – Alvin F. Rymsha (2006)
- "The Giant Rat of Sumatra" *The MX Book of New Sherlock Holmes Stories: XII – Some Untold Cases (1894-1902)* – Nick Cardillo (2018)
- "The Giant Rat of Sumatra", *The Oriental Casebook of Sherlock Holmes* – Ted Riccardi (2003)
- *Sherlock Holmes and the Limehouse Horror* – Phillip Pullman (1992, 2001)

- *Lestrade and the Giant Rat of Sumatra* – M. J. Trow (2014)
- "No Rats Need Apply", *The Unexpected Adventures of Sherlock Holmes* – Amanda Knight (2004)
- *The Shadow of the Rat* – David Stuart Davies (1999)
- *The Giant Rat of Sumatra* – Bob Bishop (2019)
- *The Giant Rat of Sumatra* – Daniel Gracely (2001)
- "The Giant Rat of Sumatra", *Resurrected Holmes* – Paula Volsky (1996)
- "The Mysterious Case of the Giant Rat of Sumatra", *The Mark of the Gunn* – Brian Gibson (2000)
- *Sherlock Holmes and the Giant Rat of Sumatra* – Alan Vanneman (2002)
- "The Giant Rat of Sumatra" – Paul Boler (2000)
- "The Giant Rat of Sumatra" [Radio Broadcast, April 20th (or June 9th), 1932, July 18th, 1936, and March 1st, 1942] – Edith Meiser (Now Sadly Lost)
- "The Case of the Missing Energy", *The Einstein Paradox* – Colin Bruce (1994)
- "All This and the Giant Rat of Sumatra", *Sherlock Holmes and The Baker Street Dozen* – Val Andrews (1997)

The list shown above is by no means a complete representation of all the Giant Rat narratives. These are simply the ones that I found when making a pass along the shelves of my own Holmes Collection. The thing to remember is that *in spite of every one of these stories being about a Giant Rat, none of them contradict one another or cancel each other out to become the only true Giant Rat adventure.*

The fact is that there are lots of different versions of the Untold Tales. Some readers, of course, don't like this and will never accept *any* of them, since the First Literary Agent didn't handle them between Watson and the light of day. Others, however, only wish to seek out the sole and single account that satisfies them the most, therefore dismissing the others as "*fiction*" – a word that I find quite distasteful when directed toward Mr. Sherlock Holmes. Quite a few are more interested in favoring one version or the other because some certain author wrote it, and they hope that naming this work as their favorite will earn them a fleeting glance for their flattery.

My approach is that if the different versions of the Untold Cases are Canonical, and don't violate any of the same rules that define what types of tales appear in these anthologies – no parodies, no anachronisms, no actual supernatural encounters, and no portrayals of Holmes as a murderous sociopathic creep with absolutely no redeeming value whatsoever – then they are legitimate.

Some people can't get their minds around the fact that there were a lot of Giant Rats (in one form or another) causing mayhem in London during Holmes's active years. In fact, each of the Giant Rat adventures listed above is very different – comedy or tragedy, police procedural or gothic horror, London-based or set in the country – and in any case – and here's the point – *Watson obfuscated!*

Not counting printer's errors or Literary Agent carelessness, Watson changed all kinds of things to make the story interesting to general readers – as compared to how Holmes wished his cases could be presented: Dry factual studies for the interested study. ("*You have attempted to tinge it with romanticism,*" he complained some months after the publication of *A Study in Scarlet,* "*which produces much the same effect as if you worked a love-story or an elopement into the fifth proposition of Euclid.*"

Watson brilliantly knew his audience, and he wrote the narratives in a way that would immediately capture the reader's attention, and yet not cloud the issue with too much of the lesser-known tedium of detective work, and also leaving out other unrelated matters which would cause confusion.

For example, when preparing a story for publication, he would often give the impression that it was the only thing currently on Holmes's plate, and possibly the only matter to occupy his attention for weeks, when in fact Our Heroes were constantly busy, and the many cases in which they were involved were truly a *tangled skein.* Watson sometimes gave the impression that Holmes went for weeks in fits of settee-bound depression between cases, when in fact he was constantly working in this or that direction upon a number of cases, each intertwined like incredibly complex threads in *The Great Holmes Tapestry*.

In spite of constructing the stories so that they were self-contained, some mentions of other cases – the Untold Cases – were unavoidable, and as students of The Master's life and methods, we can only be grateful for the small bits that we've been given and what we can glean from them. And one thing that we know by way of stories from Watson's Tin Dispatch Box is that sometimes he obfuscated by naming different cases with the same general catch-all title – an obfuscation that, for whatever reason, was important to him.

For example, there have been many different and varied stories about Holmes and Watson's 1894 encounter with Huret, the Boulevard Assassin, as mentioned in "The Golden Pince-Nez". Confusing? Contradictory? Not at all. Holmes simply rooted out an entire nest of *Al Qaeda*-like French assassins during that deadly summer. There are a lot of tales out there relating the peculiar persecution of John Vincent Harden in 1895. No problem – there were simply a lot of tobacco millionaires in London during that time, all peculiarly persecuted – but in very different ways – and Watson lumped them in his notes under the catch-all name of *John Vincent Harden.* Later Literary Agents, not quite knowing how to conquer Watson's personal codes and reverse-engineer who the real client was in these cases, simply left the name as written.

There is no need, as some do, to pick a favorite version of the Giant Rat or the Abergavenny Murder. There's no reason to think that only one of the variations is true, thus negating or neglecting the others. A previous favorite iteration doesn't have to be scrapped because some other later Literary Agent's attention and approval must be sought and curried. Watson took the time to record *all* of these versions, and all can be respected and enjoyed as part of the overall life of Sherlock Holmes. There are many already out there to read, and over sixty more of them in this collection, and still others to come in days ahead. Enjoy, and take Watson's Obfuscations as an important part of playing The Game.

* * * * *

"Of course, I could only stammer out my thanks."
– The unhappy John Hector McFarlane, "The Norwood Builder"

As always when one of these sets is finished, I want to first thank with all my heart my incredible wonderful wife of over thirty-two years, Rebecca, and our amazing son and my friend, Dan. I love you both, and you are everything to me!

Also, I can never express enough gratitude for all of the contributors who have donated their time and royalties to this ongoing project. I'm constantly amazed at the incredible stories that you send, and I'm so glad to have gotten to know all of you through this process. It's an undeniable fact that Sherlock Holmes authors are the *best* people!

The contributors of these stories have donated their royalties for this project to support the Stepping Stones School for special needs children, located at Undershaw, one of Sir Arthur Conan Doyle's former homes. As of this writing, these MX anthologies have raised nearly $70,000 for the school, with no end in sight, and of even more importance, they have helped raise awareness about the school all over the world. These books are making a real difference to the school, and the participation of both contributors and purchasers is most appreciated.

Next is that group that exchanges emails with me when we have the time – and time is a valuable commodity for all of us these days! I don't get to write as often as I'd like, but I really enjoy catching up whenever

12

we get the chance: Derrick Belanger, Brian Belanger, Mark Mower, Denis Smith, Tom Turley, Dan Victor, and Marcia Wilson.

There is a group of special people who have stepped up and supported this and a number of other projects over and over again with a lot of contributions. They are the best and I can't express how valued they are: Larry Albert, Hugh Ashton, Derrick Belanger, Deanna Baran, S.F. Bennett, Craig Stephen Copland, Matthew Elliott, Tim Gambrell, Jayantika Ganguly, Paul Gilbert, Dick Gillman, Arthur Hall, Stephen Herczeg, Craig Janacek, Mark Mower, Will Murray, Robert Perret, Tracy Revels, Roger Riccard, Geri Schear, Brenda Seabrooke, Shane Simmons, Robert Stapleton, Kevin Thornton, Charles Veley and Anna Elliott, I.A. Watson, and Marcy Wilson.

I also want to particularly thank the following:

- *Otto Penzler* – I've been aware of Otto for ages, and I owe him so much in so many ways. When I was a lad, I obtained, by way of my parents as gifts, two of his reference books, *The Private Lives of Private Eyes, Spies, Crime Fighters, and Other Good Guys* (1977) and *Detectionary* (1977). These books provided incredibly useful information to me, an urgent mystery fan living in a part of the country where such information was rare. Later, when I had my first job, I used my very first pay check to purchase *The Solar Pons Omnibus* from Otto's justly famous Mysterious Bookshop.

  In the mid-1980's while in college, my deerstalker and I were able to visit New York and the store (in its original location) for the first time, and it was something of a religious experience. At some point I was brave enough to correspond with Otto (back in the days of letters instead of emails), and later, when I wrote my own first book of Holmes pastiches, *The Papers of Sherlock Holmes* (2011), he sold copies of that mostly unseen original edition in his store.

  Over the years I've been back to New York on a few occasions, always stopping in at The Mysterious Bookshop – which, along with West 35th Street to see Nero Wolfe-related locations, and the same for Ellery Queen's house on West 87th Street, were really the only places I cared about visiting in NYC. In January 2020, I was able to visit Manhattan again, for the first time in

13

over a decade, for my first journey to the Sherlock Holmes Birthday Weekend celebration.

Each year at that time, there's an Open House at The Mysterious Bookshop for Sherlockians, and that, along with the famed BSI Dealer's Room, were the main reasons that I'd always wanted to go during the January event. The Open House was planned for Friday, but I went to the store on Thursday afternoon, so I could look around at my leisure – particularly along the entire back wall of the store, covered entirely in Sherlockian shelves – in order to accumulate a stack of Holmesian items for my collection.

When I was finished, I rather timidly asked an employee if Otto was there, and if I could say hello. In a moment the man himself came out and greeted me most wonderfully, making me feel at home and as if I'd been a weekly in-person visitor to the store for decades. Before that afternoon was over, he had me sign a massive stack of books that I'd written or edited – fulfilling a personal bucket list item of being able to autograph books at The Mysterious Bookshop – and he'd also taken me down to the incredible basement collection of still more Sherlockian items. I was also able to visit with him some the next day during the more hectic official Open House.

I'd tried for years to recruit him to write a foreword for these books, and I'm very happy that I've finally succeeded. Otto Penzler is a living legend, and has done so much for so many. It's wonderful to have him be part of these books, and a personal thrill for me. Thank you, Otto.

- *Roger Johnson* – I'm more grateful than I can say that I know Roger. His Sherlockian knowledge is exceptional, as is the work that he does to further the cause of The Master. But even more than that, both Roger and his wonderful wife, Jean Upton, are simply the finest and best kind of people, and I'm very lucky to know both of them – even though I don't get to see them nearly as often as I'd like, and especially in these crazy days! In so many ways, Roger, I can't thank you enough, and I can't imagine these books without you.

14

- *Steve Emecz* – When I first emailed Steve from out of the blue back in 2013, I was interested in MX re-publishing my previously first book. Even then, as a guy who works to accumulate *all* traditional Sherlockian pastiches, I could see that MX (under Steve's leadership) was *the* fast-rising superstar of the Sherlockian publishing world.

  The publication of that first book with MX was an amazing life-changing event for me, leading to writing and then editing more books, unexpected Holmes Pilgrimages to England, and these incredible anthologies. When I had the idea for these books in early 2015, I thought that it might, with any luck, be one small volume of perhaps a dozen stories. Since then they've grown and grown, and by way of them I've been able to make some incredible Sherlockian friends and play in the Holmesian Sandbox in ways that I'd never before dreamed possible.

  All through it, Steve has been one of the most positive and supportive people I've ever known, letting me explore various Sherlockian projects and opening up my own personal possibilities in ways that otherwise would have never been possible. Thank you Steve for every opportunity!

- *Brian Belanger* – Brian is one of the nicest and most talented of people, and I'm very glad that I was able to meet him in person during the 2020 Sherlock Holmes Birthday Celebration in New York. His gifts are amazing, and his skills improve and grow from project to project. He's amazingly great to work with, and once again I thank him for another incredible contribution.

And last but certainly *not* least, **Sir Arthur Conan Doyle**: Author, doctor, adventurer, and the Founder of the Sherlockian Feast. Present in spirit, and honored by all of us here.

It was particularly unusual editing this collection through the spring and summer of 2020, as the world faced a deadly globe-spanning pandemic. Many people ended up being stuck at home, and my first thought was that a number of them will take advantage of that newly carved-out time – although for terrible reasons – to write. However, it soon became apparent that everyone's lives were turned upside down to greater or lesser degrees, and even if they had the *time* to write something, they didn't necessarily have the *heart* to do so. I was concerned that this set of anthology volumes might not have enough stories – at least not to the level which many have come to expect and look forward to.

But as people found their footing and their spirits, the stories began to arrive, more and more of them – both for these books, and also for other Sherlockian anthologies that I'm editing at the same time. It's been amazing, and it showed that in these dark times, people have found great comfort in writing about Holmes and Watson and those bygone days, and also that they want to share those tales with others who will find comfort as well.

For everyone who dug deep and found a way forward and is a part of this collection, and for all of you who will be reading it, thank you so much.

As always, this collection has been a labor of love by both the participants and myself. As I've explained before, once again everyone did their sincerest best to produce an anthology that truly represents why Holmes and Watson have been so popular for so long. These are just more tiny threads woven into the ongoing Great Holmes Tapestry, continuing to grow and grow, for there can *never* be enough stories about the man whom Watson described as *"the best and wisest . . . whom I have ever known."*

David Marcum
September 25th, 2020
The 132nd Anniversary of Holmes
asking Watson what he makes of
Dr. Mortimer's walking stick . . . .

Questions, comments, or story submissions
may be addressed to David Marcum at

thepapersofsherlockholmes@gmail.com

Foreword
by Otto Penzler

Everyone reading this extraordinary series of books discovered Sherlock Holmes in his or her own way. No one wrote of that magic moment more compellingly than Ellery Queen (in this case, Frederic Dannay, one of the two cousins who collaborated under that memorable pseudonym) in his essay collection, *In the Queen's Parlor*.

When I was ten years old, P.S. 9, my elementary school in the Bronx, offered what I imagine was common in those long-ago days but which I fear may be less common now: A library class. Once a week, our teacher would walk us down to the school library, where Miss Gibson would talk about how to use about books. We were shown the proper way to open a book, learned the rudiments of the Dewey Decimal System, and absorbed her cheerful talks about the wonders of reading.

For the second half-hour of the class, we were allowed to take any book we wanted off the shelf and read. I pulled down an anthology (title unknown, now), scanned the table of contents, and was intrigued by the title "The Red-Headed League."

I was instantly captivated by this Sherlock Holmes fellow and by the utterly bizarre notion of someone with a particular hair color being hired to copy the *Encyclopaedia Britannica*. Totally immersed, I was crushed when the bell rang, signaling the end of the class.

No, no, no. Wait. I have to know what this all means.

Mercilessly, the class was herded back to home room. Never was a class so eagerly anticipated as the following week's library hour.

Eventually, I learned that there were more stories like this one. I bought *The Complete Sherlock Holmes*, the Doubleday edition with that magical introduction by Christopher Morley, read it more than once, and lamented that there weren't more stories about that odd but curiously likable detective.

Happily, I was wrong. There *are* more stories, and this volume – all the volumes in this worthy series – prove that life always offers hope.

Otto Penzler
New York
April 2020

"Fond of Queer Mysteries"[1]
by Roger Johnson

We're all fond of queer mysteries, of course, or we shouldn't bother with this book. And among the queerest (strangest, oddest, most curious) are those that are merely referred to by John H. Watson in the chronicles of his friend Sherlock Holmes. We're familiar with sixty of the great detective's cases – the number of which we know nothing is potentially infinite, of course, but these particular volumes are concerned with the investigations that are tantalisingly hinted at, sometimes with a little detail.

That detail can provide the spark that our imagination needs to re-create one of those unpublished stories. Who among us hasn't wondered what could possibly link a politician, a lighthouse, and a trained cormorant? Or just why Holmes claimed that world was not yet prepared for the story of the giant rat of Sumatra?

Some of the hints relate to the solving of a crime. There's the Camberwell poisoning case, "*in which, as may be remembered, Holmes was able, by winding up the dead man's watch, to prove that it had been wound up two hours before, and that therefore the deceased had gone to bed within that time – a deduction which was of the greatest importance in clearing up the case.*" That's reasonably straightforward. More problematic is the "*dreadful business of the Abernetty family, which was first brought to Holmes's attention by the depth which the parsley had sunk into the butter upon a hot day*". Naturally we wonder what was so dreadful, and what the parsley in the butter had to do with it – but more puzzling yet is how the "*dreadful business*" was *first* brought to Holmes's attention by that seemingly trivial matter. (The essential clue, I fancy, is that the parsley *did* sink into the butter. Real parsley would tend to float, even on melted butter, which suggests that there was something very wrong with one or the other on the Abernetty dining table.)

A few of the unpublished accounts fall into the category of the seemingly impossible, such as that of the cutter *Alicia*, "*which sailed one spring morning into a patch of mist from where she never again emerged, nor was anything further ever heard of herself and her crew.*" Or the enigma of Mr. James Phillimore "*who, stepping back into his own house to get his umbrella, was never more seen in this world*".

Even more nightmarish is the mental image of "*Isadora Persano, the well-known journalist and duellist who was found stark staring mad with a match box in front of him which contained a remarkable worm said to*

18

be unknown to science". (The female name *"Isadora"* has encouraged more than a few to assume that Mr. Persano was a cross-dresser, ignoring the obviously correct explanation that it's a persistent mis-spelling of the male *"Isadore"*.)

The hints that Watson offers range from the sensational to the apparently mundane. On the one hand, for instance, are the "shocking affair of the Dutch steamship, *Friesland*, which," he says, "so nearly cost us both our lives", and *"the repulsive story of the red leech"*, which may or may not be connected with *"the terrible death of Crosby the banker"*. On the other are the case of Mrs. Etherege, who recommended Holmes to Mary Sutherland because he had found her husband so easily *"when the police and everyone had given him up for dead"*, and that of Mary Morstan's employer Mrs. Cecil Forrester, whom he helped *"to unravel a little domestic complication"*. They all offer the opportunity to take up residence at 221b Baker Street, where we can let our imaginations work in tandem with the logical methods of Sherlock Holmes

Roger Johnson, BSI, ASH
Editor: *The Sherlock Holmes Journal*
July 4th, 2020

NOTES

1. "Well, Mr. Holmes, what do you make of these?" he cried. "They told me that you were fond of queer mysteries, and I don't think you can find a queerer one than that." (Hilton Cubitt, in "The Dancing Men")

Conan Doyle's Legacy in 2020
by Steve Emecz

Undershaw
Circa 1900

The MX Book of New Sherlock Holmes Stories has now raised over $65,000 for Stepping Stones School for children with learning disabilities and is by far the largest Sherlock Holmes collection in the world.

Stepping Stones is located in Undershaw, the former home of Sir Arthur Conan Doyle and the fundraising has support many projects continuing the legacy of Conan Doyle and Sherlock Holmes in the amazing building.

One of the amazing projects we have funded is to enable Stepping Stones to be a broadcast location for video using Zoom, including live events. This has proved to be incredibly timely with the global pandemic restricting movement and access. We have even broadcast a live Sherlock Holmes play *A Scandal In Nova Alba* by Orlando Pearson from Undershaw, including fans from over a dozen countries around the joining live!

The Doyle Room at Stepping Stones, Undershaw
Partially funded through royalties from
The MX Book of New Sherlock Holmes Stories

MX Publishing is a social enterprise – all the staff, including me, are volunteers with day jobs. The collection would not be possible without the creator and editor, David Marcum, who is rightly cited multiple times by *Publishers Weekly* and others as probably the most accomplished Sherlockian editor ever.

In addition to Stepping Stones School, our main program that we support is the Happy Life Children's Home in Kenya. My wife Sharon and I have spent seven Christmas's with the children in Nairobi. Due to the global pandemic we won't be visiting Africa this year.

It's a wonderful project that has saved the lives of over 600 babies. You can read all about the project in the second edition of the book *The Happy Life Story.*

There are very interesting parallels between our work in Africa and the UK – we have Zoom video enabled Happy Life, saving them tens of thousands of dollars in saved travel between their locations. In 2020 we're very proud of our *#bookstotrees* program where every book bought on our *www.mxpublishing.com* website results in a tree being funded at Happy Life. We reached our target of 1,000 trees (and still going) in August.

Our support of both of these projects is possible through the publishing of Sherlock Holmes books, which we have now been doing for twelve years.

You can find out more information
about the Stepping Stones School at:

www.steppingstones.org.uk

and Happy Life at:

21

www.happylifechildrenshomes.com

You can find out more about MX Publishing
and reach out to us through our website at:

www.mxpublishing.com

Steve Emecz
August 2020
Twitter: *@steveemecz*
LinkedIn: *https://www.linkedin.com/in/emecz/*

A Word From
Stepping Stones
by Jacqueline Silver

Undershaw
September 9, 2016
Grand Opening of the Stepping Stones School
(Photograph courtesy of Roger Johnson)

*"Life is infinitely stranger than anything which the mind of man
could invent."*

– Arthur Conan Doyle

Apt words to describe current times.

Amidst the uncertainty and ongoing challenges, I have been fortunate
enough to have recently joined the wonderful community here at Stepping
Stones School, where we spend our days in this wonderful building,
steeped in literature and history. Now that the school has re-opened after
lockdown and we are reunited at Undershaw, we appreciate our school,
our surroundings, and each other even more than ever. It is a privilege to
lead the school and its students into the future in this most treasured
setting, and we remain ever-grateful to you for your ongoing support.

Jacqueline Silver
Headteacher, *Stepping Stones,* Undershaw
September 2020

"Undershaw," Hindhead. Conan Doyle's House.

Sherlock Holmes (1854-1957) was born in Yorkshire, England, on 6 January, 1854. In the mid-1870's, he moved to 24 Montague Street, London, where he established himself as the world's first Consulting Detective. After meeting Dr. John H. Watson in early 1881, he and Watson moved to rooms at 221b Baker Street, where his reputation as the world's greatest detective grew for several decades. He was presumed to have died battling noted criminal Professor James Moriarty on 4 May, 1891, but he returned to London on 5 April, 1894, resuming his consulting practice in Baker Street. Retiring to the Sussex coast near Beachy Head in October 1903, he continued to be associated in various private and government investigations while giving the impression of being a reclusive apiarist. He was very involved in the events encompassing World War I, and to a lesser degree those of World War II. He passed away peacefully upon the cliffs above his Sussex home on his 103rd birthday, 6 January, 1957.

Dr. John Hamish Watson (1852-1929) was born in Stranraer, Scotland on 7 August, 1852. In 1878, he took his Doctor of Medicine Degree from the University of London, and later joined the army as a surgeon. Wounded at the Battle of Maiwand in Afghanistan (27 July, 1880), he returned to London late that same year. On New Year's Day, 1881, he was introduced to Sherlock Holmes in the chemical laboratory at Barts. Agreeing to share rooms with Holmes in Baker Street, Watson became invaluable to Holmes's consulting detective practice. Watson was married and widowed three times, and from the late 1880's onward, in addition to his participation in Holmes's investigations and his medical practice, he chronicled Holmes's adventures, with the assistance of his literary agent, Sir Arthur Conan Doyle, in a series of popular narratives, most of which were first published in *The Strand* magazine. Watson's later years were spent preparing a vast number of his notes of Holmes's cases for future publication. Following a final important investigation with Holmes, Watson contracted pneumonia and passed away on 24 July, 1929.

Photos of Sherlock Holmes and Dr. John H. Watson courtesy of Roger Johnson

The
MX Book
of
New
Sherlock
Holmes
Stories

Part XXIII: Some More Untold Cases (1888-1894)

The Housekeeper
by John Linwood Grant

That girl there has a ruined jaw,
Matches stolen
From the line;
Sweet phosphorus is her downfall.

The boy beyond has bloodied lips,
Nails as filthy
As these streets,
Where sovereign is always king.

That woman, now, she doubts her will,
To lift a hand,
And by so,
Knock firm upon that fateful door.
.
The man who paces is all three,
Bereft of rights,
Short of hope,
And hesitant upon the stair . . . .

But these lost souls are swept away, by
Sudden hansoms,
Noble brows,
And hurried words, affairs of State.

The moment's gone, their courage lost;
Why would he listen,
Even care,
When war and murder seek his eye?

She brings him toast and devilled eggs;
The air in there
Is fouled,
And most unjust upon her chest.

"I have no challenge!" he bursts forth,

Intemperate,
And in that,
A victim of his logic's grasp.

"Excepting Justice, sir," she says,
And opens wide
The window;
To show where clients lose their faith.

"What stimulus lies there, what clue?"
He snaps his pipe.
"What intrigue,"

The Uncanny Adventure of the Hammersmith Wonder
by Will Murray

If I hadn't called Sherlock Holmes's attention to the newspaper article, I imagine that he would have in due course discovered it for himself and the events I'm about to relate would have progressed in much the same manner in which they did. So I take no especial credit for setting the admirable sleuth-hound on the scent.

The year was 1888. April was stormy that year in London, but the most recent thunderstorm had abated overnight. A monotonous drizzle dampened the day. Before a cheery fire, Holmes and I were reading the morning newspapers. He *The London Times*, and I *The Morning Herald*.

I have no doubt that *The Times* also contained a notice about the remarkable phenomenon which Fleet Street dubbed *"The Hammersmith Wonder"*.

I spoke up sharply. "Here is a mystery for you to solve, if only you had a client to hire you to solve it."

Holmes looked up from his reading, his pipe clinched firmly between his teeth. He reached up and took it out of his mouth before speaking.

"What is it? What have you found for me?"

"According to this report, last night lightning smashed a tree in Hammersmith. An ancient wych elm tree, if I'm to believe this report."

"Why would you question such a commonplace fact?"

"I'm coming to that, my good fellow. As I was saying, the tree is ancient, and the thunderbolt shattered it most distressingly – so much so that its surviving branches burned for a time, until the rain doused the woodsy conflagration."

"Nothing remarkable thus far," sniffed Holmes.

I continued as if I weren't interrupted. "A portion of the horny bark was burnt away, revealing something remarkable. A gaping eye."

"That *is* remarkable. Kindly hand me that page."

Holmes took the newspaper and found the item. He read it carefully, his pipe back in his mouth and smoke dribbling towards the ceiling. "Hmm. Now this *is* a puzzle. Trees do not conventionally possess eyeballs."

"In my experience, my dear Holmes, trees *never* possess eyeballs."

"This orb is said to be green."

"Were a tree to grow an eyeball, green would be an appropriate hue."

35

"As would brown, I daresay."

"It is a humbug, of course."

"I fully understand your skepticism. Other than the green eye, there is nothing remarkable about the story. Yet the eye stares out from its barky orifice nonetheless, demanding our attention, if not its due."

"This presents a knotty problem."

"I congratulate you upon your sly humor on this dreary day," said Holmes. "Assuming your choice of words wasn't inadvertent. Now I wonder if you're willing to brave the elements and meet the Cyclopean gaze of this remarkable elm."

"Do you think it will profit us to do so?"

"I don't think there is a shilling in it for us. But as a mystery, it surpasses anything in recent memory. I would greatly enjoy plumbing its depths."

"In that case, let us be off."

We donned our waterproofs and were soon rattling across Hammersmith Bridge in a rain-punished hansom cab.

I attempted to pry from my good friend some of his preliminary thoughts on the bizarre matter, but he remained tight-lipped while smoking furiously. Well did I understand his past admonitions against spinning theories out of half-baked newspaper reports in advance of substantial facts. Therefore, he didn't see fit to remind me of his unwavering ways.

Holmes's deep silence made it obvious that his brain was already fastened upon the mystery and was attempting to examine it from every conceivable angle. Given its confounding nature, I privately doubted he was getting very far. A close examination of the unearthly tree itself would be necessary.

Presently, we pulled up to the courtyard where the stupendous tree stood starkly blackened and moistened by the elements, several of his age-gnarled limbs strewn broken upon the ground. A few desiccated leaves clung to the outspread boughs, stubborn remnants of the previous year's growth.

There was a crowd, as I imagined there would be. A solitary police officer was holding them at bay, and a wide-eyed knot of them clustered to the northern side of the blackened bole.

This, I took it, was the side from which the impossible orb glared forth.

Holmes at once made himself known to the police officer. The latter displayed the customary and expected diffidence that London's constabulary show to the city's most celebrated consulting detective.

"I should like to examine the miraculous tree without interference," Holmes told the man.

36

"I would be pleased if you would, sir. Perhaps you could make something of the abomination. This tree has stood in the spot for many generations, providing shade and disturbing no one. Now look at it. It's a disgrace to its genus."

"Thank you," said Holmes. Moving towards the north side of the tree, he rounded the blackened trunk, coming to a halt before that side.

I followed him gingerly. I couldn't see why my attitude was so timid, but I imagine the uneasy mood of the crowd had crept into my consciousness. Huddled and gawky, they nonetheless kept a superstitious distance.

When I drew alongside Holmes, I beheld the uncanny eye.

"My word!" I exclaimed.

For the orb was shockingly human in its configuration. The pupil was as black as my own, but the iris gleamed with an emerald light that was quite striking in its coloration. Despite its human appearance, there was something unreal about it.

The orb was fixed at a point perhaps one-quarter of the way above the tree's many exposed feeder roots. Bark had fallen away, as if to reveal it to human inspection. The surrounding corkwood was charred black. But the eye was as clear and unblemished as if newborn.

As we observed it, rainwater that had gathered around its blackened rim came together at the base and dripped down, as if the eye was shedding a tear.

Taken altogether, the sight made one imagine that the thunderbolt that had all but shattered the upper boughs of the hoary elm had shocked it out of some primeval hibernation.

"The orb doesn't appear to be organically integral with the tree," mused Holmes. "I see no sign of an eyelid or natural socket."

"Rather a precipitous observation," I remarked.

"Perhaps. Let us see what a closer look reveals."

Removing a clasp knife from his pocket, Holmes exposed the blade while stepping forward. With its tip, he dug around the staring eye and showed clearly that the surrounding sapwood held the orb fixed in place.

I noticed that the eye didn't react to his digging. Then Holmes touched the unresponsive pupil with the blade's tip, producing nothing more than a clinking noise, suggestive of something hideously familiar.

"Holmes! The orb appears to be made of – "

"Yes. Glass. It is a common glass eye."

"But who could have inserted it so deeply into the trunk that the wood appears to have enveloped eye?"

"Not appears. There is no question that the sapwood has grown around the eye. I should judge that it has nestled in that spot for easily a century or more."

"Then this may be nothing more remarkable than some prankish person inserting a glass eye into a knothole long ago, permitting the tree to close around it until this calamitous event."

As he spoke, Holmes inserted the blade and excavated the unnatural eye. The effort expended in prying the thing out of its woody socket demonstrated the accuracy of his assessment. For it wasn't a fully-formed orb, but a convex shell, further attesting to its artificiality.

"I don't think that is the correct explanation," said Holmes, pocketing his blade and scrutinizing the glassy object in his palm. "No. In fact, certain of it. This isn't the work of a prankster of yore. There is more to this story. And I mean to get to the bottom of it."

Holmes commenced stamping around the tree, inspecting the broken and charred bark, stepping over the fallen branches when he came upon them.

At length, he halted at a spot where the fire hadn't scorched the elm's outer bark. There were discernible two old hash marks that might have been made by an axe, although a small one. They stood at oblique angles to one another, barely touching at the lower limbs.

"What do you make of that?" Holmes asked me.

"Not very much at all. Someone carved or cut two intersecting lines. I daresay this was a very long ago, for the lines show indications of distortion consistent with the natural growth of the tree."

"If I were to make something of these marks," mused Holmes, "I would conjure them to form the letter *V*."

"If so," I stated, "it is a rather rude *V*."

"Made with a hand axe, if I'm not mistaken," decided Holmes. Under the watchful eyes of the nervous crowd, he continued his promenade around the tree. Here and there his name was whispered. The tones are respectful. It is a tribute to my friend's renown that a great deal of nervousness had departed from the crowd. They were very interested in his every movement and watched him closely.

After Holmes had examined the tree from every angle, his discerning gaze fell upon the visible roots. They were many and multiform, like questing tentacles of gnarled wood radiating out from the central trunk. A great many bulged above the topsoil, a certain indication of great age and weakness in a tree.

Once Holmes completed his circuit, he stood upon one bloated root that had bulged up through the soil. It lay more or less beneath the former location of the gaping green eyeball.

"This tree will have to be pulled down, I should judge," he murmured. "It is too far gone to long survive."

"It will take a team of strong draft horses to do so," I remarked, "for I doubt that a group of men welding axes could accomplish very much towards finalizing its destruction."

"I concur. But the poor condition of the surface roots will permit this to be accomplished where otherwise it might be impossible."

Abruptly, Holmes rejoined the police officer, saying, "I've seen that all that there is to be seen. Do you know when the tree is scheduled to be pulled down?"

"This hasn't yet been decided. But I don't imagine it will be very long."

"I would like to be present to witness the operation."

"I'm sure that you can be accommodated, Mr. Holmes. Now, if I may ask, what did you make of the horrid gaping eyeball?"

"Mere glass. But well-made. The owner, whoever he was, selected a costly specimen."

"Glass, you say? Well, now, that *is* a relief to hear. The rumors that have begun swirling – well, they would keep one up at night."

"Kindly inform the locals that a glass eye caught in the matrix of the tree is the explanation for the wonder."

"But how did it get into the tree in the first place? And why was it exposed in such an startling way?"

"These are excellent questions," said Holmes. "I should very much like to know the answer to the former question. As for the latter, this may be one of the mysteries that don't have a ready explanation, but I intend to pursue both lines of inquiry, for I'm not satisfied that I fully understand the Hammersmith Wonder, as it has been revealed to us. Good day, Officer."

"Good day to you, Mr. Holmes."

Holmes stalked off. His stride was purposeful and he seemed to have a definite destination in mind.

"May I inquire where we are bound?"

"To the local parish. I would like to delve into its records. I won't require your company for this endeavor. Let me suggest that you return to Baker Street and await my own return."

"I see no reason why I shouldn't," I remarked. "Shall I see that a cold supper is prepared for you?"

"It will do no harm to have Mrs. Hudson set something out. But I may be very late. Don't wait up for me."

With that, we parted.

After I had walked away, I chanced to turn around and saw that an individual I recognized from the crowd was following Holmes. The fellow soon caught up with him, bracing Holmes rather forwardly.

Holmes stopped, and the two engaged in a short conversation. As I watched, Holmes broke away from the man and continued along.

The other stood on the pavement where the conversation had taken place. He had an air about him that was at once bewildered, but also wracked with concern.

I had traveled too far along to have made out any parts of the conversation, but I noted the man's appearance and continued along my way.

Evidently Holmes had satisfied the fellow on whatever point he had brought up. He didn't return home that evening. Nor did I see him at breakfast. Knowing his capacity for keeping late hours, as well as his stubbornness when on a trail of inquiry, I wasn't entirely surprised.

Whatever records into which he was delving, no doubt they held his attention all through the evening. And into the morning hours.

After breakfast, I received a caller.

This was a street urchin of my acquaintance, rowdy and unkempt of appearance. He was nothing less than one of Holmes's Irregulars, young boys who acted as spies for his endeavors.

"Dr. Watson," said this one rather breathlessly. "Mr. Holmes has asked that you come to St. Thomas's Hospital right quick."

"What is the matter, young fellow?"

"Poor Mr. Holmes has been laid low, for he was struck down in the night. He has come to consciousness and is asking for you."

"Thank you," I said, handing the fellow a shilling.

Due to the urgency of the matter, I took a hansom cab without delay, directing the driver to proceed at his best clip to Lambeth.

It wasn't long before I presented myself to the staff of St. Thomas's Hospital. A Dr. Colvin greeted me, saying, "Mr. Holmes has a sturdy skull. The blackguard who attempted to dash out his brains should have put more English into his swing."

"Has he suffered a concussion?"

"Unarguably. He appears to be a trifle foggy. But the stout fellow is recovering. He has been asking for you, Dr. Watson."

"Direct me to him, then."

Colvin escorted me to a private room where Holmes sat up, his head swathed in bandages.

"My good fellow!" I cried upon seeing him. "What has happened to you?"

"A footpad cast me down as I was leaving St. Paul's Church."

"Did you see him?"

"I didn't, for he stole up behind me. I felt only the blow, then my face encountered the cobbles without me being cognizant of the impending ignominy."

"Were you robbed?"

"Significantly, I wasn't."

"That is most peculiar," I remarked. "What do you make of it?"

"I hurl that question back in your face, for my wits aren't quite what they should be. What do *you* make of it?"

Without hesitation, I said, "I make no sense of it. But if your pocket wasn't picked, the devil must have harbored of other reasons for striking you low."

"That was my thought. I only wished to hear your good opinion."

"Did you encounter any difficulty in your inquiry?" I asked.

"Other than the tediousness of sifting through musty old church records, no. I was fortunate in that I made the acquaintance of the Vicar, a grand old man named Belsham, who knows a great deal about Hammersmith of old. He regaled me with many stories which I was very glad to hear, but one in particular struck me as significant."

"Do you have any inkling as to origins of the glass eye in the elm tree?"

"More than an inkling. A certain path that only needs to be traversed to its natural terminus. But at the moment I'm more interested in my assailant."

"Of course."

"Although I have no idea as to the nature of the cowardly attack, I cannot help but feel that it relates to the Hammersmith Wonder in some way yet to be unearthed."

"It's unfortunate that you caught no glimpse of the blackguard."

"No glimpse, but I recall the mingled odors of horseflesh and saddle soap just before I lost my wits."

"That impression could point in a great many directions," I ventured. "From a cab driver to a stable boy."

"A cab driver doesn't ride his horse and therefore wouldn't be redolent of the saddle. I think we can omit that possibility."

"Undoubtedly. I say, do you recall the man who accosted you after we had parted?"

Holmes's face looked momentarily perplexed.

"I seem to, after a fashion."

"After a fashion! You spoke to him for easily five minutes. Perhaps longer."

41

"Did I?" Holmes muttered. "Do you recall the conversation?"

"It transpired out of my hearing. I heard none of it. But the fellow had an urgency about him. He appeared to be pressing you rather closely."

A fresh alertness came into Holmes's keen eyes. "Tell me more of him."

"He was uncommonly barrel-chested, yet on the wiry side withal."

"What would you reckon his weight to be?"

"Twelve stone, but no more. He was the rangy type. A common workman, I would venture to say."

"A blacksmith, perhaps?"

"Not that sort at all, for he lacked the broad shoulders of a smithy. Why would you think that?"

"I'm deleting possibilities. Tell me – was he bowlegged?"

"Now that you mention it, he was indeed. Well done!"

"You thought him rangy. Would you suppose the fellow to be horsey?"

"I might. Yes, he had rather a horsey air about him."

"Then that's the man who struck me down. I would wager my modest fortune upon it. I only wish that I could better recall our conversation."

"No doubt that is the concussion," spoke up Dr. Colvin. "In cases of this sort, the memory often returns belatedly. No doubt you will recall all of it in another day or so."

"Watson, if we locate that man, I'm certain that the mystery of the uncanny glass eye in the elm will be settled for all time."

"How do you connect the two?"

"I have an impression that the fellow followed me from the crowd thronging the lightning-blasted elm. No doubt there was something about my presence that excited him."

"According to my recall," said I, "virtually all of the crowd was excited by your presence, for they recognized you and expected you to perform some miracle of deduction before their very eyes."

"I did deduct certain things from an inspection of the unfortunate tree. But a great deal more was gleaned from speaking with the vicar. I have an excellent theory as to how the glass eye came to be embedded in the elm, and whence it came. All that remains in that wise is to identify the scoundrel who placed it there."

I looked at Holmes, somewhat aghast. "I was under the impression the glass eye came to enter the tree when it was much younger."

"I'm convinced that that is a fact."

"Therefore that individual must be long deceased."

"Long deceased, and as yet unidentified. But the man who struck me down did so for reasons that to him were sound, even if to us they might seem mad. Once we locate him, we may have the final strand in a very, very old cobweb."

Holmes's features grew firm with resolve. For a moment, I thought he was about to leap from his bed and resume the hunt. Instead, his head fell back upon the pillow and he closed his eyes. A weary look crossed his sharp features, seeming to soften them.

His voice was very low when he spoke. "Watson, I fear that I'm not ready to leave my bed. I beg of you a favor."

"Name it."

"Find out when the elm tree is to be pulled down. Bring this information to me. I must rest now, so that I'm strong enough to attend the ceremony. I have no doubt it will be very revealing."

"As you wish."

"That will be all. Good of you to come."

I left Holmes's room accompanied by Dr. Colvin. We spoke for several minutes in the corridor.

"How long must you keep him?"

"A day, perhaps two. He has an excellent constitution and the crack on his skull did no permanent damage. Close observation over the next few hours will tell the tale, of course. But I hope to send him home by the weekend."

"Thank you, Dr. Colvin."

Leaving the hospital, I went to Hammersmith Hall and made inquiries on Holmes's behalf. I had only to speak his name and shut-tight doors opened and all municipal reluctance evaporated.

The fantastic elm tree was to be torn down two days hence. The time was ten o'clock in the morning. The only delay had to do with mustering a team of draft horses sufficiently strong and powerful to do the job of work.

I returned to Baker Street with that information. Penning a brief note, I handed it to the postman when he came round at five o'clock. I knew that it would reach Holmes before nightfall. I thought it unnecessary to visit him again. Rest is what he most required, and rest he would have for me.

The next morning I received a letter in return:

My dear Watson, (it began)

I beg of you to meet me at the fire-blighted elm tree at the hour appointed for its final destruction. Be punctual. Until then, Baker Street and my ordinary affairs remain in your capable hands.

Yours,
Holmes

A dreary rain drummed the canopy of the hansom cab that was conveying me to the courtyard in Hammersmith on the morning selected for the removing of the ruined wych elm.

True to Holmes's admonition, I arrived ten minutes before the operation was to commence.

A crowd was already gathering. I stepped out, paid my driver, and sought Holmes in vain. I fully expected him to have arrived before me, but there was no sign of him.

A team of draft horses had been brought up. A great chain was wrapped around the middle part of the stricken elm, which dripped moisture from every surviving branch, for the rain had slacked to a drizzle. The chain was affixed to a stout pole and tackle lying on the sod, which was in turn tethered to the team.

I saw that the side of the trunk facing the horse team had been attacked by axes by way of preparing for the tree's removal. They had bitten quite deep and exposed the inner heartwood.

Fretfully, I moved among the bustle, but of Holmes, I saw nothing.

A drayman was setting the team into place, and the pulling down of the Hammersmith Wonder was soon to start.

As I watched the man prepare, he struck me as familiar.

It quickly dawned on me that this was the barrel-chested, bow-legged individual who accosted Holmes before his unfortunate downfall.

I watched him. He was a rough-hewn sort, as befitted his trade. I didn't care for the glowering expression on his square-cut face, nor the way he spoke to his young assistant as the horses were set in place.

There was nothing I could do about him, so I simply stood among the close-pressing crowd as the snorting horses were steadied.

From behind me, I heard a thin voice. It was cracked as if with age.

"Hullo, Watson. Don't turn around. I'm here."

Although I failed to recognize the voice, I had once realized that it was Holmes. He was here! No doubt he was in disguise. As genuine a fellow as one could ever meet, he was a clever master of artificiality when it suited him.

I nodded my head ever so slightly to show that I had heard every word.

"The blackguard. Do you see him about?"

Again, I nodded.

"Excellent. Don't give yourself away. But kindly indicate the man with a finger if you would."

Lifting one hand casually, I pointed in the direction of the burly drayman.

"Ha-ha," said Holmes. "I don't recognize him, for I fear that my brain is still in an addled state. But I see that he is on familiar terms with horses. Queer that he should be the one in charge of pulling down the stricken tree. But let us stand easy. We shall soon see what comes of this."

A police officer seemed to have charge of the operation. He signaled that the horses should commence pulling. And this they did, bringing the pole and tackle off the ground.

They struggled and strained, for they stood upon muddy ground. But their combined horseflesh was a formidable thing. The lofty tree began groaning, its few shriveled leaves quivering, surviving upper branches quaking as it in fear of what it all portended.

The awful eye had been dug out, of course. There was only a charcoal-rimmed cavity. Otherwise, the scene would have been one of anthropomorphic horror.

The horses' hooves dug in as they leaned into their collars, while the drayman cracked his whip. He didn't spare the team.

A crackling of wood came. The crowd murmured in expectation.

But strain as they might, the broken elm held in part.

The horses were scourged again, and they dug in harder. Neighing and whinnying, they pulled mightily and so began to win the day. With a tremendous sound, the elm abruptly began keeling over. Yet in the act of falling, it frozen place. Something had arrested its toppling.

Behind me, a voice whispered, "What ho!"

This was Holmes.

I didn't see what impressed him so, only that a great gnarled root stood exposed and suspended, stretched up at an angle and shedding clods of dirt. This alone refused to release the soil.

It was a bloated, noisome thing, thick with root-hairs. I recalled that this was the root that had bulged directly beneath the glassy emerald eye that had no business reposing in the bark of an elm tree. I had thought then that the growth comprised two adjacent roots, but now I could see the truth of the matter.

Partly excavated, it showed nearly its full length, which forked dramatically mid-way along, forming two parallel root branches. The terminus of this fork appeared to be clinging to the earth, as if reluctant to surrender its remaining life.

The horses struggled and strained noisily, but could gain no further traction.

45

Reluctantly, the drayman let them rest while he walked around the ancient elm and inspected the problem at hand.

While he was doing so, an elderly man whose thin features were dominated by a generous mustache which closely matched the unruly shocks sitting atop his head slipped up beside me and pushed out of the gathering. I didn't immediately recognize him as Holmes. That realization came later.

The oldster walked up to the drayman and engaged him in conversation.

"Stubborn root, I would say."

"Kindly step away, sir!" the man growled.

"Hmm. The soil is rather greasy at this spot. Whatever could that mean?"

"It means nothing." Lifting his voice, the drayman called for an axe, saying, "We will chop it loose. Then it will be properly done."

A stout axe was fetched. The oldster continued studying the suspended root as if it was a fascinating thing. Addressing the drayman as he took possession of the axe, he remarked, "Note how the root swells into a ball and then takes on a shape almost akin to that of a man – short neck, wide trunk, and long legs all in their proper order."

The drayman turned abruptly and blurted, "What now? What is that you said?"

"This root reminds me of a giant man. A mouldering corpse, to be precise."

Hotly, the other spat, "I see no such thing! Now be off with you!"

The axe was lifted as if to strike a blow, not at the root but at the curious old man.

What transpired next was remarkable.

The old man seized the axe by its handle, took it from the drayman, and brought it down on the two tendrils where the forked root refused to let go of the soil. His aim was true and his blows precise.

"Here now!"

"It is done," proclaimed the oldster. "Vigor is free."

"What did you say?" The drayman was as white as a sheet. All the blood had drained from his features. "What name did you just give?"

"Vigor. Do you know it?"

For no reason that I could imagine, the glowering drayman reached out with both strong hands and attempted to throttled the oldster. Whereupon the latter defended himself rather adroitly.

With the flat of the axe, he struck the aggressor at the side of his head, felling him instantly.

A commotion immediately resulted. The police officer barged in. But before he could intervene, a familiar voice rang out resoundingly.

"Officer, I wish you to take this man into custody. This is the second time he has attempted to do me harm. In case you don't recognize my voice, I am Sherlock Holmes!"

A public uproar resulted. But the officer did his duty. The insensate drayman was dragged away from the partly-toppled elm tree and his bewildered confederate proceeded to finish the job he started.

The team of horses were encouraged to make one final pull. This they did with little effort.

With a crackling commotion, the old tree came crashing down and the job was satisfactorily done. A tangle of anchor roots lay exposed, from which dribbled ancient soil.

I was soon at Holmes's side, saying, "Upon my word! I don't understand what has just transpired, but I'm certain you will have explanations sufficient to quench the thirst of my curiosity."

Holmes peeled a drooping white mustache from his upper lip. "More than quench, Watson. Extinguish for all time. Now that this tree has fallen, let us get out of this damnable drizzle and I will make explanations."

That evening, Holmes and I sat before a cheery fire at 221b Baker Street. The odd green eyeball rested upon the ticking clock on the mantelpiece, staring out rather forlornly, I thought. The events of the day were largely behind us. I needn't relive them in detail. The drayman who had attempted to brain the disguised Holmes was arrested and duly charged. He presently languished in jail, where he was likely to stay for quite some time.

Holmes were speaking in between fragrant puffs of his favorite pipe. "I imagine, my dear Watson, you would like to hear the story in detail."

"I can make neither head nor tail of the whole of it," I admitted.

"Much of my knowledge I credit to the vicar of St Paul's Church, for he gave me the entire story, although he himself admitted that certain facts remain in question to this day. Let me begin with the arrival in London of a veritable Viking of a man named Vigor over a century ago. His last name hasn't come down to us, nor his origins. It is thought that he hailed from somewhere in the Carpathian Mountains, but that hasn't been established to anyone's satisfaction, then or now.

"This fellow set up shop as a blacksmith in Hammersmith. According to the vicar's account, he was a formidable fellow, towering over every man who encountered him. Seven feet tall, if I can believe the legend, which I am disinclined to do. He was likable in his way, although his

English was rather poor. Vigor, however, proved to be an excellent blacksmith and soon attracted a great deal of steady business.

"Regrettably, Vigor also attracted the resentment of an established smithy by the name of William Bamber. This Bamber resented the loss of business to his new rival, and the two felt to quarreling. Blows were struck, with the result that poor Vigor lost his right eye. He replaced it eventually with one fashioned of glass – made either in Venice or Paris, according to different recollections. From a study of its workmanship, I would say Paris, which squares with the dates of vicar provided, Paris taking up the trade of glass-eye making years after the Ventians established it.

"Now here the story becomes *outrè*. Vigor's eyes were naturally brown in color, but he chose a green replacement for the lost orb. According to the vicar, this was either calculated to annoy Bamber, or it was a result of a miscommunication between the poorly-spoken blacksmith and the maker of the glass eye. In any event, Bamber became incensed, for every time he laid eyes on his rival, the man stared back at him with one brown eye and one green eye. No doubt this was a reminder of his crime.

"No charges were brought against Bamber, and the two blacksmiths continued to ply their trade over the years, with Vigor steadily gaining trade even as Bamber lost ground. It wasn't definitely known that Bamber had been the cause of Vigor's affliction, for the victim made no declaration. But sympathy as well as skill seems to have worked in Vigor's favor.

"A time arrived where Bamber was verging on destitution. One day, he simply packed up and moved away, never to be seen again. That would appear to have been the end of the rivalry, except that Vigor disappeared mysteriously sometime later. Nothing could be found with him. Since he was unmarried and without children, eventually his disappearance ceased to be of concern to Hammersmith parish.

"A considerable period passed in which Bamber returned to Hammersmith and set up shop once again. While suspicions were naturally cast his direction, absent a body and official charges, nothing could be done. The matter has remained a mystery all these long years, although a largely forgotten one in our present age.

I spoke up. "It would seem obvious to me in retrospect that Bamber did away with Vigor and, after a suitable interval, returned to reclaim his due."

"Of that, Watson, I have no doubt," remarked Holmes. "For his body has been disinterred in the most remarkable manner."

"I fail to follow."

"You heard my exchange with the drayman."

"I did. Something about one root of the tree resembling that of a corpse."

"I'm sure the drayman will confess to his own knowledge of the past. But allow me to present my theory: Bamber returned to Hammersmith and struck Vigor down. I imagine an axe might have been the murder weapon, but that is only supposition. No doubt this took place in the dead of night. Having created an inconvenient corpse, Bamber planted it under a young wych elm. Over time, the roots of this tree, in reaching out for nutrients held in the soil, encountered the interred body of Vigor and began to feed."

"Good heavens!" I exclaimed. "Are you saying that the root consumed the body?"

"Consumed, and took on something of the semblance of its shape in doing so. You recall that stubborn root, which refused to surrender to the team of horses. It began close to the trunk as a bulge suggestive of a cranium and then spread out, rather like a human trunk, and then formed two branches mimicking human legs."

"A ghastly thought."

"Ghastly, yes, but more gruesome still was the fate of Vigor's glass eye. As all botanists know, the roots of a tree leach water and nutrients from the soil, which are then transported up into the trunk itself by natural conduits known to science. Somehow – and this is a remarkable but also undeniable fact – Vigor's glass eye, not being subject to decay or dissolution, somehow worked its way up into the sapwood and lay concealed for decades unsuspected behind the corkwood of elm tree's bark."

"Extraordinary! I know of no such oddity like it."

"Nor do I. Nor can I account for the mechanics of the progress of the artificial eye so high into the trunk. The matter of the orb's outward orientation we shall have to put down to one of those infrequent freaks of nature."

"But Holmes," I implored, "how can you be certain that the tree root wasn't coincidently formed in the shape of a dead man?"

"Two sound reasons, both incontrovertible. The first is that uprooted ground around the root was greasy in texture, which is a certain sign that a human body had laid there for many years. The second was the position of the eye in the trunk. It stood directly above the unusually elongated and bloated root, a sentinel cyclops with perpetually closed eye. Until the decisive lightning strike, of course."

"And the hash marks cut into the tree – what did they signify?"

"They formed the letter *V*, as I surmised. The vicar informed me that the tree stood decide Vigor's blacksmith shop and that he often toiled beneath its shade. *Ulmus glabra* is a montane species, as you know.

Possibly the elm reminded Vigor of the Carpathians. I cannot state with certainty who inscribed the marks, but either Vigor did so out of a sense of possession, or Bamber cut the *V* in a macabre gesture to mark the spot under which his defeated Nemesis lay interred in an otherwise unmarked grave. It doesn't matter."

"All of this forms a satisfactory explanation," I allowed. "Except for the strange actions of the drayman."

"Not so strange when you consider that his name was Wallace Bamber. You see, he was a great-great grandson of the murderer and knew the secret, down to the very spot at the victim rested unsuspected. His motives are clear to me. Discovering that I was investigating the uncanny eye in the tree, and knowing that the elm must be pulled down, he feared the discovery of the long-missing Vigor's body. He couldn't know with certainty that the body had already been consumed, but he knew that if it wasn't, the surviving skull or skeleton would show signs of the death blow. And there was the unique glass eye. Some spare details of my conversation with Bamber, which you observed, but didn't hear, come back to me now. Bamber the drayman was keen to hear if I had arrived at any ideas as to the origins of the artificial eye. I told him that I'd formed a theory, but had no conclusions, but I was confident that I could determine the origins the green eye of glass. I seem also to recall remarking that the embroidery of the extraordinary often concealed the commonplace."

"Hence his attack upon you later. But what was the motive?"

"A personal one. He didn't wish the shame of murder to become attached to his great-great grandfather and blacken the family's good name – for the Bambers have been upstanding citizens in Hammersmith since the day blacksmith William Bamber returned to the parish from his brief exile."

"How very ironic," I said. "In seeking to avoid shame sticking to his family name, he has by his own actions brought an equivalent shame to the modern Bambers."

"Had he left well-enough alone, he would today be a free man, for he imagined that evidence of murder lingered under the blasted elm. In truth, it had migrated into the tree trunk, only to be exposed to plain sight by a violent miracle of nature."

"So the matter is at last ended," I remarked.

"Not quite, Watson. I've arranged with the vicar to see that the root that consumed poor Vigor be interred in the church graveyard with his name carved into a proper headstone. It isn't much after all these years, but I feel it is appropriate to give the fellow a proper burial."

I peculiar thought struck me. "Wherever are you going to obtain a coffin sufficiently long enough to encompass such a prodigious root?"

"Nowhere. The remarkable root will be buried as it is, to disintegrate in time, as would the human corpse in the natural order of things."

"Will you attend the services?"

"Normally, I wouldn't care to, but this is such a remarkable burial that I wouldn't miss it for the world. A man is born only once and buried but once. Vigo will have been buried twice, but in two entirely different states of matter. I daresay such a thing will never happen again for as long as this strange old world spins on."

I glanced up at the emerald eye whose awakening had started the affair.

"Will you hold onto it as a keepsake?" I inquired.

"I think not. Such a loyal and watchful possession deserves a proper disposition, along with its master."

To this very day, one may visit the parish graveyard and pay one's respects at a certain headstone. Having no last name to carve into the granite, nor dates of birth and death, the inscription reads simply:

Here Lies Vigor
The Hammersmith Wonder

At the crown of the slab, set perfectly in its center, gapes the lidless green glass orb, watching over its owner for what I imagine will be all eternity.

> *I leaned back and took down the great index volume to which he referred. Holmes balanced it on his knee, and his eyes moved slowly and lovingly over the record of old cases, mixed with the accumulated information of a lifetime.*
>
> *"Voyage of the* Gloria Scott," *he read. "That was a bad business. I have some recollection that you made a record of it, Watson, though I was unable to congratulate you upon the result. Victor Lynch, the forger. Venomous lizard or gila. Remarkable case, that! Vittoria, the circus belle. Vanderbilt and the Yeggman. Vipers. Vigor, the Hammersmith wonder. Hullo! Hullo! Good old index. You can't beat it*

> – Dr. John H. Watson and Sherlock Holmes
> "The Adventure of the Sussex Vampire"

Mrs. Forrester's
Domestic Complication
by Tim Gambrell

The account of how I met and fell in love with Mary Morstan is widely known to the world. By now, the time between us meeting and marrying seemed but the blink of an eye. Yet several weeks had to pass to avoid any thoughts of impropriety by others. Plus, I needed time to set myself up for a life with Mary as a practising doctor.

I recall that one October afternoon, I was walking out with Mary in Kennington Park, which still held some late Autumnal charm. It would have been a Sunday, most probably after Church, when the Forresters released her from her services as governess for the remainder of the day. It suddenly came upon me to enquire about the affair, which Mary had mentioned upon first arriving at our abode in Baker Street the previous month. She'd told us that Mrs. Forrester had recommended Sherlock Holmes to her, as he'd previously assisted the lady with a domestic complication, and she'd been impressed with his services.

It had, at times, troubled me since that this was a case about which I was unaware. I had mused over whether Mary and I would still have fallen immediately in love if we had met at that earlier time, under different circumstances. Alas, we are wont to afflict ourselves unduly at times in matters of the heart. It was probably nonsense, but I couldn't shake my curiosity over the matter.

Mary could see that something was troubling me, and I was prompted to lay bare my soul. She laughed, of course, in that sweet, melodic way of hers, and then explained to me that the "complication" had occurred earlier that very year, 1888. It had something to do with Mrs. Forrester's butler, Mr. Fulford. However, Mary wasn't aware of the precise details as the matter didn't involve her and it was not her business to pry.

I felt somewhat ashamed at the implication, as I was anything but a gossip. Mary softened the situation by explaining, with a smile, that she'd been away at the time with James, Mrs. Forrester's son, to whom she was governess. They'd been visiting relatives on the Sussex Downs – an annual pilgrimage for the young lad. By the time they returned to the house at Camberwell, the situation, as it were, it had all blown over.

It was shortly after this point in the conversation that I returned Mary to Camberwell myself. Mrs. Forrester invited me to stop for tea. They were a lovely family and I was always loth to pass up an opportunity to spend more time with Mary. However, I felt it somewhat inappropriate to surround myself with Mrs. Forrester's domesticity after the conversation that Mary and I had just had. I politely declined the invitation on the grounds of a prior engagement in town.

I made my way back to Baker Street by foot, better informed although admittedly none the wiser about the case. As I traversed Vauxhall and Pimlico, I held out a hope that Holmes would be willing to fill in the details I craved. He was often thorny about requests to revisit past events with anything but a cursory mention when not related to a current case.

For my part, I began by endeavouring to think when it might have been that he'd undertaken an investigation without me at his side. Alas, in our years of friendship and co-habitation, there had been any number of occasions when he had disappeared for periods of time without fully accounting for his whereabouts. I would need to ask him, and either he would tell me, or I would have to satisfy myself that the case would forever remain a mystery.

The daylight was beginning to fade as I made my way up the stairs at 221b Baker Street. I was feeling exhilarated after walking so far on a not-inclement autumn afternoon, along with the natural positivity which came from having spent time with Mary. No doubt it wouldn't be long until dinner was served, if the aromas wafting around the stairs were anything to judge by. I entered the sitting room to find Holmes leaning on the chimney breast, reading a letter by the light of the lamp. He looked up with mild amusement as I entered and raised the letter by way of greeting.

"I commend you on your timing, Watson. This letter I've been reading is all about *you*."

"It is?"

He handed it to me. "It arrived while you were out a-wooing. From Mrs. Cecil Forrester, no less."

I gave a chuckle. "I could have brought it myself."

Mrs. Forrester had written to Holmes, thanking him for doing her another fine service and finding a noble suitor for Mary, but also gently chastising him for losing her a wonderful governess. I read the lady's words and found myself struck, yet again, at the good fortune of coincidence that occasionally blessed our strange lives there in Baker Street. This charming letter had provided me with the perfect bridge by which to raise the very subject of the small domestic affair, and ask Holmes if he could explain how he'd assisted Mrs. Cecil Forrester, which made her recommend him to Mary.

As expected, Holmes responded with vehement reluctance, despite his high spirits from receiving the letter. However, something of my disappointment – or possibly my yearning to discover the truth – must have told on my face, for he paused midway through his diatribe, sighed and grinned at me fondly.

"But I can see it writ large that plenty hangs upon this, and I am feeling in *la bon humeur*, so I shall acquiesce, my dear Watson, and gratify you this once."

I gave a hearty chuckle at my condescending friend before taking a brandy and a seat.

"And," he continued, as though addressing a group of witnesses, "I shall also temper my enthusiasm. I could sum up the affair in a mere few sentences, but I know how much you enjoy allowing a story to open up as the narrative progresses. So in honour of that, and assuming that this may one day find its way into print, I shall do my best to tell it all from start to finish, as you would yourself."

I nodded graciously, and he told me this particular tale . . . .

I don't recall the exact date *(Holmes said)* but I do remember that you were away at your club on the day in question, Watson, which was why this became a solo venture for me. I'd been about some business here when you left, but I soon grew tired and restless and took myself off for a walk. It was a grey day, but dry, after a period of a week or more of persistent heavy rain. London was damp and soggy, its businesses mired and bespattered with sodden, cloying filth. And it was cold, I remember that much – cold, but without the cutting chill that makes walking unpleasant.

I wandered, lost in my thoughts. I don't recall, now, where precisely I'd crossed the Thames, but by the time I emerged from my internal ruminations, I was surprised to find myself out near Kennington Oval. I heard a great cry and assumed, initially, that there was a cricket match in progress – paying no heed to the time of year, the weather, or the ambient light. It soon became obvious, however, that the sound had originated from somewhere ahead of me. I continued onwards now with purpose and more haste. The great cry had a tragic edge to it, and I suspected that a group of people had stumbled upon some upset or other, to have raised such a commotion.

When I reached Warham Street, off Camberwell New Road, I found a great deal of water at street level. A drain had burst and flooded – sadly a likely occurrence due to the recent heavy rainfall. An assorted crowd of respectably dressed persons and servants milled around, no doubt having ventured from the residences to either side. But, as I made my way further through the crowd, I found that this flooding wasn't directly weather-related.

Some men were endeavouring to haul a body from an open manhole cover. It was clear to me in an instant that the person – a man – was dead, and further that he hadn't died investigating the cause of the flooding – he had himself been the cause of it. The body was somewhat bloated and swollen from taking on water, hence the difficulty in removing it. I rushed forward and was able to provide some much-needed assistance to those undertaking the task.

As we raised the body up and laid it to the side, I saw evidence that the deceased had been gnawed at by rats in several places. Indeed, one or two unfortunates escaped from the poor wretch's trousers as we lowered him. This was the final straw for the remaining women in the crowd, and I was left to stand with the body while the men assisted the swooning ladies and more tender female servants back into their houses. A fortunate occurrence, as it turned out. I made several telling observations – but more of them in their place, I feel.

Holmes delivered this last with a sly grin and paused to take a sip of his whisky. I raised my brows and inclined my head in acknowledgment. He was thoroughly enjoying playing the dramatist, that much was clear to me – JHW

The dead man looked to be of an age similar to us, Watson, dressed decently, but his shoes were rather more worn than the rest of his apparel. Besides the kerfuffle around the rats escaping, there had been a tearing sound as we lowered the body to the ground. The back of his jacket had given way, causing us to unbalance and drop him the final few inches. Now left alone with the corpse, I rolled him onto his side. It was evident from the state of the man's shirt beneath that the jacket had given way because it was full of holes – or cuts, to be precise. He had been stabbed in the back numerous times. He carried no identification or personal effects of any kind. It is rare to find anyone without anything in their pockets at all, is it not?

Our good friend, Inspector Athelney Jones, arrived as I finished checking the pockets. I heard the cab pull up, but paid it little heed until I heard the Welsh wizard's scuffed footsteps approaching.

"Oh, you got him out, did you?" Jones grumbled, with all the grace of a man who's just missed the last slice of cake. "That's a shame, Mr. Holmes. You could at least allow me to try to do *my* job before you start doing *yours*."

Before I could respond to the challenge, one of the local gentlemen returned – A Mr. Palmer, a well-respected local haberdasher.

He readily explained my presence to Jones as a passing Samaritan, along with all the circumstances prior to the inspector's arrival. This did nothing to calm Jones, who, in turn, informed Mr. Palmer as to my identity and calling. Palmer then shook me warmly by the hand and blessed the street's good fortune that I had been passing.

Thankfully to alleviate Jones's blood pressure, Palmer then turned the conversation back to police procedures. As far as I could gather, someone had alerted a local constable when the body was first discovered. The fellow had reported this back up the line. Jones had issued strict instructions that nothing was to be disturbed – hence his displeasure upon arrival.

Mr. Palmer had the air of a man not used to having his actions queried. He informed the inspector that he had instructed that the body should be removed. The body was discovered in the first place because some of the residents had chosen to investigate why the drains continued to back up on their street now that the rains had subsided. Palmer wasn't prepared to wait for the police to arrive, as there was a risk of localised flooding to peoples' property. Knowing how unhappy Jones would be about this may have explained why the constable in question wasn't currently in attendance.

Palmer asked Jones if he had an issue with protecting private property from damage. I fully expected the inspector to arrest the good Mr. Palmer out of sheer spite, but wonders never cease, it seems. Jones held his temper, and instead simply asked Palmer if he knew the dead man. As I mentioned earlier, the body had taken on water and was puffy and swollen, but not beyond recognition by any means. Palmer believed he was an itinerant salesman, known to frequent the area.

"Salesman, eh? Not a very successful one, judging by the state of his clothes."

Jones was, if anything, being uncommonly adept on this occasion – but not always for the right reasons, I must say. His comment about the man's worn attire was more of a judgmental sneer, for example, but the point was noteworthy, nonetheless.

I continued with my own line of constructive enquiry, and asked Mr. Palmer when he had last had the man call at his door.

Palmer stroked his chin, thoughtfully. 'Now you come to mention it, Mr. Holmes, I don't recall having seen him hereabouts for some time.'

The vagaries of human perception, Watson! I probed the haberdasher for more precision, but, frustratingly, he couldn't confirm if the "some time" was a few days ago, or even a few weeks.

Meanwhile, Jones moved his attentions to the open manhole. A lamp was obtained and lowered inside. We could see nothing untoward down there. Anything that might have been there to assist us, such as a murder weapon, had presumably been washed away by the receding floodwaters after the body's removal. I had my reasons already, by this stage, but I felt confident that no murder weapons would have been left with the body anyway.

Jones scratched his head and voiced his incredulity that the body could have been forced down there in the first place. Then he asked where the nearest telephone could be found. The Forresters was the only household at that end of the street to have one, and it so happened that we were outside their very house.

By now, Watson, you know the Forresters' residence very well and have, no doubt, walked numerous times over or past that same manhole from which we withdrew the dead body I followed Jones to the house, while Mr. Palmer went to check on his shop, which he'd left under the supervision of a junior. Two constables replaced the manhole cover and remained with the corpse.

"Worrying business, this, Mr. Holmes," the inspector confided in me as we stood waiting for the door to be answered.

When the door was eventually opened, I recognised Mrs. Forrester's butler – Fulford, as his name turned out to be – from the earlier crowd on the street. Mr. Forrester was away on business, we were told, and Mrs. Forrester was receiving a restorative in the drawing room. But she was prepared to receive us if we so wished. I accepted the offer, while Jones was directed to the telephone by a maid.

I need not describe Mrs. Forrester to you, Watson, nor any of the household, since no one has changed in the seven months or so since that day. Needless to say, it was a pleasant meeting, and I undertook to reassure the lady that the inspector and I would do all we could to clear up the situation outside with all haste.

It was at this point that something unexpected happened. There was a minor struggle outside the front of the house, and then Jones burst into the drawing room. He gave some apology to the lady and advised that he was taking Fulford into custody. When asked why, he claimed that the maid had told him she'd overheard Fulford talking to the salesman on the doorstep, and Fulford had threatened to kill the man if he ever came knocking there again. She hadn't seen him since, until today. That was enough evidence for Jones. I think it a matter of some relief that he didn't arrest the whole house!

(*I laughed at this. – JHW*)

57

Poor Mrs. Forrester was understandably agitated at this, although she admitted that Fulford had seemed a little flustered of late. I impressed upon the lady that I would sort everything, which appeared to give her some reassurance. I then spoke myself with Ettie, the maid.

The salesman had come knocking at the house only once – according to her, a week before. Ettie had been at the far end of the hallway, out of sight. Fulford had answered the door, the two men had spoken in low tones, and Ettie repeated what she'd then heard, spoken more forcefully, before the front door had been slammed in the man's face. No one else in the household knew, as far as Ettie was aware, and she hadn't spoken to Mrs. Forrester about what she'd overheard. Several of the staff had subsequently commented to Fulford that he seemed out of sorts, but he'd gruffly told them to mind their own business and leave him be. And that was all of any substance that I could obtain from the girl.

At a call from the inspector, I was alerted to the cart having arrived to take the body to the mortuary. On my way out, I found that the laundry collection was due, and the hallway had been lined with baskets. As I made my way past them, I caught my cuff button on one of the basket labels, which gave way and came off in my hand.

"Sorry, sir," said Ettie. "The garment isn't damaged, I hope?"

"Not at all," I confirmed, slipping the label that I'd also taken into my pocket and continuing out to join Jones in the police cab. "Whitehall Place?" I asked as I clambered aboard. Fulford was seated opposite between the two constables. He'd been handcuffed, but it clearly wasn't necessary. The man looked broken.

"Of course," Jones replied. "Joining us, are you?"

"And the body?" I said, deliberately not answering his question.

"Same. I think it's best if we have everything under one roof until we've got the answers we need, don't you, Mr. Holmes?"

"Capital!" I replied. For once he'd done the right thing.

The cab pulled away after the horse and cart. I leaned from the window and called for the driver to take us via the Green Dragon, where Denmark Hill meets Peckham Road.

Jones baulked at this. "Really, Mr. Holmes," he said. "You've come along just so that we can drop you at a public house?"

I'm sure I've said it before, Watson, and I'm sure I'll say it again: The man's an idiot. I told him The House of the Green Dragon is the nearest Chinese laundry, before addressing the butler.

"Isn't that right, Mr. Fulford?"

The prisoner nodded and answered quietly. "They're very good, too. Most households on our street use them."

It did nothing to appease the inspector, who continued to huff and puff about taking matters seriously and not picking up clean linen on police time. Thankfully, it was only a short ride there, and as the cab pulled up, I dashed out and jumped back in again before the horse had even come to a complete standstill.

"Walk on," I yelled, banging my cane against the underside of the cab roof.

"Was that it?" grumbled the Welshman.

I nodded and held up a label on a tie string, which I'd ripped from one of the baskets standing outside the establishment.

Fulford spoke again. "Mr. Holmes, if you wanted their details you only had to ask. I know them by heart."

"Everything in its place, Mr. Fulford, everything in its place." Then I sat back quietly and waited for the journey to pass.

When we arrived at Whitehall Place and Scotland Yard, Jones immediately instructed that Fulford be locked in a cell to await questioning. I had been turning things over in my head during the journey, and I was convinced this wasn't the correct way to proceed. I asked the constables to hold and led Jones quietly to one side.

"Mr. Holmes," he still sounded fed up and I'd barely said a word. "Please just let us follow procedure."

"My dear Inspector," I said, trying to inject some charm you always use to maximum effect, my good friend.

(Here, I blushed. – JHW.)

"I feel that this case would be better served, and more quickly resolved, if Fulford were allowed down to the mortuary with us, to examine the body."

"What, so he can gloat over his victim?"

I glanced back at Fulford, handcuffed and standing forlornly between the two constables.

"Trust me, Inspector. If I haven't solved the murder within the hour, I'll willingly step aside, and you can do what you like."

I watched as he chewed over my proposition in his head. I could almost hear the rusty cogs and mechanisms as they rotated there.

"All right, Mr. Holmes," he finally said. "One hour it is."

You know as well as I do, Watson, the charms and aromas of any mortuary, and I know there would be little to benefit the story in trying to recapture that atmosphere for you now. Jones was unwilling to get too close to the body, and seemed to actively shy away from its sunken-eyed gaze, but this was my hour and I was happy to take the lead. The body and clothing were still slowly releasing retained water. No blood, though. Clearly that had all drained away during however long the body had been discarded underground, washed clean by the recent storms. As the body lost water and the skin dried, it began to take on more of a gaunt, cadaverous appearance. This was matched by the putrescent stench which escaped from the open mouth as I flipped the body over onto its front. Even I was forced to step back momentarily to allow the noxious cloud to pass. The man's back was the focus of my attentions. I carefully removed the torn jacket and partially shredded shirt, placing them to one side, should they be required in evidence, at a later date.

Some of the stab wounds on the back had been targeted by rats, but enough remained intact for my purposes. The swelling had caused the sides of the wounds to rise up like lipless mouths, eager to call upon the identity of their perpetrator, but singularly lacking in voice. Yet what they did was show clearly that a number of different blades were used. The wounds were of a variety of sizes, and I pointed this much out to Jones, in case he might miss the obvious.

"More than one assailant, then," the inspector confirmed, matter-of-factly. "Our chum here had an accomplice or two." He turned to Fulford. "You going to tell us how you did it, then?"

I looked at Fulford. He still wore a forlorn expression. "I did nothing."

Jones nodded and sneered. "Have it your way, but we'll figure you out in the end, mark my words. These knife wounds – all domestic-size blades, by the look of them. If we searched the house, no doubt we'd find a match for each."

"No doubt you would at most houses, Inspector," I replied.

"Do you have anything else, Mr. Holmes?"

I had. Plenty. "Our victim is – what would you say? – five-foot-ten-inches tall?"

The Welshman urged me on with a dismissive waft of his hand.

"There or thereabouts," I said. "And Mr. Fulford, here, is over six feet. In fact, he and I are pretty much eye to eye, height-wise, I think."

"Your point?"

I took a deep breath to maintain my temperament before continuing.

"The angle of wound, my dear Inspector, the angle of wound."

The effect was like someone switching on an electric light behind the man's eyes. Jones's whole face lit up and he came to stand next to me at the slab.

"The swelling is revealing everything in greater detail, thankfully." I pointed to a couple of the larger cuts. "Here you can see at the top of the wound, in particular, the mottled after-effects of bruising."

Jones nodded. "So the skin was punctured with the point of the blade on an upward thrust, and then the flesh beneath was sliced with the cutting edge as the blade entered."

"And by my reckoning, the assailants would have needed to be around five-foot-five or five-foot-six inches tall to thrust in at that angle." I played out the move on Jones, for effect. "There is no way that Mr. Fulford, at his height, could have stabbed this man in that way."

"I thought we'd already agreed that there had to be an accomplice. Surely this is more evidence of that?"

"You agreed it, Inspector, not me," I replied, patiently. "And I'm saying Fulford couldn't have made *any* of these wounds."

"I'm one step ahead of you, as usual, Mr. Holmes."

The sheer audacity of the man. Even recalling it now, Watson, the gall rises in my throat. "Are you indeed?" I asked.

The inspector nodded. "Accessory to murder. The victim was addressing our Mr. Fulford, distracted by him, while the shorter assailants came up behind and stabbed him." He turned to Fulford. "I would bet that you're enjoying this. You have two of the finest detective minds in the country working out how you did it."

I rolled my eyes and tried to rein Jones back in. "All right," I conceded. "But the victim was a door-to-door salesman, as far as we know. So where are his wares?"

"Stolen? Hidden? Burned?" he said, glancing at Fulford ever more closely with each word. "We'll search Mrs. Forrester's. They'll be there somewhere – hidden below stairs no doubt."

"But why shove the body in the public drain outside the house?"

"Panic. Pure and simple."

"All right, Inspector. If that's the case, where was the blood? People would notice that."

"Mr. Holmes, you said yourself earlier, the storm water down the drains washed it away."

"That was once he was down there! Inspector, you aren't suggesting, I hope, that they shoved him down the drain, stabbed him, then flipped him over onto his back and left him, blocking the pipes so that the drain water would back up through the manhole cover and cause a flood? As a murderer, you're drawing an awful lot of attention to the scene of the crime that way."

"I said before, it was unplanned. We see this sort of thing all the time."

"But it doesn't explain this." You will recall, earlier, Watson, that I mentioned I'd made several discoveries while examining the corpse on the road. Well, this was my final one, my *coup de grace*. I produced a brown paper laundry label with a tie string from inside my pocket handkerchief and help it out for all to see.

Jones dismissed the label. "You got that from the Chinese laundry on the way here."

"No, Inspector. That was *this* one." I produced another, identical label. "There is also a third," and here I produced the label which I'd successfully snagged with my jacket cuff in Mrs. Forrester's hallway. All three looked identical.

"Where d'you get that first one, then?" the inspector asked.

"It was caught just here, Mr. Jones." I raised the corpse's right arm and indicated the buttons on his jacket cuff. "It had looped around this button here. A solid bit of stitching, this. The thread held where the string connecting the label to the laundry basket gave way. I noticed it as the corpse was raised from the manhole."

"And you didn't think to mention it before?" Jones now appeared annoyed. I took some small pleasure in that.

"Everything in its place, Inspector," I said. "We've been considering all the evidence, so far, before making a judgment." I raised the sheet over the corpse at this point, certain that we would no longer need to refer to the body.

"What does the label say?" I held it out on my palm for him to see that it was blank. He looked up at me questioningly.

"It was submerged for a time. Washed clean. But it's clearly a laundry label, and it's remained intact enough inside my handkerchief for me to match it against two others."

"Most laundries use those, though. Who's to say it's the same establishment?"

I lined the three labels up and turned them over. There was a Green Dragon Laundry ink stamp on the reverse of the two fresh labels obtained today. On the reverse of the label from the corpse there was a smeary mark of identical size. The water hadn't been able to wash that away fully.

"Persuasive, Mr. Holmes," the inspector admitted. "But not the conclusive proof we need. He could have been attacked in Mrs. Forrester's hallway and snagged the label the same way you did today."

"So we look for more evidence to fill in the gaps," I said.

Jones chewed his top lip. "What I want to know is why you think the Chinese would want to kill a door-to-door salesman anyway?"

"Well, that's simple, for a start. Because he wasn't a door-to-door salesman." I turned to look directly at the butler. "Was he, Mr. Fulford?"

"No, he wasn't," Fulford answered, with a heavy heart.

"But what I don't yet know is why you threatened to kill him."

Fulford now looked directly back at me. "Because he was my son-in-law, Mr. Holmes."

(Whether by direction or by design, Holmes paused here in his narration to have a drink. I was spellbound. – JHW)

One of the constables uttered an oath. Jones barked at him to watch his language before asking the butler to explain.

Fulford continued. "He married my Susan against my will. My only child, she was. All I had in the world. And she died young. I've always held him to blame. No life for a sweet girl, what he gave her."

"And what did he give her? I mean, what did he do if he wasn't a door to door salesman?"

"He was a detective," Fulford confirmed.

"With the police?" Jones glanced at the over-turned corpse once again, as if this revelation would make him more likely to recognise the man.

Fulford shook his head. "Private."

"Oh, like this one." The inspector flippantly cast his eyes my way.

"More of an enquiry agent, I would say, Mr. Fulford. Wouldn't you?" I asked. "Investigating queries that were, perhaps, too banal for the authorities, yet not sufficiently challenging for a consulting detective such as myself."

"All I know is," Fulford replied, "it was no job for a man who enjoyed the drink too much, and had a loving wife to provide for."

"Fairbrother was his name, was that not the case?"

A sullen nod. "That's the name he gave my little Sue."

"Have you not heard the name doing the rounds, Inspector?" I asked, this knowing full well that our Welsh wizard was likely to know only the names of his immediate colleagues and those superiors he had to keep happy, but no one else. He didn't even attempt to answer me, opting instead to cross-question.

"You knew him, then, Mr. Holmes?"

"I make it my business to know who else is out there, undertaking similar work," I replied, perhaps a little archly.

Jones didn't bite. "And let's not forget, Mr. Fulford," he said, "no matter what the personal history between you and this Fairbrother chap – whatever his occupation – you still threatened to kill him."

The butler took a long breath before explaining. "I hadn't seen him in a long time. He came knocking, pretending to sell cleansing fluid and embrocation. Then we had a mutual moment of recognition. Told me he was undercover, investigating the local Chinese laundry. They were up to no good, according to reports. He was working his way around local residents, a few streets at a time, to see what they'd seen and heard. I hadn't seen him since my poor Susan died. I didn't care what he was up to. I told him flat out what I'd promised myself I'd tell him ever since that day. Yet I take no pleasure from having seen him there, today, on the slab, I can assure you gentlemen."

"I'm glad to hear it, Mr. Fulford," I said. "There is often something of a gulf between what we believe we desire and the true realisation of that desire. Having recognised the man myself, I erroneously assumed that he had confided in you at the door as to his true vocation, and you had objected to his proposals in some way. I had no inkling that your connection ran so deep, so I must apologise sincerely if leaving you exposed to his corpse has caused you unnecessary trauma and remembrances."

Jones brusquely interrupted. "Not that you're a suspect in this, Mr. Holmes, but when did you last see Mr. Fairbrother alive?"

"He chanced to call on me late last year, as it happens. He advised me that he'd been tasked with an enquiry, by several clients, regarding the behaviours of a certain door-to-door service industry. He hadn't been gifted such a sizeable task before, and, without revealing specific details, he sought my guidance on undercover work. We discussed the matter over half-a-bottle of brandy, since he took some reassuring."

Jones looked at me as a cat does a mouse. "So, you put him up to this, Mr. Holmes? That's quite an admission, when the fellow's lying there dead."

"Not in the least, Inspector," I spat, irritably. "He had a plan already in mind. I considered his suggestions and advised that he would be better posing as a customer himself, rather than trying to gain people's confidence on their doorsteps. There's no accounting for how frightened people may get, and what they may give away to the wrong person."

"As presumably happened here." Jones's face showed he was less-than-happy that a fellow detective would come to me for advice, rather than seeking it from his professional colleagues.

"The Chinese laundry got wind of him, that much is certain. The height of the wounds would fit. Your average Chinaman is somewhat shorter than an Englishman. They could have stabbed him at the laundry, then taken him out in one of their baskets on a delivery. Most probably they masked their actions as they shoved the corpse down through the open manhole. His cuff must have caught one of the laundry basket labels as he was dragged out."

"Why put the body down the drain, though?"

"A subtle warning to the residents, perhaps? I've no doubt you'll find something untoward going on with that Green Dragon laundry, Inspector. Extortion, racketeering, or something of the sort. I'll leave that to you. I'm sure you'll get to the bottom of it – and with many plaudits to your name."

"Right," he said, somewhat surprised that an opportunity had fallen into his lap. "Yes. We'll raid the place."

"And in the meantime, I assume I'm free to escort Mr. Fulford back to Mrs. Forrester's?"

"Indeed, Mr. Holmes. Thank you. And thank you for your assistance, too, Mr. Fulford."

Jones smiled broadly at Fulford – imagine that, Watson. Fulford, for his part, neither returned the smile nor inclined his head in acknowledgment. He merely raised his cuffed wrists and his eyebrows.

Fulford and I shared a solemn return journey to Camberwell. It was clear to me that the butler was struggling to come to terms with his feelings on the whole matter. I made a mental note to apprise Mrs. Forrester of this, in case she wished to send him away for a few days of compassionate leave. Indeed, the lady was overjoyed to see us upon our arrival. She immediately ushered me into the drawing room, whereupon I was bound without delay to inform her of all that had passed.

Ah, Watson, what a thrill it is from time to time to bask in the light of an avid listener, to witness the ups and downs of fortune reflected in their very eyes as they grasp at each word falling from our lips. I saved the lady from some of the more macabre details surrounding the case, but also recommended that she change her laundry firm at the soonest opportunity. She thanked me greatly for my tact and perspicacity – those qualities which, I think you'll be aware, led to our involvement with the case of the Agra treasure and, of course, your forthcoming nuptials.

However, my duties were as yet incomplete. In compliance with Mrs. Forrester's request, I left her to speak alone with Fulford while I held an audience with the household in the kitchens. I apprised them of what had occurred, as far as was possible, without subjecting poor Fulford thence to a life of endless gossip.

(And that, I thought, was where my darling Mary, being away in Sussex at the time, missed out on meeting Holmes and learning the details of the affair. JHW)

After that, I paid a visit to Mr. Palmer, who had been of so much assistance earlier in the day. Again, I informed him of certain particulars surrounding the murder case, and laid waste to any careless thoughts over Mrs. Forrester's butler being responsible, should Jones in his overzealousness earlier in the day have been overheard. Which indeed he was. I called upon several of Mrs. Forrester's neighbours before the hour became impolite. I was sure that I'd done all I could to bolster the good reputation of Mrs. Forrester's household, as well as ensuring that the Green Dragon laundry lost its monopoly with the residents of Warham Street.

I finished the day by, once again, cataloguing my activities for Mrs. Forrester, and receiving, once more, her everlasting gratitude and appreciation. And a rather splendid dinner, also, as I recall. Bream, in a white wine sauce. Upon which deliciously fishy note, Watson, I believe my tale comes to an end.

I felt my stomach rumbling at the mention of food.

"You will understand, I'm sure," Holmes said, "why I didn't then feel a desperate desire to inform you regarding that day's activities when we reconvened in this very sitting room later that evening."

"Indeed, Holmes, indeed," I replied. "And I feel obliged to repeat how grateful I am to you, now, for filling that gap for me today, so long after the event."

I couldn't wait to see Mary again and inform her that my mind had been thoroughly settled on the matter.

The sitting room door opened at this point, and like a shining angel, Mrs. Hudson entered with our dinner.

"Splendid timing, as ever," Holmes said.

No domestic complications here, I thought, with a smile.

> *"I have come to you, Mr. Holmes," she said, "because you once enabled my employer, Mrs. Cecil Forrester, to unravel a little domestic complication. She was much impressed by your kindness and skill."*
>
> *"Mrs. Cecil Forrester," he repeated thoughtfully. "I believe that I was of some slight service to her. The case, however, as I remember it, was a very simple one."*
>
> *"She did not think so . . . ."*

– Mary Morstan and Sherlock Holmes
The Sign of the Four

The Adventure of the
Abducted Bard
by I.A. Watson

A light dusting of snow turned the soaring spires and gothic frontages
of Oxford's Colleges into fairy castles. Holmes and I crunched over Hythe
Bridge from the railway station, over the desolate and icy Castle Mill
Stream, and turned left into Walton Street. The University city was
unfamiliar territory to me, but Holmes had spent two years in study at
Christ Church. [1] We turned into Walton Street, cut across Gloucester
Green, and passed the Martyrs Memorial under the shadow of the
Ashmolean Museum.

I struggled to keep up with my companion. Holmes's long strides
betrayed his impatience to arrive at our destination. Across St. Giles' lay
the turreted bulk of Goneril College, [2] where we were greeted by a lodge
porter and hastened to the Master's chambers.

"Mr. Holmes," the Master greeted us, rising from his desk to shake
hands. "And Dr. Watson. Thank you for coming down from London so
quickly." He introduced his colleagues, the College's Dean and Bursar,
and a flustered-looking academic who was Reader in Elizabethan
Manuscripts.

"Given the nature of the problem, I felt I should come at once,"
Holmes replied.

"You come highly recommended from the Master of Christ Church.
He said you had the sort of mind that comes along only a few times in a
generation. Your decision to leave your studies unfinished was a great loss
to academia."

"My studies continue," the self-appointed consulting detective
answered. "I elected to pursue them in a different manner in a secular
venue."

The Master was forced to accept that, although it was clear to me that
none of the dons in the room could really conceive of a study life outside
the confines of their University.

Holmes had little time for pleasantries, though. "You have lost a
manuscript," he said, "A manuscript of potentially great significance."

"A manuscript of substantial value," the Bursar answered, fretting.
"And it is not lost, it is ransomed."

Holmes held up one long thin finger to stem the tide of indignation.
"I would prefer to hear the facts presented in sequence in a logical and

orderly fashion. One of you must bring to bear that academic regimen in which you are tutored and recount for me the case as it developed."

The Master nodded acknowledgement and gestured to the Dean to begin.

The Dean polished his spectacles and replaced them carefully. "Some three months ago, one of our alumni contacted the College in some excitement. He had recently been given the opportunity to examine his late grandfather's library, with a view to cataloguing it. Amongst the documents and papers there, misclassified as an eighteenth-century pamphlet, were two pages of a seventeenth-century folio, crudely printed possibly as proof sheets, and an additional two of handwritten material, all stitched together with twine. The cover-sheet pronounced it to be *The History of Cardenio*, published in 1652 by Humphrey Moseley of The Prince's Arms, St Paul's Courtyard."

Holmes breathed in hard, like a man who has smelled his Sunday dinner about to be served.

"This *History of Cardenio* is held to be a lost play by William Shakespeare," I mentioned. Holmes had spoken of little but it on our train up from Paddington.

The Reader in Elizabethan Literature burst in with agitated footnotes. Dr. Chadbury was a stick-thin scholar of advancing years with huge bushy eyebrows that seemed to belong on a different face entirely. "It was attributed to Shakespeare and John Fletcher, one of the late collaborations like *Henry VIII* and *Two Noble Kinsmen*. But it is mentioned only once, in a 1653 entry in the Stationer's Register, reported there in assertion of ownership by the sometimes-unscrupulous Moseley."

Holmes has also covered that in his lecture. "Moseley was a major printer at the time. He had already printed several compilations of Shakespeare's works without the author's permission, and was not above padding out his editions with works now thought to have been borrowed from other writers."

"Yes," Chadbury agreed. "But that was standard business practice in the day, it seems. He was well-considered enough that his peers elected him Warden of the Stationer's Company in 1659. His imprint exists on three-hundred-and-fourteen surviving editions, including the works of Francis Bacon, René Descartes, and the alchemist Robert Flood. It is possible – entirely possible – that he produced, or planned to produce, an issue of *Cardenio*, with or without sanction."

Holmes dismissed a century of academic debate in favour of the present narrative. "You heard from your former student," he prompted Chadbury.

"I did," the Dean clarified. "Dr. Chadbury was at that time visiting Salisbury to consult certain archives of relevance to his researches."

"I should never have left Oxford," Chadbury mourned. "This might never have happened."

"What happened, though?" Holmes demanded, as impatient as any senior wrangler with a derelict undergraduate.

The chastened Dean cleaned his spectacles again and carried on. "Our alumnus expressed a certain concern he had about his discovery. In the first place, he could not certainly verify it. The provenance seemed sound as best he could determine, but he freely admitted that he has not the scholarly expertise to determine if his find was actually what it seemed."

"He took History," Chadbury interjected, as if reporting a shameful deficiency. "He achieved a Second."

The Bursar chipped in. "A further complication was that the entire collection was now in the hands of his grandfather's heir, our scholar's uncle, who was somewhat indifferent to the library and was considering selling the whole of it to an American investor."

Chadbury shuddered. "The entire assemblage might be lost to British scholarship. And if the existence of the *Cardenio* was known, even suspected . . . ."

"I gather that there is little love lost between our scholar and his uncle," the Dean confessed. "Anyhow, our alumnus undertook to borrow the document so that it could be properly examined here at the College. If the discovery was verified, then some arrangement might be made to endow the manuscript here at Goneril – to purchase it if sufficient funds might be raised. But much depended on secrecy. One might admit to deception."

"Under such circumstances, there is some justification for precautions," Holmes judged. "What arrangement was finally agreed upon?"

"A two-week loan," The Dean explained. "I don't believe the uncle ever really understood the agreement he made, or even glanced at the contract of indemnity. Conditions were laid upon the transportation of the *Cardenio* – if *Cardenio* it was. A guard was to be kept upon the item during transportation. A special display stand was commissioned that might protect the manuscript from harm. Only certain named scholars would handle the document, under the supervision of Dr. Chadbury himself."

"The manuscript arrived under guard yesterday?" I verified.

"Under escort," the Dean agreed. "We set the stand up in the Cresswell Library and the Master and I were present as it was locked into its case."

"Describe the item," Holmes instructed.

69

Dr. Chadbury laid his head in his hands. He had been absent when the papers had arrived. They had gone before he returned. He might never now see the document that could have been the crown of his academic career.

The Dean had made closest observation, since he had been signatory of the receipt. "There were two printed sheets and two handwritten ones. The typeset ones were bifolia, two eighteen-by-seven inch pages printed side-by-side front and back, intended to be folded to make four pages. The paper was fibre pulp, rather frayed and discoloured, with one corner of the top-sheet broken off and missing. The holographic paper was very faded and nigh illegible, but appeared to be a cast list."

"There is better detail in our scholar's correspondence," Dr. Chadbury promised.

"You have been careful not to name your benefactor," Holmes observed.

The dons looked uncomfortable. "Anonymity was a part of the request," the Master answered for them at last. "As the Dean has said, there was a delicacy to the loan. Our graduate preferred to remain in the background lest he incur the wrath of his relative."

"It is relevant data and must be laid before me. You cannot expect me to untangle your affair blindfolded with my hands tied behind my back."

"That's fair," the Dean judged, glancing in consultation with his colleagues.

They assented to name their student, who had graduated two years earlier. At that time the name of Mr. John Clay was not familiar to us.[3] "He is a grandson of the Earl of Montguerre, and it was his Grace's library collection wherein the manuscript was found," the Master told us.

"The old Earl was a dedicated bibliophile," Dr. Chadbury added. "His son, the present peer, has shown no such interest."

"An agreement was made with Mr. Clay and the Earl, and the manuscript was delivered," Holmes summarised to continue the account. "What time yesterday was this?"

"About four in the afternoon," supplied the Dean. "The *Cardenio* travelled across from Hampshire. It was installed as required by five."

"And then?"

"There was a certain degree of furtive admiration through the glass top of the display case. At six, the cover was locked over the glass – I believe by the senior porter – and the Cresswell Library was closed."

"Locked?" Holmes checked.

"Yes. The Cresswell houses a number of rare exhibits. It is secured by our night staff. No one could enter the room past the porter's desk without being seen or heard."

"When was the library reopened and the manuscript missed?"

"The Cresswell is unlocked at eight, although seldom used before ten. But on this occasion – "

"I was very eager to see the *Cardenio*," Dr. Chadbury interjected. "I returned by the late train the night before and came down as soon as I could to inspect the find. Except . . . it was gone."

"Was the case lock forced?" I enquired. "Or was a key used?"

"The key was still on the senior porter's fob," the Dean assured us, "but there was no sign of forced entry. The windows were sealed, fastened closed for the winter. The door was still locked. But the manuscript was missing."

"A search was made," I supposed.

"Of course. That was when we found the note."

Holmes leaned forward.

The Master produced a folder and passed across a single sheet of bonded writing paper. Inscribed upon it in good penmanship was the message:

> *I have your* Cardenio. *Except it is not yours, and when its loss is discovered it will bring disgrace upon Goneril and financial ruin. Who will afterwards trust your stewardship or value your scholarship? There will be scandal. There will be litigation. Imagine the response of the broadsheets and the good name of the College dragged through the mire.*
>
> *I have your* Cardenio. *It is nothing to me whether it survives or not. I might burn it as a whim, or return it shredded to prove its destruction. I consider it sport to threaten the loss of such a literary treasure. Unless I am diverted from my ends I will be pleased to deprive the world of the Bard's lost work.*
>
> *I have your* Cardenio. *Though I might dispose of it to unscrupulous collectors for a small fortune, I am minded instead to hold it against the College's future co-operation. For the moment I shall expect a daily fee, a retainer to preserve the work in good condition. Five-hundred guineas is a good start. You will tape the bag near the base of the Martyrs Memorial beneath the statue of Hugh Latimer. Deliver the fee by noon today. Keep no watch.*
>
> *I have your* Cardenio. *I have your hopes, your futures, your academic and financial well-being, your whole lives at my disposal. I am without scruple and disposed to*

vindictiveness. I urge you not to test my capacities, for I own an excellent box of matches.

I have your Cardenio. *You shall hear from me again forthwith.*

"Well," I breathed, "that's an unpleasant sort of missive."

"Where did you come by this paper?" Sherlock Holmes asked.

"There is a cupboard in the pedestal of the document case. This was on the upper shelf," the Bursar told us.

"You paid the ransom?" I asked. "Or at least an instalment of it?"

"What else could we do?" The Master despaired. "But five-hundred pounds – even that is a large sum to render at such short notice."

"Was a watch actually kept?" The tall memorial [4] is in one of the most public spots in Oxford, overlooked by Balliol, the Taylorian [5] and many other buildings. At midday it is an important meeting point and junction, whatever the weather.

"A judicious eye was kept from a safe distance," the Dean admitted. "The bag was taken up by a rough-looking tramp of a fellow. He shuffled off with it along Beaumont Street, turned right into St. John Street, and vanished in the warren of back alleys off there."

Holmes took a description, but it might have fitted any itinerant beggar. Nor could we be confident that this scruffy fellow was anything but what he seemed, employed for a few shillings to deliver the bag to some other party.

"We proved to the thief that we are tractable to his demands," the Bursar grumbled gloomily. Evidently there had been previous debate upon the point.

The Dean was evidently of the contrary camp. "We yielded to allow us time to think, to consider our next course."

"And that course is you, Mr. Holmes," Dr. Chadbury concluded.

"We are rather desperate," the Master continued. "If you would name your fee . . . ."

"Pecuniary matters are trivial," Holmes rejoined. "What is money compared to the possibility of another fragment of Shakespeare? "

I have noted my friend's usual indifference to literature and the arts, but there are certain exceptions about which he feels passionately. He is entranced by the female soprano, [6] by the well-played violin – and by the plays of the Bard of Avon. Indeed, he was intimately familiar with the plays of Shakespeare, having performed several of them on stage during an eccentric youthful tour with a theatrical troupe. [7]

"Of what value is the missing material?" I wondered. "I mean, what would it sell for at auction?"

72

"It is priceless," Chadbury insisted.

The Bursar looked a little sick. "Some two-hundred or more copies still exist of seven-hundred-and-fifty editions of Shakespeare's *First Folio*, issued in 1623, seven years after the playwright's death. When new they sold for the princely sum of one pound. Now they are exchanged for more than a hundred-and-seventy-thousand."

"A unique item such as the *Cardenio* might fetch a lot more," the Master added disconsolately.

"But would be very traceable," Holmes pondered. "Yet that does not seem to be the motive of our villain. Or not his *only* motive." He pressed his index fingers together as he thought. "There is more to discover. The play's the thing . . . ."

The Cresswell Library was a small annex beyond the larger repository, reserved for post-graduate study and as a display room for rare books.

Holmes halted us at the door. He took time to examine the lock and hinges of the library entrance, even kneeling to study the scuffed worn floorboards. The Dean and Dr. Chadbury had escorted us to the scene of the mystery. Now they stood uncomfortably with nothing to do while Holmes shuffled about without explanation.

"There may be signs of illicit entry," I offered explanation. "Holmes has made a scientific study of the marks of burglary: Scratches on the tumblers, oil-spots around the keyhole, that kind of thing."

Holmes snorted at my inexpert witness. "There are few signs that can help us. Any useful evidence has now been destroyed by the passage of many visitors." He looked up at the Dean. "Your domestic staff are to be commended. They have wax-polished this floor quite thoroughly. Had I been called in at once when the manuscript vanished, I might have read from this floor whether anyone had crossed it after that night's domestic work was done. As it is, a day later, such traces are useless. Nor has any mark been left on the lock. I would not have expected a real professional to do so."

He rose and ventured into the library. The room had but one exit and was lit from the east by five tall mullioned windows with ancient leads and coats of arms, presumably of the Cresswell benefactor who had endowed the College. A series of glass-topped display cases were positioned out of direct sunlight. Three long study tables were positioned centrally, with desks against the far wall. A huge early fireplace dominated the rear wall, but only a smaller, more modern grate lighted the wide hearth.

I saw at once the lectern that had previously housed the stolen document. It stood in pride of place between two of the windows, a heavy

73

mahogany stand some four-feet high, topped with a wide box. The security flap had been folded back to reveal the interior glass cover.

"The stand is specially made," the Dean assured us. "It looks to be wooden, but the upper compartment is actually protected by steel plate. The base is weighted with concealed lead to make it too heavy to be easily manhandled off. The lock that holds the solid top-flap in place overnight is specially designed and is supposedly thief-proof."

Holmes examined the furniture, taking special interest in the cupboard in the pedestal. A simple hinged front allowed access to a small interior space, too small for anyone to hide in, with a single shelf dividing it. The upper shelf was where the unpleasant note had been discovered after the theft.

"The ransom demand," Holmes checked. "How was it laid out here? Foursquare, or simply as if it had been tossed in anyhow?"

The Dean frowned to remember. "It was the Bursar who discovered it," he recalled. "I believe it was stood up on one end, as if leaned on the back panel."

Holmes nodded, apparently satisfied. He leaned right inside the cupboard and called for a light to inspect it by. Then he opened the glass top and rummaged around the velvet-lined display box.

"When the manuscript vanished, I called the manufacturer," the Dean assured us. "I wanted to know if some duplicate key existed that might have been used to access the lectern. They claim not. Indeed, they sent one of their craftsmen down to check that nothing had been tampered with."

"Who was the manufacturer?" I asked.

Holmes tapped a discrete brass nameplate on the interior side of the cupboard door, engraved with the name "*A. Fischer and Sons*". "Albert Fischer is a well-known quality cabinet-maker on Cornwall Road off Waterloo," he instructed me. "He is the shop fitter of choice for many of the superior London establishments, and his cabinetry is also used by the British Museum and Library." He paused for a moment before adding, "I might have expected better tenon and mortise work from him, though."

"You have discovered something, Holmes?" I ventured.

"When was this furniture delivered?" my friend asked the Dean.

"The day before the manuscript arrived – that is, three days since. I'd need to ask the chief porter for details."

I looked more carefully at the lectern, suddenly suspicious. "Are you saying that this is not Fischer's work?" I checked. "That this is another cabinet – the wrong cabinet?"

"A thief substituted the real display case for a facsimile!" Dr. Chadbury exclaimed in outraged tones. "The delivery was somehow thwarted and a different lectern brought to Goneril – one for which the thief had the key!"

"That is certainly a conclusion that our adversary would wish us to make," Holmes scolded the scholar. "Let us, however, consider all the evidence before postulating a theory."

Chastened, Chadbury fell silent as Holmes grubbed around the floor at the base of the cabinet. "There are water stains here," he said aloud.

That did not lead me to any immediate deductions. "How would water come to be spilled in this place?"

Holmes brought his magnifier to bear, following minute traces on the base of the polished lectern and damp patches on the carpet beneath. "Not spilled. Trickled."

The Dean shook his head in perplexity.

"You are not following," Holmes understood. "Find me a stack of papers, as like in size and shape as the missing manuscripts as you can. And also two small plugs of blotting paper from the desk there."

We hastened to obey, and watched as Holmes fumbled about in the cupboard for a few moments with the screwed up scraps of blotter. Eventually he rose, closed the lower cabinet, and laid our facsimile documents in their place under the glass.

"Fasten and lock the top, Watson," he instructed me.

I did as requested, then stepped back.

"I cannot adequately demonstrate the full method of this. We lack the time," Holmes told us. He opened the cupboard again and invited each of us to stick our heads inside and look up at the small tabs of folded blotting paper he had wedged into holes at either side of the rear of the compartment.

I took my turn. Holmes's strange additions were mere twists of sugar-paper no larger or thicker than a child's fingertip, lodged like pegs in circular indentations I had not previously noted.

"You must imagine," the detective told us, "that those wedges are not paper, but actually made of ice. Ice that gradually melted over the course of the day since their installation, trickling down and leaving the minor traces on base and carpet that I have just discovered. Eventually, when both plugs were fully gone, *this* would happen."

Holmes removed the blotter-rolls. Something moved inside the cabinet. We all heard it.

"Look for your papers," Holmes instructed me. I unsealed the top and peered through the display glass. The sheets we had laid there were gone.

"Some concealed mechanism?" the Dean blurted.

"Indeed." Holmes obligingly demonstrated his discovery. "Look carefully. When the ice-pegs melted, this section of the top-box hinged down under its own weight. The papers that lay atop the velvet slid down as if on a chute, vanishing through this slot at the rear of the pedestal. There is a concealed section a mere inch deep behind this cupboard, and that was where they fell. At the same time, a hidden note was released into the cupboard proper, to drop down at the rear of the upper shelf. That was how the ransom letter was delivered. There was a third, larger plug of ice here at the front. When that finally melted, perhaps an hour or two later, a counterweight drew the trap-door back to its horizontal position and a small snap-latch secured it there permanently."

"No burglar was required!" I ejaculated. "The whole thing was done automatically with cunning machinery and chips of ice!"

"Then . . . the document is surely not lost, but hidden in the compartment of which you spoke!" Dr. Chadbury exclaimed hopefully.

"It may be," Holmes answered him, "but I suspect not. Dean, when you contacted Fischers about the key, they expressed sufficient concern that they sent a man down to inspect their cabinet yesterday. To what address did you wire your request?"

"The . . . the workshop address on the delivery sales docket," the pale-faced don answered, recognising his error. "The note said to use that contact in case of concerns."

"The fellow they sent . . . He was from the rogue outfit who supplied this rogue contraption!" I realised.

"And thus he was well-positioned to inspect the cabinet and extract the manuscript as he looked the lectern over," Holmes suggested. "But we can easily check. Here is the hidden catch that releases the cupboard backboard. And here, behind this panel, the blank papers of our recent experiment. But no *Cardenio*."

"It was taken later," Dr. Chadbury raged. "From right under our noses!"

"But it was taken," the Dean mourned. "He has our *Cardenio*, as he boasted. What ever shall we do now?"

Holmes did not linger in Oxford, but instead took the Great Western Railway straight back to London, despite the lengthening of the day.

"You are eager to begin the hunt, Holmes," I observed. I was pleased to see my friend distracted from the morphine bottle and the cocaine syringe.

He looked up from the notes written by John Clay about the find in the Earl's library, as if surprised that anyone sat in the carriage compartment with him. "Either this is a fascinating forgery or a remarkable discovery. Do we have a hoax of Irelandian proportions, a revenge like Hamlet's, or a genuine revelation of undiscovered work from the world's finest author? Any would be worthy of study, but of course one must hope for the latter."

"You think the thief may have stolen a fake?"

"Men have deluded themselves before with fool's gold, Watson. The Samuel and William-Henry Ireland Affair of spring 1795 proved that. Did not the greatest literary men of the age gather at the home of the antiquarian Ireland to examine the Shakespearian documents he claimed to have unearthed? James Boswell, Samuel Johnson's biographer, was amongst those present who examined the proffered papers and considered them genuine, including the previously unheard-of play *Vortigen and Rowena*. [8] Francis Webb, then-secretary of the College of Heralds, pronounced that the play either came from Shakespeare's pen or from heaven."

"It proved to be neither," I surmised.

"It proved to be the work of Samuel Ireland's nineteen-year-old son William-Henry – but not until many professional reputations were ruined. The bloom came off the rose at a debut performance of *Vortigen* in the West End, where the audience were moved to revolt and the critics to derision. Eventually the work and all the accompanying correspondence, poems, and drawings were proved to be forgeries."

"Surely expert examination of the documents would have exposed the fraud immediately?"

"It was an age before forensic investigation, Doctor. And young William-Henry had been quite clever. He had cut and reused the blank fly-leaves from books of appropriate age. He used specially-mixed ink, which when heated over a fire took on a convincing brown colouration like authentic aged iron-gall ink. He rehearsed his penmanship until he was perfect. And he was clever enough to provide a scattering of authenticating papers and original errors to help sell the illusion." [9]

"Such a thing would not pass today, though," I insisted.

"You would be shocked and appalled by the extent," Holmes warned me. "When collectors will pay massive sums for rare manuscripts, there is every incentive for the cunning artificer to take trouble in creating such things. Our chemistry is now better at discerning the age and composition of paper – there are tests to determine whether modern rag was used in the mix – and of breaking down the composition and age of inks, but the test are not infallible. There has been considerable study of the calligraphy of forgeries also. I am considering a monograph upon the subject. The slant of the character, the crush of pen on paper, the quality and spacing of the lines can all be telling. But the detection of literary fakes remains an art, not a science."

"You only have John Clay's initial reports and observations to go on."

77

"Yes. He conducted as thorough an examination of paper, ink, and script as one might hope from an amateur, but one must rely upon his observations as accurate. He likewise examined the provenance of the papers in the Earl's collection as best he might, given his resources. His reports are thorough and coherent, belying the poor showing he made at his finals."

"Does he speak of the contents of the manuscripts?"

"Not much. He was wise enough to recognise the extreme fragility of the materials and not to try and separate the chap-book without expert intervention. Hence we only have the front and back pages to consider. The first is a frontispiece announcing the name of the play, publisher, and authors – '*Mr. Fletcher & Shakespeare*' – and featuring a fine engraving of the presumed protagonist and his *inamorata*. The rear of the bundle is the obverse of the hand-written notes, which Clay posits as a foul paper for the play."

I was not familiar with the term "foul paper". Holmes instructed me that it was an Elizabethan writer's term for a first-draft hand-written copy, as opposed to a fair copy written out in a clean clear hand without additional corrections or abbreviations. Very few examples of foul papers from that period are now extant. [10]

"Clay is hardly an expert in this field, however," Holmes cautioned. "His assertion of authenticity is not guarantee of veracity."

"So this *History of Cardenio* may well be spurious."

"Its theft is convenient," Holmes suggested. "It at once intensifies interest in the find and denies the opportunity to verify it."

"You cannot think the Earl or his nephew might perpetrate such a fraud."

"There are many crimes committed in the drawing rooms of the rich and powerful, Watson. But we need not yet impute such deeds to his Grace or his kin. *The History of Cardenio* may have lain unregarded in the late Earl's collection for many years, bought in with some job-lot or another and never recognised until Mr. Clay's recent appraisal. It may have been purchased in good faith, either by old Montguerre, or by whomever he acquired it from. This may not be a recent fraud but an historic one, dating back to the time when every forger aspired to be another Ossian." [11]

"You also mentioned revenge," I prompted Holmes. "It's certain that the manuscript theft has put the whole College foundation under a shadow."

"I am intrigued by our thief's monograph to Goneril," Holmes owned. "Whether it is intended to divert our understandings of motive from pecuniary to personal or as an actual act of malice, twisting the knife, it is a singular feature. Few robbers leave well-penned notes in good English outlining their intentions."

"I know that you can read much from a man's writing."

"Indubitably. But in this case my reading is that the correspondent has gone to some trouble to disguise his nature by disguising his script. He would have me think him a man educated some fifty years ago, taught his cursives on the old school, tutored in childhood with an old-fashioned quill, and retaining those habits into the era of the fountain-pen. It is a master-class in deception, and I doubt many would have seen through it to question its veracity."

"A forger might attempt such a dissembling. But that returns to the unlikelihood of a peer of the realm perpetrating such a fraud."

"If the document cabinet could be intercepted en route and substituted, then so might the manuscript," Holmes pointed out. "There are several possibilities. It is too early to draw conclusions. But if revenge is the issue, the choice of forged manuscript is telling."

"How so?" I was unfamiliar with the background of *The History Of Cardenio.*

"Shakespearian scholars remain ignorant of the nature of the supposed lost play," my thespian comrade instructed me. "The other unknown play listed in the same early source is *Love's Labours Won,* which might be presumed to be a sequel or bear some relationship to *Love's Labours Lost,* a play that *has* come down to us in the First Folio. But nothing in the early literature gives any clue as to the content of *Cardenio.*"

"Another reason why even a few sheets of the text might be invaluable," I supposed.

"A simple cast list would make and break scholarly theories. But there is only one other known instance of a literary character named Cardenio, a relatively minor player in Miguel de Cervantes's *Don Quixote.* The first part of that work was published in 1612. Shakespeare's collaborator Fletcher made use of Cervantes in several of his later plays. Scholarship favours *Quixote* as the source of the lost play, and that would present some basic idea of the plot."

"It is about revenge?"

"Quixote and Sancho Panza encounter the ragged mountain madman Cardenio and hear an account of the events that led to his condition. Cardenio was to wed his true-love, but was betrayed by his rich friend who also desired her, despite having contracted to wed a girl he had previously violated. Cardenio's heroine was to enter a forced marriage but planned suicide. Cardenio went to interrupt the marriage but fainted when the bride relented and said '*I do*'."

"And then it got bloody," I assumed.

"No. Cervantes' version ends with unlikely happiness, when the bride flees to find and rejoin the madman and the rich friend relents and weds his ravished previous love. It is a comedy."

I ventured that the subject matter did not appear that humorous to me.

"There is little amusing about this entire plot," Holmes brooded, staring out of the train window at the Oxfordshire countryside. "A stolen Shakespeare work is not funny. A literary hoax is not amusing. Our perpetrator, whatever he has actually perpetrated, thinks himself insouciant and clever. The jest does not sit well with me."

I have seen Holmes be cordial with murderers whose methods he has admired, but against the thief of *The History of Cardenio* he showed no such signs of mercy.

It was past ten in the evening when we emerged from the station onto Praed Street, our collars turned up against the new flakes of snow that were attempting to improve the grime of London. I had expected us to return to our quarters until we could make visits in the morning, perhaps beginning with the cabineter Fischer. Holmes had other ideas.

"There are some places and people we can only visit at this hour or later," he assured me as he directed our cabbie towards Shoreditch.

Holmes has a comprehensive knowledge of the back-alleys of our capital. I do not. I was lost less than two minutes into our foray on foot from Great Eastern Street. Either the Borough of Hackney does not spend its income on street signs or the residents of that parish delight in removing them.

We passed under several old brick arches, through grimy courtyards that looked like they had not been changed much since Jacobean times, spaces filled with old rotting barrels and collapsed carts and piles of stinking refuse. A couple of times Holmes turned and carefully lifted his walking cane as if signing to someone I did not see. I confess that I was concerned about footpads and wished that I had been able to go home and retrieve my bull-terrier and my service revolver.

At last we arrived at a worn staircase down to an anonymous cellar entrance. Holmes rapped upon the heavy door, an odd tattoo that might have been a code. A small hatch opened in the upper panel, and shortly afterwards the portal was unbolted to admit us.

It was the nest at the heart of the rookery. Stacked under the low barrel-roof were crate after crate of tangled clothing and building materials, china jars and piled furniture. A narrow passage through the detritus led us to a vast, cluttered desk lit by an old oil lamp, and the Dickensian character who crouched behind it.

The ugly bruiser who had opened the door padded behind us, too quiet for my liking.

"Mr. Shaddock," Holmes greeted the sparse-haired, hook-nosed creature who awaited us.

"Mr. Holmes," our host responded. "You has done me the honour of coming in your own persona tonight."

"I'm hoping this need not be a visit regarding the disappearance of a remover's wagon of goods destined for Rosebery Avenue, or the contents of the Clerkenwell Cricket Club's trophy cabinet," my friend replied. "I have come tonight seeking information."

"I don't peach to the coppers, Mr. Holmes. You knows that."

"Nor am I a member of Her Majesty's Constabulary. They wouldn't be allowed to offer you a one pound banknote for your valuable assistance."

Shaddock settled back. He stretched out a booted foot and nudged a rancid old tomcat off the chair opposite so that Holmes could sit. There was no third seat, so I took station to Holmes's left, where I could keep an eye on the doorman to his right.

"If I wished to dispose of a valuable historic manuscript that had been acquired by unscrupulous means, whom would I best approach at the moment?" my companion asked. "Old Granger? Peacock and Stone? The Chinaman? Meadowlark is out of the country just now, and Pullen is incarcerated."

"What period?" Shaddock asked carefully.

"Elizabethan. Ah, I see by your attempts to conceal your reaction that you know of the item to which I refer."

"I never said nothing like that."

"Come now, Shaddock. You would prefer to deflect my professional attention. I would prefer to get on with my present investigation. Let us collaborate."

There was more to-and-fro, more evidence that my friend could do irreparable damage to the goods-fence's business and possibly his liberty, and eventually the old rogue had to submit.

"As it happens, Mr. Holmes, I am aware of such an item being offered for sale. Well, not for sale, exactly. For *auction*."

"What do you mean?" I blurted, though I'd intended to stay out of it. I was picturing some dark room filled with criminals each holding up a numbered card to bid as the stolen *Cardenio* was demonstrated.

"A sealed-bid sale," Shaddock clarified. "Each of the men Mr. Holmes just named and a few others will contact their clients, the ones they know has a special interest in items of this type. The one as will pay most, they'll write his blind bid in a sealed envelope. When the bids are

81

opened, the winning middle-man will pay the promised sum and pass the manuscript on to their principal – with a handsome surcharge."

"None of the bidders are ever in the same room," Holmes told me. "None of them are known to the others. Their clients remain completely anonymous. What is the deadline for bids, Mr. Shaddock?"

"Nine p.m. tomorrow," the fence admitted.

"And how may additional bids be entered?"

Shaddock evidently considered denying that knowledge, but under the perceptive gaze of Sherlock Holmes his nerve faltered. He confessed that he was the agent to whom each of the bids was to be sent.

Holmes secured agreement for the College to make an offer to regain its stolen goods. Since the item was not on the premises and never would be, and there was no evidence that might secure any conviction, we accepted reality and took our leave.

"You knew he would be involved," I accused my friend as we departed that Aladdin's cave. [12] "That was why you came here."

"Shaddock was the most likely to be broker," Holmes agreed. He had us stand in a shadowed alcove where we might watch the old fence's door for a time. "If not him then Granger. Shaddock doesn't have the rich contacts to bring in the high-bidders on a stolen manuscript, but he is trusted by the men who do. Someone has been doing their homework, Watson."

"The thief has no intention of returning the document to Goneril College. Or of destroying it."

"The thief is playing a complicated and dangerous game. Entertain the possibility that the *Cardenio* manuscript is and has always been a forgery. Why forge one copy of the document only? Why not make six or eight identical duplicates, impossible to tell apart because they were all made by the same hand at the same time? Why not let each auction bidder believe that he and none other submitted the winning blind bid – and sell a fake to all of them?"

"The winner – or winners – would conceal their ownership of the stolen document. No other bidder would ever know of the multiple successes. And even if they did, what recourse would they have when they were knowingly purchasing purloined goods?"

"*Caveat emptor*," Holmes agreed with me. "Of course, that is speculation, but a possibility worth a little trouble to verify."

"We do not have long to do so," I pointed out. The sealed bids would be opened in less than twenty-four hours.

"We must hurry. I shall . . . ah, excuse me a moment, Watson." He paused and turned to address the shadows of the alley behind us. "I am Sherlock Holmes. My companion and I are armed and well able to defend ourselves, using lethal force if required. I suggest you leave off your inept pursuit and find other more productive means of income. In any case, I would be obliged if you either come out now and make your futile attempt to assail us or else go away and cease to bother me."

He waited a short while to meet any response to his challenge, but none ever came. Eventually we went home.

I slept later than I had planned the following morning, but Holmes had clearly been awake for hours. Mrs. Hudson had already supplied a second rack of toast and another plate of breakfast meats.

I staggered yawning towards the table and only then became aware that Holmes was conferring with our houseboy Billy, receiving messages and sending others.

"What are you up to?" I asked our young page.

"Telegrams an' favours," he replied.

"Urgent ones," Holmes impressed on the lad, dispensing him a rasher of bacon to reward him for his efforts so far and to see him on his way.

Billy clattered out, earning a reprimand from our landlady on the stairs. I settled behind a plate of scrambled eggs and kedgeree and enquired again as to Holmes's doings.

"I have been gathering my evidence," Holmes announced as if lecturing at the Royal Society. "No single point is conclusive, but together they are suggestive."

I saw the pile of telegram message papers discarded beside his chair and a number of Holmes's big clipping files opened on a buffet.

"I have borrowed sales ledgers from A. Fischer and Sons of Waterloo," the detective told me. "The signature commissioning the Cabinet was the Dean's, as was the note of hand that outlined the agreed specifications for the loaned document. Those specifications were for a robust lectern of the kind eventually delivered, identical in measurements, but not one of such mechanical cunning."

"That's how the case was substituted, then," I recognised.

"Another letter was received at Fischer's, in a hand very like the Dean's and signed in his name, directing the new cabinet be delivered to a different address. The cabinet was received there and paid for, at a furniture shop in Headington, a few miles from Oxford proper. I have just received a wire back from the proprietor informing me that a gentleman paid for him to take delivery of the item and store it until called for."

"Can he describe the gentleman?"

"Billy is dispatching my supplementary enquiry even now, along with another seeking a better description from a carter in Aylesbury who hired his cart and team to a carpenter's work-crew to deliver some furniture to

Oxford on the day that the false cabinet was delivered. A special hire-fee was paid because it was supposedly an urgent job."

"The thief had to have accomplices."

"The sheer weight of the cabinet would require that, yes. I will be interested if the descriptions of the diligent carpenter and the Headington gentleman match up with that of Fischer's supposed craftsman who examined the 'emptied' case. Meanwhile . . . ." He handed me another note.

"The thief has sent another message to the College! Or is he a blackmailer?"

The letter had evidently arrived at Goneril with the last post yesterday, and the Dean had forwarded it hastily with the first collection today, which meant that by eleven it was on our doormat. I scanned the contents of the new message, written in the same neat hand as before on the same bonded paper.

> *I still have your* Cardenio, *your reputations, and your College's future. Another £500 proffered by noon in the same way as before will stay my malice for another while, but we must consider what is going to become of Goneril and the manuscript in the longer term. What of the word and bond offered to poor Montguerre? What of the academic liabilities? What of the treasure you are like to lose?*
>
> *I have your* Cardenio. *Further instructions will follow.*

"This fellow is decidedly unpleasant and a gloater to boot," I commented.

"Do not underestimate the value of gloating, Watson. It is that flaw which has caused the downfall of many a malefactor. Indeed, this second missive with its triumphal tone helps confirm the solution to our mystery. No, pray do not ask me yet to unfold the story. You know I prefer to have my solutions neatly assembled before presentation."

"Very well. You have your methods. May I at least enquire about your other messages this morning?"

My breakfast companion gestured to the papers under the sugar basin. "Some financial and biographical material on the main people associated with the case. A few theses from the Goneril College archives, couriered up overnight. Opinion from a couple of the best forgers I know, men at the top of their profession, on what would be required to create a credible Shakespearian facsimile."

"Forgers? Holmes!"

"I have had some strange apprenticeships to develop my clinical skills, Doctor. You had to cut open cadavers. I had to make other experiments no less unpleasant. Anyhow, I am now more confident in the likely way that any forgery might be made."

"Do you still fear that the original *Cardenio* might have been diverted between the Earl and the College?"

"I fear . . . well, we shall see when we examine the document, Watson. We shall go and review it once you have finished your breakfast."

I almost choked on my mouthful. "You know where it is?"

"I know the present address of the man who is selling it," Holmes told me. "I hope that will suffice."

Dunn's Mercantile Hotel was an unremarkable lodging house off Seymour Street. It offered twenty-two bedrooms for travelling salesmen, mostly catering to ambassadors of the pharmaceutical and dentistry companies, but its best room had been booked for six weeks by a gentleman who was evidently in town filling in for a colleague who had suffered a light stroke.

"Mr. Theobald is no trouble," the landlord's caretaker assured us. "A proper gentleman, he is, with nice manners indeed. A cut above, really."

"And he shares his name with the eighteenth-century editor and author Lewis Theobald,"[13] Holmes noted wryly. "The fellow who claimed to have obtained three Restoration-era manuscripts of an unnamed Shakespeare play, which he edited, 'improved', and published under the name *Double Falshood, or the Distrest Lovers*. The plot is the same as that of Cardenio in *Quixote*, but the names are all changed. Most scholars dismiss the works as lacking veracity.[14] The original material may have derived from John Fletcher – few see Shakespeare's genuine hand. But it is a telling choice of pseudonym for our quarry."

The caretaker didn't follow Holmes's literary digression. "His name is not apt," he valiantly tried to keep up, "because he is far from bald. Indeed, he has a fine mane of ginger-red hair."

"I suppose he left early this morning, having received a telegram."

"Why yes, sir," the caretaker puzzled. "Strange you might guess that. And stranger still the message, which was all nonsense words, all letters just jumbled up like. It happens I oversaw it when Mr. Theobald came for his post." He hastened to explain that occasionally his gentlemen guests received racing tips from pals, and that a couple of times he had ventured a "gainful flutter" on some message he had "overseen". He surmised that on this occasion some racing-savvy sporting friend of Theobald's had chosen to use some secret code.

"This was the telegram you tracked," I guessed.

85

Holmes now revealed the detail to me. "Once I had verified Shaddock as the handler of the stolen property and let him know that I was on to him, it was only natural that he would wish to warn his principal. Our vigil last night was in vain, so it was evident that he would wish to send a warning telegram first thing today. I placed Billy to hand around the nearest post office, to read off the address that Shaddock's hulking thug wrote on the sending slip. And here we are."

"And if Shaddock had chosen some other way to communicate his alert?"

"There were other measures in place too, but I need not bother you with such commonplace precautions. They will hardly make for a compelling narrative in your notebook. Sufficient that we have located the temporary digs of our manuscript thief, while he is in Oxford collecting fees at the Martyrs Memorial."

The threat of police attention bringing disrepute to Dunn's Mercantile and the exchange of a crown were sufficient to win us entry to Theobald's "best room in the house". Holmes dismissed the caretaker and proceeded to examine the place.

Everything was neat and tidy. Three shirts were hung in the wardrobe, but most of Theobald's possessions were still in a suitcase. "He is not here much," I deduced.

"This is merely a mailing address and changing room," Holmes told me. "Look at this theatrical make-up kit, similar to my own. Doubtless the hobo outfit left with Theobald. Here in this satchel is a Fischer and Sons delivery smock. And here – hidden under the bed – a sealed document box."

Holmes found a roll of precision tools in a bedside drawer, and proceeded to use Theobald's own lock-picks to open his chest. Inside were not one but nine identical bundles of documents.

"The *Cardenio*!" I exclaimed. "Or . . . *Cardenios*."

"Our villain does not think small, Watson. And each of these is indistinguishable from the others. Let me see . . . yes, the paper appears authentic at first inspection, and the writing on the foul page is of appropriate style." He sighed unhappily. "They are most excellent forgeries."

"Might not one be genuine? Or all of them copies of some real original that is not here?"

"The holographic script is well done. The printing facsimile is excellent. But alas, Watson, the language – ! Shakespeare's genius is much harder to forge."

He flipped the engraved title page and the *dramatis personae* and intoned some lines of the prologue:

> "'*True love brings joys and virtues with its bloom*
> *But sorrows and misfortune when it's lost*
> *And so Cardenio comes upon his doom*
> *And learns of love's damnations at his cost* . . . .'"

Holmes shook his head. "Fool's gold. Dross." He seemed more offended by the odd Shakespeare than by the thefts or blackmail.

"We have discovered all, then," I consoled him. "This man calling himself Theobald . . . ."

"Thinks he has been very clever. Thinks himself a genius to match the Bard! He believes that by taking a false name and hiring temporary rooms he can insulate himself, another faked identity like those he used to execute each of the other elements of his plot. But nobody can make a fool of himself like a clever man."

Holmes rose and pointed to the wardrobe. "He has erased the laundry marks on his shirts, as if I could not name the laundry by touch and smell alone. He has left us ample samples of his style of prose, not only in his execrable *faux*-Cardenio, but also in his rambling ransom demands. He has shown a knowledge of College procedures and of the weaknesses and responses of its dons."

"You know this Theobald's actual identity, then?"

"I have read his graduate thesis, Watson. It was adequate, but afflicted with the same arrogance of opinion and overconfidence that we saw in his demand notes, and in his hubris at emulating Shakespeare. You will recall that this entire project was initiated by correspondence from the manuscript's alleged discoverer, Mr. John Clay."

"The late Earl's grandson? The alumnus of Goneril?"

"The fellow who might be best positioned to turn the screw on the unfortunate and disgraced academics who dared to give his work a second-class degree, and whose finances might benefit from an input of eight or nine sales of black-market Elizabethan dramas. I have investigated his affairs, Watson – he no longer receives any stipend since his grandfather died. He is under a cloud for some family business that I have not yet discovered."

"We must have him arrested."

"We must catch him in the act. No other evidence will do here, Watson. Clay has been cunning in distancing himself from his plans. No point of proof exists good enough for a jury unless we can catch Theobald returning for his masterpieces."

"If he picks up the money from the statue as he did before, will he not next return here?" I anticipated. "His planned auction is tonight."

"We can but settle in and hope," Holmes told me.

We hunkered down to await John Clay.

But John Clay did not come.

"He is gone," Holmes told me the following day, after whatever exhaustive enquiries he had sent in train were completed. "Clay scented the wind and knew that the game was up. He has cut his losses and departed."

"Leaving us with no firm proof of his misdeeds," I complained.

"Leaving us with the supposed *Cardenio*, for return to Goneril College and verification as a fake. The University's reputation will be untarnished and duplicates and original documents alike are worthless. And do not forget that Clay's name is now known, not just to the College authorities, but to the Earl and his people, and to the Detective Branch at Scotland Yard. A vigil will be kept. Clay will not walk so anonymously in future."

"But he does walk away. He walks off with a thousand pounds extorted from Goneril to encourage him in his criminal career!"

"Rather say he hastens offstage, pursued by a bear. [15] Old Shaddock knows of the deception now, and how he almost risked his reputation in support of a confidence trick. Shaddock and his large friend do not require the same standards of evidence as Her Majesty's courts. Mr. Clay had better lie low for a time if he cares for his health."

I supposed that was better than no consequence at all. "What will happen to the forged manuscripts now?" I wondered.

Holmes told me that Dr. Chadbury intended to keep one for the College as a curiosity, believing it to be a superior facsimile.

But Holmes had no interest in a souvenir himself. The documents offended him.

"[John Clay and I] have had some skirmishes, but we had never set eyes upon each other before."

– Sherlock Holmes
"The Red-Headed League"

NOTES

1. Holmes recounts his first detective case in his Oxford days to Watson in "The Adventure of the Gloria Scott" (*The Memoirs of Sherlock Holmes,* 1893). Sherlockian biographer W.S. Baring-Gould offers additional detail in *Sherlock Holmes* (1962), explaining that Holmes was studying mathematics at his father's behest with a view to becoming an engineer, that Holmes's encounter with fellow student Victor Trevor and his subsequent investigation of Trevor's problem convinced him to instead become a consulting detective, and that Holmes quit his studies after his second year against his father's wishes, to take up his new profession. Baring-Gould also postulates an acquaintance between Holmes and Christ Church Don Charles, Lutwidge Dodson (Lewis Carroll). According to this biography, Holmes later completed a course of study in science at Gonville and Caius College, Cambridge. Baring-Gould further suggests that Watson was educated at Melbourne College in Australia and makes a case for Watson's upbringing in the Antipodes, but there is no Canon evidence for this part of Watson's history.
2. Watsonian misdirection appears to be masking the identity of the academic institution he and Holmes visited. Given his description of the geography, it was most likely either Balliol or St John's College, or possibly Trinity.
3. It was well known to Holmes by the time he investigated "The Red-Headed League" in *The Adventures of Sherlock Holmes* (1891).
4. The gothic memorial was raised to completion in 1843 to commemorate the "Oxford Martyrs" Hugh Latimer, Bishop of Worcester and Nicholas Ridley, Bishop of London, who were burned to death nearby for their Protestant faith on sixteenth October, 1555, and Thomas Cramner, Archbishop of Canterbury, who was executed shortly after. The edifice closely resembles the peak of a church spire, and for much of the early twentieth century, Oxford undergraduates were pleased to inform tourists that it was the top of a sunken underground cathedral and to accept small fees to allow access through a nearby staircase entrance. These steps actually lead to a Victorian public toilet.
5. The Tailor Institute is the Oxford University Library for European Languages, established in 1845.
6. One such performer was the gifted and notorious *Mme*. Irene Adler.
7. Baring-Gould suggests that Holmes toured America as part of Sassinoff's Troupe in 1878-80, and that *"his Malvolio offered the most adequate presentation of that character that America had ever seen up to that time."* This tour may account for Holmes' occasional Canon reminiscences of the United States and for his knowledge of its people and customs.
8. Vortigen was a fifth-century English warlord, described by Geoffrey of Monmouth as the King of England and as a usurper tyrant. His marriage to the Saxon princess Rowena opened the way for the Saxon and Angle invasions and occupations of southern Britain. Vortigen is best remembered

89

now for his early part in the story of Kings Uther and Arthur Pendragon, and for his unfortunate encounter with the youthful Merlin.

9. After eventual exposure, Ireland shamelessly continued to exploit his forgeries in extra-illustrated printed confessions, incorporating copies of selected forgeries along with other materials, "*aimed not to deceive, but rather to provide entertaining fare for bibliophile collectors*". "Miscellaneous Papers and Legal Instruments under the Hand and Seal of William Shakespeare . . . ." (1796), is interleaved with mounted forgeries of the complete *King Lear*, a small fragment of *Hamlet*, and an assortment of forged letters and documents. "The Confessions of William Henry Ireland: Containing the Particulars of his Fabrications of the Shakespeare Manuscripts . . . ." (1805) includes manuscript sheet music for songs from *Vortigern and Rowena*.

10. One such example from Folger Shakespeare Library, Ms.J.b.8, containing lines from Christopher Marlowe's *The Massacre at Paris* (1593), is reproduced at:
https://en.wikipedia.org/wiki/Foul_papers#/media/File:Handwriting-Marlowe-Massacre-1.JPG

11. From *Fragments of Ancient Poetry* collected in the Highlands of Scotland, and translated from the Gaelic or Erse language (1760) to *The Works of Ossian* (1765), Scottish poet James MacPherson published the English-language text of purported works of an early Gaelic bard named Ossian, son of Finn MacCool. These texts, supposedly gathered from native folk-accounts, were later believed to have been almost entirely fabricated by MacPherson himself. Samuel Johnson condemned him as "*a mountebank, a liar, and a fraud . . . the poems were forgeries*" and dismissed the story of Ossian as "*as gross an imposition as ever the world was troubled with*". By Holmes's era, Ossian was generally dismissed as a work of eighteenth-century fiction. Some twentieth-century scholars prefer to argue for authenticity in MacPherson's source material. Experts continue to publish on the matter and nothing can apparently stop them.

12. The tale of Aladdin, from "Alf Laylah wa-Laylah", the Arabic corpus of Middle Eastern folk tales compiled during the Islamic Golden Age, was first introduced to European readers in *Les Mille et une nuits, contes arabes traduits en français*" (1707-1717, 12 volumes) and was popularised in Britain in Edward Lane's *One Thousand and One Nights* (1840). However, Watson is likely to have picked up John Payne's *The Book of the Thousand Nights and One Night* (1882, nine volumes) or Sir Richard Francis Burton's *The Book of the Thousand Nights and a Night* (1885, ten volumes), which were much in vogue in the latter part of the Victorian era and influenced a fashion for Turkish and Arabic art, fictional settings, and architecture.

13. Theobald (1688-1744) earned the enmity of playwright Alexander Pope, who wrote him as "Theobald the Fool" into his first release of his scathing satirical poem *The Dunciad*, a mock-epic about the goddess Dulness and her faithful servants.

14. The 2010 Arden Shakespeare included *Double Falsehood* in its series of scholarly editions of Shakespeare's collected works, and its editor, Professor Brean Hammond, made a case for Theobald's play having Shakespearian origins. It has since been produced on stage several times, beginning with a 2011 performance by the Royal Shakespeare Company.
15. Holmes refers to the famous stage instruction to Antigonus in *A Winter's Tale*, Act III, Scene 3.

The Adventure of the Loring Riddle
by Craig Janacek

August is often the most stagnant and oppressive month in the twisting alleys of London, when everyone who can manage is out in the countryside or on the shores. Mr. Sherlock Holmes was in a perpetually impatient mood, for he had no work during the last few weeks, and his mental engine was always unhappy with idleness. It was thus with a sigh of relief when I opened the door one morning and found the district messenger-boy with a letter for my friend.

Holmes sprang from his arm-chair, where he had been listlessly scratching some notes on his violin, and plucked the jack-knife from the wooden mantelpiece. Slicing the envelope with a violent stroke, he studied the paper inside closely, and then looked up at me. "Ah, Watson!" he cried. "We walk in fashionable circles. This invitation might interest you." He handed me the letter, which ran in this way:

My Dear Mr. Sherlock Holmes,

It is said by certain trustworthy individuals that I may set unreserved confidence upon your acumen and prudence. I, therefore, request your presence at the Reform Club in hopes of consulting you in regards to a concerning family matter. I assure you that this will be a matter worthy of your time. I trust that you will be able to call today, and that no other engagement will preclude our meeting. I shall be lodging at the Club. As you surely know, the Reform never closes and should it be late, the footman can summon me from the gentlemen's chambers.

Yours faithfully,
Sir Neil Loring-Edricson

"Will you go?" I asked.

He shrugged. "I do not see why not. I have no other case to occupy me at the moment. The odds are that it will prove to be some minor scandal, such as what once befell Lord Arnsworth. However, no matter how frugal one may be, I cannot live upon intellectual stimulation alone, so as long as the matter is not completely devoid of interest, my cheque-book will be gratified if I hear him out. Will you join me?"

"I have no patients this morning, so I see no reason to forgo such an opportunity. It is not every day that the hallowed doors of Pall Mall are opened to a humble former Army surgeon."

Despite the early hour, the weather was stifling, and Holmes suggested that we engage a hansom cab. This quickly whisked us through Marylebone and Mayfair until we came to our destination, which lay in the most fashionable area of London.

The exterior of the three-story palatial building was a comprised of a rather plain stone facing with rows of severe windows. There were no markings to note that the black doors belonging to Number 104 were the entrance to the Reform Club. This bastion of progressive thought comprised the Liberal Party's *de facto* headquarters. However, once Holmes had knocked, and our names checked against a list, we were whisked into the impressive central Saloon. Two stories of Italianate marble columns rose up to a high glass-domed ceiling. We stood on intricate tiles, as the men responsible for the direction of the Empire strode past the various marble busts and oil paintings representing the club's past members. [1]

"Mr. Holmes," called a voice. This belonged to a slight man, of roughly five-and-sixty who was approaching from down a massive staircase to our left. His features were delicate and regular, with a clear-cut, curving nose. His blue eyes protruded forward from the lids, which gave him a permanently surprised impression. His dress was simple and yet spruce. "Thank you for coming so quickly," he continued. His soft voice had a curious lisping tone, which suggested a man of gentle ways. "I am Sir Neil Loring-Edricson." He glanced over at me, questioningly.

"Of course, Sir Neil," said Holmes. "This is Dr. John Watson, my close partner and helper in many of my most successful cases. He has been of the utmost use to me, and his discretion is unparalleled. I trust that it was acceptable to include him?"

Sir Neil considered this request for a moment before nodding. "Certainly. If you would join me in the Stranger's Room," said he, motioning to a door to the right of the entrance. Inside this luxurious bookcase-lined room, a number of men were sitting about on burgundy leather armchairs and reading papers. He waved us to an empty trio of chairs near the mirror at the far end. Once we were settled in, our host began to relate the reason for his meeting request. "I have it from my friend that you are a clever man, Mr. Holmes," said he.

"Oh, and who would that be?"

"Lord St. Simon."

Holmes's eyebrows rose with interest. "I thought Lord St. Simon was rather put out by the final result of my inquiry."

Sir Neil smiled. "I am certain that Robert was less than gracious in the heat of the moment, but – as the old saying goes – time heals all wounds. He has since realized that you saved him, Mr. Holmes, from the sad fate of never knowing what happened to his erstwhile wife. Far better to realize immediately that their union was never a legal one. And Lord St. Simon is in a rather jollier mood of late, for he has found a new object for his affections." He passed a copy of *The Morning Post* to Holmes, its pages turned back to the personal column.

"I see," said Holmes, handing it to me. I read the beginning, which ran:

> *A marriage has been arranged and will, if rumour is correct, very shortly take place, between Lord Robert St. Simon, second son of the Duke of Balmoral, and Miss Henrietta Vanselle, the only daughter of Mr. Anthony Vanselle, the railway tycoon of Manhattan, New York.*

"And do you share a similar problem to his Lordship?" Holmes continued. "Has your bride vanished?"

"No," said Sir Neil, with a frown. "My wife passed on two years ago and I have no intention of remarrying. Instead, I find myself pondering loftier matters. We had no children, Mr. Holmes. When I pass on from this mortal world, I would like to know whom amongst my relatives I may trust with my estate."

"Are you dying, Sir Neil?"

"Not rapidly, but I am no longer a young man. The reaper will eventually come for me, as it comes for all."

Holmes nodded. "Wiser words were never spoken. So what is your problem, Sir Neil?"

The man puffed silently upon his pipe. "You see, Mr. Holmes," said Sir Neil, "my family has a peculiar riddle, which has been handed down from father to son for many centuries, to be read aloud on St. George's Day. [2] The legend holds that the riddle was devised by my ancestor, Sir Alleyne. He had been raised in the great Cistercian Abbey of Beaulieu, where he had received an education on the level of that of any clerk of Cambridge or Oxford. Sadly, the meaning of it – presuming there was once a meaning – has been lost."

"May I see it?"

Sir Neil smiled. "I will do you one better, Mr. Holmes," said he. "I will recite it for you. Here are the questions, if you would be so good as to ask them of me." He handed over a sheet of paper, upon which I could see typewritten words.

"If this riddle has been passed through your family for generations, then this is not the original," said Holmes.

"True. The original is too fragile to handle. It is now preserved under glass. I assure you this is a faithful copy. Would you please read it aloud?"

Holmes shrugged and handed it to me.

"*To whom did it belong?*" I read.

"*The head of the free,*" answered Sir Neil.

"*Who bequeathed it?*"

"*The prince who is captive.*"

"*Where does it rest?*"

"*In the Wild Wasteland.*"

"*How may we find it?*"

"*The pall wavy reversed.*"

"*What is in the east?*"

"*The Beautiful place.*"

"*What is in the west?*"

"*The foe of George.*"

"*What is in the north?*"

"*The flow of Red blood.*"

"*What is in the middle?*"

"*The Sight skewbald.*"

"*Where does it lay?*"

"*Eight furlongs from the North.*"[3]

"*Who guards it?*"

"*All the Saints above.*"

"*What protects it?*"

"*The blessed rood,*" concluded Sir Neil.

"Ah, yes, I have seen something of it's like before," said Holmes. He turned to look at me. "You recall what transpired down at Hurlstone, Watson."[4]

I nodded, "Yes, it is remarkably similar."

"You may keep it, Doctor, if you are interested," our host continued. "I have another copy. I suppose that many ancient families have developed similar rituals in order to strengthen the chain that links back to their honoured past," said Sir Neil, wistfully. "My family is no different. Moreover, my lineage, while not particularly elevated, can be traced all the way to one who bore the shield for the first William at Senlac.[5] Sadly, that is all about to end, unless I were to adopt one of my sister's children and make them a Loring-Edricson. So that is what I have proposed to do."

Holmes shrugged. "And how may I be of assistance in such a matter?"

"My family has long lived at Tilford Manor House, which is situated a few miles southeast of Farnham in Surrey. The estate once possessed rather vast land holdings throughout the South Downs, but is no longer as large as it once was. It would be foolish to attempt to split it up, for divided it would be worth almost nothing. Fortunately there is no entail, so I may pass it on to whomever I choose. My sister Maude was a lovely girl, if a bit naïve. She fell in love with a wool merchant by the name of Walter Cooper. Sadly, she died decades ago in her labour bed, giving birth to the second of her children. Walter did his best to raise them on his own, before he too died a few years back. I had far too infrequent contact with my niece and nephew when they were young, but have endeavoured to rectify that mistake of late. Therefore, they knew relatively little about our family's long history. A few months ago, I asked them to come down to Tilford for St. George's Day. When they arrived, I read them the riddle again, but this time request that they actually attempt to solve the meeting of it. To sweeten the pot, I informed them that the individual who first did so would become my heir."

Holmes's right eyebrow rose with interest. "Ah, was that wise?"

"Perhaps not," said Sir Neil, nodding slowly. "But it has long been the way with my family. We have always loved to contest. There may no longer be any chivalric tournaments with swordplay and jousting, but the spirit of competition remains strong."

"Tell me about your niece and nephew," asked Holmes.

"Well, Trudy is the elder. She is an author of some repute."

"Oh?" said I, with interest. "Anything I would have read?"

He shook his head. "*The Table Round*? No? *The Furious Horn*? Ah, perhaps that is not surprising. Sadly, her works are well reviewed but rarely read, for they are serious historical novels, and not some tawdry popular fiction. She lives in London, of course. The younger is Allen. He is a major of Artillery, based at Woolwich."

"So what is the problem?" said Holmes, plainly growing uninterested in this trivial family matter.

"The problem, Mr. Holmes, is the dead man in my library."

Holmes sat up with sudden interest. "Ah! Well that is something altogether different. If you would be so kind as to elaborate."

"Yesterday was my birthday. To celebrate with me, I invited the two of them down to Tilford again, along with my friend Dean Adams from Canterbury, who was fascinated in my family's peculiar catechism when he first heard it. To be honest, I was interested whether either of them had made progress on the family riddle."

96

"And had they?" I interjected.

"Not that I could tell. Of course, the problem is that I myself do not know the answer and thus it may be difficult to prove that one potential solution is the correct one."

"How did you intend to deal with that possibility?" I inquired.

Sir Neil shrugged. "I assumed that it would simply feel correct when I heard the proper elucidation."

"Pray continue," said Holmes.

"Well, we had a pleasant dinner and conversation afterwards. Some minutes after eleven o'clock I had tucked in for the night. The next thing I knew I was being shaken awake by Allen. The sun's rays were just beginning to appear in the east, so I knew it was not yet five in the morning. As the fog cleared from my brain, I listened to Allen's fevered whispers. He had risen early, per his usual military routine, and gone into the library to read until the rest of the household had begun to stir. To his vast surprise, there was a man lying upon the Wilton carpet, a paper-knife buried in his heart. Allen confirmed the man's lack of pulse, and then went to wake me, so that we could decide what to do. By the time my nephew had completed his tale, I had thrown on a dressing-gown and descended the stairs. Crossing the foyer to the library, I confirmed that there was indeed a dead stranger in my house."

"So you do not know him?" interjected Holmes.

Sir Neil shook his head. "No. I am confident that I have never seen the man before."

"Can you describe him?"

Holmes's client closed his eyes, as if to help him remember. "He was about forty years of age, middle-sized, with curly brown hair and a handlebar moustache."

Holmes nodded. "And what did you do next?"

"I called in the Inspector Booker of the Surrey Constabulary. He looked about for a while, but could make neither heads nor tails of the matter. No one in the house knew the man."

"And no one admitted to stabbing him, I presume?" asked Holmes.

"No. That is what is so odd, Mr. Holmes. If the dead man was a burglar, whoever stabbed him might simply acknowledge their action. Under the Castle Doctrine, they could not possibly be held accountable for his death." [6]

"You know your common law, Sir Neil," said Holmes, plainly impressed.

"In my youth, I spent some time at Inner Temple. Therefore, I was bewildered why no one would admit to confronting the burglar, especially after I explained the stance of the law is such a situation. That is when I recalled Lord St. Simon relating how you had located his first intended bride by studying a hotel receipt, while Scotland Yard was busy dragging the Serpentine. I realized that if anyone could deduce why there was a dead man in the library, it was you. As there were no trains running at that early hour, I had my driver bring me up to town. Despite my excitement, I lay down for an hour upstairs, and sent that note round to you as soon as seemly."

"And what do you propose?"

"I wish for you to return with me to Tilford forthwith, while the trail is still warm, as they say. Inspector Booker will be glad of the assistance, for certs."

"One more question, Sir Neil. Besides your family and Dean Adams, who else was present in the house? You must have servants?"

"Of course. Such a place as Tilford requires considerable maintenance. Besides the garden and stable staff, there are two maids, a cook, butler, and footman. But they do not reside in the house proper. You see, Mr. Holmes, the manor house is perhaps the oldest inhabited building in the county. It has been much added to and altered over the centuries, but with great age comes great peculiarities not present in a building purposely designed all at once. The main house is a rather simple pile of rude blocks of stone, framed in heavy beams of wood, with two stories. The upper floor is all sleeping rooms, while below there are only two rooms, the smaller of which is the library. The larger is the hall, which has served as the living room and common dining room since the days of the Conqueror.

"The dwellings of these servants, the kitchens, the offices, and the stables are all represented by a row of houses and sheds behind the main building, clinging to the old house as barnacles to some old vessel. To enter the main building, they would need come through either the main door, the opening of which is loud enough to wake the dead, or through the back entrance, to which only the butler holds the key. Therefore, there is no reason to think that any of them would be in the library at night."

"Surely the dead man gained entrance in some fashion?" asked Holmes. "Unless you are proposing that he slipped in while the main door was open?"

"No, I am not. You are correct, Mr. Holmes. In fact, Inspector Booker noted that one of the windows leading to the library was jimmied open."

"Ah, so a common burglar, perhaps?" said Holmes. "But who killed him and why do they not come clean?" He shook his head. "It is a pretty problem, Sir Neil. I would be happy to come down to Tilford and take a glance about."

That is how several hours later, we found ourselves disembarking the Waterloo-train at Farnham Station. From there, Sir Neil's trap drove us through a series of lovely Surrey lanes and villages. While the heat of London was oppressive, here amongst the trees and wayside hedges a pleasant breeze and pillows of massive white clouds provided respite from the bright sun's rays. As we came over a slope, I saw beneath us a winding river with an old high-backed bridge across it. On the farther side was a village green with a fringe of cottages and, upon the side of the hill, a dark manor house, its grey gables and machicolations visible above the trees.

"That is Tilford," said Sir Neil, with evident pride. "The bridge was rebuilt in the reign of Mary and William, but it was upon an earlier structure that my ancestor once tilted against the knights of Edward III, in hopes of making a name for himself."

A keen-faced young man was waiting for us in the hall of the Manor House, which looked as if it had little changed since the days when knights errant roamed the medieval forests and fields seeking adventure. The floors were stone, and covered with plush carpets of deep scarlet and azure. A long wooden buffet loaded with plates and dishes filled one end of the room, some old benches lined the walls, and one old table was littered with chessmen and a great iron candelabra. A quartet of more modern chairs gathered about a large empty fireplace, above which were displayed a myriad of coats-of-arms, all grouped around a silver shield painted with red roses.

The room was spanned sideways by heavy oaken beams from which a great number of objects were hanging. There were mail-shirts of obsolete pattern, several shields, one or two rusted and battered helmets, bowstaves, lances, and other implements of war or of the chase. Higher still amid the black shadows of the peaked roof, great iron hooks gave testament to an age when the room would have been hung with the salted hams, venison, geese, and other forms of preserved meat that formed the mainstay of the medieval diet. After we had taken in our surroundings, Sir Neil introduced the waiting man as Inspector Booker.

"You found no identification upon the body?" Holmes asked the policeman.

"None."

"Anything of note in his pockets?"

"Only a pouch of paper and tobacco."

"Ah!" exclaimed Holmes. "May I see it?"

Booker produced the pouch and handed it to Holmes, who proceeded to shake some of the loose leaf onto one of the tables. "Look, Watson! Surely, that is no Cavendish or Grosvenor mixture. No, unless I miss my guess, these are the leaves of the Gros Caillou manufactory, on the left bank of the Seine."

"French tobacco?" said I.

"Indeed. An odd choice for the common burglar." He turned to the inspector. "The body is undisturbed?"

"Yes, Mr. Holmes. If you will step this way . . . ." Booker waved his hand towards a door leading off the hall. This opened into a bookcase-lined room, filled with tomes that were plainly ancient. I noted that many of the older ones were secured to iron rails by chains of sufficient length to reach the table in the middle of the room. My attention was immediately drawn to the body upon the rug, which was exactly as described by Sir Neil. Holmes knelt beside it and his nimble fingers began to examine the corpse. His eyes took on a far-away expression. Finally, he nodded and stretched back up to standing.

"What do you see, Watson?"

I considered this. "His nails are heavily stained, as I would expect from a heavy tobacco user."

Holmes shook his head. "No, no, you are missing the most important clue of all. Look at his flannel topcoat. It has peaked lapels, a flat back and no belt. Its double-breasted six-by-two button arrangement has its top buttons placed wider. Could you find such a thing on Savile Row or Bond Street? Of course not, for this is what is known as a *paletot*, and it is distinctly French in cut."

"So the dead man is French?" exclaimed Inspector Booker.

"So it seems. While at first blush this finding may not seem to be of much utility – as we have merely narrowed it to some thirty-five million souls – the one defining feature of these individuals is that most of them are presently residing in France. You might inquire at Newhaven and Dover for anyone who meets his description, though the odds are . . . What is this?" he suddenly exclaimed, starting at the floor. Holmes looked sharply at the man. "Why did you not mention the dead man's candle, Inspector?"

Booker frowned. "He had no candle, Mr. Holmes."

"Do you see this?" said Holmes, pointing to a splash of wax. Using a small blade, he scraped it from the floor and held it out for the three of us to examine.

"What of it, Mr. Holmes?" asked Sir Neil.

"Do you see the deep ruby colour of the spermaceti? It is unlike any other which I have thus far seen in your house, which are made from golden tallow."

"So it was brought by the dead Frenchman?" asked Booker.

"Or the person who killed him," replied Holmes. "For there were two individuals in this library last night. Since men who vanish are invariably missed in time, the dead man we will inevitably identify. But the other is the more interesting. Did he or she bring his or her own candle? If so, why? Why not use the ones in the house? If not, why did they take the Frenchman's candle with them when they fled?" He shook his head. "It is most puzzling." He looked up at the policeman. "Inspector, I assume you have your men asking at the local towns and villages for men who have recently taken rooms there?"

"Yes, Mr. Holmes. That is standard practice."

"You might instruct them to clarify their question that they are looking for a Frenchman. It is possible that his accent was so minimal that his nationality was not evident, but it's worth a shot."

"Very good, sir," said Booker, before stepping out.

Holmes turned to his client. "Now then. Plainly, our Frenchman was looking for something in this room when he was interrupted. Is there anything of note in the library?"

Sir Neil considered this. "Well, we have been acquiring books for five-hundred years, and rarely – if ever – part with them. There might be some of value, I suppose. There is a fine copy of Golding's *Ovid* on the third shelf from the door, for example. [7] But no First Folio that I am aware of."

"Unless you believe that our Frenchman chose your house at random, there must be something that is unique in this room."

"Well, there are the old family records," admitted Sir Neil. "They were begun by an ancestor of mine, Lady Maude, who first united the houses of Loring and Edricson. She was quite a remarkable writer and chronicled the varied adventures of both her father and her husband in a series of now dusty volumes. I believe that Lady Maude's tomes were even the basis for one of Knyghton's late chronicles, which was called the *Gestes du Sieur Nigel*. [8] Though it is a rather broken narrative, I fear, for she only reported on certain events. To be honest, I haven't glanced at them since I was a boy, though I recall them being a rather vivid account of what has become known as The Hundred Years War. We even have had scholars down from Oxford upon occasion to consult her notes."

"May I see them?"

Sir Neil led Holmes over to a row of ancient tomes and left us alone in the library. Holmes spent some time pulling each from its spot on the shelf and turning through them. I watched him for a while before growing restless. I occupied myself with a book about the Monmouth Rebellion, in which I became quite engrossed, until I heard Holmes slam close the final volume. [9]

101

"I believe, Watson, that it is time to speak with the other people who were present at Tilford Manor on the night in question."

We went back out into the hall, where we came upon a man wearing a military uniform who could only be Major Allen Cooper. Sir Neil's nephew was a tall, handsome, yellow-bearded man of thirty, with cool eyes and steady hands.

"What can I tell you, Mr. Holmes," said Cooper after Holmes had introduced us and we had taken seats before the cold fireplace, "that I have not already told Inspector Booker?"

"Major Cooper, I understand that you are based at Woolwich."

"That is correct, sir."

"What made you join the Gunners?"

The man smiled. "Look about you, Mr. Holmes. I might not be a Loring-Edricson by name, but this place is in my blood. And it was built on the back of men who loved to fight. Of course, my illustrious ancestors made their name in the saddle of a destrier, which is all well and good for the lover of medieval romance. However, as any student of history knows, the English armies were victorious not because of the armoured knight, but thanks to the archers. Our Ordnance twelve-pounders are just modern versions of their longbows."

"You discovered the body in the library?"

"Yes, sir."

"And you have no idea of his identity?"

"None, though I imagine that he is one of those wandering gypsies. They encamp all over Surrey, pitching their tents on whatever benighted estates will give them leave. Sir Neil would never hear of it, and one of them likely got in his head to rob the manor house in revenge. I already suggested to Inspector Booker that he should round some up of that thieving lot for questioning."

Holmes shook his head. "Little good of that. The roaming gypsies always have their ears to the ground. They would have cleared out at the first hint of trouble, for they have little love of the police."

"Too bad," said Major Cooper. "You may never learn his identity."

"Possibly," said Holmes. "However, that is only half the mystery."

"Oh?"

"Well, Major, who do you propose killed your hypothetical gypsy?"

The man's eyebrows furrowed. "Surely you do not think it was one of us?"

"Who else?"

"That is plain, sir!" cried Cooper. "There were two of them. One of them convinced the other to join him, and when the second realized that

102

there was little of value in the library, he knifed his fellow burglar in anger."

"That is an interesting theory, Major."

"What other explanation could there be? If any of us had killed an intruder, there would be no reason to deny it. No jury would have touched us."

"The strain of a trial is no small matter, even if the final acquittal is highly probable."

Cooper shook his head. "No, I do not believe it, Mr. Holmes. Despite his advancing years, my uncle is fully capable of such a violent act, but he would be the first to admit it. I woke him that morning and saw his face. Sir Neil is no actor. And I doubt that my sister is strong enough to do such a thing. Of course, the thought of poor Dean Adams knifing a man is laughable. No, it could only have been another gypsy."

Holmes nodded and indicated that the man was free to depart, but not before asking him to request his sister to step in. He went through the archway, which I presumed led to the stairs.

As we waited for her, my friend glanced at me. "What do you think of Major Cooper's explanation?"

"It seems plausible. It would explain why no one knows him."

"You are forgetting that we believe the dead man to be French, and not one of the Romany. Furthermore, of all the individuals present at Tilford Manor last night, Major Cooper is undoubtedly the one most qualified to kill a man with a single blow."

Any further discussion on this was forestalled by the appearance of Miss Trudy Cooper. Sir Neil's niece was tall and slight and dark, with a lithe, graceful figure and clear-cut, composed features. Her jet-black hair was gathered back with a ribbon, her head poised proudly upon her neck, and her step long and springy, like that of some wild, tireless woodland creature.

"Miss Cooper," said Holmes, "your brother will have told you who we are and our purpose."

"That is correct," said she, reservedly.

"You must be fascinated by your family's riddle?"

She shrugged. "Not really, Mr. Holmes. I am a historian and – in case you had not noticed – a woman attempting to have her work recognized in a field dominated by men. I seek after cold hard facts, not legends or treasure hunts."

"So you believe the questions to lead to a treasure?" he asked.

"I believe they once did. But Sir Alleyne Edricson lived over five-hundred years ago. Anything he hid has either long-since been recovered, or the passage of time has erased the physical clues from the face of the earth."

"So you do not intend to try to solve the riddle?"

"No, Mr. Holmes. I have, of course, consulted Lady Maude's notes from time to time for the sake of my research, but I would have nothing else from the House of Loring."

"And do you have any theory as to the identity of the dead man?"

Miss Cooper shook her head. "An adventurer of some sort. My uncle hasn't been shy about telling his friends about the riddle, and word must have gotten round."

"Surely your uncle doesn't associate with men of such poor reputation, Miss Cooper?"

"Surely not all who wear spurs are true gentlemen, Mr. Holmes?" said she, in rebuttal.

Holmes smiled in acknowledgment of this point. "If you think of anything to add, here is my card. Please do not hesitate to write."

After she left, Holmes turned to me with a gleam in his eyes. "What do you think of Miss Cooper?"

"She seems a very driven woman. She hardly strikes me as someone who would be knifing strangers in the dark."

"Oh, there I disagree. I think Miss Cooper is one who very much could coolly dispatch an assailant."

"But why hide it?"

"Precisely. I do not doubt her word that she has little desire to decipher the riddle. I fear Miss Cooper is somewhat lacking in her appreciation for the romance of history. I doubt that she would much care for your little brochure on the Jefferson Hope case." [10]

"Then she would agree with you," said I, with some small annoyance at Holmes's constant dismissal of my efforts.

Holmes looked as if he were about to say something, but was interrupted by the arrival of an older, grey-bearded man wearing a light tweed suit with white tie. He was holding a broad black hat, which he twirled by its brim. He had sympathetic blue eyes and a benevolent smile.

"Ah, Dean Adams – Come in sir!" cried Holmes.

"Yes, Mr. Holmes? What can I do for you?"

"I wondered about your friendship with Sir Neil."

"We have known each other for many years. I believe we met at the Athenaeum. He prefers the Reform, but when in a less political mood, he wanders next door."

"Sir Neil remarked that you have an especial interest in his family's riddle?"

The man shrugged. "Well, it is a fascinating bit of history, do you not think, Mr. Holmes? I've always found the past to be of more interest than the present. You might call me something of an amateur antiquarian."

"Can you recite it for me?"

"Excuse me?" said Adams, his brow furrowing.

"The riddle," explained Holmes. "Can you recite it?"

Dean Adams pursed his lips. "Not by heart, of course. Something about a wild wasteland and red blood. It is all rather Tennysonian, like something out of his *Idylls*." [11]

"Watson, may I have the copy of the riddle given to you by Sir Neil?" When I had taken the paper from my coat pocket and handed it to Holmes, he passed it over to Adams. "Is this it?" he asked the clergyman.

The man pulled out a pair of thick pince-nez and peered at the paper. After a minute of reading through the questions and answers, he nodded and looked up. "Yes, this is what Sir Neil recited the other night." He handed the paper back to Holmes. "I am afraid that I don't see what these ancient verses have to do with the dead man."

Holmes shrugged. "Likely nothing, Dean Adams. In fact, I'm planning to pursue Major Cooper's theory that the dead man is a gypsy."

The clergyman's eyebrows rose. "Ah, I had not thought of that. He was stabbed, was he not? I understand the gypsies are fond of their blades. Well, if there is nothing else, Mr. Holmes?"

When Holmes had dismissed Adams, he leaned back in his chair and closed his eyes. If I didn't know him better, I would have worried that he had dropped off to sleep. Instead, his lids flipped open at the sound of approaching steps. He sat up and we both looked over to see our host.

"What have you discovered, Mr. Holmes?" asked Sir Neil.

Holmes shook his head. "It's too soon to say. There are one or two theories, but without knowing the identity of the dead man, it will be more difficult to learn who might have wished him harm."

"Perhaps Inspector Booker's inquiries in the local towns will turn up something?" said I.

"I fear that our dead Frenchman would have been too notable in a quiet little English village. No, he would have come down from London, much as we did. There, he could melt into one of the innumerable comfortless private hotels along the Strand, where he would remain perfectly anonymous. It's possible that the Farnham station master might have remarked on him, but we should prepare for disappointment on both fronts."

"So what do you suggest?" asked the Lord of Tilford Manor.

"We might put an account about in the newspaper."

Sir Neil frowned. "My estate is a poor one, Mr. Holmes, but we still have our pride. I would hardly fain to parade this misfortune about before the press."

"We need not include too much information, Sir Neil," said Holmes. He paused and jotted a few lines into his pocket notebook. "How about this?" He proceeded to read:

> *An intimate dinner party at Tilford Manor in Surrey was interrupted by an attempted robbery. Sir Neil Loring-Edricson, his nephew Major Allen Cooper, niece Trudy Cooper, and Dean Justin Adams of Canterbury, had gathered to celebrate Sir Neil's birthday. Fortunately, nothing of value was taken. However, a reward of fifty pounds is offered to learn the identity of the intruder. The man in question is approximately forty years of age, middle-sized, with curly brown hair and a handlebar moustache. His nails are heavily stained from tobacco, and he wore a French-style topcoat of dark flannel. Apply for the reward at 221b Baker Street.*

The man seemed unhappy. "There is no way to leave our names out of it, I suppose?"

"I don't believe that this was a random robbery, Sir Neil. There have been no reports of a gang of burglars doing jobs in this area. We must work under the hypothesis that Tilford Manor was purposefully targeted. If so, then the dead man must have been familiar either with you or one of your guests, and may have put your name about. Divulging the combination of names and description, with the possibility of a reward, is the best chance we have of learning the identity of your dead man."

"Very well," said Sir Neil, with obvious reluctance. "You may proceed."

"Holmes," I said, "I wonder if there is another approach we may also take?"

My friend smiled. "Indeed, Watson. For once, we are of the same mind. While we wait to discover who the man was, we shall simultaneously endeavour to determine what it was that he sought."

"What do you mean?" asked Sir Neil.

"You said yourself, Sir Neil, that there are no items of intrinsic worth in your library. Therefore, the man must have sought after something else. I believe this to be information related to your family riddle."

"My riddle?" cried Sir Neil. "There is no reason to kill over such a thing!"

106

"On the contrary, I have seen just such a thing before. You would be surprised to learn what sorts of things have been concealed by ancient catechisms. Do you know the de Mohun family?"

"Of course," said Sir Neil, nodding. He pointed to a coat-of-arms over the fireplace. "Do you see the black engrailed cross? They were allied to us by blood, and Sir Thomas de Mohun fought the Spaniards with my ancestor Nigel. The Barony became abeyant after his death."

"I recently had a remarkable conversation with a man named Falkner, who learned that the line was revived by John Mohune. His descendent hid clues to the location of an enormous diamond once belonging to Charles I in a series of Bible verses." [12]

"You believe the Lorings once possessed a great treasure?" said Sir Neil, astonished.

"I think it the most likely reason why your home was targeted."

"We could follow the clues ourselves," I cried. "We can solve it first!"

"But where would you start?" asked Sir Neil.

"We must assume that it has to do with your ancestor's battles during The Hundred Years' War," I concluded.

"Not necessarily," said Sir Neil, considering this. "In many lands did Nigel carve his fame. Whenever there was a brief truce in the wars between England and France, he offered his sword to the Teutonic knights for their ceaseless battle with the Lithuanian heathen. As Lady Maude reported, he once gazed from the battlements of Marienburg on the waters of the *Frisches Haff*, and endured the torture of the hot plate when bound to the Holy Woden stone of Memel. [13] Nigel was the epitome of the medieval knight, roaming wherever his services were needed."

"We will consider the matter further, Sir Neil," said Holmes. "There is no more to be learned here. We can pursue these two angles from London. You may check with Inspector Booker, but I believe that your guests should be free to return to their homes."

We took our leave of Sir Neil, though Holmes availed us of the man's offer of his trap to carry us back to Farnham Station.

"So we are returning to London?" I asked, as we rode along through the splendid Surrey scenery.

"Yes, Watson. But only long enough in order to change to Victoria, where we must catch the first train to Canterbury. The turnpikes will take far too much time to traverse by carriage."

"Canterbury? I exclaimed. "So you believe that Dean Adams is involved?"

"I have been sure of it from the first. Trudy and Alan Cooper have heard this riddle before. Only when Adams became involved did it progress to the state where a dead man was found in the Manor House library. And Lady Maude's tomes were recently consulted, for the layer of dust was disturbed."

"So who is the dead man?"

Holmes shook his head. "That I still do not know. I am counting on our use of the press to reveal that part of the mystery."

"Then what do you hope to find in Canterbury?"

"We need to know what Adams knows. That is how we will find our entry into the riddle."

"The Black Prince!" I exclaimed.

"What of him, Watson?"

"He is buried in Canterbury Cathedral! He would have known Sir Nigel and Sir Alleyne. Perhaps the Prince entrusted his treasure to the Loring family for safekeeping?" [14]

Holmes shook his head. "No, Watson. Edward passed his jewels onto his son Richard, for his Ruby still adorns the front of our Gracious Majesty's imperial crown. [15] It is something else entirely which we seek."

When our train reached Waterloo, Holmes sent me to purchase tickets for Canterbury while he perused the wares at a lime-green Smith's newsagents shop. Several hours later, our train pulled into our destination and we alighted. It was a short walk from the station to the Christchurch Gate, which permitted ingress to the cathedral close.

Approaching the ancient structure, I admired how the warm Caen stone glowed in the afternoon sun. Entering via the carved Southwest Porch, I was immediately struck by the grandeur of the tall naïve and aisles, bright with the sun's rays beaming through the Gothic tracery windows. Crossing over, we walked along the northwest transept, passing the spot where Becket was slain and his shrine stood until it was destroyed on orders from the eighth Henry. [16] Holmes paused at a side chapel and pointed to a row of candles.

"Note the ruby-coloured tallow, Watson."

"The same from the library!" I exclaimed. "Adams must have brought them!"

"Indeed. I think it likely that Adams, whose vision is rather poor, prefers to read by the light of these specific candles. However, this is not sufficient to prove that it was his hand that struck the killing blow. Adams could claim to have spilled the tallow earlier. No, we must complete our quest in order to build a complete case."

We continued to circle about the ambulatory until we came to the element we sought. I studied the bronze effigy of the armour-clad prince, laid to rest some five centuries ago. Around it was inscribed his epitaph, which Holmes read aloud:

> *Such as thou art, sometime was I.*
> *Such as I am, such shalt thou be.*
> *I thought little on th'our of Death*
> *So long as I enjoyed breath.*
> *On earth I had great riches*
> *Land, houses, great treasure, horses, money and gold.*
> *But now a wretched captive am I,*
> *Deep in the ground, lo here I lie.*
> *My beauty great, is all quite gone,*
> *My flesh is wasted to the bone.*

"The wretched captive!" I cried. [17]

"Precisely, Watson. Now we have our definitive link to the Loring's riddle. From here, we may attempt to trace the path laid out by Sir Alleyne. Let us adjourn to a spot where we might think for a minute."

Walking back along the south aisle towards the entrance, I sensed that Holmes was distracted by something. Suddenly he sprang away from me. I turned in astonishment to see him chasing after a fleeing figure. Hurrying after him, we followed the man through the maze of ancient corridors until they opened into the exit-less cloisters. There, the man was plainly trapped, though at the moment he cowered behind one of the marble pillars.

"Hello, Major Cooper," said Holmes.

After a moment of hesitation, the man in question slid out into the open. "How did you spot me, Mr. Holmes?" he asked, shaking his head in embarrassment.

"Your hiding spot behind the massive pier was excellent, Major, save for one exception. While the sun was to our left – so we could not spot your direct shadow – the bright sun bouncing off the interior of the northern windows created a rare double shadow. It was this that I witnessed and deduced that someone was following us."

The man shrugged. "That is scarcely a crime."

"No, but killing the man at Tilford might be."

"I had nothing to do with that!" Cooper cried. "I overheard you and Sir Neil talking about treasure and decided that it could not hurt to see what you had in mind."

Holmes stared at him for a moment. "I believe you. However, cheating will get you nowhere, Major. If you cannot solve your family's catechism on your own, you hardly deserve whatever awaits at the end. Is your sister with you?"

"Trudy?" said Cooper. "Hardly. She decided that she had enough of our mother's family and was headed back to London."

"Very well. May I suggest you do the same, Major? Return to Woolwich. Abandon all thoughts of fame and fortune, for they can drive even the sanest man to acts of madness."

The man nodded and departed us. Holmes watched him go and then chuckled to himself. "I think that Major Cooper can be trusted to cause no more mischief. Come, Watson. Let us apply ourselves to the riddle and see if we can learn where Adams might be headed."

As we took seats at the Black Boy, a coaching inn across from the gateway leading to the cathedral's enclosure, a question occurred to me. "If you suspected Adams from the start, Holmes, why did you not just follow him? Were you concerned about being spotted?"

He snorted in amusement. "Unlike Major Cooper, when I follow a man, you may trust that I am not easily seen." He proceeded to stuff shag into his old briar-root pipe before continuing. "In fact, I considered just such a stratagem. However, I could not be certain that Adams had puzzled out the entire path of the steps laid out in the list of questions. I might be following him for weeks, waiting for him to finally determine his destination. No, I thought it simpler to deduce the answer myself – it should be no real difficulty – and to catch him at the end."

"It does not seem simple to me," said I, worriedly. "I wish we were back in London. Lomax would be of great assistance." [18]

He shook his head. "It may come to that, but for now we must act as if Adams has a head-start on us. If we turn our attention back to the riddle, we plainly see that the first question is not essential to the final answer – for it merely asks to whom it belonged. Furthermore, we now know the answer to the second. Consequently, let us start, Watson, with the third question about where it rests. What do you propose is the '*Wild Wasteland*'?"

A thought occurred to me. "It sounds like the Weald!" [19]

Holmes considered this. "An interesting suggestion. Before vast sections of it was cleared to turn the Royal Navy into the mightiest in the world, that great forest was a notorious hiding place for bandits and outlaws throughout the Middle Ages." He took a folded paper from his pocket and flattened it out before us. "This is a map of southeast England. I also have acquired several of Mr. Murray's helpful handbooks. [20] Let us look it over and see if any of the places appear to satisfy some of the other clues. Recall that we are looking for something beautiful in the east, something related to George in the west, and something bloody in the north."

My eyes wandered over the map trying to find a place that matched one of these requirements.

"Here is something," said I, pointing at the village of Thursley. "I have heard this village takes its name from the Norseman's god of battles, and upon Thor's stone were sacrifices made to him. Surely '*Red blood*' once flowed there."

"Perhaps, though the direction is wrong, for that is in the far western edge of the Weald, not the north. Let us keep looking."

After a few minutes, a question occurred to me. "Which George?" I asked. "There have been four."

"Not one of our former kings. They are far too late for this medieval mystery. No, I would wager that Sir Alleyne could only have been referring to one man. As the Bard once said: '*Follow your spirit, and upon this charge / Cry 'God for Harry, England, and Saint George'*.'" [21]

"Then his foe is a dragon!"

"Yes, that is how I read it."

After a few minutes, I realized that we had a problem. "There is nothing in the Weald which seems to match any of descriptions."

"I concur," said Holmes. "Let us see what Mr. Murray has to say." He flipped through the book until he came to the relevant section. "Ah! We have been going about this all wrong, I think. The Weald is Old English for 'woodland', not 'wasteland'. No, we must look elsewhere."

"Where else in England would be considered a 'wasteland'?" I pondered. "One of the moors? Should we look at Dartmoor or Bodmin Moor?"

He considered this for a minute. "Hold a minute, Watson. I have it in my head that medieval English knights such as Sir Alleyne were more likely to be found roaming the great forests rather than the moors." He set down one of the books and flipped through the other. "By Jove! Listen to this, Watson: '*One of the ancient kingdom of the Jutes was called "Ytene", which meant, the "Wild Wasteland"*.' That sounds promising, does it not?"

"Indeed!" I exclaimed. "Where was Ytene?"

"It occupied an area in Hampshire, which would eventually take on another name as part of the Conqueror's Domesday Book, after it was declared a royal hunting preserve. Ytene is the ancient name for the New Forest." [22]

"The New Forest!" I cried. "How I love striding through its pleasant glades. Wait! I have it, Holmes – Beaulieu Abbey is literally a '*beautiful place*'. Here," said I, stabbing my finger on the map."

"And it is in the east. That seems promising. What else do you recall of your visits, Watson?"

"The Rufus Stone!"

"Which is?"

"The marker of the very spot where a man – reputedly acting on behalf of the future Henry I – killed with a wayward arrow King William II. He was also known as William Rufus – or 'the Red'!"

Holmes smiled. "Surely a location where '*Red blood*' flowed. And it is in the north. Now, what have we in the west that relates to the foe of St. George?"

I ran my eyes over the villages in the western part of the forest. "The Bisterne Dragon!"

"What, pray tell, is the Bisterne Dragon?"

I shook my head. "I do not recall the story, but I know that there is something about a green dragon in Bisterne."

Holmes flipped through his guidebook. "Your memory is correct. As legend holds, a dragon was chased from his den and slain by a Sir Maurice Berkeley, who soon thereafter died of his wounds from the battle. The dragon's corpse became a hill, and many of the local inns are named after this famous event. Excellent. We now have three of the cardinal directions, but we are now at an impasse, for the riddle does not speak of a southern marker, but rather one in the middle. And the clue is most vague," said he, irritably. "'*Sight skewbald*'. What the devil does that mean?"

"Well, skewbald is a pattern of white and brown colours, of course," I reasoned. "I once lost half-a-month's pension at Newmarket Heath betting on a skewbald horse to beat Lord Singleford's Blackbird." I trailed off, for my friend had developed a strange look in his eyes. "What is it, Holmes?"

"The word '*Sight*' is capitalized, Watson. What does that suggest to you?"

"I do not know."

"It suggests that it is a proper name. Much like 'Beautiful', 'George', or 'Red' were. Blackbird, Watson, blackbird," said he, enigmatically. "Do you know the French word for 'blackbird'?"

"*Merle*," I replied.

He smiled. "Even today, those who possess the power of sight are said to come from the old blood of England's greatest wizard."

"Merlin!" I exclaimed, as my eyes ran over the map. "But I see nothing related to Merlin in the new forest."

Holmes chuckled. "No, it is unlikely that it would still be there after all of this time. But I recall that in the chronicles of Sir Nigel, there was a forest inn on the outskirts of Lyndhurst, later run by Nigel's archer friend

Samkin Aylward during his retirement. And it was called the 'Pied Merlin'. [23] Only someone familiar with the chronicles could know to what that clue referred. This is the data for which Adams was searching!"

Holmes proceeded to circle each of these locations upon the map, which when combined led to an irregular pattern almost like a Greek lambda. I said as much.

He shook his head. "No, Greek was not a language much in fashion during the Middle Ages, Watson. We are missing something."

And then I saw it. "'*The pall wavy reversed*'," said I. "A pall is a heraldic device, rather like a '*Y*'. When it has irregular edges, it's 'wavy', and – "

"When it is upside down, it is '*reversed*'," concluded Holmes. "Capital, Watson! You have solved it. So, if we run our finger eight furlongs south from the Rufus Stone, we come to . . . *Minstead*! Of course!" he cried. "Before Sir Alleyne Edricson married the only daughter of Sir Nigel Loring, he was the Socman of Minstead." He flipped through his guidebook. "Would you care to hazard a guess as to the name of the village church?"

"All Saints?"

He smiled. "The game is afoot!"

Glancing at his pocket-watch, I watched as Holmes performed some mental calculations "If the sea be calm, and the tide is full upon the straights, Watson, the fastest route will be by water."

We raced back to the station and caught the first train for Dover. There, Holmes engaged the captain of the *Marie Rose*, the swiftest steamer in the port, to take us half-way across the southern coast of England. As evening began to fall, Holmes shook his head.

"It will take us at least six hours to our destination, Watson. We must hope that Adams has not beaten us to Minstead."

"And what are we looking for there?"

"The blessed rood, of course. Presuming that the church's original crucifix has somehow lasted through the deprivations of Cromwell's troops – if the Loring Riddle is accurate – it should have been built with some sort of secret compartment."

"And inside this?"

He smiled. "We shall see. It does not do to get one's hopes up. Five centuries is a long time for anything to remain hidden. The Plantagenets, Tudors, and Stuarts have all come and gone, notwithstanding a pause for the Interregnum. It would be a miracle if something is still waiting to be found."

We stole a few hours of rest before our ship docked at Lymington. While I paid a king's ransom to a sleepy carriage driver to take us deep into the woodlands of the New Forest, Holmes wired to London to learn if his advertisement had garnered any leads. He returned with a satisfied look upon his face, though I knew better than to ask for any details before he was fully ready to share them.

The path which we rode along lay through a magnificent forest of the very heaviest timber, where the giant trunks of oak and of beech formed long aisles in every direction, shooting up their huge branches to build the majestic arches of Nature's own cathedral. Beneath lay a broad carpet of the softest and greenest moss, flecked over with fallen leaves, but yielding pleasantly to the wheels of the carriage.

An hour later, dawn was breaking when we finally entered the village of Minstead, where I noted a square tower catching the rays of the rising sun above the trees upon the right. I felt this must surely be All Saint's Church. Holmes motioned for the driver to stop and we alighted. I followed Holmes along a path through the woods to the front of the building, where we noted that the doors were ajar.

"Come, Watson!" Holmes whispered.

We rushed into the church and my eyes were drawn immediately to the space above the altar, where the cross should have been.

"We are too late!" I cried.

"No, Watson!" exclaimed Holmes. "The cross is too large to have been carried far." He raced up to the space behind the altar. "Look! There are footprints in the dust." He pointed to where they led to a small door at the rear of the chancel. Opening this, we found ourselves in the deserted churchyard.

"There!" said Holmes, his voice a tense whisper. He pointed to a stone sarcophagus off to the side, behind which we could just see a head poking up. Motioning for me to circumnavigate this from the other direction, he set off in a silent sprint to one side. I followed Holmes's orders and we soon surrounded the kneeling Adams, who was so engrossed in his task that he initially failed to become aware that he was no longer alone. The dean had flipped the cross on its face and located a seam in the black wood. It appeared that – using a house-breaker's jimmy – he had managed to separate it, which revealed a crevice. From this space, he was busy extracting a mouldering velvet sack.

"That is far enough, Adams!" said Holmes, his voice stern.

The man startled and dropped the sack, which split apart, spilling flashes of colour onto the grass. He looked up shamefacedly at Holmes. "What?"

114

"I know all, Adams. I know that you killed Bertrand de Bras so that you could claim the Loring treasure for yourself."

The man shook his head. "No, it is not like that at all!"

"Then tell us."

The man shook his head. "I don't know what to say, Mr. Holmes. It began several months ago, when I attended Sir Neil's house-party and heard him read the riddle to his niece and nephew. I was not expecting it, so I took little note of the precise words at the time. However, after I returned home, I became obsessively preoccupied by it."

"An *idée fixe*," said I.

Adams nodded. "Yes, that is just it, Doctor! I recognised at that moment that the Loring's funny old catechism had a deeper meaning. It could only be a map to a great treasure, long hidden. I was consumed with thoughts of what I might do with such wealth. While it would be impossible to fully decipher the riddle without hearing it again, one line stuck with me."

"'*The prince who is captive*'."

"Exactly, Mr. Holmes. I walk by the Black Prince's tomb every day, and knew those lines by heart. Since both Sir Nigel and Sir Alleyne had fought under Edward of Woodstock, I realized that he must be the one referred to in the riddle. And that is where I went wrong. I consulted various libraries here in England to learn where the Lorings might have stumbled upon great wealth, but none held the information I sought. So many of the old accounts were scraped and reused as palimpsests."

"So you finally wrote to the Archives Nationales in Paris?"

"Indeed. They possess documents which date all the way back to the Merovingian Era. Nigel Loring spent most of his career fighting in Brittany and Aquitaine against the forces of John the Good. I thought that if there was nothing from the English point of view, perhaps there would be from the French side."

"But instead, you attracted the attention of Bertrand de Bras?"

The dean nodded sadly. "I believe he was once an academic of some repute, but he lost his position over a scandal. If his stories are to be believed, de Bras spent his days pouring over dusty manuscripts in hopes of becoming the next Schliemann. [24] When he heard about my injudiciously worded inquiries about French treasures looted around the time of the Battles of Poitiers or Nájera, he became curious and decided to seek out what I knew. [25] A week ago, de Bras accosted me in the close behind the cathedral and I admitted to him what I knew about the Loring riddle. But I couldn't tell him all of it, as I couldn't recall it myself."

"So he left you alone after that," said Holmes.

"Yes. I thought he had given up and returned to France."

"Instead he broke into Tilford Manor and surprised you as you poured over the Loring family chronicles, by the light of the candle which you so prefer for reading."

Adams nodded vigorously. "He had come up from behind me and seized my shoulder. When I turned, I was so shocked to see him, Mr. Holmes, that I grabbed the closest thing at hand to defend myself. It was a terrible misfortune that my blow happened to strike directly home to his heart."

"Perhaps that is true, Dean Adams. And yet you refused to admit it. You had returned to Tilford under false pretences. You wished to hear the riddle again and study their records, in hopes of stealing their lost fortune for your own uses."

The man sunk his head in shame. "I swear that I went with the full intention of telling Sir Neil what I had learned and what I suspected. But I am a weak man. Once I arrived at Tilford, I realized that I wanted it for myself. I was tempted, and failed to resist."

"Moreover, when de Bras's body was found, you pretended not to know him. You carried on with your obsession to solve the Loring riddle."

"I cannot deny it, Mr. Holmes."

"Hand me what you have found in the Minstead rood," ordered Holmes.

The man gathered roughly a dozen enormous gemstones from the ground and, rising to his feet, passed them to my friend, who held them out for me to admire. I noted a couple of deep purple amethysts, a red carbuncle, three blue jacinths, four scarlet sardonyxs, and a pair of curiously cut diamonds. All were of a remarkable size, worthy of display on the finest crown in the kingdom.

"The Treasure of Charlemagne," said Holmes.

"The head of the Franks," replied Adams, nodding.

I recognized the first answer from the riddle. "What do you mean, Holmes?" I asked.

"There were three possible treasures mentioned in Lady Maude's chronicles, Watson. One: The remains of the House of Loring guarded by Lady Ermyntrude, and bequeathed to Nigel so that he could purchase his first set of armour. Two: The plunder kept in the treasure chamber of Oliver, the Butcher of La Brohinière. But this was mainly carried away by the English archers. Three: The buried treasure they found at the village of Les Andudes, in the Pass of Roncesvalles."

"Roncesvalles," said I. "Where Roland fell?" [26]

"Precisely. If you recall the legend, Roland led the rear-guard and baggage train, which carried the vast treasures that Charlemagne had extracted from the Moorish governor of Zaragoza. When Roland blew his

Oliphant and summoned Charlemagne back to where he had fallen to the Basques, his looted treasure was nowhere to be found. Now, if Lady Maude's chronicles are to be believed, at least some of it was buried under a nearby hostel, only to be dug up centuries later by Sir Alleyne and his companions. Alleyne carried some of it back to Hampshire, but ultimately decided that it would be wise to lock it away for some future nadir in the fortunes of the House of Loring-Edricson. He and his wife left the riddle behind as a guide to their descendants."

"But none ever solved the riddle until Dean Adams came along," I said.

"Well, he had the advantage of an intimate knowledge of Canterbury Cathedral and the Black Prince. Without it, he too would likely have not been able to pluck at the initial thread that unravelled the skein." Holmes turned to the man in question. "You have confessed your misdeeds to me, Dean Adams, and I have little doubt that you would be acquitted as acting in self-defence, much as a matter was handled was handled down at Birlstone earlier this year. [27] Thus, I see no reason to bother passing your case to the Courts of Assize. If you truly repent of your greed, we shall not condemn you. But neither shall we forget, I warn you. Return to your home, sir, and look to your own work, but always remember those men who loved honour more than life, and who would die rather than allow such a stain upon their reputation."

Adams face shone with relief and gratitude. I thought it probable that he would henceforth stay on the straight and narrow. [28]

When Adams had gone, I turned to my friend. "What now, Holmes?"

"Well, we must fit this poor rood back together and hang it back where it belongs before anyone is the wiser."

"And the treasure?"

"What of it, Watson?"

"What shall we do with it?"

He shrugged. "I trust in your judgement, Watson," said he, handing me the pile of gems. "To whom does such a thing truly belong? The Moors of Zaragoza, who were driven out of Iberia centuries ago? The Carlovingians? They have been extinct for nearly a millennia. [29] The Basques who stole it from him? Could we ever hope to trace them through the mists of time? Perhaps at this late hour, it does best belong to Sir Neil. However, I suspect that we can persuade him not to separate this rare find by dividing it up at Hatton Garden for the sake of some ready sterling. [30] Instead, I think that he'll appreciate the idea of the Loring-Edricson Bequest for the Department of Britain and Europe, located at the British Museum. [31]

I nodded my agreement with this wise decision and thrust the stones into my pocket. I then assisted my friend in the reassembly and re-hanging of the cross. Fortunately, we managed to accomplish this task before anyone came along, and once complete, I was certain that no one would realize what had transpired in this sleepy church. Our duty complete, Holmes went carefully about the place making certain that there were no other remaining signs of its recent despoliation.

Recognizing that I was unlikely to catch anything that Holmes's meticulous attention to detail missed, I made my way back out to the rear of the church. Stepping outside, I felt the heat of the sun on my face. I reached into my pocket and pulled forth the shining stones, tiling them forth to allow the light to glow through them. I marvelled at the notion that I held in my hand the relics of centuries-old struggles, yet which still reached out to touch us in our present day. The tales of noble lives, the record of the valour of the men who fought for honour, shall never die, for they live on in the soul of the people who remember their names, and play their own little part on this green stage of England.

So distracted, my steps led me away from the church along a gravel path, until I stopped under the old yew tree and sat upon the stone bench that I found there. I gazed out at the field of tombstones which lay before me, each little mound marking the spot where a man or woman went back to that good soil from which they sprang, nourishing forever the great old trunk of England, which still sheds forth another crop and another, each as strong and as fair as the last. I felt that I too would someday like to rest my bones in just such a spot. No mouldering chancel or crumbling vault for me. Just a simple country churchyard in the pleasant glades of the New Forest.[32]

Lost in my thoughts, I did not hear Holmes approaching until he laid his hand upon my shoulder.

"Come on, Watson," said my friend, smiling. "Further adventures await."

> "I am glad to meet you, sir," said [Mycroft], putting out a broad, fat hand like the flipper of a seal. "I hear of Sherlock everywhere since you became his chronicler. By the way, Sherlock, I expected to see you round last week, to consult me over that Manor House case. I thought you might be a little out of your depth."
>
> "No, I solved it," said my friend, smiling.
>
> "It was Adams, of course."
>
> "Yes, it was Adams."
>
> "I was sure of it from the first."
>
> – Sherlock Holmes and Mycroft Holmes
> "The Adventure of the Greek Interpreter"

NOTES

1. While the Liberal Party's leader was William Gladstone, who served as Prime Minister for twelve years in four stretches from 1868 to 1894, they were out of majority power at the time of Holmes's visit to the Reform. In August 1888, Robert Gascoyne-Cecil, 3rd Marquess of Salisbury, of the Conservative Party was in office, making Watson's remarks somewhat incorrect.

2. The 23rd of April. St. George was promoted as Patron Saint of England by Edward III after the Battle of Crecy (26 August, 1346). As he was not patron saint of Scotland or Wales, the traditional celebration of St. George's Day had waned somewhat during the days of the Empire, but it was revived by the Royal Society of St. George (founded 1894).

3. A "furlong" is an old measure of distance corresponding to an eighth-of-a-mile.

4. Holmes is obviously referring to "The Adventure of the Musgrave Ritual", the events of which occurred in 1879. The story was told to Watson during the winter of 1887-1888.

5. Senlac Hill is the generally accepted location where Harold Godwinson deployed his army for The Battle of Hastings (14 October, 1066) against William the Conqueror.

6. Sir Edward Coke (1552-1634) was considered the greatest jurist of the Elizabethan and Jacobean eras. He is considered the coiner of the legal concept of "Castle Doctrine": "*For a man's house is his castle*, et domus sua cuique est tutissimum refugium *[and each man's home is his safest refuge]*."

7. Arthur Golding (c.1536-1606) is remembered today for his translation of Ovid's *Metamorphoses* (1567), which was highly influential on the works of William Shakespeare.

8. Henry Knyghton, or Knighton (d.1396), was an Augustinian canon in Leicester who wrote a history of England from the Norman Conquest up to his death. Sadly, his *Gestes du Sieur Nigel* has been lost. Fortunately, Watson's first literary editor, Sir Arthur Conan Doyle, published his versions of Lady Maude's chronicles as *The White Company* (1891) and *Sir Nigel* (1905). Some traces of those works can perhaps be found in Watson's words herein.

9. The Monmouth Rebellion was an unsuccessful attempt to overthrow James II. It would become the setting for Sir Arthur Conan Doyle's historical novel, *Micah Clarke* (1889).

10. From this, we may conclude that this case took place no earlier than August 1888, given that *A Study in Scarlet* was not published until December 1887.

11. Alfred, Lord Tennyson (1809-1892) retold the Arthur legends in *Idylls of the King* (1859).

12. It is unknown where Holmes became acquainted with J. Meade Falkner, who would later go on to write the tale of *Moonfleet* (1898).

13. The Marienburg is a castle in Malbork, Poland. The Frisches Haff is the German name for the Vistula Lagoon on the Baltic Sea. A Woden Stone was an altar upon which human sacrifices were offered to the Teutonic deity Woden, or Odin. Memel Castle was another castle built by the Teutonic knights, in what is now Klapeda, Lithuania.

14. Edward of Woodstock (1330-1376), eldest son of Edward III and father of Richard II, died of either dysentery or poison before he could take the throne himself.

15. The Black Prince's Ruby, actually a large irregular red spinel, was seized in 1367 by Edward from Don Pedro the Cruel as payment for services rendered against Henry of Trastámara. It is one of very few pieces of the Tudor-era Crown Jewels to survive the plunder of Oliver Cromwell. It is well known that Holmes assisted in the recovery of several other stones in the Stuart Crown from the cellar of Hurlstone.

16. Thomas Becket (c.1119-1170), Archbishop of Canterbury, was assassinated by followers of Henry II, after hearing him ask: "*Will no one rid me of this turbulent priest?*" This was most famously depicted in T.S. Eliot's *Murder in the Cathedral* (1935), which included a deliberate homage to "The Adventure of the Musgrave Ritual" in the interplay between Becket and the second tempter:

> *THOMAS: Whose was it?*
> *TEMPTER: His who is gone.*
> *THOMAS: Who shall have it?*
> *TEMPTER: He who will come.*
> *THOMAS: What shall be the month?*
> *TEMPTER: The last from the first.*
> *THOMAS: What shall we give for it?*
> *TEMPTER: Pretence of priestly power.*
> *THOMAS: Why should we give it?*
> *TEMPTER: For the power and the glory.*

17. Edward of Woodstock, called the Black Prince only starting in Tudor times, was most particular about his burial. He requested to be buried at Canterbury Cathedral, and chose his own epitaph, specifying that it should be readable by all passers-by. The words (written in French) are derived from a text written in Latin by Petrus Alphonsi, physician to King Henry I and suggest a man seeking repentance for his earthly deeds, recognizing that death is the great leveler of men.

18. Lomax, the sub-librarian at the London Library in St. James's Square was one of Watson's old friends. During the events surrounding the cancelled marriage of Violet de Merville, Lomax assisted in finding Watson a book, the study of which facilitated Watson becoming a temporary authority on Chinese pottery (The Adventure of the Illustrious Client).

19. Holmes and Watson had recently visited the Weald during the investigation into the tragedy at Birlstone.

20. John Murray III (1808-1892) began to publish guidebooks for tourists in 1836. Holmes must have been reading from his *Handbook for Travellers in Surrey, Hampshire, and the Isle of Wight* (1876).

21. From *Henry V* (Act III, Scene I). Clearly one of Holmes's favourites, he omitted the prior two lines, which run: "*I see you stand the greyhounds in the slips, / Straining upon the start. The game's afoot.*"

22. *The Domesday Book* is the manuscript record of "The Great Survey" completed in 1086 by order of William the Conqueror to take stock of the country he ruled.

23. "Pied" is a term meaning having two or more different colours. In this case, the Merlin refers to the small falcon used for hunting other birds, rather than the legendary Wizard.

24. Heinrich Schliemann (1822-1890) was the amateur discoverer of the legendary sites of Troy (c.1873), and Mycenae (c.1876). In the popular accounts, his discoveries were made by simply reading *The Iliad* and *The Odyssey* and comparing Homer's descriptions to what he saw while walking about the Ottoman Empire and Greece.

25. The Battle of Poitiers (19 September, 1356) was where Nigel Loring won his spurs, while Alleyne Edricson was knighted after the Battle of Nájera (3 April, 1367).

26. A further sign that Watson was well-read, for most would have only known Roland in the form of the Orlando of Edmund Spenser's *The Faerie Queen* (1590) and George Frideric Handel's *Orlando* (1733). However, in 1835, a manuscript of *La Chanson de Roland ou de Roncevaux* was found in the Bodelian Library at Oxford. It was written in the Anglo-Norman dialect and translated into French in 1837, where it became quickly recognized as the national epic. Despite this, it was not translated into English until 1907, suggesting that Watson read it in French, much as he did Murger's *Vie de Boheme*.

27. In January 1888, John Douglas was acquitted of the murder of Ted Baldwin as having acted in self-defence (*The Valley of Fear*, Chapter VIII).

28. This explains why no official conclusion to the Tilford Manor House case was ever published in the newspapers.

29. The Carolingian descendants of Charlemagne lost their hold on the throne of France in 888, only seventy-four years after his death. The last known Carolingian, Adelaide, Countess of Vermandois, died c.1124.

30. Hatton Garden has been famous as London's jewellery quarter since the early nineteenth century.

31. Sadly, the Loring-Edricson Bequest is no longer on display at the British Museum. Inquiries have suggested that it was not dispersed in August of 1939, when most of the Museum's most valued collections were moved to bombproof tunnels below the National Library of Wales at Aberystwyth. If that is true, it may have been destroyed in the same October 1940 Nazi bombing which severely damaged the Duveen Gallery.

32. Sir Arthur Conan Doyle was originally buried in July 1930 at his home of Windlesham Manor, Crowborough, East Sussex. When his family sold that

house in 1955, he and his wife Jean (who had died in 1940) were disinterred and their remains transferred to the churchyard of All Saint's in Minstead.

To the Manor Bound
by Jane Rubino

The latter part of the summer, and into the autumn of '88, will be remembered for events much darker and more gruesome than the Manor House matter, and yet that problem did present certain features so out of the common that, had it not been overshadowed by the Whitechapel Murders, the Manor House affair would be singled out as one of my friend's more remarkable, if not entirely successful, investigations.

I can clearly recall September 2nd as the commencement of the case, for the date was only two days after the first of the Whitechapel atrocities.

I came down early that morning to find the table not yet laid for breakfast, and Holmes lounging upon the settee with his clay pipe between his lips, meditating upon the wreaths of blue smoke curling above his head.

"That Whitechapel murder has had you up all night," I said.

"It is hardly a matter that is conducive to sleep, Watson."

"And you have gone more than three months without a case of any consequence, so I suppose – " I gave a nod to the litter of yesterday's newspapers scattered 'round the carpet. " – even a simple murder – "

"Murder is never simple."

"'Commonplace', then."

"Yes, it is that." He puffed silently at his pipe for a few minutes more, and then let out a sigh, rose, and set it on the mantel. "It had been my observation that the darker the crime, the more transparent its motive. Think of Roylott or Blessington. And yet, to take a knife to a woman in such a brutal fashion is not done out of those commonplace passions such as vengeance or greed."

"There is madness."

"Yes, there is madness," replied Holmes with a shrug of his shoulders. "I suppose where other motives are wanting, madness will have to serve. Inspector Spratling has been given the case, and I would not be at all surprised if I am called upon to – Ah! Perhaps this is my summons now!" he cried as a wire was handed in.

Holmes snatched the sheet and ran his eyes over it eagerly. "It is not the Whitechapel business," he said, and then read aloud:

> *Might I prevail upon you to run down to Surrey? Your opinion*
> *as to how Edgar Adams, of Manor House, Redhill, got his*

123

head bashed in while alone in his bedchamber with door and windows bolted from inside, would be invaluable.

Inspector John Forrester

"Forrester," said Holmes, as he tossed the telegram to me. "The Reigate matter last year. A sharp enough fellow as I recall. Well, what do you say, Watson? Shall we attempt to determine how the unfortunate Mister Adams got his head bashed in, or shall we proceed with our breakfast?"

"What is your opinion?"

"That I have gone more than three months without a case of any importance."

"Surrey it must be, then."

Holmes threw on fresh clothes and pocketed his cigarette-case, and in ten minutes we were inside a hansom, rattling toward Waterloo, where we had time only to dash off a reply to the inspector and swallow a cup of tea before we boarded our train.

"There will be nothing of value in the Sunday editions," Holmes observed as we sped toward Surrey. "But that is just as well. So early in a case, a rush to get something into print will often result in too much material and very few facts."

"We are not without facts. We know the victim's name."

"Edgar Adams," Holmes muttered. "Something about that name is familiar – I can't think why."

"We know that he died from a blow to the head."

"Quite so."

"And if Forrester is correct when he states that the victim was found alone in his bedroom, we know that it was a murder and not a suicide. A fellow may retreat to his bedroom and take his own life by way of a knife or a gun or poison, but he does not go into his room and then bash in his own head."

"And how do you explain the locked windows and doors?"

"Forrester was mistaken. Or misinformed, perhaps, if he was not the first one at the scene."

"We shall know soon enough. See there!" Holmes tapped upon the window as our train drew up to the platform. "Our friend has come to meet us."

Inspector Forrester, who had brought Holmes into the Cunningham matter at Reigate, rushed toward us as we alighted. "Mr. Holmes! And you have brought Doctor Watson!" the young inspector cried as he shook our hands. "Well, two heads are better than one, as they say, and I will be happy to have your views of the matter, for I am quite out of my depth! But come – I have a trap, and we had best hurry. The coroner's van arrived just as I set out, and the household is all in a state."

"You gave orders, I hope, that nothing is to be touched?"

"Yes. And you will find it a strange scene, Mister Holmes. It is as strange as any I have witnessed!"

"Is the household a large one?"

"A housekeeper, two maids, a footman, and a cook – but when I say 'household', I include the guests as well. Last evening, there was a small dinner party, and all but the Mortons, who live only two miles off, stayed the night. I have sent word to him of the tragedy, and it will be a blow, for he was the victim's solicitor and oldest friend."

"But for the Mortons, all of the other guests are at the house?"

"All but for Mrs. Walker, the housekeeper, and the victim's nephew. They left very early this morning for Salcombe, well before the victim was discovered. I have dispatched a constable to wire the next station and have them intercepted and brought back."

"What was the purpose of their journey?" Holmes asked as he climbed into the trap.

"Mister Edgar Adams owned two homes, Manor House here in Surrey and a villa at Salcombe, and it was his practice to pass half the year at each residence. He was to leave for the villa this afternoon, and it was customary for Mrs. Walker and the nephew to travel ahead of his arrival to see that everything was in order."

"Other than the Mortons, who else dined with the victim last night?"

"His late brother's widow, Mrs. Hugo Adams, her son, Hugo Adams – "

"The young man who was traveling to Salcombe?"

"Yes. Her daughter, Miss Mabel Adams, and Mrs. Walker and her son, Ned."

"The housekeeper and her son dined with the family?" said Holmes. "That is rather unusual."

"Well, Mister Adams was a rather unusual character. A *very* unusual character, in fact."

"In what way?"

"Last night's affair, for example. Every year, on the eve of his departure for Salcombe, Edgar Adams gave a dinner party."

"I see nothing particularly unusual in that," observed Holmes.

"But on these occasions, he insisted that it must be a party of eight. Not six, nor nine, nor twelve. In fact, it was not until five years ago, upon the death of Adams' elder brother, that Ned Walker was invited to take the eighth chair, though in other respects, Adams always seemed to be quite fond of the lad – provided him with a home, and even paid for his schooling. And then, only two years ago, Mrs. Morton fell ill and could not attend, and the prospect of dining with only seven had Adams so near panic that at last, the new schoolmistress was prevailed upon to make up the deficiency."

Holmes raised his eyebrows. "Were you acquainted with the victim?"

"No. I grew up in these parts, but Adams was a very wealthy man, a bachelor, and nearer my parents' generation – fifty or thereabouts – so we moved in very different circles. The great-grandfather had made a fortune in ship-building and the importing of wine and spirits, and then bought the most out-of-the-way tract of land in Surrey and built the first Manor House. Of course, younger generations often have no use for those big old fire-traps, especially not ones where there is little society to be had, and yet, it was said that the original Manor House was designed by Nash, and the grounds laid out by Repton, and so it was thought to be a great shame when Mister Edgar Adams had it pulled down and something quite plain put up in its place."

"I would not call that 'eccentric'," I remarked. "I would call that 'excessive'."

"The property was not entailed then," said Holmes.

"No. It was not long after Adams left university that his father died, and though the fortune was equally divided, Manor House was left, by will, to the elder brother, Hugo. Neither had a turn for trade, and so Hugo Adams persuaded his younger brother that they should sell off the business interests. Edgar Adams agreed and applied some of his money toward the purchase of a villa at Salcombe – it was said that he had visited there as a lad and had great affection for the place. As time passed, the younger Adams enriched himself through his own labor and some very shrewd investments, while the elder impoverished himself and his family by taking his portion to the card tables and the races. When Hugo had gambled away what might have gone toward keeping up Manor House, he prevailed upon his younger brother to take it off his hands. It was said to be more out of family feeling than any liking for the place that induced Edgar Adams to agree to the purchase – he much preferred Salcombe to Surrey – but he gave his brother a fair price, took possession, pulled the old Manor House down, and built a new one more to his liking."

"And was the elder Adams any more prudent after he had disposed of the family home than when he had occupied it?"

Forrester shook his head. "Five years ago, he died, leaving his wife and children head-above-ears in debt. If it were not for the – well, you may call it charity or you may call it constraint – exercised by Mister Edgar, his brother's family would have found themselves in a very bad way. He

126

settled his brother's debts and payed a small allowance to the wife and daughter, enough for them to live in reasonable comfort – but not so much that they might squander."

"And he does nothing for the nephew?" asked Holmes.

"Young Hugo Adams was given a post in lieu of allowance. The uncle was persuaded that his nephew must earn his way in life, and so gave him a post as a sort of valet and secretary, whose chief task is managing the uncle's eccentricities."

"Seeing to it that there were eight at table and so forth?"

Forrester nodded. "Edgar Adams was a creature of habit. So are we all, to some degree, but we do not allow them to rule our lives. For Adams, every object must be in its proper place, every daily activity is carried out in the same manner, and any alteration to his surroundings or any variation to his routine was said to cause him acute distress. Many of the simplest actions that you or I might perform without thinking – pulling a window shade or locking a door or shaking someone's hand – he would not perform save in a particular fashion, often accompanied by some ritual that could not, under any circumstance, be omitted."

"I have read of such conduct," I said. "It is often addressed as a form of monomania or intermittent insanity. Dagonet called it the *folie impulsive.*"

"And yet, Adams was said to be quite clever and with an extraordinary head for numbers. He took a degree in mathematics and fashioned an occupation for himself, auditing the accounts for a number of banking firms. The ledgers are brought to him, he works on them in the setting where he is most at ease, and then a courier is summoned to take them away again."

"Ah, yes!" said Holmes. "Adams! I believe I've heard the name from someone who is in a similar line."

"Of course, he might have lived very handsomely on his inheritance and investments alone," countered the inspector. "But some fellows – if they are not kept busy – they go all to pieces."

"I am familiar with that conduct as well," I said.

"At any rate, he built up a comfortable fortune, which allowed him to live as he liked and indulge eccentricities that would have sent a poor man to Bedlam. It is rumored that he leaves a quarter-million behind."

Holmes let out a low whistle. "A fortune of a quarter-million provides a man with more than comfort, Inspector. And it also provides us with a very powerful motive for crime. The nephew and niece are his only heirs, I presume?"

"Well, I assume they are, as they are next of kin, and I daresay they assume it as well. But you would have to ask Morton where the money goes, for it was he who drew up the will. We have all heard tales of eccentric fellows who leave the entire fortune to a favorite cat."

"Nine lives may test the patience of the one who comes next after the cat," I observed.

Holmes gave a dry chuckle. "I think we may rule out the cat as a suspect."

We had, during this conversation, splashed through tree-lined Surrey lanes, the thick, green foliage glossy from a long period of heavy rains that had only ended hours before. Our journey took us toward an isolated region, quite apart from any village shops or neighboring houses, until we came upon a stout hedge-row that formed a border around our destination.

"Manor House," announced the inspector as we approached a wrought-iron gate at the head of a long, single-carriage sweep. The gate had been left open and Forrester worked our trap through it and toward a plain, two-story structure of exacting symmetry, the front door precisely at the center, the windows set in a regular pattern, and the house itself flanked by barren lawns that were unrelieved by any sort of foliage or ornamentation. Only the coroner's van disrupted the rigid uniformity of the image before us.

"I see little that I would attribute to Repton," Holmes remarked, glancing at the broad expanse of lawn.

"Oh, the trees and flower beds were pulled up and some raised fountains were given away, and a pond filled in as well," said Forrester, as he drew up to the house. "It was said that Mister Edgar Adams found the original design too cluttered for his taste."

"I think the rains will have erased anything useful to me upon the grounds," said Holmes as he sprang down from the trap. "I should like to have a look at the scene first, and then interview the household."

The constable posted just inside the front door admitted us to a grand hallway, with glossy marble floors, a dozen or so portraits upon the walls, and a broad staircase at the center. On either side were identical doors, one opening into the dining room, the other to the drawing room and library. From the latter, the subdued tones of fretful conversation could be heard.

The inspector waved us toward the staircase and led us up to the bedroom of the deceased. Here, the constable posted outside of the room was attempting to pacify the impatient mortuary attendant, who was clearly unhappy with the delay.

The door, a heavy oak affair, had been knocked clean off its frame with enough force to dislodge four sturdy hinges and a stout iron bolt. Holmes ran his hand along the splintered frame, and then knelt to examine the hinges and bolt, first with his naked eye and then with his lens. "The door has a keyhole," he said as he rose. "Did you find a key?"

"Yes, it was lying there." The inspector pointed to the night table nearest the door.

"And the door was locked. Was it the only key?"

"Yes, but even if there had been another, the door was bolted from within. It had been Adams' habit to lock and bolt his door as soon as he retired. The bolt is a stout, iron one, and the door is solid oak."

During this exchange, we three had remained at the doorway, Holmes's penetrating gaze taking in the details of the chamber as he spoke. The room was a large, high-ceilinged affair, with pale walls, polished floors and a pair of windows, the shades half-drawn, overlooking the front of the house. Identical night tables, a lamp upon each, were on either side of the wide, four-poster bed, and at the foot of the bed lay a woven rug that extended to a fireplace. It was rather deep and at least six feet in height, and both its hearth and its projecting mantelpiece had been fashioned from a solid block of gray marble. Bookcases were set into the walls on either side of the fireplace, and the arrangement of books was a peculiar one, for they did not appear to be laid out by subject or author, but by their height and the color of the spine. In front of each bookcase, and precisely at its center, were low pedestals, which bore the marble bust of some Roman emperor, and beside these pedestals were identical armchairs, end tables, and lamps.

I give these details to provide a picture of the gentleman's chamber, before I must go on to the terrible sight that we beheld immediately upon entering the room. For, as I have said, each pedestal bore a large marble bust, and yet only one of them was in its settled place. The other had been the weapon used upon Mr. Edgar Adams. That unfortunate man lay on his back upon the carpet in a ghastly pose, his arms flung outward, the carpet beneath his head soaked with the blood from the savage blow of the cumbersome object that still lay upon his crushed skull.

"It is all as it was when the door was brought down," said the inspector.

"Bed turned down, pajamas and slippers laid out – was that the duty of one of the maids?"

"Yes."

"Door locked and bolted and the key laid upon the night table," Holmes muttered, almost to himself. "He is still in his dinner clothes, so it cannot have been long after he entered the room the murderer struck. We must, of course, account for everyone's whereabouts at the time that Adams retired for the night. If that hour was a constant in his fixed routine, it was certainly known to the household. Is it possible that the murderer had slipped into the room beforehand and lay in wait when Adams entered? And yet, how was it that the door was locked from within?"

"There is one other complication, Mister Holmes," said the inspector. "It is true that the victim kept very regular hours, but last night there was a departure from his routine. It had been customary for one of the maids to come up at ten o'clock, turn down the bed, light the bedside lamp, and lay out the master's pajamas and slippers. Then shortly thereafter, nephew Hugo would step in to make certain that all was as the master wished, and that nothing had been left out of place. He would inform his uncle that the room was ready, and then, promptly at ten-thirty, Adams would retire."

"And last night?" asked Holmes.

"According to Saunders, the footman, Adams appeared somewhat dull at dinner. Half of his meal and wine were left untasted, which surprised Saunders, as the prospect going to Salcombe always seemed to animate his master, who was it seems, much fonder of his villa than of Manor House. 'Manor House was his duty – ' (It was more convenient to his banking clients, I believe) ' – and Salcombe was his pleasure.' That was how Saunders expressed it."

"But his master was not animated last night."

"No. Not long after nine o'clock – the gentlemen had only just left the table and joined the ladies in the drawing room – Adams asked Mrs. Walker to have his room prepared. The Mortons, seeing that their host was all in, excused themselves, and Mrs. Walker went down to give the orders. The maid went up to prepare the room, the nephew followed not long after to examine the arrangements, and then went down to the drawing room to inform his uncle that his bedchamber was ready. Adams bade good-night to his guests, came here, and – " Forrester gestured toward the body in bewilderment.

"Who discovered the body?"

"The same maid who prepared the room. Bessie is her name. It was Adams' custom to breakfast in his room, and for the tray to be brought up promptly at six-forty-five. Bessie would knock twice and twice again, whereupon Adams would unlock the door and take in the tray. When he didn't come to the door, she knocked once more, and then spoke his name, and when there was still no response, she laid down the tray and peeped into the keyhole and could just see her master's feet sticking out from behind the bed. The poor girl's screams roused the entire household, and threw the ladies into hysterics. Ned Walker and Saunders tried the door, but couldn't budge it, and so Walker said they must have at the windows. The two of them ran to fetch a ladder, and Walker climbed up, tried the windows, but they were locked from within. He then peered into the room – the shades were only half drawn – and saw the victim. One glance told him that Adams was gone, and so he decided that they would do better to leave everything as it was and call for the police."

As Forrester spoke, Sherlock Holmes approached the body and squatted down to examine it. "You examined the windows yourself?"

"Yes. They were securely locked."

"And the door was locked and bolted?"

"From the inside. It took two stout constables and myself to bring it down."

"And you searched the room? There was no possibility that anyone was hidden under the bed, or in the wardrobe."

"Every inch was searched! There was not a soul in the room but the poor devil lying upon the carpet!" the inspector cried. "It is possible, as you say, that the murderer may have slipped into the room before Adams entered it, but I am ready to proclaim you the greatest detective who ever lived, Mister Holmes, if you can tell me how, in the name of all that is holy, he got out again and locked up the room behind him!"

"How indeed?" Holmes lifting the victim's right hand by the shirt cuff and examined it intently, then did the same with the left hand. "Singular cuff-links. You observed, of course, that they are fashioned from pennies."

Forrester nodded. "Dated 1864 and 1866. Souvenirs, I expect, and another of his peculiarities, for according to the footman, they were the only ones he ever wore."

"You noted the abrasions and bruising on his palms?"

"Yes – I daresay he gave a good fight."

"Hmm! His height and build are no better than average, he was near fifty years of age, he does not appear to be in the best of training, and he was weary enough to retire well before his usual time. I would be surprised if he had any fight in him at all. Yet, even if we suppose that he made some attempt to defend himself, where is the evidence of a struggle? No furniture has been overturned, no windows are broken, there are no signs of disarray. Did no one report hearing sounds of a scuffle, or a cry for help?"

"I believe that everyone was downstairs at the time."

Holmes was silent for a few minutes and then asked, "Save for the fact that Mister Adams retired somewhat earlier than usual, did anything else occur last night which may be said to be out of the common?"

"No. Well, one of the girls did complain of some indisposition or other and was sent off to her bed. She is quite well this morning."

Holmes's rose and glanced around the room once more. Then he went over to the fireplace, sat upon the hearth and, leaning inward, he peered up the chimney. "I suppose that a small person could manage it, a girl or a child," he muttered. "And yet, there were heavy rains last night. I cannot conceive of the girl or child who could climb up to the roof and down the chimney, use that unwieldy marble bust to dispatch poor Adams, scale the chimney back to the roof, descend to the ground and escape. Not in fair weather, much less in last night's wind and rain."

Holmes pulled himself to his feet and returned to the victim. "The coroner's man grows impatient. If you allow it, I will remove the weapon so that the body may be taken away." He stooped down as he spoke, gripped the marble bust. With the greatest of effort, he was able to stand and carry it two or three feet toward the pedestal before its weight compelled him to lay it down once more.

"Poor devil!" muttered Forrester as he looked upon the blood-streaked waves of fair hair above the wreckage that had once been the victim's face. "No ordinary man could have done this."

"The crime presents singular features, certainly," said Holmes as he stepped aside for the attendant. "And yet the absence of any significant disorder, the calculation that must have gone into sealing the room, argue against a crime of impulse. Calculation is always suggestive of motive, so I believe, Inspector, that we ought to take our researches toward those who might enlighten us as to what that motive might be. The servants first, I think, if you would be so good as to have them assemble in the dining room."

"Not the family?"

"Not until Mrs. Walker and Hugo Adams return."

The servants who came up from the kitchen were of the type that one finds in any prosperous household: The cook was round, the footman was angular, one maid was rosy, and the other was wan. All four regarded us with wariness and trepidation, and though the footman seemed composed enough, it was evident that the three women had been crying.

"This is Mr. Sherlock Holmes," said Forrester, "and his associate, Doctor Watson. They will be assisting in my investigation. If you are truthful with us, you have nothing to fear. You, Saunders," the inspector addressed the footman, "I believe you said that you have been with Mr. Adams the longest?"

"We – Mrs. Porter and myself," he said, with a nod to the cook, "have been at Manor House for nearly twenty years, from the time the master pulled down the old house and put up the new. Bessie," he indicated the rosy one, "has been here four years, and Alice, nearly two. But Mrs. Walker has been with Mr. Adams longest of all. She kept house for him at Salcombe, before he purchased Manor House, and still does, when he travels there."

"And do all of you remain here?" Holmes asked.

"Yes, sir. I understand that Mrs. Walker brings in one or two local girls to look after the villa, and Mister Hugo travels there as well to assist

132

Mrs. Walker in opening the house, and then he is sent back here to attend to the list of repairs and matters of maintenance and such things as would be a distraction if they were done when the master was here."

"Still, it would see the four of you very little to do for six months of the year," said the inspector.

"There is less than when the master is here," replied Saunders, "unless Mrs. Adams and her daughter should come. The master allows them to visit when he isn't here, so long as his rooms – his study and library and bedchamber – are left alone. Miss Adams isn't especially fond of Manor House – nor, to be frank, is her brother. But it must be superior to the pair of bedrooms and sitting room that Miss Adams shares with her mother in town. And yet, I have heard her complain that she finds Surrey dull, and when she is here, she always seems anxious to get back to London."

"Well, for a young person, London offers diversions that the country does not," Holmes observed. "Tell me, Saunders, what sort of person was your master? In twenty years' service, you must have become well-acquainted with his character."

"He was particular, sir, but not unkind. His affliction, or whatever his odd ways may be called, seemed to trouble him more than it ever gave trouble to any of us, and I say if you cannot do with a bit of queer behavior, you best not go into service. Still, I don't know how we should manage without Mrs. Walker – she knew him longest, and had quite the knack for smoothing things over should anything in particular ruffle him."

"Her son has lived here?"

"Well, he lived with his mother when he wasn't at school. Here, or at Salcombe."

"And was your master not ruffled by the noise and antics of a young child?"

"You would think he would be, sir, and yet it was Mister Ned was the only one who could be counted on to make the master laugh at his odd ways, and even forget them for a time."

"Now as to yesterday – you say that Mrs. Walker was adept at smoothing things over – Did everything go smoothly yesterday? Were there any unexpected changes in routine, perhaps, or family quarrels?"

"Not quarrels, no. Of course, there is always a bit more fuss and bother when Mrs. Adams and her daughter visit, for they have no maids of their own, so there will always be a little something more asked of Bessie and Alice. And the allowance the master gives them was due and Mrs. Adams, who is a nervous sort, is never easy until she and Miss Adams have it in hand. And there was the business of the wine glasses – but the master was never made aware of it, so there was nothing to vex him."

"The wine glasses?" asked the inspector.

It was Bessie who spoke up. "After the table is laid, Mister Hugo will come in before the others to take stock."

"'Take stock'?"

"He takes a look around the room to make certain nothing is out of place that might rattle the master's nerves."

"Was that his usual routine?" Holmes asked.

She nodded.

"And was something out of place?"

"Mister Hugo said he spied a nick upon the rim of the master's wine glass and told me to take it away and put another in its place. He must have eyes of an eagle, for I saw nothing at all."

Holmes glanced at the display of gold-rimmed plate and etched crystal goblets in the china cabinet, and then opened the cabinet door and took one of the glasses. "It would take a very sharp eye indeed to spy a small nick upon such a heavily engraved object," he said. "If he was concerned that your master might notice it, I would think you might simply exchange it for one of the others at the table."

"Which *I* said," she declared. "But Mister Hugo ordered it taken away, and he looked good and hard at the one I put in its place."

"Well, well – I daresay he was only acting according to your master's wishes." Holmes replaced the glass. "Now, I understand that the gentlemen did not remain at table long after the ladies withdrew."

"Not as long as is usual," said the footman.

"Because Mister Adams complained of fatigue."

"He seemed a bit done in."

"And you, Bessie, were sent to prepare his room somewhat before his usual time."

"A good half-hour before. Mrs. Walker came down to tell me that Mister Adams wished to retire right away and sent me up to make his room ready."

"And so you went up, turned down the bed, laid out the night-clothes, lit the lamp, and at some point, Mister Hugo Adams came in to take stock, as you put it."

"Yes."

"Did anyone else come upstairs?"

"Mrs. Walker."

"Did she enter the room?"

"No, she only stopped to say that the master gave her leave to retire, as she had an early train in the morning, and then she wished us good-night and went on to her room."

"No one else?"

"No – well, Miss Adams passed by, but only to fetch her mother's bromide. As Mister Saunders said, Mrs. Adams is a nervous sort and takes something for sleep."

"Anyone else?"

"I saw no one, but not long after, Mister Hugo dismissed me, so I went to the kitchen to see if Mrs. Porter or Mister Saunders needed my help putting things to rights, as Alice had gone to bed, but they didn't want me, so I went up to the drawing room to see if there was anything the ladies wished done before they retired."

"And who was in the drawing room?"

"Mister Hugo and Miss Adams came in just as I did, and Mrs. Adams and Mister Walker and the master were there together, though the master left after a minute or two."

"To go to his room?"

"Yes, sir."

"Leaving everyone except Mrs. Walker in the drawing room?"
She nodded.

"Did the ladies have anything they wished done before they retired?"

"No. They said that I might go, but I don't believe they meant to retire right away, for I heard Miss Adams say something about bringing out the card table."

"And then you went to bed?"

"Yes, sir."

"And Alice, you had already gone to bed?"

The girl, who had stood with her eyes cast down throughout the interview, gave a faint nod.

Holmes was silent for several minutes. His gaze seemed fixed upon the dinner service once more, but with the far-away, introspective look which suggested that he was making a methodical catalogue of the facts presented to him. "Whose task was it to clear the table?"

"I take the silver," said Saunders. "Bessie takes the table linens and plate, and Alice sees to the glasses."

"Quite so. Was it a good dinner?" he asked, abruptly.

Inspector Forrester directed a startled glance toward me, and Mrs. Porter bristled and declared, "A *very* good dinner, sir!"

"I only meant that Mr. Adams didn't finish it. Well, I have nothing more. You may go – all but Alice, please. I have one or two questions more."

The girl cast an anxious look toward the departing servants, her hands fidgeting with her apron.

"I understand that your master's family had once been in the business of importing wines and spirits. I daresay he was something of an authority

135

on the subject. He might even be called a *connoisseur*. And yet it seems he scarcely touched his food and wine last night. To leave a glass of expensive wine half-full seems wasteful, don't you agree?"

"It's not for me to say, sir."

"Quite so. Now I understand that you were indisposed last night."

"Just a bit tired, sir."

"And you were allowed to retire early."

"Mrs. Porter said that I might."

"Well, I imagine that you had a great deal to occupy you yesterday – there were preparations for Mister Adams' journey to Salcombe, the dinner party, and Saunders hinted that you were expected to look after Mrs. Adams and her daughter as well."

"We were kept busy."

"It's no wonder you were a bit tired. I imagine that by the time the master's dinner had ended, you would have found some restorative quite welcome."

This interrogation was interrupted by a knock on the door. The constable who had been posted at the entrance hall poked his head in to inform us that Mrs. Walker and Hugo Adams had just arrived and been directed to join the others in the drawing room. "He holds up well enough," the constable told us. "But the housekeeper is in a bad way."

This announcement seemed to dispense with any interest Holmes had in the girl. "Well, you appear to have made a full recovery, Alice," he said, and dismissed her with a wave of his hand.

"I don't understand, Mister Holmes," declared the inspector when the maid had gone. "Do you say the girl drank some of her master's wine? It seems a trivial offense, and gets us no closer to resolving the mystery before us."

Holmes shrugged his shoulders. "There are incidents that are thoroughly trivial, and others that only seem so, but which may guide one toward what might have been overlooked. Come, I think we may now turn our attention to the late gentleman's guests."

We passed through the hallway and approached the drawing room door and, as we did so, a woman's passionate sobbing could be heard from within. Upon entering the room, our attention was immediately drawn to a lady who sat in an armchair weeping uncontrollably. Her simple attire, and the plain gray mantle thrown across her lap, pronounced her to be the housekeeper, Mrs. Walker. I should have put her age somewhere in her middle forties, and though her countenance was distorted by grief, she was a remarkably lovely woman. Beside her chair knelt a fair-haired lad of twenty-two or -three, who must be her son. This unhappy young man pressed her hands in his and attempted a few words of comfort with a solicitude that did him credit, particularly when contrasted with the conduct of the other two young people in the room toward their own fretful, fidgeting mother, who sat upon the sofa, one hand plucking at her bodice, the other clutching a vinaigrette.

Though close to Mrs. Walker in age, Mrs. Adams appeared many years older, and I found myself wondering, rather uncharitably, whether it was her brother-in-law's murder that had produced the sickly pallor and the trembling hands, or whether she feared for the loss of her allowance.

Her son and daughter took no notice of her distress, but stood apart, engaged in some private conversation that ceased abruptly when we entered. In contrast to Mrs. Adams, who was a small, colorless creature, the victim's nephew and niece were tall and imposing – indeed, Miss Mabel Adams was near to her brother in height – with piercing dark eyes and resolute features. There was a hint of dissipation about the brother's mouth which suggested that indenture to his uncle had not kept him from those private indulgences which had been his father's ruin, and I suspected that Miss Mabel Adams, though some years his junior, was the more formidable of the two.

She stood before us with her arms crossed, and her lips compressed, the picture of cold intolerance for delays that had kept her at Manor House when she clearly wished to be gone. Though her mother still wore the dressing gown and slippers that she had donned when the alarm was first raised, Miss Adams' traveling costume, and the hat, umbrella, and valise laid beside the door, suggested that she did not intend for the morning's tragedy to put off her return to town.

Inspector Forrester had scarcely introduced Holmes and myself when his remarks were interrupted by a commotion in the outer hallway, and after a moment, a portly, bespectacled gentleman burst into the drawing room.

"Margaret!" he cried, hurrying to Mrs. Walker's side. "I have just heard! Murdered! I cannot believe it! Why, it was only last night that we all dined together! And Hilda!" He went over to Mrs. Adams and pressed her hand, and then returned to Mrs. Walker and sat beside her. "Inspector Forrester – what is being done? And who are these gentlemen?"

"Mr. Josiah Morton," said the inspector, "this is Mr. Sherlock Holmes and Doctor Watson. They have been good enough to come down from London to offer their assistance."

"Yes, yes! I have heard of you, of course, Mr. Holmes. You are said to be very good at what you do. But Adams? Murder!" He looked around the room, in disbelief. "Who could have done such a thing? Why, Adams had not an enemy in the world!"

"*How* such a thing could be done would seem more to the point," said the inspector. "He was found in his room, which was locked from the inside. It took three of us to break down the door."

"Why – that is impossible!"

"Inexplicable, perhaps," said Holmes. "But clearly not impossible."

"Then what is your explanation, Mr. Sherlock Holmes?" asked Hugo Adams. "I understand that theories are your forte."

"A provisional theory," replied Holmes, imperturbably. "inclines me toward a domestic offender rather than a stranger."

"'Domestic?'" sputtered Mrs. Adams, as she waved her vinaigrette back and for the beneath her nose. "Surely you do not accuse one of us!"

"I have made no accusation, madam. But it is often useful to view a problem not only by what did happen, but by what did not. Mr. Adams had not yet undressed. The room was not ransacked, nothing appears to have been stolen, there have been no reports of burglary in the district – "

"You state the obvious, Mr. Holmes," said Mabel Adams, coldly.

"It is the obvious, Miss Adams, that is often overlooked. I know that you have all had a very trying morning. If you will allow one or two more questions – "

"I daresay you have more than one or two," was the girl's retort.

"Perhaps I do," said Holmes with a polite smile. "Was it your uncle's habit always to lock himself in at night?"

"Yes." It was Hugo Adams who replied. "I'm certain that the servants have already told you – my uncle was a slave to his routines."

"But last night, there was some alteration to that routine when Mr. Adams complained of fatigue and decided to retire early. You, Mr. Morton, and your wife, took your leave, and you, Mrs. Walker went to give orders to the maid that Mr. Adams' room was to be prepared immediately. Not long after that, you, Mr. Hugo Adams, went upstairs to assure yourself that Bessie had not overlooked anything. I understand that there had been some earlier oversight, something about a scratch upon a wine glass, so I'm certain that you took particular care to ensure that everything was as it should be."

"We were all slaves to my uncle's routine," said Hugo.

"Now, Mrs. Walker, after you had sent Bessie upstairs, did you return to the drawing room?"

"Not immediately. Mrs. Porter had a few questions about breakfast – Hugo and I needed to be up before six to catch our train, and Mrs. Adams and Mabel were to leave later in the morning. We spoke for several minutes and then I came back here."

"And who was in the drawing room when you returned?"

"Everyone. Well, not the servants, of course, and Hugo had gone upstairs to see to Mr. Adams' bedroom, but everyone else."

"Who retired first, you or Mr. Adams?"

"I did."

"Because you had to catch a very early train. You went upstairs, stopped to wish good-night to Hugo Adams, and went on to your room. I understand, Miss Adams, that you also had occasion to go upstairs."

"Mother wanted her bromide," said the girl. "She cannot sleep without it."

"And then the two of you returned to the drawing room together, while your mother, your uncle, and Mister Walker had never left it. Not long after, your uncle bade you all good night, went up to his room, locked his door as was his custom, and it was not long thereafter that the attack took place – that much we know from the fact that he was still in his dinner clothes. So it is vital – as the circumstances argue in favor of a domestic offender – to establish where everyone else in the household was when Mr. Adams retired."

A look of comprehension passed over Ned Walker's features, and he displayed the first signs of temper. "I hope that you don't mean to imply that my mother – !"

"I imply nothing," Holmes replied, evenly. "I simply state facts. All of you – Mr. Morton excepted – were in this room. Mrs. Walker retired first, and not long after Mr. Adams went up to his room. The two maids had also gone to bed, but I think we may eliminate them as suspects – "

"You may eliminate my mother as well," declared young Walker. "If you must know, I also retired, not ten minutes after Mr. Adams did. The others talked of cards, but I don't play, so I got a book from the library and took it up to my room."

"I caution you, Mister Ned," advised Forrester, "that anything you say may appear in evidence against you."

"It would be best to hold your tongue, lad," said Morton, firmly.

Our attention had now focused on the young man, so it was surprising to us all when Holmes turned back to the Adamses. "When Mr. Walker left the room, did the rest of you sit down to cards?"

"Yes," said Mabel.

"How long did you play?" Holmes asked.

"Until midnight, perhaps."

"Almost two hours?"

"Yes."

"I'm surprised, Mr. Adams, that you played on so late when you had to be up before six."

"I wasn't tired."

"You weren't tired," Holmes echoed. "Not tired," he muttered again. "Mrs. Adams, your daughter had gone up to fetch your sleeping draught. Did you take it immediately, or did you wait until you were about to retire?"

"Why . . . immediately."

"And yet you remained alert enough for two hours of cards? Well, well – you may wish to have a word with the dispensary. In the matter of sedatives, both too little and too much may produce undesirable results."

"If you have no other advice for my mother, Mr. Holmes," said Miss Adams, "I think that she would like to be excused so that she may go upstairs to dress."

Without waiting for a reply, the girl reached down, took her mother's elbow, and helped her to her feet. The woman swayed unsteadily as she rose, and Hugo gripped her by her other arm. With her son on one side, and her daughter on the other, the frail woman was guided toward the door.

As they crossed the room, Holmes gaze fixed on them with that far-away look which I recognized as a symptom of profound reflection. "One moment!" he cried and, striding past the three, he threw open the door and called to the officer posted in the hallway. "See that no one leaves this room! Watson, Inspector – Come!"

Holmes dashed up the stairs, Forrester and I at his heels, and sprang over the toppled door at the victim's bedchamber. He went straight to the fireplace and ran his palms along the mantelpiece, which was level with his forehead.

"Ha!" He stood upon tip-toe so that he might examine the surface and then cried, "Come, Watson! Inspector! Run your hands across the surface!"

I swept my palm across the expanse of marble, and at one end, felt a deep groove scored into its otherwise unblemished surface.

"Why – how odd," muttered Forrester, as he probed the abrasion. "For the nephew to carry on over a nick in a wine glass, and yet leave this as it is. Of course, Edgar Adams was no taller than I, and the mantelpiece was above his head and that of the maid, so it's likely this gash escaped their notice – though the nephew ought to have seen it easily enough."

Holmes, meanwhile, had knelt down beside the marble bust which lay where he had left it on the carpet. He ran his fingers along the underside of the base, and then took out his lens and examined it closely. "There is a graze mark at the base here, which corresponds with the one on the mantelpiece."

"Do you mean to say," asked Forrester, "that mark and the scratch on that mantelpiece are clues of some sort?"

"They support a theory, at least. An uncommon one, I will admit, but one that accommodates what we know thus far."

"Does that theory tell us who the murderer is, and how he escaped this room and left it securely locked behind him?"

"I am afraid that it does."

"Afraid? Do not make a riddle of it, Mr. Holmes!" cried the inspector in exasperation. "If you have solved this puzzle – "

"A *solution* does not always bring about *resolution*," my friend replied. "I do not mean to make a puzzle of it, Inspector, only to prepare you for disappointment."

"Disappointment?"

"You can make no arrest – not one that will hold up, in any case."

"Give me the name, Mr. Holmes, and I will have him in handcuffs in three seconds!"

"Ordinarily, that would be so, but this is no ordinary crime. Come, Inspector, lift up this marble bust, and set it back on its pedestal."

Forrester looked from Holmes to myself, and then with a shrug of his shoulders, he squatted down and gripped the object. With a visible effort, he lifted it a foot or two and wobbled unsteadily, before its weight compelled him to lower it to the carpet once more.

"You were prepared to charge young Walker with taking up that object and hurling it at Adams' head. Now that young man is not a particularly bulky fellow. Do you think that he could lift that bust?"

Forrester scowled, and shook his head. "No. I can't think of one person in this household who could lift it."

"Nor can I," said Holmes, with an enigmatic smile. "And, of course, there is the matter of the bolted door and locked windows to be addressed. Is our culprit a robust fellow who could lift that block of marble, or a shadow who passes through walls?"

Forrester threw up his hands. "I confess, Mr. Holmes, that I'm as much in the dark as I was when I wired you this morning."

"Perhaps, then, we should turn our attention to the factor that might offer us a glimmer of light. What was the motive for this crime? Unless Adams uncovered some sort of criminality in a client's bookkeeping – which I think unlikely – we must look to the most obvious motives: Vengeance or greed. Now, for all of his peculiarities, Adams seems to have been a rather inoffensive fellow. His affliction might try the patience of those around him, but I daresay he had no active enemies."

"But he was a very wealthy man," said Forrester. "Which leaves us with greed."

"Correct. And greed is a powerful lure. You said that it was Morton, the victim's solicitor and friend, who drew up his will. Let us go down and see if that gentleman would have any objection to divulging its terms."

Our absence had only aggravated the atmosphere of tension which was already at a high pitch, and Miss Adams all but sprang upon us as we entered the room. "Inspector!" she cried. "This is intolerable! We will not be kept here any longer! As soon as Mother has dressed, I am going to have Saunders order a trap – "

"I am afraid," interrupted Holmes, calmly, "we must trespass upon your patience a few minutes more. Mr. Morton, if I may ask – you were charged with drawing up your friend's will, correct?"

"His will? Indeed, I was."

That single word – "*Will*" – seemed to pique Miss Adams' interest and she dropped back onto the settee beside her mother.

"Would you have any objections to answering a few questions regarding its contents?"

The solicitor looked around the room. "It is a bit irregular," he said.

"But not improper, surely. I assume that those in this room are the principle beneficiaries, and the terms will be disclosed soon enough."

"Yes, I suppose you are right." Morton cast a nervous glance from the housekeeper and her son to the victim's relations. "Mr. Adams left a thousand to each of the maids, and also to the girls who saw to the villa at Salcombe, and three-thousand each to Saunders and to Mrs. Porter. Mrs. Adams and Miss Mabel Adams are each to receive five-thousand." The man paused to clear his throat, and avoiding everyone's eyes, he continued. "The villa at Salcombe and thirty-thousand pounds will go to Mrs. Walker."

I will not describe the look of astonishment upon the face of Hugo Adams, nor the fury upon that of his sister. I daresay, if a stare had the force of a dagger, Mrs. Walker would not be long for this world.

"This house – Manor House – goes to Mr. Hugo Adams, and he will receive as well an annuity of five-hundred pounds a year, for thirty years, or until his death, should that unhappy event occur beforehand. Those," he concluded, "are the particulars, but for several thousand that will go to some public charities."

"And the residue? It was said that Mr. Adams' fortune was near a quarter-of-a-million, so unless he was inconceivably generous to those charities, there must be more than a hundred-fifty or so remaining."

"A bit more." Again, Morton hesitated, and then said, "The residue will go to the nearest blood heir. That is how Mr. Adams wished it expressed – 'my nearest blood heir'."

It was, of course, Adams' right to dispose of his fortune wherever he wished, and yet, when I thought of the uncle who lay upon a slab in the mortuary, I could scarcely conceal my disgust at the complacent look that passed between his nephew and niece.

"Singularly expressed, to be sure," said Holmes, "but in keeping with his character, I daresay, Inspector, that I agree with Miss Adams. Her mother – indeed, none of them – need to be detained any longer. You may take your mother to her room, Miss Adams, and Mr. Adams, your sister spoke of ordering a trap to convey them to the station – In fact, it may be best if you escorted the ladies back to London. And, Inspector, I think we must think of our return to London as well."

"Do you mean to say that your investigation is finished?" Hugo Adams looked from Holmes to the inspector.

"Not every case an end in success," said Holmes, with a shrug of his shoulders.

"Perhaps something more will come out at the inquest."

"I am not hopeful. But we will take up no more of your time."

The dead man's solicitor, his housekeeper, and her son looked at one another in bewilderment as the three left the room, and the inspector was fairly dumbfounded. Indeed, the expression of incredulity upon his face would have been comical if the matter before us was not so grim.

"Mr. Holmes, I don't understand," said Morton. "You had said that you favored a domestic offender. If you dismiss them," he gave a nod toward the door, "then do you accuse one of us?"

"Oh, no. I am convinced that Hugo Adams is guilty, and the sister as well."

"What? Hugo and Mabel!" cried Ned Walker, while his mother went white to the lips.

"Why did you not have the inspector arrest them?" asked the solicitor.

"Because all I can offer is a theory, not proof, and without proof, the charges would break down. Twelve unimaginative British jurymen do not want theories, Mr. Morton, they want facts, and those, I am afraid, I cannot supply. But I observe, sir, that you are not surprised to hear me accuse young Adams and his sister."

"I am bound to say I am not," said the lawyer. "If Hugo has been kept from the indulgences that were his father's ruin, it is only by way of those constraints, imposed by his uncle, that have deprived him of opportunity and means. And the girl is a cold, unfeeling sort. But what theory, Mr. Holmes, can possibly explain how they managed to murder Adams, when they were known to be here inside this room, at a time when he was locked inside his own?"

143

"It's true, Mr. Holmes," said Ned Walker. "Hugo and Mabel had been upstairs, but they came back to this room before Mr. Adams left it, and they were here still when I went up to bed."

"Oh, proof be damned!" declared Forrester. "I am ready to hear any theory at all, no matter how far-fetched it may be!"

"It may be far-fetched, but if I am right, it was an ingenious piece of business," said Holmes. "Mister Hugo and Miss Mabel had the ill luck to be at the mercy of a profligate father who squandered his inheritance, the profits from the sale of his family's business and, finally, his home, leaving his family dependent upon the charity – and constraints – of his younger brother. The mother, as you see, is a meek, passive sort who resigned herself to this reversal of fortune, but the son and daughter did not. They resented the loss of money and the status and diversions it will purchase, and began to view their eccentric uncle as the only obstacle between themselves and his quarter-million pounds – for it was inconceivable to them that Adams would ever dispose of his fortune upon anyone but his only relations. But their uncle was not yet fifty, and might live another thirty years. Or, perhaps, his eccentricities might lure him into temptations that had been their father's ruin, and he would squander what they meant to inherit. So it would be suit their ambitions much better if he were dead."

At this, Mrs. Walker began to weep once more.

"Now, Adams' affliction – his *folie impulsive* as Doctor Watson calls it – demanded that every item – every wine glass, every book upon a shelf, every stick of furniture – be arranged in a particular and unaltered manner. Should something be out of place, Adams would suffer acute distress and a sense of urgency to have it set right, and to prevent any such occurrence, Hugo Adams was charged with inspecting the household arrangements to ensure that all was as it should be. It is quite likely that, in the course of discharging such duties, the designs upon his uncle's life took root, and unfortunately, it was the victim's own affliction which suggested how the murder might be carried out while providing the murderer with an alibi.

"Both Adams' affliction and his occupation, which required a keen attention to detail, had given him an acute awareness of everything about him, and so, as a precaution, the murderer thought it best to suppress his uncle's natural vigilance – "

"The mother's sleeping draught!" I cried.

Holmes nodded. "Hugo found some occasion to take a measure of it, diluting the remains so that his mother would not take note of any lessening of the contents. He then played the little parlor game with Bessie, which enabled him to slip several drops of the bromide into the uncle's glass, which would be well concealed by the vessel's elaborate etched design and perhaps some distraction when the wine was being poured."

144

I saw Morton give an unconscious nod, as if recalling an incident at the dinner table that would concur with Holmes's statement.

"As the dinner progressed, Mister Adams begins to feel the effects of the drug – he appeared fatigued, and did not finish his meal – "

"Nor his wine!" cried Forrester. "The maid!"

Holmes nodded. "As she cleared away the table, little Alice helped herself to the remainder of her master's wine, and succumbed to its sedating effects. Adams, meanwhile, had decided to retire earlier than usual, and so you, Mrs. Walker, sent Bessie to see to the room, and Hugo went up not long after to look over her preparations, as was his custom. While Bessie was waiting to be dismissed, she saw two people come upstairs – Mrs. Walker, who stopped to say good-night, and Miss Adams, who was going to fetch her mother's bromide. I wonder – did Mrs. Adams *send* her daughter for the drug, or did Miss Adams *offer* to fetch it."

It was Ned Walker who spoke up. "That's right! You weren't in the room, Mother, but it was Mabel who raised the subject, not Mrs. Adams. Mrs. Adams said she might well wait until she retired to take it, but Mabel reminded her mother that they had a morning train to catch and that it was always harder to rouse her when she took the bromide very late in the evening."

"Now," continued Holmes, "after Miss Adams had gone upstairs, Bessie was dismissed, and returned to the kitchen. It was in that period, when brother and sister were upstairs together, that they made the critical alteration in their uncle's room. When I saw Mrs. Adams being walked out of the drawing room with her children supporting her on either side, I recalled what you had said, Inspector, when I arrived with Doctor Watson this morning – that two heads were better than one. Well, so are two pairs of arms. You had also said that you did not know of one person in this house who could lift that cumbersome bust, and you were quite right. One person could not."

"But two people could!" gasped Forrester.

Holmes nodded. "It required considerable effort, to be sure, but the brother and sister were young and fit, and greed is a powerful motivation. Together, they lifted it from its pedestal and raised it onto the mantel. They then returned to this room before their uncle left it. After a few minutes, Adams bade his family good night and went upstairs to his room. He immediately locked and bolted his door, as was his habit, whereupon he saw the object out of its usual place. What happened next, we can only imagine, but I would venture to say that a powerful urge to put matters right, which was a symptom of his affliction, overtook him. The busts had never been moved from their pedestals, and it was unlikely that Adams had ever lifted one or had any notion of their weight. He was not a tall man, so the effort required him to reached above his head. He pulled the unwieldy object toward him dragging a deep score mark into the marble as he did so, and the object's weight and the force of gravity caused him to stumble backward, which sent the object plunging upon him as he fell."

"And while it crushed the life out of him, Adams' niece and nephew sat here calmly playing cards?" demanded Forrester.

"Ah, yes – the cards. Did you not find it rather suggestive, Inspector, that Mrs. Adams, despite having taken her sleeping draught, was not too tired to play until midnight? Her potion had been diluted, you see, by her son after he had taken a measure of it some hours before."

"I have known Hugo and Mabel since they were children," said Mrs. Walker in a tone that expressed her anguish and disbelief. "I knew they were discontented and ambitious for a style of living above their reach – but what you describe, Mr. Holmes – is heartless. *Evil!*"

"Indeed," declared the inspector. "In all my career, I have never come upon anything so cold and unfeeling! And you say they will get away with it?"

"I say that they will escape the reach of law," Holmes replied. "Surely, you see your own difficulty – it is one thing to kill a man, quite another to stage-manage the particulars which bring about his death. What did they do, after all, but rearrange the *décor*? And even that cannot be proved. A jury will want more than surmise and conjecture."

"The law? What of justice?" cried Forrester. "She will have five-thousand and he will have the house and an annuity and, as his only blood kin, they will divide up the residue. A hundred-fifty-thousand or more!"

Holmes could not repress a smile. "I also have had occasion to make a distinction between justice and the law. What is your opinion on the subject?" he asked Morton. "For I observe that you looked somewhat conscious, as you addressed the nephew's bequest. There is a contingency that you withheld, I think."

"There is. I saw no point in stirring things up at such a time, and I am bound to say that I am not looking forward to the reading of the will. It is true," he addressed Forrester, "that Hugo Adams will have an annuity of five-hundred for thirty years, but only so long as he resides here. It will be forfeit if he ever abandons, mortgages, or disposes of Manor House. As for Miss Adams and her mother, five-thousand, if prudently invested, may yield enough for an income of a few hundred a year. I think that would satisfy the mother – she is a humble sort – but it will not satisfy the daughter's ambition to move upward in society."

"She may find employment," said Holmes. He walked to the window and drew the curtain aside. I glanced over his shoulder to see Hugo Adams handing his mother into a hired trap, while Miss Adams climbed in

146

unassisted and took the reins. "Or perhaps her fond brother will allow her to make a home here at Manor House."

"You forget that they will divide more than a hundred-fifty-thousand," I reminded him. "The interest on each share may bring in a few thousand a year, a sum that may make Hugo Adams willing to forfeit his modest annuity and a house that it hateful to him. Or he may declare that he alone is the nearest blood heir and lay claim to the entire fortune."

"From what I have seen, I would not make an antagonist of Miss Mabel," said Holmes. "But Mrs. Walker, it is your bequest that I find interesting. Mr. Adams was far more generous to you than he was to his brother's family. Thirty-thousand alone would have been extraordinarily generous, but he provides you with his villa as well, one that he acquired even before he took Manor House off of his brother's hands. It seems he had a fondness for that place than he did not have for this one."

"Yes – everything is much more tranquil at Salcombe."

"I noted that Mr. Adams wore an unusual pair of cufflinks, fashioned from pennies dated two years apart. You, Mr. Walker – I should put your age at twenty-two or thereabouts."

"Yes – last June."

"That would make the year of your birth 1866, which was the date of one of those pennies – the other date being two years earlier. But, perhaps, I should say no more."

"You can say nothing that Ned has not known since he was old enough to understand. If it pleased Edgar to have us present ourselves as we did – if he believed that it would prevent any strife among his brother's family, and provide the order and tranquility that were so necessary to him – I was not unwilling to comply. I *was* Miss Margaret Walker, and took on a more respectable 'Mrs.' after Ned was born. But if anyone had troubled to look at the parish registry at Salcombe, they would see the record of Ned's baptism – we always called him 'Ned', but it was 'Edgar', of course – in '66, and my marriage to Edgar Adams two years before that."

"Marriage!" cried Forrester.

"But then," I said, astonished, "it is your son who is Adams' nearest blood kin."

Mrs. Walker nodded.

"What if his cousins attempt to contest the will?"

"Oh," said Morton, "like your friend, I am also very good at what I do. They will find they have no grounds under the law. You see, Inspector, there are times when the law and justice do come together as one."

With no more to be said, Holmes gave his card to Mrs. Walker and promised that he would always be at her disposal, if she should ever need

147

his aid or advice, and then we left the lady and her son in the solicitor's able custody.

"I gave my word, Mr. Holmes," said Forrester as we left Manor House, "that I would pronounce you the greatest detective who ever lived if you could tell me how poor Adams met his death, and though it cuts my pride to have those two walk free, I will swear it to anyone who will hear me."

"Well, I must give some credit to my conductor of light," Holmes said, laying his hand upon my shoulder, "for his interesting observation that no man takes his life by crushing his own skull. He was stating the obvious, of course, but it is precisely the obvious that is too often overlooked."

"I am glad to meet you, sir," said [Mycroft], putting out a broad, fat hand like the flipper of a seal. "I hear of Sherlock everywhere since you became his chronicler. By the way, Sherlock, I expected to see you round last week, to consult me over that Manor House case. I thought you might be a little out of your depth."

"No, I solved it," said my friend, smiling.

"It was Adams, of course."

"Yes, it was Adams."

"I was sure of it from the first."

– Mycroft Holmes and Sherlock Holmes
"The Adventure of the Greek Interpreter"

The Crimes of John Clay
by Paul Hiscock

A week had passed since the successful conclusion of the case of the Red-Headed League, yet one detail still vexed me.

"Holmes," I said to my friend, as we sat drinking brandy after supper, "I'm sure the name John Clay never came up in any of the adventures we've shared before last Saturday, yet I cannot escape the feeling that I recognised him when he emerged out of that tunnel. Am I imagining it, or did I, by chance, just see him on the street one day?"

Holmes smiled. "John Clay was one of the most elusive criminals I have ever hunted," he said. "Peter Jones had never seen him, and I only caught glimpses of him over the years when our paths crossed. It would have been quite a coincidence if you had seen him around London."

"Then I am just imagining it?"

"I didn't say that. You once stood as close to him as we are now, closer than I ever had, and even exchanged words with him. However, once I realised, it was too late and he had flown the coop. It was the closest we had ever come to capturing him. Back then, I still hadn't learnt his real name, just a multitude of aliases that he would adopt for a time before discarding them at the end of each scheme."

"But when was this?"

"Do you recall the Norris case?"

"Of course. How could I have forgotten?" I said, as I remembered the tragic sequence of events that had taken place two years earlier.

The case began, as so many have over the years, when a young woman called upon us in Baker Street. As Mrs. Hudson showed her in, we stood to greet her.

"Good afternoon, dear lady," I said. "How can we be of assistance to you?"

"Are you Mr. Holmes?"

"No, that would be my friend over there," I replied.

She turned to Holmes. "Then I hope that you can assist me," she said and sat down in the visitors' chair, placing the large carpet bag she'd been carrying on the floor next to her.

"I am Miss March," she continued, "and I'm informed that you handle matters that the police are unable, or unwilling, to investigate." She paused for a moment and sighed. "Gentlemen, please sit down. My feet are too tired for me to stand any longer, and I will strain my neck if I have to look up at you while we speak."

I found myself complying with her instruction without a thought. She had an air of authority that few women possess, and which is mainly found in the aristocratic classes. However, it was clear from her accent and drab clothes that she wasn't from that part of society.

I was pleased with this observation, but as always Holmes saw far more than I did.

"Please forgive us," said Holmes. "Of course you must rest after your long journey. You began your day in Norfolk, if I'm not mistaken."

For the first time, Miss March's composure slipped. "How did – ?" she started to say, but then stopped herself and began again. "That is an impressive deduction."

"It is quite obvious. Your clothes are far more practical and hard-wearing than the fashions favoured by ladies who live in London. Yet they are clean and of good quality. You clearly take care of them and would have brushed off the mud around the bottom of your skirt had you been here for more than a few hours."

"But how do you know she is from Norfolk?" I asked. "You cannot have memorised the consistency of the mud in every part of the country!"

"No," Holmes replied, "but the yellow flower stuck in that mud on her left boot is quite distinctive. I recognised it immediately as a hoary mullein – common in Norfolk, but rarely seen anywhere else in the country."

"I can see that I have come to the right man," said Miss March.

"Yet, you didn't travel to London to see me," said Holmes. "You planned to stay here for a few days, but something unexpected happened – something that prevented you from dropping off your heavy bag at your intended destination, and distressing enough to cause you to seek out our assistance."

"I was planning to stay with my friend, Miss Fairfax, but sadly that has proved impossible."

"She must be a good friend for you to travel so far to visit her," I said. "What happened?"

"Rosemary – that is Miss Fairfax – and I were neighbours and school friends. However, just before we completed our education her father died. This tragedy was compounded by the fact that her mother had died when she was born. Having no other relatives in Norfolk to care for her, she moved here to live with her uncle from her mother's side of the family. We promised to stay in touch, but while we've corresponded diligently, we have been unable to meet.

150

"I secured a post as governess and hoped that Rosemary might visit me, but she always had a nervous disposition and, since her father's death, it has only grown worse. She no longer feels comfortable travelling and, from what she has written in her letters, I fear that she barely leaves the house anymore."

"And so you decided to visit Miss Fairfax in the hope that you might coax her out into the world?" said Holmes.

"That's right," said Miss March. "I was finally able to take a few days of leave and we arranged that I would spend them with her here in London."

"So she was expecting you?" asked Holmes.

"I thought so, but when I arrived at her home a couple of hours ago, her uncle seemed surprised and told me that he wasn't aware that I had planned to visit."

"What did Miss Fairfax say?" I asked. "Had she forgotten to tell him, or maybe up her dates?"

"That is the mystery I need you to solve," said Miss March, "for if I had been able to speak to her, I'm sure we could have resolved the matter in good humour. However, her uncle claimed that she wasn't there.

"'Has she gone out to the shops?' I asked. 'I can wait, or come back in a couple of hours if you would prefer.'

"'No,' he replied. 'She has gone to York to visit her cousin. I don't expect her back until next week.'

"As I'm sure you can imagine, his response troubled me greatly. I couldn't believe that Rosemary would have travelled all that way to visit a cousin that she'd never mentioned before. Such a long journey would've been far too much for her."

"Are you sure that it was the journey that prevented her from visiting you in Norfolk?" I asked. "Perhaps the cause of her anxiety was the idea of visiting a place that held so many memories of her deceased parents?"

"I'm certain that she would have told me if that were the case. We shared every confidence. Besides, just last week she wrote how much she was looking forward to being together again. She would never have abandoned me without warning."

"How then did you proceed?" asked Holmes.

"I demanded to see for myself that she wasn't there."

"You thought that her uncle might be holding her prisoner in the house?" I asked.

"I worried that he might have been, and that maybe that was the true reason why she had never visited me. I know that she was concerned before she moved because she knew that he had once been involved in some sort of scandal."

"What kind of scandal?" I asked.

"She didn't know, but apparently they didn't speak to him for many years."

"Did he let you search the house?" Holmes asked.

"He was reluctant at first, but soon realised that I wouldn't be dissuaded. Besides, he had received me in his jewellery shop, as their home is situated above the business, and I think he feared that I might scare away his customers. However, he was telling the truth about her absence at least, and in the end I was forced to apologise for the intrusion and leave."

"You must be disappointed to have missed her," I said, "but I don't understand why you felt the need to ask Mr. Holmes for help."

"I'm certain that he was lying," said Miss March. "The fact that she wasn't there made me fear even more for her safety. So I went to the police."

"But they didn't share your concerns?" said Holmes.

"No, they told me that they would send a message to York and ask if someone could make enquiries there, but I could tell that they thought I was worrying about nothing. When I suggested that they might come with me to speak to Rosemary's uncle, I was told that everyone was too busy. However, one officer then said that it might be a case for Sherlock Holmes. I suspected that he might be mocking me, but I needed help and had nothing to lose. So I asked him where I might find you and travelled straight here."

"It sounds like they were trying to waste your time," I said to Holmes.

"You're probably correct," he replied, "but I'm glad that they did. A missing woman is a serious matter and deserving of our attention. We should visit this jeweller and see what we can discover for ourselves."

However, just then there was a loud knock at the door and, a few moments later, the sound of heavy feet hurrying up the stairs. Then the door opened and a police constable entered. He was clearly not the fittest man on the force, as climbing the stairs had left him out of breath.

"Mr. Holmes. Thank goodness you are here. You're needed at King's Cross Station. Mr. Jones says he has a lead in the Mayfair counterfeiting case and needs your help."

"I don't recall that case," I said.

"It is an old matter," said Holmes, "from before we met. Sadly the man behind it slipped through my fingers. We should go and see what Jones has found."

I looked at Miss March and could see that she wasn't at all happy at the prospect of a delay in the search for her friend.

"Maybe I should visit Miss Fairfax's uncle while you assist the police?" I said.

Holmes hesitated for a moment, torn between his desire to help Miss Grant and eagerness to finally resolve an old case.

"Very well," he said. "Take a look, but try not to alarm him. It would be better that you visit anonymously under some pretext. Maybe you could buy something for Miss Morstan."

I felt my cheeks redden at this public discussion of my private life. Then, after I had composed myself, I asked Miss Grant for the address of the jewellery shop. She handed me a business card from Norris's Jewellery and Clocks in Camden Town.

I turned back to Holmes, but he was already heading for the door.

"Remember, Watson, discretion. Whatever this man has done with his niece, for her sake we must not arouse his suspicions too soon. We will both attend to our business and meet back here later, so you can tell me how the land lies and we can make a plan."

Then he ran out the door and raced down the stairs, followed more slowly by the constable who was still recovering from his previous exertions.

It was a bright autumn afternoon and so, rather than hailing a cab, I decided to walk across Regent's Park to the jewellery store. Miss Grant had wanted to come with me to confront Mr. Norris once more. However, I reminded her of Holmes's final injunction and eventually persuaded her to go to a small boarding house nearby, where she could stay while we investigated.

I almost walked straight past the shop. It had no window displaying its wares and no painted sign advertising its presence. Instead there was just a matte-black door and a small brass plaque with the business name, opening hours, and an instruction to ring the bell for entry. I did as directed and, after a few moments, a man opened the door and let me in.

I had been thinking of this business as a jewellers, but as soon as I entered it was clear that Mr. Norris's primary passion was timepieces. They lined the walls on both sides of the shop – shelves full of carriage clocks, cabinets stuffed with pocket watches, two grandfather clocks that stood like sentries to either side of the door, and even a cuckoo clock. They were all ticking, but not quite synchronised so that their beat sounded disjointed and uneven. It was most disconcerting and I wondered how anyone could stand to spend more than a few minutes in there.

The man who had admitted me made his way to the back of the shop where he took up a position behind a glass counter. He was elderly and almost bald with just a narrow band of remaining hair, like a monk's tonsure. His shiny head was sweaty and every few minutes he wiped it with a pocket handkerchief. I followed him, excusing myself as I passed another customer.

"That's alright," said the other, a young man who moved to let me through. "It's a bit tight isn't it?"

I turned and nodded, and a white mark on his forehead caught my attention. I'm ashamed to admit that I stared at him for longer than was polite before I caught myself and resumed my progress to the back of the store.

When I reached the counter, I saw that this was a display cabinet housing the shop's collection of jewellery, a paltry selection of rings and necklaces and other small items. I would've been ashamed to present any of them to Miss Morstan and wondered what alternative excuse I might concoct for being there.

"Can I help you?" said the man behind the counter.

"Are you the proprietor?" I asked.

"I'm Mr. Norris. This is my shop. How can I help you?"

I took out my pocket watch and placed it on the counter.

"I hear you are the man to see about a faulty watch," I said, "but I can wait if you would like to serve this young man first. After all, he was here before me."

Mr. Norris looked at the other customer and wiped his brow again.

The young man laughed. "Don't worry about me. I'm not in a hurry. How could one be short of time in a place like this?"

He gestured around the shop and laughed at his own joke. I chuckled slightly, out of politeness rather than genuine amusement. However, Mr. Norris didn't react.

"I guess you must have heard all the clock jokes many times," I said.

He looked at my fellow customer once more and then nodded slightly. He seemed very nervous and I wondered why. I thought that maybe it was the young man's earrings. They were hardly an indication that he was a respectable gentleman, but he seemed friendly enough. It was more likely that Miss March had been correct in her fears and there was some dark explanation for Miss Fairfax's sudden disappearance. Maybe he had her tied up somewhere and was afraid that she might make a noise alerting us to come to her rescue?

A large part of me wanted to push past the counter and start a thorough search. Even if he could harm a young girl, this old man would hardly pose a threat to me. However, I remembered Holmes's instructions. I had learnt in our time together that he never asked me to do anything without a good reason. Therefore, I decided to maintain my pretence, at least until I knew more.

"My watch seems to be losing time," I said. "I keep it well wound, but it is losing more time every day."

"It's a nice piece," said Mr. Norris, and for the first time since my arrival he looked happy. "It probably just needs a good clean. It won't take me long."

For a moment I thought he was going to start the work there and then, but then my fellow customer asked, "How much is this one worth?"

I looked around and saw he was holding a small clock, intended for a mantelpiece, in his hand. I looked back at Mr. Norris and saw that he had turned quite pale.

"I don't think that one will suit your needs, Mr. Courtenay. Just let me give this gentleman a receipt and I will assist you."

"Excellent," said Mr. Courtenay, and replaced the clock back on the shelf.

Mr. Norris took out a pad and quickly wrote a receipt for my watch. "It should be ready tomorrow afternoon. Will that suit you?"

"That would be acceptable," I said, but I got the impression he wasn't really interested in my answer, almost as though he was waiting for approval from Mr. Courtenay.

There was clearly something rum going on in that shop, but while I was confident of tackling Mr. Norris, the younger man gave me pause. Although short, he appeared stocky and strong. Better to wait, as Holmes had advised, and to return together.

"Here is my card," I said to Mr. Norris. "Please let me know if there are any problems."

"Of course, Doctor," he replied. "Now, let me show you out."

He came around the counter and, placing his hand on my shoulder, guided me towards the door. I wondered if I could come up with any other pretext for staying and, possibly, getting access to the residence above the shop. However, before I could devise any sort of plan, the door was open and I found myself being ushered out on to the street.

I wandered up and down the road for a short time, trying to find a way to see into Mr. Norris's, but the upstairs curtains were drawn and the shop was in the middle of a long terrace with no obvious way to get around to the other side of the building.

My last thought was that I should follow Mr. Courtenay when he left. There was something suspicious about the relationship between those two men. I waited, although I wasn't sure for how long, as I no longer had my watch, but he never emerged.

Eventually, I decided that my best course of action was to return home and wait for Holmes.

155

"A most frustrating waste of time," said Holmes upon his return to Baker Street. "Our suspect was apparently seen near King's Cross this morning. Jones was convinced he had arrived on the Edinburgh train and wanted me to employ some of my 'little tricks', as he called them, to pick up the trail. He seems to think I'm a conjuror who can produce a criminal out of thin air. However, none of the station staff seem to have seen our man. They seemed far more concerned with the arrival of the opera singer, Mme. Valliere. She and her entourage drew quite a crowd. The Pinkerton agent in charge of her security even suggested that we should pause our investigation until they had passed through.

"I doubt we will ever learn if our man was ever there, much less manage to apprehend him this time. I hope you had more luck at the jewellery store."

"I'm not sure I learnt much," I said. "Certainly not the whereabouts of Miss Fairfax. I was only able to see inside Mr. Norris's shop, and there was nowhere one could possibly hide a woman in that cramped space, unless she is small enough to fit within the case of a grandfather clock."

Holmes started muttering to himself and went over to where he kept his records.

"This Norris," he said. "Was he a young man?"

"No, elderly. He was a curious fellow. Seemed to be obsessed with clocks."

"Clocks, you say? Well that would fit."

Holmes continued flicking though his files and I was wondering whether I should continue telling him about my visit when he suddenly shouted out in triumph.

"A-ha, Watson – I thought that I recognised that name."

He waved a piece of paper at me.

"Miss March was right to be concerned for her friend. It appears she has been living with a career criminal."

"Is he very dangerous then?"

"Not dangerous, but highly skilled. Christopher Norris is a master cracksman. There wasn't a safe secure enough to keep him out. The list of unsolved crimes that I'm confident he's had a hand in is far longer than the list of charges that were brought against him. I thought he might have died in prison, as I haven't seen evidence of his unique style at any burglary scenes since he was locked away."

"Maybe he is a reformed character," I said. "He certainly didn't look like a master criminal. I was far more wary of the other man in the shop."

"Another employee?" asked Holmes.

"No, he was a customer – a Mr. Courtenay."

I described the young man, and watched Holmes's eyes light up when I mentioned the mark on his head. Then his face fell again.

"Curse Jones's wild goose chase. I should have been there with you. You had all the luck when I had none."

"Do you know the man I described?" I asked.

"I believe Mr. Courtney is the man that I was seeking this afternoon. If I had been with you, Jones would have him in custody by now. Still, if we hurry back, we could still catch him."

"It is late and the shop will be closed. The police will need to break down the door."

"We aren't taking the police with us," Holmes said. "Jones's incompetence has kept me from my quarry once today already. I won't allow him to distract me a second time."

"Are you sure that this is wise?" I asked.

"I'm certain we can handle him, although our man has a violent streak, so I would be obliged if you would bring your revolver, just in case."

This time, the journey to Camden Town was by hansom. However, when we were still a street away, Holmes instructed the driver to let us out.

"We should walk the rest of the way," he said. "Drawing up directly outside will attract too much attention."

I climbed down and followed him to the corner of the road, where Holmes put out his hand to stop me.

"Is that the shop we're heading for?" he asked, and pointed down the street.

I immediately saw what had drawn his attention. A delivery cart was waiting outside Norris's shop, and there were three rough-looking men standing next to it smoking.

"That's the shop," I confirmed. "Do you think that they're with Courtenay and Norris?"

At that moment, the shop door opened and the two men in question emerged. For a moment, Norris hesitated when he saw the men congregated outside until Courtenay nudged him from behind.

"What is your plan?" I asked. "We cannot hope to subdue all these men on our own, and it looks like they are getting ready to leave."

"We should still be able to gather help in time to catch them in the act," said Holmes. "The type of safe-cracking that Norris specialises in is slow, painstaking work. The police should reach the hotel before they have finished."

157

"Hotel?" I asked. "What makes you think that's where they are heading? Surely a bank would be a far more likely target."

"Mr. Norris doesn't appear to have engaged in his criminal profession for many years, turning his skill with delicate mechanisms to more honest work. There are two obvious reasons to rouse him from his retirement. First, if a safe is of an older model, with which he is familiar, and second, if there is a high chance of discovery and stealth is paramount. Norris is of the old school that relies on the skill of his hands, while his younger successors seem to prefer drills and explosives."

"That still doesn't explain why you think they are going to a hotel."

"A luxury hotel is a location which requires particular stealth as, unlike a bank or shop, there will be people around at all hours of the day and night. Its safe could be a treasure trove for a thief, particularly if a guest with lots of valuables, such as a famous opera singer, is known to be staying there. It turns out that my excursion earlier wasn't quite the waste of time that I'd first supposed. It's significant that the man you know as Courtenay was never seen inside the station. It suggests he was in the area for another purpose, such as surveilling the Midland Grand Hotel next door."

Just then, we were interrupted up a commotion from down the street where the criminals had gathered.

"I won't do it!" shouted a man, and I recognised the voice of Mr. Norris.

"Please, let's not have this argument again," said Courtenay. "I shouldn't have to remind you of the consequences if you don't do as you are told. Adam here will be keeping your niece company this evening. If you don't co-operate, or we fail to return as expected, then she will pay the price."

"Very well," said Norris. "Just don't hurt her." Then he allowed one of the men to help him up into the cart.

"Her fate is in your hands," said Courtney. "Remember, if you open the safe, she will live. If not, her body will be dumped in Whitechapel where the police will assume that she is just another of The Ripper's victims."

Holmes had been writing quickly in his notebook. Tearing out a sheet, he said, "Quickly, Watson!" Then, thrusting a piece of paper into my hand, he added, "Find a hansom and tell the driver to deliver this note to Peter Jones at Scotland Yard. It contains everything he'll need to know. Then hurry back here."

I did as he instructed and hurried off. I was worried that it would take me too long to find a cab, but I was in luck and came across a driver who was just dropping someone off a couple of streets away. The cabbie was reluctant to help me at first. He had been driving all day and had been planning to take a break. However, an offer of three times his regular fare convinced him to take the message.

I rushed back to Holmes and was relieved to see that I had made it in time, as the cart was just setting off.

"Are we going to follow them?" I asked. "If so, I'll need to find another hansom."

"I would dearly love to, but in this instance I must rely on the police to apprehend them. The person we must not lose sight of is that man."

He pointed to the member of the party left standing by the side of the road.

"We must follow him to where they have detained Miss Fairfax. Otherwise, the cost of preventing the robbery will be her life."

"I could find her, while you go to the hotel. He is just one man and I'm sure I could handle him."

"Watson, you are brave as a lion and I don't doubt you for a second, but we have been caught out by superior numbers once this evening already. We don't know how many men might have been left with Miss Fairfax. No, it is better that we tackle this together."

"If she is inside Norris's home, we might be able to accomplish both," I said.

"If that is the case, I will be grateful," said Holmes, "but I don't doubt Miss March's account of how she searched the premises."

Sure enough, as soon as the cart had departed, the man identified by Courtenay as Adam set off down the road in the opposite direction. We waited a moment and then followed at a discreet distance.

We pursued Adam through the streets for about a quarter-of-an-hour, and he led us into a less-reputable area of the city. It was hard to keep our distance in some of the smaller winding alleyways, and more than once I thought we might have lost him. However, Holmes was like a bloodhound on the hunt and always managed to pick up the trail again.

Eventually, Adam stopped at a run-down building and went inside.

"I wish that we had more information," said Holmes. "I can make out four distinct sets of footprints around the front door. I would assume that one set belongs to Mr. Courtenay, probably these smaller ones here, so we can discount him. So we could be facing up to three men, all of whom are probably armed. Still, we have no choice. Are you ready?"

I took out my revolver and double-checked that all the chambers were filled. Then, at my nod, Holmes opened the door and we stepped inside.

From what I could see in the gloom, the building was just as dilapidated inside as out. There didn't appear to be anyone on the ground floor, but Holmes pointed out a flickering light at the top of the stairs. He led the way over there and we started to ascend.

I was trying to be stealthy, but about halfway up a board creaked under my foot. I winced and tried to hold as still as possible.

"Did you hear something?" said a voice at the top of the stairs.

"It was probably rats," someone said in reply. "They're all over the place. One of them bit me earlier. A massive great brute."

"Serves you right for sleeping on the job. Go check it out anyway. We don't want anyone, even your giant rat, disturbing us."

There were mutters of indistinct complaint at this, but I heard a chair being pushed back and a man standing up. I looked to Holmes and saw that he had ascended further up the stairs, crouching so that his head remained just below the level of the upper floor. He slowly reached up and then, fast as a cobra, he struck, grabbing a man by both legs and pulling him over.

The unfortunate criminal was caught completely unawares and tumbled down the stairs, almost knocking me over.

"Come on, Watson!" shouted Holmes as he bounded up the stairs.

I followed as quickly as possible. When I emerged at the top, the first thing I saw was a woman, whom I presumed must be Miss Fairfax, tied to a chair with a rag shoved in her mouth to prevent her from speaking.

I looked around and saw that Adam was on the other side of the room. He was holding a knife and seemed to be deciding whether he should tackle Holmes or move to threaten Miss Fairfax. When he saw me he made up his mind and headed towards the young woman. He wouldn't prevail against us both in a fight, but with a hostage he could hold us both at bay.

Without hesitation, I raised my revolver and fired. The shot caught Adam in the leg and he fell, sprawled at Miss Fairfax's feet. Holmes ran over and stamped his boot down hard on the man's hand, making him drop the knife, which Holmes then kicked towards me. I picked it up, went over to Miss Fairfax, and used it to cut through her bonds. She tried to stand up, but her legs were weak from lack of movement, so she stumbled. I caught her and she clung to me like a child, weeping uncontrollably.

"Thank you. Thank you, kind sirs," she eventually managed to say through her sobs. "However did you find me?"

"We followed this man from your uncle's house," I said.

"Oh, uncle. He must have been so worried. Did he ask you to find me?"

"No," I said, "it was your friend Miss March."

"Darling Emilia! I had forgotten all about her visit. I have lost track of time while I've been kept here. What day is it?"

"It is Monday," I said.

"It has been that long? They took me on Friday."

Holmes interrupted us. "We should leave immediately. The man who fell down the stairs has run away and I fear that he might return at any minute with reinforcements."

He tied Adam to the chair and I stabilized the man's wounded leg. Then we helped Miss Fairfax down the stairs.

We weren't going to be able to find a cab in this part of town, so we had to walk. I kept looking over my shoulder for someone pursuing us, but thankfully no one found us.

"Is it much further?" asked Miss Fairfax. She was able to walk unaided now, but she was obviously weary and keen to rest. "Uncle will be so worried about me."

"We aren't going to your home," said Holmes. "It isn't yet safe. Besides, your uncle isn't there."

"Not there?" she asked anxiously. "Is he out searching for me too?"

"No," I said, "I'm afraid he is in the clutches of the rest of the gang that took you."

She started crying again. "Why would they want him? He is just a harmless old man. Is it about the jewellery shop? I know it sounds grand, but really there is little of value there."

It seemed as though Miss Fairfax was unaware of her uncle's criminal past. I considered whether to tell her, but decided that knowledge would only distress her further.

"Don't worry," I said. "The police are on the case and I'm sure he is safe with them by now."

We took Miss Fairfax to the boarding house where Miss March was staying and watched as the two women were tearfully reunited. Then, with her safe and cared for, we dispatched a constable to check on Adams and then made our way to the Midland Grand to see how the police had fared.

There was a lot of fuss around the entrance as we approached, with constables trying to keep the crowds back and under control. For a moment, I wondered if we would be able to get through, but then Jones spotted us and sent someone to clear a path.

"Wherever have you been, Mr. Holmes?" asked the police agent.

"We were saving the life of a young woman," I said, indignantly.

"Well, that is very fine, I'm sure," said Jones, "but it cost us dearly. I'm afraid your message came too late."

"Too late!" Holmes's rage was a sight to behold. I have rarely seen him so angry before or since.

"Well, your message was handed to the officer at the desk, but I was out, so they put it aside until I returned."

161

"Did nobody think to check what it was about?" I asked.

"That's not how things are done. It could have been some confidential matter. You should have indicated it was urgent."

"Bumbling fools!" said Holmes. "We had all but tied them up in a parcel for you."

"Anyway, there's no point arguing about it now," said Jones. "However it happened, the fact is that, by the time we arrived, the deed was already done. You'd better come and see."

He led us into the hotel and to the manager's office, where the safe on the wall stood open. All the contents had been removed.

"Was much stolen?" I asked.

"The takings and personal items belonging to a number of the guests, including those of the opera singer we saw earlier. She was most upset. It seems that she was carrying a large amount of money and valuable jewellery. She is already threatening to speak to the Home Secretary, who is apparently a personal friend."

"They all got away then?" I said.

"Not quite," replied Jones. "There's one less villain on the streets tonight. Seems there was some kind of falling out amongst the gang."

He led us around the manager's desk and to where the body of Mr. Norris lay in a pool of blood, his throat slit from side to side.

"Poor Mr. Norris," I said. "I know he had committed crimes, but he didn't deserve this."

"I knew we were taking a risk leaving him in their hands," said Holmes, "but there was no other way. He was a liability to them once the safe was open. Come, Watson, there is nothing more we can do here. We should leave Mr. Jones to clear up his mess."

We returned to Baker Street with heavy hearts. The next morning, after retrieving my watch from Norris's shop, I went to break the news to Miss Fairfax. I tried to persuade Holmes to join me, but he had fallen into one of his dark moods and wouldn't come.

Miss March took charge as soon as she heard the news, both comforting and organising her friend. She decided that they would return to Norfolk together and I wished them both well.

Recalling the case now, I wonder once again whether we could have saved both the girl and her uncle, if we had acted differently? However, such speculation is pointless. I'm mainly glad to have known that the man behind these foul deeds has finally been brought to justice.

"[John Clay and I] have had some skirmishes, but we had never set eyes upon each other before."

– Sherlock Holmes
"The Red-Headed League"

The Adventure of the
Nonpareil Club
by Hugh Ashton

In my experience of humanity, I have discovered that there are few forces as powerful as that of egotism. When I mentioned this to my friend Sherlock Holmes, the celebrated consulting detective, I was heartened to find him in general agreement with me on the matter.

"It is," he said to me when I had expounded my thesis, "a commonly held belief that the root of much crime is romantic passion. Though it is certainly true that a large number of crimes have this as their cause, it seems to me that injured pride is often at the root of the passion that supposedly prompted the commission of the crime. I would therefore have to agree with you that egoism and pride are the cause of much of the wrongdoing in this country."

Never, in my experience, was this more vividly demonstrated than in the case of Colonel Upwood.

"Sir Thomas Ridgson," Sherlock Holmes remarked to me in conversational tones one November morning as we sat at breakfast. The dense fog which enveloped London like a shroud had deadened the noise of the sparse traffic that made its cautious way down Baker Street, and I confess that I had become drowsy with the almost anaesthetic effects of the enforced solitude.

Holmes's words jolted me awake. "You were saying?" I asked.

"Sir Thomas Ridgson," Holmes repeated. "You are aware of him?"

"Of course. The famous African explorer, the first Englishman to see the upper reaches of the Niger River, and the only white man to enter the city of Bamako. He was knighted two years ago for his achievements, was he not?"

"Indeed he was. He is also the president of the Nonpareil Club, and it is in that capacity that he intends to visit us this morning. A message was awaiting me as I awoke this morning, telling me that it is about this extraordinary society that he wishes to consult me." My bemusement must have shown in my face, for he added, "Perhaps Sir Thomas will be willing to explain the workings of this singular institution when he calls, if the details are unfamiliar to you."

I should perhaps mention here that the Nonpareil Club, the name of which was to become a household word as a result of the events that followed, was at that time virtually unknown to anyone who was not a member.

"Have you any idea of the matter on which he wishes to consult you?"

"None. He is expected here at eight-thirty."

At the appointed hour, Mrs. Hudson announced the arrival of Sir Thomas and showed him into our sitting room.

The famous African explorer presented a fine figure as he entered. Our doorway was scarcely tall enough to admit him, and his rugged frame seemed to fill our room with an impression of primaeval energy. His voice, rather than the booming tones that one might expect from such a man, was surprisingly quiet and weak.

"Thank you for agreeing to see me on this matter, Mr. Holmes," he greeted my friend. "I take it that you," turning to me, "are Doctor Watson?"

I admitted my identity and invited him to take a seat.

Once he was settled comfortably in an armchair with a warming and stimulating cup of coffee, Holmes invited him to explain his visit to us.

"It concerns the Nonpareil Club," he explained. "Since we are a somewhat private – some might almost call us secretive – group, it may be that you are unfamiliar with the Club and its conditions for membership."

"I have heard a little," Holmes told him, "but would appreciate hearing more."

"And for my part," I added, "I know nothing."

"Very well then. I am the President of the Club, whose membership consists of those men who have achieved a unique success in life. Such a success may be similar to mine in being the only white man ever to have visited the African city of Bamako. It might be in the realm of science or medicine, such as being the only man to have brought about the cure of a patient suffering from a disease thought to be incurable, or in the world of music, such as having one's composition played by a famous European orchestra not usually given to playing works from outside its own country. Hence the name of the Club, the *Nonpareil* – all members are without equal in their individual fields."

"May I ask who determines what constitutes an achievement worthy of membership?" asked Holmes.

"Certainly. A prospective member must be proposed by an existing member, and the nomination seconded by two more. A ballot of all members is then taken to determine whether the prospective member and his achievements are eligible for membership. A quorum of half the membership is required for the vote to be valid, and a simple majority of those voting is sufficient to determine the result."

"This sounds like a remarkably parliamentary procedure," I smiled.

"Our membership does indeed include a few Members of Parliament and a few noble lords, who are members for reasons other than their political achievements. It was they who were responsible for this system."

"A question, if I may, Sir Thomas," said Holmes. "Your members are selected on the basis of having performed some sort of unique feat, are they not? What happens if that event is duplicated by another?"

"In that event, which happens frequently, given the pace of change in this modern age," replied our visitor, "a process similar to that of a new member's joining takes place. To take an example, should another man prove to have visited Bamako, any member of the Club could then call for my resignation, seconded by two members, and a ballot conducted along the same lines as I described previously. However . . . I should mention that a man may qualify for membership on account of more than one achievement. In my particular case, I may also lay claim to be the only man to have been made an honorary chief of the Soninké people – indeed, of any group in that region. There are other claims that I may make, which I will not bore you with at this time. Many of our members have some similar claim or claims, and so our membership is not as fluid as one might at first suppose."

"A very exclusive group of men, then?" I remarked.

"Indeed, that is the case. And not only that – these men are jealously proud of their membership in the Club. Pride is a sin to which they are all – myself included on occasion, I confess – subject, and jealousy of others, particularly those they see as competitors in their field, forms another failing in many."

"Ah, Watson and I were speaking only the other day of such matters as being the cause of much crime," said Holmes. "Indeed, I gave it as my opinion that they were the primary cause of such wrongdoing. May I hazard a guess that it is in connection with this that you have come to us today?"

"Indeed, you are correct, Mr. Holmes. We are faced with a situation that is unprecedented in the seven years of the Club's existence. It concerns a certain Colonel Constantine Upwood."

"I have a recollection of that name," Holmes interrupted. "Watson, if you would be good enough to pass me the Index containing the letter '*U*'. Ah, thank you." He received the appropriate scrapbook in which he filed any items of interest, and started to leaf through its pages. "Ah yes, my memory does not betray me. Formerly of the Greenjackets – that is too say, the Rifle Brigade – served in Afghanistan and North India – decorated for actions in the Battle of Ali Masjid – Ah! This is why the name seems familiar – court-martialled for his part in the death of a native woman and

166

her husband. Acquitted, but from my reading of the accounts of the case, there is no doubt in my mind that he was guilty as charged."

"That is the man, Mr. Holmes. I confess that I find the man's company to be distasteful, but by the rules of the Club, unless anyone can be proved to have duplicated the feat that gained him his membership, or unless he has been found guilty by a court of having committed a criminal offence, he cannot be expelled from the club."

"And the feat that gained him his membership?"

"The slaying of two tigers within seconds of each other with the use of a double rifle. Personally, I am against the taking of animals' lives simply to gratify one's vanity, but there was a sufficient number of members to secure his election."

"And now?"

"A certain Captain Vernon Banford reports that he has achieved the same feat – however, claiming that he was on foot when he dispatched the beasts, whereas Colonel Upwood was seated on an elephant howdah when his tigers were killed. He is also the only man known to have swum across the Hooghly River in Calcutta, and is for that feat that he was recommended."

"Then with regard to the shooting of the tigers, are these not different feats, then?" said I. "Is there not a way in which both can be members?"

"There are certainly those who believe that to be the case. On the other hand, there is a substantial proportion of the membership feel they have been insulted by Upwood, and would prefer to see his membership terminated. However, under the rules that I mentioned earlier, his membership cannot be revoked so easily as they would like. There is clearly bad blood between Upwood and Banford – Upwood resenting the man he sees as a potential usurper who would deprive him of his membership, and Banford regarding Upwood as a man who is unworthy to be a member of the Nonpareil Club since he, Banford, has duplicated his feat.

"Matters came to a head two nights ago. Both men had been imbibing freely, and strong words were spoken. At one point, some witnesses claim that Upwood challenged Banford to a duel with pistols. Upwood denies this, and asserts that his words were misinterpreted, claiming that he told Banford that if these events had taken place at a different time in history, he would have challenged Banford to a duel. In any event, both men were apparently extremely angry, and physical violence between the two appeared to be a real possibility, according to some who were at the scene."

"Excuse me," interrupted Sherlock Holmes. "Were you present while this was taking place?"

"I was not present at the start of the argument. However, as matters became more heated, one of the senior Club servants had the presence of mind to dispatch an urgent message to me at my lodgings, which happily are only a few minutes away from the Club. I immediately made my way there with the intention of acting as some sort of umpire or referee to settle the dispute."

"I see," said Holmes. "Pray continue."

"By the time I reached the Club, matters had cooled to the extent that the argument was to be settled, not with pistols, but with playing cards. As decided by other members of the Club who might be seen as acting in the role of seconds, there were to be eleven hands of *chemin de fer*, each man starting with a stake of one-thousand pounds. At the end of the eleventh hand, the player with the most capital would be free to impose his conditions on the other: Upwood would retain his membership of the Club should he emerge as the victor, and Banford would be able to claim that his tigerish exploit had invalidated Upwood's, should he come out on top, and Upwood would be forced to resign.

"I confess that I was not in favour of this game, but I felt I had no authority to prevent it, and to be frank, little wish to do so, given the threatened alternatives. A coin was tossed to determine who should be banker, and Banford won. He held the bank for three hands, and the bank passed to Upwood, who retained the bank until the end of the eleven hands. Over that period, he had gradually taken almost all of Banford's thousand pounds, with only twenty-five pounds left on the table. He announced that he would wager one thousand on this final deal, and a murmur went up, as this went against the original agreement that only one-thousand pounds should be the amount staked. However, Banford coolly accepted this challenge, and seemed almost in a dreamlike state as the cards were dealt.

"Upwood triumphantly showed his hand – an eight and a king, but Banford slowly turned his cards up to show a six and a three. Upwood's face turned black with fury, and he pushed over the counters representing the one-thousand-nine-hundred-and-seventy-five pounds, together with five five-pound notes which he withdrew from his wallet, before storming out of the room, and indeed, out of the building.

"Despite his winnings, which had left him in sole possession of the field, as well as a wealthy man, Banford was in a downcast mood. I drew him to one side and, as gently as I could, enquired if there was any way in which I might be of assistance to him.

"His reply was an almost tearful admission that his fiancée, to whom he had been betrothed for the past two years, and to whom he was to have been married in two days' time – that is to say, today – had that very afternoon informed him of her intention not to marry him, giving no reason for this change of heart."

"Dear me," I said. "The poor fellow."

"He told me that he was ready to lose all his money, having already lost everything in the world that he held dear – that is to say, his betrothed."

Holmes sat in silence a while, his hands with the fingertips pressed together in that familiar steepled position which I knew betokened thought. At length, he spoke. "Sir Thomas, you have given us an admirable account of the facts, but I am unsure of what you require of me."

"I have not reached the point of the story, I fear. Last night at half-past-ten o'clock, I was once more summoned from my lodgings to the Club. The messenger was agitated, but refused to tell me the reason for my summons. On reaching the premises, I was greeted by Sir Archibald Milton-Harbury – "

"The eminent surgeon?" I asked.

"The same. He is a member of the Club following a unique surgical procedure which he and only he has been able to carry out successfully. He informed me that Captain Banford had been discovered dead some thirty minutes earlier in one of the private dining rooms."

Holmes sat up straight. "Dead, you say? How had he died?"

"According to Sir Archibald, it appeared that the poor man took his own life by cutting his throat."

I shuddered. "What a horrible method to choose."

"Indeed it is," Holmes agreed. "Of course, it has the advantage of being silent."

Sir Thomas and I looked at him in a silent entreaty for him to continue, but he simply asked, "The police were called, of course?"

"Of course. A constable was on the scene within minutes."

"And which officer is in charge of the investigation, do you know?"

"An Inspector Gregson. He specifically asked me to call on you."

"Ha! Do you hear that, Watson? I predict that Gregson will go far in his profession. A man, capable and competent as he is, who nevertheless knows and recognises his limits. Something must have seemed amiss to him, or he would not be asking for my assistance."

"You know him well, then, and you will be able to help us get to the bottom of this matter?"

"Indeed I do, and I believe we will be able to work together to solve whatever mystery is involved. Do you know if the body has been moved?"

"Other than Sir Archibald, I believe no one has touched the body, or indeed, anything in the room."

"Excellent," said Holmes. "We should strike while the iron is hot. Watson, you may bring with you whatever medical instruments you feel may assist us. For myself, if you will wait for a few minutes while I collect my impedimenta, Sir Thomas, we will travel with you to the Club. I fancy," he added, looking out of the window at the fog outside, "it will be more convenient and quicker to go on foot, as I perceive you did when coming here, rather than to entrust ourselves to the tender mercies of a jarvey."

Accordingly we groped our way from lamppost to lamppost through the London streets to the premises of the Nonpareil Club, a handsome townhouse in Lower Berkeley Street, where a doorman greeted Sir Thomas and admitted us to the building.

Inspector Tobias Gregson was waiting for us in the hallway and greeted Holmes and me with what appeared to be genuine pleasure.

"Very happy to see that you are available to help us on this one, Mr. Holmes and Doctor Watson. This is a strange affair, and no mistake," he greeted us, extending his hand. "You'll see what I mean. Follow me."

He led the way up the stairs to the first floor, where a constable was standing by a door. "Thank you, Jarvis," he said, as the uniformed officer stepped aside. "Now, take a look for yourselves, gentlemen," he proclaimed.

The scene inside was as shocking as any I have ever encountered. The body of a man sat in a chair at a table, both these pieces of furniture covered in congealed blood. Another chair stood on the other side of the table, and a piece of paper lay on the table beside the man's hand. But for the ghastly wound to the throat, visible even from the doorway, it might almost be thought that the occupant of the chair was dozing while in the act of composing a letter. A curiously-shaped blade lay on the floor beside the table.

"There are bloody footprints on the carpet, leading out of the room," I remarked.

"Indeed there are," Holmes confirmed. "Two sets that I can see, and if you will take the trouble," he continued, lying at full length on the floor, and looking over at the desk from that position, "you will notice several more distinct sets of footprints – three in this case, leading to the desk. Have you or any of your men entered?" he asked Gregson.

"No. We have left the room untouched until now," said the police officer.

"Capital, Gregson. Then we may assume – "

"Excuse me," interrupted Sir Thomas. "Sir Archibald Milton-Harbury entered to examine the – the body."

"Then I will wish to see the boots he was wearing at that time, in order to compare them with these prints," said Gregson. "Sir Thomas, can

170

you please dispatch one of the Club servants to Sir Archibald, so that we may confirm this."

Holmes clapped the inspector on the shoulder. "Excellent, Gregson. If you continue in this way, I expect to see you at the head of Scotland Yard before too long."

Gregson flushed at the praise, but merely asked Holmes if he now felt it appropriate to enter the room.

"So long as we take the obvious precautions," said Holmes. As he and Gregson made their way along the edges of the room, keeping to the walls in order to preserve any clues that might lie in the path from the table to the door, I followed in their wake.

"Excellent," Holmes said. We proceeded to the grisly centre of the room, where blood seemed to cover every surface. The paper which we had remarked from the doorway lay on the table, its edges stained with blood, and an inkwell stood on one corner of it. A tumbler such as might be used for a whisky-and-soda was to the right of the paper. Holmes bent over and sniffed at it without touching it.

"Poor beggar," remarked Gregson.

"Carotid artery severed," I said, following a brief examination of the body. "Cause of death: Shock following massive blood loss."

"Sir Archibald's conclusion also," remarked Sir Thomas from the doorway.

"And here we have the suicide note," said Gregson, pointing to the piece of paper.

"I think not," said Holmes.

"But look, man," expostulated Gregson. "Here it is, as clear as can be."

"Precisely my point," said Holmes. "Inspector, may I have your permission to examine this paper before it passes into the hands of the police? I anticipate that it will not take more than half-a-day before I'm done with it."

Gregson and I exchanged glances and shrugs as Holmes moved to the blade that was on the floor beside the chair on which the body sat.

"A *kukri*," I said. "The traditional knife of the Gurkhas of northern India. They are said to be able to remove a man's head with one stroke."

"Exactly the sort of knife one would expect a man such as Banford to have in his possession following his time in India," remarked Gregson.

"I would remind you, my dear Inspector, that Banford is by no means the only member of this Club who has spent time in India."

"Good God, Mr. Holmes!" exclaimed Sir Thomas. "Are you saying that poor Banford was murdered by another member of the Club?"

"If, as I strongly suspect, he did not kill himself, he was killed by another. I believe we may accept this as being true, may we not? This state of affairs hardly seems to be the result of an accident. And I'm sure that no one except members and Club servants would be in the building at the time you mentioned – that is, ten o'clock in the evening."

"Our Club servants are all above reproach," Sir Thomas told us. "I will personally vouch for that."

"I notice," Holmes said in a low aside to me, "that he does not make the same claim concerning the members of the Club."

"Have you seen all that you need, Mr. Holmes?" asked Gregson. "May we move the body? I'm sure that the Club will wish to clean this room and make it fit for use again."

Sir Thomas nodded his agreement, and Holmes also agreed.

He turned as if to leave, but instantly stopped in his tracks.

"There!" he exclaimed, pointing to a small grey object that stood out against the crimson of the carpet. He dropped to his knee and used tweezers to transfer the item into one of his ever-present envelopes which he carried about his person for purposes such as this. "Cigar ash," he pronounced, "though at present I don't know of what kind." He continued to scrutinise the carpet minutely, at times concentrating on individual tufts, which he probed with the tip of his mechanical pencil. After a few minutes of this, he turned to Sir Thomas, who was still standing in the doorway. "These rooms are cleaned regularly?"

"Indeed they are. Once in the early morning, and once following luncheon. We maintain a very high standard of cleanliness here."

"I had observed that," said Holmes. "Can you tell me whether Banford smoked cigars?"

"Indeed he did. Trichinopoly – I assume he acquired the taste for them in his time in India."

"Thank you." Again, to avoid disturbing the clear footprints which marked the carpet, we made our way around the edge of the room. As we reached the door, the well-known figure of Sir Archibald Milton-Harbury appeared.

"I understand that you wish to view the boots I wore last night," he told us. "They are on my feet now."

"May I?" asked Holmes, and without waiting for an answer, he once more dropped to one knee and proceeded to examine the boots through his ever-present magnifying glass and compare them with the footprints in the carpet. He thanked Sir Archibald as he rose.

"I think that has made matters quite clear," he told Gregson, who nonetheless appeared more than a little mystified. "Dear me," he added, patting his pockets. "I need a cigar to clear my nostrils of the smell of blood, but I seem to have left my cigar-case at home. Watson?" he said to me, turning towards me and giving a wink together with an imperceptible shake of the head which would have been invisible to any other person. I took Holmes's silent hint and reported that I too had neglected to bring any of the weed with me.

"Allow me," said Sir Archibald, bringing out a cigar-case and offering one to Holmes.

"Many thanks," said Holmes as the famous surgeon lit Holmes's cigar before applying the vesta to his own.

Sir Archibald turned to me. "You would concur, Doctor, with my diagnosis of the cause of death? Severe shock following extreme loss of blood?"

"Certainly," said I.

"Poor lad," said Sir Archibald, nodding towards the corpse in the room.

"Poor lad indeed," said Holmes. "Watson, we must be off. Thank you once again for the cigar, Sir Archibald. Sir Thomas, do you happen by any chance to have the name and address of Banford's fiancée?"

"I believe he signed her in as a guest on one of our social evenings, and her details should therefore be in our guestbook."

"Thank you. Gregson," he called as we moved away, "do not write your report until I have contacted you later today. I hope to have some more information for you by this afternoon."

After obtaining the name and address of Miss Emily Sallerton, we stood outside the portals of the Nonpareil Club. The fog of the night had partially lifted, meaning that we were able to hail a cab.

Holmes was in a sombre mood. "Murder is a foul thing," he remarked, apropos of nothing, as we jolted slowly through the streets.

"Murder?" I said. "I was under the impression Sir Archibald and Gregson believe it to be a suicide."

"I have at least sown the seeds of doubt in the good Inspector's mind," he answered me. "As for Sir Archibald, he may be a famous and competent, even brilliant surgeon, but he lacks my extensive experience of investigating violent death. Let us take one trivial, but telling, example to illustrate my point here: Suppose you were to take it into your head to cut your own throat – an event that I sincerely hope will never come to pass, I may add. With which hand would you hold the knife?"

"My right, of course, since I am right-handed."

"Naturally. And with which hand did Banford supposedly cut his throat, based on the wound that you observed?"

I had to reflect for a minute, but eventually answered, "With his right hand."

"Indeed that is so. Now tell me why a left-handed man should cut his throat with his right hand."

"How do you know that he was left-handed?"

"Tut, man. Think back to where the inkwell was on the table."

"To the left, if I remember correctly."

"You do indeed remember correctly. And the tumbler?"

"To the right of the paper."

"Indeed. In a position where it would seriously inconvenience anyone attempting to write with their right hand." He fell silent for a few minutes, and the cab stopped, with the driver informing us that we had reached our destination. Holmes paid him, and then tipped him a half-crown to wait for us. "I fancy that this will not be a long visit," he said to me as we rang the bell.

A maid answered, and told us that, "Miss Emily is with Colonel Upwood," and that if we cared to wait, she would let her know of our presence.

"Thank you, there is no need for that," said Holmes, and we turned and walked down the steps to the waiting cab. "I had marked Upwood as a cad," he remarked, "but this latest is quite a surprise to me."

"You mean?" I asked.

"I think we may safely assume that Upwood has been involved for some time in stealing the affections of Miss Emily Sallerton, detaching her from the unfortunate Banford. It is quite possible that Banford knew of this when she announced her intention not to proceed with the engagement."

"And now the scoundrel has the nerve to visit her on the day after her former betrothed's death? This is infamous, Holmes!"

"Indeed it is, but it is not the worst. This business is a foul one."

Once at Baker Street, Holmes placed the cigar ash that he had collected from the carpet under his microscope. "As I thought," he pronounced after about a minute's examination. "This is not ash from a Trichinopoly, such as we are informed that Banford smoked, nor is it a Panetella, as enjoyed by Sir Archibald. Now, recall that the carpet showed us three sets of footprints entering the room, and two leaving. Your conclusions?"

"Given that we know Sir Archibald to have entered and left the room, we must assume that the footprints which enter and fail to leave are Banford's, leaving another set unaccounted for."

"Precisely. And I was able to determine that the prints made by Sir Archibald's distinctively square-toed boots were made following the staining of the carpet with Banford's blood, while those of the unknown were produced before that time on entry, and afterwards on leaving. We may therefore deduce that the unknown, who incidentally smokes a Havana Robusto, of a very different quality to that smoked by Sir Archibald, was present when Banford lost his life."

"That would seem to be clear."

"Now we come to the letter that we discovered on the desk. In full it reads: '*I am in despair. I cannot go on. V. Banford.*' Short, sharp, and to the point, and a clumsy attempt to divert us from the truth. We saw the register in which guests were entered, did we not, and where Banford's signature was to be found. In the first place, that signature was not '*V. Banford*', but '*Vernon Banford*', and in the second, the formation of the letters differed significantly. In particular, the capital *B* was formed in a completely different fashion. Furthermore, we agreed that Banford was in all probability left-handed, and that supposition was borne out by the entry in the register. This, on the other hand, was written by a right-handed man."

"But how did you initially come to suspect the authenticity of the letter?"

"Elementary. Do you remember Gregson's saying that it was clear as could be? And so it was – clear of blood, when everything else on the table was saturated. It was obvious that it had been placed on the table *after* the death of Banford. There is also the amusingly minor point that the ink in the inkwell appeared to be blue ink, while this is written in blue-black ink. And you may also recall the pen on the table."

"I saw no such item."

"There was none. Now, it is just possible that Banford wrote the note in blue-black ink, using his own fountain-pen which will be discovered on the body, with his handwriting and signature being made less than typical by the emotion of the event, and placed the finished note on the table following the cutting of his own throat – "

"So improbable a sequence of events as to be impossible," I interrupted.

"Exactly. I think we must therefore conclude that our smoker of Havana Robusto cigars penned this short missive before entering the room, and dropped it on the table following the death of Banford."

"And how was that death accomplished?"

"As a medical man, you may be in a better position to give me the details."

"Very well, then. The carotid artery was severed. I would say that, given the angle and depth of the wound, the head was bent back at the time that the wound was inflected."

"Good. And?"

175

"The depth of the wound was excessive. It did not appear to me to be a wound inflicted by an action usually inflicted in the cutting of a throat." I shuddered. "In my time in India, I saw enough such, inflicted on our brave lads by their Afghan captors. This wound seemed to be more in the nature of an attempted decapitation. A swinging slashing cut, rather than the slicing action whose results I have seen in the past."

"Such as might be expected from the wielder of a *kukri*, such as we saw by the body?"

"Just so. The design of this weapon makes it suitable for such an attack." I paused. "Are you suggesting, though, that Banford allowed his unknown assailant to attack him in this manner without putting up any resistance?"

"There is another piece to this puzzle which I have not yet explained to you. You remember the tumbler on the table?"

"Naturally. I had assumed that it had contained a whisky-and-soda, or similar."

"Indeed it had, but there was also a faint, but yet distinct, smell of chloral hydrate, which, as you probably know, forms a powerful sedative when mixed with alcohol and water.

"Let me reconstruct the scene for you as I see it. The murderer – I think we may now both agree that Banford's death was no suicide – arranged a meeting with Banford in that private room. Banford arrived first, and brought with him a whisky-and-soda which he had previously ordered from one of the Club servants. When the murderer arrived, already armed with a concealed *kukri* and the forged suicide note, he managed to distract Banford's attention sufficiently to add the hypnotic to the drink unnoticed. Once the chloral had taken effect, he pulled poor Banford's head back, out came the *kukri*, and – " Holmes brought his hand down in an energetic gesture.

I shivered. "And the weapon itself?"

"I think the *Army List*, or maybe *Who's Who*, will provide us with the answer." He stretched out a lazy arm towards the bookcase and pulled out the latter volume. "Upperby, Upton, ah! Upwood. Here he is. Yes, indeed, Watson, here it is. Seconded to the Fourth Gurkha Rifles for a year some time back. I am sure that ghastly weapon is a souvenir of his time there."

"What do you intend doing?"

"We will go and see him now. And if he is not at home, we will wait for him. You may care to bring your revolver and one cartridge."

I did not question this extraordinary request, but did as I had been bid.

We arrived at Colonel Upwood's rooms at three o'clock and were informed by his valet that the Colonel was expected to return at half-past the hour.

On our informing the valet that we would wait for his master, we were conducted to a small sitting room, furnished with Oriental knick-knacks, including various native weapons. A space on the wall clearly indicated where one such ornament had been removed and not subsequently replaced. I silently indicated this to Holmes, and he responded with a nod.

At length we heard the sound of the front door being opened, and shortly thereafter, Colonel Upwood fairly burst into the room.

"Dobbs informs me that you two have been waiting for my return. Infernal impertinence! Why could you not have left a card?"

Holmes, still seated, responded. "This is an urgent matter that requires your personal attention."

"Very well. I will give you two minutes of my time to state your business, Mr. . . . ?"

"The name is Sherlock Holmes, and my friend here is John Watson."

"The nosey-parker busybody? The police spy?"

"I am no spy for the police, Colonel. If I were, you would now be handcuffed and in the cells. I am giving you a chance to clear a man's name, and at the same time to restore a little honour to your own."

"Damn you, you miserable meddler in other men's affairs! You and your friend may leave instantly." He pointedly held the door open and stood by it, but Holmes remained seated. "Are you going of your own free will, or shall I make you go?" he shouted as he advanced upon my friend with a look of fury on his face.

There was a flash of steel, and Holmes was on his feet, his swordstick unsheathed, with the point at the Colonel's throat. "You would do well to sit, and to listen to what I have to say to you. No, do not consider calling for assistance. It will serve no useful purpose. Sit." He moved the swordstick in a meaningful fashion, and Upwood half-fell into the chair behind him.

"There is little point in denial," Holmes told him. "I have been informed of the circumstances surrounding this business at the Nonpareil Club. I have investigated the matter, and can now present enough evidence to convict you many times over in a court of law. Did you really think that your clumsy efforts could persuade even our Scotland Yard police to believe that Banford killed himself? Your efforts at forging a suicide note were laughable in the extreme. And the carelessness with which you left a clear clue as to your identity in the form of a half-inch of cigar ash is almost unparalleled in the annals of crime. My only question to you is why you behaved so abominably?"

The fight seemed to go out of Upwood's body as Holmes spoke, but his eyes burned. "My reputation, Holmes. As a member of the Nonpareil Club, I was accorded some respect. Should I lose that membership, my creditors would come flocking around like vultures to a Parsee Tower of Silence." He paused. "Young Banford would have seen me out of the Club, and I would have been ruined. His fiancée, young Emily Sallerton, would have brought with her some ten-thousand pounds upon her marriage to him, and with that money, he could have easily bought the votes to expel me from the Club.

"I therefore determined to woo her away from his side, and was successful to the extent that she broke her engagement to him and entered into an understanding with me. And that same evening, we had words."

"I heard about that and about the card game."

"That thousand pounds that I paid him when he won that final hand – that was money I did not have. I would be ruined even more thoroughly in the eyes of society. So . . . I knew he was in low spirits over the breaking of the engagement. I suggested that we talk together over the tiger business – you know of that. He was in the room, waiting at the table. I brought two whisky-and-sodas with me, and I had added a few drops of chloral to the drink that I gave him. In a few minutes he was practically asleep, and I – I am ashamed to describe what I did."

"I think we know," Holmes said, almost gently.

"I never imagined there would be so much blood. My God! I have seen men die in battle, and I have also seen the inside of a surgeon's tent, but . . . ." He paused and drew a deep breath. "I arranged the glass and the inkwell and hurriedly placed the note I had written in his writing on the table."

"You neglected to notice that Banford was left-handed," Holmes remarked, almost negligently.

"Maybe I did," said Upwood, a new strength in his voice. "But it doesn't really matter, does it?" He held out his hand, a small revolver pointed at Holmes held in it. "You will drop that stupid pig-sticker, and if you believe in a God, you will say your prayers before I dispose of an intruder whom I discovered in my rooms."

He seemed to have forgotten my existence. I was seated in a position invisible to him as he faced Holmes, and it was the work of a moment for me to use the butt of my revolver to knock him senseless with a blow under the ear.

"Good work, Watson," said Holmes, removing the unconscious man's revolver from his hand, and removing five of the six cartridges. "Do you think you can guard him while I get the servants out of the house?"

I agreed to this, and Holmes left the room. Our adversary stirred, and moaned as he opened his eyes to find himself staring down the barrel of my pistol.

"Do not move," I told him. I have no doubt that I would have shot and killed him, unarmed as he was, had he attempted to make any resistance. He was a dangerous man, and had threatened my friend with death.

After a few minutes, the sound of the front door opening and shutting reached us, and Holmes re-entered the room.

"Now, Colonel, I wish you to sit at that bureau and to write to my dictation."

"The devil I will."

Holmes clapped the revolver he was holding to Upwood's temples. "Very well, then. I shall be forced to take you to the police."

"Damn you, I'll write."

He struggled to his feet and seated himself at the desk while Holmes dictated a detailed confession of how he had arranged Banford's death.

"My congratulations. You are the devil himself to know all this, even given what I have told you already," said Upwood when he had signed the document and placed it in an envelope.

"Some have said so," smiled Holmes, pocketing the envelope.

"And what now?" asked Upwood.

"I think you know what is expected of an officer and a gentleman," Holmes told him. "We will leave the room, leaving you with the revolver, which, by the way, has one cartridge in it. There is therefore no point in attempting to attack us, armed with our own revolvers and my swordstick. If we have not heard the shot within five minutes, we will carry out the task that you have failed to do."

Holmes and I left the room, Holmes placing Upwood's revolver on the floor as we closed the door.

The sound of the shot reached us less than one minute later, and on opening the door, we beheld Upwood seated at the bureau, a bullet through his brain.

"Pride," said Holmes, looking at the ruined head. "Damnable pride. Come, let us to Gregson, and present him with this," waving Upwood's confession. "It will provide him with invaluable assistance in the writing of his report. And then to Sir Thomas."

Sir Thomas listened gravely to the account that Holmes gave of events. "Shocking, shocking," he said, shaking his head. "And yet, I can hardly claim to be surprised. Our members, as I mentioned, are beset with that most invidious of the deadly sins. I can see it in myself, in the very founding of the Club."

It came as no surprise to either Holmes or myself when a few days later the daily newspapers provided a full account of "The Upwood Scandal", as it became known, together with a full account of the card game that had preceded the killing of Banford. Inspector Gregson was given the majority of the credit for the exposure of Upwood's atrocious conduct, and the same accounts also reported that following this scandal, Sir Thomas Ridgson was dissolving the Nonpareil Club.

"A welcome move," I said as I read the story to Holmes over our breakfast that day. "The fewer opportunities for these peacocks to strut and display their feathers, the better for us all."

"I entirely agree," said Holmes. "How elegantly you phrase things," he mused.

And then and there the Nonpareil Club became a nine days' wonder, and then sank, as these matters invariably do, into the marsh of history.

> *Since the tragic upshot of our visit to Devonshire he had been engaged in two affairs of the utmost importance, in the first of which he had exposed the atrocious conduct of Colonel Upwood in connection with the famous card scandal of the Nonpareil Club . . .*

.

Dr. John H. Watson
The Hound of the Baskervilles

The Adventure of the
Singular Worm
by Mike Chinn

"Well, Watson? Are we to assume it is someone of your acquaintance, or not?"

I turned away from the window to glance at my friend, Sherlock Holmes. He was relaxing in a chair, noisome pipe hanging from his thin lips, his eyes apparently closed as though enjoying a post-prandial nap.

"Who is that?" I asked.

He removed his pipe and favoured me with a faint smile, although he didn't deign to open his eyes. "You have been gazing down from that window for two-and-a-half minutes," he said. "Your head has tracked back and forth repeatedly during that period, so I must conclude that you're watching someone pacing the pavements below."

So much was true. A gentlemen, dressed in a fine suit, head uncovered, had stepped down from a cab almost directly opposite our Baker Street rooms a short while ago. Since then he had walked no more than a dozen yards before turning about and retracing his steps – an action he had repeated many times. On occasion he would cast a glance in the direction of our door, but make no attempt to cross the road.

"Furthermore," continued my friend, "that you have observed our indecisive visitor without comment all this time suggests either he or she is known to you, and you have no wish to see this person for you own reasons, all the while silently praying he or she will depart quickly, or you're uncertain as to whether you recognise him or her at all and are loath to acknowledge this person's presence until you are certain." Holmes finally opened his eyes fully and removed his pipe, waving the stem to accompany his words. "Your face betrays none of the tension I might expect from the sight of an unwelcome acquaintance – and you are so often an open book, Watson – but it does reflect an honest curiosity. Therefore I must conclude that whomever is stalking Baker Street strongly resembles someone you know – although not, I would hazard, so intimately that this person's features are instantly recognisable. Thus, you do not feel comfortable enough in that recognition to announce his or her arrival."

I smiled at his deductions. "It is Sir Preston Baggott, or so I believe. I attended his lectures on the comparative uses of ether, chloroform, and nitrous oxide in surgical anaesthesia whilst a medical student. His researches at the time were quite revolutionary, although he is no longer so famous that his image is routinely displayed in the newspapers, and it is difficult to be sure how time has worked on his features." I looked down again. The figure had completed yet another transit along the pavement and started another. "Still, I'm certain it is him."

Holmes raised a bushy eyebrow. "Then I hope he eventually agrees to throw himself upon our hospitality. I'm intrigued at to what would cause vacillation in such an eminent personage."

The figure appeared to reach a decision. Throwing back his shoulders, he abandoned his aimless back-and-forth and crossed Baker Street, heading directly for our door. "We should know shortly," I said. There was a loud, staccato rapping downstairs. "That will be him now."

Moments later the door to our rooms was opened, and a tall, portly figure entered. Now that I saw him clearly I was left in no doubt – this was indeed the pre-eminent Sir Preston Baggott, although he had gained some considerable weight in the years since I saw him last. A mane of thick, iron-grey hair was brushed back from a florid, clean-shaven face. Matted black eyebrows dominated brown eyes which were outlined by puffy red lids, eyes which scanned the room restlessly. Indeed, his entire frame seemed to vibrate with barely-suppressed energy. Having made the decision to come up to our rooms, I had the strong impression he was already regretting doing so.

Holmes came to his feet, indicating a chair. "Sir Preston, if you would be so kind."

The surgeon stared at my friend for a moment, before lowering himself into the proffered armchair with a deep groan. He rubbed at his eyes. "You recognise me, then."

Holmes folded his frame back into his chair. "Not I," he said. "But it is my belief that you made quite an impression on my colleague, Dr. Watson, back in his student days."

Sir Preston glanced my way, his thick brows drawing down as though he was trying to recall my face. After a moment his features relaxed and he managed a tentative smile. "I am gratified to be remembered, Doctor, after all these years."

"Your lectures were always of deep interest," I said, offering him a cigarette, for by his manner I imagined he was in sore need of one. He accepted gratefully, lighting it with a match of his own.

"Well," began Holmes, tapping out his pipe against the fireplace and slipping it into a pocket, "now you have finally made up your mind, may I ask why you are here?"

Sir Preston drew deeply on his smoke and smiled again. This time it was almost bashful. "I confess – Mr. Holmes, Doctor – that I am not sure whether my visit is necessarily prudent. Or even that the matter which perplexes me is within your purview. It is – too odd . . . ."

"I assure you that this agency relishes the odd, Sir Preston, and as a doctor yourself, you will appreciate that Watson is the most discrete man I know."

"Indeed." He puffed again on his cigarette, finally coming to a decision. "You will have heard, I am sure, of Isadora Persano."

"The celebrated Italian journalist?" I knew of the man, and had read some of the essays that he'd published in British newspapers. Although I had to admit his writings were incisive and fearless, I found his style somewhat florid and self-congratulatory.

"And an equally famous duellist," added Holmes. "A man whose opinions must frequently be defended with a sabre – a weapon in which I believe he is most proficient."

Sir Preston nodded. "His reputation has always preceded him. Indeed, I cannot be sure if he wrote those inflammatory articles to provoke the duels, or he fought the duels to increase his readership. I have known Isadora for almost five years, off-and-on, but I cannot say that I'm close to him. He wouldn't allow it."

"You used the past tense," remarked Holmes.

The surgeon frowned, crushing out a cigarette he had smoked remarkably quickly. "You lose me, Mr. Holmes."

"You say 'wrote' and 'fought'. Are we to assume Signor Persano no longer pursues those activities?"

Sir Preston nodded his leonine head. "Five years ago Isadora settled in England, here to retire and commit his memoirs to paper. During that time his bouts with sabre were generally confined to practise within a small, rather ugly garden to the rear of his house."

"Not least because duelling is generally frowned upon within our shores," I observed.

Sir Preston sighed. "As you say. But just because something isn't considered legal doesn't mean that it is does not take place."

"There I must heartily agree with you," said Holmes, his eyes twinkling.

"So Signor Persano continued to duel?" I asked.

"I think that his blood demands it. Each bout was carefully managed – I seconded several myself – and honour was always considered satisfied at first blood. Isadora never lost. Up until recently his stamina and reflexes were unequalled – his body sustained barely a scratch."

Holmes shifted impatiently. "Sir Preston, so far you have spoken only of Signor Persano and your somewhat qualified admiration for him. What you have so singularly failed to tell us is your reason for being here."

"I apologise." Sir Preston stared at the floor for a moment. "It is hard for me, for the matter is beyond my training and experience." He drew in a deep breath. "He has been suffering from chronic insomnia for many months. You will know, Doctor Watson, how debilitating that can be. I have been prescribing a series of sleeping draughts, and at first they seemed to help . . . ."

Holmes gave an irritable sigh. "At first? You are obtuse, Sir Preston."

"Isadora has always been a man of tremendous nervous energy. It infuses all aspects of his life – his writing, his duels. However, lack of sleep has, I believe, been eroding that energy, leaving him irritable and snappish. And by temperament he has never been the most accommodating of men. His maid, Faith – who is the most devoted creature – has increasingly become the subject of his deteriorating character. Isadora will always apologise profusely when the fit has left him, but it is distressing to witness – almost like watching a man whipping a puppy.

"Then, three days ago, Faith discovered him sitting in his garden – unusual in itself, for apart from exercise and a shrinking number of duels, Isadora had no time for that barren patch of ground. Sometimes I imagined that he actively abhorred it." Sir Preston shook his head. "It is not a term I use lightly, Mr. Holmes, but when she found him, he was quite insane. Aside from the twitching of his lips and a faint, continuous mutter of sounds – I cannot call them words – he was almost catatonic."

Holmes frowned at the man. "A medical matter, surely? Certainly not within my purview."

"There is more, Mr. Holmes. Clutched within Isadora's grasp, held so tightly that it was all but impossible to extricate, was a closed matchbox. And inside that box was a remarkable worm, a quite hideous creature, and one that appears to be quite unknown to science!"

Holmes steepled his fingertips and leaned back. "You think the two events – your friend's sudden insanity and this curious worm – are related?"

The surgeon shrugged helplessly. "I cannot say. Certainly he was rational enough a few hours earlier – aside from his usual bad temper and nervous state."

"Then what do you imagine I might be able to do about it?"

Sir Preston ran a hand through his unruly hair. "I am plagued by doubt. What if Isadora's increasing mania was not the result of insomnia? Was he, in fact, a man living in dread?"

"You consider there may have been someone threatening him? Surely he would have challenged such a person to a duel and be done with it, rather than let the matter fester."

"Perhaps I am too close and need a fresh perspective." He looked as us both with imploring eyes. "At the least there is the question of how a worm – no matter how grotesque – may have driven him insane. Will you both at least consent to examine Isadora and the frightful creature? Any fresh insights will be more than welcome."

Holmes was silent for some time. As he pondered, I felt compelled to point out that I was not an alienist. Sir Preston waved aside my concerns, saying a second opinion would still be welcome.

At length Holmes spoke. "You have kept the worm?"

"It is in a jar, preserved in alcohol."

My friend pursed his lips. "Unfortunate. I would have preferred a living specimen. Still. And Signor Persano?"

"Remains at his house, under the care of Faith. His condition has shown no change since that fateful day."

"Then we shall attend. There is little to distract me at the moment. The criminal classes have been woefully unimaginative these past months." Holmes glanced at me, his eyes kindling with the fire of a new curiosity. "What of you, Watson?"

I smiled back. "As ever, I am at your disposal."

Persano's house was one of several standing in misleading isolation among the fields of Neasden, far enough away from the encroaching city for the eye to be fooled. As we stepped down from the cab that Sir Preston had hired, the air smelled fresh and clean – it was hard to believe that London was so close. We had observed that much of the creeping urbanisation on our journey – the new estates, following the line of the Metropolitan Railway as it edged north. It was with a pang of regret I silently acknowledged that even these farmlands would soon fall to the pick and spade, be paved over, and covered with bricks and mortar.

The house itself was a large white building, parts of it clearly dating back a century or more, with recent brick extensions to one side and the rear. It had a grey slate roof, and a confusion of mullioned windows punctuated the rendered sides as though placed there by the original builder as the whim took him. An air of genteel decay overhung its shabby, unpainted exterior and it was clear that the owner – for I surmised Persano was a tenant – had spent nothing on the building's upkeep in many years. A line of overgrown hedgerows ran along the lane off which it stood, leaving a narrow entrance onto a small, weed-dotted drive. A narrow, ivy-choked porch enclosed the main entrance.

Sir Preston asked the cabbie to wait. Clearly he didn't expect us to be staying long.

As we approached the door it was opened, and a young maid greeted Sir Preston, and nodding to Holmes and me. Strands of dark hair had escaped from her cap, and her pleasant, open face was too pale, with shadows underlining black, feverish eyes. Persano was clearly not the only one within that house whom sleep eluded.

"Mr. Holmes, Doctor Watson," spoke the surgeon, "this is Faith, of whom I have spoken. How is he, my dear?"

The maid gave him a brief, weary smile. "No change, sir. I tried to tempt him with some broth earlier, but he wouldn't take it. He simply stared past me, his eyes unseeing, murmuring all the while."

Sir Preston patted her shoulder. "Thank you. Will you take us to him?"

The girl led us inside the house. It was dim, the irregular windows providing little in the way of illumination. The walls and floor were mostly of dark wood, and the scent of polish thickened the air.

We entered a room that was just as dark as the corridor outside. Curtains had been drawn, further deepening the gloom. Faith parted them only a little – for there were no ties to hold them open, just bare hooks – allowing a chink of daylight to enter and fall upon a bed. A lone figure lay there, still as death, his face aimed up at the dim ceiling. I heard a low monotone issuing from him, too soft to be sure if he spoke in English, Italian, or neither. Sir Preston stepped close, peering down, and waved a hand before the staring eyes. He sighed.

"Little response."

Holmes stood at the foot of the bed, his head bowed in thought. "Watson – would you care to examine Persano?"

Sir Preston nodded his agreement and stepped aside, allowing me to approach the muttering figure whilst not blocking the scant light. I was alarmed at how emaciated Persano looked, and for a minute was unable to locate a pulse. His skin was cold, pale, and clammy. Originally I had thought his immobility due to catatonia, but I noted broad leather straps looped around his wrists, passing over his gaunt chest, and under the bed. Aside from his ever-moving white lips, an irregular facial tic would pull at an eyelid, or tug at the corner of his colourless lips. His breathing was slow and shallow. Even now, standing so close, I could make no sense of his mutterings.

"How is his blood pressure?" I asked.

"He has been hypotensive since his collapse," said Sir Preston. "Faith, quite sensibly, managed to get him to bed and – as you heard – has attempted to give him fluids on a regular basis. With mixed results. I have treated him as best as can, but he remains unresponsive."

186

"You said Signor Persano has been suffering from insomnia," said Holmes. "Would you expect such a condition as we see to result from severe sleep deprivation?"

"It is possible that nervous collapse might result from prolonged lack of sleep."

"And the facial tics?" I asked.

"Another symptom," replied the surgeon. He gazed at us both. "Isadora has a small catalogue of established symptoms – but none that add up to a recognised condition. All that I can surmise is that the singular worm is at the bottom of it."

"Ah – the worm." Holmes raised his head. "You said you had preserved it. Might we see it?"

The surgeon seemed to be stricken with indecision once again. "Yes. Very well, I will fetch it." After a moment's hesitation, he quickly left the dim room.

Holmes immediately turned to the maid. "Now, in the days prior to his collapse, how was Signor Persano?"

She frowned. "He has always been of an excitable nature – one moment complaining that his breakfast eggs are overcooked, the next apologising for his manner. In the past months he has grown worse, more . . . grandiose, if that's the word. He has been increasingly irritable and obsessed with silly details. Sir Preston has told you that the Signor is writing his memoirs? Small things such as whether a certain duel was fought on a Wednesday or a Thursday would drive him to distraction. Quite often his mood would go from being outrageously generous – like when he insisted on paying for me and my family to see some opera by Verdi and would not hear of me saying no – and a murderous rage minutes later when the grocer's boy brought some spaghetti that his employer thought the Signor would like, him being Italian and all. In fact he has little taste for pasta. Isn't that odd?" She tried to smile – a pale, weary thing. "I feared for my life, sir."

My friend nodded thoughtfully. "I observe that your employer is quite thin. How is his appetite?"

"It used to be quite healthy," she replied, "but of late it too has grown erratic. He will often go for more than a day without a morsel, then demand an enormous meal. I flatter myself I have grown quite handy preparing Italian food, but he will eat only a few bites before losing all interest again."

"Does that remind you of anyone, Holmes?" I said.

He faced me for a moment, his mouth twitching briefly. "Your concern is noted and touching, Doctor."

"There is one other thing, sir," said Faith. "Those spasms that Doctor Watson drew attention to – tugging at the Signor's face. I have noticed them over the past weeks, too – growing worse, I'd say. Quite disturbing. He often looked uncomfortably hot as well – sweating."

"Excellent!" Something like a thin smile touched Holmes's features. "Faith, you have been invaluable – Ah, Sir Preston!"

The surgeon had bustled back into the room, carrying a liquid-filled glass specimen jar. He stepped into the light thrown by the partly-opened curtain and raised it. The rays angling through the gap lit up its strange contents.

The creature within was coiled around several times and difficult to see clearly. I asked if I might remove it from the jar, but at that moment, Persano began to moan and wrench at his bonds. In seconds he was in the throes of a fit, yelling and screaming incoherently. Sir Preston handed me the jar and went to his charge, imploring us to remove the bottled worm out to the rear garden.

Holmes and I found it easily enough. It was a simple, paved rectangle, about the area of a tennis court, surrounded on three sides by brick walls which reached a height of several feet. There was not an inch of grass to be seen. This would be Isadora Persano's duelling and training ground, no doubt.

As Holmes held the specimen jar I carefully opened it and scooped out its contents. The sharp smell of spirits assailed my nose as I held the preserved worm in an open hand. It was bright orange, with a fringe of what may have been legs or tentacles running down either side of its body, which had a thick, scaley exterior. It was almost six inches in length, while the main body was over an inch thick.

"I might suggest it is some peculiar hybrid of *nereidae* – the ragworms – and *polynoidae* – the scale worms, although I am at a loss as to explain how such a thing is possible." I brought the creature closer, ignoring the astringent fumes coming from it. For a moment I was seized by the fancy it was actually a chimera created for a carnival exhibit – like the absurd Feejee Mermaid perpetuated by the American showman P.T. Barnum. I could see no obvious fakery, however. One end – which I presumed to be the head – had small palps or jaws, lined with tiny pseudo teeth. From the tail ran two long antennae or feelers of some kind. Certainly it was nothing I had seen before.

"I didn't realise you had such an intimate knowledge of the *annelida*," said Holmes with a degree of amusement. I offered the worm for his own examination, but he declined with a shake of the head.

I returned the specimen to the jar. "I was once a boy," I said, quietly. "With an older brother whose consuming passion was, at one, time fishing."

Before we could return to the house, Sir Preston joined us in the garden. "A grotesque creature, is it not?" said he.

I handed over the specimen jar. "Certainly unusual," I replied. "How is Signor Persano?"

"I managed to administer a little calmative by syringe. He will sleep for a while." He turned his attention to Holmes. "Have you any opinions?"

My friend shook his head. "There are aspects I must consider further before I will commit myself. It seems to me this case is quite a simple one – one you may have shone some light on yourself, if you had thought on it longer."

Sir Preston looked offended. "Mr. Holmes, I am a surgeon. The mind is not my speciality."

"Quite so." Holmes produced his cigarettes and offered them. Once I was confident that the alcoholic fumes had dispersed, I took one. "Watson and I will return to Baker Street. If you will be good enough to call on us tomorrow morning . . . ?"

The surgeon lit his own cigarette and stared at us thoughtfully. "You will have an opinion for me by then?"

"As I said, the case is vexingly simple – but I must consider everything, if not merely for my personal satisfaction."

After a moment, Sir Preston nodded. "As you wish. I will see you tomorrow."

We walked through the house and out to the cab awaiting us. Once we were aboard and moving, Holmes barked out an abrupt laugh. I wondered what was so amusing. He shook his head, still smiling, but wouldn't answer. Instead he called out to the cabbie, instructing him to take us to Simpson's, rather than Baker Street.

"We're dining out?" I said, surprised. It was more usual for my friend to celebrate at one of his favoured restaurants when a case was fully resolved. "Are there not still details to be explored?"

"My dear Watson, nothing that a quick search of a suitable pharmacopoeia and my own files cannot resolve." He laughed again, but would speak no more on the subject.

The following morning, Sir Preston arrived at our rooms while we were finishing our breakfast. He looked more refreshed than on his first visit, his great grey mane carefully brushed, his eyes bright. Clearly he believed Holmes would present him with good news.

My friend bade him make himself comfortable, offering a smoke and coffee. The surgeon declined both, producing a large cigar, which he puffed into life. Holmes lit his pipe, while I contented myself with a cigarette.

"What news, then, Mr. Holmes?" asked Sir Preston, leaning forward in his seat.

"My conclusion was reached easily enough," began Holmes, "although the sources I required were a little harder to lay hands on than I had first anticipated. Perhaps that is not a surprise."

The surgeon looked intrigued, while I could attest to Holmes being awake most of the night, searching through his filing system.

My friend puffed slowly on his pipe a while longer. Eventually he spoke. "Are you aware of the condition known as *scoleciphobia*?"

Sir Preston frowned. "It is not familiar to me," he admitted.

Holmes glanced my way. "Watson?"

I shook my head.

"No? Well, perhaps it not such a common dread – such as that of heights or crowds. It is the morbid fear of *worms*, gentlemen, also known as *helminthophobia* or *vermiphobia*. In short, a sufferer may experience extreme anxiety or even severe attacks of panic – perhaps manifesting as rage – at the sight of a worm, or anything resembling a worm. Were you aware that Isadora Persano was inflicted by this ailment, Sir Preston?"

The surgeon shook his head. "As I said, I had never heard of it before."

"Indeed. It was an easy deduction. The garden paved over so no soil was present, the brick walls mortared into the ground. No soil – no worms."

"Isadora had that garden designed for his duels," Sir Preston pointed out.

"I have no doubt – but a neatly cut lawn would serve just as well as stone slabs, surely?" Holmes tapped out his pipe and laid it aside. "Then there is the lack of ties for the curtains, only the hooks. A curious omission. And the rage he flew into at the sight of the spaghetti delivered by a thoughtful grocer." His lips quirked. "Very suggestive. All things of a wormlike appearance."

Sir Preston grunted. "Now you highlight these facts, they are curious."

"And the most obvious fact of all: Signor Persano being driven to madness by the sight of what I must admit is a singularly ugly worm."

"But why would that take him to madness and beyond?" I wondered.

"His nerves have been deteriorating for many months – so much the maid and Sir Preston told us. It is not inconceivable the singular worm, found so unexpectedly, would be the breaking point for a man already teetering on the precipice of nervous collapse."

Sir Preston leaned back and took a long draw on his cigar. "Then your conclusion is that Isadora, already suffering from a phobia of which I was unaware, his nerves in a dreadful state and deteriorating, was literally scared out of his wits?"

"So it would appear. As I said, the resolution was, in the end, quite simple. Insultingly so."

"Perhaps to you, Mr. Holmes." The surgeon gathered himself, ready to stand. "I'll admit I would never have divined that conclusion."

"You do yourself a disservice, Sir Preston. I am sure you reached the very same supposition months ago."

The surgeon paused in the act of standing, his expression perplexed. "You have lost me, Mr. Holmes."

"I stated quite clearly: So it would appear. I am always wary of appearances, as Watson will tell you. They are all too often a disguise thrown over inconvenient questions."

Sir Preston sank back into his chair. His air of casual satisfaction had dissipated somewhat. "Which questions?"

"Most obviously: How did a worm of an apparently undescribed family of *annelida* come to be in a matchbox? Even a common earthworm could not have found its way there unaided. So who placed it there, and why? Less obviously, what has caused Signor Persano's woeful mental state?"

"Other than insomnia? I did speculate on the possibility of some threat – "

Holmes was scornful. "The man was fearless! There has been no threat in his history that, once received, was not confronted with a blade or exposure in his writings."

The surgeon drew himself up. "Then what are you implying?"

"I never imply, Sir Preston, any more than I will theorise without data – both are the actions of a lazy brain. Instead I draw now on my own experiences. There are compounds available – some less legally than others – that, while a boon for a while, over time have a deleterious effect. But this you know, of course, from your own researches into anaesthesia."

"I fail to follow you."

"Then I will make it plainer. Two years ago the Romanian chemist Lazăr Edeleanu synthesised a new compound which he named *phenylisopropylamine*. It is one of a series of compounds related to the plant derivative *ephedrine*, which was also isolated in same year by a Japanese chemist, Nagayoshi Nagai. Although overlooked by the medical profession so far, it has been noted in some of the more obscure pharmacopoeias as a stimulant for the central nervous system. Experimental data suggests *phenylisopropylamine* can be used to promote a sense of well-being and exhilaration, and lessening the sense of fatigue."

"This obscure compound does indeed sound like a boon," said Sir Preston.

"If only it was so simple. Experimental data on prolonged exposure in mice and rats – and, I regret in less enlightened quarters, on men – suggests there may be a woeful litany of less-welcome effects." He pulled a sheet of paper from his pocket. "I have noted some of the more pertinent down, for it is a lengthy catalogue. I quote: '*Both loss of appetite and weight, profuse sweating, tics, irritability and restlessness, mood swings, insomnia, an exaggerated sense of one's own importance, and obsessive behaviour. In severe cases, psychosis may occur*'." Holmes folded the sheet and replaced it in his pocket. "Do those symptoms not sound familiar, Watson?"

I agreed that they did. Sir Preston however, was dismissive.

"Are you suggesting that Isadora has somehow found access to this substance and been using it to excess?"

"But of course I am. As the supplier, you must know it to be true."

The surgeon's normally florid expression grew redder with furious incredulity. "Mr. Holmes! I came to you in good faith, hoping you may shed some light on a curious occurrence – !"

"On the contrary, you approached me knowing I would easily deduce Signor Persano's *scoleciphobia* from your clumsily placed clues: The missing ties, the spaghetti, his violent reaction when you so obviously held the dead worm up before him, illuminated against a darkened room by a ray of sunlight. As you played the confounded close friend, you hoped the suggestion of myself – along with that of Watson – would be to have the man committed to a mental institution for a total mental breakdown brought on by overwork, lack of sleep, and his peculiar phobia. You would finally have your revenge against one who has offended your family, even though you are not man enough to face him on the field of honour!

"It is really too bad, Sir Preston, that you imagined I would fall for such a transparent plan. Better men than you have tried, and failed."

The surgeon continued to bluster, although I could see his outrage was beginning to deflate in the face of Holmes's conviction. "What is this offense to my family? Isadora have been friends for only five years – !"

"The case of Fulford Weatheroak. You may recall the name, Watson?"

I thought carefully. "Indeed I do. A brilliant orthopaedic surgeon, he was briefly considered as a Physician to the Queen until an accident damaged his right arm – some twenty years ago. He retired and vanished from public view."

"The same – except it was no accident robbed him of his skill and future. It was a severe injury, taken on the field of honour. The details have always been carefully suppressed in Britain, as indeed was the original libel, for no scandal must ever be allowed to stain the character of one potentially so close to the Queen-Empress."

Sir Preston's face had gone quite pale. "How did you know?"

"When such a figure suffers an unexplained injury and backs out of public scrutiny it will always be of interest to me," said Holmes, a note of censure in his voice. "That the whole incident is hidden behind official obfuscation merely whetted my interest the more. I long ago satisfied myself as to the reality behind your uncle's premature retirement – yes, I am aware of his maternal relationship to you – and consigned it to my files, alongside many others of greater and lesser prominence."

Sir Preston looked shrunken, a ghastly shade of his earlier self. "Then you know – ?"

"The details of the scandal need not concern us," said Holmes. "Even Signor Persano, in the original offending article, published in an obscure Australian newspaper that has long since ceased publication, chose to hide behind hints and innuendo. He retained just enough information for Fulford Weatheroak to be identifiable to those who knew him. Of course, your uncle could not let the matter lie, and confronted Signor Persano. A rash manoeuvre."

The surgeon shook his head. "The duel was fought in Switzerland, in as much anonymity as could be arranged. Although to describe it as a duel is to give it too much gravity. My uncle had no skill with a blade, and Persano struck him within seconds, stating that honour had been satisfied and the matter closed. The wound was deep, and treated incompetently by seconds whose medical knowledge was minimal. By the time my uncle returned to England the damage was irreversible – no amount of surgery could save his arm. And so he retired, in disgrace, albeit a private one."

"Whereupon you decided to have your vengeance upon Signor Persano, befriending him when he came to these shores to write his memoirs – memoirs which, I have no doubt, would have been less discreet than his original newspaper article. He would not necessarily connect you to Weatheroak – "

Sir Preston laughed bitterly. "I doubt he would have cared! The man had fought, and won, so many duels he could no longer remember their details. The evenings I have endured as he recounted his triumphs, as he saw them, and so often could not even recall the names of the vanquished.

And he thought to commit such poor scholarship to paper. I even told him I would aid his research, filling in such gaps as his memory had left."

"No doubt formulating the idea that you would reveal who you were as a final twist of the knife."

"Indeed, I entertained some such plan. Of course, his abrupt descent into madness made the concept worthless. He would not have understood, even if I had revealed every detail."

Holmes's lips drew tight. "No doubt you consider yourself cheated. I have one question, however: How did you administer the *phenylisopropylamine* to Signor Persano? By stealth, or was he a willing, albeit unwitting, victim?"

The surgeon actually smiled. "I described the compound's rejuvenative qualities. He is at heart a vain, shallow man who was not taking the ageing process well. His reactions were slowing, he was gaining weight. He continued to antagonise in print, and thus risked challenges he might no longer be able to surmount. It took little persuasion on my part for him to try a series of doses, suspended in wine. His reflexes sharpened rapidly – as the daily practice in his garden could attest – and after a while his excess weight began to lessen. He was more than willing to continue taking *phenylisopropylamine*. Indeed, I believe the compound may even be addictive."

"Then you admit it?" I asked. I was disconsolate that a man I had considered a giant of the medical fraternity was little better than a murderer.

"Admit to what, Doctor?" he asked. "*Phenylisopropylamine* is not a recognised compound and the administration of it is not a crime – especially when the one taking it does so willingly, as Persano did. I cannot be held accountable if the symptoms of an already existing condition – the existence of which I say I was unaware, and no one can prove otherwise – were exacerbated or exaggerated."

"In that you are partially correct," said Holmes. "But it is likely you may be found guilty of conspiracy to cause harm. You introduced a man to a potentially dangerous substance in revenge. You awaited a time when his mind was so unbalanced that the sight of a hideous worm crawling from a matchbox – a box into which you placed it, for such a unique specimen could hardly have found its way there by accident – would almost certainly drive him to madness. It is possible that, with the aid of a skilled barrister, you would escape conviction, but you will be ruined. You will never practice medicine or perform surgery again."

Sir Preston nodded after a moment's thought. "There is that, of course." He sighed. "I should not have allowed the maid Faith to be involved. She has such a simple-minded devotion to that blackguard. I would not be surprised if he has not seduced her. I might have dismissed her, except then she would have been totally beyond my control, and there would be too many questions as to why I had done so. She gave you a full account of his symptoms, of course."

Holmes nodded.

The surgeon sighed again. "It was always a risk. I was reluctant to leave her alone with you while I retrieved the specimen, and hurried back as swiftly as I could. Clearly I was too long."

"Where did you find it?" I asked, genuinely curious.

"A young colleague of mine came across it, dead, lying on the sands at Brighton. He has a childish interest in such curiosities. I asked if I might borrow it – for a prank. I knew it would work on Persano – it certainly gave me the shivers. I dread to think from what hideous abyss it crawled." He actually shuddered. "Naturally my colleague had already preserved it in spirits, but I reasoned Persano would be in no state of mind to notice." He took a deep breath, composing himself. "And now, Mr. Holmes? What now?"

"I cannot detain you," said my friend. "You may flee, or you may throw yourself upon the mercy of Scotland Yard. Lestrade and his ilk are frequently out of their depths, so this case should come as no great shock to them." His thin lips twitched a bleak smile. "I would recommend the latter course, for if you make any attempt to abscond, both Watson and I will have no choice but to reveal all we know to the authorities. A chance of redemption or to be hunted like a dog – the choice is yours."

Sir Preston stood, tugging at his coat. "And Persano?"

"I will see to it that he receives the best care available, no doubt with the maid at his side. His life – what remains of it – is ruined, if you wish to take any form of satisfaction in that. So, I suspect, is hers."

Sir Preston looked about to add something. Instead he made a stiff bow and left.

Holmes fished out his pipe and relit it with a spill. "An ugly case, Watson," he remarked between puffs. "Lacking the happy endings you so love to chronicle."

"There is misery a-plenty in all of the cases I have recorded," I pointed out. "For every happy outcome there is a dismal one."

He grunted. "You are in a profound mood today, my old friend," said he, closing his eyes and settling back in his chair. "I am unsure as to whether it suits you."

Somewhere in the vaults of the bank of Cox and Company, at Charing Cross, there is a travel-worn and battered tin dispatch-box

195

with my name, John H. Watson, MD, Late Indian Army, painted upon the lid. It is crammed with papers, nearly all of which are records of cases to illustrate the curious problems which Mr. Sherlock Holmes had at various times to examine. Some, and not the least interesting, were complete failures, and as such will hardly bear narrating, since no final explanation is forthcoming. A problem without a solution may interest the student, but can hardly fail to annoy the casual reader . . . A . . . case worthy of note is that of Isadora Persano, the well-known journalist and duellist, who was found stark staring mad with a matchbox in front of him which contained a remarkable worm, said to be unknown to science.

– Dr. John H. Watson
"The Problem of Thor Bridge"

NOTE

Romanian chemist Lazăr Edeleanu isolated *phenylisopropylamine* (amphetamine) in 1887. This tale in is set in 1889.

The Adventure of the Forgotten Brolly
by Shane Simmons

The Disappearance of Mr. James Phillimore, as the headlines called it, was one of them mysteries what gets the public all perplexed and interested and discussing what might have happened based on little to no facts. It grabs them by the imagination and won't let go for a day or three. And then, when there's nothing else to report, they forget all about it like it never happened, and they're on to the next bit of news that promises a better ending.

But Mr. Sherlock Holmes don't forget these unsolved mysteries so easy. Nor, I suppose, does Scotland Yard, who like to have enough answers so they can shut an open case file and stick it away in a cabinet where no one will ever look at it again. It was only after the headlines stopped talking about the vanished James Phillimore, and police decided they wasn't ever going to turn him up, that they went knocking on 221b Baker Street to see if Mr. Holmes could sort it out for them.

Mr. Holmes had been living alone for the first time in years and hadn't taken well to it by my estimation. As much of a lone wolf as he was most times, I think his type benefits from having someone around, sharing rooms with him, and keeping him connected to other humans. But times move on and things change, as they do, and Dr. Watson, after a good long stretch, had up and relocated with his new wife to another address in London, leaving his old friend to do most of his detecting alone.

Times had changed for your humble narrator as well. After running with the Baker Street Irregulars as their fearless leader for about as long as the Holmes and Watson partnership lasted, I'd been tripped up by internal politics. The problem with being in a gang of rough-and-tumble young lads is, no matter if you're the roughest of the bunch, and always up for a tumble, eventually you're going to age out of the part. I found myself stuck in an impossible spot. Not old enough for anyone to see me as a man, but too old to be considered a child – at least, not by the Irregulars, who went about their business as spies and infiltrators because nobody saw them as anything more than street urchins unworthy of notice or consideration. The more years I got on me, the more I found I weren't so inconspicuous no more. Eventually, as I should have expected, a younger upstart began eyeing my role as leader, and the rest of the lads started acting as though we was in a democracy. Without so much as a ballot cast, I lost an election I never knew was happening.

Retired out due to old age, and before I'd so much as sprung my first chest hairs! So it goes. Not for the first time, nor the last, I learned my lesson that life ain't fair to no one.

Adrift, I weren't so sure what my future prospects might be. I suppose I could have gone looking for normal work, but after acting as the eyes and ears of the greatest detective in the world, it's a bit of a letdown to go slumming for wages scrubbing guts off a butcher's floor, or ratting for a ha'penny per rat. Luckily, Mr. Holmes still summoned me on occasion, when he had a use for two helping hands, instead of a whole army of Irregular hands. And now, with Dr. Watson gone, this former Irregular was in regular demand.

Once Mrs. Hudson let me up to his rooms, Mr. Holmes sat me in Dr. Watson's old chair and reminded me of all the details of the Phillimore case. I must confess, like the rest of the public, the mystery had captured my imagination for two or three days, but I hadn't thought twice about it since the papers stopped spilling ink on the story.

The sparse details were simple enough: Man leaves his house one morning. Man goes back in because he forgot his umbrella. And poof! He's never seen again. James Phillimore never came out, with or without his umbrella. Once he was reported missing, the whole house was searched, top to bottom. It's like he fell through a hole in the world. The man was gone, just gone. Everyone had a theory. Nobody had an answer.

Now the case fell to a man who made a point of coming up with answers no one else could.

"So much has been made of the disappearance and the umbrella, Wiggins," said Mr. Holmes, pacing the room, "a terribly obvious consideration has been overlooked by everyone in the subsequent days."

"What's that?" I asked.

"Read it for yourself," said Mr. Holmes, and threw a stack of newspapers down on the seat of the armchair next to me. "It's all there in black-and-white. Each and every publication concurs unanimously."

Every London newspaper was represented in the stack, and the first thing I noticed is that they was all from the same day, now nearly a fortnight in the past.

"Why so interested in the papers from the day *before* he vanished?" I wondered. "Do you think he read some news that made him want to go and hide hisself?"

"Not in the least. There's nothing that would provoke such alarm in the man."

"What then?" I wondered, flipping through a few sheets of the top daily, with no idea of what I should be looking for in all that pulp.

"The forecast," said Mr. Holmes.

"The what now?"

"I cannot claim to remember the exact weather on that day. There is little to hold my interest when it comes to English precipitation unless I find myself out in it, or if I need to track footprints in the mud. As it so happens, I was alone in my rooms that entire week, distracted by a new shipment of chemical compounds. For my experiments, you understand. I took no notice of the weather, nor the passage of day and night for some time. But the newspapers all assure me the day James Phillimore vanished was sunny without so much as a cloud in the sky. Why then would a man, already outside and capable of seeing this fact for himself, step back inside for an umbrella that he clearly would not need?"

"There was something hidden in the umbrella that he forgot?" I guessed.

"No, no, Wiggins. If he had something so secret that he needed to hide it away in an umbrella or an umbrella stand, it's unlikely he would forget it. Think simpler than that."

Mr. Holmes's solutions were complex more often than not, but I went for as simple as I dared get.

"It was an excuse to go back inside."

"Precisely!" agreed Mr. Holmes. "And what would compel the man to go back inside?

"Something outside."

"Well done, Wiggins! If only Scotland Yard were so astute!"

"Doctor Watson has arrived," Mrs. Hudson announced from the open doorway.

"Ah," declared Mr. Holmes, "tell him to come up at once. I'm confident he remembers the way."

"I came as soon as I got your message, Holmes," said the doctor a few moments later, once he'd clomped his way up the steps.

"An hour-and-a-half ago," said Mr, Holmes, unimpressed.

"There was a patient," apologised Dr. Watson.

"Wiggins was summoned nearly a full hour later, he came from farther away, and still beat you here by eighteen-and-a-half minutes."

"I ran," I said, by way of explanation.

"The streets were full," said Dr. Watson. "The cab made slow progress."

"You should try running," I suggested.

"You're in my chair," was Dr. Watson's reply, prodding my shoulder with his cane. I didn't move.

"You, my dear friend, do not live here anymore," Mr. Holmes reminded him. "As such, the chair rests abandoned and unclaimed. If my guest, Mr. Wiggins, wishes to partake of its comfort, he is most welcome to do so. As a later arrival, you may indulge yourself with whatever unoccupied surface remains."

Dr. Watson did not look pleased to take the seat by the window, but he opted for it rather than be presumptuous enough to remove the stack of newspapers from Mr. Holmes's armchair and claim it for himself as the detective walked the room.

"The James Phillimore missing-persons case," said Mr. Holmes briskly. "You are familiar with it?"

It was my understanding that Dr. Watson was at least trying to keep current with London criminology. It can't have been easy though, doing that, seeing patients, and fulfilling his duties as a newlywed.

"Right. Phillimore," he said, struggling to remember the details as quickly as Mr. Holmes expected him to. "Went back for his umbrella, never seen or heard from again."

Dr. Watson seemed pleased with himself for having remembered so much from so obscure a bit of news, now lost in the tide of crimes and misdeeds that had swamped the papers in the days since. Mr. Holmes was not so impressed.

"Your conclusions?"

"Well, obviously, there was something terribly important about that umbrella to compel Mr. Phillimore to go back for it. Something worth kidnapping him for, perhaps?"

The next few seconds of silence were torture, and it weren't even directed at me.

"Oh, Watson . . . ." said Mr. Holmes, shaking his head sadly and clicking his tongue. "You used to be better than this. Marriage has ruined you."

"It's only been three weeks!" protested the doctor.

"Such is the destructive nature of the institution," replied Mr. Holmes solemnly.

"I suppose that I have become a touch rusty on the deduction front."

"Rusty, is it? You have been entirely absent."

"I have been occupied," countered Dr. Watson. "With my practice – with life in general!"

Mr. Holmes ignored the doctor's protests and placed a commiserating hand on my shoulder.

"Wiggins, of late, has suffered a similar split. A company broken up, a partnership dissolved."

"I been usurped," I told Dr. Watson.

200

Mr. Holmes elaborated.

"He has parted ways with the Irregulars. They have cast him out."

Dr. Watson didn't seem particularly concerned by my plight, I have to say.

"Yes, well, I am very sorry to hear of any misfortune that has befallen young Wiggins, but it bears no comparison to our standing."

"Does it not?" said Mr. Holmes.

"Our partnership – unofficial and unbinding as it may be – has not been dissolved, surely!" protested Dr. Watson.

"No?"

"Of course not, Holmes! I got married and have taken up residence with my wife. It is a normal and healthy thing for a man to do, and it changes nothing between us. I remain at your side as you need me."

"And when some desperate client, perplexed by a pressing intrigue, comes pounding on my door in the middle of the night, are you ready to spring into action? No. You are asleep in bed with your wife across town."

"If the intrigue is as pressing as that, I can be roused," the doctor assured him. "Mary will understand."

"I cannot claim the same wisdom about married life as you, doubtless, have accumulated in the last several weeks. But if there is a married woman who will understand and tolerate her husband being recruited out of bed after midnight to go adventuring in the dark, I have yet to encounter this mythological creature."

Mr. Holmes retrieved his coat from the rack and began pulling it on.

"Where are we going?" asked Dr. Watson.

"We?" responded Mr. Holmes.

"Yes, of course. You and I."

"Wiggins and I are going to the last place eyes were ever laid upon James Phillimore," he was informed.

"You're taking Wiggins?" sputtered the doctor.

"Wiggins is up to speed on the case. You, dear doctor, are lagging behind. Of course, if you wish to come along, that is your own prerogative, assuming that Mary permits you. But be quick about it before you fall any further in arrears. We are late to this hunt, and James Phillimore's discovery grows ever more unlikely with each passing minute."

It was all three of us what took the hansom cab to the last known whereabouts of the missing man, with me perilously hanging on next to the driver's sprung seat. The whole way, Dr. Watson pressed for more details, but Mr. Holmes was not in a talkative mood. By the time we arrived, the doctor was no further enlightened.

"That is the door there," said Mr. Holmes, pointing at an address across the street. "The Phillimore residence is upstairs."

"Who lives below him?" asked Dr. Watson.

No longer pushed to repeat himself, Mr. Holmes was more forthcoming with new facts.

"That tenant has been abroad for the last two years, but permission to search the lower residence was obtained from the landlord and it was likewise gone through by police on several separate occasions."

"There is no connection between the two residences, hidden or otherwise?"

"Not according to the owner, nor the plans to the building. There have been no major alterations to either residence since the block was first erected."

The police had been in and out a hundred times over, from the day the disappearance had been reported to now. But over the course of the last week-and-a-half, the number of officers involved had steadily reduced, until now there was only one lone bobby set to keep an eye on the address as part of his local rounds. Mr. Holmes led us to the uniform on duty, and we saw he was standing with another man.

"Good day, Constable," Mr. Holmes said. "I trust things are unchanged since the last watch."

"Ah, Sherlock Holmes, is it?" said the bobby. "Inspector Lestrade told me you'd be by. He sent this gentleman to meet you."

"You must be Derick Neame," said Mr. Holmes to the man stationed next to the bobby. "I perceive you work as a clerk in a law office – the same one as the vanished James Phillimore."

"Yes, sir," said the man. "I suppose Inspector Lestrade told you as much."

"He didn't need to."

"Then how did you know I worked in a law office?"

"The same way I know you are left-handed, have not had a raise since you started at the firm, and are currently engaged to young lady of simple tastes who prefers red wine to white, enjoys dancing to traditional folk songs, and has a pet bird."

"How could you possibly – ?" stammered Neame. "Are you some sort of mentalist?"

"It is merely a talent for observation," Mr. Holmes assured him.

"He does rather a lot of it," said Dr. Watson. "Do not let it perturb you."

"You were the last person to see the missing man?" asked Mr. Holmes.

"I suppose I was," said Neame. "There has been no word of him?"

202

"None," confirmed Mr. Holmes. "You were friends?"

"We have been well acquainted since we both started at Holst, Hammer, and McGillicuddy nearly a year ago, and often walked to the office together. His home is along the route I take each day, so it was nothing to ring his bell and share the rest of the journey."

"As this was a matter of routine, you were well placed to notice any inconsistency on that day."

"There was nothing particularly unusual," said Neame. "I rang his bell and he came to the door presently. We began our walk after our common morning greeting."

"But the walk was cut short," prompted Mr. Holmes.

"James stopped no more than a few steps from the door," Neame nodded. "He looked momentarily stricken. As though something of utmost importance had occurred to him. Then he told me he had to go back because he had forgotten his umbrella."

"Was he in the habit of carrying an umbrella?"

"When it was raining."

"But it was not raining."

"I suppose he expected that it might."

"What happened after he went back inside?"

"I waited," said Neame. "For a good five minutes. Then I rang the bell and knocked several times."

"There was no answer?"

"None. Even after I tried to call to him through the door. I thought he must have taken ill."

"What was your next move?"

"I checked – the front door was unlocked. I recruited a neighbor and a passing constable, and we went upstairs. He wasn't there. There was no other way out than past me at the front door. Finally I had to go to work.

"I thought it best to avoid getting my pay docked. I made excuses for James, sure he would arrive shortly. But he never did. After the work day, I returned here and spent at least half-an-hour knocking on the door – it was locked by then, by the constable I suppose. I rang the bell and walked all around the house, trying to get a look in the windows. I knew something was dreadfully wrong," added Neame. "I only wish that there was something that I could have done."

"You did all that could be reasonably expected of a friend and colleague. There was no way you could know matters were so dire."

"I do hope you find him, Mr. Holmes. James was just getting started in his legal career, and I know his parents had such high hopes for him."

"I shall search under ever stone," Mr. Holmes assured him. "Thank you for your assistance in the matter."

"Good luck with your pending nuptials," Dr. Watson added, as the witness turned to leave.

"My colleague is enamoured with wedded bliss," Mr. Holmes told Neame. "I caution against it, but I wish you all due happiness, whatever your choice may be."

We watched Derick Neame slip away around the corner, on his way back home.

"I don't trust him," said Dr. Watson, once he was certain Neame was too far away to hear his suspicions.

"Nor do I," Mr. Holmes concurred.

"You think him capable of – " Dr. Watson began.

"Murder? Absolutely."

"So James Phillimore is dead," said the doctor, gravely.

"We have no evidence of that," said Mr. Holmes. "I was referring to Derick Neame's private life."

"You think his finance is in danger?"

"I do not fear for the lady, but her bird is in mortal peril. Her new husband is likely to choke the life out of it one night."

Mr. Holmes noticed that both Dr. Watson and I looked completely lost.

"An Eleonora," elaborated Mr. Holmes. "Quiet piercingly loud. I'm afraid Mr. Neame's patience with it is running short. You see, there were feather barbs on his . . . ."

"Yes, yes, I'm confident there were!" Dr. Watson interrupted. "But how does this help us with the disappearance of James Phillimore?"

"It doesn't. I was only making an observation."

"Is this man not a suspect in the disappearance?" Dr. Watson asked with growing frustration. "If he was the last person to see James Phillimore in the flesh, perhaps he had cause and motive to see him gone."

Of course Mr. Holmes had already considered this himself – and dismissed the possibility.

"No, Watson," he said. "There were other witnesses in the street who concur with Mr. Neame's general account. James Phillimore went back inside alone, and Neame waited for him to emerge for quite some time before heading on his way. No one was seen coming or going all that day until Neame returned after work and continued to attempt to rouse his friend. Once his concern reached its peak, police were involved, the landlord contacted, and a search conducted. The situation has remained unchanged since that moment. It falls to us to push this investigation out of the mud where it remains mired."

"So we're going into the house to look for the bloke?" I asked.

"Quite right, Wiggins," said Mr. Holmes. "Let us see what the police missed, for it is certain they missed something. No man vanishes into thin air."

"How do we get inside?" asked Dr. Watson.

"Want I should pick the lock?" I offered.

"No need, Wiggins," said Mr. Holmes. "And I shan't inquire where you learned such a trick, nor how many occasions you've had to employ it. When Lestrade brought the matter to my attention, he also entrusted me with the key."

Mr. Holmes produced the bit of cut brass from his pocket and showed it to us.

"We're just going in for a quick look, Constable," Mr. Holmes informed the copper.

"Right you are, sir," the bobby replied, raising a finger to the brim of his helmet.

Through the front and into the hall, we climbed the steps up to the first floor and let ourselves into Phillimore's rooms.

"You will note the umbrella that James Phillimore did *not* go back for."

Mr. Holmes pointed to the stand near the door that contained exactly one unclaimed umbrella that James Phillimore had never needed or wanted, despite his claims to the contrary.

"Do you suppose there is any evidence to be found amongst his other possessions?" asked Dr. Watson.

"Nothing that hasn't been trampled by the herd of policemen who have passed through here at regular intervals. No, Watson, it is the mysterious means of egress I seek. If the man was seen entering and is nowhere to be found now, dead or alive he had to have been removed from the premises somehow. And in such a way that it would go unwitnessed."

"Surely he must have slipped out back," said Dr. Watson.

"A reasonable proposition, but the lane behind these houses is well travelled and, more importantly, paved."

"Why is that an important detail?"

"Even hanging from a window, a drop from this high would, at the very least, result in a twisted ankle. More likely a broken leg. That would not facilitate an escape, and certainly not one that went unnoticed."

"There is an interior flight to the second floor," Dr. Watson noted.

"His bedroom, and a reading room fit for a law clerk studying for the bar," said Mr. Holmes, already familiar with the basic layout of the place thanks to Inspector Lestrade's description. "Let us see what else is up there."

The stairs to the second storey of the building let out on a tight corridor that was capped by matching rooms at the front and back. We tried the front one overlooking the street first. A tidy desk was the main piece of furniture, but Mr. Holmes was more interested in the shelves of thick tomes.

"Law books all," Mr. Holmes said, as he blew a small cloud off their bindings, "but not as well-studied as they might be. This is more than a fortnight's collection of dust."

The room at the rear was even more sparse.

"Simple bedroom furnishings for a young professional," noted Mr. Holmes. "They could have fit anywhere, so when he first moved in a choice was made. Two rooms. One of quiet solitude at the back, another subject to street noise in the front."

"Seems reasonable to want to sleep in relative quiet," said Dr. Watson.

"Rather than study for the bar in silent concentration," countered Mr. Holmes.

"Some of us value a good night's sleep, Holmes. You should try it sometime."

"It was not meant as a criticism of Mr. Phillimore. It was merely an observation as to his priorities."

"I still see no means of escape from these modest rooms," said Dr. Watson. "Not unless he learned how to melt through walls."

Mr. Holmes threw open the two sides of the bedroom window and leaned out to have a look at the lane that ran behind all the houses on the block. Close residents and closer neighbours were out and about, using the lane as a short cut, tending to small planter gardens, or hanging wet laundry. The drop down to ground level was sheer, with no possible landing a good one.

"You said it yourself, Holmes," said Dr. Watson, joining Mr. Holmes at the window and looking down. "It's a devil of a fall with nothing but hard stone to catch him."

"Yet it appears someone has attempted a leap of faith."

Mr. Holmes ran his finger along the exterior edge of the windowsill until he hit a rough patch where the green paint was scuffed, exposing the bare wood beneath.

"I measure the mark at about six inches wide," judged Mr. Holmes.

"Looks new," I noted. "What caused that scrape do you think?"

"A man's shoe, I venture," said Mr. Holmes. "It is well short of a footprint, but it nevertheless points us to a path."

"So he did drop down to the lane," said Dr. Watson. "How did nobody notice? And how could he have avoided serious injury?"

206

"Because he did not go down, Watson. He went up!"

Before we could say a word to stop him, Mr. Holmes was out the window and standing on the ledge, feet pointed inside, as he hugged the brick wall and reached for the roof above him. It was only being so tall that allowed him to hook is long fingers over the top. Like James Phillimore before him, his shoes scraped at the windowsill paint as he shifted his weight off his feet and committed to his handhold.

"Careful Holmes!" was all Dr. Watson could say, his eyes shifting from his dangling friend to the deadly tumble that awaited him below if he lost his grip.

With one mighty chin-up, Mr. Holmes brought his head above the roof and was able to get an elbow over the top. It anchored him and let him pull himself up enough to swing a leg over as well. With a final scramble, he made it to the roof and was gone from sight.

A moment later, Mr. Holmes reappeared. He had turned himself around and now, braced on his belly, stretched an arm down towards the window directly below him.

"Reach Watson," he said. "Take my hand."

Dr. Watson looked down at the precipitous drop and thought better of it.

"You'll be asking a man troubled by his war wounds to do a trapeze act next!" shouted the doctor.

"Wiggins, then!" replied Mr. Holmes. "Up you go."

I stretched for his hand and found it just out of reach. Never one to fail Mr. Holmes, I leapt up, and we were able to seize each other by the wrist. I would have been in for it if we'd missed the catch, but it's hardly worth considering since we didn't.

Once I'd been hoisted up and set on my feet atop the roof, Mr. Holmes seemed strangely saddened.

"At least we haven't all lost our nerve," he said.

I knew he was on about Dr. Watson's shortcomings of late, and I felt inclined to make excuses for him.

"I guess his shoulder's been bothering him."

"That is not Watson speaking," said Mr. Holmes. "It is, rather, the concerns of a fussy and fearful wife coming out of Watson's mouth."

"You sound disappointed," I said, which was not a tone I'd ever heard out of Sherlock Holmes.

"Disappointed? Perhaps. Yet it cannot all be laid at the feet of Watson. My true disappointment lies in a mystery unsolved. Looking across the skyline, I can see many avenues of escape, and many possible answers denied me. The probability of a definitive outcome diminishes rapidly."

"Well, Phillimore isn't up here, sure enough," I observed.

"He was, but he is long gone. See there!"

Mr. Holmes went to stand at the very edge of the north side and looked across to the next building over. Most of the houses in the area were in tight rows, but the one James Phillimore had lived in was more isolated than the others, standing on the corner, with an alley branching off the back lane and separating it from its neighbour.

I came over and looked at the opposite rooftop, and there was a distinct dent in the tar.

"A point of impact," concluded Mr. Holmes. "And on this side you can see a hint of heavy footfalls, spread wide apart, suggesting Phillimore made a running jump of it."

The gap between buildings was broad enough to challenge a professional athlete, and offered a fall upon failure that would handily break a neck. Climbing up to the roof had been enough danger for one day. Even Mr. Holmes wasn't keen to risk life and limb trying to trace the path of James Phillimore across such a canyon.

"How many other rooftops did he hop to in order to remove himself from the place unseen? How many other broad gaps and deadly drops did he risk? I shall have to employ your former compatriots to scour the entire neighbourhood. Every alley and lane and backyard of it. James Phillimore may well be lying in any nook or cranny, his body undiscovered since missing a final, fatal jump."

"What if he got away?" I asked.

"Then the odds of finding him again are precipitously reduced."

"I have another question," I said. "It might sound a bit thick."

"Consider me forewarned," said Mr. Holmes. "What is it, Wiggins?"

"How do we get back down?"

At that moment, we were startled by the sound of two prongs hitting the edge of roof from the rear. We looked at the twin nubs of wood that were poking up from below, and they bobbed slightly for several moments until a man's head appeared between them. It was Dr. Watson.

"There's a fire house just around the block," explained Dr. Watson of the tall ladder we found him perched atop. "A rather more practical solution, don't you think?"

"Well done, Watson!" commended Mr. Holmes. "There may be hope for you yet."

Once we were done and down, we saw to returning the ladder. The crew of firemen were only too glad to have helped move along an investigation by Sherlock Holmes, but Mr. Holmes hisself was less pleased with the progress we'd made.

"Phillimore is on the move if he has survived his daring flight thus far," said Mr. Holmes. "I fear that a man so motivated to flee will not make himself easy to find. It's a big world, with many places to lose oneself. The best we can do is to locate him if he remains in London, and even that is a dim prospect. Do not expect a satisfactory resolution to round out one of those case histories you're working on, Watson."

"Maybe I could try my hand at it?" I suggested, happy to take any scraps of adventures the doctor didn't fancy writing about.

"I am afraid, Wiggins, that dangling from rooftops will be the extent of your involvement. You have my thanks for your assistance, but canvasing the entire district must now fall to the manpower the Irregulars can provide. And as you are *persona non grata* of late, I think you will agree that your participation in the next leg of the investigation will not be welcomed by the troops."

I tried not to look bitter in the face of my dismissal. I probably failed.

"What awful thing could the man have laid eyes upon to bolt in such a fashion?" Dr. Watson wondered, his mind still turning over the biggest unanswered question of the day.

"Not a thing, Watson," said Mr. Holmes. "A person. The moment James Phillimore stepped outside, he saw someone that struck terror into his heart. Of that I'm certain. Someone from whom he is still running, even now – assuming he lives."

"His bookie," I said, firmly.

"A bold proposition, Wiggins," said Mr. Holmes. "What evidence do you have?"

"Nothing," I said. "It's just in my experience – every time a man makes hisself this scarce, it's because he owes money to his bookie. Or he's up the spout with the missus. And since this Phillimore bloke weren't married, it's got to be a bookie."

"You may well be right. Better to risk a broken leg running away, than assure one over the settlement of a gambling debt. For my part, however, I prefer a more definitive answer based in knowable fact."

As the coming days would show, though, facts don't present themselves so easy when you don't know where to look for them.

By the time another week had passed, all hope of discovering the fate of James Phillimore had vanished as thoroughly as the man. It never came up again in the papers, even if you went digging through the rear-most back pages. Word on the street was that even the Baker Street Irregulars hadn't managed to come up with a single clue. Not for lack of trying. The boys had comported themselves well in the hunt, and had found plenty of bodies hidden away. In the span of seven days they had come up with no less than three dead men, two of them murdered, and more drunks sleeping it off than could be accurately counted. None of them were James Phillimore.

I tried to forget about the case, but it picked at the back of my mind like a hungry nit. Even so, I had a living to make, and I was earning my way by scrounging what I could and selling my finds at rag shops all over town. Only a day after I'd been kicked off the Phillimore case, I found myself a nice overcoat that fetched me a whole shilling. It had been left out to dry at the back of a laundry, but finders-keepers is the law of the land in the East End, and no one was around to claim they was in charge of that coat, so there you have it.

The next time I was by the same shop, I noticed that someone had snatched it up – probably for twice what I got paid for it. I asked after the coat, and the rag lady at the stand told me about the well-dressed gentleman who had been by and wanted to swap all his finery for some dingy work clothes. He'd also been quick to buy the overcoat when he saw it, and then off he went.

Call it a hunch, but I asked to see the clothes he had traded. Most of the pieces had already sold, but there was a tie still hanging from a nail stuck in the stand. Not much call for fancy ties amongst the working class in the East End. When the rag lady showed me that silk neck choker, I knew I was onto something. It was personalised – embroidered with the initials *J. P.*

By happenstance, it seemed I had just picked up the trail of James Phillimore, but there were no indication of where his next stop might be. I sat down to give it a good hard think, and try to put some of that deductive reasoning Mr. Holmes was always on about to work.

Assuming Phillimore was still on the go and now dressed to blend in somewhere, the question was what was he trying to blend in with, and how was that going to help him get to wherever he was heading? He didn't need a warm coat with the arrival of spring in London and a long summer to follow. So where might he get a chill put in his bones? The answer came to me at once. If he was running, where better to run to than a place no man could follow?

I must have walked up and down the London Docks a dozen times that day, my eyes peeled for any steamers ready to ship off, and any crew returning to port to leave with the high tide. It was times like this that I really wished I still had a crew of my own to cover all the ground that needed watching. As it was, I had to rely on my own two feet, and one big stroke of luck. I had it at in Wapping, where I found a fifty-footer set to leave for Estonia by way of the cold waters of the North Sea and Baltic. Seated on a cargo crate, taking a break during the final load, was a junior seaman who caught my attention. He looked like he must have been newly signed on, because he wasn't the least bit weathered like the real sailors get after a voyage or two.

I didn't know what the fellow I was searching for looked like, but I recognised the coat at once. The man tucked inside it could only be one person.

I sat down on the box next to him and said, "You're a hard man to find, James Phillimore."

He was startled to hear the name spoken aloud, but relaxed slightly when he saw it was only an urchin, and not some uniform.

"You know me, boy?" he asked.

"You're famous. The whole city has their eye out for you. Or had. The heat's off now. But the file is still open."

"Scotland Yard would like to have a word, I imagine," he smiled.

"You've got more than them after you."

"Who else?"

"Consulting detective. Sherlock Holmes," I said. "And me, of course. Wiggins is the name."

Those names rang a bell and he nodded slowly, remembering our claim to celebrity.

"I've read about Sherlock Holmes. In a book, I believe. I seem to remember a Wiggins in it. Anyway, I'm afraid you're all out of luck. We cast off in an hour, and I don't expect to see London ever again."

It's not like he'd committed any crime that I could report, and I wasn't big enough to tackle him and hold him down at any rate. James Phillimore was free to come and go as he pleased, and he seemed intent on going – as far away as he could. Still, there was a mystery to solve – a question to have answered,

"Mr. Holmes thinks you're running away from someone," I said. "Someone you saw when you stepped out of your house that day."

"He is not wrong, your Mr. Holmes. I saw someone that put the fear of God into me, and I've not had a moment's peace since then."

"Who was it?" I asked, eager to know the truth at last. "I said it was probably your bookie. Was it a bookie? Is was a bookie, wasn't it?"

"No, boy. I owe no debts to anyone except, perhaps, one man alone."

"Who was it you saw then?"

"It was *me*. I saw myself, as though someone had held up a mirror an inch from my face. I saw the life I was living, and I saw it was not my own life at all."

"How can your own life not be yours?" I asked, truly confused.

"I grew up with everything," he said. "Money, family, a home."

"You're one of the lucky ones."

"Yes," he agreed, "but with it all came expectations. So many expectations. Especially from my father, who planned out my entire existence for me, from the very moment it was announced that he had a son. He wanted me to follow in his footsteps. The same education in the same schools, and a bright future practising law in a firm of his choosing. Beyond that? A wife, a family – all subject to his approval, of course."

"Some of us don't have a father."

"And some of us wish we didn't," he said. "On that day I saw that I was not my life and it never was. It was *his*. I was heading out to that blasted law office once more, to do a job that I hated, to study for advancement that I didn't want, to strive for a career that would make me miserable for the rest of my days. A panic took hold of me, and I had to get away at once. Leave it all behind and never look back! So I left, just like that, with nothing but the clothes on my back and the money in my pocket."

"You chose a funny way to go about it," I said.

"I didn't want to explain myself. Not to anyone. I only wanted to vanish without a trace. I didn't know it would cause such a fuss."

"The fuss has died down," I told him. "The only person who knows you're here is me."

"Then I am free," he announced, taking a deep breath, like it was his first taste of clean air – even though it was full of smog.

The waiting vessel let out some of its steam through the ship's whistle. Several long blasts called the rest of the crew in, and the few remaining boxes were brought aboard. As I was swept off my claimed seat, Phillimore lifted his own box to one shoulder and balanced it there with both hands.

"It is an enormous thing to change the entire course of your life," he said to me. "To remove yourself from all that you know, and dare to walk a new path of your own making."

He thought twice about the words he had just said. Not their meaning, but their audience.

"No, I supposed you wouldn't understand. Not at your age."

He started to walk up the gangplank, but hesitated when I spoke.

"Maybe I do," I said.

He saw how serious I was in that moment, and shifted the weight on his back long enough to spare me a look of camaraderie.

"Then count yourself lucky you were able to grasp it so young."

He boarded the ship and set the crate next to the hatch that led down to the cargo hold.

"Where do you think you'll end up?" I shouted after him.

"I don't know," said James Phillimore. "For the first time in my life, I have no idea where my destination may lie. And it fills my heart with great satisfaction to not know it."

As the ship left port, I followed it out of Shadwell and then stood at the river's edge, watching it steam away down the Thames, until it was a dot lost in the haze on the water. I considered if I should report my findings to Baker Street or Scotland Yard the whole time. And, in the end, I decided to stay silent.

The fate of the man was of his own choosing. It weren't none of my business, nor that of any policemen, doctors, or consulting detectives. That piece of information is a private matter between James Phillimore and the sea.

Somewhere in the vaults of the bank of Cox and Company, at Charing Cross, there is a travel-worn and battered tin dispatch-box with my name, John H. Watson, M.D., Late Indian Army, *painted upon the lid. It is crammed with papers, nearly all of which are records of cases to illustrate the curious problems which Mr. Sherlock Holmes had at various times to examine. Some, and not the least interesting, were complete failures, and as such will hardly bear narrating, since no final explanation is forthcoming. A problem without a solution may interest the student, but can hardly fail to annoy the casual reader. Among these unfinished tales is that of Mr. James Phillimore, who, stepping back into his own house to get his umbrella, was never more seen in this world.*

– Dr. John H. Watson
"The Problem of Thor Bridge"

The Adventure of the Tired Captain

by Dacre Stoker and Leverett Butts

For Arthur and Bram

"I am sure you will not think it an impertinence if I write to tell you how very much I enjoyed reading Dracula *. . . The old Professor is most excellent."*

– Letter from Arthur Conan Doyle to Bram Stoker, August 20th, 1897

Chapter I

I have mentioned the irregular sleeping habits of my friend Mr. Sherlock Holmes. In the early days of our association, when we shared rooms in Baker Street, I would often hear him pacing the floors well into the early hours of morning, and on such days, assuming he slept at all, Holmes would retire as the sun rose, often not rising until it had passed beyond the western horizon. At other times, when the fit was on him, he would take to bed as late (or as early) as the first hour after noon, sleeping three or four hours to rise again for some activity before once more returning to his rooms around dusk to sleep until midnight or the following sunrise, depending on his whim.

It was no surprise to me, then, when I detoured by Holmes's rooms on my way to the surgery early one morning in the summer after my marriage to see the lights on in his windows. I had intended only to leave a book on anatomy, which I had borrowed from his library, with Mrs. Hudson, but I found Holmes not only already among the living, but meeting with a client at the ungodly hour of six!

The client was a tired-looking elderly gentleman, well-dressed in a dark suit, though not of English cut. He had about him a military air, though he seemed to slouch in a decidedly unmilitary manner in my old armchair.

I tried to make my excuses, waving the book, saying that I had assumed it would be too early to find Holmes awake, and attempted duck out without further interruption of his conference.

Holmes would have none of it.

"Come," he nodded to the divan by the window and motioned for me to remain. "Allow me to introduce Captain Brutus Morris, late of the Army of the Confederate States of America, and currently renowned Texas rancher and oil baron."

I shook the man's hand before settling onto the divan.

"It would appear," Holmes continued, "that his son was murdered."

"As Mr. Holmes said," Captain Morris began after I settled, "I served in the Confederate Army during the War of Northern Aggression."

I looked quizzically at my friend, who interjected, "The American Civil War."

"There weren't a thing civil about it." Captain Morris grumbled before continuing. He spoke with the slow drawl associated with his region of the Colonies. "I served from '61 all the way to the end. I saw action in just about every one of the bloodiest battles there was, from Manassas to Shiloh to Sharpsburg, all the way down to Chickamauga, and I seen more'n my share of violence and bloodshed and needless cruelty to last me a lifetime. When it was over, I found I didn't relish the thought of returning to Virginia and seeing what the Yankees had done to my homeland, so I lit out for Texas like so many others.

"I made me a new life out there, bought me a piece of land for a song, and tried cattle ranching just outside of Nagodoches. After few years of that, I struck oil in one of my fields while digging a well. Before I knew it, I had enough income to settle down and start a family.

"We wanted to have a whole passel of children, my wife and me, but the Good Lord didn't see fit to give us but the one."

Captain Morris paused to gather himself, and I was struck by the stark contrast between this well dressed, comfortable American, exuding an air of confidence, with his red-rimmed eyes and lines of grief stamped on his forehead. "He was good boy, my Quincey, and a better man. Wasn't nobody in the county could touch him when it came to any kind of weapon, be it rifle, pistol, or Bowie. And he was smart as a whip. Top of his class at the A.M.C., and all ready to take over the business when he got back from his European tour.

"We sent him over here when he graduated, and he wasn't supposed to be gone but six months. But durned if he didn't get caught up in the social circles here. Made friends with an Arthur Holmwood, the son of one of your lords out here."

"Lord Godalming, yes," Holmes added.

"The very one." Captain Morris nodded his head. "Well, he and this Arthur toured the Continent, for sure. Got involved in a few military squabbles – with the Legion, I believe. And six months turned into a year, then more. When he got back to England, he got involved with a woman, Lucy Something-or-Other, and next thing we know, he wasn't sure when he'd be back."

"Indeed," Holmes nodded sagely and threw me a glance, "The members of the fairer sex often throw our lives into disarray."

"You're speaking God's own truth there, Mr. Holmes, for a fact." Captain Morris smiled thinly, but his eyes remained weary. "Well, it wasn't long before his mother and I got a telegram asking if we'd have any objection to him bringing a wife home. He was aiming to ask this Lucy for her hand, but it wasn't no sure thing on account of she'd been sparking two other fellas, this Holmwood and some doctor, name of Seward."

Captain Morris stopped again to take a deep breath. "And that was the last we heard from Quincey until a few months later when this Arthur Holmwood wrote us that our boy was killed in a hunting accident way out in Transylvania where he'd gone with him and this Doctor Seward, along with some other folks we hadn't ever heard of: A lawyer and his wife, and some professor."

"Transylvania?" Holmes caressed his chin and leaned in towards the captain.

"Yes, sir," Captain Morris nodded.

"And your son died there?"

Captain Morris shrugged. "That's what the telegram said. Attacked by a wolf and – " Captain Morris paused to collect himself. " – and torn limb from limb. But we never did get the body. They said he was torn up so, they couldn't risk the return journey and buried him there."

I leaned into the conversation, apologizing for interrupting. "And this was two years ago?"

"Yes," Captain Morris replied. "My wife and me, we grieved for our boy and we never did get over it. He was our only one, you see. Martha was worse off than me – I had my work to draw me, but Martha, she couldn't do a thing all day but sit and ruminate. It affected her health, and she's been withering away ever since."

"What's wrong with her?" I asked.

"The doctor thinks it's cancer," Captain Morris looked at me with his red-rimmed eyes, "and it may be, but if it is, it's from her grieving so, I'm sure of it. Doc says that's just claptrap."

"Your idea is not without merit." I shrugged. "There is evidence of a relation between the body's physical health and that of the mind and emotions – at least according to several doctors in Germany and at least one in Vienna."

"She just spends her days sitting in her chair, staring out the window. 'If I could just see my boy again,' she says. 'Just to say goodbye to him proper, I could go on, but it's a hole in my life I can't fill.' So I thought if I could get this Holmwood to tell me where Quincey's buried, I'd pay any amount of money to bring him home and bury him near us. I thought maybe that would help his mother find peace."

"Surely he agreed to help you." Holmes interjected.

"That's just it, Mr. Holmes. He ain't answered my telegrams or letters, so I came here to ask him in person, and he won't see me."

"Curious way to treat the father of one's deceased friend," Holmes muttered.

"That was my thought, too." Captain Morris nodded his head vigorously, "and the more I thought about it, the more I couldn't see any logic in his story about Quincey's death."

"Indeed not." Holmes looked the captain straight in the eye. "There's a good many things wrong with his tale." He began counting with his fingers. "Why Transylvania? Surely, they could have hunted wolves closer to home – in Germany, perhaps, or France. Who were these others in the hunting party? It seems an oddly specific crew: The son of British royalty, a doctor, a lawyer, and a professor? What were their relationships to your son? And why the lawyer's wife?"

Holmes paused to light his pipe and drew slowly on it. "The most damning part of their story, though, is the matter of your son's death. Certainly, if he had been attacked by a wolf, even if the beast knocked his rifle away, your son would have drawn his pistol or knife before suffering such a fate, and surely his friends would have interceded."

"Mr. Holmes, you are a marvel." Captain Morris shook his head wonderingly. "Those were my very own thoughts, too. So I went to the police here, your Scotland Yard, and Inspector Colford allowed that even if there was foul play, since it happened out of country, there was nothing he could do, so he referred me to you."

"Well, that shows considerably more initiative and resourcefulness than the average Yard inspector," Holmes said, rising and placing his pipe on its stand, "with one or two notable exceptions." He extended his hand to Captain Morris as the older man rose. "I will be delighted to take your case."

"Mr. Holmes," Captain Morris sighed, "if you can just find my boy's body so I can bring him home, I will be more than satisfied."

"You will have your son," Holmes assured him, "and I sincerely hope it brings your wife comfort."

"What are your thoughts?" Holmes turned to me after the captain had left. "I can tell by your sighing and your twitching knee that you have them."

"I have followed you on numerous cases, and I feel I have grown my own deductive skills significantly under your tutelage."

"Indeed you have."

"But how on earth did you know Quincey had a spare pistol and a knife?"

"Simplicity itself." Holmes settled back in his chair. "The man was an American, and from the Western states, as well. Of course he had more weapons. Captain Morris told us his son was skilled in rifle, pistol, and knife – obviously, those would be his back-up arms of choice. Now, can you clear your schedule for the next few days? I'd very much appreciate your company on this case."

"I'm sure my colleague, Dr. Anstruther, would be more than happy to step in."

"Excellent." Holmes smiled around his pipe. "After Mrs. Hudson brings us our breakfast, then, we should call on Arthur Holmwood, I think."

Chapter II

It was no simple thing to procure an audience with Arthur Holmwood, especially since his installation as Lord Godalming after the death of his father a few years previous. It was, however, much easier for Holmes than it would be for an American tourist, even one as well-off and distinguished as Captain Morris, though it did require Holmes to request the assistance of his brother Mycroft of the Foreign Office.

"So you're going to try to find the American's son are you?" Mycroft asked when we met him in his Whitehall office, asking him to arrange a meeting with Holmwood.

"How on earth . . . ." I exclaimed but was cut short by Holmes's lightly nudging my arm.

"Why else would you be asking?" Mycroft smiled thinly at me before returning his attention to his younger brother. "I keep track of our customs agents. It is, in fact, one of the primary responsibilities of my department, you understand. Not three days after a Captain Brutus Morris arrives on our shores, my own dear brother graces me with a visit, begging me to set him an appointment with Lord Godalming. This is the same Captain Morris whose son disappeared in Transylvania two years ago, hunting with the same Lord Godalming. I may be older than you, Sherlock, but I am not yet doddering. I am afraid," Mycroft turned to me, "this will not be a case you can send to *Beeton's Christmas Annual*, Doctor. I fear it's quite out of my brother's scope."

"I hardly begged," Holmes muttered after Mycroft left us to send a telegram.

When we were led into the office of Arthur Holmwood, Lord Godalming, on his ancestral Ring Estate later that afternoon, I was surprised to find it as large as all of the Baker Street rooms put together, including Mrs. Hudson's. At the far end of the spacious room, Holmwood sat at his desk as his servant poured tea.

"I must say, how honored I am to be visited by the premiere consulting detective of London," he said after we introduced ourselves, and took our seats. Holmes smiled thinly and nodded as he sipped his tea. Holmwood looked at me then. "And his friend." I nodded my head. "Now tell me," he continued after sipping his own tea, "how may I be of service?"

"We've been hired by Captain Brutus Morris to help him locate the body of his son, who was, I believe, known to you," Holmes explained.

"I was as close to Quincey as a brother." A cloud passed over Holmwood's face, but it quickly disappeared. "And his passing hit me as hard, as if my own blood had died."

"Indeed?" Holmes glanced fleetingly at the portrait of the late Lord Godalming, Holmwood's father, over the fireplace. Holmwood caught the glance and nodded.

"I loved my father deeply, Mr. Holmes, but I'd be lying if I didn't admit that I felt worse for Quincey's death than I did for his." He nodded at the portrait. "After two years, it still haunts me."

"And yet Captain Morris' communications go unanswered?"

"What could I say to the man?" Holmwood sighed, running his hand through his thinning light brown hair. "That I feel responsible for his son's death? That I never should have allowed him to accompany us on our trip? Nothing I could tell him would bring the old man an inkling of peace."

"Who else joined you in the hunting trip?"

Holmwood stared blankly at Holmes for only a few seconds before answering. "Jonathan Harker and his wife, Mina. Jonathan is a lawyer in London, the head of the Hawkins firm."

"Surely it is the Harker firm, then?" I asked.

"No, Jonathan inherited the firm from his previous employer, Peter Hawkins, when he passed away a couple of years ago."

"And how do you know the Harkers?" Holmes asked, removing his pipe from his pocket and gesturing inquiringly.

Holmwood waved his hand permissively and even drew from his drawer a tobacco pouch, which he offered to Holmes, before pulling a cigar from his own pocket and cutting of the end. "Jonathan's wife, Mina, was the best friend of my former fiancée."

"That would be Lucy?" Holmes asked, packing the pipe's bowl.

"Westenra, yes."

"And who else went with you?"

"Two other people." Holmwood lit his cigar and drew on it. "Dr. Jack Seward and his mentor." Holmwood paused to draw on his cigar again. "Professor Abraham Van Helsing."

Holmes sat quietly for a moment, drawing on his pipe and studying Holmwood's desk.

"You're fiancée, Miss Westenra?" Holmes looked again at Holmwood. "She had other suitors? Quincey and this Dr. Seward both courted her, did they not?"

Holmwood's face became granite, and he began to rise from his chair. "Now look here, Mr. Holmes, if you are insinuating . . . ."

Holmes raised his hands placatingly. "Please, Lord Godalming, I insinuate nothing. I am merely attempting to get as clear a picture as I can of the relationships."

This seemed to calm Holmwood somewhat and he settled back into his seat with a sigh. "I apologize. As I said, I am still haunted by the death, especially as it came so soon after my father's passing." He drew on his cigar again, collecting himself. "Yes, the three of us courted Lucy – in fact, all three of us proposed to her within the same week."

"Yet you three remained friends after she rejected the other two," I interjected. "Quite unusual."

"And quite laudatory as well," Holmes added before Holmwood's dander rose again.

"The three of us had been friends well before we met Lucy," Holmwood explained, "and we swore that we'd remain so regardless of which one of us she chose." Holmwood looked at the clock on the mantel beneath his father's portrait. "And now, gentlemen, if there's anything else I can help you with, I do have a few other appointments this afternoon."

"Why Transylvania?" Holmes asked suddenly.

"Pardon me?"

"Why hunt wolves in Transylvania when there were so many other places closer to home?"

"We were invited there," Holmwood studied his desk, "by a local Count of Harker's acquaintance, or Van Helsing's." He waved his hand as if this information were the merest trivia. "Besides, there was a particular breed we wanted."

"I see." Holmes nodded. "I have only one other question before we take your leave. Captain Morris only desires to bring his son's remains home. If you can tell us where in Transylvania the body was buried, we can relay the information to the captain and be done with it."

Holmwood drew again from his cigar and exhaled slowly, the smoke curling up to the ceiling. "I am afraid I cannot help you there," he said directly. "Jonathan and Van Helsing took care of him, as I was quite too shaken by his death to help."

"Well," Holmes said as we sat beside each other in the hansom on our way back to London, "what did you make of that?"

"He's hiding something," I replied. "His answers were mostly measured. He drew from his cigar each time you posed a question as if giving himself time to formulate the best response."

"Very good." Holmes said. "And what is he hiding?"

"I'm sure I have no idea."

Holmes sighed. "Nor do I, I'm afraid. But it has to do, at least partly, with Miss Westenra."

"How do you know that?"

"Did you see his desk?"

"I did, and noticed nothing out of the ordinary."

"There's no picture of Miss Westenra – not on the desk nor anywhere in the house that I saw."

"He did say she was his 'former' fiancée." I shrugged. "Perhaps the engagement was cut short."

"Yet, we do not know how the engagement ended," Holmes smiled without humor. "But, judging from the shadow that passed his face every time she was mentioned, it is safe to say it ended tragically. He avoided discussing it, and even feigned outrage whenever the conversation drew too close to his engagement. Curious."

"So where do we go from here?"

"I believe," Holmes looked at the countryside passing outside, "we may have just enough time to meet the Harkers before we get you back to your wife and your dinner."

Chapter III

Jonathan Harker's appearance surprised me – if it did Holmes, he made no indication. We were ushered into his office at the Hawkins firm by his wife, Mina, who was also apparently his personal assistant, a kind of secretary, typist, and stenographer. As we entered, he rose from his desk and proffered us his hand.

From the doorway, he seemed ancient with snow-white hair and beard, but as we approached his desk, I saw that his face was free of the wrinkles that settle upon us with age. Indeed, other than his hair, he seemed no more than twenty-nine.

"You have suffered a great shock," observed Holmes, taking his hand and then settling into one of two chairs arranged before Harker's desk.

Harker seemed confused at my friend's brusque words and looked to me questioningly.

"Your hair, dearest," Mrs. Harker prompted gently as she took a seat at a smaller desk equipped with a shorthand machine beside his.

"Ah, yes." Harker replied with a mirthless smile as I shook his proffered hand and took my seat beside Holmes. "I suffered a bit of an upset and a lengthy recuperation a few years ago during a trip to Transylvania."

"Was this the same trip that ended in Mr. Morris' death?" Holmes asked.

"No, no," Harker shook his head. "It was . . . it was a different trip."

"A few months earlier," Mrs. Harker interjected. "The previous summer. Mr. Harker had been sent there by the firm to finish work his predecessor, Mr. Renfield, had been unable to complete."

"This is predominantly a real estate firm, is it not?" Holmes asked.

"Yes." Harker replied.

"Though we also do other work," Mrs. Harker added. "Criminal defense, business law, divorce."

"But predominantly real estate." Harker said.

"Why on earth would your firm send you to Transylvania, then? Surely that country is a bit far from your purview."

Harker stared at Holmes, thinking.

"Mr. Harker was sent to secure signatures from a gentleman there who wished to purchase several properties here in London." Mrs. Harker explained.

"And this Mr. Renfield was unable to secure these signatures from a man who clearly wanted to purchase them?" Holmes looked from Mr. Harker to his wife.

"Mr. Renfield was – " Harker began before his wife interceded.

"Mr. Renfield had several health issues that prevented him from completing the journey. Jonathan was sent to relieve him of the responsibility so the man could return home and seek medical attention. I'm sorry, Mr. Holmes," Mrs. Harker continued, "but surely you didn't come all this way to discuss our firm's confidential business and my husband's coiffure."

Holmes smiled slightly at Mrs. Harker. "Quite so," he said, "I do apologize for the diversion." He turned to Mr. Harker again. "I have been asked by Quincey's father to locate his son's remains so that the old man

222

may return them to the family grounds in Texas. You and your wife were, I am told, part of the hunting party organized by some Transylvanian Count? Is that correct?"

Harker's face grew paler at the mention of the Count, but otherwise showed no change in manner. "Yes," he said. "We accompanied Quincey, Lord Godalming, Dr. Seward, and Professor Van Helsing on the trip."

"And how are you acquainted with these men?" I asked.

Again Mrs. Harker answered. "I was Lucy Westenra's dearest friend. She was Lord Godalming's fiancée."

Holmes turned his attention to Mrs. Harker. "A hunting trip is not traditionally a desired holiday destination for one of the fairer sex, especially when accompanied only by men."

"I was accompanied by my husband, Mr. Holmes." Mrs. Harker bristled, but her voice remained calm. "What precisely are you suggesting, sir?"

"Nothing untoward, I assure you," Holmes explained. "I only wonder that your husband brought you, but Lord Godalming did not bring his fiancée, whom you tell us was your dearest companion."

"Miss Westenra died," Mrs. Harker's voice was subdued, almost a whisper, "of anemia. She had been ill, and she perished after an unsuccessful blood transfusion." She paused to dab at her eyes with a handkerchief. "It was horrible. The shock of it killed her mother. This coming so soon after Arthur, Lord Godalming, lost his father – the grief was simply too much. We took the trip as a means of escaping our sorrow and removing ourselves, if only temporarily, from the scene of so much sadness."

I sighed heavily. I admit the young woman's story greatly affected me, bringing to mind a litany of my own sorrows: The loss of my father and brother, the war, and so many others. "And the expedition itself," I interjected, "such a shame that it, too, ended in more unhappiness."

"Indeed," Mr. Harker said with a glance at his wife. "I am afraid," he continued, "that I cannot help you, Mr. Holmes. I do not know where Quincey is."

"But surely you assisted in the burial?" Holmes asked.

"After the attack," Mrs. Harker replied, "we deemed it best for two men to stay behind and protect me, should more wolves come while the other two put Quincey to rest."

"Lord Godalming," I interjected, checking my notes, "told us that, and I am quoting here, 'Jonathan and Van Helsing took care of him, as I was quite too shaken by his death to help.'"

"Perhaps you misheard Arthur." Mrs. Harker smiled gently at me. "He was shaken by Quincey's death, as he was closer to Mr. Morris than any of us, and he did stay behind with my husband and myself. Dr. Seward – that is Dr. John Seward – assisted Professor Van Helsing with Quincey's burial. So you see," Mrs. Harker smiled gently at both of us, and I was reminded of my own dear wife waiting for me at home, "we really cannot help you. We are sorry to have wasted your time here."

"On the contrary, my lady," Holmes rose from his chair and bowed to Mr. and Mrs. Harker, "this has been a most illuminating conversation, and it is we who should apologize for taking up so much of your time."

Holmes stopped at the fireplace, apparently taken by the portrait over the mantel depicting a stately older gentleman in the same chair Harker now occupied. "This is, I presume the late Peter Hawkins?" As he gestured, the pipe fell from his hand and hit the hearth with a clatter.

"Yes," Mr. Harker replied. "He founded the firm. We were sorry to lose him."

"How did he die?" Holmes asked, bending over to retrieve his pipe.

"It was a heart attack," Mrs. Harker replied, "two years ago."

"A shame," Holmes said as he pocketed his pipe. "Well, as I said, we won't take up any more of your time today." He turned to Mrs. Harker. "Before we take our leave, though, could you provide us with the address of Dr. Seward's offices?"

"A truly amazing woman," Holmes exclaimed as we once again entered the cab to carry us home. He sighed with a wistful smile. "Mrs. Harker has surprising spirit." He sank into thought before continuing. "She's lying, of course."

"About what exactly?"

"Everything." Holmes chuckled. "And she lies in the best possible manner: By sprinkling the falsehoods among truths. Did you note how she refused to let her husband speak and instead seamlessly modeled her narrative to the information you gave her?"

"I did not."

"My dear Watson, when it comes to women, you are simply besotted. Take, for example, her manipulation of the burial story. You told her plainly that Godalming said Mr. Harker helped bury Morris. And without missing so much as a breath, she explains that either you misheard or Godalming misspoke, that it was not Jonathan Harker who assisted the professor but John Seward."

"Perhaps Godalming did misspeak."

Holmes shrugged. "Perhaps, but you clearly missed the look she gave her husband before relaying that information. No, they know more than they're telling, and she either doesn't trust her husband to keep to their story, or she fears another mental break if he stays too long in the past."

"A mental break?" I exclaimed. "Surely you jest."

"When in our association have you ever known me to jest about the art of deduction?" Holmes removed his pipe from his pocket and lit it. "How else to explain his premature grey? What but distress of the most devastating sort would engender such a drain of pigment that severe in one so young? No, this is was no mere 'bit of an upset' our Mr. Harker suffered. It was something so disturbing that it permanently overturned the poor man's entire understanding of the world. Did you notice his face when the Count was mentioned?"

"I did."

"Mark my words: The two trips to Transylvania were related, and this Count was at the center of it."

"But how?"

"I do not yet have adequate information to answer that, but perhaps tomorrow." Holmes drew on his pipe. Letting its smoke drift out of the window. "For now, we need to get you back to your home and hearth. I'm certain we can get you there before your wife's roast is out of the oven."

"What are we doing tomorrow?"

"If you can join me, we are going," Holmes removed the slip of paper Mrs. Harker had handed him as we left the offices and handed it to me, "to Purfleet to talk with Dr. John Seward at his sanitarium."

We rode the rest of the way in silence, but when the carriage stopped in front of my house, Holmes spoke again. "Something to think about."

I turned to him as I opened the carriage door.

"Why did Holmwood not tell us that his fiancée had died, do you think?"

Chapter IV

My wife does not habitually wake me when she rises. While I have always been a light sleeper, she had been a governess before she met me and thus had developed the skill of rising from the bed with minimum disturbance so as to keep her young charges secure in the Land of Nod, a talent that was equally of use in the marriage bed. I rarely, as a result, stirred as much as a whisker when she rose each day well before the sun to begin preparing the morning meal. It was a shock then, the next morning, to feel her hand on my shoulder shaking me awake in the darkness.

"Darling," she murmured as she gently roused me, "you are needed downstairs."

I rose to sit on the edge of the bed, reaching for my trousers folded on the chest at the foot. "Is it a patient?" I asked groggily. Mrs. Partridge,

225

I knew, was approaching her time, and her pregnancy had been a troubled one. I also feared it might be Mr. Gilstrap, who had recently taken a fall while replacing some shingles damaged in a recent storm. He suffered from a comminuted femoral fracture: His leg had been broken in three places, and I feared we might have to amputate before it was all over.

"It is," she replied, handing me my shoes, "Mr. Holmes."

I found my friend sitting at the head of our table, sipping a cup of tea. "Ah, you're up. Capital." I noted with some displeasure that he was wearing a pair of worker's coveralls and was covered from head to toe in soot. "I took the liberty of pouring your tea. A splash of cream and a hint of cinnamon, yes?" He gestured at a china cup steaming to his right, then nodded to his left at a similar cup. "And Mrs. Watson, you take yours black if I'm not mistaken."

Mary thanked Holmes with a smile and took a seat, wrapping her hands around the warm cup.

I sighed, looking at the state of Holmes's dress, and sat. "I suppose you deduced my wife's preference from the lack of cream scent on her breath when she greeted you at the door, combined with the unmistakable aroma of Earl Grey and the warmth of her hands as she took your coat, suggesting that she had already had her first cup and would be ready for a second?"

"Excellent deduction." Holmes beamed like a proud father watching his child do his sums correctly for the first time. "But no, I saw her empty cup on the table and noted the dregs were black." His smile widened. "And do not worry, my dear fellow, about your chair. I put a towel down before sitting."

"Our laundress will be ecstatic." I stifled a yawn. "Why on earth are you dressed this way?"

"Wiggins and I have spent the entire night at the Hawkins firm."

"Why?"

"You did, of course, note that Mr. Harker's office smelled strongly of burning wood, despite the lack of fire?"

"What of it?"

"When I bent to retrieve my pipe, I noted that the flue was crusted with creosote." Holmes shrugged. "I'm afraid the Harkers have been negligent in their chimney maintenance, so Wiggins and I took it upon ourselves to rectify that for them.

"I had no idea you were familiar with the upkeep of fireplaces," I said drily, sipping my tea.

"Really, Watson, you've not yet read my monograph on the classification of fires, ashes, and their various byproducts? It's only been almost nine years."

"It's on my list," I replied. "Eventually, I'm sure I will have insomnia."

Holmes shook his head, smiling thinly then continued. "We arrived an hour after the firm had concluded business for the day and approached the cleaning staff with a document instructing us to clean and repair the fireplace and chimney."

"And they let you in with nothing more than a forged work order?" I asked.

"Of course they did." Holmes smiled. "Most people will let you anywhere as long as you appear to know what you are doing, and if you have a piece of paper that says you know what you're doing, all the better." Holmes shrugged. "Once in the office, I picked the lock to Harker's desk and looked through his papers."

"Holmes!"

"I put everything back in order when I was finished." Holmes waved his hand dismissively at me. "Mrs. Harker will never know I was there."

"And Mr. Harker?"

Holmes chuckled. "I assure you, the only person we need concern ourselves with is Mrs. Harker. I could have left the papers scattered across the floor and the desk open to the wind, and Mr. Harker would only wonder why the cleaning lady didn't tidy up."

"But what if someone had come in and found you rifling through the papers?"

"Wiggins was keeping watch at the door and would have alerted me to anyone nearby. Besides," Holmes shrugged, "it was the work of perhaps five minutes."

"And what did you do for the rest of the time?"

Holmes gave me a withering look.

"Cleaning chimneys, dear." Mary said between sips of her tea.

"Of course." I could not help smiling at my wife, as she in turn winked at me over the brim of her cup. "And what did you find?" I asked Holmes. "You clearly found something of interest or else I'd still be in bed."

"I found a medical invoice." Holmes replied. "Dated two years ago and addressed to Peter Hawkins."

"Did he suffer from some malady other than a weak heart?"

"Possibly," Holmes replied. "I've no idea. The medical invoice listed the charges for the care of a Roderick M. Renfield."

"The original lawyer sent to Transylvania?"

227

"The very same." Holmes nodded. "And would you like to know where he was treated?"

Holmes handed me a piece of paper with an address written in his own scrawling hand for the Seward Sanitarium in Purfleet. Then, as if to make things doubly clear, he slid the calling card he had received from Mrs. Harker with Dr. John Seward's address written on the back.

The two addresses were identical.

"Mrs. Watson," Holmes turned to Mary, "Could you get by without your husband tonight? I suspect we will need to stay overnight in Essex."

"I'm sure I can muddle through, Mr. Holmes."

Chapter V

Rather than return to my bed after Holmes left, I packed an overnight valise and broke my fast with Mary. She offered to notify my morning appointments and reschedule, but I demurred. Holmes would sleep away most of the morning I was sure, and my two appointments, the aforementioned Mrs. Partridge and Mr. Gilstrap, were both scheduled for before noon. As for new or unscheduled patients, I simply asked Dr. Anstruther, my colleague and neighbor, to cover for me again.

Noon found me at Holmes's rooms, but I wasn't the first visitor he had received that morning. Mrs. Hudson warned me that Holmes had a guest as she let me in, but that he had insisted I be brought directly up upon my arrival.

I found my friend engaged in a heated discussion with a slovenly man in his late thirties. Holmes sat in his favorite chair while his guest stood over him. The man wore a shabby, brown Macintosh, with elbows frayed almost to the point of uselessness, over a rumpled suit that appeared at least one size too large for him. His shirt collar was unbuttoned and his cravat was slightly askew. Though he sported no mustache or beard, it seemed he may had given it a thought three days ago, decided against it, and lost his razor. His light brown hair didn't seem to have seen a brush or comb in just as long.

"We are talking," Holmes was saying as I entered, "about nothing short of cold-blooded murder, and you tell me there's nothing we can do?"

"I'm quite aware of the subject of our discourse, Mr. 'Olmes, and that's exactly what I'm saying." The man spoke with slight Cockney accent. "The murder of an American by a Dutchman in Transylvania is not in the purview of the Yard. My God, man, you can't even provide me a shred of evidence that an actual murder occurred."

"My deductions are sound." Holmes's voice grew chill, then he noticed me in his doorway. "Ah, Watson, have you met Inspector Belton Colford of Scotland Yard?"

"I have not," I reached my hand to Inspector Colford who wiped his on his trouser leg before taking mine. "I recognize the name, however. He's the inspector who recommended you to Captain Morris, is he not?"

"The very same. A good thing he did, too." Holmes turned his attention back to Inspector Colford. "If left to his own devices, I'm afraid the good inspector here would refuse to arrest Judas for lack of evidence."

"To be fair, Mr. 'Olmes, Judas didn't murder our Lord and Savior. He only sold 'Im out to the Romans."

"A fine distinction." Holmes murmured.

"Look," Colford continued, ignoring Holmes's jibe, "Bring me evidence of a crime committed on our shores, and I'll make sure the culprit meets justice, whether he's English, American, Dutch, or Roman, but I can't take 'deductions' to the Crown Prosecutor and 'ope for more than keeping my job."

Holmes rose from his chair and walked Colford to the door. "Look for me tomorrow evening, then," he said as the inspector exited, "and be ready with your handcuffs."

"A tedious man," Holmes muttered after closing the door before looking at me. "Well, if we leave now we just have time to make the one o'clock train to Purfleet."

"You have a suspect?" I asked as Holmes grabbed his valise and ushered me through the door. "He mentioned a Dutchman."

"I have a murderer," Holmes sighed, "but I will not discuss it yet. Let us first visit Dr. Seward and gather actual evidence for the intrepid Inspector Colford – perhaps even a confession if we're quite fortunate." Holmes closed the door and followed me down the stairs to the street, muttering. "Since he won't be bothered to come with us to catch a murderer, I suppose we'll simply have to bring the murderer to him."

Chapter VI

It was well past two o'clock when we arrived at the sanitarium. It was situated just outside of Purfleet and next to an abandoned abbey. Before entering the building, however, Holmes wanted to explore the grounds, so I followed as he walked the perimeter, staring at everything from the grass to the stonework of the building itself. We also spent a few minutes wandering the grounds of the eerily empty abbey.

Eventually we returned to the gates of the asylum, where we were met by a rather gruff-looking attendant who glared at us suspiciously as

229

we left the abbey grounds. "And who might you be skulking about like that?" He asked looking askance at us. "I seen you looking around over yonder – in the abbey that was bought by that foreigner."

"I am Sherlock Holmes," Holmes handed him a calling card, then nodded to me, "and this is my associate Dr. Watson, Mr. – ?"

"Name's Simmons." The attendant took the proffered card and stuck it into a breast pocket without looking at it, "and none of that tells me what you're doing prowling around here."

"We are here to speak with Dr. Seward about a case, Mr. Simmons," Holmes explained. "Is he in?"

Simmons crossed his arms and looked sidelong at us. "Is he expecting you?"

"Oh, I'd be surprised if he was." Holmes smiled.

"Not half as surprised as he'd be, seeing as he ain't here." Simmons' manner grew more furtive, and he looked around the yards before continuing. "Is this about that poor Mr. Renfield? It was his window you were peering in."

"You're familiar with Renfield's case then?" I interjected.

"Well, I ought to be, I reckon." Simmons nodded towards the window, his voice growing softer. "I'm the one found him the night he died, all bleeding and blabbering about the 'Master' coming."

"He was injured?" Holmes asked.

Simmons looked at us as if Holmes had asked the most idiotic question imaginable. "Poor man had been beat up something awful. Broke nose, head just about bashed in from being slammed to the floor, neck snapped, arms all wrong, and back most broke in two." Simmons chuckled without mirth. "Yes, Mr. Holmes, in my professional opinion, I'd say the man was injured."

"And Dr. Seward attended him?" Holmes asked.

"Sure." Simmons paused. "Well, him and that foreign fellow, Van Helsing, what was visiting that night."

I glanced at Holmes, but his face remained impassive.

"And this 'Master' Renfield spoke of," Holmes asked, as if this had been the subject all along. "Do you know of whom he was speaking?"

"Mr. Holmes, the man was crazy." Simmons smiled and shook his head. "He spoke of this 'Master' from the day he was brought in. Never gave him a name. Perhaps he was praying."

Holmes sighed. "Perhaps."

"You'd have to speak to the doctor if you want to know any more. I've said enough already."

"Do you know where we might find Dr. Seward," I asked, "if he isn't here? Does he live nearby."

"Lives here when he's here."

"I see."

"You could talk to Dr. Hennessy," Simmons added as an afterthought. "He runs things when Dr. Seward's away."

"Was he here during the Renfield confinement?" Holmes asked.

"He was."

"Then yes, Mr. Simmons," Holmes said, "we'd very much like to speak with him."

Chapter VII

Simmons led us into the asylum and to a door just off the main atrium, upon which was attached a brass plaque reading: *Patrick Hennessey, M. D., M. R. C. S., L. K. Q. C. P. I., F.R.A.M.I.*. Asking us to wait, he lightly knocked on the door before entering. After a moment or two, he returned and ushered us into Dr. Hennessy's office.

Patrick Hennessey was a hawk-faced man with a smile that seemed to stretch across his face but fell just short of his eyes. "The Famous Mr. Holmes and his associate," he said, rising from his desk and offering his hand. "Simmons tells me you are investigating a case involving our Mr. Renfield, God rest his soul."

"Only tangentially," Holmes replied, taking the proffered hand and giving it a single quick tug. Hennessey offered me his hand, but gave it only a perfunctory shake before turning to face Holmes.

"Well, I am happy to shed what light I can on the fate of that poor man and help in your investigation." Hennessey took his seat and gestured Holmes to one of the two before his desk. I took the other.

"What can you tell us about the patient, Dr. Hennessy?" I asked as I settled into my chair and Holmes stuffed his pipe.

The doctor glanced at me fleetingly, then turned his attention to Holmes, striking a match and holding it out. "A tragic case," he replied finally, as Holmes leant to the fire and took several pulls from the pipe stem to light the tobacco. "The poor man suffered from delusions of grandeur far outside his station."

"How did these delusions manifest?" I inquired. "Did he see himself as a king, or an emperor?"

"A god?" Holmes added after taking a long and thoughtful drag on his pipe.

"No, no," Hennessey chuckled and leaned back in his chair, "nothing so obvious. Renfield came to us after a breakdown in Munich."

"What," Holmes asked, "was he doing in Munich?"

"Losing his mind." Hennessey chuckled, then turned serious. "I believe was employed as a law clerk or something for a London firm and was on his way to Romania or Transylvania, one of those primitive territories where they kiss crosses to ward against demons, to sell some half-literate princeling some property in and around London. Maybe Whitby, I'm not sure."

"Was it the same foreigner who purchased the abbey next door?" Holmes asked.

"I'm sure I don't know," Hennessey replied with dismissive wave of his hand. "Jack . . . Dr. Seward thought so, but I failed to see the importance." He scratched his chin before returning to Renfield's case. "Renfield came to us convinced that he was the slave to some diabolical 'Master'."

"How is this a delusion of grandeur?" I interrupted. "Surely the shift from solicitor – for he was solicitor, Dr. Hennessy, not a clerk – to a slave would be a delusion of triviality?"

Hennessey glared at me, but again spoke to Holmes. "The favored servant of a master destined for world domination, would be, at least in Renfield's estimation, a decided shift upward on the social scale."

"And this is who he imagined his master to be?" Holmes asked, exhaling a long plume of white smoke. "A megalomaniacal despot?"

"In a manner of speaking, Mr. Holmes, yes." Hennessey smiled, then altered his voice, to a near frantic quivering, as if in mockery of another. "'To rule, Dr. Hennessy, to rule,' he said to me once. 'That is the only thing worth living for, whether it be over the will of people or their hearts, preferably both.'

"'But,' I returned, 'you don't wish to rule? You wish to serve the one who rules the world?'

"He grew restive at this and began fidgeting with his hands. Then he answered while looking furtively out his window. 'No, Dr. Hennessey. To serve at the right hand of he who rules is quite enough ambition for me. Yes, quite enough for me. The world must bow before the strong ones.' Then he smiled and crept back to his bed as if dismissing me, refusing to reply to further questions, picking flies from the air – You know, we suspected that he ate them, and other things besides."

Holmes made no reaction to this last statement. "He looked out of his window?" he asked instead.

Hennessey seemed confused by the question. "Yes."

"And this window opens upon the grounds of the abbey?"

Hennessey seemed on surer ground here. "Oh yes. He was fascinated by the abbey. He escaped there at least twice. We had to drag him back screaming. Dr. Seward tried to trick him into escaping once so we could follow and see what he did there, but he didn't take the bait."

"Why do you think," I asked, "he went to the abbey? Surely if escape was his plan, he'd have fled down the road or through the fields."

Hennessey surprised me by addressing me for once, though his tone was almost as patronizing as Holmes's could be when I attempted my own deductions. "He thought that his master lived there. Clearly the man saw himself in thrall to the Almighty, not just some tin-pot despot."

"What can you tell us about Renfield's death?" Holmes asked pulling again from his pipe.

"Not much, I'm afraid. I was not present that night. You would have to ask Dr. Seward . . . or his friend."

"His friend?"

"Van Helsing," Hennessey spoke the name as if it reeked of something unpleasant. "He is a professor from the Netherlands. Strange fellow. Erratic, laughs at the oddest things, but apparently an absolute genius. He taught Dr. Seward in medical school, and they have been thick as thieves ever since."

"And why should we ask him about Renfield's death?" I asked. "Surely he wasn't on staff here."

Hennessey snorted derisively. "One wouldn't know it by looking." His voice rang with wounded pride. "He came to visit Dr. Seward around the time of Renfield's admission and was here more than he was elsewhere. Though to be fair, Jack was in a bad way then as well. He'd been rejected for marriage and then the girl fell ill. I believe they called Van Helsing in to consult, but she died under Jack's care, and it hit him hard. Then the disastrous Renfield case, and finally, his American friend, who'd wooed and lost the same girl, died in a hunting accident. If I'm being generous, Van Helsing has remained so long to comfort his friend and protégé."

"And if you're being ungenerous?" Holmes prodded.

Hennessey hesitated. "I'd really rather not say, but the man spent an awful lot of time here."

"You think he had designs on your position?"

Hennessey's face grew hard, as if Holmes had struck a nerve. "I'd really rather not say," he repeated, "but he certainly seems to act as if he owns the place. Dr. Seward has even given him his own key."

"And why should we ask Van Helsing about Mr. Renfield?" I attempted to bring us back to the subject at hand.

"Because he was one of the last men to see Renfield alive. He and Dr. Seward. They both filled out the certificate," Dr. Hennessey smirked. "The poor man fell out of bed, apparently."

233

"And where might we find either of these two?" I asked.

"Van Helsing? I have no idea, but if he isn't returned to the Netherlands, you'll generally find him near Jack."

"Where would you look for Dr. Seward then?" Holmes asked, tapping his bowl into the ashtray on Hennessey's desk.

Hennessey sighed. "His hours here have grown increasingly sporadic the last two years. I haven't seen him at all in at least two weeks, in fact."

"That doesn't answer my question, Dr. Hennessey."

Hennessey leaned across his desk to speak to Holmes and lowered his voice as if there were others in this room, empty save for us three, that might listen. "It pains me to say this," his tone that implied quite the opposite, "but I'd look for him in the Limehouse district."

"The opium dens." Holmes said it as a statement rather than a question.

"He never fully recovered from his losses. He began taking laudanum when Miss Westenra denied him his proposal. After her death . . . ." Hennessey shrugged. "His habits expanded to other, more powerful opiates." He paused to let this sink in. "I have taken over the lion's share of running the sanitarium in his absence. Otherwise, the doors would have been shuttered, and what would happen to these poor men and women?"

"Yes," Holmes said drily, "you're quite the saint to worry so."

"I do try my best, Mr. Holmes." Hennessey smiled as he rose from his desk, our meeting over.

"The case is drawing to a close." Holmes said on the train back to London. "It is, not surprisingly, more complex than we were led to believe, but I have almost all the information I need."

"You know where Captain Morris can find his son's body?" I asked, incredulous.

He looked at me strangely. "No, but I suspect we will have that information by this time tomorrow.

Holmes said nothing the rest of the ride back. He merely peered out his window, first on the train, then in the hansom. It was late when we arrived at Baker Street. Holmes rose from his thoughts and looked at me.

"Why not stay the night here? You've already made arrangements for your appointments tomorrow, and you told Mrs. Watson you'd be away anyway."

"I suppose I could," I replied, stifling a yawn.

Chapter VIII

Any hopes I had for a quick fall into my old bed, however, were dashed when we alighted from the carriage and found Inspector Colford approaching our door.

"Ah," he said seeing us leave the hansom. "Just the two men I was looking for."

Holmes seemed unsurprised to find the inspector waiting for us at this late hour. "You have discovered something," Holmes said with a self-satisfied smile, "that has altered your view of the case."

"To be fair, Mr. 'Olmes," Colford replied, running his fingers through his unkempt hair, "I never doubted your theory, only the probability of getting the Crown to prosecute a crime committed outside of the country."

"You have, I take it, changed your mind then." Holmes spoke this as a statement, not a question as he held open the door to 221 and ushered us inside. "Come in then, and I will ask Mrs. Hudson to prepare some tea for us as you relate your tale."

"To be fair," Colford continued once Holmes's landlady had brought us our refreshment, "there is still little chance that we can prosecute anyone for the American's death. 'Owever, I've done a bit of digging since we last spoke, and I've found an interesting piece of information that may open new avenues for us."

Holmes motioned for him to continue as he took a sip from his own tea.

"I went 'round to the probates when I left your rooms earlier." Colford smiled ruefully. "I was curious about the death of Lord Godalming's fiancée and her mother. You said Mrs. 'Arker claimed Miss Westenra's mother died of shock at her daughter's passing?"

"Such was her claim." Holmes admitted.

"Well, according to her death certificate, she died at least an hour *before* her daughter."

"Indeed?"

"And d'you know who she left her property to?"

"One would assume," I said before Holmes could answer, "her daughter."

"Aye, one would assume that, considering her husband was gone already," Colford nodded. "She left her estate to Arthur 'Olmwood. Her will stated explicitly that her estate went to 'Olmwood, even if she predeceased her daughter."

"Well, surely she expected her daughter to be married before she died," I suggested, "so Miss Westenra would still receive the benefits of her estate practically, if not technically."

"You'd think that," Colford nodded with a wry smile, "except the will was dated before ever 'Olmwood proposed to Miss Westenra."

"And what was the elder Mrs. Westenra's cause of death?" Holmes asked as he sipped his tea.

"'Eart failure," Colford shrugged, "though there were traces of laudanum in her system. Miss Westenra's as well."

"A common enough sleep aid," Holmes admitted.

"Not in these levels." Colford eyed Holmes over his cup. "Seward and your Dutchman signed both death certificates, Lucy's and her mother's."

Holmes made no indication he heard. "It is curious," he continued setting down his tea, "the number of bodies piling up around these people." He began counting on his fingers. "Holmwood's father, the elder Lord Godalming passes, just before deaths of Miss Westenra and her mother, leaving Mr. Holmwood with not only his father's lands and titles, but all the assets of the Westenras." Holmes raised another finger. "Then Peter Hawkins, senior partner of the Hawkins law firm, dies suddenly, leaving his professional and personal estate not to his family or the next senior partner, but to Jonathan Harker, who was, as far as I can tell, merely a junior member of the firm before his trip to Europe." He raised a third finger before continuing. "Next the patient Renfield, Harker's predecessor in the Transylvanian transaction, who dies mysteriously under the care of Dr. Seward, Holmwood's close friend, raving about a 'Master' coming to rule the weak." Holmes raised a fourth finger. "Finally, Quincey Morris, ostensibly the close friend of both Holmwood and Seward and rival for Miss Westenra's affections, dies in the wilds of Transylvania hunting wolves of all things, yet no one who was there can say definitively who buried him or where."

"We haven't yet spoken with Seward," I reminded Holmes. "Perhaps he may shed light on Morris' death."

"Perhaps," Holmes shrugged, signifying no similar hope for enlightenment from that corner. "There is one man, however, who lurks at the periphery of the entire case." Holmes paused. "This Doctor or Professor – the Dutchman Van Helsing. He treated Miss Westenra for anemia before she died. Two witnesses place him at the scene of Renfield's death, and everyone we've questioned agrees he was present for Morris' burial, yet he remains elusive. No one can tell us where to find him. Perhaps he's in London, maybe he's in Purfleet. It's possible he has returned to the Netherlands. The man is a will-o-the-wisp."

236

"You reckon this Van 'Elsing is the center of it?" Colford asked.

"If he isn't our man," Holmes stated firmly, "he knows who our man is." Holmes paused. "He certainly knows where Captain Morris can find his son. Of that I'm dead certain. Mark my words, though," Holmes eyed the clock on the mantel. "This Dutchman is at the center of something far exceeding mere murder. If the arrogant Dr. Hennessey's report of Renfield's rantings are to be believed, there is a more insidious conspiracy afoot, one more far-reaching than strange beneficiaries to final testaments. Now, gentlemen," Holmes rose from his seat, "if you will excuse me, I have a man to see in the Limehouse District. Don't wait up for me."

Chapter IX

I was awakened the next morning by Holmes, wearing a false nose and eyebrows, shaking me. "Come, Watson," he said as the scent of bacon, eggs, and strong tea assailed my nostrils, "Mrs. Hudson has prepared our morning repast. Let us break our fast together, and I will tell you what I learned from the good Dr. Seward."

"You found him?" I asked, wiping the sleep from my eyes and sitting up.

"I did," Holmes removed his prosthetics then clapped his hands, altogether too loudly for that hour of the morning. "He has helped me break the case, in fact. Come come, cold eggs are of no interest to anyone."

"How on earth did you find him?" I asked, pouring my tea. "There must be dozens of opium dens in Limehouse."

"As I suspected I would," Holmes said around a forkful of eggs. When Holmes is distracted by a case, I have found his table manners go straight out the window. "In one of the less seedy houses. As you know, I am not unfamiliar with the establishments in that district. A man of Seward's stature would be more discerning in his choice of den, preferring one whose management could be depended upon for discretion. That narrowed the field considerably, and I found him in the first place that I looked." Holmes swallowed. "I spied him already deep in Morpheus' arms, curled on a mattress in the back."

"How did you recognize him?" I interjected. "No one has described him to us in all our interviews."

"His portrait was right there in the sanitarium's lobby." Holmes sighed, speared a sausage with his fork, and put it in his mouth. "Honestly, if you don't train your powers of observation to work instinctively, why bother training them at all? Dr. Seward has grown a bit more emaciated and greyer since the portrait was painted, but otherwise the likeness was perfect.

"I knelt by his side and nudged his shoulder to draw him from his doze. He looked at me blearily and asked who I was.

"'The professor sent me,' I told him and, in his addled state, this seemed to satisfy him. 'He's afraid you might speak out of turn the more time you spend in these places.'

"He had trouble focusing his sight on anything, so he stared into the middle distance. 'I come to these places to forget, not to remember. Van Helsing knows that.'

"I filled my voice with all the sympathy I could muster as Seward tried to blink back slumber. 'What are you trying to forget, Jack?'

"He tried again to focus on my face, but his eyes remained bleary and tears formed at the corners. 'Her,' he replied almost in a whisper. 'My Lucy.'

"'The one who died?'

"'Died?' He laughed without even a hint of amusement. 'We killed her.' He stifled a sob. 'We gave her four bodies' worth of blood and still she needed more. Van Helsing near drained me twice for all the good it did.' His voice faded. 'We took the wrong precautions, you see? Merely fattened her for slaughter. Died?' he laughed again grimly. "No sir, we killed my poor Lucy as surely as if we had stabbed her with Quincey's Bowie.'

"'Quincey?' I asked, and I placed my hand comfortingly about his shoulder. 'He died, too, yes? In a hunting accident?'

"For a moment, Seward's eyes grew clearer and glared at me. I feared I had overplayed my hand. But then weariness overtook him, and he stared blankly upward, chuckling. 'Yes, a hunting accident. The Count did for him. Well, his allies.' He held his hands above him in front of his face. 'Right before my eyes. Stabbed in the back.'

"'The Count?'

"'Ask Van Helsing.' Seward stifled a yawn and tried to roll over, but my hand on his shoulder prevented him. 'He knows all about the Count. More than anyone,' the yawn came, 'except maybe Renfield.'

"'What happened to Quincey's body?' I asked, moving my hand soothingly over his shoulder, and hoping the spell of opium still held sway over his reasoning faculties.

"Seward blinked several times, and I thought he might descend back into oblivion. Then he sighed heavily. 'Van Helsing knows all about that. We couldn't carry his body back through Borgo ourselves, so Van Helsing buried him. He and . . . I don't remember. Somebody else.'"

Holmes paused his monologue long enough to shove a piece of toast whole into his mouth, washing it down with his now-lukewarm tea. "Well," he continued, suppressing a slight belch, "I supposed I had gotten all the information from the good doctor that I was likely to without arousing even his drug-addled suspicions, so I drew the interview to a close.

"'You really must return to the professor,' I said, gently lifting him up. 'You know where he is?'

"Seward chuckled. 'I would assume so,' he murmured. 'He's not left my side since,' he waved his arm languidly, 'everything.'

"By now we had left the den and were standing by the road. I flagged down a cab, and as I helped Seward into the carriage. I heard him ask the driver to take him to Brown's Hotel. I paid the cabbie, and then made my way further down the street before flagging another cab.

"When I arrived at Brown's, Seward was nowhere in sight. I went to the front desk and left a note for Van Helsing."

"What did the note say?" I asked placing my napkin on my empty plate.

Holmes gave me a mischievous smile. "I wrote this address and added, '*It is urgent I speak with you about the Count. 6 p.m.*' It is now just past eleven, so that should give us ample time to gather the tired captain and Inspector Colford, and you enough time to let your wife know you're safe."

"Do you really think he'll come?" I asked.

"I will be quite surprised if he doesn't," Holmes responded dabbing the corners of his mouth with his napkin. "However, we know where he is staying, and Wiggins has some of his boys keeping constant watch. If he doesn't come here, we'll know where he went."

Chapter X

Holmes's precautions proved unnecessary. Precisely at the appointed hour, we heard a knock upon the street door.

"Is that him?" Captain Morris asked from the divan. "The man who can tell me where my boy is?"

"If anyone can, it is he." Holmes said as he took his seat in his armchair. "Colford, have your shackles ready."

Colford stood by the fireplace with his hands in his coat pockets. He said nothing, but the sound of linked metal jingled in his right pocket.

"Good then," Holmes smiled. "We are ready, and I hear an older gentleman on the stair who is, if the weight of his step is any indication, rather strongly built for a man of average height."

At the knock on Holmes's parlour door, he bade the visitor enter, and we beheld a man just as Holmes had described. His shoulders were set back over a wise, deep chest, and his neck was as well balanced on the trunk as his head was on the neck. His head was broad and large behind the ears. His forehead rose almost straight, then sloped back above two ridges wide apart, forcing his reddish hair to fall naturally back and to the sides. His clean-shaven face had a hard, square chin, a large, resolute mouth, an impressive nose, rather straight, that seem to broaden as his big bushy brows came down and his mouth tightened. His large, blue eyes, set widely apart, glared at our party as he entered.

"Professor Abraham Van Helsing, I presume?" Holmes rose and gave the man a slight bow before motioning to an empty chair between my own and his.

"I vould rather to stand I think," Van Helsing chuckled nervously, hooking his thumbs into his waistcoat and eying the four of us suspiciously. "To who am I speaking, please?"

"I am Mr. Sherlock Holmes, and this is my associate Dr. John Watson," He motioned to me, and I nodded before Holmes continued. "The man there by the fireplace is Inspector Belton Colford of Scotland Yard, and this gentlemen," Holmes indicated the captain, "is Captain Brutus Morris, whose son Quincey, I believe, you knew."

"*Ja*," Van Helsing nodded. "A good man. Very noble. A son for which you should to be proud."

"Tell me what happened to him." The Captain said, barely containing his emotion. "Where is my boy now?"

Van Helsing looked at the tired captain with a blend of pity and, I daresay, remorse. "Killed by wolves in Transylvania."

"Where you were," Holmes interjected, "hunting at the behest of a local Count, I take it."

"Count Dracula's hunt, *ja*."

"You and Quincey?" Holmes continued.

"Yes, and Jack Seward and Lord Godalming and Jonathan Harker and his wife Mina, yes." His voice grew irritated. "What is your point, Mr. Holmes? Why have you called me here today under, how do you say, false pretenses?"

"On the contrary, Professor Van Helsing," Holmes replied. "There was nothing false about them. I wish to speak with you about the Count. You know him well?"

"*Ja*," Van Helsing chuckled again. "We were . . . old friends."

"You were deep in his counsels then?"

"In his counsels, *nein*." Van Helsing seemed to choose his words carefully, "but I knew what he wanted. And well I knew the consequences should he attain his desires."

"And you abetted him in those desires?" Holmes said. "Once Mr. Renfield proved inadequate to the task?"

At the mention of Renfield's name, Van Helsing shot a look at Holmes that would have killed him had they been knives. "I do not think Herr Count would have seen it that way." He chuckled. "I did only what had to be done."

"Did you kill Renfield?" Holmes asked.

"*Nein*."

"You and Doctor Seward were last ones to see him alive."

"Perhaps."

Holmes gave Van Helsing's powerful arms a pointed look. "He was, according to reports, beaten to death, and I have met Dr. Seward. I daresay he'd have trouble beating a corpse to death."

Van Helsing shrugged. "He fell out of bed."

"What is your relationship with the 'Arkers and Lord Godalming?" Colford interrupted from behind us.

"We are comrades." Van Helsing smiled and lifted his fists in a fighting stance. "Comrades in arms, fighting side by side, yes?"

"Against what, exactly?"

"Why against tyranny and oppression, and the wiping away of all freedoms," I could not tell whether the old Dutchman was being sarcastic. "We fight for God, you see."

"Well," Holmes chuckled. "Your fight for spiritual freedom has certainly yielded your crew their share of worldly rewards. The Harkers got a law firm. Lord Godalming his father's estate, as well as the Westenra holdings. Seward – well he hasn't fared so well, but you . . . you have almost free reign over Seward's facilities. Tell me, did this mysterious Transylvanian Count help you in all of this? Did Quincey balk at participating in these crimes?

At this Van Helsing burst into laughter. "Mr. Holmes, you see the clues, but you do not understand."

"Well, then," Holmes leaned back in his chair with a satisfied smile, "by all means enlighten me."

"Ah, but I cannot, you see." Van Helsing shrugged. "These things that you claim I did, you cannot prove. Because you have a science mind, you can only see science." He chuckled again. "It is the fault of our science that it wants to explain all – and if it explain not, then it says there is nothing to explain. You do not think that there are things which you cannot understand, and yet which are." He paused here collecting himself. "But

241

I? I try to keep an open mind – and I understand the things that make one doubt if they be mad or sane. No, Mr. Holmes, I cannot explain to you with your too scientific brain, me and my friends."

At this, Colford moved from the fireplace to stand behind Holmes's chair. "Tell me about Lucy Westenra." Holmes said.

Van Helsing shrugged. "She fell to evil and died."

"How?"

"She lost her blood, and the transfusions we gave her did not help."

"You used Dr. Seward for the transfusions, did you not?" Holmes asked.

"*Ja*, and myself as well, and Lord Godalming, and even your son, Quincey." Van Helsing looked at the old man who had remained seated during the previous exchange, lost in his own thoughts.

"How many times did you use Dr. Seward?" Holmes continued.

"I remember not well." Van Helsing sighed. "Twice, maybe three times."

"Even though you knew he took laudanum regularly?" While Holmes questioned Van Helsing, Colford moved around Holmes's chair until he stood very near the professor.

"Yes. The young girl was dying, and we had to do something. He was there, and we needed blood."

"Surely," Holmes said, "there were servants in the house."

"Certainly," Van Helsing said dismissively. "And?"

"And you never thought to use them?" Holmes asked so softly that Van Helsing strained to hear him. "Several servants in the house, and you chose instead to fill the girl up with opiate-poisoned blood, not once but twice, on top of the laudanum you prescribed her." Holmes sighed. "And you wonder why she died."

"No." Van Helsing was so focused on Holmes, he did not notice Colford moving closer, "I know for how she died. It is you who wonders. I know what killed her and why, but you cannot know, because of your science brain." He looked to his right as Colford closed on him, slipping a shackle over the professor's wrist. "And now," he added with a resigned tone, "I think it best I say no more until you speak with my barrister. Mr. Harker, yes?"

"I'm arresting you, Professor Abraham Van 'Elsing, on suspicion of murdering Lucy Westenra." Colford's tone was firm.

"What about my boy?" Captain Morris said from his seat. "Does he not get justice?"

Colford turned regretful eyes to our American guest. "As I told Mr. 'Olmes, I can do nothing for a crime in another country. I'm sorry, truly I am." He turned Van Helsing towards the door as Holmes and I stood.

"You ain't taking him nowhere yet."

We all turned to find Captain Morris, standing behind us with a revolver pointed at the professor.

"Captain Morris," Holmes said, "please put away your gun."

"Not until that man at least tells me where Quincey's buried." Captain Morris' voice was steady, but I could see water welling in his eyes. "I didn't come halfway around the world to help you solve some other girl's murder. I came to bring my boy home, and I aim to."

"Please." With a shrug of his shoulders, Van Helsing nodded to Holmes's writing desk. "May I?"

Holmes nodded, and Colford led the professor to the desk, where he scratched something on the writing pad with Holmes's pen. "Please to give that to Captain Morris." He said to Colford who ripped the top sheet from the pad and handed it to the old man. As he took it, I noted the message: "*47° N Lat, 25.75° E Long.*"

Van Helsing looked again at the grieving captain and smiled. "If you follow those coordinates, just south of the Borgo pass, you will find a giant, ancient oak with roots tangled in the shape of a cross. That is where your much brave son was laid to rest after losing his sore trial." Van Helsing sighed deeply and shook his head. "Take him home, Captain Morris. He deserves to be with his people."

Chapter XI

The next afternoon, I stopped by Holmes's rooms after my rounds and found Mycroft with him.

"Ah, Doctor," Mycroft greeted me, "Sherlock here was just explaining how he cracked the case."

"It was, I admit, an interesting affair," I replied.

"Indeed," Holmes added. "I would speculate that the professor and the Transylvanian Count were clearly in league the entire time. They were, as he said, 'old friends', and they devised a plan to benefit themselves, as well as several of their friends. They ensured that Holmwood became Lord Godalming, and sweetened the deal by manipulating his future mother-in-law into altering her will, making Holmwood not only Lord of the Godalming estates, but of the Westenra holdings as well. Thus, through him they would have even gained a foothold in government.

"Next they installed Harker as the head of an influential law firm. They had originally enlisted Renfield, but he proved unstable, and they had to alter their plans, locking him away in the sanitarium until Van Helsing could dispose of him."

"How on earth could they have known the elder Lord Godalming and Peter Hawkins would die in time for their plans?" I asked.

"They ensured it." Holmes replied, "With the help of Dr. Seward, they induced a heart attack by drugging the elder Godalming, probably through his sherry. They did the same with Peter Hawkins and Miss Westenra's mother – her blood had traces of laudanum, you recall. And then poor Lucy."

"Oh, come now," I sighed. "Why would Doctor Seward commit murder?"

"Jealousy and grief." Holmes shrugged. "He had been rejected by his love, and so in his drug-addled mind, Van Helsing helped Seward see a way to make Holmwood feel the same loss."

"And how would they have convinced him to kill Lucy's mother?"

"Perhaps Holmwood did it, or Van Helsing." Holmes shrugged. "Harker or his wife, of course, would have taken care of Hawkins. I do not think, however, that Seward meant to kill Miss Westenra. Van Helsing used Seward's tainted blood to kill the girl, and thus strengthen the bond of the conspirators through their shared grief.

"Yes, Professor Van Helsing proved a worthy opponent," Holmes sat back with a satisfied sigh. "I've known few with an intellect as sharp."

"And what," Mycroft interjected, "of his ravings about 'things which you cannot understand, and yet which are'? Your 'too scientific brain' and what-not?"

Holmes scoffed. "One may have a brilliant intellect and still have a disordered mind."

"Quite," Mycroft continued. "Though, to be fair, unless the professor decides to give up his friends, we haven't much legal standing to do more than simply observe them. A shame you could only arrest him for medical negligence."

"Miss Westenra," Holmes's voice seemed tinged with an irritation only his brother can evoke, "was the only victim of Van Helsing's malfeasance that the Crown could prosecute, since it was the only crime on British soil of which we had tangible evidence. Besides," Holmes waved his hand dismissively, "my only concern is that my deductions were solid, which they were, and that Captain Morris found his son. The rest I leave in your hands, brother."

Mycroft nodded, looking at me. "Still, Doctor, as I said before, I'd think twice about publishing this little adventure. I'm afraid it would not paint your subject in a glowing light."

"Why not?" I asked. "Holmes solved the problem and caught the culprit."

"You did indeed solve the captain's problem – " Mycroft turned to his brother with an almost sad smile. " – but I'm afraid that this time you absolutely missed the mystery."

The July which immediately succeeded my marriage was made memorable by three cases of interest, in which I had the privilege of being associated with Sherlock Holmes and of studying his methods. I find them recorded in my notes under the headings of "The Adventure of the Second Stain", "The Adventure of the Naval Treaty", and "The Adventure of the Tired Captain".

– Dr. John H. Watson
"The Adventure of the Naval Treaty"

The Rhayader Legacy
by David Marcum

The heat was already stifling when I stepped outside that morning – a Tuesday, as I recall, in late July – but it was nothing like what I'd experienced a decade earlier in India and Afghanistan. As I don't find those conditions particularly unpleasant – at least at that time of day, and not long after breakfast – I decided to walk instead of hailing a hansom, which was never a problem that close to Paddington Station.

In my pocket was a letter from an old school chum, only just recovered from nearly ten weeks of debilitating brain fever following the shocking loss of a naval treaty that had been left in his care. I recalled him quite well from many years before, although our contact since then had been quite minimal. However, he knew of my connection to Sherlock Holmes – likely learned by way of his own position within the office of his uncle, Lord Holdhurst – and as soon as he had regained his senses, he'd sent a letter to me, begging that I obtain Holmes's assistance.

My wife and I agreed that there was something quite pitiful in his plea, and I resolved to bring it to Holmes's attention immediately. After arranging that my friend and neighbor Dr. Anstruther cover for me, I set out for Baker Street.

The doors were thrown wide for some early morning meeting at the Baptist Trinity Chapel, and as I passed I nodded at the minister. He did the same, but with a certain wariness. Although he seemed to respect me as a physician, we'd had an uneasy accord at best since the night that I'd helped Holmes force the church's side door to prevent young Alice Welwyn from hanging herself in the vestibule, convinced while drugged by her step-father that her death was the only way to save her reputation and expiate her sins – while simultaneously giving him control of the vast fortune left to her by her real father. We had only been just in time to prevent the tragedy, but the minister would probably never forgive himself for losing his temper when he learned the story, revealing to Holmes and me his own violent (and poorly suppressed) tendencies when he temporarily forgot the tenets of his faith and beat the step-father within an inch of his worthless life.

A turn along Chapel Street led me into the bustle of Marylebone Road, and I made my steady way, nodding here and there to strangers and the occasional familiar face. Soon I reached Baker Street Station and turned toward 221. As I walked, I considered how to place the matter before Holmes in such a way as to gain his interest. I knew well that he loved his art, and that usually he was as ready to bring his aid to a client as the client was to receive it. But there was always the possibility that he was already engaged.

And this concern seemed to be justified, as I observed upon my arrival. Letting myself in with the key that I'd retained at both Holmes's and Mrs. Hudson's insistence, I climbed upstairs to find my friend seated at his chemical table, absorbed in some investigation. He was clad in a dressing gown, and I wondered if he'd been up all night. Then I observed his dirty breakfast dishes on the dining table and concluded that he'd only recently become involved in his chemical research, as he would have otherwise ignored the food if he was carrying out his experiments when Mrs. Hudson brought it up.

I tried to see what he was doing, but the arrangement of glassware on the deal table was indecipherable. A large curved retort was boiling furiously in the bluish flame of a Bunsen burner, and the distilled drops were condensing into a two-litre measure. Holmes hardly glanced up as I entered, although he waved in my direction, and I seemed to have an indication that he would be finished shortly. I dropped into my old armchair, watching as he swirled the container around with one hand while drawing up a few drops in a glass pipette with the other. Eventually he stood, a test-tube in one hand and a slip of litmus paper in the other.

I could see that he looked rested, again confirming that he hadn't been up all night. Whatever he'd been doing hadn't taken much time.

"You come at a crisis, Watson," he said, as if we were in the middle of an ongoing conversation, instead of having not seen each other for a couple of days. "If this paper remains blue, all is well. If it turns red, it means a man's life."

He dipped it into the test tube and it immediately turned red. There was no doubt – whatever was in that test tube was acidic.

"Hmm," he said. "I thought as much!" Then he looked for a few more seconds at the paper before adding, "I will be at your service in an instant, Watson. You will find tobacco in the Persian slipper."

He placed the test tube in the rack on his chemical table and then stepped to his desk. After shifting through the various stacks of documents and journals, he found a pad of telegram forms and proceeded to scribble on several of them. Then he went to the landing door, threw it open, and called for the page boy. After handing over the slips of paper with instructions as to their disposition, he threw himself down into the chair opposite and drew up his knees until his fingers clasped round his long, thin shins.

Acknowledging my inquiring expression, he smiled and said, "A very commonplace little murder. You've got something better, I fancy. You are the stormy petrel of crime, Watson. What is it?"

I then handed him the letter from my old school chum, which he studied with great care.

I've recorded elsewhere the events of Holmes's subsequent recovery of the naval treaty, and the saving of the career of my friend Percy Phelps, as well as the great service that was performed for the country. As usual, Holmes was able to perceive the truth where it remained hidden from the rest of us, successfully revealing the stolen document and exposing a scoundrel in the process. And it was just two mornings later that Holmes and I, along with Percy, were back in that same room where the matter had first commenced.

As the three of us sat around the breakfast table, Holmes was able to explain the truth to a startled Percy. It had been a wearying couple of days, and during that time we'd made two trips to Briarbrae, Percy's family home in Woking, had interviewed several people of vastly diverse social stations in London, and Holmes had received a nasty knife cut across his knuckles. Now, with the treaty again in his possession after a long ten weeks, Percy would – in theory – be able to return to his position at the Foreign Office, under the aegis of his noted uncle.

When Holmes had revealed the truth of the matter and seen the treaty into Percy's hands, the nervous fellow had been beside himself, not knowing whether to rush home and tell his fiancé of his good fortune, or instead notify Lord Holdhurst that the treaty had been found. I advised the latter, going to Whitehall immediately to deliver the document back into responsible hands. I considered accompanying him, but instead felt that Percy should take care of this business on his own. And in truth, I was a bit raw and weary from having cared for him since the previous day while Holmes carried out his investigations.

I watched Percy's cab trundle down Baker Street and out of sight before climbing back upstairs to thank Holmes. Surprisingly, he had poured a bit of brandy for each of us, although the remains of breakfast were still on the nearby table. I raised an eyebrow.

"It seemed," he said, "that you could use this after so many hours spent with your quarrelsome and jittery friend, and I find that the pain in my knuckles is a bit more than I let on. I need a bracer before you look after the wound."

Although I didn't have my medical bag with me, there were sufficient supplies still in Baker Street to adequately fix up the cuts across a couple of his knuckles. They were clean with no underlying damage and would heal well. When I was finished, I poured another brandy for each of us and we retired to our chairs by the empty fireplace to discuss those features of the case which would have held no interest for Percy Phelps.

By then it was the first day of August, and the heat was already quite noticeable. It was the beginning of a long hot month in which the capital would feel like an oven, and the sunlight on the bricks would be painful to the eye. I was considering whether to rise and open the windows to a greater degree in order to catch the morning breeze. Yet even as I set down my glass to do so, the front doorbell began to ring with great ferocity. This was followed immediately by someone pounding upon the door.

Holmes raised an eyebrow, but he seemed tired and willing to wait for whomever had caused the commotion to come to him. I was more cautious, recalling past times when these rooms had been invaded by men – and the occasional woman – with an angry score to settle. I remembered one such only six years earlier, when a giant of a man – who had less than a day to live at that point, although we didn't know it then – had charged into the sitting room in a most abusive way. The brute had grabbed the iron fireplace poker, bending it and tossing it aside as an example of what he would do to Holmes if he didn't step out of the case. Holmes, in a rather amazing bit of strength of his own, had retrieved the ruined poker and straightened it back out – not perfectly, of course, but at least to a level of functionality. As we heard Mrs. Hudson and another voice speaking downstairs, I confirmed that I had my service revolver with me, as always, but I also glanced at the misshapen poker, still standing beside the fireplace, and considered whether I should take it up as well.

We heard the sound of one person ascending to the sitting room, indicating that Mrs. Hudson (by methods known only to her) had reasoned that her presence wasn't required. The footsteps were light and quick, and clearly those of a young woman. While that in itself didn't lessen any possible danger – as there were quite a few ladies who wished for an end to Holmes's life, and not quite as many (but some) who felt the same way toward me – I felt that the extra use of the poker would not be required.

There was a quick knock and then, without waiting for a reply, the door was thrown open to reveal a girl who appeared to be in her early twenties. (We were soon to learn that she was in fact only nineteen, but quite poised for her age.) She had neither hat nor gloves, as if she had just left home without preparing to properly pay a visit. She was angry, as evinced by her expression and stance, and her words quickly confirmed this observation.

Identifying Holmes immediately, she cried, "You have destroyed my father!"

We both stood, but Holmes didn't seem to feel threatened in any way. I, however, didn't immediately lower my guard.

"I'm sorry," replied Holmes. "You seem to have the advantage of me, Miss – ?"

"Natalie Rhayader," she replied, her tone filled with contempt. "Walter Rhayader is my father."

An understanding look crossed Holmes's face and he nodded. "Miss Rhayader, I'm very sorry that my conclusions implicated your father, but the experiment simply verified the official idea that the substance painted onto the metallic fittings, causing them to break loose and fall on Oswald Scampton, held traces of hydrofluoric acid – and your father was apparently seen painting near there a short time before. As I understand it, he admitted that he had been working nearby. I did nothing more than confirm what the police already suspected, and made my conclusions known to them day before yesterday."

She took a step closer. "And they arrested my father soon after they received your telegram. I've only just this morning learned that you were involved in gathering the evidence against him. I rushed over her to ask if you might investigate further, rather than simply sending a telegram and then washing your hands of the matter. He'll die, Mr. Holmes – long before his trial! He isn't well – He hasn't been for years! – and he's an innocent man, placed there because of your misreading of the evidence."

I thought back to the morning that I'd arrived two days before, waiting as Holmes finished his chemical experiment before telling me that the result might mean a man's life. The litmus paper had turned red, indicating the presence of an acid, and Holmes had then sent his wire to the Yard. Sadly, with my own story to tell, and in the rush to help my friend Percy Phelps, I hadn't given any more thought to that other "commonplace little murder", nor to any of the implications involved. Now this young lady stood before us, desperation and anger emanating from her in equal parts.

Holmes glanced my way. "Dr. Watson isn't aware of the facts of this case, Miss Rhayader. Won't you sit down while we discuss it? Perhaps I can clear up some of the confusion surrounding the matter."

She struggled with her decision – whether to remain standing in outrage, or capitulate and join us. Finally she did neither, instead saying, "Will you come with me? To speak with my father? He's being held at Scotland Yard."

Holmes glanced my way to see if I was free. I nodded that I was, for I hadn't known how long Holmes might take to resolve the matter of the missing naval treaty, and I had arranged with Anstruther to look after my practice until he heard otherwise.

Miss Rhayader said nothing, simply watching with her mouth tight while we retrieved our hats. Then we went downstairs, and soon we were in a growler headed south.

"Have either of you read of the case in the newspaper?" asked the young lady when we were underway. "There is a full account of it in yesterday's *Times*."

I shook my head. "We've been involved in another matter, and my time over the last day or so was spent caring for our client, who was ill. Mr. Holmes has been in Woking, related to the same affair."

"I did read *The Times*," Holmes stated, "as I had a number of empty hours yesterday as I waited for nightfall, and was able to examine several newspapers. From my understanding of the case, based on what has been reported, I had already intended to involve myself further in the matter. From the limited information conveyed to me by Inspector Gregson two days ago, your father is employed at the family glass factory in Hoxton, where the murder occurred."

"That's correct," replied Miss Rhayader. "The company was started by my grandfather."

"Three days ago," continued Holmes, "on July 29th, in the late afternoon, one of the long-time employees, Oswald Scampton, died horribly when a load of iron fittings, to be used by him in the framing and construction of industrial windows, fell from where it was suspended above him, killing him instantly."

"Oswald had worked there his whole adult life," Miss Rhayader said. "He was trained to do any task, but he had specialized in the last few years in the design and assembly of heavy windows with metal framing. He was fitting together one of them at his work table when the chain holding the iron works broke loose and crushed him. He should have known better than to leave them hanging there like that."

"May I ask," I interrupted, "if it was typical that he should be working in such a dangerous location?"

She closed her eyes. "Oswald was . . . willful. He often cut corners where safety was concerned. We have a series of tracks with rollers suspended from the ceiling throughout the factory which can be used to hoist and then shift various materials from one location to another. Earlier that day, Oswald had arranged to have the metal forms that he required chained together and loaded onto the hook. They were then pulled to his station, but he must have decided that he didn't need them quite yet, and they were left hanging while he worked on something else. They were directly above him when they broke free."

"At first," said Holmes, "it was believed that the chain simply snapped."

She nodded. "But my cousin, Brian Rhayader, who owns the factory, insisted that such a thing was impossible. The police had been called because of the accident, and when they examined the broken chain, they found a great deal of unusual corrosion."

"The chemist from the Yard suspected hydrofluoric acid," added Holmes, "but knowing that I had done some research in that area, he asked for me to confirm it. That was the limit of my involvement, I'm afraid. I had meant to follow up and ask a few additional questions, but then the other matter presented itself, and Dr. Watson and I have only completed it shortly before your arrival. The newspapers indicated that your father, Walter Rhayader, was arrested the day after the death occurred – on July 30th."

"That's right," she said with obvious bitterness. "That morning, soon after your wire arrived."

"The press accounts stated that a witness placed your father on the suspended walkway above the dead man's work area just an hour or so before the chain failed. He claimed to have been painting a rusty spot on the railing – one of his regular chores around the factory."

"If that's what he said he was doing, then that's what he *was* doing!"

"Did the police give any indication as to what they believed your father's motive would be for committing such a crime?"

"They said . . . they learned that my father and Oswald had been arguing. It has been going on for several weeks."

"What about?"

"I . . . I would prefer not to say."

"Miss Rhayader," I said gently, "we can easily determine from the police whatever motive is ascribed to your father. Your reluctance to discuss it will not prevent it from being discovered."

"It's not that it's a secret. It's simply that I find it . . . distasteful. You see, Oswald – that is, Mr. Scampton – had been pressing a case to ask for . . . to ask for my hand in marriage."

"I see. And your thoughts on that were – ?"

"It was ridiculous!" she snapped at me. "He's twice my age, and he thinks . . . *thought* . . . that simply because he was a valuable member of the business and a key employee, and that he had known me since I was born, that he had some special connection that would make him a legitimate suitor."

"And do you already have someone in your life to hold such a position?" I asked.

"I do. A major in the Army. He's out of the country at present, in Gibraltar, but I assure you – "

She stopped herself suddenly. "What, Miss Rhayader?" asked Holmes. "What were you about to say?"

"Only that if Thomas – that is, Major Stroud – were here, he might have . . . he would have already thrashed Oswald Scampton quite soundly long before things came to this point!"

She fell silent, her mouth tight with anger, and Holmes chose to leave off questioning her for the present. We continued to make our way south and then east. Our pace was steady, but not so fast that I couldn't observe the various people going about their business on the partially crowded streets. They moved with lethargy as the air grew warmer. Throughout our passage, Miss Rhayader didn't say another word.

We traversed Trafalgar Square, still somewhat empty at that time of morning. The spray of the fountains danced in the morning light, and the heat of that first day of August continued to build. When we entered the shade of the eastern side of the square, the morning sun was blocked by the tall buildings, and the sudden feeling of coolness was both palpable and welcome.

Turning along Northumberland Avenue, our cab soon released us within that warren of streets and buildings layered around Scotland Yard. At that time the men (and occasionally women) who made up the Force were still several months away from their planned move to new digs at the large handsome building beside Westminster Pier, but already there was a sense that plans were afoot to transfer elsewhere – for instance, there were boxes and crates standing in hallways between office doors that weren't normally left there. I wondered how all of this sprawl would somehow manage to fit into the new building.

Holmes and I were both well-known at the Yard, and we had been given unofficial free run of the place for years. We nodded at acquaintances and friends as we moved ever-deeper into the building, headed for the bank of modest offices which housed the various inspectors. We passed Lestrade's closed door and heard him reading the riot act to someone, his words indistinguishable through the aged oak door, but his tone unmistakable. A turn around the next corner and we found ourselves at Gregson's office, where the door was standing open.

The big fair-haired inspector looked up from a stack of papers and, when recognizing us, he stood and gave a smile of welcome. His eyes narrowed a bit when he identified Miss Rhayader, but he was no less gracious, seeing us all to chairs, inquiring if we wished for tea – we did not – and then closing the door with his large hands and reseating himself, asking how he could assist us.

Miss Rhayader took a breath, seemingly ready to voice a list of grievances, but Holmes spoke first. "Following my incidental involvement in the Scampton murder, by way of my chemical experiment a couple of mornings past, Miss Rhayader has now approached me with some dissatisfaction in regard to her father's arrest. I decided that, with your agreement, I would add a bit to what I've since learned by way of the newspapers."

Gregson leaned back, his aged chair complaining. "I'm not sure that discussing this in the presence of the suspect's daughter is wise, Mr. Holmes, but I can give you a limited amount of information – none of it is secret, after all. The iron that crushed Scampton was foolishly left suspended over his work station – specifically over the very stool where the man was laboring. Apparently he was often careless that way, regularly having materials loaded onto the hook that he'd pulled there, although he didn't necessarily always leave them directly over where he would be working. In fact, the men who chained the iron onto the hook swear that they left it positioned to one side of the work table, and that someone – possibly Scampton himself, or – (Here he cast a glance at the young lady.) – someone else pulled it further along the suspended track so that it was directly over where the dead man was working.

"We checked, and both track and hook were well-maintained, and loads hanging from them are easy to move, and can be done so silently. More importantly, they can also be moved easily by anyone standing on the suspended iron walkway that runs beside the track, so that someone could have come along there, reached over, and pulled the hanging iron-works directly over Scampton and – with the continuous hellish noise in that place – he might not have even been aware of it.

"There were a half-dozen of the iron frames chained together, comprising nearly half-a-ton of metal. As you know, when the load fell and killed Scampton, the first officers on the scene found signs of unusual corrosion on the remains of the chain wrapped around both them and the remnant suspended from the track." His scowled. "Constable Naughton handled the chain quite a bit before someone told him to stop."

"Oh no," I breathed, and Holmes shared my grim expression.

From her gasp, it seemed that Miss Rhayader understood the implications as well. Hydrofluoric acid can be absorbed by the skin, and while not immediately damaging to surface tissue, it can cause cardiac arrhythmia or pulmonary *oedema*, and other irreversible internal damage that can lead to death within days.

"How much of his body touched the acid?"

"Both hands – he had tugged the chain loose from the iron pieces for a better look before some of the workers could stop him."

"I assume that he has been treated with calcium gluconate injections or calcium chloride infusions?"

"He has. But – " Gregson added, "if the constable dies, an additional charge of murder will be laid upon . . . " Looking at Miss Rhayader, he finished, ". . . upon the person who tampered with the chain."

He shifted forward, twining his large fingers and placing his hands on the desk before him. "The owner of the factory is Brian Rhayader – your cousin, I understand, Miss?"

She nodded. "He and my father are both about the same age, but strangely my father is Brian's uncle. They are of the same generation, but not cousins as one would expect, due to the vast difference in years between when Brian's father and my father – brothers – were born. Brian is the only child of my grandfather's older son, while my father was the younger of those two sons. My grandfather . . . didn't feel that my father was capable of helping run the business, or even inheriting a share of it, so he instead left everything to his older son, Brian's father.

She lowered her head. "My father is . . . simple. He never had a head for business. His father – my grandfather – Bryn Rhayader, came from Wales and founded the business seventy years ago. He recognized my father's weakness and never expected anything from him, although he loved him in his own way and took care of him. When he died, his older son, Rhys – Brian's father – continued to do so.

"Somehow, twenty years ago, my father met my mother, and they married in secret. A year later I was born, and my mother died in childbirth." She said it without grief – a simple fact that had always been part of her life, and something sad that happened to someone whom she had never met. "Her death caused my father to further retreat from his responsibilities. He cared for me in his own way, but I was raised by a fine woman hired by my Uncle Rhys. Through my whole life, my poor father has simply been like a pleasant ghost. He's been interested in me, to be sure, but he is . . . distracted. When Oswald Scampton asked for my hand – " She stopped herself suddenly, afraid to give fresh emphasis to the possible motive that her father would have for committing murder.

Instead, she continued, "My cousin Brian has continued to care for my father since his father passed. He allows my father to carry out small jobs in the factory. It keeps him happy, and makes him feel useful."

Gregson nodded, but one could see that the history of the Rhayader family held no interest for him. "Brian Rhayader," he said, "was the one that told us that the metal looked as if it had been eaten through by acid, and that hydrofluoric acid is used a great deal in the factory for glass etching." He glanced at Holmes. "We had a good idea of what had happened, but Dr. Mayes in the laboratory wanted your opinion."

Holmes nodded. "Would it be possible to speak with Miss Rhayader's father?"

Gregson unlaced his fingers, and a pained expression crossed his face. "Umm, he is in the infirmary at present." Miss Rhayader gasped, and Gregson quickly raised a hand to placate her. "Purely precautionary, I assure you, Miss. He became rather . . . agitated after you left this morning, and considering what you'd told us about his health, we felt that it would be safest to move him there and sedate him."

Miss Rhayader rose to her feet. "I demand that I be allowed to see him immediately!"

Gregson stood as well. "Of course. I understand that he's asleep, but you may sit with him." He turned toward Holmes and me. "I suspect that you wished to question him, but I'm afraid that will have to wait."

"We understand," I said. Turning to Miss Rhayader, I added, "I personally know the physicians here at the Yard, and can vouch for every one of them. Your father will receive the best of care."

Holmes added that we would be in touch, and Gregson summoned a constable to take her to her father. Then, when she was gone, Gregson said, "It appears to be cut-and-dried, Mr. Holmes – although we both know that I've said that before, and you've revealed that it wasn't necessarily so. I'll be happy to hear whatever you learn. I admit that I'm of two minds – it seems likely that Rhayader did do something to the chain. A couple of witnesses place him on the metal walkway an hour or so before, although he says that he was painting – doing touch-ups is one of his duties – and several people knew that he and Scampton have been overheard arguing of late. It's fairly certain that Walter Rhayader gambles, and that Scampton had a hand in it – possibly placing bets for him, and no doubt skimming a hefty cut off the top.

"It wouldn't be too difficult to do. As you've gathered, the girl's father is rather simple-minded – a gentle-seeming soul, but just the type that might react stupidly and violently if he thought that he had a grievance. I talked to him last night, and one can see why his own father, the founder of the company, left him out of the inheritance. He'd be no use whatsoever at running a business.

"Now that other one, Brian Rhayader, unlike our suspect, is a right canny fellow. He only inherited the business a year or so ago, and even though his father Rhys was quite capable, the new owner has already doubled the production, and has a number of expansions planned. It seems that he had a lot of good ideas that he was prevented from implementing until his own father passed away."

"I believe then that Mr. Brian Rhayader is the next person that we should visit," said Holmes. Gregson agreed and wrote the address for the glass-works on a slip of paper. We thanked him and then wended our way back to the street, where we settled into one of the many cabs that are always waiting in that quarter.

Holmes was quiet as we traversed London, making our way toward Hoxton. I glanced his way. "Do you see anything definite that leads you to believe that Walter Rhayader is innocent?"

"It's too soon to tell, and I would certainly like to hear his story. But this certainly reminds me that I need to have all of the data before making conclusions."

"But you did what was asked of you as a consultant – you verified the presence of hydrofluoric acid. That was the extent of what was requested."

"True, but obviously there is more to it than simply watching a piece of litmus paper change color and declaring that a man's life depends upon it. By agreeing to conduct the test, even if only to verify another's conclusions, I attached my reputation to the outcome. I did so without any thought to the bigger picture. I called it 'commonplace'. Now that I understand the case better, I realize that something isn't right. For instance, hydrofluoric acid wouldn't eat through a chain like that in such a quick manner. Instead, it would form an upper layer of iron fluoride and free hydrogen. If those chains failed, then there was something else going on besides the mere application of acid."

He became silent again, and I left him to his thoughts. Once as we moved along Farringdon Street he shifted his position, and I thought that he might have decided to say something else, but instead he simply settled a different way and continued to brood.

The steady pace of the horse, the rocking of the cab, the tedious monotony of the city around us as we passed through it, along with the absence of engagement from my companion, all acted upon the lack of rest that had defined my previous night when Percy Phelps, recovering from his brain fever and attempting to sleep without the benefit of his medication, had kept me from sinking into a steady doze. I must admit that I fell asleep sometime past the halfway point of our journey, and when I awakened, I found myself in a very unpleasant place indeed.

We had pulled to a stop alongside a plain gray factory building, the same as any number of others up and down the narrow and dark street. There was a steady cacophony coming from every direction, although it took different forms depending upon which direction one focused – here was a loud metallic pounding, while there was the high whine of some kind of saw, ululating in terrible shrieks when the teeth encountered some kind of resistance. But worst of all was the smell – a mixture of chemicals, heat, and burning, and a terrible rotten stench that one usually only encounters along the worst parts of the Thames. It was exacerbated by the rising August temperatures. Only a little later did I learn that we were amongst the factories lining the west side of the Wenlock Basin.

I visited there another time several years later in connection with another case – the sad affair of the misplaced newborn and the midwife's crab sleamery – and had a chance to observe the place in greater detail, approaching that time in a state of wakefulness. Running south off the Regent's Canal and not far from the Islington Tunnel, at the very western edge of Hackney and almost in Hoxton, the basin is a thousand feet long, but only forty or so feet wide. Just to the west is the larger City Road Basin, and surrounding the two are a number of very busy factories, all contributing to the disagreeable noise and stink of the region. We were standing in the Wharf Road, which runs between the two canals, and nearby were several iron and zinc foundries, a couple of sawmills, and perhaps most objectionable, a gutta percha factory, which took up many hundreds of square feet and was probably responsible for a great deal of the terrible odor hanging in the air. However, as bad as it all was, the overhanging reek coming from the canals was worse, a miasma that settled most in the back of one's throat and made one's eyes water. It was almost a relief to enter Rhayader's glass-works and shut the door behind us. The mephitis and clamor were awful here too, but relatively it was more pleasant within than without.

We immediately had to step back as a couple of cursing and sweating laborers pulled a large piece of glass past us, wrapped in padded fabric-covered chains and hanging from a pair of hooks. These in turn were attached to a pair of heavy chains that led up to a wheeled track system suspended from the ceiling. Here, then, was the same type of device that had been used to place the iron window pieces above Oswald Scampton's work space. I could see over us that a network of tracks was spread all across the underside of the building's roof and support beams, allowing workers to move loads, by clever manipulation, from here to there nearly anywhere in the building in the same way that a specific train car could be shunted and routed through a crowded yard, ending up exactly where it needed to be.

A wizened fellow passed us, and we managed to catch his attention and convince him to lead us to Brian Rhayader's office, which was actually quite close, in a suite of rooms to our left, tucked along the front wall of the building. As we reached the door, I heard a mighty crash of broken glass somewhere behind us in the vast structure and wondered if some new tragedy had occurred, but our guide showed no concern, and I began to realize that such sounds were probably heard all day long in this place, and simply an expected cost of doing business.

At the door, our guide turned and departed without a word. Inside the offices it was marginally quieter, and a man behind a desk near the door nodded when we asked for the owner and led us back through a short hallway. He knocked and opened a door, stating as he did so, "More police."

We hadn't identified ourselves, but we didn't bother to correct the man's assumption until the door had closed and we introduced ourselves to Brian Rhayader. He was a solid fellow of around forty, wearing an expensive-looking suit that somehow didn't fit with these surroundings. His hands were square and blunt, and his dark features were topped by hair that was black and rather shiny. It was combed back in a sleek flatness that gave him the appearance of a sly otter. He seemed distracted, which was to be expected, and waved us to a pair of chairs before his desk.

We introduced ourselves and he nodded, saying, "I take it that Natalie has hired you." He had a sour expression. "Well, I don't blame her, I suppose. But it was only a matter of time until Walter did something stupid like this. I only wish that he'd thought of a way to do it so that it didn't happen here at work, but he's always been impulsive."

"We learned from Inspector Gregson that there were disagreements between your Uncle Walter and Oswald Scampton."

"First I'd heard about it was when the inspector mentioned it to me, after the body had been taken away. He must have learned something from the men on the floor. It was probably about money, though. Walter has had a weakness for gambling the last few years – nothing substantial, you understand, as he doesn't have that much money of his own – and Oswald encouraged it."

"Miss Rhayader – your cousin – stated that Mr. Scampton had been pressuring her father to allow the two of them to be married.

"Indeed. Well, that's news to me as well. Did she want to? Marry him, I mean?"

"Apparently not."

"I wouldn't think so. Oswald was fifty if he was a day, and I believe that Natalie has been flirting with some army major for a year or so."

The more he spoke, the more I found myself disliking Mr. Brian Rhayader, but I held my tongue. I could see that Holmes agreed with me, although to anyone that didn't know him, he appeared to be unaffected by the factory owner's unpleasant mien.

"What can you tell us about the factory?" said Holmes, changing his questioning into a seemingly unimportant direction. It might have been to simply have a greater understanding of the business, or perhaps he was backing away from some point to be explored, lest he show too much interest in it and give away something that he wished to remain hidden for the present.

"Hmm? Let's see." Rhayader seemed to relax, as if he were more willing to have this discussion instead of what he'd expected. "The business started by my grandfather, Bryn Rhayader, seventy years ago – 1819, as a matter of fact. He'd come here from Wales, and there's some rumor that Rhayader wasn't his real name, although we've never bothered to find out. He was around twenty years old and had just two coins in his pocket, but he was blessed with quite a bit of physical strength. He never told anyone where he learned to work with glass, but he started in a small loft in Whitechapel, and by the time the basin here was constructed in 1826, he was ready to locate his own building here – this very factory.

"My father, Rhys, was born in 1830, and Walter – grandfather's only other child – wasn't born until twenty years later, around the same time as me. It's been fairly well accepted in the family that Walter wasn't planned – or wanted. He was always rather – well, weak and simple, but good-hearted enough. Or so we thought until the other day. My own father was invaluable at growing the business, and it was his pride and joy, but he always went out of his way to make a place here for Walter, his very much younger brother. Walter married about twenty years ago – he somehow found a girl willing to have him – but she died when the baby was born. I didn't really know Walter's wife, as he and I have never been close, but I suppose that Natalie takes after her mother – she's a smart girl, and nothing like her father.

"I grew up working here, like Walter, but unlike him, I was groomed to take over some day – which happened just a couple of years ago, when my father passed suddenly, and far too soon. He was only fifty-seven. I kept Walter on as father had done, paying him a good living, but not too much, as he wouldn't know how to manage it. I see now that letting him handle his own affairs was a mistake. He allowed his own problems grow until he tried to do something about it, and he did it here at work, which is unacceptable. Oswald Scampton will be difficult to replace."

Holmes chose then to pivoted back to Scampton's death. "The chain was compromised by use of hydrofluoric acid," he said.

"That's seems to be right. We use it here for etching the glass. When I saw the corrosion on the chain links, I suspected what might have happened. Then a couple of our workers remembered that they'd seen Walter on the walkway where the chain was hanging, just a few hours before it broke. He confirmed that he'd been painting that morning – it's one of his little jobs that gives him something to do – and there was fresh paint on the railing at that spot."

Holmes asked if we could see Scampton's work table where the death had occurred, and Rhayader seemed happy to be rid of us. He called to the man in the outer office and instructed him where to take us. Then, without another word, he returned to the papers on his desk.

We were led through the factory and along a round-about path to a wide work-table, about eight-feet square, near the rear wall. Overhead was an iron walkway, and above that was a track where the chain-and-hook system could pass overhead when necessary. Holmes asked where the hook was now.

"The police took the corroded chain that fell," replied our guide, who had introduced himself simply as Morrison, "and had a few of us cut off the other part still hanging from the track." Holmes nodded and then turned and made for a set of nearby stairs leading to the iron walkway. Morrison started to object, but then desisted, seeing that Holmes was only working his way slowly to a spot ten feet or so directly above us.

Holmes looked carefully at the railing. When he was finished, he rejoined us.

"Before the iron fell, had anything unusual happened that day? Any unexpected visitors?"

"Not a one. There are about fifty of us that work here, and we're told to keep an eye out for anyone uninvited."

"How often did Walter Rhayader's daughter visit him?"

"Occasionally, but I don't think she'd been here in weeks."

At Holmes's urging, we were introduced to several of the workers who might have relevant testimony – the two men who had seen Walter on the walkway, and another who had been first on the scene after the iron fell. The former confirmed that Walter had been at different locations that morning, painting as he sometimes did, but they couldn't place him for certain at the exact spot over Scampton's table. The man who had first found the body clearly enjoyed telling his version of the gruesome story, and had likely had a great deal of practice in the past few days in order to have so colorfully embellished the details of Scampton's terrible death in such a short amount of time.

At that point Holmes seemed satisfied and, with nothing further left to see, nor any other individuals to meet, we were taken to the front door and released.

It was quieter outside to a certain degree, but not necessarily more pleasant. "Let us walk for a few minutes," said Holmes, leading me north along Wharf Street, and so across Regent's Canal to the north bank. There he turned west along the tow-path, and we ambled as the stink and noise of the basin and the industries that had leeched onto it faded. The canal itself was none too clean, but compared to the Wenlock Basin, it was a like a pastoral brook.

"What did you find on the upper walkway?"

"Some evidence of recent painting – just a dab. Black enamel, to match that already there."

"Which confirms Walter Rhayader's story."

"Possibly. But the spot showed no signs of requiring additional paint. And that doesn't negate whatsoever the idea that he could have also been up there to spread acid on the chain – and to do whatever else was done to cause the fall of the iron-works – for hydrofluoric acid alone wouldn't have destroyed that chain so easily." He tapped his lip with a finger. "I feel as if something is missing – that there is some unknown fact."

"But surely it's too soon to know that. You've barely begun to investigate. And perhaps it's exactly as it looks – Walter Rhayader decided to kill Oswald Scampton, and he did so with a very poor and obvious plan, thinking that no one would actually notice him or investigate the damage to the chain."

"By all accounts he may very well be that naive. And yet, I observe that this crime not only removes Scampton from the board, but Walter Rhayader as well, and I have to wonder whom that benefits, and how."

We had reached the end of the towpath, where the canal continued west through a brick archway and into the dark Islington Tunnel. From somewhere inside we could hear the echo of calling voices, and then the sharp sudden peal of a woman's laughter. It stopped as suddenly as it had begun, with an almost hysterical quality, as if its effort to quell the nervousness and possibly terror that some might feel in such a place had failed suddenly and completely. We stood there at the end of the path for a moment, both frozen and alerted by some atavistic impulse when hearing a woman express fear. We waited for several long minutes to see if a boat would appear, but it never did, and we eventually came to the mutual unspoken conclusion that our concern was unfounded, and we retraced our steps back to a point where we could make our way up to Danbury Street and so find a cab.

Holmes directed its course toward the Strand. When we reached Somerset House, he disembarked, telling me that he had some facts to ascertain, and would it be possible to meet in Baker Street at seven o'clock that night. I agreed, and then requested that the cabbie take me on to my Paddington home.

My wife, having not seen me for two days, wanted to know all of the details related to Percy Phelps' difficulties. I found that I had to force myself to remember specifics, as my mind was already distracted by the current problem related to the curious death of Oswald Scampton.

I spent a portion of the afternoon conferring with Anstruther to learn whether any of my patients had special concerns, and then I made my rounds, planning my route so as to end up in Baker Street at nearly seven o'clock. As I approached the front door of No. 221, I noticed a hansom cab waiting nearby. In the early evening light, I identified the cabbie as Bert Deacon, the former Houndsditch ramper who had been proven innocent by Holmes of a murder seven years before. Since that time, he had been part of a steady group of cab-drivers that were generally available when Holmes had need of them. We nodded to one another and I looked up to see that the sitting room windows were lit. Using my key to let myself in, I climbed the stairs, where I found Holmes looking rather grim.

"You're just in time, Watson. Word has gone out that Walter Rhayader is not long for this world. Do you have your revolver?"

He knew that I did, as I'd learned long before never to leave home without it. I often wondered at the curious dichotomy of carrying out my duties as a physician while armed, but as I'd done the same in the army, nothing had really changed except the location and the sorts of enemies that I regularly encountered.

"What has happened to him?" After our recent encounter with Percy Phelps, the thought of brain fever was at the forefront of my thoughts. "We've heard nothing of any serious health problems. Did he have some sort of attack?"

"I shouldn't worry. I understand that he'll make a full recovery very soon. But be sure to wear your best concerned-doctor face."

Within moments we were ensconced in the hansom and to my surprise, Holmes directed Bert Deacon to make haste to Charing Cross Hospital. Then, in contrast to the quiet stretches that had characterized our earlier trips across the city, Holmes began to speak, but instead of explaining why we were going to the hospital, he said, "As I mentioned, I found it curious that the death of one man also effectively removed another as well, with the arrest and likely conviction of Walter Rhayader for the murder of Oswald Scampton. From the little we've heard, it didn't seem likely that Walter would be able to provide an adequate defense, and if someone was framing him, it would proceed without hindrance.

"But who might do such a thing?" I asked. "If we assume that Walter is innocent, then there is someone still unknown to us who wished to kill Scampton for entirely different reasons. Walter Rhayader would make an excellent scapegoat. We know from his daughter that Scampton was pressuring Walter regarding arranging a marriage with her, and that he also had some kind of leverage over him, if the story of Walter's gambling problem is true. It's likely that these facts are more commonly known than is believed, and they would serve to incriminate Walter and deflect attention away from some other motive."

"But it's equally possible," Holmes replied, "that someone with a reason to get rid of *Walter* made use of his dealings with Scampton. Thus, Scampton's death was for no other purpose than to except incriminate Walter."

Holmes turned somewhat to face me. "You are correct – the facts of Walter's gambling, and Scampton's pressure upon him to encourage a marriage, are rather well known. And Walter Rhayader does have a problem with gambling. I verified it. At one point this afternoon, after my earlier researches were complete, I disguised myself and returned to Wenlock Basin. You may have noticed a rather shabby pub near the glass factory, just on the other side of one of the saw mills. I arranged to be there at the end of the work day, garbed as a workman from one of the nearby factories, and managed to ingratiate myself with a number of the employees who stopped there for a quick pint before continuing homeward. For the price of a few drinks, I quickly confirmed all that we'd heard – Walter is a known gambler, and Scampton served as something of a middle-man for him, all the while manipulating Walter terribly. The men in the factory didn't like it very much, as they feel no ill-will for Walter, but they also considered it none of their business if the uncle of the owner loses money to someone smart enough to take it from him – namely Scampton. I also found along the way that the employees don't like Mr. Brian Rhayader very much at all – although being liked is certainly not a part of his job.

"Well, I can understand that, as I didn't like him either, but what were their reasons?"

"They feel that he's been reckless with the business – taking on debt to expand while concurrently making excessive requirements of the employees in the process – increased output, longer hours for the same pay, and so on – in order to give the impression that the business is a greater success than it actually is. It is their perception that it's all being done to overvalue the business in order to obtain loans – and if something in Brian Rhayader's house of cards goes wrong, their livelihoods will be at risk."

"How would the employees know of this – these maneuverings to increase the company's resources? That isn't the sort of thing that is common knowledge among factory workers – or so it seems to me."

"That fellow who showed us the factory – Morrison – appears to pick up a lot of details from his position in the office, and he subsequently uses what he learns as currency amongst the workers, trading private information for whisky. I saw him in the pub, letting several men buy him drinks while he blithely chattered away about various business-related facts that were probably not anyone's proper concern."

"So is Brian Rhayader financially unsound?"

"Unquestionably. That fact was verified by a few simple telegrams."

"But what does that have to do with Oswald Scampton's murder? Unless Scampton were blackmailing him somehow, I don't see how that the man's death could benefit him at all – or why he would frame his uncle for the crime."

"Ah, but Watson, you forget that before I went to the pub, I mentioned that I had undertaken some 'earlier researches'. When we parted in the Strand, I made my way to Somerset House, where I was able to take hold of one end of a thread that revealed a most interesting motive indeed.

"You'll recall that we heard several times that Walter Rhayader is around the same age as his nephew, Brian – both around forty. It was an easy assumption to picture Walter, the uncle, as the elder of the two, even if only by a small amount. But we also had an intimation of Walter's age when Brian stated that his own father was born in 1830, and that Walter was born 'twenty years later', or in 1850. That could have been an approximation, or it might have been precise. I was able to verify without any difficulty that Walter *was* born in 1850, and therefore next year he will turn forty."

"And since you've gone to the trouble to explain it, I'm sure that you will tell me the significance of it as well."

Holmes smiled. "Indeed. I looked at old Bryn Rhayader's will. The founder did leave the factory to his son, Brian's father Rhys, as well as the bulk of his fortune. But what hasn't been mentioned – and what no one may know except Brian – is that Bryn also left a substantial amount in trust for his second, much younger, son, Walter – an amount that, through careful investment by an independent financial counselor, has grown tidily over the previous decades to nearly three-quarters-of-a-million pounds."

I believe that my jaw had literally dropped open in amazement. There had been no mention of this factor, which led me to believe that –

"Is it possible," I said aloud, "that Walter isn't aware of this inheritance?"

"He didn't know it, and his daughter didn't either. I asked them when I stopped by the Yard. He was awake, and they were completely unaware that upon his fortieth birthday, in less than nine months, both the principal and accumulated interest that has been held in trust since the old man's death will be released to him, without strings or strictures, and he will go from being a tolerated and rather pitiful handy-man on the periphery of his own family's business to a fellow who is soon-to-be vastly more wealthy than his nephew – that same nephew who is now financially leveraged to the hilt, and who is quite aware of this possible source of future revenue, on the horizon and drifting ever closer to him."

"So," I said, "if Walter were to die before the designated age . . . ."

"Once again, Watson you have put your finger on the heart of it. The trust was set up by old Rhys care for the younger son whom he perceived as 'slow', and to make sure that he did in fact receive his share of his father's fortune, but only if he lived to the designated age – otherwise it reverts to Bryn's line of the family. One of the requirements was that Walter be given employment in the factory – which has been done. Thus, keeping him around was not simply an act of kindness by Brian or his father before him. Likewise, a small salary is generated by the trust for Walter's employment – and I believe that when this is settled, we'll find it quite likely that Walter never received the full amount of it that was designated for him."

"So Brian has an excellent reason for removing his uncle from the board – to gain control of the fortune that was so far out of reach. But why kill Scampton in the process? Why frame Walter for that murder, and then hope that Walter would be executed, rather than simply killing Walter?"

"I'm not yet certain. Perhaps the keepers of the trust are canny folk, and Brian was afraid that they would be suspicious if Walter were to simply die so close to coming into his inheritance. And knowing that Oswald Scampton was pressuring one Rhayader, isn't it likely that he was doing the same to Brian for some reason as well? He had worked at the glass factory his entire adult life – that's over thirty years – and he would have known Brian's father Rhys, and possibly old Bryn Rhayader as well. He would have kept his eyes and ears open, and if Brian was up to anything dodgy with his finances while trying to expand the business, who better than Scampton to notice – and then try and use that knowledge to his advantage? An excellent reason for him to die."

I raced to piece together what I had learned. "So it was well known that Oswald Scampton had leverage over Walter, apparently because of gambling debts, and also that he was trying to use this to marry Walter's daughter. While she is certainly attractive, is it possible that Oswald also had another reason to become her husband – Perhaps he had knowledge that in a few months the girl's father would become a rich man, and therefore as Walter's heir, perhaps she would eventually inherit that wealth."

"That's one way that I read it. In any case, Brian saw a way to take down two birds with one shot – he could kill Scampton before he somehow pressured Walter into approving of the marriage and diverting the fortune another way, although in truth the young lady would never have gone along with it, and more importantly he could frame Walter, and get it done now, months before the inheritance was to be released. He had to do it before Walter turned forty, or after Walter's death it would next go to Walter's daughter, and thus be lost to Brian forever, one way or another."

"Diabolical," I muttered.

"And subtle. Ah, but we've arrived."

Bert Deacon had brought us along a route through various byways to avoid the crowded main streets, depositing us at the front entrance of the hospital on Agar Street. Gregson and two constables were waiting just inside the door. Holmes looked expectantly and the inspector nodded.

"We sent a constable to retrieve him, timing it so that you could be here before he arrived."

"And Miss Rhayader?"

"On her way with her father from the Yard. He's improved quite a bit – especially after you spoke with us a few hours ago. She wanted to come along now and perform in your little drama, but I could see how angry that she was, and I believe that she would have given away too much."

I started to speak, but Holmes smiled and raised a hand. "Watson and I didn't have time to discuss the plan. Mr. Brian Rhayader has been told that Walter is near death, and has been transferred here, to the hospital. A constable was sent for him – as a courtesy. When he arrives – ah, but you shall see, for that is them I see now, walking in the door." I glanced over and saw an officer following the nattily dressed factory owner, who recognized us immediately and quickly stepped our way. Remembering Holmes's earlier warning, I put on a grave face, as if ready to impart grim news.

"Is he . . . is Walter . . . ?"

Holmes shook his head sadly. "I'm afraid that he passed ten minutes ago."

Rhayader glanced my way, and I added, "The stress of his arrest brought on some sort of attack."

I might not have seen it if I wasn't prepared to look, but the flash of triumph that seemed to cross Rhayader's eyes, if only for the briefest of instances, seemed too definite to ignore. And yet, it was immediately replaced by a look of profound sorrow. "This is terrible. He had such a sad and . . . unfulfilled life in so many ways, and for it to end so abruptly, and so soon . . . . If only he hadn't chosen to resolve his conflicts with Oswald in such a violent manner."

Gregson nodded and cleared his throat. "So true. Tell me, Mr. Rhayader, were his affairs in order?"

"What? I suppose so. There wasn't much to manage, and either I or his daughter did what was necessary. I paid for his lodgings, and for the housekeeper who essentially raised Natalie."

"We'd uncovered some mention of gambling debts, you see," added Gregson. "I wouldn't want you to be bothered about those, now that your uncle has passed."

"Thank you, Inspector. That's very kind."

"And did he have a will?" Gregson continued, glancing toward the door where a man with a crutch was being helped inside, as if the question held no great interest for him.

"No, he didn't. He'd never had any true assets to dispose of, you see."

Gregson nodded. "That tallies with what his daughter told us. But before he died, he became quite alert, if only for a little while. He wouldn't rest until he'd written a will. It was a very simple thing – he left everything – every last asset – to his daughter. It was properly fixed up by a lawyer associated with the Yard that we hold in high esteem. It was signed and witnessed not a quarter-hour before he died – although as you say, he had nothing to pass onto the girl, so getting it fixed up really did no more than give him a little piece of mind."

As Gregson said this, a slight frown pulled down Brian Rhayader's brow. I could see his thoughts racing – Did this affect anything? Would he still be able to take control of the trust as he'd planned, thinking that his Uncle Walter would die without a will before his fortieth birthday, or did the circumstances now send the fortune down a different track, forever out of his grasp?

While the man was still distracted by these questions, Holmes spoke. "I was wondering about the use of acid for etching glass," he said, in a conversational tone, and rather loud when discussing the recent death of a man. I noticed that he'd taken a step toward Rhayader, just a bit too close for the man to feel comfortable. "You use hydrofluoric acid, I believe?"

Rhayader looked at him, as if only then abandoning his worries about the will and noticing that Holmes had stepped so close. "Hmm? Yes. It's dangerous stuff, but we're careful and get good results."

"And of course that's what was used to corrode the chain holding the iron window pieces above Oswald Scampton."

"That's right."

"How much would one need to use in order to eat through a heavy iron chain like that?"

"I'm . . . I'm not sure. It's very destructive, you know. Intentionally applying it to the chain in that fashion was quite malicious."

"Indeed." Holmes edged even closer to the factory owner. "I'm something of a chemist, and generally the reaction between iron and hydrofluoric acid is rather topical – the reaction forms a paste that can be wiped away. I was curious about that, and went back and reexamined the corroded chain, which was taken was taken as evidence by Scotland Yard."

Holmes shifted another inch closer. "Were you aware that one of the constables who initially arrived on the scene mistakenly touched the chain coated in acid?"

"I . . . I heard something of the sort."

"Do you know what happens when hydrofluoric acid is absorbed into the body?"

"Of course. It doesn't initially burn, as would happen if handling hydrochloric acid."

"Correct. By some curious property, the acid passes through the skin intact, penetrating and spreading through the body and, only when located in the dermis does it separate into free hydrogen and fluoride. After some time passes, and the victim begins to think that possibly he will emerge unscathed, the fluoride combines with other chemicals in the body to destroy tissue in a most terrible manner, almost liquefying it while causing extreme pain. Death follows – almost as a blessing."

Rhayader's voice cracked. "Why are you telling me this?"

"Why, simply because whomever slipped up there and painted the chain with hydrofluoric acid is now also responsible for the death of Constable Naughton, who passed away this afternoon. That's three deaths on someone's conscience."

"Three?" asked Rhayader, his slicked hair now looking somewhat ragged and a nervous sheen on his face. "But Walter only killed Oswald – and now, I suppose, this constable . . . ."

"No, the killer wasn't your uncle. He was another victim. This crime was beyond him. Knowledge that the acid wouldn't have caused the damage needed to make the chain break made us go back and reexamine the corroded links. Underneath the resultant material formed by the acid and the iron, we found evidence that the links had been filed part-way through beforehand. And there's no indication that your uncle would have had the opportunity to carry out something with that added complexity. But *you* could have."

Rhayader started to back away, only to realize that one of the constables was quite close behind him. He whipped his head around, and then back again toward Holmes.

"Several of your employees have been questioned. It was common for you to be seen on the work floor, so no one would have particularly noticed if *you* were the one to pull the iron works over Scampton's work space. No one else acknowledges doing it – "

"He did it himself!" Rhayader interrupted, but Holmes ignored him.

"You could have filed the chain ahead of time, even the night before. The acid wouldn't have been enough by itself, but applying it to already weakened links did guarantee a failure. A dab of paint on the railing above the work space – in a spot that clearly didn't need it – would be enough to imply that your uncle had been there. And you were the one who told your uncle to touch up the paint around the factory that day."

"What? You can't know that. The only one who knew was – "

"Your uncle? Yes, that's right. That's what he told us." And Holmes raised a hand, signaling a pair of constables who were now standing off to one side to open a door, allowing a tall man, his arm gripped by Miss Rhayader, to make his way awkwardly in our direction.

Brian Rhayader turned as white as a ghost. It's a literary cliché to use that expression, but in this case it was completely true. Except for his widened eyes and slight nervous twitch, he might have been a corpse pulled from the Thames.

"How – ?" he asked. "You said – "

When Miss Rhayader and the man who was clearly her father were quite close, she dropped his arm and took the remaining couple of steps to her cousin. Then with a mighty swing, she slapped him, the resounding crack echoing across the room.

"Mr. Holmes told us of grandfather's will!" she cried, and would have slapped him again, but Brian Rhayader took a stumbling step backward and tripped on his own feet, landing before the constable standing behind him.

Instead of responding to his cousin, he stared up at his uncle. "You're alive?" he said, not with wonder or joy, but barely concealed anger. "Walter – how?"

The other man, nearly the same age as Brian Rhayader but looking twenty years older, provided a gentle smile. I could see that the gravity of the situation didn't affect him. "Thank you for saving Natalie from marrying Oswald," he said, "but you didn't have to kill him. I had a plan. I would have taken care of things in my own way . . . ."

His voice drifted, and his daughter turned her attention from the man on the ground before her to her father, her expression changing from anger to sadness in an instant. Brian Rhayader used that time to scramble to his feet. Whatever he'd intended was arrested by the solid hand of the officer standing behind him.

"You can't prove I did anything!" he snarled. "Anyone might have killed Oswald. Walter here could have done it, just like you first thought. He just admitted that he intended to!"

"It isn't just Scampton's murder," rumbled Gregson. "We prevaricated about Mr. Walter Rhayader's death, but not so about

270

Constable Naughton. He apparently received a worse dose of the acid than we'd first known. He died today in agony. And while we don't yet have every duck in a row in terms of a case against you, Mr. Brian Rhayader, thanks to Mr. Holmes we know exactly how to start rounding them up. You're under arrest for the murders of Oswald Scampton and Constable Thomas Naughton." He turned away as if he didn't trust himself, his great hands clenched. "Get this Son of Cain out of my sight."

We chose to walk home, and we were somewhere on along Wardour Street, avoiding the busier thoroughfares, before either of us felt like speaking. Then a thought occurred to me. "Miss Rhayader's fiancé – the major from Gibraltar. Have his whereabouts been verified?"

Holmes shook his head. "He is still out of the country. I confirmed it early on. But I see that you're thinking he might have made his way back to England surreptitiously kill the man who was pestering his bride-to-be – somehow managing to sneak into the factory and inadvertently implicating his own future father-in-law. Rest assured – he had no involvement in the case."

We paused before crossing a street, and Holmes continued. "It's an ugly business, and it went on for far too long. Rhys Rhayader apparently kept the knowledge of his brother's inheritance a secret long before the son, Brian, chose to do so as well. They both withheld funds from Walter, and also knowledge and necessary assistance, in spite of giving the impression that they were generously providing for him. I've seen evidence this afternoon that Walter's young wife need not have died, but she didn't receive any help from Rhys, even when Walter asked for it.

"Both Rhys and then Brian cared for Walter in the same impersonal way that they would have nurtured an investment, with the certainty that someday when needed they could collect his inheritance. Perhaps Rhys loved his brother just enough not to go ahead and kill him, but as the event of Walter's birthday came closer, and Brian found himself in dire financial straits after over-extending himself to build the business, he decided to find a way to make sure that the fortune came to him. Hearing of Oswald's own machinations simply gave him the excuse to remove Walter. I expect that if Walter hadn't been convicted, Brian would have found a way to poison him, perhaps during a prison visit, in such a way that he would still die without ever knowing what his father had left for him."

"Still," I said, "it was such a clumsy plan. Why didn't Brian simply strike Walter down some night, as if he'd been attacked by a stranger in the street?"

"He couldn't risk the kind of attention that might bring to Walter's background. If he was killed outright, the police would begin to investigate his past with an eye as to who might have a motive, possibly discovering the large inheritance that was coming his way. Better that Walter should be implicated in killing someone else, so that his death – by execution or simply the inability to survive arrest and imprisonment – would be the cause. Oswald Scampton made it easy for him."

In the coming weeks, the resources of Scotland Yard were able to gather a substantial case that was more than strong enough to convict Brian Rhayader without any difficulty whatsoever. Near the end, in some sort of attempt at easing his conscience, he signed over all rights to the business to his cousin Natalie. I understand that she consulted with her new husband, the major, but he had no interest in running a glass factory, so she sold it lock, stock, and barrel. The she and her husband, along with her father, departed from England with her father, gone long before Brian Rhayader was hanged in Newgate Prison.

I became aware that the unpleasant heat of the day had faded, and that there was now a pleasant-enough breeze from the south, carrying a curious spiced scent with it, possibly from as far away as south of the river. The sun was dropping in the sky, causing long shadows and giving the light a sentimental and brassy aspect. I'm not sure why, but instead of turning aside and continuing to my own home in Paddington, I continued to walk with Holmes toward Baker Street. We had both returned to the silence which had marked the first part of the journey, and I was unprepared when Holmes suddenly spoke, as 221 Baker Street came into view.

"Ho! What's this? I wonder what events have transpired to bring *this* particular visitor to my door. You don't recognize the crest on the carriage door? Well, no matter. Come upstairs – all we be explained soon, I expect."

In truth, I did not recognize the smart little brougham parked before the door, pulled by a pair of fine horses. The crest did look familiar, and yet the name of the owner escaped me.

The question was soon answered when we reached the top of the stairs and Holmes threw open the door of the sitting room to see a man pacing along the bearskin rug placed before the empty fireplace. I recognized him immediately. We had met with him only two days before, and his thin, tall figure, with sharp features, thoughtful face, and curling hair prematurely tinged with gray, was instantly recognizable. It was Lord Holdhurst, uncle of Percy Phelps, and the man ultimately responsible for the stolen naval treaty which had just been recovered that morning.

"Mr. Holmes!" the man cried. "I have been waiting for over an hour. Your landlady had no idea how to reach you, and could only say that she expected you back tonight, but with no guarantees. I need your help!"

272

Holmes calmly divested himself of his fore-and-aft cap, worn year-round in both the city and countryside with complete disregard to society's fashion requirements. Standing calmly before the revered nobleman, he asked, "What is the problem, sir?"

"It's that damned treaty!" cried the man, his clenched fists shaking before him. "It's been stolen from my own office, not eight hours after it was returned to me!"

"And Percy Phelps – ?" I asked, concerned for my old friend.

"Completely uninvolved," was the reply. "I had sent him home for more rest, He was obviously completely wrecked." He turned back to Holmes. "Can you help me?"

"Yes." Then Holmes glanced my way.

I nodded. "I'll send a note to Mary. And to Anstruther as well . . . ."

> *Holmes was seated at his side-table clad in his dressing-gown and working hard over a chemical investigation. A large curved retort was boiling furiously in the bluish flame of a Bunsen burner, and the distilled drops were condensing into a two-litre measure. My friend hardly glanced up as I entered, and I, seeing that his investigation must be of importance, seated myself in an armchair and waited. He dipped into this bottle or that, drawing out a few drops of each with his glass pipette, and finally brought a test-tube containing a solution over to the table. In his right hand he held a slip of litmus-paper.*
>
> *"You come at a crisis, Watson," said he. "If this paper remains blue, all is well. If it turns red, it means a man's life." He dipped it into the test-tube and it flushed at once into a dull, dirty crimson. "Hum! I thought as much!" he cried. "I will be at your service in an instant, Watson. You will find tobacco in the Persian slipper." He turned to his desk and scribbled off several telegrams, which were handed over to the page-boy. Then he threw himself down into the chair opposite and drew up his knees until his fingers clasped round his long, thin shins.*
>
> *"A very commonplace little murder," said he. "You've got something better, I fancy. You are the stormy petrel of crime, Watson. What is it?*

– Sherlock Holmes
"The Adventure of the Naval Treaty"

The Adventure of the
Tired Captain
by Matthew J. Elliott

*T*his script has never been published in text form, and was initially
performed as a radio drama on October 21, 2012. The broadcast was
Episode No. 107 of The Further Adventures of Sherlock Holmes, *one of*
the recurring series featured on the nationally syndicated Imagination
Theatre. *Founded by Jim French, the company produced over one-*
thousand multi-series episodes, including nearly one-hundred-and-forty
Sherlock Holmes pastiches. In addition, Imagination Theatre also
recorded the entire Holmes Canon, featured as The Classic Adventures
of Sherlock Holmes, *the only version with all episodes to have been*
written by the same writer, Matthew J. Elliott, and with the same two
actors, John Patrick Lowrie and Lawrence Albert, portraying Holmes
and Watson, respectively.

This script is protected by copyright.

CHARACTERS
- SHERLOCK HOLMES
- DR. JOHN H. WATSON
- MARY WATSON
- INSPECTOR LESTRADE
- EMILIA HOLYWELL – Early forties. Strong-willed to the point
  of being stubborn
- PERCIVAL HOLYWELL – Forties. A gentleman with a very
  Bohemian outlook

SOUND EFFECT: OPENING SEQUENCE, BIG BEN, STREET
     SOUNDS

ANNOUNCER: *The Further Adventures of Sherlock Holmes* . . . .

MUSIC: *DANSE MACABRE* (UP AND UNDER)

WATSON: My name is Dr. John H Watson, friend and biographer of Mr.
     Sherlock Holmes. By the summer of 1889, I had been married less

than a year, and not even Holmes himself would have expected me to spend any great amount of time away from my new wife. But unbeknownst to me, back at our old Baker Street rooms, matters were being set in motion which would result in Holmes and me reuniting over a matter involving the friends I had made during my married life . . . .

MUSIC: OUT

MARY: It's quite some time since I visited these rooms unaccompanied, Mr. Holmes.

HOLMES: And on that occasion, Mrs. Watson, you provided me with one of the most fascinating cases of my career.

MARY: And I, in return, rather selfishly deprived you of your colleague.

HOLMES: (AIRILY) Oh, I've barely noticed the Doctor's absence, I assure you.

MARY: And yet hardly a day goes by without John mentioning your name.

HOLMES: Really? Well, that's – (HURRIEDLY CHANGING THE SUBJECT) If you expected to find him here this morning, I'm afraid I shall have to disappoint you, Madam. I imagine he's on his rounds in his capacity as a physician.

MARY: It's precisely because John is *not* here that I've come to see you, Mr. Holmes.

HOLMES: (SLIGHTLY UNCOMFORTABLE) Mrs. Watson, I can assure you that the Doctor is the most devoted of husbands. Why else should he have abandoned a life filled with the thrill of the macabre –

MARY: I've come to see you because I wish to consult you. Again.

HOLMES: My services are always available to anyone who has genuine need of them. And Watson cannot know?

MARY: No one can know. Not even your client, Mr. Holmes.

HOLMES: *You* are not my client?

MARY: I will pay your fee, of course –

HOLMES: There is no fee.

MARY: – but you are not acting on my behalf. The person I wish you to represent is Captain Holywell.

HOLMES: Captain Holywell? I don't believe I'm familiar with the gentleman. Pass me my index, Watson. (A BEAT) *Mrs.* Watson. (A BEAT) Please.

MARY: Captain Holywell is no gentleman, Mr. Holmes.

HOLMES: How strange – a disgraced military officer is all the more likely to be known to me.

MARY: *Emilia* Holywell is a captain in the Salvation Army.

HOLMES: Ah.

MARY: You may, however, have heard of her husband, Dr. Lucien Holywell.

HOLMES: Of course – former Professor of Clinical Surgery at Edinburgh Royal Hospital for Sick Children. Your husband was much impressed when he saw Holywell deliver a lecture some years ago, if I remember correctly.

MARY: It's my understanding that you *always* remember correctly.

HOLMES: Quite so. And if you are familiar with the Holywells, the association must have occurred *after* your marriage – your husband would certainly have mentioned the fact, at length.

MARY: I became friends with Emilia through my charity work. She persuaded her husband to set up a charitable clinic in Whitechapel, near her soup kitchen.

HOLMES: A not-inexpensive gesture. Dr. Holywell is a wealthy man, then.

MARY: (SLIGHT UNCERTAINTY) I believe he and his brother inherited the wealth of a third of the coal-producing mines in Wales.

HOLMES: Forgive me, Mrs. Watson, but you don't sound entirely certain on that point.

MARY: I've met Percival on a number of occasions – if he's as rich as his twin brother, I see no sign of it in his clothing.

HOLMES: You've always possessed greater observational skills than your husband, so I don't doubt you on that point. Please go on.

MARY: I was assisting at the soup kitchen one evening last week . . . .

BACKGROUND: MUCH CHATTER, ALL MALE

SOUND EFFECT: (IN BACKGROUND) SETTING DOWN OF METAL PLATES, SPOONS

EMILIA: Mary . . . I can speak to you in confidence, can't I?

MARY: Of course, Captain.

EMILIA: Just "Emilia". This doesn't concern my duties.

MARY: Then what *does* it concern?

EMILIA: The entire family.

MARY: Including Ernestine? Such a lovely child, a credit to you both. So poised, and so like her father. John and I always hope one day –

EMILIA: I think he's going to kill me, Mary!

MARY: Kill you?

EMILIA: Mary, I'm so afraid! I don't know what to do!

MARY: John can help.

EMILIA: No one must know of my shame, no one.

MARY: If your life is in danger, something must be done. If not the police, perhaps Mr. Sherlock Holmes –

EMILIA: Not Mr. Holmes, no.

MARY: Emilia, come with me. You're staying with us tonight. John need never know the reason.

EMILIA: Forgive me, Mary, I made a mistake. Please forget everything I said to you.

MARY: I can't.

EMILIA: You must! Hush now, my husband's coming. Swear to me that you'll never speak of this to anyone – swear to me!

BACKGROUND: OUT

HOLMES: And *did* you swear?

MARY: I did, Mr. Holmes. And may God forgive me, I'm breaking the most sacred of promises in telling you any of this.

HOLMES: Why?

MARY: Because this morning I received word that Dr. Lucien Holywell was murdered in his home – and his wife Emilia has been arrested for the crime.

MUSIC: STING

LESTRADE: And may I ask what brings you here today, Mr. Holmes?

HOLMES: Curiosity, Lestrade, plain and simple. I thought you might be having some difficulty with this one.

LESTRADE: That's just what Dr. Watson said.

HOLMES: (SURPRISED) Watson is here?

LESTRADE: And I'll tell you what I told him – there's no mystery here. We have the culprit under lock and key.

HOLMES: Captain Holywell.

LESTRADE: *Mrs.* Holywell. And I'm not entirely satisfied that the maid didn't have a part to play in this somewhere.

WATSON: (OFF-MICROPHONE) . . . save for the fact that their stories differ. Good afternoon, Holmes.

HOLMES: Watson.

WATSON: You got my telegram, I see.

HOLMES: (LYING) Of course.

LESTRADE: It's not uncommon for criminals engaged in a conspiracy to fail to get their stories straight, Doctor.

HOLMES: Perhaps if I knew those stories, I might be able to participate in this discussion, gentlemen.

SOUND EFFECT: PAGES OF LESTRADE'S NOTEBOOK FLUTTER

LESTRADE: No fear, Mr. Holmes. I've got it all written down. The maid, Alice, says she left the house at ten to pick up a box of Dutch Panatellas for Holywell. Her mistress was reading in the library. He was in his . . . his . . . .

SOUND EFFECT: LESTRADE WAGS HIS NOTEBOOK ABOUT

LESTRADE: What's this word?

HOLMES: *Armamentarium.*

WATSON: It means the gun room.

LESTRADE: I know what it means, Doctor, I just wanted to know how to pronounce it. Well, when the maid returned, she found Mrs. Holywell fast asleep on the chaise longue. So she carried on with her duties for another hour or so before looking in on Dr. Holywell in the *ar* – the gun room.

WATSON: Only to find him dead, from a gunshot to the head.

LESTRADE: (MILDLY IRRITATED AT BEING INTERRUPTED) Yes, thank you, Doctor. I was just getting to that part.

HOLMES: It would appear, then, that the crime occurred while Alice was out of the house. Otherwise, she would surely have heard the shot.

LESTRADE: Mrs. Holywell didn't hear it – so she says. In fact, she contradicts the maid by denying ever being asleep.

HOLMES: But she is insistent that she heard no shot?

LESTRADE: An obvious lie, wouldn't you say, Mr. Holmes?

PERCIVAL: (FAR OFF-MICROPHONE) Let me in! For God's sake, let me in!

HOLMES: The scene of the crime is becoming rather crowded, Lestrade.

PERCIVAL: Where's my brother? Who's in charge here?

WATSON: Percival!

LESTRADE: Good Lord! You look just like –

WATSON: Dr. Holywell's twin brother, Inspector – Percival Holywell.

PERCIVAL: Is it true, John? Did Emilia kill him?

WATSON: That's what Mr. Holmes here is trying to determine.

LESTRADE: I'm afraid it's true, Mr. Holywell. We have evidence to prove it.

HOLMES: May I be permitted to see this evidence, Inspector? Solely in order to verify your conclusions, of course.

LESTRADE: Well, you've been of assistance once or twice in the past, so I don't see why not. It's all gone back to the Yard.

PERCIVAL: I knew she was unhappy with Lucien, desperately unhappy, but how could Emilia do it?

WATSON: We've yet to determine if that really is the case, Percival.

LESTRADE: *You* may not have determined it, Doctor . . . .

HOLMES: You came here by train from Brighton to Victoria, Mr. Holywell?

PERCIVAL: (CLEARLY UPSET) Is this . . . is this one of your celebrated deductions, Mr. Holmes?

WATSON: You still have a Southern Cup racing programme in your pocket.

PERCIVAL: You're right, of course. Damn stupid – won the first prize at the International Chess Tournament last night, lost all three-hundred pounds of it in one morning. None of it really matters now, of course. Oh, Emilia! How could you do it? And what's to become of little Ernestine? Where's poor Ernestine?

LESTRADE: She was at a friend's house when all this occurred. A police matron is looking after her now.

PERCIVAL: Oh, thank God. I must see her. That poor child.

HOLMES: Mr. Holywell, would it be convenient for you to call upon me in my Baker Street rooms this evening? Number 221b.

PERCIVAL: I, er . . . I suppose so. Say, six o'clock?

HOLMES: Six o'clock, then. In the meantime, Lestrade, I like to examine the armamentarium, and then to the Yard, to look over this evidence you spoke of . . . .

MUSIC: BRIDGE

LESTRADE: Here it is, then. The murdered man's typewriter, Mr. Holmes.

HOLMES: Dr. Holywell was typing in his armamentarium? Why not in the study?

LESTRADE: For protection, no doubt.

HOLMES: A pretty poor sort of protection.

LESTRADE: The paper hasn't been removed from the machine – read it.

HOLMES: A letter to his brother. (READS) *"My Dear Percival, I find it almost impossible to believe my own words, but I wish you to know that, in the event of my sudden death, I will almost certainly have been murdered. Emilia's delusions have reached the point where she imagines that I am plotting her own demise, and I fear that she believes her only salvation is to strike first. I ask only that you ensure the safety of the child, Ernestine –"*

LESTRADE: And there it stops. Probably because, at that point, he was surprised by his wife – and she did just what he feared.

HOLMES: And having killed her husband, Captain Holywell –

LESTRADE: *Mrs.* Holywell.

HOLMES: – didn't think to read what her husband had been writing?

LESTRADE: No doubt she imagined he was typing up his notes from his previous day's work at the clinic. It was his habit to do so, according to Alice the maid.

HOLMES: Telling. Extremely telling.

LESTRADE: Before you ask, Mr. Holmes, there's no possibility that someone else typed this letter. It's been checked for fingerprints, and they all match the dead man.

HOLMES: And this burgundy-colored powder beneath the keys?

LESTRADE: Probably not important.

HOLMES: As you say. I'll nevertheless take a small sample back to Baker Street, if you don't mind.

LESTRADE: Please yourself. But it doesn't change a thing – she killed her husband, all right.

HOLMES: The letter indicates only her *intention* to commit murder, Lestrade. It is hardly definitive.

LESTRADE: (CONFIDENT) Oh, there's more, Mr. Holmes.

SOUND EFFECT: THE DOOR OPENS

HOLMES: Ah, Watson. Completed your examination so soon?

WATSON: I have.

SOUND EFFECT: HE SHUTS THE DOOR

WATSON: (GRIM) Never had to examine the body of a friend before . . . (RECOVERING SLIGHTLY) Anyway, star-shaped wound to the head, indicating a weapon fired at close quarters. And I retrieved the bullet from his brain.

HOLMES: May I examine it, please, Watson? Thank you. Very small – fired from a derringer, no doubt.

LESTRADE: Ladies' gun.

WATSON: (HARSHLY) Not always, Inspector. Both the Holywells are my friends, I don't believe Emilia is capable of such an act.

LESTRADE: You'd be surprised what goes on in other people's marriages, Doctor. I used to be – but not anymore. And when I said it was a ladies' gun, I meant it.

SOUND EFFECT: HOLMES SETS A SMALL GUN DOWN ON A TABLE

LESTRADE: You see?

HOLMES: A two-shot derringer. With blood on the barrel.

LESTRADE: Mrs. Holywell's two-shot derringer. I found it in her needlework bag.

WATSON: I'm not aware of Emilia ever owning a weapon.

LESTRADE: She admits to it, Doctor – says her husband bought it for her, to keep her safe while she did God's work in Whitechapel. Apart from that, she has nothing to say – won't admit or deny her guilt.

HOLMES: The lady is helpful and evasive in equal measure. Most interesting. If only I could speak to her . . . .

WATSON: Why shouldn't you, Holmes?

HOLMES: (UNCERTAIN AT FIRST AS TO HOW TO RESPOND) Because . . . Because I'm expecting Percival Holywell at Baker Street shortly. Do you think you could lay your hands on some of Dr. Holywell's typed reports from the clinic?

WASON: I suppose so.

LESTRADE: I don't know what it is you hope to prove, Mr. Holmes. I honestly don't.

SOUND EFFECT: INTERIOR OF A MOVING CAB. HOLMES IS FLICKING THROUGH SHEETS OF PAPER

WATSON: Holmes?

HOLMES: (BARELY PAYING ATTENTION) Hmm?

WATSON: Things have been happening so quickly, I haven't had a chance to thank you.

HOLMES: (STILL NOT REALLY LISTENING) Thank me for what, old chap?

WATSON: For responding to my telegram.

HOLMES: Telegram? Oh, yes, the telegram.

284

WATSON: I should prefer if it you treated me like an ordinary client in this instance. What I mean is, I'm happy to pay for your services.

HOLMES: As I told you earlier, Watson, there's no charge.

WATSON: I don't think you *did* tell me that earlier, Holmes.

HOLMES: (RAPIDLY CHANGING THE SUBJECT) These reports are really very interesting, you know. Very interesting indeed.

WATSON: Perhaps Lestrade was right.

HOLMES: Unlikely. Although he *has* been persuaded of value of fingerprints, so the world *does* turn.

WATSON: I'm thinking of what he said about what goes on in another person's marriage – I've only known the Holywells a short time, and all we every really talk about is my adventures with you.

HOLMES: Understandable.

WATSON: Who knows what resentments lurked under that serene surface? What secrets were being kept? Thank heavens Mary and I are always so honest with one another.

HOLMES: (CLEARS HIS THROAT)

WATSON: I've been giving some thought to this case, Holmes.

HOLMES: Always advisable.

WATSON: And I was wondering . . . Could Lucien Holywell have killed himself? And perhaps typed that letter to incriminate Emilia?

HOLMES: There was blood on the barrel of the gun, Watson. You examined the body – were there any traces of blood on his hands?

WATSON: No. No, of course not, I should've thought of that. Foolish of me.

HOLMES: This case has caused you some distress, old friend. Think nothing of it.

WATSON: I did have another notion, but it's so fanciful, I hesitate to mention it. Lucien and Percival Holywell were twins. Identical twins, in fact. Is it even remotely possible . . . ?

HOLMES: That the body you examined is in fact that of Percival and that Dr. Lucien Holywell is alive and has merely taken his brother's identity?

WATSON: Yes!

HOLMES: No, Watson. It is not remotely possible.

WATSON: Oh.

HOLMES: Percival's hands are not those of a doctor. From the callosities on his thumbs, he's occasionally worked as a manual labourer. Rest assured, Watson, the dead man is indeed *Dr.* Holywell.

WATSON: Of course. I apologise again, Holmes. I'm not in my right mind today.

HOLMES: No apologies necessary, Watson.

WATSON: I just wondered whether that might be the reason you'd invited Percival to Baker Street – to unmask him.

HOLMES: No, Watson. It was to ask him about his thumbs.

SOUND EFFECT: OUT

MUSIC: STING

PERCIVAL: You mean why does a man who inherited half the wealth of so many coal-mines in Wales spends so much of his time working as a gardener?

HOLMES: Precisely so, Mr. Holywell. I notice, by the way, that you take snuff. Watson and I do not indulge, but please, feel free.

PERCIVAL: It's hardly the time, Mr. Holmes. And to answer your question, there are two reasons. Firstly, because I happen to enjoy working.

HOLMES: And secondly?

PERCIVAL: Because I didn't inherit anything.

WATSON: How is that possible?

PERCIVAL: My father's will was quite specific. His money was to go to his first-born. And I arrived a good half-an-hour after Lucien.

WATSON: That must have made you extremely angry.

PERCIVAL: Not as much as you might think, John. I fend for myself most of the time because I wish it that way. Lucien helped me out from time to time. When I needed it.

WATSON: But not always, Percival. Forgive me, but – didn't the two of you row a couple of weeks ago?

PERCIVAL You heard that, did you? And is that why you suspect me of my brother's murder? My own twin –

WATSON: I didn't say –

HOLMES: I regret that there is no time at present for the finer feelings. A man has been murdered and a woman's life is at stake. If Captain Holywell is hanged for shooting her husband, you will inherit all your brother's money.

PERCIVAL: (DISGUSTED) I don't care about money!

HOLMES: Your argument with your twin seems to indicate that you're lying, Mr. Holywell.

PERCIVAL: Tell me, John, did you happen to overhear what I needed the money for?

WATSON: Something about an astronomer's telescope.

287

PERCIVAL: At the peak of Mount Snowdon.

HOLMES: An expensive venture.

PERCIVAL: I'm a man of many interests, Mr. Holmes – gardening, astronomy, chess . . . .

WATSON: Gambling. The Southern Cup, remember?

PERCIVAL: I'm no more of a gambler than you are, John. Less of one, in fact. And Lucien refused to even countenance such a notion. He viewed it as a spectacular folly.

HOLMES: One that you will now have the opportunity to indulge.

PERCIVAL: I'm already indulging it. The Earl of Evesham is a keen amateur astronomer. He's generously offered to fund the construction. I expect there'll be an announcement in *The Times* tomorrow morning. (TERSELY) If that's all, gentlemen . . . .

SOUND EFFECT: HE OPENS THE DOOR

PERCIVAL: I've already spent far too much time away from my niece. (A VERY MINOR HESITATION OR GULP BEFORE THE WORD "NIECE". THEN, GOING OFF-MICROPHONE) Far, far too much.

SOUND EFFECT: HE SHUTS THE DOOR BEHIND HIM

WATSON: Well, Holmes, it seems Percival has no motive. I never really considered him a likely suspect, to be honest.

HOLMES: (DEEP IN THOUGHT) It's not complete, Watson. There are indications, yes, but . . . It's not complete. There's nothing for it – I must visit Dr. Holywell's wife in custody.

WATSON: About time, if you don't mind me saying – (SOMETHING'S CAUGHT HIS ATTENTION) Holmes, is this the telegram I sent to you?

HOLMES: Yes, I imagine it must be.

288

WATSON: It's unopened. So how did you know I'd asked you to look into the case?

HOLMES: I won't bore you with my process of deduction, Watson. All that matters is that I am on the case, and that if I receive the answers I expect, the good Captain will soon be free to pursue her duties for the Salvation Army!

SOUND EFFECT: SLIGHT ECHO DURING DIALOGUE THROUGHOUT

EMILIA: I'm afraid there's been a misunderstanding, gentlemen.

HOLMES: I'm bound to agree with you, Captain.

WATSON: You can rely on Mr. Holmes, Emilia.

EMILIA: (FIRMLY) I mean that I didn't wish to see you. I have nothing to say.

HOLMES: You will not deny responsibility for your husband's murder?

EMILIA: Inspector Lestrade seems satisfied that I'm guilty.

HOLMES: And what of your daughter, Ernestine?

EMILIA: I don't wish to talk about Ernestine.

WATSON: If you're found guilty, you'll almost certainly hang.

EMILIA: I'm aware of that.

HOLMES: You would prefer for her to think of her mother as a murderess than to know –

EMILIA: (ALMOST A SHRIEK) Mr. Holmes!

HOLMES: (SIGHS) Very well. A simple question, then. Your husband was murdered in his armamentarium.

EMILIA: So I understand.

WATSON: And you were asleep at the time.

HOLMES: I'm getting to that, Watson.

EMILIA: Our maid Alice told the Inspector that I was asleep. I have no memory of that. I suspect she was simply trying to be helpful.

HOLMES: To return to my original point, your husband was typing a letter at the time of his death. Why was his typewriter not in his study? (NO REPLY) Surely you can have no objection to answering that?

EMILIA: (BEGRUDGINGLY) I don't know. Lucien always did all his typing in the study.

WATSON: Then what was he doing in the gun room?

EMILIA: From time to time, he liked to admire his collection.

WATSON: And he never thought to use any of them to protect himself?

EMILIA: He never kept any of them loaded, Doctor.

HOLMES: No. I examined every one. And now perhaps you would now permit Dr. Watson to examine *you*.

EMILIA: What?

HOLMES: Doctor, would you oblige?

WATSON: Of course, Holmes. Just hold still, Emilia – I'd like to see your complexion in the light . . . .

HOLMES: You see it, Watson?

WATSON: I do . . . A blue-ish tinge to the complexion . . . You've been drugged.

EMILIA: Drugged?

WATSON: And if I can just look at the back of your neck. Yes . . . there's a small puncture there.

EMILIA: (BEWILDERED) This is all impossible!

HOLMES: Watson, what drug causes unconsciousness *and* a loss of memory?

WATSON: Hyoscin.

EMILIA: What's hyoscin?

WATSON: It's a hypnotic, derived from henbane – deadly nightshade. It's used in small doses to treat *delirium tremens*. In large doses, it results in symptoms that are often mistaken for a stroke.

HOLMES: There is a glimmer of light penetrating the gloom that has surrounded this case.

WATSON: When Alice thought you were asleep, you were actually under the influence of the drug. Someone wanted to make sure you wouldn't interfere – perhaps even to implicate you in the murder of your husband.

HOLMES: Watson, I believe Lestrade should know about this immediately.

WATSON: Of course.

SOUND EFFECT: HE BANGS ON A METAL DOOR

WATSON: Guard! (TO HOLMES) Aren't you coming, Holmes?

HOLMES: I have a few more questions.

SOUND EFFECT: THE DOOR OPENS

WATSON: As you wish. Ah, thank you.

SOUND EFFECT: CELL DOOR CLOSES AGAIN

EMILIA: Mary sent you, didn't she? She gave me her word.

HOLMES: Your restrictions were foolish, Captain. You would honestly prefer your child to believe you a murderess than to know that you

291

lied to her about her parentage? Percival Holywell is the girl's father, not Lucien.

EMILIA: Most perceptive, Mr. Holmes.

HOLMES: I was struck by the fact that in the letter found in the gun room, Dr. Holywell referred to Ernestine as "the child", rather than "*my* daughter". Someone else typed it, of course – someone who could not bring himself to have his victim claim Ernestine as his own, even in a forged letter. You told Mrs. Watson that your problem concerned your shame and your *entire* family – not only you and your husband, but your daughter and your brother-in-law. Or perhaps I should refer to him as your lover.

EMILIA: You are a very harsh man.

HOLMES: The truth is often harsh. But you encourage those poor beggars in the soup kitchens to face it every day. You feared that Percival was planning to kill you, but you couldn't give Mrs. Watson any further details once your husband appeared. Why would you not tell Inspector Lestrade?

EMILIA: I feared for my *own* life, Mr. Holmes, not that of my husband. Yes, Percival had threatened me – he was enraged that I refused to acknowledge that Ernestine was his – but as you can see, I am very much alive.

HOLMES: Not for much longer. It's Percival's intention that you should be hanged for your husband's murder. He told Dr. Watson and myself that he had no interest in money, and that was quite true. With both her parents dead, he will end up with the child – that's what he really wants.

EMILIA: I will admit that it is a possibility, Mr. Holmes.

HOLMES: Good.

EMILIA: But without proof, I will not speak.

HOLMES: This is foolishness!

EMILIA: I will not speak, Mr. Holmes.

HOLMES: Very well. Then I shall have to acquire some proof.

SOUND EFFECT: ECHO OUT

MUSIC: BRIDGE

LESTRADE: I just popped round to say – well, to say how very grateful I am to you, Mr. Holmes. Oh, and to you too, of course, Doctor.

WATSON: You're welcome, Lestrade.

LESTRADE: Yes, it might have been a considerable embarrassment. Considerable.

HOLMES: I imagine that the inconvenience would have been greater still for Captain Holywell.

LESTRADE: *Mrs.* – Er, yes, yes, *Captain* Holywell. Most regrettable. Still, she's been released now, and reunited with that little girl of hers.

WATSON: Ernestine. She'll be a continual reminder of Lucien – the child takes after her father.

HOLMES: So I believe.

LESTRADE: Tell me, Mr. Holmes, just when did you know Percival was the killer?

HOLMES: The very moment I set eyes upon him, Inspector.

WATSON: Surely not that soon!

HOLMES: The hair on one side of his head was flattened, and it contained threads from the red velvet cushions one finds in train carriages. Clearly, he'd slept on his journey here.

WATSON: How could he do that, knowing that his own brother had just been murdered? Of course. Had he ever actually been to the Southern Cup?

LESTRADE: Oh, yes, Doctor. Then he came to London to commit the murder, went back and came here *again*. *And* he forgot to throw the tickets away.

HOLMES: Tell me, Lestrade. Did Percival say why he'd killed his brother?

LESTRADE: No, he just admitted to the murder once I showed him the evidence against him, but that was all.

HOLMES: I see. Well . . . .

LESTRADE: But I think we can make an educated guess.

HOLMES: Oh?

LESTRADE: The money, obviously.

HOLMES: (SLIGHT RELIEF) Obviously.

WATSON: Presumably, the tickets weren't the only evidence against him.

LESTRADE: He provided the rest himself, with that typewriter trick. Tried to be too clever by half.

HOLMES: I examined Dr. Holywell's reports – he placed an even pressure on keys when writing. His brother was not an accomplished typist, however, using only one finger and varying amounts of pressure. In addition, I found traces of snuff beneath the keys – a maharini brand created by the East India Company. The same type I observed beneath Percival Holywell's fingernails.

WATSON: Wait a moment, though – I thought *Lucien* Holywell's fingerprints were on the typewriter keys. How can that be, unless he –

HOLMES: Yes?

WATSON: Unless he wiped the keys clean, and placed his dead brother's fingers on them.

HOLMES: That is how I read it. And, of course, the killer had to be familiar with the routine of the householders, including the fact that Dr. Holywell provided his wife with a two-shot Derringer.

WATSON: Ghastly.

HOLMES: The presence of the typewriter in the armamentarium clinched the case. His brother kept his typewriter in the study, but Percival had his heart set on planting the letter. After shooting Lucien, he was faced with a dilemma – move the body into the study with the typewriter . . .

WATSON: . . . or bring the typewriter into the armamentarium.

HOLMES: Inevitably, he took the path of least resistance.

LESTRADE: And while he wiped his fingerprints off the keys, he didn't remove them from the base of the machine. There really is no such thing as the perfect crime, is there?

WATSON: Not so long as Sherlock Holmes remains in practice.

LESTRADE: Yes, yes, I have to admit it. That was a very nice piece of work, Mr. Holmes.

HOLMES: Why, thank you, Lestrade. Though I fear that people will think less of my powers if they believe this is a case of which I'm proud.

LESTRADE: Well, I'd better be getting back now.

WATSON: I'll share a cab with you, if you don't mind, Inspector – Mary will be wondering what's become of me.

HOLMES: Which reminds me, Watson . . . .

WATSON: Yes, Holmes?

HOLMES: Please pass on my very best wishes to your wife. She is a splendid woman in every regard.

MUSIC: *DANSE MACABRE*

The July which immediately succeeded my marriage was made memorable by three cases of interest, in which I had the privilege of being associated with Sherlock Holmes and of studying his methods. I find them recorded in my notes under the headings of "The Adventure of the Second Stain", "The Adventure of the Naval Treaty", and "The Adventure of the Tired Captain".

– Dr. John H. Watson
"The Adventure of the Naval Treaty"

The Secret of
Colonel Warburton's Insanity
by Paul D. Gilbert

The asylum of St. Jude's had always held for me the most harrowing of memories and had forever been associated with the conclusion of the Isadora Persano affair.

As my more diligent readers might recall, my friend Sherlock Holmes had inveigled his way into that awful establishment and had subjected himself to the most awful sights and sounds in his efforts at obtaining the truth and thereby saving a man's life. His experiences that night had had the most profound and detrimental effect upon his own mind, and it was to be some considerable time before he would allow me to finally commit "The Mumbling Duellist" to print *.

Therefore, my consternation upon our receiving a letter from Mr. Nathaniel Brewer, the custodian of St. Jude's at the time of Persano's incarceration, might be well understood. The significance of the name had not been lost on my friend either, but despite the threat posed by his suppressed memories, Holmes had been willing to accept Brewer's request for help and advice with barely a moment's hesitation.

Once Holmes had penned and dispatched his brief reply, he offered the request from Brewer for my perusal. It had been as brief as it had been lacking in detail, and yet the name of the inmate, to whom he had referred, shook me to the core and the look of disbelief upon my face had not been lost upon my friend.

"So, Watson, I see that the name of Colonel James Warburton is familiar to you," Holmes stated simply.

I shook my head slowly back and forth before replying.

"It is inconceivable to me that a man such as he has come to so sorry a pass," I replied gravely.

"You know, I can think of only two other occasions on which you have had prior knowledge of a case upon its inception and I have a feeling that your military background might well prove to be invaluable to me. Pray, what do you know of the man?"

Holmes had undoubtedly been referring to the matter of the Naval Treaty and the strange case of the engineer's thumb, both of which had found their way into my journals of our cases. However, at this stage I could not see how my knowledge of Colonel Warburton could possibly shed any light upon his current plight.

297

I finally placed Brewer's note back down again upon the table and glanced up at my friend who was eager for my response.

"Although we had both served in Afghanistan with the Berkshires, our roles within that illustrious regiment had been so disparate that we had never actually come into direct contact. His orders quite often culminated in an increase in my own duties, but I held little resentment for that. I would say that of all of our commanders, his decisions were the most rational and sound." I paused once I had recognised the irony of my choice of words.

"In short, he carried the reputation of being a brave and honourable soldier who had earned the respect of his men by leadership and deed. His current situation is irreconcilable to the man under whom I had once served," I concluded.

Holmes rubbed his long chin slowly and thoughtfully.

"Perhaps our friend Nathaniel Brewer is of a similar opinion to your own?" Holmes mentioned speculatively as he picked up the note once more. "See here, Watson, how he refers to 'the peculiar matter of the incarceration of Colonel Warburton'. If he is referring to Warburton's incompatibility with an establishment such as St. Jude's, he might well be seeking the wrong consultant when once he arrives?" Holmes suggested.

"I can assure you that although I am a man of medicine, the vagary of the human mind is more of a mystery to me than it is to you."

"Hmm. Perhaps . . . ." By now we had both pulled our chairs up closer to the fire, for the grey dampness of a late October morning had slowly seeped its way towards the centre of the room. Holmes lit his pipe and drifted away into one of his more meditative states of mind, while I dived into the morning papers.

I noticed a strange transformation take over my friend as the appointed time for Brewer's arrival drew ever closer on the following morning. He seemed to be suppressing a pent-up emotion that caused him to pace up and down the room relentlessly, and I could only assume that those dark, distant memories of that night at St. Jude's were suddenly resurfacing.

Nevertheless, Holmes had managed to contain himself by the time of Brewer's arrival, and he was sitting calmly in his chair from where he directed Brewer to the seat opposite to his own with the long and elegant stem of his cherry-wood.

Although our guest had the bearing and deportment of a military man, Nathaniel Brewer assured us that he had been civilian all of his life. He was tall and thick-set and he sported a thick bushy moustache that seemed to conceal much of his upper face and gave him a most severe demeanour. It was easy to see why such a strict and austere regime prevailed at St.

298

Jude's, although Brewer's concern for one of his inmates belied his gruff exterior.

"Mr. Brewer, I trust that the conditions within your appalling establishment in Hanwell have improved somewhat since my own unique experience of the place?" Holmes asked sharply.

Brewer visibly blushed and seemed incapable of a coherent reply. Finally he cleared his throat and gathered his thoughts.

"That I truly cannot say, Mr. Holmes, for your view of St. Jude's was taken from a most exceptional perspective. However, I would certainly hope that we have integrated some of the more progressive treatments, which seem to be so prevalent nowadays, into our regime," Brewer concluded breathlessly.

"I would certainly hope so, but please explain to us the nature of the concerns that you are undoubtedly harbouring for your illustrious inmate, Colonel Warburton, and his incarceration within the dark halls of St. Jude's."

"I must tell you at once, Mr. Holmes, that my initial misgivings regarding the admission of Colonel Warburton were not based upon his state of mind at all. No sir, it was the *manner* of his admission that caused me the gravest concern. Nowadays, the majority of our patients are diagnosed with either a form of mania or dementia, and these assessments are certified by a Medical Officer and a Justice of the Peace, prior to the patient's admission." Brewer paused for a moment while he lit a small, evil-smelling panatela.

"I take it that neither was the case when it came to the admission of Colonel Warburton?" Holmes conjectured.

Brewer found it impossible to suppress a deep cough, induced no doubt by his poisonous cigar. He turned bright red and replied to Holmes's inquiry with several emphatic nods of his head. I offered our client a glass of water, which he eagerly accepted.

"The circumstances of his arrival were certainly most singular and, I must say, highly irregular." Brewer finally replied. "I had been awoken in the dead of night by two of my orderlies, just as a violent electric storm was reaching its thunderous climax. I could barely make out their words through the repetitive explosions, but I was left in little doubt as to the urgency of the situation, and they led me to my office while I hurriedly pulled on my robe.

"Upon our arrival, I was confronted by the sorry sight of a tall man, of late middle-age, reeling from side to side while a torrent of nonsensical mutterings tumbled from his quivering lips. The pathetic creature had been flanked by two men, of obvious military bearing, who would broker no

299

protest of mine until I had read and thoroughly digested the contents of a sealed white envelope that bore the crest of the Foreign Office."

Holmes stretched out his long bony fingers, while Brewer fumbled in his inside pocket to extract the envelope in question. Unfortunately, the officials from the Foreign Office had insisted on reclaiming the original letter, once Brewer had read and fully digested its contents. Consequently, all that now resided within the envelope was a rough *précis* that Brewer had put together after the officials had departed. Holmes then retained the envelope for examination, while handing to me the letter for my perusal.

Holmes ran his glass over the envelope, but he was only able to confirm the size of one of the men, by virtue of his enormous finger-prints, and that the water mark indeed established its source of origin. In disappointment, Holmes flung the offensive envelope to the floor and indicated that I should now read from the single piece of paper that it had contained. We both filled and lit our pipes before I did so. Unfortunately, Brewer lit another of his poisonous cigars!

Initially I read the scant missive silently to myself and in disbelief.

"Mr. Brewer, is this truly an accurate resume of the letter that accompanied the unfortunate Colonel Warburton?" I asked incredulously.

Nathaniel Brewer nodded his head solemnly while emitting a plume of his noxious brown smoke.

"Why, this is nothing short of the most scandalous set of instructions that I have ever heard of!" I exclaimed.

Holmes suddenly jerked forward and, while resting his elbows upon his knees, demanded that I elaborate upon my declaration. I waved the slip of paper excitedly in front of my friend's face.

"Mr. Brewer has been left in no doubt that should he waver from his instructions – even ever so slightly – his position at St. Jude's would be in the gravest jeopardy. It says here that Colonel Warburton is to be kept secluded from the other inmates, at all times and at all costs. He is to receive no visitors. Even those from a medical professional are forbidden, and he is to be constantly sedated, ostensibly for reasons of his own safety, under the strongest dose of chloral hydrate that his health will allow! Mr. Brewer," I asked rather forcefully, "do you appreciate how deadly chloral hydrate can be, unless accurately administered?"

Brewer could not look me in the eye and his voice dropped to a whisper as he replied in the affirmative.

"In all good conscience, Mr. Brewer," I insisted, "you surely cannot expedite these draconian measures, despite the very obvious threat to your position."

"I have had very little choice, Doctor Watson, for one of the men who brought Colonel Warburton to me on that sorry night, known simply as

Leverton, has remained at St. Jude's ever since, all the while maintaining a threatening and watchful eye over all proceedings. That is why I have come to you today, gentlemen, in the hope that you might suggest a way in which I can end the poor man's suffering and explain the reasons behind his inexplicably inhumane treatment at the hands of those whom he once so nobly served." Nathaniel Brewer seemed to be sincere in his entreaties and he cast my friend an importunate glance.

Holmes slapped the arms of his chair violently as he leapt to his feet and strode over to the window, a place of solace and reflection to him on a grey melancholy day such as this. He gazed out into the shadowy swirling mists before turning towards the centre of the room once more.

"Mr. Brewer, as worthy as your cause undoubtedly is, I fail to see what effect you expect my intervention to have upon a supposed medical injustice such as this. There are no clues that I might glean, no criminal that I might apprehend – "

"Is it not a crime to incarcerate someone without going through all due processes?" Brewer interjected, with enough passion to stop Sherlock Holmes firmly in his tracks.

"Obviously this gentleman from the Foreign Office is not going to take too kindly to the notion of Sherlock Holmes interviewing the object of his supervision and observation," Holmes muttered softly, almost to himself.

I saw Brewer gaze expectantly at my friend, but I motioned to him to hold back from any further inquiry, for I could tell that Holmes was already generating a germ of an idea. In that I had been correct. However even I, with all my experience of Holmes's unique method, could not have anticipated his next question!

"Mr. Brewer," my friend asked with a glint in his eye, "would you not say that the interior of St. Jude's is somewhat overdue a coat of paint or two?"

Brewer received nothing more than a shrug when he shot me a shocked and questioning glance and so, after a deep swallow or two, Brewer decided to answer.

"I suppose so. There are few long established institutions that do not, I should imagine. However, I fail to see how – "

"Excellent! Then Doctor Watson and I shall be with you tomorrow morning, promptly at nine, although I should add that you may not immediately recognise us." Holmes indicated that I should usher the hapless Nathaniel Brewer towards the door, while he began scribbling a brief note for Mrs. Hudson to deliver to the page boy.

Once our client had made his hasty and confused departure, I turned upon my friend with a mocked indignation.

"I assume that I have just been cajoled into undertaking some form of unnecessary decorating work?"

"Indeed you have, friend Watson, but also much more than that! That is, of course, if you don't object to such a mission?"

"If my services will help to alleviate the suffering of Colonel Warburton," I proclaimed, "then not at all."

Holmes was clearly pleased with my vigorous response and he spent the rest of the day in putting his preparations into place. The page boy was constantly going back and forth, each time bearing either a pot of paint or some other item of decorating equipment. All the while Holmes busied himself within his room, pulling out various appropriate items of clothing and other means of altering our usual appearances.

Then, upon my insistence, Holmes finally condescended to explain to me the reasons behind our masquerade. As usual there proved to be an irrefutable logic behind his plans.

"There is no doubt that the gentleman designated by the Foreign Office, this Leverton, is there for one reason and one reason alone, and that is to ensure that nobody should discover the true motives behind the incarceration of Colonel Warburton. Therefore, the chances of our being able to interview the Colonel in our usual guises, without interruption and interference, are slim indeed.

"Consequently, we will infiltrate St. Jude's in a manner that should arouse the least suspicion, while allowing us the opportunity to glean from the Colonel whatever we may."

"I still do not see how this might be achieved, even within our elaborate disguises."

"It is simple enough, Watson: You see, I shall create a diversion that will distract this fellow Leverton long enough for you to be able to interrogate Colonel Warburton."

"You wish *me* to conduct the interview?" I asked while feeling somewhat aghast at the prospect.

"Most certainly I do. You have the advantage of possessing some knowledge of the man, not to mention the fact that you shared the experience of the same campaign, albeit from a different perspective."

"Perhaps you would care to share with me the form that this diversion is likely to assume?" I suggested, although I had been unsuccessful in eliminating any of my misgivings from my tone. Holmes had not been slow in perceiving that, and he hesitated before replying.

"I am afraid that in this respect we shall have to trust to a moment of improvisation."

"No, Holmes," I protested. "I do not like leaving this to chance, not when there is so much at stake."

"You must see that I have no other choice – unless you would have me go on my own?" Holmes suggested mischievously.

"Well, of course I would not!"

"Ha! Then it is agreed!" Holmes clapped his hands gleefully and we finally completed our arrangements.

Consequently, after joining Holmes for a rushed breakfast the following morning, he and I were fully prepared for Alperton. We asked our driver to pull up and remain a half-mile from St. Jude's, so that we were seen to arrive there on foot.

During the journey I had asked Holmes if he had any qualms about returning to the scene of the traumatic night that he had once spent there. He did not reply until we passed under the stalwart old red bricked archway that led to the inhibiting, similarly built edifice in front of us.

"In the cold light of day and under this entirely different set of circumstances, I would say no qualms whatsoever. After all, on this occasion I am in the reassuring company of that renowned artisan, Doctor Watson!" Holmes declared while striding purposefully towards the front door with his paint and brushes in hand.

We were met at the door by Brewer himself and, once he had assured himself that Leverton was nowhere to be seen, he led us discreetly through to his private quarters.

Holmes pressed his lips with his left forefinger to ensure our silence, but did not speak until he was certain that we had not been observed.

"Are the arrangements unchanged from those you described to us yesterday?"

"Sadly yes. The Colonel still sits in his depressed solitude, mumbling incoherently to himself. Needless to say," Brewer warned, "Mr. Leverton is in constant attendance, so you will need to be at your most vigilant."

"Very well then. We shall continue as planned. Are the other members of your staff alert to our arrival and the nature of our work?"

"Yes, indeed Mr. Holmes. You are free to begin at once."

"Excellent! Perhaps you would be good enough to direct Doctor Watson towards Colonel Warburton's room, while I shall start painting on the upper corridor. My only previous experience of this place was at night, and from what I've seen so far, the need for a coat of paint should not be lost on Mr. Leverton either!"

"Well, you both certainly look the part, I must say."

"You will, of course, discreetly indicate to me the moment Leverton comes into view?" Holmes suggested, and once Brewer had agreed, Holmes and I buttoned up our overalls and set to work.

I soon lost sight of Holmes as he climbed the stairs, but within a short while I could hear him opening his paint pot and begin to whistle. We had arrived shortly after the residents had been served their breakfasts, and many of them had started trooping out into the gardens, where the more able among them had been designated their own small allotments.

The doors to each of the individual rooms and the large dormitories had all been unlocked and left ajar, with one notable exception. For many years there had been a running debate within *The Lancet* as to the merits, or otherwise, of solitary confinement within a modern and enlightened asylum. To the advocates of a small solitary cell, it represented a calm and quiet atmosphere in which a patient might be able to avoid the loud or violent behaviour of the other inmates.

However, the other side of the argument told a disturbing story of the opportunity for abuse and maltreatment of difficult patients, a lack of observation, and the neglect of basic hygiene. One school of thought also broached the notion that an extended time in a solitary cell might actually induce a form of insanity in a patient where none had previously existed! It had been this notion that had disturbed me the most – especially once I had observed the size of Colonel Warburton's room.

I began applying my whitewash to the wall at the end of the corridor and the one closest to Warburton's room. His door was shut and there appeared to be no light seeping out from under the door. I spent an agonising age in ensuring that I was not being observed, before sidling over to the Colonel's observation plate.

There had been a dim light at the far end of the room and it revealed the sorry sight of a once noble and honourable warrior seated dejectedly on the edge of a small bunk bed, with his shoulders hunched and rounded, his toilet sadly neglected. Fortunately they had stopped short at encumbering the Colonel with a restraining device and so I quietly called him over to me, while giving his title its due respect.

He uncurled himself and rose to his feet with a measured and deliberate unease. His steps towards the observation plate were painfully slow and uncertain. Yet, as he grew ever closer, I could see that something had glimmered within those sad and forlorn eyes – a narrow portal of recognition.

We had never previously met, so therefore that realisation had clearly been born of his proud rank and the knowledge of whom and what he had once been. Colonel Warburton drew himself up to something approaching his true height, and I was certain that he was about to speak, when the sound of heavy and official footsteps began to echo down the corridor towards us.

I had not the time to retreat to my work-station before a voice of warning rent the previous unnatural silence. Clearly Brewer had not been able to warn me in advance, for I was in little doubt that this voice belonged to none other than the aforementioned Leverton, of the Foreign Office.

"Hey! You there – get back to your work at once!" Leverton's voice was more reminiscent of that of a harsh Regimental Sergeant-Major than that of a civil servant. I doffed my cap apologetically and moved quickly back to my work. To my dismay, it appeared that Mr. Leverton was an individual who was not so easy to placate.

He strode aggressively towards me, pausing only to glance briefly through Colonel Warburton's observation plate. That look alone was enough to convince him that I had attempted to communicate with the wretched Colonel, and Leverton was on the point of raising the alarm when a terrible commotion from the upper corridor temporarily diverted his attention away from me.

Leverton moved towards the source of the uproar and he was raising his head just as a large pot of whitewash came cascading down upon him from the upper corridor where Holmes had been painting! Although Holmes had earlier asked me to trust to the notion of improvisation, I could not have foreseen him resorting to a ploy as clumsy as this one, even in my wildest imaginings.

Nevertheless, Holmes's feigned clumsiness seemed to have the desired effect, and Leverton had little choice other than to run off and attempt to remove the paint from his hair and clothes. His chorus of expletives echoed around every room and corridor of St. Judes, and as Leverton disappeared into Brewer's office, I could hear Holmes beating a hasty retreat back to our waiting vehicle.

This diversion presented me with my only opportunity to communicate with Colonel Warburton, for I knew that as soon as Leverton had completed his sponge down he would have me dismissed without a moment's hesitation.

"Colonel Warburton!" I called through the open plate. "I must speak to you at once, as I have very little time!"

Fortunately he still hadn't returned to his bunk, no doubt stirred by the clamour that had just occurred and he didn't hesitate in answering my summons. I could see that his last sedation had been some time ago, for there was a certain lucidity in his voice and manner that I hadn't been expecting. I introduced myself at once and I could tell that he appreciated my motives for being there.

Nevertheless, his attempts at articulating his thoughts and feelings upon the reasons for his hospitalisation weren't so successful. Even then, from the other end of the corridor, I could hear Leverton mobilising some assistance in having me removed and I knew that I would have no more than a moment or two alone with the Colonel before that occurred.

As it transpired, I was only been able to extract four recognisable words from the otherwise nonsensical ramblings of that poor man. I committed them to memory as I was being unceremoniously ejected from the building, and I could just make out the horrified and apologetic look upon the face of Nathaniel Brewer while he was actually orchestrating my removal.

By the time that I arrived at our waiting carriage, Holmes had already removed all traces of his decorator's guise and was sitting back contentedly in his seat, smiling smugly to himself while he pulled gratefully upon his cigarette.

"So, Watson, what did you think of my little solution?" he asked mischievously.

I was aghast at my friend's trivialisation, and as our carriage began the journey back to Baker Street, I told him so.

"Well, I had expected something a little more subtle from you. The repercussions could have been far worse than the result."

"You cannot deny that we should have been lost, had my ruse been less successful?"

"Well, I suppose so," I conceded grudgingly, "but I do wish that I could have been forewarned at least,"

Holmes then tried to console me with his most winning smile, although I tried to ignore this as I pulled out my notebook and pencil.

"Ah, I see that you did have some success with your brief interview," Holmes observed.

"If you can call it that, after all I only managed to extract four recognisable words from the poor fellow before my untimely ejection," I complained while hurriedly jotting them down.

I would have passed the piece of paper to my friend, but as was his wont, he preferred me to read them to him.

"*Stewart, Massy, Timothy,* and *Sherpur.*" I read them slowly and deliberately, but I could see at once that they meant somewhat less to Holmes than they had to me.

Holmes squeezed his eyes tightly shut, I assumed in the hope that he might muster the depths of some distant memory to our cause. However, when I had attempted further discussion, to my great surprise I received no response from my friend. Whether the emotional effort of having returned to St. Jude's had caused an exhaustive sleep to wash over him or that he was in a state of the deepest meditation, I could not tell. In any event, I can confirm that we spent the remainder of the journey in a surprising but total silence.

Once safely back in Baker Street, Holmes poured out two unusually large cognacs and spurned Mrs. Hudson's offer of a late lunch in a most dismissive fashion. Fortunately I was able to confirm my own intention to dine before she bustled from the room!

"So, the names upon your lamentably short list seemed to mean a great deal more to you than they did to me," Holmes stated invitingly while putting flame to his old clay pipe.

"Three of them certainly do," I confirmed. "As one would have thought, they are connected most notably to the Afghan Campaign of 1879 in which Colonel Warburton was actively involved. Major General Frederick Stewart and Colonel Massy, of the newly created Kabul Field Force, led a relief column to the recently besieged Sherpa Cantonment.

"A long and hard fought battle then ensued, from which the British forces emerged victorious and the remnants of the Afghani forces were dispersed to the hills!" I proudly proclaimed.

Holmes appeared to be unmoved by my jingoistic recounting of events, and we were momentarily interrupted by the arrival of my small platter of cold meats. Holmes was lost in deep thought and remained oblivious to my demolition of the landlady's meagre offerings.

"As rousing as your account undoubtedly is, I am surprised to note that you have made no mention of Colonel Warburton or his role at the battle of Sherpur."

"Why, he was at that time in command of my regiment," I replied. "The Berkshires, and was so even a few months later at the fateful battle of Maiwand, where I received my wound and consequent discharge."

"Nevertheless, whilst under the terrible strain of having to fight off the effects of his sedation and under the most lamentable of conditions, the Colonel summoned up the last of his strength to utter four words that are apparently unrelated and irrelevant to him. Rather curious, would you not say?" Holmes seemed to be asking himself this question, rather than addressing it to me.

"Yes indeed, but there is also the possibility that my assessment of his condition was ill-judged and that the use of those names was merely random?" I speculated. "After all, he is under a most debilitating form of sedation."

Holmes pursed his lips with his left forefinger and arched his eyebrow, as if he was accusing me of self-deprecation. Then he shook his head emphatically.

"No, we are working upon the hypothesis that Warburton's internment was for reasons other than medical ones, and that Mr. Brewer's concerns are genuine and well-founded. After all, he doesn't seem to be a man who would be prone to flights of fancy, and he came to us in spite of the very real threats that hang over him.

"I am, therefore, very much of the opinion that the Colonel holds information that is a threat to the British military, but they couldn't resort to his elimination due to the prominent nature of his position and reputation. His internment at an establishment such as St. Jude's would garner sympathy for the Colonel rather than arouse any kind of suspicion.

"Now think, Watson," Holmes asked intently of me, "apart from the rousing success enjoyed by the British, were there any other features of the Battle of Sherpur that were worthy of note?" I lit up my pipe while I considered my reply, all the while trying to ignore the loud grunts of impatience emanating through my friend's clenched teeth.

"You must remember that these events took place a very long time ago, and that I had been otherwise engaged in a different part of the country. As I recall, the engagement at Sherpur came about as a direct result of the assassination of a number of British citizens in Kabul. Consequently, the column's mission to Sherpur was more of a punitive nature than a strategic or political one.

"The retribution was considered to be excessive at the time and the phrase, 'No quarter was given to all Afghans bearing arms' seems to resonate with me. However, there was a rumour that even found its way to the Berkshires, which quantified the phrase 'All Afghans bearing arms' in a most chilling aspect. The rumour had been regarded in a most dismissive manner, and it hadn't even found its way into the most sensational of newspapers." By now Holmes had been leaning towards me so acutely that I feared he was about to fall upon me.

"You have a tendency to prevaricate that is agonising in the extreme." Holmes exclaimed.

"The words are hard to say, Holmes, but we were told that amongst those supposedly bearing arms were both women and even a number of young children . . . ." I broke off suddenly and Holmes emitted a long but almost silent whistle.

"Evidently Colonel Warburton knew considerably more about the validity of those rumours than did his subordinates," Holmes gravely concluded.

"I suppose so, but why would Stewart and Massy have waited so long before deciding to silence Colonel Warburton?" I asked.

"Perhaps the threat posed to them by Warburton's knowledge has only recently become apparent. We will probably have the answer to that once we have identified this 'Timothy' to whom the Colonel also attaches so much importance," Holmes surmised.

Holmes gave the matter much silent thought as he drew heavily from his pipe.

"Watson, please pass me down our edition of *Who's Who*." Holmes grabbed the tome eagerly from me and took it over to the window. He hurriedly rifled through the pages of that well-fingered volume before finally slapping his right palm down upon the relevant page in triumph.

"Ha! We have it!" Holmes brandished the book before me and thrust it into my eager hands. Not surprisingly, the page contained a large entry for Colonel Warburton.

Holmes isolated the reference to Warburton's family with his index finger. Sure enough, there was a brief mention of his son, Lieutenant Timothy Jeffrey Warburton, late of the Kabul Field Force.

"As you are only too fully aware, I am loath to theorise before the facts. However, it would not be too much of a leap into the dark to suppose that anything untoward witnessed by Timothy would have found its way to his father. Sadly, Timothy was mortally wounded by a stray bullet during a field exercise last year and it would have been most remiss of him had a letter to his father not be found amongst his papers, would you not say?"

"Indeed it would have been, especially if he possessed even a tiny proportion of his father's sense of honour. Doubtless the Colonel would have raised the issue with the powers that be, and his immoral confinement proved to be the reward for his sense of justice and duty. Nevertheless, even when armed with this knowledge, I fail to see how we can achieve his release without bringing a similar fate upon ourselves."

Holmes smiled to himself while he considered his next response.

"There is but one man who possesses enough power and influence to bring about Colonel Warburton's release."

"Of course – you mean your brother Mycroft!" I exclaimed, but even before I had finished speaking Holmes was pulling on his overcoat and rushing to the door.

"Look at the time! He might still be at his desk."

Anyone who has ever read my accounts of Mycroft Holmes will recall that he was a man of the most singular habits and an immovable daily schedule. Therefore, I knew exactly what Holmes meant by his urgency, and a moment later, I could hear the street door crashing shut behind him.

I spent the next three hours taking an early supper and extracting as much as I could from the morning papers. Nevertheless, the time went slowly and I could only speculate as to Holmes's success, until I observed his glowering face upon his return. He threw his coat to the floor and immediately lit a cigarette with trembling hands.

I thought it prudent to maintain a silence until such time as Holmes was calm enough to broach the subject, which he did upon completing his cigarette.

"As you may have observed, the meeting with my brother was not entirely a satisfactory one. Although he did not deny that the carnage at Sherpur took place, he did not confirm it either. Nevertheless, once I explained the nature of my deductions and our inevitable conclusions, he felt duty-bound to admit that had he known of the details at the time, he would not have condoned such atrocious action, or the internment of Colonel Warburton. It was at this point that the politician within my brother manifested itself. He will not allow the tragedy of Sherpur to become public knowledge! Consequently, and against my better nature, I was forced to arrive at an awkward compromise with him, as you will now see for yourself."

With that Holmes pulled two sheets of official paper from his inside pocket and threw them down disdainfully on the table in front of me. At a glance, I could understand the cause of my friend's great frustration. The first sheet was nothing less than an authorisation for Colonel Warburton's unconditional release from St. Judes. However, before I had a moment to celebrate this heartening news, this was somewhat blunted by the contents of the other sheet.

This required the signature of Colonel Warburton, at the foot of a disclaimer, to the effect that he would never again make mention, either publicly or privately, of the incident at the Sherpur Cantonment. Obviously the contents of the first sheet were entirely dependent upon the completion of the other. I was aghast at this realisation. To a man of honour, this proposal would be entirely unacceptable and we were, therefore, certain that the Colonel's internment was to continue indefinitely.

Nevertheless, on the following morning Holmes and I made our way back to Alperton in our usual guise, doubtful of Warburton's concurrence, but determined to provide the Colonel with that opportunity. Although Brewer was delighted to see the release, the same could not be said of the abhorrent Leverton. Naturally enough, once he had seen the signature, he grunted a reluctant acceptance, pulled on his coat, and stormed out of the room without uttering another word.

It was decided that the disclaimer should not be shown to the Colonel until such time as we were certain that all traces of his sedation had left his system and that he was fully cognisant. Brewer explained that this would require a minimum of twenty-four hours, and so Holmes and I returned to Baker Street, certain in the knowledge that all of our efforts and hopes would come to nought.

Immediately after breakfast the following morning, we received a wire from Nathaniel Brewer that Holmes tore open with great reluctance. To our great surprise, the brief note confirmed that the Colonel had in fact signed the disclaimer and that a carriage was even now conveying him home.

We heard nothing more of the matter for several days, but when we did it was with news of a most remarkable nature. A distraught and irate Mycroft Holmes had sent a private message to the effect that both Major General Stewart and Colonel Massy had resigned their commissions under the darkest of clouds and that there was no doubt that our interference would inevitably lead to a calamitous scandal! The current political atmosphere would not broker such behaviour from the British armed forces, and Mycroft was certain that in the light of Warburton's revelations, many more prominent heads would roll.

Holmes and I sat in a stunned silence for what had seemed to be an eternity, while the notion of a man of Warburton's integrity ignoring the terms of the disclaimer slowly sank in. It was inconceivable to me that he had immediately broken those terms, thereby bringing further disgrace upon himself.

The following afternoon, however, the answer to that conundrum was brought to us in the most tragic of circumstances. On the previous evening and in full dress uniform, Colonel Warburton, formerly of the Royal Berkshires, had put his revolver to his head and pulled the trigger. To a man such as he, it must have seemed to have been the only solution. He could not tolerate the thought of those responsible for the massacre going unpunished, and yet his revelation of the facts had left his own position as untenable.

I put this chain of thought to my friend, for I could see that he had been greatly moved by this awful news.

"You know, Watson, sometimes I feel as if my successful pursuit of justice does, on occasion, do more real harm than any good that might be achieved."

"You cannot hold yourself responsible for Warburton's final solution, Holmes. We make our own paths, and therefore our ultimate destination is by our own design. Besides which, you can be comforted with the knowledge that, thanks to your intervention, the tragedy of Sherpur will likely never be repeated."

My friend attempted a brave and appreciative smile, but as he turned his ashen face away from me, there was undoubtedly something in his eyes that I hadn't seen there for some considerable time. I left the room glancing anxiously towards the locked drawer of his bureau, wherein he kept his Moroccan syringe case . . . .

Of all the problems which have been submitted to my friend, Mr. Sherlock Holmes, for solution during the years of our intimacy, there were only two which I was the means of introducing to his notice – that of Mr. Hatherley's thumb, and that of Colonel Warburton's madness. Of these the latter may have afforded a finer field for an acute and original observer . . . .

– Dr. John H. Watson
"The Adventure of the Engineer's Thumb"

NOTE

*   For more about Isadora Persano, "The Mumbling Duellist", see Paul Gilbert's *The Chronicles of Sherlock Holmes* (2008).

The Adventure of
Merridew of Abominable Memory
by Tracy J. Revels

"I hope you'll forgive me for knocking you up so early this morning," Inspector Lestrade said as we made our way through a bitterly cold London metropolis. "I would have waited until a more decent hour, but the family is anxious to move the corpse, and I know your obsession with viewing the scene before – as you once put it in the Doctor's hearing – a 'herd of buffaloes' tramples it."

My friend Sherlock Holmes chuckled. "You need not apologize to me, Inspector, but Watson may be, at this very moment, deeply regretting his decision to return to his bachelor abode for a few days. I am certain that when he crossed my threshold last evening, carpetbag in hand, he had no inkling that he would be drafted into service again on such short notice."

Truthfully, I was not in the proper mood to appreciate Holmes's sly wit. Circumstances which delicacy prevent me from recording had necessitated a reoccupation of my old rooms. It had been kind of Holmes to never seek out another flatmate, or to transform my bedroom into a chemical laboratory or a shooting gallery. However, renewing my residency had come at the cost of being shaken awake at five in the morning. Lestrade had appeared on our doorstep only moments previously, asking my friend to assist in looking into the tragic death of Professor Lawrence Whittle, who had been found dead inside his greenhouse. I pleaded a terrible headache, for I had imbibed a bit too liberally the night before, but Holmes would have none of my excuses.

"What? Are you no longer an old campaigner, Watson? Come now, there's no time for you to malinger."

And with that pronouncement, Holmes simply whisked the covers off the bed with the flair of a magician who removes a tablecloth without upsetting any of the crockery. I had little choice but to dress and follow. I might have been a soldier in the cause, but rather mutinous thoughts curdled in my brain on that exceptionally bitter morning.

"Whittle," Holmes mused. "A strange name, yet oddly familiar. Why do I know it?"

"Because I read his *Index* article aloud while you shaved," I muttered.

Lestrade was clearly amused by my lack of enthusiasm for the work. "Cheer up, Doctor. Perhaps one day some great inventor will come up with a machine to do the job for you. Just push a button and a voice will read to Mr. Holmes every article ever published!"

Holmes scowled. "Let us leave such idle fantasies for Mr. Verne and his ilk. According to the *Index*, Professor Lawrence Whittle is – or rather, was – a relic of the Enlightenment, a gentleman naturalist and an early advocate and defender of the theories of Charles Darwin. If the date given in the *Index* is correct, Whittle missed his ninetieth birthday by less than a week."

I wondered if I had heard Holmes correctly. Even though I had read the words aloud, I had been so groggy and befuddled I had made little sense of them.

"Ninety! Inspector, what makes you think that his death was anything other than natural?" I asked, perhaps with a bit more heat than I intended. It might have been the darkness of the carriage, but it seemed to me that a hint of smugness crossed the man's ferret-like features.

"Oh, let's just call it a bit of intuition. When one has as many years on the job as I do, one develops a sixth sense about these things."

"And Sir William Paltrow insisted that I be consulted, because the death is suspicious," Holmes said.

"Well, that too, but – wait!" Lestrade jerked as if his seat had just been electrified. "How in the blazes did you know about his involvement? I didn't tell you!"

Holmes tilted his head, looking out the window of our elegant conveyance. "Just an intuition, I suppose. One does develop these things after so much time in the game."

For a moment I thought the inspector might toss us from the carriage, which bore the coat of arms of the gentleman Holmes had named. Even with a slowly receding headache, I had worked out who was truly behind the summons.

"Very well. I might as well tell you all I know," Lestrade muttered. "You are absolutely insufferable at times."

Holmes accepted this as a compliment. "But I am always willing to give you the credit, Lestrade. We should have another half-hour before us. Do inform me of the particulars."

Though his feathers appeared well-ruffled, the representative of Scotland Yard launched into a thorough recitation.

"Professor Whittle was indeed a naturalist, a chum of Darwin's and other great men, though he never made much of a splash in the academic world himself, or so I'm told. Only taught for a few years at Cambridge. Then he inherited money, published a large volume on exotic animals, and spent the rest of his life puttering around in the jungles of the empire, collecting specimens for his scientific friends. His home is called

Hallowhill, and as best I could tell from the two times I was there, you'd be more comfortable sleeping in the greenhouse or the barn or the groundskeeper's cottage than the house itself. Old, run to seed, needs repair. I'd guess it costs too much to keep the plants warm to mind about the family."

Holmes raised a hand. "You've been to Hallowhill before today?"

"Yes. A week ago, Sir William made a complaint to my superiors and I was sent out to open an investigation. Sir William is Professor Whittle's neighbor, and rather fond of the old gentleman, which is more than I can say for Whittle's kith and kin. Seems that Whittle claimed to have seen a shadowy figure skulking around his greenhouse at night, and a pane of glass in the roof had been shattered. But when I got there, of course, there was no clue. The glass was broken but there were no discernible footprints, or ashes, or – "

"Inside or outside?"

Lestrade huffed, annoyed to be interrupted. "What do you mean?"

"Was the glass broken from the inside or the outside of the greenhouse?"

The inspector scowled. "I don't know. From the outside, I assume."

"You assume?"

"Well who would break glass from the inside? It's not as if a person is being kept prisoner in there. Nothing inside that greenhouse but fancy tropical plants, a few birds, that kind of thing. Sorry to disappoint you, Mr. Holmes, but there's no murderous pygmy running around."

Holmes sighed and signaled for Lestrade to continue.

"The nephews said their uncle was growing daft. He'd been that way, they claimed, ever since he came back from Brazil a year ago with Beatrisa in tow. He was always seeing shadows, hearing spooks, thinking someone was out to steal his prizes."

"Was anything missing from the greenhouse?" I asked.

"Not that the Professor could account for," Lestrade answered. "And I can't imagine why anyone would creep out into this lonely neighborhood just to swipe an orchid or two. You know how bad the weather was last week. A storm probably broke the glass."

"Is the greenhouse near any trees?" Holmes said. "Was there any debris found around it?"

Lestrade frowned again. "No . . . none at all."

Holmes rolled his eyes. "Then the storm is an unlikely culprit, unless it was far more intense than what we felt in London. And surely if lightning had struck the dwelling, the entire household would have been buzzing. Speaking of household – who is Beatrisa?"

"The source of much of the mischief, if I'm any judge," Lestrade said. "Whittle never married, but he adopted his two great-nephews, Jason and Reginald Whittle, when their parents were killed in a railroad accident. He sent them to Eton, then Oxford – hoped they'd amount to something, but they've been nothing but wastrels, at least to hear Sir William tell it. Half-a-dozen times, Whittle threatened to cut the lads out of his will, but they'd mend their ways just long enough to weasel back into the old fellow's good graces. There was also the advantage that Professor Whittle was rarely about long enough to admonish them. Then, when he returned from his trip to Brazil, it was with more than butterflies and palm trees in his baggage. He brought home a young woman – Beatrisa by name – who claims to be his daughter by a native lady he met while in the Amazon hunting butterflies, two decades ago."

"You doubt the validity of her claim?" Holmes asked.

Lestrade shrugged. "It's not my business to judge a man for his adventures in foreign fields. I suppose he knew she was his daughter, or at least believed it likely when he took responsibility for her. But I must say I don't see any English in her features. She's barely more than a savage, too dark-skinned, with markings on her cheeks and chin. She is the right age, though, and the professor was quite fond of her."

"Fond enough to change his will?" I said.

Lestrade smirked. "You have an evil mind, Doctor, and you may well be on the right scent! Sir William confided to me that Whittle said he had recently revised his will. But the professor wouldn't tell his noble friend exactly how he reworked it. I suppose that only the old man's solicitor knows the truth, and he is currently in France! Otherwise, I would have woken him up as well – spread the suffering around a bit."

Holmes noted that we were approaching Hallowhill. "One final question – how is the lady's English?"

"Broken at best. As I said, she's still trying to learn our ways. According to the nephews, she'd never even worn decent skirts before the professor took her in."

"She has no maid or companion?"

"None that I am aware of."

The wane winter's sun had just begun to throw weak illumination as the carriage pulled up to the front of a rather decrepit Georgian house, all soured bricks and slate grey tiles, the entry flanked by a pair of lichen-coated statues of dogs. The steps were warped, the door needed paint. A butler with a long, sad visage ushered us inside.

"Best we speak with briefly Sir William and the family first," Lestrade said, after refusing to surrender his greatcoat. "But I know your ways, Mr. Holmes. You'll be eager to see the body. I've stationed two of my men out there. We threw a blanket over the corpse for decency's sake, but nothing else has been moved or altered."

Holmes nodded his acquiescence, though I could tell by his expression that he would have preferred to go directly to the scene. The butler, who gave his names as Yates, directed us to a downstairs parlor.

I knew Sir William from his pictures: He was a tall, regal man with a mane of silvery hair, formerly a royal official in India, and a noted writer of travel pieces for the best magazines. Though his eyes were red-lined, he had clearly subdued his own distress to hold mastery over the situation. This was perhaps a blessing, as the two other gentlemen in the room appeared incapable of any respectable emotion. They were perhaps in their thirties and bore every sign of dissolute living, from their long, unkempt hair to their sagging bellies and pasty skin with broken veins tracing unwholesome red maps across their noses. Neither had bothered to properly dress, but instead lounged about in dressing gowns and carpet slippers. Reginald puffed on a cigarette, while Jason had to quickly put aside a glass that contained some libation much stronger than coffee or tea. Neither offered a hand as introductions were made.

"I do regret that you were be brought into this matter, Mr. Holmes" Reginald drawled. "It was only at our *friend's* insistence."

"And surely, Sir William," Jason added, with a curled lip and a dark look at his elder, "you knew Uncle's advanced age?"

Sir William's expression made it clear he would like nothing better than to turn both of the nephews over his knee and administer a sharp caning, despite their years.

"I knew your uncle was in remarkable health for a man of his decades, with a clear mind and a strong will. True, he had begun to show some frailty in his legs, and his eyes were bad, but there was absolutely nothing wrong with his wits."

Jason snorted. "He was jumping at shadows, imagining that someone was out to destroy his life's work – as if anyone actually cared about that queer collection besides himself."

"You are referring to his greenhouse?" Holmes asked.

"Yes, and there's nothing in it except – Oh, there you are! About time! How long does it take to fetch a few biscuits, you stupid wench?"

A young woman had entered the parlor, bearing a tray of food and a pot of coffee. Reginald snatched it away from her. She simply dropped her head and drifted, ghost-like, to a chair in the corner.

She was a remarkable figure, completely at odds with the frayed carpets, tarnished mirrors, and worn furniture of the room. Her dress was in the latest fashion, brilliantly colored in purple and green, with a sapphire broach at her throat and delicate boots peeking out beneath her voluminous

317

skirts. But her thick, coarse black hair was worn loose and flowed almost to the floor, with a distinct curtain of it cut across her brow. Her skin was red-brown, and her features were those of a South American aboriginal, with inky black eyes and a compressed mouth. Strange tattoos drooped from her lips and accented her sharp cheekbones. Her earlobes had been stretched and deformed, so that they hung almost to her shoulders. As Lestrade had observed, there was nothing English about her, no hint of mixed blood. Indeed, the only thing that marked her as belonging to our nation was her dress.

Holmes stepped forward, executing a polite bow and reaching for her hand.

"Miss Beatrisa Whittle, I presume? I am most sorry for your loss."

She flinched instinctively, then looked up at my friend with wondering eyes as he kissed her fingertips. Her lips trembled. I sensed that no one in the house, besides her father, had ever treated her with any of the kindness or the civility due her sex.

"Thank you . . . sir."

"We'd better be getting outside, to view the scene," Lestrade muttered. "If I could ask everyone to remain in this room, we will be back shortly."

"Sir William could be of assistance to us," Holmes said, "if he does not mind going out in the cold?"

"I will be glad to help," the gentleman said, signaling for the butler to retrieve his coat. As we walked down a long central hallway, he pointed out the great age of the house, and how it had been in the Whittle family for six generations. Once we had passed through the rear doorway, his words became frank and focused.

"It wouldn't surprise me if one or both of those ingrate nephews killed Lawrence. They've been furious ever since he came back with the girl. You see how they treat her, now that they are at liberty. Lawrence wouldn't tell me what exactly he planned to do with his will, but I have every suspicion he was finally cutting them out."

"Sirs!"

We all turned at the cry. It was Beatrisa, who had clearly run after us, huddling in the doorway without so much as a shawl. "Please . . . find Merridew. Cold . . . for him . . . very bad."

"And who is Merridew?" Holmes asked. Jason Whittle suddenly appeared, snatching the lady back inside. Sir William frowned.

"No doubt one of the exotic birds. Whittle had a dozen or more in the greenhouse. Come along."

The greenhouse stood in the middle of a courtyard formed by the wings of the home. It was not as large as I had expected, only about the size of a significant gazebo or bandstand. One large pane above the door was shattered, allowing the sharp wind to whistle in and whirl about the roof. A burly, gnarled man in a canvas coat stood just outside the door, stamping his booted feet against the cold.

"Beggin' your pardon, sirs, but when can I get about with cleaning up and replacing that pane?" he asked. "Professor Whittle might be dead and gone, but I know he'd want his life's work taken care of. Bunch of them sensitive plants will freeze if I don't get started."

Sir William waved the man aside. "We shall be done shortly, Burton. Go and tell the footmen to get ready to transport their master's body to his bedroom and summon the undertaker."

The man favored us with a sour look but trudged away obediently.

"The groundskeeper," Sir William said. "He's thoroughly unpleasant and has done nothing but complain since Lawrence returned from Brazil. I advised Lawrence to sack him a dozen times – he drinks excessively, but Lawrence said he was a good worker and could keep the greenhouse in order."

Holmes digested this information with a slight nod as we moved inside. With the large pane of glass above the door broken, the area had grown bitterly cold. There was a strange odor in the air, an unpleasant smell that assaulted my senses before a chill wind whirled through the broken glass and bore it away. I lifted my head and noted two bright parrots on a tree limb, huddled together, pitiful in their distress. I wondered which of them was Merridew. Holmes pointed toward the central burner.

"Why is it not ignited?"

"I asked the same question," Lestrade said, puffing out his chest a bit. "The groundskeeper said a part broke yesterday afternoon. He was supposed to go to London today, to find a replacement."

Just a few paces inside the doorway was the sad scene. Inspector Lestrade's men were standing at a respectful distance to a figure covered with a darken woolen cloth. The body rested below the broken glass pane, in the shadow of a sturdy palm tree. At a signal from the inspector, the policemen lifted the blanket.

The cause of death seemed obvious: Large, jagged shards of glass had fallen into a long tray of soil, some of them coming to rest in an upright and perilous position, especially should an elderly individual be stumbling around in the darkness. Whittle's cane lay a short distance from his left arm, and his outstretched right hand showed that he had clearly tried to catch himself but failed. He had collapsed atop the largest of the broken glass pieces, which had sliced into his carotid artery. The amount of dried blood was conclusive, as was the wound. Elderly and frail as he was, death had come quickly.

"Who discovered him?" Holmes asked, crouching beside the corpse. The old man had was clad in nothing more than his flannel nightshirt and a loose Indian silk robe, with threadbare velvet slippers on his feet.

"The woman," Lestrade growled. "Her bedroom is across the hall from his. She said that he heard him leave his room at about three in the morning and became concerned when he didn't return in a few minutes. He had taken to the habit of going to the rear door of the house to check for 'prowlers' and 'ruffians'. Usually, a quick glance and a few deep breaths of cold air brought him back."

Holmes looked up at the broken pane and inquired as to the positioning of the old man's chamber. Sir William pointed it out. The professor's room had a large window overlooking the greenhouse.

"Perhaps he heard something that gave him the alarm," Lestrade added. "If only he had roused his nephews, this all would have been avoided. What is it, Mr. Holmes?"

My friend had gently brushed back the collar of the dead man's robe. Holmes gave a low whistle and, with great delicacy, pulled the fabric further down, directing our attention to what was revealed.

At the juncture of the professor's neck and shoulders were several distinctive marks, deep and small incisions, as if someone had driven sharp fingernails into his pale, fragile skin.

Lestrade hovered over Holmes. "My God! Why did I not see that? This changes everything!"

"And how so?" Holmes inquired, pulling out his lens to better examine the wounds.

"Why, it is as clear as day. Beatrisa must have followed him outside and hit him, knocking him onto the glass. That is the mark of her nails! The savage! I will arrest her immediately! Come along, men."

"Lestrade, wait!"

There was no use to protest. The inspector was racing through the greenhouse, slapping at the branches and vines, setting panicked parrots into flight. I saw one disappear through the broken glass. With a loud "See here!" Sir William gave chase toward the house. The policemen shrugged and languidly followed.

"Intriguing," Holmes whispered, returning to his examination of the marks. "Oh, let them go, Watson. I need just a few more moments to close my case."

I frowned, thinking that this was very damning to the lady. Perhaps she had learned that she was indeed an heiress and was tired of enduring abuse at the hands of her ungracious cousins. An accident to the old gentleman might be readily accepted by all, and Beatrisa would be in control of the house, able to remove her obnoxious relations.

"Did she also break that glass?" Holmes asked me. There was no point in asking him how he had followed the trail of my thoughts. "Admittedly she seems strong enough, but to do so would have required a ladder and some blunt instrument – the glass above the door is much too sturdy to have been shattered by the mere throwing of a stone. And there is the curious incident of the conveniently malfunctioning burner. But come – there is no need to wait any longer. Lestrade will have worked himself into a frothing fury by now."

Lestrade, Sir William, and the two constables had entered the house, but Burton remained just outside the greenhouse door, along with the shivering footmen.

"Can we move things along now, Mr. Detective?" he growled. Holmes halted.

"This is the second time greenhouse glass was shattered," my friend said. "What is your sense of the first time it occurred? Was it deliberate?"

The man tugged on his scraggly, tobacco-stained beard. "Probably the work of those tramps about the neighborhood. Seen a few of them sleeping rough. Guess they thought it would be warm enough in that greenhouse. 'Course, once they got a whiff of it, they changed their minds."

His comment caused Holmes to raise a brow, but my friend did not speak. I wondered how strong the odor I had noted upon entering the greenhouse would have been, without the chilly air diffusing it.

Giving a curt nod, Holmes led us back into the house. We could hear raised voices, the sound of a terrible row.

"Let us hope your medical services are not required," Holmes said, gently tugging me into the lead. With some reluctance, I pushed through the door.

The poor young woman was prostrate on the rug, sobbing as if her heart would break. Sir William had interposed himself between Beatrisa and Inspector Lestrade, while the two policemen stood awkwardly in a corner. Jason and Reginald Whittle lurked behind the sofa, glaring down at their young relative. If murder could have been accomplished with eyes alone, the woman would have been lying in a pool of blood.

"Of course, she did it!" Jason shouted, just as we stepped inside. "Look at her – she's nothing but a damned savage. Her people are headhunters, I've heard!"

"Headhunters and cannibals," Reginald echoed. "Have you checked for a weapon? Father brought clubs home with him from Brazil – maybe she used one of those."

"No! Me love Papa!" the pitiful creature cried. She had to struggle for her words between hiccups of terror. "Love Papa! No hurt him! He dead when I find him!"

"A likely story," Lestrade said. "I've seen the wounds. A woman's nails made them. You clawed at his back and knocked him into the glass."

"This – this is an outrage!" Sir William said, his long face now flushed with emotion. "This poor child has lost the only person she has in the world, and you accuse her of his murder! I suggest you look a bit more closely. If there was anyone who had a motive to kill my friend, it would be one or both of his nephews."

The men began to sputter protests in unison. Beatrisa curled up, the picture of misery, clasping her knees to her chest like a child. I looked for Holmes, and found him standing by a bookshelf, peering down at a ponderous work on biology. This hardly seemed like the time for reading.

"Well, I know what my eyes tell me," Lestrade said, "and they say I see a murderess before me. Constable, give me your darbies."

Holmes snapped the book's sides together. The act rang like a pistol shot in the room.

"Lestrade, if you lay one finger upon this lady, your men will have to arrest me as well," my friend said.

"On what charge?"

"For assault on an officer. Touch her and I will put you on the floor."

A terrible silence descended in the small room. Lestrade stepped back from his victim.

"Here now, Mr. Holmes," he snarled. "I give you more latitude than I should, but there is no reason – "

" – For you to inflict any more distress upon this poor lady," Holmes finished. "I am going to step back outside. I will return shortly. Watson, please see to her comfort. And someone get the fire stoked up."

With that, my friend was gone from the room. I gently raised Beatrisa to her feet, helping her to the sofa. She eagerly claimed the fresh handkerchief I pulled from my sleeve.

"The man is mad," Jason Whittle whispered to the inspector. "He threatened you!"

"Aye," Lestrade said, and I could sense his discomfort. He did not appreciate Holmes's words, but their relationship had been a long and, for him, profitable one. He dared not react out of pique and ruin a case. As ineffective as Lestrade was, he wanted justice for the poor old man in the greenhouse and knew that Holmes was his best means of acquiring it. He turned and snapped at his underlings to stoke up the fireplace, which had been woefully underfed.

Sir William moved to the sofa, offering his hand to Beatrisa.

"Do not worry, child. Mr. Holmes may seem an odd person, but he will get to the truth."

Reginald grumbled a curse, then caught his brother's arm and towed him into a corner, their heads nearly pressed together. I wondered whether I should part them, to prevent some dark plotting of mischief or revenge. But at just that moment, Holmes strolled back into the room. He had something in his arms, covered by the blanket that had once shielded Whittle's body.

"What the blazes is that?" Jason demanded.

"It is the murder weapon. Or, if you prefer, the murderer himself."

Holmes threw back the cloth, revealing what he held.

It was a large, hideous lizard, with green scales and a thick hide, it's back covered with evil-looking fins. The monstrous thing's whip-like tail dragged almost to the floor. Its feet were capped with long, frightful nails, and even from a distance I could smell the unpleasant odor that its body emitted. It was as if Holmes held a dragon's hatching in his arms. Beatrisa gave a cry.

"Merridew!"

The beast appeared dead. It was stiff and made no response to Holmes's handling of it.

"A green iguana, native to South America, and an unusually large one. No doubt it was Whittle's greatest prize, as he had organized his greenhouse to its comfort. Indeed, the hot glass box was paradise for the creature – until the pane of glass was broken, and the cold air came in. Iguanas are not inclined to English winter."

Holmes set the fiendish lizard before the fireplace.

"Had anyone bothered to give the professor's wounds more than a cursory examination," my friend continued, "they would have noticed that their spacing and depth prevented them from having been made by a woman. However, they are a perfect fit for the claws of this species."

Jason peered around the sofa. "The lizard killed him?"

"Not intentionally," Holmes said. "If you will observe, our cold-blooded friend has gone into something of a catatonic state. This is a survival mechanism, which – according to Whittle's own book upon the subject – allows them to endure the occasional dip of temperature within their environment. However, once the lizard goes into this strange stupor, he loses his grip upon a branch or tree trunk. Surely, Lestrade, you noted the palm tree just above the professor's body? Our lizard friend was perched there. The professor was roused by the sound of breaking glass and came out in hopes of finding his pet before it perished. As he crouched, no doubt calling to it, the iguana slipped into unconsciousness and plummeted onto the frail old gentleman's shoulders, knocking him into the glass, with fatal consequences. The fall jarred the creature from his sleep, and as the lizard scrambled away, his claws bit into the professor's back, leaving those incriminating marks. But the greenhouse grew colder and so the lizard returned to his hibernation. I found him tucked beneath a large fern, which has also been a casualty of the cold weather."

Beatrisa rose from the sofa and knelt beside the ugly creature, stroking its repulsive hide.

"Poor Merridew, poor . . . look!"

The lizard's eyes had opened. A long, slimy tongue flicked out of his jaws.

"Ah, he rouses," Holmes chuckled. "Will you arrest him, Lestrade?"

The inspector snorted. "I'd be the laughing-stock of Scotland Yard. Clearly, this was all a tragic accident!"

"In which case, I believe you owe Miss Beatrisa an apology. I trust you are gentleman enough to make it. Watson and I must take a quick detour, and then we shall be ready to depart."

"Where are you – "

Lestrade did not get to finish his question, for at just that moment Merridew came fully to life and scrambled across the floor. The Whittle nephews screamed louder than any terrified pair of maidens, leaping onto chairs to avoid the clumsy beast's attack. The constables made for the bookcase ladder and the window seat. Lestrade scrambled onto the back of sofa with the agility of a circus rider mounting his steed.

I think I would have enjoyed watching the farce, but Holmes was escorting me from the room with a grim warning.

"Our job is not finished," he said softly.

"But you said the lizard caused Professor Whittle's fall."

"Yes, but who caused the lizard's fall? The greenhouse window didn't break itself. I think, Watson, that a brief interview is in order."

"But . . . who are we . . . ."

Holmes was walking fast, and my question was lost in the howling winter wind. We made our way down a wide lawn and over to a cottage that was tucked into the shadow of the forest behind the house. Holmes halted for a moment and, with the merest flick of a finger, drew my attention to a stout ladder and a mallet that had been abandoned beside a shed, just a short distance away from the cottage. Silently, Holmes pressed on and knocked on the door, opening it before he could be properly answered.

Burton sat inside at a rough-hewn table, still wrapped in his canvas coat. He glared at us as we entered.

"What do you gents want? We brought the professor up. There's nothing more that can be done for him . . . God rest his soul."

"Yes. *Requiesce in pace*."

Holmes sat in the chair opposite to Burton, stretching his feet toward the fire. "I have it from good authority that you have an appreciation for a refreshing libation, Mr. Burton."

The man grunted, clearly uncomfortable and uncertain of what Holmes was implying. My friend drew a silver flask from inside his coat.

"I also am something of a connoisseur of invigorating beverages. I have, in this flask, a sample of a rather potent Irish whiskey. I employ it to 'keep out the cold', and we must both admit that it is an exceptionally chilly morning."

Holmes took a rough mug from the table and poured the flask's contents into it. Burton licked his lips, his eyes beginning to shine. Holmes lifted the mug but paused before drinking. He put it down on the table before Burton's eager gaze.

"It is yours, if you can but confirm a few deductions of mine."

"I – I will do my best."

"Very well. You gained a comfortable position here at Hallowhill after your wife died. You did very little in the way of maintenance of the grounds, but your employers didn't care, for they were far more interested in carousing in London than in the appearance of the family estate. Unfortunately, a year ago the true owner, Professor Whittle, returned. He ordered you to make repairs to the greenhouse. You worked night and day, and at the end of your labors, the professor installed his exotic plants and birds into the chamber. This was acceptable – it would be far easier to tend to a garden inside a warm room than scattered about the manor. There was just one problem, and that was Merridew."

The rough man started. His shoulders began to quiver.

"You hated the creature. It was monstrous in appearance, foul-smelling, requiring constant care and cleaning of its limited space. The reek of the thing was more than you could stand. But you dared not leave – you are well past your prime and have a bad reputation in the neighborhood for your drunkenness. No one would hire you. Yet the lizard was – "

"An *abomination*," Burton growled. "I told the professor, nothing that ugly could be of God. The devil made it – it was an unholy beast – it was Satan's lapdog! But the professor wouldn't listen."

Holmes nodded slowly, inching the mug toward Burton's curled, crabbed fingers. "Somehow – perhaps an overheard conversation – you learned how cold could kill this 'abomination'. You thought how easy it would be to break a pane of glass and blame it on a tramp. You were trying to murder the iguana, not its master."

Burton sniffed. "I thought the first time, when the copper came, that the beast had slipped out, had maybe run off in the road and been killed. But the professor found it under the bushes. The damned thing – it was just . . . sleeping."

Holmes pushed the earthen cup into Burton's hand. "You never meant to harm your master."

"No. No, I swear to God and all the saints . . . I just wanted that damned beast to die!"

"Drink," Holmes urged, and the man swallowed the draught in one gulp. "You will be relieved to know that Miss Beatrisa Whittle has been cleared of the crime."

The man began to weep. "I wouldn't have let them take her away, I promise. She's a good girl, for being from a savage race. She's always been kind to me. I promise, I would have spoken out, just . . . . Does the devilish thing still live?"

Holmes rose. "I suggest that if you wish your actions to be dealt with leniently, you take a vow never to harm Merridew again. The lady, like her father, is much attached to him."

I followed my friend from the cottage, leaving Burton weeping into his folded arms. I looked toward the sad edifice of Hallowhill. The sun had just begun to clear away the thick clouds, and a tepid ray of light shown down into the glass panes of the greenhouse. A brightly colored bird flitted overhead, and I was relieved to see it find its way back through the opening into the meager shelter of the tropical chamber.

"Holmes," I asked, "how did you know Burton was a widower?"

"A magician must not reveal *all* his tricks, Watson. But you see what becomes of a good man, inclined by nature to matrimony, who loses a spouse? You see how easily he falls into snares, loses his way, even takes to drink? It is a pitiful tale."

My eyes narrowed. It was difficult at times to be Holmes's friend, to accept that he would always understand more about me than I knew about myself. But I digested the words in the spirit they were offered, for Holmes was, indeed, the wisest man I had ever known. By the next morning, I had returned home, and could sleep until almost noon in my own warm, good bed. My dear wife smiled when I told her the entire story.

"I will not write this one, I fear," I said to her. "Sir William Paltrow swore Holmes to secrecy for the sake of the family name, and Lestrade is unwilling to tell his superiors that he nearly arrested an innocent heiress when the cold-blooded murderer was actually the intended victim!"

"But what a fascinating tale it would make," she said, her smile lighting her entire face. I touched her soft cheek, thinking of how Holmes had described the culprit in his *Index*.

"Holmes referred to the creature as 'Merridew of abominable memory'! Shall I write this story just for you, my dear?"
"Yes, John. Please do!"

> *"My collection of M's is a fine one. Moriarty himself is enough to make any letter illustrious, and here is Morgan the poisoner, and Merridew of abominable memory . . . ."*

> – Sherlock Holmes
> "The Adventure of the Empty House

The Affair of the
Hellingstone Rubies
by Margaret Walsh

It was a warm summer's afternoon when the messenger came from Mycroft Holmes that led us into one of the strangest cases of my long association with Mr. Sherlock Holmes.

I was once more residing in our rooms in Baker Street, as my wife had ventured to the countryside to nurse an ill friend. Holmes and I had slid back into our congenial relations of old and were perusing the newspapers when the messenger arrived.

It seemed there was nothing in the papers except for reports the extraordinary jewel thefts from Calcroft House in Dorset. It was a puzzle, I felt, that would interest Holmes, but so far he had shown little inclination to pursue it, nor had his assistance been sought. That was about to change.

The young man that Mrs. Hudson showed to our door was dressed in the livery of the Diogenes Club. He handed the envelope he was carrying to Holmes without a word. Holmes read the contents then looked at the lad. "Tell my brother that we shall be there as requested."

The lad nodded, turned around and marched out of our rooms.

I looked to where Holmes had carelessly discarded the missive. It bore Mycroft's distinctive handwriting and simply read: "*Diogenes Club. Six o'clock.*"

"Short and to the point, eh Watson?"

"Not very informative," I agreed.

Holmes glanced at the clock. "Well, we haven't long to wait." With that he returned to reading the papers and, after a moment, I did the same.

At six o'clock precisely we arrived at the Diogenes Club and were shown into the Stranger's Room, where Mycroft was waiting for us, along with a tall, well-dressed man with dark blonde hair and well-trimmed beard, and with a worried, careworn, expression on his otherwise handsome face.

"Sherlock! Doctor! Good of you both to come." Mycroft handed us both a glass of brandy and waved us to the chairs set out for us. The unknown man was already seated, toying absently with his own glass of brandy.

Mycroft took his seat before saying, "This is Percival Calcroft, M.P. He has a problem that needs your skills, Sherlock."

"You mean the mysteriously disappearing jewellery." Holmes said.

I noted that the man, Percival Calcroft, flinched perceptibly at Holmes's words.

"Indeed," Mycroft said.

"Why are you interesting yourself in jewel thefts, Brother, no matter how mysterious?" Holmes asked. His tone was curious. "After all, it is hardly a matter of grave importance to Her Majesty's Government."

"Not to Her *Government*," Mycroft agreed.

Holmes looked sharply at his brother. "But of importance to Her *Majesty*?"

Mycroft nodded. "The last theft was of a ruby necklace – "

"The Helingstone Rubies," I said, pleased to be able to add something to the conversation. "It was in the paper today. A matched necklace of exquisite blood red rubies. "

Mycroft nodded. "The necklace was gifted to Her Majesty by the late Colonel Bertram Helingstone. Her Majesty had loaned the necklace to a distant cousin of hers to wear at a ball at Calcroft House."

Percival Calcroft groaned and placed his head in his hands. "I am ruined!"

"When was the necklace last seen?" Holmes asked.

"Just before the ball," Calcroft replied, his voice muffled by his hands. "Lady Alexandrina's maid had taken the necklace from its safety box and placed in on the dressing table prior to dressing her mistress. The girl was called into another part of the suite to fetch something for her mistress. When she came back, the necklace had gone."

"No one came to the suite?"

Calcroft raised his head. "No, Mr. Holmes. Nor could anyone have got into the room via the windows. Lady Alexandrina had the Coral Suite on the fourth floor. The window was open to catch the sea breeze, but no one could possibly have climbed up the wall. They would have been seen, for one thing."

"Interesting," Holmes commented.

"Will you take the case, Sherlock?" Mycroft asked.

"When I thought it to be simply a case of jewel theft, I would have said no," Holmes admitted. "But your story intrigues me greatly."

"You will come to Calcroft House?" Percival Calcroft was almost pathetically eager.

"I will come." Holmes looked at me, eyebrows raised.

"And I also," I said. "If you think I can be of use to you, Holmes," I added.

"I doubt there will ever be a time when you aren't of use to me, my friend." He turned to his brother. "Can you get me a list of all the other jewellery that has also been stolen?"

Mycroft took a folded sheet of paper from his pocket and handed it to his brother without comment.

Holmes tucked into his own jacket pocket. "I shall study this at my leisure. Mr. Calcroft, if it suits you, Watson and I will come down to Calcroft House in a day or so."

"Certainly, Mr. Holmes." Percival Calcroft looked as if a great weight had been removed from his shoulders. "You can take the train to Swanage and I will send a carriage to collect you from the station. Calcroft House is near Worth Matravers, which is west of Swanage. A cab would bring you out, but it would cost you a fortune."

The man got to his feet, now smiling, and with a definite spring in his step, took his leave from us.

When he had gone, Mycroft looked at his brother. "Thank you, Sherlock. Her Majesty is most upset."

Holmes waved a hand in a self-deprecating manner. "The puzzle interests me, Mycroft, no more than that. Pray do not read any unnecessary altruistic motives into my agreement." He looked more closely at his brother. "What do you know about the inhabitants of Calcroft House?"

"Apart from Percival Calcroft, there is his wife, Annabelle. She is the youngest daughter of Lord Aubrey Derwent. No children." Mycroft paused to gather his thoughts. "The other permanent resident is Percival's younger brother, Peregrine. Peregrine was a bit of a scapegrace as a youngster. Went to Asia to make his fortune."

"And did he?" Holmes asked.

Mycroft nodded. "He came back with a fortune made from trading in Oriental art from China and Japan, and he continues to deal in artworks on the Continent. Peregrine travels several times a year to France."

"Interesting," Holmes commented, "But probably not useful."

We took our leave from Mycroft and headed out into the gathering dusk. Holmes was in a hurry to return home, so, much to my regret, we hailed a cab rather than walk. I felt it a great pity. Whilst London can be dangerous, and is almost always noxious, there are few places as pleasant to walk about in as the capital on a pleasant summer's evening.

Back in the Baker Street rooms, Holmes settled himself in to study the list that Mycroft had supplied to him. I contented myself with finishing the newspapers that I had begun before our summons.

Finally, Holmes threw the papers onto the table with a sigh.

I looked up. "Did you gain anything?"

"Not a thing, except for the fact that the pieces taken were all quite large. Heavy necklaces and bracelets."

I frowned. "Wouldn't those be the logical things to take?"

Holmes shook his head. "Too hard to smuggle out of the house. Jewel thieves tend to take things that are easily concealable, such as rings and ear-rings, or even tie-pins. Things that can be tucked into coat linings without creating a noticeable bulge." He looked across at me. "This case should prove to be extremely interesting."

Holmes spent the next day finding out what he could about the occupants of Calcroft House from sources other than Mycroft, though he wasn't inclined to share his information with me. Due to his reluctance to confide in me I suspected that what little he had found had come from Langdale Pike.

Langdale Pike – not his real name, you can be quite sure of that – was a society gossip-monger of whom I disapproved. Gossip has never interested me and I find the mere idea of dealing in it as if it was some form of commodity extremely distasteful. Holmes had no such reluctance. Indeed I suspected his friendship with Pike, if that is what it was, predated his friendship with me. At this remove, I'm prepared to admit that there may have been a slight tinge of jealousy in my attitude towards Pike.

The day after that we woke early and headed to Waterloo Station to catch a London and South Western Railway service to Swanage. The train took us through Surrey and through England's ancient capital of Winchester. We couldn't go directly to Swanage – the Dorchester line on which we were traveling bypassed it. We alighted at Wareham and got on a branch service that took us to Swanage.

It was originally little more than a fishing village, and a supplier of fine Purbeck marble, but under the encouragement of local businessmen John Mowlem and George Burt, it had flourished into a charming tourist town akin to Eastbourne. There were more than a few people on the branch line train, and the platform was extremely crowded when we arrived.

Gathering our luggage, we hastened out of the station. I paused to breathe in the cool, crisp, sea air. Holmes was looking around for Percival Calcroft's coachman. As it turned out, Calcroft himself came to meet us. I spotted him striding towards us.

He held out his hand to both of us. "Thank you for coming, gentlemen." We were led to where a fine carriage waited nearby. The coachmen loaded our luggage and we joined Calcroft inside. It took him a while to extract us from the crowd around the station, but we soon set off at a brisk pace out of town.

"I thought it best to come with Alfred," Calcroft said, a wave of his hand indicating that Alfred was the coachman. "With the nice weather bringing so many people out, I felt he wouldn't easily find you. I, at least, have the advantage of knowing what you both look like."

Calcroft was practically beaming with delight. "I cannot tell you how relieved I am that you've both come. Everything will be all right now." His childlike confidence in my friend was as endearing as it was worrying.

Holmes held up a hand. "As my good friend Watson here will tell you, I'm not infallible. There is no guarantee that I'll find the jewel thief, though if I can discover how the thefts are carried out, then I'll know who is responsible."

"Just your being here, Mr. Holmes, takes a great weight off my mind," Percival Calcroft replied.

We passed through the village of Worth Matravers. It was a pretty place, with cottages and farm houses constructed out of limestone built around a large duck pond. It was the sort of place that poets tend to call idyllic. The people seemed prosperous and content. More than one waved cheerfully when they spotted the coach.

Once through the village, the carriage swung off the main road and bounced down a slightly less-well-maintained one. We passed through a charming wooded park, and I could tell that we were heading towards the sea. As we came out through the trees, I gaped in astonishment at the sight that met my eyes. A large manor house sat on a prominent position near the cliffs. It was built of some light-coloured stone that gleamed in the sunlight. It was so bright that it almost hurt to look upon it.

Calcroft noticed my reaction and chuckled softly. "That is Calcroft House, Doctor Watson. What do you think of it?"

To be truthful, I couldn't see it clearly enough to form an opinion, honest or otherwise.

"It is certainly bright," Holmes commented.

"The locals call it Calcroft's Lighthouse, or simply, the Light House, because of the way it reflects the sunlight," Calcroft said. "My great-great-grandfather built it out of local limestone and chert. It has more than the usual number of windows as well. He wanted plenty of light and sea air inside. I believe he was troubled by his chest. At least, that's what my father said." He gave the house a look that was almost affectionate. "It is a monster to heat in the winter, but the rest of the year it's pleasant enough."

The carriage drew up in front of the building, which was, thankfully, not nearly so bright as when one was close to it.

We climbed down from the carriage and Calcroft took us inside, where his wife was waiting to greet us, along with a man, who by his resemblance to our host, I took to be his brother, Peregrine. Introductions were made and the butler, a stiff-spined, stone-faced individual by the name of Hopkins, showed us to our rooms on the third floor.

The room I was given was spacious, bright, and airy. I saw what Percival Calcroft meant about an unusual number of windows. The exterior wall was comprised almost entirely of several extremely large windows that gave out onto views of the English Channel. The air was filled with the cries of sea birds, and I noted that there seemed to be a colony of shags or cormorants, along with seagulls and terns, making their homes on the cliff and in the rocks below.

Hopkins tapped upon my door and I accompanied him back downstairs, where we joined the Calcrofts in a comfortable parlour where tea was waiting. I allowed Hopkins to serve me a cup of tea and a selection of sandwiches, and settled back into a well-upholstered chair.

It was then that I observed the presence of another person: A well-dressed young woman with dark hair, brown eyes that sparkled with merriment, and a well-placed dimple, who sat beside Mrs. Calcroft. She was introduced to us as Miss Cynthia Taverner, the cousin of a colleague of our host who had come to Dorset for the benefit of her health. I couldn't forebear raising my eyebrows. In truth, there seemed to be little, if anything, actually wrong with the woman. She appeared to be the picture of rude health. I looked at Holmes who, when our hosts weren't looking, winked at me. I made a mental note to myself to ask him what he knew about Miss Taverner, as he didn't seem at all surprised by her appearance.

After tea, our host excused himself and handed us over to his brother for a tour of the house. Holmes gave every appearance of being interested in the furnishings and ornaments, but I knew him well enough to know that all he was really interested in was solving the puzzle.

Peregrine Calcroft was a genial man, bluff and hearty, as he showed us around, and every inch the English country gentleman. "It's a fine house, what? A grand place for a lad to grow up, that is for sure." He beamed at me and swept his arm in a wide arc towards the cliffs. "Can you think of a finer place for a boy, Doctor Watson?"

"In truth, Mr. Calcroft, I cannot," I replied. "The sea air would be most beneficial."

We were standing just inside Peregrine Calcroft's own rooms, which were on the same floor as ours. He had shown us everywhere within the house, including the suite that comprised the personal apartments of his brother and his wife, which I for one, felt was a trifle odd. He had even dragged us through the servant's quarters.

Holmes had wandered towards the window and was staring at something just outside it. We joined him and I saw, with some puzzlement, that the object of Holmes's interest was a smallish wooden platform that had been affixed to the windowsill.

Holmes turned to Peregrine Calcroft with raised eyebrows.

The man fidgeted and looked faintly embarrassed. "I feed the squirrels, Mr. Holmes. They live in the trees in the park. But there isn't much food around for the poor things, so I help out a bit."

"That is very kind of you," I said into the awkward silence.

"Not very manly, though, is it, Doctor?" Peregrine said.

"I have never been one to subscribe to the theory that kindness is an exclusively feminine attribute," Holmes said. "Thank you for the tour, Mr. Calcroft. I think Watson and I will take a short walk before dinner." He turned and walked out of the room.

I hurriedly took my leave and hastened after Holmes.

It wasn't until we were walking in the park that I was able to get him to speak.

"What on earth was that about?"

"Hmm?"

"Your behaviour in Peregrine Calcroft's rooms was quite odd. Feeding squirrels on a platform outside his window may be unusual, but it is hardly a crime."

Holmes stopped and looked at me. "I may not know much about the natural world, Watson, but I do know one thing."

"What is that, Holmes?"

"Squirrels do not eat fish."

On that cryptic note he continued walking and refused to say another word on the subject.

I refused to allow Holmes's odd behaviour to disturb me. I walked beside him in the warm afternoon sunshine and found myself relaxing with the combination of gentle warmth and refreshing sea breeze. We walked for perhaps an hour, with Holmes pausing from time to time to examine a tree or two. I assumed he was looking for signs of squirrels and refrained from commenting. I was sure that if I said something, I would receive a statement along the lines of, "You see, but you do not observe".

We had turned back from the woods and by unspoken mutual agreement headed for the cliffs. The view was spectacular. If I squinted, I could discern a vague smudge on the horizon that I took to be France. I had to agree with Peregrine Calcroft – this was indeed a fine place for a boy to grow up. Relaxed and feeling somewhat content, regardless of the reason for our being here, I begin to whistle a merry air – an old Scots song: *"Charlie He's My Darling"*. It had always been a favourite of mine.

As we turned back towards the house, a flash of black swooped at me. I swore loudly and ducked as a large black bird came at me. Then it flew away. I admit I was shaken. Holmes came and stood beside me, gazing after the departing creature with an odd expression upon his face.

"God knows what possessed the blasted thing," I grumbled.

"Perhaps it didn't care for your whistling," Holmes said with a faint smile.

"An avian music critic?" I asked, brows raised.

The smile grew a hairs breadth wider. "There are stranger things, my friend, as we both well know."

I was in no mood now to continue with a walk. Holmes, sensing my mood, turned his steps back towards the house.

Even from close up, it was easy to see why the locals called it the Light House. In the late afternoon sun, it fairly gleamed. I was looking at the building and didn't notice Holmes stop and bend down and, as a consequence, I almost tripped over him.

Holmes straightened up and gave me an irritated look.

I glared at him. I was heading into an increasingly foul mood. I opened my mouth to snap at him, and then stopped when I perceived that he held something in his hand.

"What on earth is that?" I asked.

Holmes turned the object in his hand. It was a strip of leather, soft and worn smooth and tied in an odd loop. At one point the aged object had snapped, leaving the loop and two fraying ends. I was puzzled by it, but I failed to see why it held such interest for Holmes. "A bootlace?" I suggested, unable to think of any other purpose for a thin strip of worn leather.

Holmes tucked it into his pocket. "Not a bootlace, my dear Watson. A very valuable clue."

"A clue? You mean you already have an idea as to how these thefts have been carried out?" I was almost shocked. To my knowledge, we had seen nothing that could possibly lead us to the thief.

Holmes chuckled drily. "Indeed. It isn't even the first clue."

"Is it not? What was the first?"

"Squirrels," Holmes replied before walking on towards the house.

I stared after him, completely bemused. Holmes looked back over his shoulder. "Hurry along. We must change for dinner."

I swore to myself and then followed after him. There were times when Holmes was the most infuriating man on earth. This was one of them.

Dinner at Calcroft House was quite a formal affair, if somewhat unbalanced with men outnumbering the women. It took place in a formal dining room that showed signs of recent renovation. New drapes of burgundy velvet hung at the windows, and the table was draped in cloths of a matching shade.

The butler, Hopkins, and assorted footmen came and went with a number of excellent dishes. The main course was a fine Baron of Beef served with roasted potatoes, carrots and parsnips, green beans, and a rich, thick gravy. English cooking at its finest. Everyone paid due attention to their meal, and there was little talk until we reached the final stage of the meal, which was a cheese board comprising some quite excellent local cheeses.

I couldn't help but see that Miss Taverner, the woman who was staying there for her health, was wearing a rather large and ornate sapphire pendant. The jewel was the size of a quail's egg and set in a heavy mount of gold on a broad gold chain. To my mind it seemed a little out of keeping with the tone of the dinner to be wearing such an ostentatious piece.

Our host was eyeing the necklace almost nervously. "I do hope you have good strong box for that, Miss Taverner. I would be quite distraught should it be stolen. Not to mention embarrassed."

Miss Taverner laughed – a gay, tinkling sound. "Don't be concerned. I'll place it on my bedside table overnight and lock it away properly before I leave. It won't be out of my sight for long. Besides, isn't Mr. Holmes here to ensure no more jewels go missing?"

Holmes briefly acknowledged the conversation before cutting himself a wedge of a very fine Stilton, taking a small bite from it before turning to Peregrine Calcroft to say, "I understand you spent time in Asia."

"Why yes, Mr. Holmes. In both China and Japan. Both countries have produced some quite good artworks that have their admirers here."

"I have a familiarity with both countries," Holmes said which, I own came as a complete surprise to me.

"Particularly around Linyi in Shandong Province in China," he continued, "and in Susaki in the Kochi Prefecture in Japan. Perhaps we may know people in common?"

Peregrine shook his head. "I'm afraid not, Mr. Holmes. In China I spent most of my time in Guilin in Guangxi Province, and in Japan I was in Asakura in Fukuoka Prefecture. Both are quite a reasonable distance from the places you mentioned." He smiled in a manner that was almost ingratiating. "But I would be delighted to hear of your adventures in those countries."

"Perhaps another time," Holmes demurred. "My reasons for being there weren't ones that are at all suitable to talk about in front of ladies." He nodded his head at our hostess and Miss Taverner.

"Another time then," Peregrine agreed.

The ladies withdrew from the table shortly afterwards, and we men went to the billiard room, except for Holmes, who pleaded fatigue and retired to bed. I saw that he stopped to have a word with a couple of the footmen before heading up the stairs. After several games of billiards with both our host and his brother, I too retired for the night.

Holmes and I were the first down for breakfast the next morning, though we were soon joined by Percival Calcroft and his wife. Good mornings were exchanged, but not another word was said as we helped ourselves to the food laid out in brightly polished silver chafing dishes on the sideboard.

I tucked into a plate of bacon, eggs, and devilled kidneys. Holmes filled his plate with coddled eggs and toast and sat beside me. I discerned that he didn't pay much attention to what he was eating. His entire focus was on the door to the breakfast room, which I thought was a little strange. I found myself watching the door as well, wondering exactly what it was that kept my friend's focus upon it. I wasn't kept in suspense for long.

Miss Taverner came to the door of the room and nodded briskly to Holmes. He got to his feet, startling our hosts.

"Is the breakfast not to your liking?" Calcroft asked.

"It is excellent, thank you. However, I think it's time that we apprehended the thief." Holmes pushed his chair back and walked to the door. After a moment of stunned silence, I followed, accompanied by Percival and Annabelle Calcroft.

Miss Taverner stood aside to let everyone out of the room and then followed us up the stairs.

Holmes led the way to a room that I recognized from the tour the previous day, that of Percival Calcroft's brother, Peregrine. Without so much as pausing to knock, Holmes threw the door open. Behind us I could hear Percival Calcroft's voice raised in complaint. How dare we intrude upon his brother! The complaints died as we all took in the scene in the room.

Peregrine Calcroft stood by the window gazing at us open-mouthed. In his left hand he held the sapphire pendant that Miss Taverner had been wearing the previous evening. In his right hand he held a fish – a fish that was taken from his unresisting hand by a large and decidedly impatient black bird that was sitting on the platform outside the open window.

Holmes strode across the room and took the sapphire from Peregrine's hand. The bird, not liking the crowd of humans around it, flew away towards the cliffs.

Peregrine Calcroft sank down onto his bed and placed his head in his hands, much as his brother had done in the Diogenes Club several days earlier.

Percival Calcroft stared at his brother. "Why?" His voice was anguished. "In God's name, why?"

Peregrine shook his head and wouldn't reply.

Holmes looked at me and tilted his head towards the door. I nodded and we quietly left the room, joining Miss Taverner in the hallway, where Holmes handed back the sapphire.

Annabelle Calcroft slipped into the room and stood staring at her brother-in-law, a comforting hand placed on her husband's shoulder.

Within the hour, Holmes and I, accompanied by Miss Taverner, had left the estate and were headed back to London.

It wasn't until several days later back in London, and in the comfortable confines of the Diogenes Club, that Holmes would deign to fully explain what had occurred. We were once again seated in the Stranger's Room with some of the club's excellent brandy.

"It was obvious," Holmes said, "that the thief had to be a member of the household. But not a servant."

"Why not a servant?" I asked.

"Too great a risk, Watson. Servant's belongings, and indeed their very persons, can be searched. In a situation like that, the only people who wouldn't be searched would be the family and guests. It was soon clear to me that it wasn't a guest."

Mycroft looked thoughtful. "Because there were never the same guests each time a theft occurred," he said.

"Exactly. Therefore, the thief had to be a member of the family. I thought it to be highly unlikely that an M.P. would be stealing from his guests. Nor his wife. Annabelle Calcroft's family is unusual amongst the English aristocracy: They are independently wealthy. Indeed, it was her father that financed her husband's run in politics. She is unlikely to be stealing jewels."

"Unless the poor lady suffers from kleptomania," I said.

Holmes waved his hand in a dismissive gesture. "Again, it is unlikely, though I admit I did consider the possibility. If that was the case, the kleptomania would most likely have manifested much earlier, and the lady's family would have placed her into an asylum rather than allow her to be married."

I thought about it for a moment, and then nodded. The class that Annabelle Calcroft belonged to was that which preferred to hide what it viewed as abnormalities behind high walls and securely locked doors.

338

Holmes was correct. If Annabelle Calcroft had been a kleptomaniac, her father would never have permitted her to wed – and he certainly wouldn't have funded her husband's foray into politics, an arena where private lives had a tendency to become public ones.

"That left the brother, Peregrine," Mycroft observed.

I frowned. "But did he didn't make a fortune selling Asian artworks? What possible need could he have to steal?"

Holmes lips twisted into a wry smile. "He did indeed make a fortune, my dear Watson. He also spent it rather quickly."

"How do you know that?" I asked.

"You know that I have contacts in interesting places," Holmes replied.

"Including clubs in St. James Street," Mycroft murmured.

"Then I was correct in my surmise," I said. "You did go to Langdale Pike."

Holmes nodded. "I did. And a pretty tale he had to tell me about Peregrine Calcroft, involving expensive brothels and even more expensive gaming clubs. The money the fellow made didn't last long."

"But the method of the thefts? How on earth did you work them out?"

"The first clue was the platform outside Peregrine Calcroft's window."

I though back. "After we left his room, you made that odd comment about fish. I admit I didn't observe any fish upon the platform."

"There was no fish," Holmes said, "but there were fish scales caught along the edge of the platform. That was the first pointer that Calcroft's brother was the culprit."

"He took a calculated risk letting you into the room, Sherlock," Mycroft said.

"Peregrine really didn't have any choice," Holmes replied. "We had been given the grand tour of the house and been shown everywhere else. If he had left his own room out of the tour, it would have looked suspicious."

Mycroft nodded thoughtfully.

Holmes continued, "Several things combined to convince me that Peregrine Calcroft had trained a *Phalacrocorax carbo*, or Great Cormorant, not to catch fish, as they do in parts of Asia, but to steal jewels."

"And those things were?" Mycroft asked.

"The size of the pieces stolen. It was only large necklaces or pendants, with the occasional large bracelet. Nothing small, such as ear-rings or tie-pins."

Mycroft frowned for a moment then expression cleared. "Of course, the bigger pieces would be difficult for a bird to swallow."

"Exactly, and Peregrine Calcroft made certain of it by using a throat snare."

"A what?" I asked.

"A throat snare. That's what we found near the cliffs. It confirmed for me what I was already beginning to suspect, that thief was familiar with the practice of fishing with cormorants. Peregrine Calcroft confirmed it himself at dinner."

I frowned as I thought back to the dinner that night. I couldn't recall anything being said about fishing or cormorants, and I said so.

Holmes sighed. "The places where Peregrine Calcroft admitted to having spent a great deal of time: Guilin in Guangxi province in China, and Asakura in Fukuoka Prefecture in Japan – both areas where cormorant fishing is common."

"There is a great deal of difference between fishing and jewel theft," Mycroft observed. "One comes naturally to the bird – the other does not."

"Very true," Holmes agreed. "I cannot prove it, but though a traditional throat snare was used to prevent the bird ingesting the ill-gotten gains, I suspect other methods were used to train this bird. For example, it seems logical that a particular song was whistled to call the bird to him."

"What song?" I asked.

"'*Charlie He's my Darling*'," Holmes replied. "Or something very similar."

"The song that I was whistling when the bird almost hit me!" I exclaimed.

"I don't think it was going to hit you, Watson. I suspect that it was coming in to *land* on you, when the poor creature realized that you weren't its master, and flew away in confusion – another thing that led me to the conclusion a bird was involved was the windows and alcohol."

I gave Holmes a bewildered look, totally unable to follow his thought processes.

"A few questions to the servants after dinner led me to understand that the common factor amongst the thefts was that the owners of the stolen jewels had all been a little less than restrained about how much they drank at dinner, leading to a certain carelessness with their belongings, and that in every instance of theft, the windows had been left open."

"So Peregrine Calcroft trained the bird to fly into the rooms and remove jewellery that was sitting out in the open." I shook my head. "It's astounding. How on earth was the bird trained?"

"How isn't germane," Mycroft observed, before Holmes could reply. "The main thing is that the thief has been caught."

Holmes nodded. "With his brother moving so swiftly after the theft of the Helingstone Rubies, Peregrine Calcroft didn't have the opportunity to get away to sell them."

"Where was he selling them?" I asked. "Surely all the thefts were covered in the newspapers? Any reputable jeweller – "

Holmes chuckled drily. "You know as well as I do that all jewellers aren't reputable, my friend. You remember that Mycroft told us that Peregrine Calcroft journeyed several times a year to France – ostensibly to visit with the contacts he made in the art world, but I suspect it was actually to sell the jewels that he had stolen. He certainly came back from each trip with more money than he left with." His lips twisted back into the wry smile of earlier, "And there is no need to remind me that when Mycroft gave me the information, I was of the opinion that it was probably not of use."

I frowned as another thought struck me, on how lucky we were that Miss Taverner had been present. I said as much to Holmes and Mycroft.

Holmes snorted. "Luck, my dear fellow, had absolutely nothing to do with it. Miss Taverner is a private enquiry agent. Langdale Pike sent me her way when it became obvious that we would need to catch the thief red-handed."

"And the sapphire pendant?" I asked.

"It did not belong to Miss Taverner," Holmes replied. "A jeweller on Bond Street for whom she had done some good work for in the past agreed to the loan of the item as bait." Holmes smiled. "She really is the cousin of another M.P., who was only too happy to help slide her into the household under false pretences."

"Freddie Taverner is game for just about anything," Mycroft commented.

"But what will happen now?" I asked. "Surely the scandal will wreck Percival Calcroft's career?"

"There will be no scandal," Mycroft said firmly. "Peregrine Calcroft has already left these shores, bound for Australia accompanied by several stalwart footmen to ensure that he doesn't disappear *en route*. Australia is still the place where inconvenient and embarrassing relatives can be safely stashed. He will not return. As for the jewels: The Helingstone Rubies were recovered and Her Majesty is content for me to deal with the thief in a manner that won't cause repercussions."

Mycroft turned his gaze on me. "It goes without saying, Doctor Watson, that this case cannot be written about – much less published."

I have adhered to Mycroft's command, but only in part. I have written up the case but I have refrained from publishing it. If it is ever published, it shall be long after all the participants are dead and well beyond fear of scandal. Indeed, it is likely that beyond being a mere curiosity what I have taken to calling "The Hellingstone Rubies" will be of little interest to anyone at all. Ah, well. Time will tell, as it always does.

I deprecate, however, in the strongest way the attempts which have been made lately to get at and to destroy these papers. The source of these outrages is known, and if they are repeated I have Mr. Holmes's authority for saying that the whole story concerning the politician, the lighthouse, and the trained cormorant will be given to the public. There is at least one reader who will understand.

– Dr. John H. Watson
"The Adventure of the Veiled Lodger"

The Adventure of the Drewhampton Poisoner
by Arthur Hall

In response to repeated requests from my publisher, I have recently approached my friend Mr. Sherlock Holmes on several occasions to enquire whether any of our past cases that have been hitherto withheld for one reason or another could now be laid open to public scrutiny. His reply was not at first favourable, nor was it enthusiastic, for he has always maintained that our exploits should be viewed as exercises in logic and reasoning, rather than as tales of the dramatic and mysterious.

At length, and with the utmost reluctance, he gave his permission. This was more, I haven't the slightest doubt, to ensure that I would press him no further than for any desire for fame or notoriety. I believe that I have mentioned the following events in passing, and only once in my writings until now. To my surprise I find that my notes are incomplete, and so I must rely on my ailing memory to assist in relating this affair to the public to the best of my recollection.

March of '91 had been a month of very mixed weather. Two weeks of intermittent storms were now succeeded by days of hot weather that suggested a pleasant spring ahead. Holmes's mood had been deteriorating for some time, despite his recent successes, as it always did when he was starved, as he put it, of mental stimulation.

On one such morning, when I was staying temporarily in Baker Street while my wife was on a short holiday with a friend, Holmes and I had left the breakfast table and were about to settle ourselves in our armchairs to enjoy our first pipes of the day, he collecting yesterday's dottles from the mantelshelf, when I chanced to glance through our half-open window to look down upon Baker Street.

"Holmes!" I called to him, and he looked towards me in response. "Unless I'm much mistaken, you are about to acquire a new client. There is a fellow running towards our door as if the devil were after him, dodging in and out of the passing traffic."

His expression lightened immediately. "If he is indeed intending to visit us, let us hope he has something interesting to offer. You may have noticed that I haven't been my most amiable self of late."

"Not at all, dear fellow," I replied with a tactful, if not completely truthful, assurance. "Ah, it seems I was right."

The doorbell rang loudly and we heard Mrs. Hudson answer almost immediately. There followed some momentary discussion, during which I formed the opinion that our landlady was enquiring whether the caller had secured an appointment. His voice rose at this, betraying the conceived urgency of whatever had brought him to our door, whereupon Mrs. Hudson allowed him to enter and preceded him on the stairs.

Holmes answered her knock with a bid to enter, and a tall man, ashen-faced and trembling, was shown in. We rose from our chairs as our landlady withdrew, for it was clear that our visitor was far from well.

"My dear fellow," my friend said concernedly, "come and rest yourself in this basket chair."

I put an arm around our new client's shoulder and guided him. He shivered violently under my touch and his expression was of someone deeply troubled.

Holmes quickly poured a measure of brandy from the decanter, and the man accepted it gratefully. When he had drunk much of it, he set the glass down on a side-table beside the top hat which he had removed before entering.

"Are you feeling any improvement?" I asked him.

"Thank you, yes. I'm most grateful to you gentlemen," he replied in a stilted voice. "Recently this strange condition has come upon me. Our local physician can make nothing of it, other than to say that it may be stomach cramps and to prescribe a powder, but I have formed my own conclusions. It is poison, you see – the cause of the deaths of several in our village, but I know not from whence it comes."

"And this is what has brought you to us?" Holmes enquired.

Our visitor glanced from my friend to me, and back again, looking confused.

"You are Mr. Sherlock Holmes?" he ventured.

"Indeed I am, and this is Doctor John Watson, before whom you may speak as you would to me. When you are feeling better, pray take a moment to consider all that you have to tell us and begin at the beginning, without omitting the slightest detail. Be assured that we will do all that we can to help you."

The man began to breathe more steadily and drained his glass before pausing to collect himself.

"I am Mr. Ahab Rampling," he began in his unsteady voice. "I hold the position of farm manager on the estate of Sir Trevill Bertram, near the village of Drewhampton, which isn't far from the Surrey border. Recently a plague has descended upon our village – or at least that is what most folk there believe, but I'm certain that there is evil afoot. I'm quite sure that someone, for reasons I cannot imagine, has in some way introduced a

344

substance that continues to claim the lives of some of the villagers. I also believe that this is the cause of my present state."

Holmes had been listening intently, with his fingers steepled beneath his chin.

"Have the victims been both men and women?" he asked.

"They have. Two men and two women have died."

A few seconds passed and both Mr. Rampling and I glanced towards the window, attracted by the curses of a cab driver whose anger was apparently directed at someone obstructing the passage of his vehicle.

"Have you made your suspicions known to the local force?"

Our client smiled painfully, as if the suggestion was ludicrous. "The nearest police station of any size is in Guildford, quite a distance away. Constable Jessop, who serves our village and works out of tiny premises with a single cell, is as puzzled as everyone else. Until now, you see, the most serious crime that has ever taken place there was when Albert Crawley allowed his horse to gallop down the high street and frighten the children outside the school."

"An admirable record," Holmes acknowledged. "But tell me, sir, is there anyone whom you yourself suspect as the cause of these unfortunate deaths?"

Mr. Rampling endured a fit of coughing, for which he apologised profusely, before replying. "I confess that there is not. However, there is an unfounded opinion among the villagers that the landowner, Sir Trevill Bertram, is to blame. He is a rather Bohemian figure, and it is believed, I understand, that he visits a witch after dark to obtain substances and spells."

"But what possible reason would he have? I presume the victims are among his tenants."

"Some of them are, sir, and the story has no sense to it. That is why I'm here, Mr. Holmes – to clear Sir Trevill's name in the eyes of our village."

"Are you acting for Sir Trevill," asked Holmes, "or on your own initiative."

"My own, sir."

"If you believe yourself to be poisoned," I interrupted, "you should seek medical attention."

"Thank you," he replied. "I have seen our village doctor."

Holmes had meanwhile lapsed into a silence that lasted so long that Mr. Rampling, like many before him, looked to me to confirm that my friend's attention was still with us. I made a reassuring gesture and our client nodded.

"Mr. Rampling," Holmes asked suddenly, "do you know of any person in your village who has travelled abroad – particularly to the tropics in, let us say, the past year?"

Our client shook his head. "I am certain that there is no one. Such an absence would have been considered an unusual event, and certainly remembered."

"As I would have expected." He turned to me. "In view of the prevailing warm weather, I think a trip to Surrey would be rather pleasant, Watson, if you would care to accompany me."

I assented at once, of course.

"It may be a day or two, I regret we are unable to visit your no doubt charming village sooner, but we will certainly look into this." Holmes rose and, seeing that the interview was at an end, our client did likewise. "And so, we will bid you good-day, Mr. Rampling, and we trust your health will be much improved when we see you in Drewhampton."

Mrs. Hudson happened to be on the stairs wielding a brush and pan, and so Holmes and I were left undisturbed as she assumed the task of showing our client out. My friend's expression had deepened and he appeared asleep or lost in thought for several minutes, before his eyes opened and he shifted his thin frame in his chair.

"We can, of course, immediately discount any involvement with witchcraft or wizardry," he murmured, "although I would like to know, given these circumstances, what association Sir Trevill Bertram has with such supposed practices."

"What then, could be the cause of these deaths?" I asked him. "Mr. Rampling's own symptoms, such as I was able to see, could be indications of anything from a failing heart to a fever."

Holmes turned to me with a glint in his eyes. "Oh, I believe our client to be quite correct. This is almost certainly a case involving poison of some sort. The mystery here is the identity of the perpetrator and, of course, why he is conducting this apparent *vendetta* against the village."

"That is why you asked Mr. Rampling whether anyone local had recently travelled abroad – you suspected that any such person might have brought back some exotic and deadly herb?"

"Precisely, but I'll form a more accurate impression when we arrive in Drewhampton. As it is, I delayed bringing my attention to this affair because it suddenly struck me that I'm now in a position to bring to a close a case I undertook some months ago which appeared to have no motive or solution." He rose from his chair and wandered to the window, and I saw his posture alter as he looked down into the busy street. "In addition, I see that our friend Inspector Lestrade has just emerged from a hansom and is walking briskly to our door. Doubtless he has need of our help, so it is as well that we didn't promise our services to Mr. Rampling immediately."

As it was, the inspector's request took up an unexpected amount of Holmes's time. It was, in fact, fully four days before we found ourselves alighting from a local train which set us down in Drewhampton after a short journey.

"How unfortunate," he remarked as we emerged from the station into a short and tree-lined lane, "that we were unable to procure a trap or cart. Ah, but perhaps such a conveyance is unnecessary, since I see that the outskirts of the village begin at the end of this avenue of elms. Do you see, Watson? There's the inn, between the grocer's shop and the bakery."

"I hope that they have rooms for us," I replied.

"Have no fears on that score, old fellow. I took the precaution of wiring ahead to reserve our accommodation."

We were shown to two fine rooms overlooking the street. At luncheon, which comprised of chicken pie followed by a rather over-sweet gooseberry fool, Holmes mentioned his observation that the manager and staff seemed rather crestfallen.

"There is to be a funeral today, sir," our waiter said in answer to my friend's enquiry. "The deceased was a man known to all of us here in the village."

"I am exceedingly sorry to hear of this. May we know the poor fellow's name?"

"Of course, but it's unlikely that you will have encountered him, seeing as you are London gentlemen. He was Mr. Ahab Rampling."

The shock from this news of the death of our client quickly passed, as I remembered his unhealthy appearance. Holmes's expression was unaltered as he replied. "We have indeed met Mr. Rampling – in fact it is because of a business arrangement with him that we are here today. I recall that he mentioned a number of unexpected deaths hereabouts when we spoke to him last, and expressed some concern regarding them. Do you, by any chance, recall the names of these unfortunates?"

The man gave us a slow, suspicious look. He brushed a stray lock of grey hair from his forehead.

"Mr. Rampling was the manager of Sir Trevill Bertram's farm, sir. Sir Trevill owns most of the property around here, and I don't know that he would like me spreading our village affairs to outsiders."

Holmes raised his eyebrows. "I had no idea that he was so secretive. Ah well, no matter. I shall be seeing Sir Trevill later, so I expect he will tell me then."

"I didn't realise that you were acquainted with him, sir." The waiter's face reddened slightly, I noticed. "As far as I can recollect, three men and two women have passed away within the last month or so, including Mr. Rampling. There was Thomas Leary, Matthew Collet, and Ben Trafford's wife, as well as Arthur Edmond's sister. We thought at first that a plague had come upon us, but now it seems as if something in our food is the cause."

"Were that so, wouldn't the deaths be more widespread?"

"Who knows, sir? Doctor Walgrave seems unable to discover the cause. Many of us are worried that we or our families will be the next to be struck down."

"Let us hope that both the cause and cure will be identified soon," I said. The waiter murmured his agreement and collected our coffee cups before leaving us.

"I think a word with Doctor Walgrave would be in order," Holmes said as we left the inn.

After asking directions from a passer-by, we made our way up the High Street, past a number of shops and the church, and turned into a narrow lane which rose steadily with occasional houses scattered around open fields. We hadn't walked far when we came to a thatched cottage surrounded by an array of colourful flowers. Holmes opened the white-painted gate and we approached the front door. As he raised his stick it swung open, revealing a stern-looking woman, probably a secretary or receptionist I thought, who peered at us silently.

"Good afternoon," Holmes began, for it was past mid-day by now. "We would like to see Doctor Walgrave, if it is at all possible."

"I haven't seen either of you before," she said haughtily.

"That is because we haven't been here before. We are visitors."

"So you are not Doctor Walgrave's patients?"

"We are not."

"Are you in pain?"

"We are not," Holmes said again, in his most patient voice.

"Then what is your business here?"

"That is for the doctor and ourselves to discuss. My name is Sherlock Holmes, and I'm in your charming village in response to a summons from the late Mister Ahab Rampling."

She looked from Holmes to me and back, clearly undecided as to whether to disturb the doctor.

"I, also, am a doctor," I added. "Kindly inform your employer that our purpose is of the utmost urgency."

"Very well." She vanished into the dim interior, leaving the door ajar.

Holmes glanced at me with raised eyebrows. He smiled faintly but said nothing.

"The doctor will see you," the woman said as she reappeared. "Come in."

We allowed ourselves to be led along a short corridor and into a small room, lined with ancient books and containing a worn desk and chairs. The receptionist announced us and quickly retreated. Behind the desk stood an elderly man of distinguished appearance with hair and beard of pure white. His eyes were clear, as was his voice.

"I have heard of you and your companion, Mr. Holmes. As you are a consulting detective, I assume you are here at the late Mr. Rampling's bidding to attempt to discover the cause of our recent unexplained deaths, for he mentioned to me that he proposed to take some action. That is the case, is it not?"

"It is indeed, sir. I'm told that it was first assumed that a plague had come upon the village."

"That was quickly disproved – at least as far as any plague that I'm aware of is concerned." He gestured towards the chairs. "Let us sit, gentlemen."

We settled ourselves, the aged leather creaking under us. Doctor Walgrave sat hunched in his chair, shaking his head hopelessly. After a moment, he looked up.

"I truly hope that you will be more successful than I. When I discounted plague from the possibilities, I turned to poison. I still believe that to be the cause, but I cannot identify it. My tests for arsenic and all other common substances of the kind have provided no answer, save that of elimination. This evening I shall take the train to Guildford, where I hope to consult a colleague who has spent some years in India. He has encountered many practices and cures that are strange to us, and may well be our last hope."

"If I may ask," I said, "what are the usual symptoms?"

"The patient appears to be extremely pale, as if drained of blood. A constant trembling, both of the body and voice, which rises and falls in its intensity. Speech becomes slow and uncertain, and movement is maintained with increasing effort. The condition worsens within a few days, culminating in the ceasing of respiratory and kidney functions. Do you know of any poison that produces such effects, Doctor Watson?"

After brief consideration, I replied, "None that produce *all* of those symptoms. In Afghanistan, I recall, several preparations that produced similar effects were common among the natives, but the paleness, especially, eludes me as to its source."

"Then we are no further advanced."

"Not as yet," Holmes acknowledged. "But tell me, do you know of any new cases in the village?"

"None have been reported to me since that of Mr. Rampling."

My friend nodded. "Thank you, Doctor Walgrave, for allowing us to take up some of your valuable time." He rose abruptly. "I wish you well in Guildford, and with your further investigations."

"As I wish you in yours," the doctor said.

We descended the hill with Holmes in deep thought. He walked with his head upon his chest and I said nothing until we were about to emerge into the High Street.

"Do you think that our friend the doctor will discover anything of worth in Guildford?"

He gave a slight shrug. "I cannot answer such a question, because we don't know the nature of the poison or where its antidote is to be found. There is another way to solve this affair, however, and that is to identify the poisoner and extract the information from him."

I was about to reply when Holmes touched my arm silently and pointed. A hearse had appeared, pulled by two black mares that seemed, from their slowness of movement, as downcast as the small procession of mourners who followed. We stood still, removing our hats and bowing our heads respectfully until the procession has passed. It had but a short distance to carry the coffin, which was visible within the brass rails of the bier, until it came to the churchyard further along the street.

Holmes looked especially grim.

"Cheer up, old fellow," I said by way of encouragement. "Though Mr. Rampling has passed on, I have every hope that you will solve the problem that he brought to you."

"I wonder: Would he still be alive if I had begun to work on this case at once?"

I shook my head. "On that you can set your mind at rest. Nothing that you, or I for that matter, could have done would have saved him. He had the appearance of a man at death's door. I fear that the poison is quite potent, even if its full effects aren't felt immediately."

We continued our walk along the High Street in silence. Some of the shops were closed, doubtless because of the funeral, but the blacksmith was busy at his anvil. From behind us we heard running footsteps, and a moment later a large and surly-looking fellow who I recognised from the funeral procession caught up with us.

"Are you the detective from London?" he asked breathlessly.

"I am," my friend answered. "My name is Sherlock Holmes."

"Well, I am here to save you some trouble. I know that you are trying to find the cause of the deaths we've had hereabouts lately, but I can tell you here and now who is responsible."

"In that event, you will have solved the case for me. Pray tell me the identity of this murderer, for that he truly is."

The heaving of the man's massive chest began to subside. "It is my employer, Sir Trevill Bertram! He has been seen at night on his way to visit a witch, and has paid her to curse our village."

"But even if that were possible, why would he do such a thing? Does Sir Trevill not own most of the village? It makes little sense to suppose that a man would deliberately bring about the end of some of his own tenants."

"That may be so, but I know it. We all know it."

"Who are you, sir?"

"I am Roland Dender, the new farm manager. Sir Trevill appointed me on the day that Mr. Rampling died."

"He is evidently not slow in managing his affairs, and this seems a curious way to show gratitude."

Mr. Dender's eyes narrowed. "I told him months ago that it is I who should take care of things on the farm. Mr. Rampling was slow with everything."

"You weren't a friend of Mr. Rampling's then?"

"We had our disagreements."

"That is largely inevitable, when men work closely together for some time."

"Well, we fought once." Mr. Dender was becoming uncomfortable I saw, now that he realised that he hadn't convinced Holmes. "I must go now. I have work to do."

With that he resumed his run, and was soon lost to our sight.

"It occurs to me," I said as we resumed our walk, "that it could be that fellow who is at the root of this. He strikes me as rather insensitive, and he is clearly ruthlessly ambitious. He assumes Mr. Rampling's position at the drop of a hat, so who is to say that he would flinch from taking over the entire farm? As he seems determined to throw suspicion upon Sir Trevill, to whom he should be grateful, it may be that there is some way, perhaps a clause in the landowner's will, that will enable him to achieve this."

"Certainly that theory is worth considering," Holmes allowed, "and it may be that we will be forced to do so before this affair reaches its conclusion. However, I'm inclined to believe that there is more to this." He stopped to examine a sign-post. "I see that the farm of Sir Trevill Bertram, whose name repeatedly confronts us, is only a mile or so further along this road. We will have a rather pleasant walk there, I think, in the morning."

With that we returned to the inn. We sat in a quiet corner, where Holmes lit his pipe and maintained a thoughtful silence. I contented myself with a local newspaper until the hour for dinner arrived. My friend ate with more enthusiasm than usual, attacking his lamb and sprinkling it liberally with mint sauce. Our stewed apple dessert attracted less of his interest, but on completing our meal he called for two pints of good ale.

We returned to our former seats in the corner, and I noticed at once that Holmes avoided any mention of or reference to our current investigation. This was a certain sign that he had formed a theory, or perhaps more than one, and was testing them in his agile mind against the known facts. After a while he smiled and we reverted to discussing some of our old adventures, and to wondering what had befallen a few of our former clients. During our conversation our glasses had become empty and I made to signal the landlord, but my companion declined, saying that it was best that we retired a little early to be at our most alert in the morning.

I slept dreamlessly and woke to the loud crowing of a cock. By the time that I'd prepared myself and dressed I had heard movement outside my door, so I wasn't surprised to find that Holmes and one or two other guests were already taking breakfast as I entered the dining room.

He greeted me cheerfully. "Good morning, Watson. I can recommend the kippers, if you are so disposed. Two of these and some toast should satisfy even your appetite until the time arrives for luncheon. As for me, I need nothing more except another pot of this strong coffee. Sit down, dear fellow, and I'll summon the waiter."

This he did, and I ate heartily. On finishing our coffee he rose at once. "I think we'll enjoy a pleasant walk to Sir Trevill Bertram's farm, as it's a bright and sunny morning. By now word of our presence will certainly have reached his ears, and I'm curious as to the sort of reception we'll receive."

As my friend had observed the previous day, it was little more than a mile from where the High Street became a tree-lined country lane to the entrance to the farm. We were then confronted with an uneven path that boasted the impression of many cart-wheels, with fields to either side in which villagers busily picked crops. Pigs, cows, and sheep looked up from feeding to peer at us as we passed, and other, more distant, fields contained goats and several fine horses. The path continued past a group of outbuildings, one of them appearing to be a dairy, until it brought us to bushes fashioned to the shapes of animals spaced around a circular lawn. Beyond that a Tudor mansion stood, almost engulfed in ivy to the extent that the windows appeared as eyes staring from behind a mask.

"This is a strange place," Holmes remarked. "Observe the flags of many countries draped across most of the windows. I doubt if many men have travelled to such an extent. Also the suits of armour are, I would have thought, of too much value to a cultured man to be left outside to rust."

I glanced about me, around the courtyard and the front of the house. "Mr. Rampling, I recall, mentioned his employer's Bohemian ways, but this isn't so much a home as a museum."

The door opened before we reached the top of the steps to reveal a smiling butler, a tall man most of whose hair had been sadly lost, who welcomed us.

"Good morning, gentlemen. You are here to see Sir Trevill, of course. He isn't at home now, but is expected back soon. Allow me to show you to the drawing room, where I will serve port while you wait."

At his invitation we preceded him. He guided us to a room in which curtains hung half-drawn across tall windows and the furniture appeared fashioned from thick upholstered cane.

"Sir Trevill is evidently an explorer," Holmes remarked.

"Ah, Mr. Holmes, you have noticed that the chairs are from foreign parts, and some of the trophies suggest this, perhaps. He has travelled much over the years, unlike myself who has yet to leave these shores." The butler bowed courteously. "My name is Morgan, gentlemen. If I can serve you in any way in my master's house, you have only to mention it."

"You know me, then?"

"Who hasn't heard of your most commendable fight against lawlessness?" He looked at me with kindly approval. "And of your excellent portrayal of these adventures, Doctor Watson. I confess to reading *A Study in Scarlet* soon after it was published."

"I'm glad that you found it entertaining," I replied.

"Oh, much more than that," he paused as he heard the clatter of horse's hooves from the courtyard. "But Sir Trevill has returned! He will be with you in a moment, I'm sure, and I will serve drinks immediately."

"A rather familiar butler, wouldn't you say?" I said when the man had left the room.

"He seems most content in his work, and lacks the aloofness to which we are accustomed."

"Quite. He is certainly well informed as to our activities."

"Doubtless your over-dramatic account of them has ensured this."

As our host arrived, I scowled my disapproval of this most out-of-place and unnecessary remark. He didn't immediately greet us, but stood still and silent in momentary appraisal. At the same time I made my own assessment of the man, concluding that he was of a most Bohemian nature, as we had been told. His riding clothes were of a colourful tweed, such as one wouldn't expect to be used for that purpose, and his greying hair touched his shoulders. His moustache was of an unusual style, his beard unkempt, and his thick eyebrows gave him a menacing appearance. Quite suddenly, he smiled and approached us.

"Mr. Sherlock Holmes and Doctor Watson! Morgan informed me a moment ago that you were here. I have just returned from a ride around the farm. Please sit, and tell me how I can assist you."

As we sank into two rather uncomfortable chairs, the butler entered with a tray. He filled three crystal glasses from a heavy decanter, handed them to us, and departed. We sipped, and I tasted port of the finest quality.

"We have been summoned here by your late employee, Mr. Ahab Rampling," Holmes began. "He reported several suspicious deaths in the village, and was convinced that they weren't accidental. If you, yourself, have any opinions on this, or any additional information, it would be of immense help in our investigation."

Sir Trevill stroked his beard. "Rampling was an imaginative fellow, I often thought, but there has indeed been a surfeit of deaths hereabouts. As far as I'm aware, neither Doctor Walgrave nor Constable Jessop have found anything amiss, but the village is alive with rumours. Sometimes, one has difficulty in separating the truth from hearsay."

"So I understand, sir. We have heard mention of witchcraft and curses hereabouts."

"Oh, that!" Our host dismissed the notion with a wave of his hand and replaced his glass on the tray. "Those stories have been circulating here since the area first became a settlement, I shouldn't wonder. In particular, Barnabas Leary, the brother of one of the victims, is quite convinced of their veracity. In your place, gentlemen, I would discount such a consideration from my enquiries. The cause of the deaths of these poor unfortunates will probably become known in time, and will prove to be of a nature that is quite unexceptional."

Holmes and I put down our glasses and rose as one.

"Our thanks to you for your time and hospitality," my friend said.

Sir Trevill smiled. "I fear I cannot have been of much help, but I found this interview most interesting. Pray feel free to visit my house again, should you acquire any insight on the situation that you feel you can share. Good morning, gentlemen."

Morgan appeared at the drawing room door as if summoned by magic and showed us out. Outside, as we were about to descend the steps, he confided to us, "You gentlemen have doubtless heard of the stories surrounding Sir Trevill, commonly discussed in the village. It seems to me that there are some ungrateful souls in the area, when consideration is given to the employment he has provided, as well as the produce from the farm that he has distributed freely."

I was rather shocked by the man's references to his employer, although they were in no way derogatory. Holmes, however, maintained a thoughtful expression, saying only, "Rumours are an unreliable basis on which to build opinions or theories, I have found. I perceive that you are content with your duties here, and that Sir Trevill appears satisfied with you. A mutually satisfactory situation, evidently."

The butler smiled and bowed as we turned away, and we soon found ourselves retracing our steps to Drewhampton.

"Sir Trevill seems like an amiable fellow after all," I said when we had left the farm behind.

"So it would doubtless have appeared, had he not lied."

I slowed my pace and turned to him, aghast. "Whatever can you mean? I saw no deceit in the man."

"As always, you saw as I did, but you did not *observe*. You will recall his mention of riding around his estate."

"The farm, I believe he said."

"Quite so. You will doubtless recall that the entire area, the farmland and the land surrounding the house, was composed of a reddish soil, possibly because of a heavy clay content."

I nodded. "Indeed."

"Then it is difficult to see how one of Sir Trevill's boots could have had a fresh piece of black mud adhering to its sole, unless he had extended his ride a little further. When I add to this the rather defensive look he adopted as he explained his absence from the house, what am I to conclude, other than that he wishes to keep his wandering secret?"

"An assignation, perhaps? Possibly with one of the village girls?"

"That is certainly a possibility, but I dispensed with it because, to begin with, Sir Trevill must be in his late fifties. He is aware of the dim view that some villagers have of him because of his supposed connection with witchcraft, even though no one can suggest a reason why he would wish harm to them. Why then, would he risk additional scandal that could cause some or all of his employees to seek positions elsewhere? Superstition is a powerful motivation, and I would wager that there are more than a few in the village that would prefer a longer journey to their work rather than the employment of a man they perceive as a wizard – let alone if he were also suspected of over-familiarity with their daughters. If sufficient resentment were caused, the farm could well face ruin."

"What, then, do you believe that he is concealing?"

We had by this time almost reached the inn. A cart, piled high with hay, made its way past slowly.

"That, we may discover tonight," Holmes replied as we crossed the road opposite the entrance. "But, as it's time for luncheon, let us now eat

355

and refresh ourselves. This afternoon we'll seek additional information about Sir Trevill's conduct from another source."

During our meal, I noticed that my friend's eyes were now filled with a look with which I was long familiar. He had, I knew, begun to piece together the disparate elements of this case, recognising clues that were quite beyond me. After our long association I should have become accustomed to his ways, but there were still many times when I felt in awe of his intellect.

"What is it that you intend for this afternoon?" I enquired as we finished our meal.

He glanced around the dining room to confirm that we couldn't be overheard. "You will recall that Sir Trevill mentioned the brother of one of his tenants, Barnabas Leary. I'm inclined to seek this man's viewpoint on the deaths in the village, and on the reason for his suspicions."

We rose then and made to leave, but Holmes waited until the waiter appeared. He asked the fellow a question, to which the answer was quickly forthcoming.

"So, we now know that Mr. Leary resides at 9 Wheatsheaf Copse," he explained. "In a small village such as this, it's certain that a person's business, and indeed where he may be found, is known to almost everyone. As with most destinations hereabouts, ours is within walking distance."

A fifteen-minute stroll, in the opposite direction to that we had set out upon that morning, brought us to a lane that was awash with wild flowers. I wondered, for a moment, if this was the place we sought, but my friend confirmed this by peering beneath the heavily-leafed branches that obscured a sign-post.

"But there are no houses to be seen, Holmes. There are nothing but fields and animals."

He viewed our surroundings. "Then we have no alternative than to follow this most scenic thoroughfare until we come upon some signs of habitation. Don't despair. I have every expectation that around this bend will be the house that we seek."

In no more than a minute, he was proven correct. After a short but brisk walk that took us around a long curve, the trees and flowers gave way to a cluster of about a dozen small dwellings. At our approach, Holmes inspected the cottages and, finding no numbers, he counted from the first before rapping on a rather dilapidated door.

Presently it opened a few inches, and an eye peered out from the gloom within.

"Mr. Barnabas Leary?" enquired Holmes. "My name is Sherlock Holmes and this is my associate, Doctor John Watson. We would be grateful if you would spare us a few minutes of your time, sir."

"What's this about?" The door opened further.

"As well as expressing our condolences regarding your brother, we would like to ask you about the owner of the farm hereabouts, Sir Trevill Bertram. He has featured greatly in our investigation into the sudden deaths that have occurred in the village of late, and we're given to believe that you hold that he's some way responsible. "

Now the door opened wider, revealing a short elderly man with wild hair and a sullen expression.

"That man is a servant of the devil!" he exclaimed. "Who else can be the cause of Thomas' death and of Ben Trafford's wife's passing, or that of Arthur Edmond's sister – not to mention Mr. Rampling and Matthew Collet? I tell you, three men and two women, all good and sturdy folk, have been taken from us."

By now it was apparent that we weren't to be invited into Mr. Leary's home but this, if it occurred to him at all, didn't deter Holmes in his questioning.

"Pray enlighten us as to your reason for this accusation."

"Thomas worked on the land for more than twenty years," the old man growled, "and he always swore that Sir Trevill went out every evening to consort with a witch, or to visit some sort of cult that worships the devil. He never told me how that became known or who confided it to him, but it's been common knowledge around here for a long time, and that usually means it's the truth. I can tell you that there's any number of folk who would leave his employ if they could, but there's no other estate within miles, and work on the land is all they know." His tone calmed slightly. "In fairness though, I don't think the wages would be as good, anyway."

Holmes nodded thoughtfully. "And you can't tell us how such a suspicion began?"

"There was a story that was heard in the village for a little while, some years ago," Mr. Leary remembered. "It was told by an animal doctor who was called to the farm to treat some sick cows. The way he put it, as he arrived one evening he walked from the station and, not being familiar with the village, went out of his way. Soon he saw a man enter the house of an old and evil-looking woman over on the Guilford Road. From what he said, it appeared as if they knew each other and acted quite familiar. The doctor stayed at the inn that night, where he related his experience to other customers who he had struck up a friendship with. The next morning, he arrived at the farm and found, to his surprise, that the man he had seen the previous evening was none other than Sir Trevill!

"Now, Mr. Holmes, when he was working late, it didn't take Thomas long to realise that his employer strode off in that direction every evening at about the same time, which was about eight o'clock. I know that us village folk are said to be simple and superstitious, but if you add to what I've just said to the well-known fact that Sir Trevill never is anything but prosperous, regardless of the richness of the harvest or anything else, and then you remember the saying that the devil looks after his own, it's easy to see, isn't it, how his reputation came to be?"

"Indeed, there is no mystery about it," Holmes said wryly. "I thank you, Mr. Leary. Your information has been most helpful. I wouldn't be surprised if Sir Trevill's activities weren't clear to all in the very near future. Good day to you, sir."

We retraced our steps with Holmes saying little. He walked with his head upon his chest, as he always did when pondering the facts and inferences of a current case. When he began to give his attention to his surroundings, at first to the colourful variety of plants and flowers and then to the passers-by in the street, I ventured to interrupt his thoughts.

"I take it that you have dismissed Mr. Leary's viewpoint on this matter. It seems to me that he believes the superstition that has been attached to Sir Trevill, which appears to be little more than local gossip. I don't feel that we have learned much here."

Holmes nodded slowly. "Gossip, yes, although I don't always dismiss this a source of information. I think that we'll return to the inn to spend an hour or two smoking peacefully before dinner. Then we'll set about ascertaining the true reason for Sir Trevill's nightly excursions. I feel that we must clarify his intentions before proceeding further, although I don't expect them to be in any way the cause of the villagers' deaths."

"You're quite certain that he is in no way connected with these occurrences then?"

"I have been, almost from the first. All opinions to the contrary, I can see no reason for such actions, despite the mud on his boots that I noticed previously. However, our exercise tonight will either confirm or deny my suppositions"

I can recall making but one remark to Holmes during a quite acceptable dinner which he regarded with little interest.

"There appear to be no hansoms around the village, but perhaps we can hire a cart for the evening."

He laced his long fingers together, after pushing his half-empty plate away.

"Why ever should we do that?"

"To follow Sir Trevill, of course."

"That won't be necessary, I think." He folded his napkin and placed it before him. "You will recall that Mr. Barnabas Leary related that his brother often watched his employer as he *strode off,* on his nightly travels. From this, we can expect that the journey is a short one. I'll wager that the Guildford Road is quite near at hand."

So it proved to be. We had hardly finished our coffee before Holmes stood up with an expression of anticipation upon his face. We set up a brisk pace as the light faded quickly, and by the time we had reached the farm, darkness was complete. The place presented no difficulty as to our entry, for the wide gate was secured only by a latch that was within easy reach. We kept to the shadows, watching for any workers who might still be nearby, and hearing only the murmur of animal sounds and the sighing of the slight wind among the trees. When the house was in sight, my friend silently guided me away from the path.

"If Sir Trevill wishes to keep his excursions secret," he whispered, "he will doubtless leave by a back door."

Accordingly, we settled ourselves in the concealment of a thick bush that grew near both a rear entrance and the path that led further into the estate. Fortunately, the night was warm enough for us to be comfortable, and very soon we heard the faint chimes of the church clock in the village. I took out my pocket-watch and saw that the next fifteen minutes would bring us to eight o'clock.

Sir Trevill was indeed a punctual man, for he appeared exactly as the clock struck the hour. We crouched still as statues, holding our breath as his indistinct form marched past with the gravel crunching beneath his boots.

My friend placed a restraining hand on my shoulder as I made to rise. "Not yet, Watson. Wait." When all sounds had ceased we rose slowly, and I followed Holmes to the rear of the estate in close pursuit. The shadowy figure of Sir Trevill strode unhesitatingly ahead, and not once did he look back. Under the trees the darkness was dense, but Holmes seemed to see ahead with much more clarity than I. It was in far less time than I expected that we came upon a low fence, and after crossing a rather dilapidated stile found ourselves in a field edged by a narrow footpath.

We halted abruptly as Sir Trevill paused, for fear of becoming close. The cry of an owl, no doubt surprised at our sudden appearance, and the rustle of leaves intruded briefly into the silence. Then he continued until another stile confronted him, before crossing into the deserted Guildford Road.

Holmes held up a hand in a silent gesture and we halted to watch Sir Trevill walk a final few yards to where a small cluster of cottages stood in

359

darkness. We hesitated while he approached, and it was only as the door of the nearest of them was answered to his knock that we emerged.

"Good evening, Sir Trevill," my friend called as we drew nearer.

The landowner turned towards us quickly. "Good heavens! Mr. Holmes and Doctor Watson." Then his expression clouded, as he was struck by realisation. "Did you follow me here, sirs?" he asked angrily.

Before either Holmes or myself could reply, a figure standing in the shadow of the doorway spoke softly to Sir Trevill. He answered soothingly, before returning his attention to us.

"I imagine that you gentlemen seek confirmation of the absurd rumours that circulate among my tenants. I know of the things that the villagers say about me, but I have yet to discover their reason, if it is other than primitive superstition. Very well then, you shall have your explanation." He paused and in that instant the shape before him moved, so that the meagre light from the candle within revealed a very elderly lady whose skin appeared yellowed and wrinkled like ancient parchment. Despite her obviously painful condition, she smiled at us as she was introduced as Miss Gwendolyn Stirk.

We replied courteously, and Sir Trevill continued.

"This lady is no witch, gentlemen. She is, in fact, my aunt. Her unfortunate condition is the result of nursing the poor in India, where she was for many years attached to a religious order. She has been a good and charitable women for all of her life, but now is in need of my help in order to survive. She chooses to live a lonely existence because she fears that the disease she carries might be passed to others, although I have attempted many times to persuade her otherwise since I'm unaffected. Far from taking offence at the locals' accusation, she finds them amusing. I, however, do not."

An expression that I have rarely seen crossed Holmes's face, to quickly disappear.

"Sir Trevill," he said then, "I cannot but apologise for this intrusion, to both Miss Stirk and yourself." He paused as I mumbled my concurrence. "But you will, I am certain, appreciate that my work demands that every avenue in question should be explored. By way of restitution I will, if you both agree, arrange for Sir James Saunders, the London specialist, to visit you, Miss Stirk, to make a thorough examination. I have some slight acquaintance with Sir James, and it's certain that this will take place before too long, and that he'll quickly ascertain whether or not your fears are justified. I beg that you consider this."

Sir Trevill looked to his aunt who, after some hesitation, nodded silently.

"Very well," he said again. "We will discuss your proposition. If you would be so good as to call on me in the morning, I'll tell you of our decision." His long hair glinted in the poor light. "Goodnight to you gentlemen."

We retraced out steps rather more slowly. I felt relieved to be back among the trees and surrounded by silence.

"I'm afraid we have committed a cardinal error there," I said presently.

"Much to the contrary, old fellow. Everything has worked out exactly as I expected."

I turned to him in surprise, hardly able to distinguish his shape in the gloom. "I cannot see how that can be."

"It is really quite simple. As you know, I give no credence to the supernatural, so the elderly woman featured in the various reports concerning Sir Trevill's night time visits seemed to me most likely to be either infirm or in some way ill. I couldn't of course define the exact circumstances, but I was reasonably certain that I would be able to offer assistance in the shape of one or other of the London specialists that have become known to me over the years. Had they declined my help, I would have found some way to insist, and if they had made an immediate decision I would have suggested they sleep on it, for it was imperative that Sir Trevill invite us to call at his home tomorrow."

I stopped, a little breathless, and placed my hand against a sturdy oak for support. "But what can we hope to discover? Is there more to Sir Trevill's part in this, after all?"

"No." Holmes stood a few feet away and lit his pipe. "But you will recall the butler, Morgan."

"Rather a forward fellow, I thought."

"That is as may be, but did you notice the tattoo on his right wrist?"

I thought for a moment. "I seem to remember the mathematical symbol, known as '*pi*', and concluding that he may have at some time been a teacher of that subject."

"Not so, but almost correct. In fact, you have mistaken the Greek letter for a Mandarin character. In spite of his assertion that he has never left this land, this shows clearly that Morgan has at some time visited China."

"But that design could have been applied to him anywhere. There are establishments in Limehouse that specialise in such things."

"Indeed there are, but his tattoo came from the Orient."

I smiled, but yet I knew that he would never joke about his observations.

"How could you know that?"

"You will disappoint me if you tell me that you've forgotten our previous client, Mr. Jabez Wilson. If you remember, from my previous study of tattoos I was able to identify his as Chinese by its distinctive colouring. The same is true of that of Morgan. Examples from elsewhere have a lighter colour."

"Yet he mentioned, for no apparent reason, that he has never been there, or to any other country for that matter. Yes, I see."

"That is why, for the purpose of confirmation, we'll visit the tiny library that I observed next to that rather luridly-painted tea shop just off Drewhampton High Street. If we set off immediately, there's a chance that someone might still be there.

To my astonishment, an elderly man was still at the library, explaining that he was the librarian and that there was no one waiting for him at home, so it was just as easy for him to remain there and indulge in his love for reading. Upon hearing Holmes's request, he led him to a volume of ancient Chinese medicine. While Holmes pored over it and the librarian returned to his desk, I contented myself with a back issue of a medical journal. Less than half-an-hour had passed before Holmes stood up, closed the book, and returned it to its place. Quietly, he thanked the librarian for his help, and then stepped outside.

"Did you find what you expected?" I enquired.

"Exactly that. Everything is now clear to me. It remains only to send a wire from the Post Office, and my case is complete."

We set off on at a brisk pace, sharing no further conversation. I knew better than to ask my friend about his discoveries in the library, or about his deductions. After the telegram was sent, we headed back to our rooms for the night.

In the morning, Holmes was in a good mood, and after breakfast we immediately set off for our appointment with Sir Trevill. He would reveal all at the appropriate time, and that couldn't be far away.

Morgan positively radiated good humour as he admitted us.

"Welcome again, gentlemen. Sir Trevill forewarned me of your visit, and instructed me to see that you are comfortable until he returns from his ride. He will not be long. I would say no more than half-an-hour."

We thanked him and allowed ourselves to be led into the drawing room as before.

"The truth is, Morgan," Holmes said as we seated ourselves, "that on this occasion we are here to see you, as much as Sir Trevill."

The butler's expression went suddenly blank. "Me, sir? How could that possibly be?"

"That I will explain presently. For now I will prevail upon you to bring to us the telegram that will arrive at any moment."

Morgan bowed. "Of course, sir. Meanwhile, I will also bring porter and some of the seed cake for which our village is famous. I trust that will be acceptable?"

"Most certainly," I answered, as Holmes nodded.

As soon as we were alone Holmes inclined his head to listen, I perceived, for the retreating footsteps of the butler.

"At all costs," he whispered, "touch nothing. Do not eat as much as a crumb, nor drink a drop."

I was about to reply when Morgan reappeared. He placed a laden tray before us, containing generous quantities of cake and port.

"I'm most curious," he said to Holmes, "as to what it is that you wish to speak of to me. I believe – but there is the doorbell ringing. Doubtless it is the telegraph boy."

He left us again, and returned in moments. Holmes tore open the envelope held out to him on a tray.

"Now I'll tell you," he looked straight at Morgan with triumph in his face, "that I have concluded my investigation. There is but one unanswered question, which only you can settle."

Some of the geniality had left the butler's face. "Whatever could that be?"

"The reason why you have poisoned three men and two women in the village of Drewhampton."

If we expected this to be received with some excitement, we were disappointed.

"I don't think of any of this as a joke, sir," Morgan said calmly. "Allow me to cut you a piece of this seed cake to sustain you until Sir Trevill's return."

"I imagine that you knew," Holmes continued, "from your travels in China, that the *gu* poison is obtained from venomous snakes which are imprisoned with lethal scorpions in a jar. The survivor of the resulting fights is used to obtain the substance which you have employed. No doubt you were a member of a cult that disposes of its victims in this way, either for revenge or money. I confess that I had no indication of this, until I eventually realised the significance of your tattoo."

Morgan glanced at his wrist. "Surely you are mistaken."

"The discovery that the same device has been the symbol of the cult from ancient times makes this unlikely, I think."

"Gentlemen." The tray was held within easy reach of both of us. "Do try this cake. I find it quite delicious."

To my amazement, Morgan then took a slice and consumed it before us, a highly unusual liberty for a servant but, I suspected, intended to demonstrate that the cake was free of poison. It flashed across my mind that it could have been the act of a guilty man cheating the hangman, but he seemed unaffected.

"We will, I think, forego that pleasure," Holmes answered.

At that moment several things occurred. Morgan's expression changed as he accepted defeat. The mask slipped. The good humour vanished in an instant, to be replaced by the grim countenance and soulless eyes of a man who feels no remorse. Behind him I saw the drawing room door open to admit Sir Trevill, who was accompanied by another. I started as I recognised Inspector Lestrade.

Morgan became very still as he realised that we were no longer alone. He turned his head slowly, and then his body seemed to sag before us.

"Good morning, Sir Trevill!" Holmes cried jovially. "I do hope you intend to accept my offer of last night. Ah, I see that Lestrade accompanies you! Your arrival is perfectly timed, Inspector. I commend you."

Sir Trevill nodded but said nothing, as Morgan squirmed visibly under his condemning stare.

"I came as soon as I could, Mr. Holmes," Lestrade said. "Just managed to catch the morning train. After receiving your message last night, I consulted the archives at the Yard, and also had one of my men wire the Chief Constable of Surrey as you suggested."

"I was right, then?" My friend enquired.

"Oh, you were, sir. It's been five years now, but I soon uncovered the truth."

"As I knew you would, Inspector. I take it that you happened to meet Sir Trevill on your way from the station, and recognised him from my description."

"That I did. I explained to him some of what has been going on hereabouts, and he brought me here at once."

"Capital! Perhaps you would care to elaborate on your findings, for the further understanding of Sir Trevill and Doctor Watson."

Lestrade acknowledged me courteously before he spoke. "The Northern Landworkers Bank robbery, of five years or so ago, was a dreadful affair. An official was shot dead, as were two police officers who attempted to arrest the robbers. The gang, five of them, fled south from Northumberland with the intention of taking a boat to escape to France. When this proved impossible because of the nation-wide manhunt and days of bad weather, they hid in various towns, always on the move, until they finally settled in Drewhampton."

"Attracted by its quietness and because it is situated off the beaten track, so to speak," I remarked.

"Exactly, Doctor. Each of the robbers found lodgings in the village, intending to remain here until things settled down. I regret that I have been unsuccessful in discovering whether any of the villagers concerned knowingly harboured the fugitives in exchange for money. This state of affairs might have continued for much longer hadn't a certain Mrs. Molly Wixted somehow discovered the truth about them. She was a married woman from Kent, who had taken refuge here from a violent husband. One of the gang is thought to have murdered her while they were in hiding, for she was found strangled after their departure."

Holmes turned to Sir Trevill. "Was it not about this time when Morgan took up his position with you?" he asked.

"It was," the landowner looked at Morgan through narrowed eyes. "His predecessor, Boone, had disappeared, failing to return from a short visit to his relatives in Bristol. After several days Morgan presented himself, explaining that he was a cousin of Boone who had died suddenly from a weak heart. I haven't doubted this, until now. Morgan claimed that he, like several members of Boone's family, were experienced in the profession, and so I accepted him on a trial basis at first, as a replacement. His references were impressive."

"Forged, no doubt," Lestrade said.

Holmes nodded. "Tell us then, Inspector, of the connection of Morgan to this affair."

"The murdered lady – this Mrs. Wixted – was his sister, and revenge for her death was the sole reason for his presence in the village, and for taking up employment with Sir Trevill. My enquiries have revealed that the first villager was murdered on the fifth anniversary of her death."

"Thank you, Inspector," Holmes said. "So you, Morgan, allowed a year to elapse for each intended victim. That, I imagine, was in order that your activities wouldn't be connected to the events of five years ago. I'm aware that you have travelled in the Orient where you became familiar with *gu,* a local poison much used by criminals thereabouts, but unknown otherwise. How, by the way, did you administer it?"

Morgan raised his head from his chest, sullen-faced. "Since you and the inspector seem to have become acquainted with my plan, Mr. Holmes, it can do no harm to tell you. One of my duties as Sir Trevill's butler was to take messages and instructions to the farm and the adjoining dairy. It was a simple matter to ascertain which milk churns were to be delivered to the villagers who had harboured those robbers, and whose actions had led to my sister's death, and then to add a little powder before they were sealed."

"But two of your victims were women!" Sir Trevill exclaimed.

"They were incidental," Morgan said contemptuously. "How was I to know if it was the man or the woman of the house who had allowed those murderers to remain there? To me, their punishment was equally satisfying."

"You may yet cheat the hangman." Lestrade murmured. "It may be an asylum for you."

Morgan smiled crookedly, an expression that made his madness evident. "But you will prove none of this, in court. I have enough money saved for the services of the best lawyers in the land. What is my confession? A fairy tale that I invented to amuse you. Nothing more."

"There is, I think, one piece of evidence that cannot be explained away easily," Holmes asserted.

"Impossible! My plan was perfect."

My friend went to the tray containing the seed cake. "It did not escape my notice that you were excessively anxious, as soon as you realised that I had identified you as the murderer of the villagers, to ensure that I consumed some of this cake." He withdrew the knife that had sliced the confection and handed it to Lestrade. "I will wager, Inspector, that it will be found that the blade is smeared with the very poison that we have been discussing."

"But Morgan himself ate some of it." I pointed out.

"It is a very old trick, dating as far back as the Borgias unless I am much mistaken. Only the unfortunate who partakes from some of the food is affected. The blade, you see, is coated on one side only."

"Devilishly ingenious," Sir Trevill gasped.

Lestrade stepped forward and firmly handcuffed Morgan's wrists. "Come on, my lad. It's the local lock-up for you, until the next train to London arrives."

"That should be in precisely two hours and twenty minutes, Inspector," Holmes said after consulting his pocket-watch.

"Thank you, Mr. Holmes and Doctor Watson, for your assistance."

"We are always glad to be of service. However, I perceive that you are about to mention that the time for luncheon approaches, and the inn is serving a particularly well-seasoned partridge. Perhaps, Inspector, after your visit to the local station, you would care to join us?"

"My collection of M"s is a fine one. Moriarty himself is enough to make any letter illustrious, and here is Morgan the poisoner . . . ."

– Sherlock Holmes
"The Adventure of the Empty House"

366

The Incident of the
Dual Intrusions
by Barry Clay

Foreword: This is the fourth account that comes from a collection of manuscripts that I accidentally discovered in the manner I described in the foreword of the book The Darkened Village. *As before, I found my word processor to be a problem. Despite my best efforts, it inexorably changed Dr. Watson's British spellings to American. I have long given up the struggle with it. Perhaps another editor would do a better job, as I am a poor one. These manuscripts fell into my hands by chance, and I am doing my best to bring them to the reading public as quickly as possible. Any anachronisms or mistakes are my own. I have been forced to patch together the unreadable portions of Watson's manuscript as best I can. As I have said before, I know I am not his literary equal.*

I did not need to wonder long why Watson left this manuscript unpublished. In Victorian fashion, he had always been meticulous in refraining from providing personal details of his life, deciding instead to highlight the exploits of his friend, Sherlock Holmes. Perhaps Watson found this tale to be too personal to be published in his lifetime, and yet too important not to record. The fact that he never referred to it in later accounts is instructive. It is obvious from some of the narration that this story was put to paper much later than it occurred.

Historians have had great debates concerning the life of Sherlock Holmes and, to a lesser extent, his chronicler, John H. Watson. To some, there appear to be contradictions in the stories submitted by Watson that make them suspicious. To others, these are only indications of mysteries to unearth. I hope this recently published manuscript provides the historian with more information about these men who, despite being so well-known, appear to be as much a mystery as anything found within Watson's accounts. – B.C.

During my long association with Sherlock Holmes, I have seen small and great, rich and poor, barons and schoolteachers, the perplexed, the puzzled, and the desperate call upon my friend. Even Scotland Yard, when faced with a baffling crime, has been known to hire Holmes to bring the case to resolution. The sheer diversity of humanity that have found themselves at 221b Baker Street has been an education in itself. That I've been able to help the great detective in a few of his cases has been an honor, and I have deeply valued our friendship. But never did I think that

I would have cause to call upon his services on my own behalf as I did in the spring of 1891.

It was one of the bright, late-March mornings that occasionally blesses even London, known for its less-propitious weather, with a promise that can lighten even the most pessimistic of hearts. I had broken my fast and was preparing to descend to my surgery for a day, caring for patients, when my lovely wife, who had answered the door to our lodgings, returned with a telegram.

"John, didn't you tell me you stopped by to see Mr. Holmes yesterday?"

"Yes, that's right. After my rounds. Why?"

My beloved was puzzled. "He has sent you a telegram."

"Indeed? What does it say? Is there a case?"

Mary unfolded the telegram and frowned at is as she read. "I don't think so. He asks you to visit him again today after you finish with your patients. But he asks that you walk rather than take a cab, and he asks that you do not start before five or after six. And further, he has a certain route that he wants you to take."

I took the telegram from her and read it myself – not that I was uncertain that she had read it correctly. I was merely puzzled and hoping to determine from something that Mary had missed why my friend would make such a request. There was nothing in the telegram to indicate his reasons. I could only comment, "This is odd."

"Could it be some kind of joke?"

"From Holmes? I should think not. No, I'm certain he has his reasons, though I don't know what they might be." I put the telegram down. "Well, I must get to my surgery before the first patients arrive." I embraced my wife warmly and descended the steps of our terrace house to the ground floor, only to re-enter by another door into the same building, where I had my practice.

The waiting room was as I had left it, and I passed the room in the hallway in which I had a small office, but I received a shock upon entering the examining room in which I saw my patients. The door that led to the back alley was open. Each and every jar of Jackson's Liniment Oil, which I stock for my patients with minor cases of arthritis, was standing by the sink, empty, except for those that had been shattered – I assumed thrown or knocked accidentally on the floor. The door to the wall cabinet in which I habitually kept them was opened, and that portion of the shelf empty.

My first thought upon seeing this was confusion and disbelief. My second was to verify that my stock of laudanum, opium-based medicines, and other more dangerous remedies were untouched, which I did quickly and found them all as I had left them. My third thought was to wonder if Holmes knew.

If he was somehow already aware of the intrusion into my surgery, why he had sent me the mysterious telegram? But why did he not tell me outright what had occurred, or come himself? And why had he provided me such odd instructions? I resisted the urge to go to him immediately. I couldn't do so. My hours were near, and I would likely have patients calling. My office hours were clearly posted, and even if I had no scheduled visitors, I made sure that I was there every Monday, Wednesday, and Friday between the hours of eight and five, for those who needed a physician, reserving house calls for the other days of the week.

I also resisted the urge to clean the broken glass. I had been with Holmes too many times when he angrily excoriated the London police for "tramping through" the remains of a crime and obscuring clues. Instead, I moved one of my examining screens in front of the sink and broken glass so that my patients wouldn't be able to see the disorder unless they were so bold as to walk around the screen. I could do nothing about the smell of the liniment, and I had no choice but to shut the back door and keep it shut by the expedient of placing a chair under the doorknob. I would need to hire a workman to repair it.

It was with great difficulty that I turned my mind to my patients that day. Fortunately, the number of visitors to my clinic was light, and their ills of a mundane nature, for I found my thoughts returning again and again to the inexplicable emptying of all my Jackson's Liniments and the wonton shattering of some of the bottles. When I broke for lunch, I didn't tell my Mary what I had found, but she was far too perceptive not to notice that I wasn't myself.

"John, what's wrong? You've hardly touched your food."

"Nothing, my dear," I responded, knowing full well that she wouldn't believe me. I disliked lying to her, but neither did I wish to alarm her. Yet I had to tell her something. "I'm worrying about the telegram from Holmes. It is most unlike him."

I'm not sure if I convinced her, but she placed a hand on my arm. "As you said, I am sure he has a good reason, which you shall know soon enough."

Which was true. My afternoon was full, but not overly so, and a little after five o'clock, I took my medicine satchel with me and started to Baker Street on the route indicated by the telegram

Prompted by Holmes's insistence that I take a prescribed path, I couldn't prevent myself from looking at my surroundings with more than my usual attention, but I saw nothing out of the ordinary. The occasional woman, often a servant, was pushing a pram along the street. Gentlemen, like myself, were walking on both sides, some with the firm step of a man who has a destination in mind, others more slowly, stopping at displays in shop windows or to examine flowers. Servants passed by on errands. There were children, both attended and unattended, the latter often running recklessly between other pedestrians, some of whom commented on their misbehavior with a remonstrance that went unheeded.

But it was only upon approaching Baker Street that I saw the beggar. While not uncommon in the less affluent areas of London, they were a rarity here, where the local constable would be inclined to intervene and perhaps even arrest one for vagrancy. This particular beggar was covered in hideous and pitiable sores, his face barely distinguishable as human under the lumping deformity. His scalp still retained wisps of hair, but it was mostly afflicted by the same unappealing lesions. He was sitting cross-legged on a tattered blanket, more a rag than a covering, with a worn hat and his paltry belongings beside him.

"A ha'-penny for a poor man, guv'nor?" he asked as I approached. I could barely believe that he saw me, for his eyes were rheumy and milky.

I paused. He could be just as he appeared, an unfortunate representative of the human race, or he could be one of the professional beggars that plague the populace of London. But even knowing the latter was possible, I could not prevent pity from welling in my heart. Despite my extensive background in medicine, I couldn't identify the nature of his affliction, but it was obviously a sore trial. Frankly, I couldn't believe this weak shadow of humanity was a member any professional class, begging or otherwise. And yet, I hesitated. Was this poor wretch the reason that Holmes had me walk this route? I quickly dismissed the notion. If that had been his motive, he could have achieved such a goal with less mystery. I reached into my pocket and withdrew a sovereign. As I handed it to him, his eyes widened in surprise and, perhaps, a little avarice.

"Coo, guv'nor!"

"Take it, my good fellow, and take my advice. Leave here before a constable sees you, and you spend a night in gaol."

"I will, guv'nor! I will! God bless you, guv'nor!"

Leaving the wretch behind, I continued to 221 Baker Street, somewhat troubled in my mind at having witnessed such suffering in the streets of London, knowing full well that in the poorer sections of our great city, there was nothing uncommon about it, except, perhaps, in his horrible disfigurement.

When I rang the bell at 221, Mrs. Hudson, who had been my landlady when I roomed with Holmes and still served as his, opened the door. "Dr. Watson, how good to see you again, though it seems it was just yesterday." Of course, as she well knew, it was. "Mr. Holmes has been expecting you.

He regretted that he had to step out, but he told me that, should you come before he returns, you should make yourself at home. He told me to assure you that he won't be long."

I was a little surprised at this, but I had only to wait to know why Holmes was acting in such mysterious ways. I ascended the stairs to the rooms that, until my marriage, I had shared with him and, as instructed, made myself at home. The morning *Times* was there, and I sat down in my accustomed armchair to read it.

After perhaps fifteen minutes, I heard steps on the stairs, and as I expected, Holmes entered the room. I arose to clasp his hand. "Ah, Watson," he exclaimed. "I apologize for keeping you waiting, but it was absolutely necessary."

"Of course. Think nothing of it."

And then he handed me a sovereign. "Here. Most generous of you. But if you keep handing sovereigns to beggars, you'll soon be out on the street yourself, and Mrs. Watson with you." His eyes twinkled with humor.

I was amazed. "Holmes, that beggar – was that you?"

"It was." He took a seat on the settee. "What did you think of my disguise?"

Bewildered, I sat opposite him. "It was utterly convincing, but why go to all that trouble? Does it have to do with the wreckage in my examining room?"

It isn't often that I see Holmes taken by surprise, but he was then. He leaned forward, keenly interested. "What's that you say? Your examining room was vandalized?"

"You didn't know?"

"I did not."

"When I arrived before my patients this morning, every bottle of Jackson's Liniment Oil was emptied into my sink. Some of the bottles were smashed. The back door had been forced. I thought that somehow you knew."

"How on earth could I possibly know?"

I was embarrassed. I was so accustomed to my friend knowing the impossible, that I had just assumed it. "Well, your telegram, and then I saw the wreckage . . . ."

"And you put the two pieces of information and assumed I knew more than I could possibly know. The intrusion must have been most upsetting to a man of your regular habits." And then he added, sharply, "You didn't tidy the mess, did you?"

"No, I left everything as it was, except that I had to position a screen between it and my patients or excite their question."

"Splendid! Then let us examine the room."

He immediately rose, and I did likewise, but my words stopped him. "But if you didn't know about the break-in, why did you request that I come here? And by that route, and why were you wearing that disguise?"

"Why, Watson, so I could get a closer look at those who were following you without them being aware that I had taken an interest in their actions."

I could barely believe what he had said. "There is someone following me?" I exclaimed in alarm. "Me?"

"Yes, and more than one man." He added after a moment, "Though I think it would be more accurate to say that one man is following you, and another man is following *that* man."

"Did you get a close look at them then?"

"I did. Beggars have every reason to stare at those who pass by and, unlike you, few people wish to examine them closely. After we investigate the break-in of your examining room, we will ask our dear friend, Inspector Lestrade, about the man following you."

"Why Lestrade?"

"Because the man following you is one of his detectives." I'm confident that I goggled at my friend. "You may remember him. Taylor? Small chap, dark hair, clean shaven, thin face, somewhat young."

"Of course I remember him. But you say he was following *me*?"

"When you visited here last night, merely by chance I had been standing at the window when you approached. I noticed a man behind you. He kept far enough behind that I was certain you were unaware of him. When you left, I purposely positioned myself at the window to watch your departure. I observed him leave after you. It was too dark for me to be sure of his identity, but I was nearly certain that it was Taylor. You may recall that he has an unusual way of holding his head. I was even more amazed when another figure left the shadows of an entryway even farther back and appeared to follow him!"

"What does this all mean?"

"That," he replied grimly, "is what I intend to discover."

We took a cab back to my surgery. In all, I had been gone nearly an hour, and I began to worry about what I should say to Mary. I broached the subject with Holmes.

"Mrs. Watson? I should tell her everything."

"I don't want to alarm her."

Drily, he said, "As I remember the former Miss Morstan, it would take more than this to alarm her."

We arrived at my home, but before I could insert the key, Holmes stopped me. "One moment, Watson," he said, laying a hand to my arm. I stepped back as he removed a magnifying glass from his coat and examined the lock. After a short time, he straightened. "This lock has been picked, recently – perhaps even today – and by a professional."

"How do you know?"

"There are faint markings. The metal is lighter in color where the picks scraped against it when they were used to open the door. An amateur would have left more scratches."

"But . . . ." I was perplexed. "But why would someone who could open a door in that manner force my back door?"

"He wouldn't. The mystery deepens." He looked at me. "Let us see if your examining room will provide more indications."

I opened the door and led Holmes through the waiting room, past my office, and into the examining room, where I received another rude shock. "Good heavens!"

"I take it this is not how you left it."

The room was now a complete shambles. All the doors to my cabinets and drawers holding my surgical equipment were open. Bottles were lying every which way – boxes of bandages, empty, lay where they were tossed, the bandages fully unwound and, it seemed, thrown at random. Notes from my practice files were strewn about. Bottles of pills were emptied and their contents scattered, some on the counter, others on the floor. My entire stock of laudanum and other medicines were moved but still present – everything wasn't simply in disarray but spread about the room. Various liquids were spilled on the floor and on the counter. My entire stock of medications, ointments, and potions was vandalized. The only thing that was undisturbed was the door to the back alley and the chair under the knob.

Watching me keenly, Holmes observed, "You seem to have secured your broken back door well. No doubt that's why your second intruder entered through the front." After a moment, he asked, "Are you all right, Watson?"

"I . . . I am shocked. What does all this mean? What shall I tell Mary?"

"Investigation will determine what this means. What you will tell your wife is more complicated." And then he shook his head. "Do I remember correctly that she has distant relatives in Cornwall?"

"You do, but why do you ask?"

"I would suggest you advise her to pay a visit to them until this is resolved."

"Do you think she is in danger?"

His response was thoughtful. "No. No, I do not. Your burglars seem to prefer you to be absent before they enter the premises, but it would be prudent measure to take in the event that changes."

"I have no intention of leaving," came my wife's voice. We both turned behind us, and there was my Mary. She was dressed in her old clothes, carrying a bucket and mop. Her hair was tied back with a scarf. I rushed to her.

"Mary, are you alright?"

She set down her mop and bucket to embrace me. "John, you had me so worried!"

"Me? You, you mean! Why me?"

Before I could respond, Holmes said, "Mrs. Watson, I can see you have come prepared to restore your husband's surgery to order, but please, not before I have an opportunity to examine it. If you will excuse me." He turned his back to us and, magnifying glass in hand, he began methodically to go through the room. We both watched his meticulous progress in silence, and then he said, "I can listen while you tell your story."

"Your story?" I asked my wife.

Without turning his attention from his examination, Holmes said, "She obviously has one, or she wouldn't be here now."

Mary nodded. "Mr. Holmes is correct. It was perhaps ten minutes after you left to leave to comply with his request. I thought I heard someone moving in your examining room. At first, I believed that you had simply returned for something you had forgotten, and I paid it no mind, but the sounds continued. After a while, they began to worry me. Some of them were quite loud. I tried to ignore them, and succeeded for perhaps half-an-hour, long after the time it would take you to find something. And, John, I knew there was something you weren't telling me. As the sounds of a search continued, I decided to ask you about it. It never occurred to me that it might not be you! I came down the stairs and then around to the front door of your office when, to my surprise, a stranger opened the door before I could do so. He was exiting as I was entering. We looked at each other, both of us startled, and then the man passed me without a word, turning his head away. He jostled me on the stoop as he passed, forcing me to hold the railing to keep from falling."

"My dearest, were you hurt?"

"No, but I was terribly frightened – for you more than for me. I caught my balance and watched his back disappear into the crowd, and then I rushed into the waiting room, fearing the worst. I assured myself you were not there, and then entered this room, and this was what I found." She took a deep breath. "I was so afraid to find you lying here, and greatly relieved when I saw that the only damage done was to things that can be replaced with a little money."

Holmes, still examining the room, called to us. "Did you get a good look at the man, Mrs. Watson?"

"Yes. He was tall, and broadly built. I would say around thirty. He had a brown mustache, and he had a small scar under his left eye. He was wearing a grey suit."

Holmes arose. "Watson, your wife would make an excellent detective."

Mary smiled at him. "I think I will leave that to you and John, Mr. Holmes."

It was clear that Holmes had finished his examination, and my dear wife began to restore my examining room to order. I asked my friend, "Did you find anything?"

"Yes, though this kind of destruction made learning about your first intruder nearly impossible. Your second intruder, however, left many indications. He is perhaps six-feet-two-inches in height to judge from his shoe size, stride, and reach. Spilled liquid doesn't leave as sure an impression as damp earth, but it serves. I was able to ascertain from a thread that caught on one of the drawers that he was well-dressed in, as your wife has told us, grey. It is a luxuriant thread, and not common. Hardly the kind of finery one would expect from a run-of-the-mill burglar, who moved your stock of opiates but didn't take them."

"Were you able to learn anything about the first intruder?"

And here his eyes took on a look of amusement. "Very little, except that he was a patient of yours that has only been here once, was under six feet in height, was left alone in the examining room for a short time, had a minor illness that you thought, to your annoyance, was not worth a visit to your surgery, who left behind a small envelope, who you have made unintentionally very angry, and that Lestrade will know his name."

"Holmes! How could you possibly know all that?"

"I deduced it from the facts, of course."

"I do not see how!"

"Well," said Holmes, "let us visit Lestrade, where we can determine if at least one, if not all, of my deductions is correct."

Inspector Lestrade of Scotland Yard was wiry and sallow, with a thin face, dark eyes, and a face like a ferret. He frequently called on Holmes when faced with a particularly knotty problem, paying him well, but often taking the credit for the solutions that Holmes provided. Despite this, and the occasional acerbic comment my friend might make of his abilities, I knew that Holmes respected him, along with Tobias Gregson, as being a cut above the average Scotland Yard inspector.

Given their working relationship, I was surprised when my friend asked at the desk to see Lestrade on a matter of some urgency and wasn't permitted to do so immediately. Instead, the constable returned to say that the inspector was otherwise engaged and couldn't see Mr. Holmes at the moment, but if he were to leave his card and reason for visiting, the inspector would return his call at his earliest opportunity.

"My goodness!" said Holmes mildly. He looked at me. "Well, Watson, there's nothing for it. We'll just have to go to the newspapers." He added, with regret in his voice, "I had been hoping to spare the Yard the embarrassment, but if the good inspector is simply too busy to see us, he will no doubt be able to explain it to his superiors after they read it in the morning." And he rose to leave.

The constable reacted to my friend's words with alarm. "Here now, sir! One moment. Let me try again." Holmes sat back down with a smile tugging on the corner of his lips, and the disturbed constable left us alone. This was a longer wait than the first, but it was more successful. When the constable returned, he said, "The Inspector will see you now." He led us to the office door on which "*G. Lestrade*" was printed on a brass plate, and let us into the office, closing it behind us.

"Mr. Holmes, what is it?" Lestrade greeted us, more than a little annoyed. "I am a busy man. What's all this twaddle about going to the newspapers?" He gestured us to seats.

"I thought they might be interested to know why Scotland Yard is expending money to follow an upstanding, British citizen like Watson rather than to keep the streets of London safe from pick pockets and purse snatchers."

Lestrade's face showed first surprise, then anger, then, finally, calculation. "I don't know what you're talking about," he said.

Dryly, and without humor, Holmes replied, "If you intend to take that tack with me, I shall go to the papers and mention your name."

Lestrade winced. "There's no need for that, Mr. Holmes."

The two men stared at each other. Finally, Holmes said, "Let us try it like this: Three days ago, you instructed one of your detectives of follow a man, probably in relation to the theft of something precious, probably gems, though I will concede it is possible it was another small article or articles of immense value. That man entered Watson's establishment during his visiting hours. When he left, the detective finally apprehended him, only to discover that the gems you thought he had stolen were not in his possession. Your superiors reasoned that he might have turned them over to Watson, and they forced you to keep Watson under observation to determine if he was in league with the thief and attempted to sell the gems."

That Holmes had struck home was obvious from Lestrade's face. "You cannot possibly know that!"

"I deduce it. Am I correct?"

"Yes, but how did you know?"

"Because I knew of the vandalism in Watson's surgery – something I dare say you do not. It indicated that a man had examined the contents of a certain brand of liniment oil stocked by Watson for his patients. Why would an intruder do that? I asked myself. And I answered it: Because he had hidden something in those bottles and had returned to obtain them. Just that fact alone told me that there was subterfuge and criminal enterprise afoot, for why would he hide anything in Watson's belongings? Whatever the man possessed must have been small enough to be placed in a bottle of liniment and sturdy enough not to be damaged by the oil. It couldn't possibly have been paper, which would have been damaged by immersion. Nor could it be anything that would dissolve in liquid. That suggested small gems. That they were of considerable value was self-evident. And, finally, you know Watson well enough to realize that he would never act as a fence for stolen gems, which meant that your superiors had forced your hand. Come, come, Lestrade. You can see the game us up."

Lestrade shook his head, but more in wonderment than in refusal, for he said, "You are correct in every aspect."

"It was gems?"

"Five diamonds, worth about five-hundred pounds."

"Stolen?"

"From the home safe of a jeweler, Albert Fenwick."

"By?"

Lestrade shifted uneasily. "There, I am not sure. We received an anonymous tip that Nicholas Walker, a known thief and burglar, had the diamonds."

"But you doubted it?"

"I regard all anonymous tips of that nature with suspicion. Walker was known to us, but he had never stolen gems before. The odd candlestick, perhaps, or currency. But gems seemed out of his league from what we knew of him. And the robbery itself was conducted with more finesse than we would have expected of him."

"I dare say you are correct. But of course, you had him followed as a precaution."

"Of course. It took no small amount of effort to locate him. I assigned Taylor to the case. Had Walker entered a pawn shop or known fence, we would have caught them both."

"But Walker entered Watson's surgery, and your detective became alarmed."

"Yes. It occurred to him that if Walker had the diamonds, he could hide them anywhere or pass them to anyone."

"And so he stopped Walker, searched him, and found nothing. When you reported this to your superiors, they insisted that you put Watson under observation."

Lestrade looked at me. "I'm sorry, Doctor, but I simply had no choice. I tried to vouch for you, but they wouldn't accept my word for your probity."

Holmes also turned to me. "Did I not tell you that Lestrade would know the name of your patient?"

"You did indeed, but why do you believe him to be my patient?"

"Surely that are obvious now."

"I am afraid not."

"Very well. First, I assume Mr. Walker did indeed have the diamonds in his possession, but he noticed that he was being followed."

Lestrade said, "Taylor admitted he suspected that was the case. It was another reason he stopped Mr. Walker."

"So, Mr. Walker notices that he's being followed, has the diamonds in his possession, and he is afraid he might be stopped at any moment. He must hide the gems, but where? Ah, then he sees your office sign. Remember, I know your habits. You are in office on Mondays, Wednesdays, and Fridays, and you make rounds on Tuesdays and Thursdays, as well as Saturday mornings if necessary. This is Wednesday, so this had to be Monday, three days ago, when this occurred. He decides on a bold move. He will hide the gems in your office, then return for them later. But Mr. Walker wasn't sick, so he had to provide you with an excuse."

"I . . . you are right. There was a man with a large, black mustache. It hung over his mouth. He was perhaps forty years of age."

Lestrade interjected, "A good description of Walker, Doctor."

"And under six foot?" Holmes asked.

I recalled Holmes's description, based on his observations in my examination room.

"Yes. He wasn't as tall as I am. He said he had a splinter in his finger that he couldn't remove without aid."

"And you left him alone in the examining room."

"Yes," I confirmed, once again astonished at my friend's ability to describe events from such small clues. "I had just taken him to the room, when he said that he'd heard a fall and a cry. I worried that an elderly patient might have entered the waiting room and collapsed."

"And while you investigated, he removed the gems from a small envelope he was carrying, opened the nearest cabinet to him that he could reach easily – which is how I knew him to be shorter, for on the shelf above were bottles that were even better suited for hiding gems that a taller man would have used – extracted a bottle of liniment oil that was contained in a nearly opaque, deep-green glass, and deposited the diamonds in it. He replaced the bottle where he had found it, but in his haste, he left the envelope that held the diamonds on the counter. There is nothing else like it in your examining room, and obviously it had been brought there from outside. You returned from the waiting room, where you found him waiting for you."

"He was standing. He said that the splinter had just come out on its own, which is poppycock, and that he no longer needed my services. I was very annoyed."

"As I knew you would be."

"But how did you know that I'd made him angry?"

"Because of your description of your surgery this morning. When Walker broke into your examining room to retrieve the diamonds, he only emptied the bottles of Jackson's Liniment Oil because it was in such a bottle that he'd placed the diamonds. Having finally thwarted his police tail, he broke into your surgery sometime yesterday when you were on your rounds. He expected to retrieve the diamonds easily, but he became angry when he was unable to find them in any of the bottles, and he dashed two of them on the floor in his anger."

Understanding flooded me. "I think I know where the diamonds are."

"I'm sure you do, for it was you who removed the bottle containing the diamonds, not knowing they were in it. Who has the bottle now?"

"I gave a bottle to Mrs. Shay. Her arthritis has been bothering her horribly, and she actually visited me towards the end of my day on Monday. She said that her own bottle was nearly empty."

"Well, Lestrade," said Holmes, as satisfied as he was amused, "shall we visit Mrs. Shay and see if, perhaps, she is in possession of a very singular bottle of Jackson's Liniment Oil, with unexpected and expensive contents?"

Such proved to be the case. Old Mrs. Shay, a garrulous, generous woman, was quite willing for us to test her bottle, and she was surprised to discover as we poured Jackson's Liniment Oil through a strainer from her new bottle into her nearly empty one, that five diamonds had been hidden in it. Lestrade was greatly pleased, for he would no doubt receive a commendation for having found them after all, and so quickly.

But as he left us, Holmes's voice called him back. "Lestrade, I would send a constable to check on Mr. Walker."

"Why?" returned the inspector. "We can't possibly prove that he had the diamonds."

"No, but you might want to assure yourself that he is well and unharmed."

"What do you mean?"

"Somehow, someone learned of Scotland Yard's interest in Watson. It is obvious that they used Scotland Yard to uncover Walker's whereabouts, and thus they learned of your interest in Watson. Whomever that someone was, they were following your Detective Taylor before Watson paid me a visit on Tuesday night. I would be surprised if Mr. Walker handed that information over willingly. I suspect that he stole those gems from whomever stole them originally from Mr. Fenwick."

I blurted, "The second man that Mary saw tonight!"

"Precisely."

"But if that were true, wouldn't that second man have known that Walker couldn't find them?"

"Perhaps, but you're assuming that Walker would have been believed, or that he survived his interrogation long enough to provide that information."

"Good heavens! That's dreadful!"

"But it is, I am sad to say, likely." He glanced at Lestrade, who nodded.

"I'll take care of it, Mr. Holmes. And thank you."

When he left us, I turned to my companion. I am certain my face showed my terror. "This was why you wanted Mary out of the way," I declared to him.

"At the time, it was merely conjecture, but now? I think that we must assure ourselves of Mrs. Watson's safety." And then he added, "But don't worry. I suspect that she is safe and well. Had there been true danger, it would have happened this afternoon before we arrived, when the second man who violated your surgery couldn't find that for which he searched."

Despite my friend's words, the cab we took couldn't travel fast enough to suit me. When we arrived at our home, I dashed up the steps to our lodgings and burst through the door, startling my wife. "John!" she cried in surprise, and I ran to her and embraced her. "John, whatever is the matter?"

After a moment, I could hear Holmes's voice behind me, wryly observing, "I think you can release Mrs. Watson now. She appears to be in excellent health." I did so, but reluctantly.

"Mr. Holmes is right, John. I'm fine. What on earth has you so worried? The case is solved, isn't it?"

I let Mary go, while Holmes asked, his eyebrows raised, "The case is indeed solved, but how do you know that?"

"Why," said my wife, "your associate, Mr. Whistler, told me."

Evenly, Holmes said, "I have no associate other than Watson here."

She seemed bewildered. "Oh. But . . . but he said . . . ."

"What exactly did he say?"

"Well, that he was a detective like you, Mr. Holmes. You just missed him. He was here not five minutes ago! He said that his man, the one I saw this afternoon, had been searching for missing diamonds in John's examining room."

"Indeed?"

"Yes. He was most apologetic. He told me that his man had exceeded his instructions, and that, now that you had recovered the diamonds, there was no need for me, or John, to worry about a reoccurrence. He told me that he had thoroughly disciplined his employee for his actions. And John – " Here Mary picked up an envelope." – he left this for you to pay for the damages. It's quite a lot of money."

I looked through it and confirmed that I was looking at more money than I had seen in one envelope in my life. I looked wonderingly at Mary, and then at Holmes.

Mary continued. "He apologized for the work that I was forced to do to clean the room, though how he knew I had done so I do not know. And, Mr. Holmes," Mary said, "he was most insistent when he told me to tell you how much he admires you and how he hopes that you and he will become friends." And then she added, "Or, at least, not enemies." Holmes looked so grim that Mary then said, "I thought that last a little odd, but he was so very polite, I didn't feel the least bit ill at ease."

"What did this Mr. Whistler look like?"

"He was very tall, very thin. Mostly bald with a very high forehead. He was quite well-dressed, in a deep blue suit, with a thin, gold bar instead of a cravat at his collar. And he had an odd manner of moving his head back and forth, but slowly." As Holmes said nothing to this, Mary asked, "Did I do something wrong?"

My friend seemed to rouse himself. "No, Mrs. Watson, you've done nothing wrong." He assumed an air of confidence that I could tell was false, and he said, "Nothing is wrong at all. At least, nothing that you and your husband need concern yourselves with. Well, I believe I should leave you both alone."

But I could tell that Holmes was holding something back. I insisted on accompanying him to the door. As we descended the steps, I asked, "Should I be worried?"

He stopped and looked at me. Finally, he said, "No. No. I should think not."

"But your concern that Walker might be dead . . . ."

"Is probably correct. As I said, I suspect that Walker stole from the original thief. Sometime on Tuesday, the original thief caught up with him and extracted sufficient information to know that he had secreted the gems in your surgery. I doubt that Walker survived the interrogation."

"But then, how can you be sure Mary is in no danger?"

"If she were in danger, it would have already taken place. No, there is a larger picture here. We have her descriptions of two different men, and there must be more of them involved, for we've been under observation. And it's observation of the first order for me to have been unaware of it. It must be so. It is how this 'Whistler' – I think that we both know his real name – knew that the case was solved. He must have come straight here after our visit to Mrs. Shay. There is something more behind this. What, I don't know, but our 'Mr. Whistler' appears determined to convince us of his good will – or perhaps rather that he bears us no ill will. For now, I believe that we can count on that declaration to hold. He says that he admires me. Well, let us trust that I am up to his admiration. He may live to regret it."

And then he placed a hand on my shoulder. "But you, Watson – I think I can tell you with confidence that you and your wife are completely safe. You have my word on it."

And with that, he left me. At the time, I remained somewhat apprehensive, but I trusted Holmes's assurance that Mary was safe, and as the day's events drew farther into the past, my concern was left behind as well.

After several months of hesitation, I decided to commit to paper what I remembered of this affair, and Mary's visitor. I'm very thankful that she was given no cause for concern, for my time with her was far too short as it was. I remain uncertain if I will send it to my publishers, for even afterwards, we never uttered the true name of the mysterious Mr. Whistler, even after the incident at Reichenbach Falls was as firmly in the past as The Incident of the Dual Intrusions.

" 'You crossed my path on the fourth of January,' said he. 'On the twenty-third you incommoded me; by the middle of February I was seriously inconvenienced by you; at the end of March I was absolutely hampered in my plans . . . . "

– Professor James Moriarty
"The Adventure of the Final Problem"

The Case of the
Un-Paralleled Adventures
by Steven Philip Jones

Note – *You never know what the postman might bring.*

In the summer of 2012, a package arrived from my friend John Ross, who lives in England. John and I collaborated on an original graphic novel sequel to Bram Stoker's Dracula *many years ago, during which time he became painfully aware of my fascination with Sherlock Holmes, who makes an important cameo in our story. When John chanced across a battered diplomat briefcase that purportedly belonged to Holmes's elder brother Mycroft at a market in Sleaford, he thought of me and sent it as a gift.*

The briefcase came with no provenance, but it was love at first sight. I am one of those guys who will hang on to an antique console radio that hasn't worked in decades because they don't make 'em like that anymore, and I thought the scruffy black leather bag with battered double gussets was as beautiful as a mint condition 1940's Underwood Champion typewriter. The briefcase didn't make the transatlantic journey unscathed, however, and a slip pocket had pulled away from the back compartment to expose two slim handwritten manuscripts and some scraps of official stationery that had been sewn in behind the fraying fabric. Imagine my incredulity when I saw "Mycroft Holmes" in the stationery letterhead and read where one manuscript was written by Dr. John H. Watson and the second reported the circumstances surrounding the "short but interesting visit" *Sherlock Holmes made* "to the Khalifa at Khartoum" *and* "communicated to the Foreign Office" *that he mentions in the* "The Adventure of the Empty House."

I will forgo presenting the (often laborious) details involved with authenticating these papers here, except to say that this would have been impossible without the tireless assistance of many American and British Sherlockian groups spearheaded by The Always Available Hansom Cab Drivers of the Midwest. *An exhaustive accounting of these efforts is in the works, but for now I offer this transcript of two incidents that transected briefly during what could have been one of the most tumultuous months in the history of the British Empire, if not the world.*

– SPJ

From the Journal of Mycroft Holmes

31 October, 1893 – Minutes of Meeting with Gladstone

I.   *Post mortem* of Lords's defeat of Second Home Rule Bill.

II.   IMRO, Thessaloniki.

III.   Communications from Walter Simonson.

        A.   Letter delivered by G. Lestrade via John Watson being deciphered. Coded dispatch delivered via Queen's Messenger confirms Khalifa agrees to speak with our agents.

        B.   Review of events preceding dispatch.

                1.   W.S. and zenko tracked Moriarty's 2nd Lieut. from Amol and Mecca to Sudan.

                2.   W.S. and zenko arrived in Khartoum last week after Maghrib prayer.

        C.   P.M. concerned about Khalifa's insistence on meeting agents in Khartoum, not new capital Omdurman.

                1.   P.M.: "Khartoum must never become an embarrassment again!"

                2.   P.M.: "Could use your brother's help. His death must not be in vain."

                3.   Concurred.

IV.   Notified P.M. of "a possible and equally embarrassing situation" involving the Moriarty brothers [1].

        A.   "Hammersmith"

        B.   Jack the Ripper

* * * *

From the Unpublished Personal Reminiscences
of John H. Watson, M.D.

Chapter I

The streets of London have always been haunted. By ghosts. Monsters. And memories.

It was October of 1893 and my wife Mary was ill. Her health had grown tenuous since the onset of autumn, and the dread of what winter would bring festered my thoughts. By this time I had all but completely devoted myself to attending to her, so when I received a request from a journalist named Daniel Kingdom with *The London Illustrated News* to speak with myself and Inspector Lestrade that evening concerning a matter involving Sherlock Holmes, I had every intention of declining. Mary, however, insisted that I accept. "You have ignored yourself too long, James [2]. Shutting yourself up and forsaking any physical or mental exercise benefits neither of us. Go to satisfy your own curiosity if for no other reason." How could I refuse my wife's sympathetic spirit? I could also not deny that I was curious, as was Lestrade, who was preparing to get in touch with me about Kingdom when I telephoned. The inspector was familiar with the journalist and felt almost certain this was no prank or gyp, although he had no inkling as to what Kingdom wanted to ask us.

Lestrade and I hadn't seen one another since early summer, and when we arrived in Dorset Street upon the requested hour, I was most grateful for both his company and the revolver I knew that he always carried in his hip-pocket. As I regarded the low, sloped, dilapidated Huguenot houses with high windows that clustered on each side of the dreary lane, I said, "It appears that the cleanup of the slums hasn't yet reached this bleak spot." [3]

"If you want to see bleak, Doctor, go down that alley to the right and walk through Miller's Court. There are advantages in allowing your worst criminals to gather themselves in one rookery, but it's a convenience that comes with perils. Constables have been patrolling there in pairs even before I was a peeler. I doubt there's a fouler, more dangerous spot in all of London."

The name Miller's Court was familiar and I remembered why an instant before Kingdom joined us. He was a slim young man, slightly tainted in the Oxford manner, with an inquisitive, clean-shaven face and alert attitude. Speaking in an unabashed tone, he pronounced, "And no spot is more notorious than Thirteen Miller's Court, where Mary Kelly was eviscerated by Jack the Ripper before he was nibbed."

"What are you about?" Lestrade growled. "We never arrested the Whitechapel Murderer."

"I disagree, Inspector. According to one of my sources, the Ripper died of Hempen Fever in Newgate Prison nearly five years ago."

"And what source is that?"

"Confidential and generally reliable, but I believe you gentlemen can help me in verifying this information."

"You mind telling me how?"

385

"You were with the CID in November 1888?"

"I was, but not '*H*' Division, and this is their district."

Kingdom cocked his head with the air of a solicitor already acquainted with the answers to his queries and looked my way. "Did Mr. Holmes's ever offer to lend Scotland Yard his assistance with the murders?"

"No," I said.

"Did the police ever consult him?"

"No."

"Did anyone besides the police ever ask for his help?"

"Yes. George Lusk of the Whitechapel Vigilance Committee approached Holmes's a week after Miss Kelly's murder, but he assured Lusk that he was more than satisfied with Scotland Yard's efforts. There were no more killings after that, of course, thank God."

"Are you sure, Doctor Watson? Some insist there were – and not just after Mary Kelly, but before Mary Ann Nichols."

Lestrade snorted. "Those opinions are the merest moonshine and nothing more."

"How can you be so sure, Inspector?"

"Because Dr. Thomas Bond assured Robert Anderson, the head of the CID, that there were only five killings. Bond has an excellent reputation with '*A*' Division, so if he says there were no more and no less than five, that's good enough for me."

Kingdom cocked his head again before asking me. "Was Mr. Holmes's working on any cases at the time of the Whitechapel Murders?"

"He was, although nothing even remotely related to them."

"Did he work on any cases immediately after Mary Kelly's murder?"

I rummaged through my memories. "None that I recall."

"May I ask what you were doing during those times?"

"I was in Dartmoor near the end of September and for a good deal of October at the request of Mr. Holmes. After that I was preoccupied with my wedding and setting up a new home and practice."

"I see." Kingdom smirked, the solicitor moving in for the kill. "Inspector, did you consult Mr. Holmes's on a murder investigation in Hammersmith that November?"

I think it unlikely that Lestrade could ever have looked more confounded. "A murder? In Hammersmith?" Then he laughed in a most unpleasant manner.

Kingdom shot an angry glance at the Inspector. "What's so funny?"

"The Hammersmith Ghost Murder was ninety years ago! A bit before even my time." [4]

Giving Kingdom the benefit of the doubt, I said, "Surely he is referring to something more recent."

"Then he can surely tottle over to west London and poke bogey with the Hammersmith Police."

Kingdom was not about to be dismissed. "Did you consult Mr. Holmes's on any murders that November?"

"I can't say that I did."

"Think again, Inspector. You must have."

Whatever patience Lestrade still possessed at this point evaporated. "Look, I don't know who put this bee in your bonnet, but you can come to the Yard and check the official files from the Factory if you want."

"I do."

"Your funeral. Coming, Doctor?" Lestrade asked me,

My own patience along with my curiosity were likewise depleted. "No. I have more pressing matters waiting at home."

A somber mien overshadowed Lestrade's irritation. "Of course. My best to Mrs. Watson."

"Thank you." I bid Kingdom good night as politely as I could and departed.

Chapter II

The hour was late by the time Mary dropped asleep. The nurse took over her care so that I could retire, but I couldn't put away Kingdom's allegation. Like the rest of London, I had spent the autumn of 1888 absorbed and repulsed by the Whitechapel Murders, and I had read and reread George Hutchinson's statement in *The Illustrated Police News* about what the man claimed he witnessed during the night of Mary Kelly's murder. I recalled the accompanying illustration of an opulently dressed man that Hutchinson described having seen accompany her inside Thirteen Miller's Court no more than three hours prior to her death. I also couldn't stop reimagining the landlord's agent Thomas Bowyer going to collect her rent the following morning, only to commemorate Lord Mayor's Day by discovering her mutilated corpse.

Unable to sleep, I pulled out my notebook for the year 1888 and located my transcript of Holmes's meeting with Lusk. My friend had had no intention of intruding without invite into a matter that was becoming a whetstone of public ridicule towards Scotland Yard. There were radical elements using the Whitechapel Murders to sharpen their arguments that the police were mismanaged and maladroit. By talking with Lusk, Holmes's hoped he might pacify one of the Yard's critics. As I scanned my notes, I was surprised to see that I'd forgotten that Lusk had brought along another member of the Committee, a young tinsmith named Minor Barnes:

>*HOLMES: I applaud your committee's sense of civic duty in patrolling the Whitechapel district, Mr. Lusk. Although not being trained as sentries or detectives, I fear your efforts may prove to be of little benefit.*

>*LUSK: We're also petitioning the government to offer a reward for information about this monster. And we've hired other unofficial detectives to interview any witnesses.*

>*BARNES: But there must be more we can do. The newspapers are right. The police are nothing but stumbling fools.*

>*LUSK: Minor! Keep a civil tongue or out with you! I'm sorry, Mr. Holmes.*

>*HOLMES: Not necessary. I share your frustration that the murderer has so far escaped justice, Mister . . . ?*

>*BARNES: Barnes, sir. Minor Barnes.*

>*HOLMES: Mister Barnes. What more would you have the police do?*

>*BARNES: Follow your methods.*

>*HOLMES: Which I can assure you they are. By all accounts they have done an exemplary job collecting and examining all the pertinent evidence. I also have every confidence in the police surgeon, Dr. Thomas Bond, and concur with his findings and opinions. A thorough search of Whitechapel has also been conducted by dozens of policemen, who have interviewed over two-thousand people and investigated over three-hundred suspects.*

>*LUSK: But Mr. Holmes, this brute kills on or near a weekend at the end of the month or soon after, and each killing has been more savage than the last. If we don't find him . . . if he isn't stopped . . . I dread to think what will happen when the calendar nears December.*

Lusk's dread was justified but never realized. The murders seemed to stop as abruptly as they began, but if Kingdom was correct this was only because the vilest villain this side of Professor Moriarty had died in prison.

Only how?

Why?

And who was he?

Apparently my curiosity was not as spent as I supposed.

I managed to nod off sometime soon after and it was long past dawn by the time I woke. Mary had already managed to eat a little breakfast and my meal was waiting, along with the first batch of morning mail. One envelope immediately attracted my attention. There was no return address, but there were four backstamps on the rear of the envelope, along with a message scribbled in Latin:

Mea gloria fides [5]

My friend Walter Simonson was fond of this maxim. It was his motto as an agent with the British Government, working through the aegis of Scotland Yard's Special Branch when he infiltrated the Moriarty organization after assuming the guise of a criminal named *Fred Porlock*. It was much the same ploy used by the Pinkerton agent Birdy Edwards when he infiltrated the Scowrers, a corrupt union operating in Pennsylvania's Vermissa Valley. [6]

Edwards succeeded in escaping the retribution of that murderous gang for over a decade until they enlisted Moriarty's aid, and after Simonson was forced to reveal himself after the Professor's death, his superiors ordered him to leave England to avoid the same fate. [7] I hadn't heard from Simonson since June of 1891, and my fingers trembled from anticipation and apprehension as I opened the envelope, but all it contained was another envelope addressed to "*G.L.*"

Inspector G. Lestrade was Simonson's liaison with Scotland Yard, so I departed for his office, only to be informed that he wasn't in. I left word for Lestrade to call at my house as soon as possible. "Please tell the Inspector that I wouldn't ask if it weren't urgent." Stepping outside, I purchased a *Morning Herald* for the cab ride home. I didn't peruse it long before coming across news that Daniel Kingdom had been shot and killed on Great George Street by a hansom driver who fled the scene and was still at large.

Chapter III

It was nearly time for lunch when Lestrade arrived. The man looked done in so I instructed the maid to bring some food as I led him into my consulting room, where I offered him a seat and some brandy.

Lestrade took a judicious sip. "Very much obliged, Doctor. Much as I hate to admit it, working all night uses me up more than it once did."

"We all get older. You haven't been home at all since we left Spitalfields?"

He shook his head before taking a second small sip. "Have you told anyone about last night?"

"Only my wife."

"I see. Have you Walter's envelope?" I presented it to Lestrade, who glanced at it then tucked it into a pocket.

"Aren't you going to open it?"

"Not for my eyes, and I have to ask you and Mrs. Watson not to discuss anything about last night with anyone. This request doesn't come from me, mind you, but from the Prime Minister and the Queen."

"Of course, but does this mean that Kingdom was right?"

Lestrade nodded with a weary frown. "What I'm about to tell must stay a secret between you and me, like that Sumatra business a few months ago. [8] Even Leather Apron was never informed that we knew who he was, although I suspect he guessed we might."

"How is that possible?"

"Chalk it up to good fortune or luck. I think they call it *kismet* in India. If the Moriartys get their way, however, it'll all be undone and the government and the throne will be the worst for it. Those curs are still up to their anarchist tricks, and not just in England, but our friend is onto them." Lestrade patted the pocket with the envelope. "That's all I can go into now about that, but Walter ought to have some tales to tell us whenever he returns."

The maid arrived with some cold beef and beer, and I waited for Lestrade to eat. Reinvigorated, he continued, "After that Baskerville business, Mr. Holmes's and I didn't cross paths again until near the end of November."

"Did he know about the Ripper?

"He did, as does his brother."

"And Kingdom, of course. And the Moriartys, you say?"

"One of them must have been his reliable source."

"But how is it they know? Was that cab driver who shot Kingdom one of them?"

"All good questions, Doctor. I took Kingdom to the Yard to look at the old files, but nothing was ever put there to find so he left. I shadowed after him to see where he went, hoping to find out how he knew to mention 'Hammersmith'."

"So there was a Hammersmith murder five years ago?"

"Nothing of the kind. Kingdom must have misunderstood that part. Anyway, it was midnight when we reached Great George Street and that hansom pulled up along the curb." Lestrade sat silently a few moments. "I couldn't see the driver, and when we tracked the cab down by its number, it turned out to be stolen. No one else was near enough to overhear the driver ask, 'Need a cab, Mr. Kingdom?' Daniel asked how the cabbie knew his name. 'Dear me, wouldn't that Yarder tailing you like to know!'" Mortified rage blotted Lestrade's features. "He plugged Kingdom twice and was off before I could even shout. By the time I was able to search Kingdom's rooms, any notes he might have kept about the Ripper were gone. Someone had been there and all they left was this." Lestrade removed a scrap of paper from another of his pockets and handed it to me. "Sound familiar?"

I read, "'*Dear me, Inspector! Dear me!*'"

"The Birlstone Murder may have been MacDonald's case, but there's not a jack who doesn't know about the note that the Professor had put in your letter-box after the Moriartys caught up with that Pinkerton agent."

"'*Dear me, Mr. Holmes! Dear me!*'" I recited. "Holmes's might have called this '*A distinct touch*'."

"Very much so, in this case."

"Why is that? I don't understand what the Moriartys gain by killing Kingdom."

"It's always been their way. 'Dead men don't bite.'"

"I'm sorry, Lestrade, but you're going to have to be more specific."

"Yes, I suppose I shall. This goes back to November 26th in 1888. Perhaps I am getting older, but I'll not forget that date, much less anything about it. A bobby found two men fighting near Saint Katherine Docks. Each swore the other had let some daylight into a dead sailor named Thomas Corder, lying a few feet away. One man, Richard Parsons, was a tailor, and the other, Minor Barnes, was a tinsmith. Corder was just back from South Africa and hadn't been in England since he signed on with the *Palmyra* in January."

Hearing Barnes's name intrigued me, but hearing the ship's name was startling. "You're sure it was the *Palmyra*?"

"The same ship that Birdy Edwards went overboard from when he was trying to elude the Moriartys? I'm sure. I wasted no time informing Mr. Holmes's and he wasted no time talking to Parsons and Barnes.

Parsons was a lousy duffer with a couple of murders in his past, although we could never prove that, while Barnes insisted that he found Corder and Parsons fighting and that he had tried to help the sailor. I was inclined to believe Barnes since he'd never even been arrested before."

"While Parsons sounds like just the sort who could have killed Edwards."

"Oh, he did, just like he killed Corder. The Pinkertons had never stopped searching for Edwards's killer, so we notified them, and it turned out they had just missed garnishing Corder in Cape Town. He probably came back to London to beg the Professor for sanctuary."

"Only dead men tell no tales."

"You'd think Parsons would have known that, but desperate men are apt to try desperate things. We weren't about to settle for half-measures with the Professor being involved, so Mr. Holmes's and I took a look about both men's residences." The hardy man's face pinched with disgust. "We found things in Barnes's rooms."

"Umm . . . what – ?"

"One of the things we found was a clasp knife. It was straight, about six inches long with a strong, sharp blade pointed at the top and an inch thick. We compared it against the victims' wounds and . . . well . . . Barnes was the Whitechapel Murderer, all right."

"My word." Several moments passed before the shock of learning the truth and how it was uncovered withered sufficiently to ask, "You never arrested Barnes?"

"Not for what he did to those five women. How could we without explaining why we searched his room? Professor Moriarty's name was bound to come up, and we had no proof against him."

"So what did you do?"

"All we could do was take the matter to Mr. Holmes's brother . . . who took it to Gladstone . . . who took it to Her Majesty, whereupon I was ordered to arrest Barnes for Corder's murder . . . release Parsons . . . and file everything about the investigation with Mycroft Holmes's under the cryptonym 'Hammersmith' after the old murder case."

"Why use that?"

"I can't claim to understand how the mind of government works, but the irony serves as a *caveat* to me of what we did." Such introspection from Lestrade was unexpected. In the Hammersmith case, George III had commuted the guilty man's sentence from hanging to one year's hard labor, but here the King's granddaughter had effectively commuted Barnes's sentence from innocent to guilty.

I said, "I understand the dilemma, but I can also sympathize how this solution doesn't seem proper, especially with Parsons going free."

"Well, you needn't fret about that. The hope was that the Professor would attend to Parsons, and from all accounts he did. Mr. Holmes, however, liked no part of the plan. He also warned that the Professor might figure out about 'Hammersmith', and it looks Mr. Holmes's was right. The way it seems to me is that the Moriartys slipped word about Barnes to Kingdom, expecting that he would just print it. It probably never crossed their minds that he'd want to dig up more about it first."

"So following his journalist's nature, he alerted you . . . which made Kingdom a possible liability to them . . . so they silenced him. But surely the Moriartys will try to expose 'Hammersmith' again."

"I don't know why they wouldn't, but they've tipped their hand so we'll keep sharp. It's just one more reason why the sooner there's an end to the Professor's organization, the better."

"Except that's easier said than done, as Holmes knew too well."

"Poor Mr. Holmes." Lestrade gave long sigh of melancholy. "I think he knew too much about some things."

"Why do you say that?"

"Doctor, jacks like me can do our job because we know this city and its people. I may not add imagination to my list of qualities, but I grew up on London's streets and I've been with the Yard over half my life. Now Mr. Holmes's knew London, but he wasn't raised here, and he grew up studying crime the way schoolboys do history. We were both doing all right for ourselves in our own ways, but then along comes Leather Apron. I've seen murders, but not like those. Neither had Mr. Holmes, but he did know about some like them from the past – some that were even worse." Lestrade stood and patted the pocket with the envelope again. "I'd best deliver this. Thank you for your hospitality. The food and drink did wonders. And, again, my best to Mrs. Watson."

Chapter IV

By myself once more, my mind was a swirl from all that I had discovered during the last twenty-four hours. As the minutes passed I found myself fixating more and more upon Lestrade's observations regarding Holmes, which eventually led to my recalling a rumination Holmes's made not long before the tragic events at Reichenbach regarding the likes of Moriarty.

"One of the burdens of my unique profession is my familiarity with the worst of mankind, both our attributes and personalities. Professor Moriarty is in some ways unprecedented as a tyrant-monster, but that has as much to do with the opportunities afforded to him by this current era as it does his personality. There have been clever criminal bosses like Worth,

393

Grady, and Mandelbaum, but they tended to be intolerant of violence. Not so much Richard Lines, proprietor of that Old House on West Street, the Red Lion Tavern, who might possibly be considered an actual forerunner to the Professor. At the other extreme are rivals to Moriarty's brutality but not his intellect. Gilles de Raise and Jonathan Wild fall into this camp.

"Perhaps worse than any of these – even Moriarty – are creatures like the unidentified brute who recently butchered seven women in Austin, Texas over a period of two years. More often than not he employed an axe. About this same time in the Netherlands, Maria Swanenburg definitively poisoned twenty-seven people, but I am far from the only person who suspects the actual number to be above ninety.

"Keeping the knowledge that such abominations exists in my brain-attic is necessary, but being aware that their existence is as inevitable as the passing of Time can be a curse. Except for those rare instances where Providence intervenes, humanity is powerless to prevent the havoc these bestial criminals cause. All we can do is remain vigilant and, if the time comes, act to put an end to their disasters at whatever cost."

* * * *

Walter Simonson's Journal

17 October, 1893 – Governor-General's Palace, Khartoum

It was well past sunset, closer to Isha than Maghrib, and there was still no sign of the Khalifa.

Had he changed his mind?

If so, what did that mean for our plans? Or us?

As more time passed, the tranquility of the courtyard seemed to grow more circumscribed than the surrounding tiers of shadowy archways and lattice-work.

I noticed that Mr. Sherlock appeared rather pensive as he gazed at some stairs leading from the ground level to the west wing's first floor, so I asked him what was on his mind.

"I was imagining what General Gordon might have been thinking that last morning. Standing right there, if Bernard Allen is correct. Had he erred ignoring orders to abandon the Sudan? Or was he more convinced than ever that he had done the proper if not the wisest thing?" [9]

"Or maybe he's still wondering, like President Lincoln's ghost wandering the White House corridors." Our voices carried in the stillness, but I decided to risk it after noticing a silhouette in an archway. "Some

394

insist that a merchant saw Gordon standing on those steps later that day, all dressed in white and just staring into the darkness."

"I've heard that, too. It would seem that Khartoum, like London, has its ghosts."

"I wouldn't know why not." I lowered my voice to a whisper. "Although I doubt that's Gordon's spirit watching us." I had assumed Mr. Sherlock was already aware of the silhouette and, judging by his blasé reaction, I was correct. In his own whisper he replied, "Unlikely. I suggest you ready your revolver." My hand was already upon the grip of my Webley, and I drew and cocked it as I barked, "You in the shadows! Come out where we can see you!" The stranger unhesitatingly stepped into the moonlight and I just as swiftly lowered my weapon. "The Khalifa! Please forgive me!"

The reply: "No, Mr. Sigerson. Or should I say Mr. Simonson? I cannot claim to be the Khalifa. I am only here at his behest." A spry, lean stranger with jade-colored eyes smiled as he fearlessly approached.

Keeping the Webley cocked, I asked, "Where is he?"

"Across the Nile in Omdurman." The stranger gazed upon Mr. Sherlock and beamed. "Is it possible you are Mr. Sherlock Holmes, of whom I have heard so much?"

I said, "Sherlock Holmes's is dead. This is my guide, Haj."

"And what a wonderful guise it is. Sir Richard Burton's could not have been better when he made his celebrated *Hajj*."

Mr. Sherlock ended all pretense of our charade with a shrug. "Well, perhaps no better than Achilles's in the court of King Lycomedes. Simonson, if I'm not mistaken, this gentleman is a *daroga*."

"A police chief?"

"From the Māzandarān providence, where, until recently, he spent some years in jail."

The *daroga* was impressed, but even more delighted. "Oh, your eyes and ears would be the envy of a soothsayer! I am Nadir Khan, just pardoned for a most heinous crime."

I asked, "What sort of crime?"

"For not killing a man as ordered by the Shah-in-Shah. Now, please, allow me to show you why the Khalifa did not come himself." From somewhere on his person Nadir drew a long single-edged gilt steel knife with a Persian recurve blade tapered to a needle-like point. "This was found stabbed beside the Khalifa's bed the morning before he received your request regarding the *majrim* you are hunting."

Mr. Sherlock asked to examine the knife and Nadir gratefully presented it. "A *pesh-kabz*?"

"Correct. An innovation of the Safavid dynasty. Its reinforced tip is designed to spread apart the links of an opponent's coat of mail so the blade may penetrate the armor."

I mentioned how leaving a knife as a present in this way was an old assassin tactic to intimidate enemies into submission, and Mr. Sherlock never paused in his inspection as he commented, "I believe the term is *hashashin*, and they always included a threatening note."

Nadir applauded twice. "Both of you are correct! However, the Khalifa found only the *pesh-kabz* and the *hashashin* . . . or Nizari Islaimis . . . were all defeated by the Mongols in 1256. Some insist that a few *hashashin* do still exist, plying their trade for personal rather than political purposes."

"You are an absolute font of knowledge, Nadir. Is your expertise of the *hashashin* the reason for your pardon?"

"In part, yes, although I like to think I still possess some small police skills."

"I would wager you possess considerably more than that." Mr. Sherlock handed back the knife. "Do you believe this belonged to a *hashashin*?"

"The Khalifa believes it's possible. That is all that matters."

"Can't you at least tell if it belonged to someone skilled in murder?" I asked.

"It's too pristine to display any tendencies of its owner."

"Which does not eliminate a mercenary *hashashin* is behind this," Mr. Sherlock said. "Leaving a new *pesh-kabz* might have been preferable to relinquishing an accustomed knife. Still, there is no note, leaving us to ponder who else might wish to threaten the Khalifa, and why. The Ashraf, perhaps?"

"The Khalifa has survived several Ashraf attacks since succeeding the Mahdi, but they wish him defeated, not cowed."

"It's also been two years since the last Ashraf attack," I added.

"Correct. During that time, however, many tribal disputes have intensified to a point where the Khalifa has had to hire Egyptians as administrators."

"So what's the motive? You don't risk leaving a knife in the Khalifa's bedroom without a reason."

"Whatever the motive, it has resulted in the Khalifa being even more cautious than usual. It is no secret that he fears assassination, although not so much by infidels as potential rivals, supporters, and even his family. Do you think this man that you seek is capable of such a feat?"

"I know him and I'd say he is," said Mr. Sherlock. "Whatever Connor Newcomb lacks in skill, he makes up for in daring, and he's no dullard.

Just the opposite. Newcomb is even more adept at learning customs and languages than I am. It was a skill that the Professor admired. Newcomb might have gone far in a number of professions, but he enlisted with the Coldstream Guards and was part of the Camel Corps at the Battle of Abu Klea. The fellow was never quite right after that. Still, if Newcomb left that knife, why didn't he simply slay the Khalifa when the man was at his mercy?"

A wry smile played over Mr. Sherlock's lips. "I once overlooked what should have been the simple explanation to an investigation by failing to recognize its similarities with an exploit of King David. [10] Somehow, though, I suspect that will not turn out to be the case here." His expression grew more thoughtful. "Sergeant Newcomb is the second most dangerous man in the late Professor James Moriarty's crumbling criminal empire, which intends to inflict as much hardship upon the world as it can with its death throes. Just imagine the chaos that the Khalifa's assassination by Newcomb would ignite throughout northern Africa, or the humiliation it would rain upon Great Britain, whose citizens have barely forgiven the Prime Minister for the fall of Khartoum."

Nadir paled. "Such horror for what sounds like futile nonsense!"

"After what I've seen," I said, "I wouldn't be surprised to find out that the Moriartys were behind the Mayerling Incident." [11]

As usual, however, Mr. Sherlock drove home the point better than I could. "I'm afraid men are rarely reasonable when their passion for power or lust for retribution is on the boil."

18 October, 1893 – Khalifa's Palace, Asr

Nadir informed us that the Khalifa had invited us to bivouac in his palace, and Mr. Sherlock and I gratefully accepted, seeing as we were in no position to demur.

The "palace" turned out to be one of five unimposing brick buildings situated around the Mahdi's tomb and Great Mosque in an unpaved compound encircled by a formidable stone wall. Omdurman had been a large village of mud hovels and straw-walled huts at the time of Gordon's death, and the Mahdi intended it to be a temporary capital before his own untimely demise. The plan was to establish the permanent capital for his pan-Arabian empire in Cairo or Damascus, but the caliphate never materialized. Since then, several desert tribes had been relocated to Omdurman by the Khalifa's centralization decrees, their numbers engorging dingy slums which had once been home to only some fishermen and the infrequent bandit.

Our hasty journey to the Sudan must have exacted more of a toll upon Mr. Sherlock and me than we realized. We slept later than we intended, but there was still time for us to formulate. The sun was on the verge of turning orange before Nadir visited us again and Mr. Sherlock greeted him, "I see you've changed clothes since arriving. Does this mean you spoke with the Khalifa?"

"I have, and he's agreed to all your recommendations."

Mr. Sherlock had suspected this would be the case, but it still struck me as impressive. "No wonder you've been gone so long. Nadir. You're a miracle worker!"

"I'm Persian. I know how to barter. Even as we speak, the number of palace guards is being increased and a review of all Egyptian administrators shall commence within the hour. Naturally the Khalifa's personal bodyguards were informed as to the reason for all this, but they are from his own Taiasha tribe, and if the Khalifa trusts anyone, it is them. After the incident with the *pesh-kabz*, they also know whose heads will pay the penalty if word leaks out."

Mr. Sherlock smiled with appreciation. "I dare say the Khalifa could teach our government a thing or two about efficiency and decisive action."

"And motivation," I added before excusing myself. "I had a bit too much coffee with my beef stew." Out of habit, I paused outside the room a few moments to listen and heard Nadir say, "I like your companion."

"As do I. His intuitiveness and courage remind me of my friend, John Watson."

"Another man I would like to meet. I pray your mission here will be over quickly so you can see him again."

"Thank you, but I'm afraid our reunion is still some time off."

"But why? Won't your task end if you intercept Newcomb?"

"There remain other tasks, not the least of which is problem posed by Newcomb's commander. He is a wily tiger prowling in plain sight with nothing linking him to the Professor, and until I can prove otherwise, returning to London would be as foolish as it would be fatal for Simonson and myself."

Later – Isha prayer came and went by the time a servant bearing a goblet approached the ante-chamber to the Khalifa's bedroom and connecting harem. Inside the harem, a regiment of eunuchs attended to some four-hundred wives. Meanwhile a dozen bodyguards stood sentry in the ante-chamber, where anyone seeking an audience with the Khalifa was required to relinquish their sword and knife. No one – not even dignitaries such as the Mahdi's one-time heir apparent Ali Wad Helu or the emir Osman Digna of the Hadendoa – were permitted to approach their leader

398

unless they first disarmed. Like the servant did each night at this hour, he told the chief bodyguard, "I bring the Khalifa's *doogh*." And like the chief bodyguard did each night, he replied, "Enter," but tonight added, "The Khalifa is in a temper. Just leave the drink and go."

"I taste all his food for poison. What if – ?"

"If you have to come back to taste it, so be it. Do as you're told."

The servant acquiesced and went in.

The Khalifa's bedroom was furnished with carpets and several pillows, like most chambers in the palace, but it was the only room in Omdurman with a brass bed. Not even the Khalifa's somewhat disobedient son Osman Sheikh el Din, who lived in a far more lavish house with its own garden, could boast of such a jewel. The Khalifa's back was turned towards the room so he could stare out a northern window towards the Kerreri hills as the servant said, "Your *doogh*, Khalifa. May I – ?"

"Put it down and then leave."

"Of course, Khalifa." The goblet was set on the floor near a pillow propped against the foot of the bed. With his free hand the servant surreptitiously reached beneath the mattress to extract an arm dagger. "So be it." Approaching the Khalifa on tiptoe, the servant drew the dagger from its scabbard before shouting in English, "For Gordon!"

His target turned around, but it wasn't the Khalifa, and the imposter wielded the *pesh-kabz*.

"*Masá alkhayr*, Sergeant Newcomb," Nadir greeted the servant.

Newcomb stopped in his tracks. Before he could recover, Mr. Sherlock and I stepped out from concealment and I aimed my Webley. "Drop the chiv or I'll fire."

The servant did an about-face to look our way. "How . . . what . . . ?"

Mr. Sherlock instructed, "Do as he says, Sergeant Newcomb."

Newcomb squinted, peering through Mr. Sherlock's guide costume. "So that's where you've been hiding, Mr. Sherlock Holmes! Out of twig as a native, eh? No wonder the Colonel couldn't track you down."

"He and I will find each other at the proper time."

"I'm sure." Newcomb glowered at me. "I've been wanting to ask if you turned nose on us, or were you always working for Holmes?"

"Oh, I've always worked for Mr. Holmes. And you might as well drop that chiv. No one's coming."

This rattled Newcomb, who seemed to suddenly realize the bedroom had not been overrun. "What's going on?"

"We have no intention of permitting you to sully England's empire at our expense," Nadir said.

"You got careless in Amol and Mecca," I explained. "We tumbled to your plan and warned the Khalifa."

Mr. Sherlock provided specifics. "Leaving the *pesh-kabz* without a note beside the Khalifa's bed was inspired. A feint worthy of the Professor. The only time you could get near enough to the Khalifa to slay him was when he was sleeping, but doing so at such an hour would hardly provide you with the spectacle required to humiliate the Empire after it was discovered that you are British. Striking down the Khalifa now, however, when his bodyguards as well as his many wives and their attendants are awake and so near, would be more than ample. And leaving no note with the *pesh-kabz* enticed people to leap to wrong conclusions and fail to search the bedroom for another knife that might be employed at a later time."

Newcomb sneered. "Very clever as usual, Mr. Holmes."

"It seemed most likely that you must have already positioned yourself within the palace. Posing as a guard would be too prominent. Better one of the servants, who are often taken for granted and are therefore invisible. But how to flush you out? Increasing the palace guards and reviewing the administrators would suggest that the Khalifa harbored suspicions against someone inside the palace, leaving you little choice but to act before he could review the servants. That is what we hoped, anyway."

"I see. A neat little trap you set. But – "

I cocked the Webley. "'But' nothing, Newcomb. Drop that chiv."

"Why should I go down without a fight? I can still kick up a little ruckus."

"No if I gut-shoot you, drag you into the desert, and leave you on some lonely anthill. Do as I say and I'll see that you that you die quick and easy."

Several seconds passed. Finally Nadir gingerly took the knife from the reluctant Newcomb. "Take it from one who knows, Sergeant. This is your best choice."

19 October, 1893 – Governor-General's Palace, Isha

At the Khalifa's request, we waited to set out for Upper River until after Maghrib, and with his permission we bided our time in Khartoum until Nadir joined us after sunset.

"Thank you so much for waiting for me," he said. Nadir had donned traveling clothes and brought along all his worldly possessions in a small ruck sack that he strapped to the saddle of the camel we had brought for him.

"It's the least we could do," I told him. "Besides, we wanted to see Gordon's palace again. Who knows if we'll ever have another opportunity."

"A pariah, even a grateful one such as myself, can be a risky travel companion in the Sudan."

"It's a risk we happily accept."

Mr. Sherlock scowled. "Now that we are across the Nile and free to speak, I must tell you that exiling you seems unduly harsh, considering you risked your life for the Khalifa."

"It is more the whim of the Shah-in-Shah than the Khalifa that I leave. Besides, I happily accepted the risk to have my sentence commuted. Better to die a free man."

I could not argue with the sentiment, but, "He used you as bait!"

"To catch a wily tiger. Mr. Holmes can appreciate that. Or else he wouldn't have adapted the Khalifa's scheme into your trap for Sergeant Newcomb." Nadir winked.

"*Touché,*" said Mr. Sherlock quietly.

"There is also the recompense of a small monthly pension I shall receive from the Persian Treasury as a member of the royal house. By the way, the Khalifa was most impressed that you – how do you say it? 'Tumbled'? – That you tumbled so quickly to his employing me as his decoy. May I ask when you first deduced this?"

"Right here," I said, "when I mistook you for the Khalifa."

"Why pardon a prisoner," replied Mr. Sherlock, "even one as qualified as you . . . to hunt a *hashashin*? Abdullah Ibn-Mohammed Al–Khalifa is a slim man, and it is not hard to see that your physique is normally a stocky one that was whittled down in prison. Using the resulting resemblance, coupled with your knowledge and skills, to lure the *hashashin* into the open seemed a more likely reason."

"And let's not forget that you changed your clothes before you came to tell us that the Khalifa had agreed to our entire plan."

"But you would have seen the Khalifa *in camera*, not in audience, so the condition of your wardrobe should not have mattered. On the other hand, if the Khalifa was in hiding in Khartoum whenever you were supposed to be in Omdurman to assure his safety, then you would have had to change clothes and wash off, or we would have seen the dust from your journey."

Nadir chuckled. "Of course. Mr. Holmes, you always make me feel like a man who doesn't know he is playing with marked cards. And, Walter – may I assume you have attended to Sergeant Newcomb?"

"Yes. He got a swift execution, as promised. Anonymous, too. Best thing for everyone."

Mr. Sherlock wasn't sure he agreed. "You had your orders, Simonson, and perhaps executing Newcomb was the wisest course. However, was it the proper one? As more and more years pass, I find

401

myself pondering more and more what terrible costs doing what is best over what is right will inevitably reap."

* * * *

From the Journal of Mycroft Holmes

6 November, 1893 – Review of W.S.'s Letter with Gladstone

The P.M. thanked me and asked me to thank "our loyal agents".

"I'll tell Simonson and Lestrade, Prime Minister."

Wistfully: "Tell me, Mycroft, do you see a cessation to this war with the Moriartys? The battles never seem to end."

"History teaches us that the bloodiest conflicts occur at the end of a war. We might take some solace in that."

"Perhaps, but these last two strikes cut especially deep. They have resurrected memories that I prayed would never haunt England again. Perhaps I'm just getting too old."

"We all dread the turning of the calendar page and what it inexorably brings. Not only for ourselves, but for the people and things we hold dear. There is nothing we can do about that, but you might find comfort in the knowledge that – thanks to Providence and acting upon the best of our abilities – we have helped to keep England on her proper course."

"We have. But at what cost, Mycroft? At what cost?"

Unfortunately, all I could do is shrug and say, "Only time can tell, Prime Minister. Only time will tell."

> *"I then passed through Persia, looked in at Mecca, and paid a short but interesting visit to the Khalifa at Khartoum, the results of which I have communicated to the Foreign Office."*
>
> – Sherlock Holmes
> "The Adventure of the Empty House"

NOTES

1. Professor James Moriarty had two brothers, Colonel James Moriarty, and another, presumably also named James, who was a station-master in the west of England. There is evidence that after the Professor's death at Reichenbach Falls on May 4th, 1891, the two remaining brothers attempted to keep the Professor's criminal enterprise in existence.

2. Mary Watson referred to her husband as James in "The Man with the Twisted Lip". The reason why is never given in The Canon, but William S. Baring-Gould provides several possible theories suggested by Sherlockians over the years in the chapter "Good Old Watson!" in *The Annotated Sherlock Holmes*. Perhaps the most popular is by Dorothy L. Sayers, the creator of Lord Peter Wimsey, who speculated that Mary was referring to her husband by his middle name, the initial of which we learn is "*H*" in "His Last Bow". Sayers proposes the "*H*" stands for "*Hamish*", the Scottish Gaelic equivalent of "*James*".

3. A cleanup possibly triggered by the murders of Malcolm and Halima Angus-Burton, recounted by Watson in "The Case of the Petty Curses" (see *Imagination Theatre* [Episode 82, Broadcast on February 24, 2008], *The MX Book of New Sherlock Holmes Stories – Part VII*, and *The Art of Sherlock Holmes: West Palm Beach Edition*).

4. In 1804, a plasterer named Thomas Millwood was fatally shot because his white greatcoat made another man, Francis Smith, think he was a specter that had reportedly been haunting the Hammersmith district.

5. "*Fidelity is my glory*"

6. These events are recounted in The *Valley of Fear*.

7. Watson, Lestrade, and Simonson thwarted the first attempt by the remnants of Professor Moriarty's criminal organization to wreak international havoc in "A Case of Unfinished Business" (see *Imagination Theatre* [Episode 114, Broadcast on March 16, 2014] and *The MX Book of New Sherlock Holmes Stories – Part XX*).

8. In June of 1893, Watson and Lestrade aided Mycroft Holmes and the British Government in preventing the Moriartys from inciting an international incident that could have started a multi-national conflict when they recovered a statue stolen from Sumatra in 1883 in "The Case for Which the World is Not Yet Prepared" (see *The MX Book of New Sherlock Holmes Stories – Part XVII*).

9. Major-General Charles George "Chinese" Gordon arrived in Khartoum in February of 1884 under orders to evacuate soldiers and loyal civilians in light of several raids in the Sudan by the self-proclaimed Mahdi, Muhammad Ahmad. Gordon remained in Khartoum, however, determined the smash up the Mahdi. A siege ensued and Khartoum finally fell to the Mahdist on January 26, 1885, two days before a British relief expedition arrived.

10. These events are recounted by in "The Adventure of the Crooked Man".

11. On January 30, 1889, the bodies of Rudolph, Crown Prince of Austria, and his mistress Baroness Mary Vetsera were discovered in the Imperial hunting lodge in Mayerling. The deaths may have been a murder-suicide or a double murder, but Rudolph, the heir-apparent of the Austro-Hungarian Empire, died without sons, so Rudolph's uncle, Archduke Karl Ludwig, and Ludwig's son, Archduke Franz Ferdinand, suddenly became next in succession. This disrupted the delicate security of the Habsburg dynastic direct line of succession, which endangered what at the time was a growing reconciliation between the Austrian and Hungarian factions of the empire. Developments arising from the Mayerling Incident worsened each year, a destabilization that would eventually lead to the start of World War I after the assassination of Archduke Franz Ferdinand and his wife Sophie in 1914.

The Affair of the *Friesland*
by Jan van Koningsveld

The year 1894 will go down in history as one of the most challenging for my good friend, Sherlock Holmes, as well as for me. After three long years believing that the great detective had lost his life in the struggle at the Reichenbach Falls with his arch enemy, Professor Moriarty, I had to deal with the new situation that Holmes had indeed risen from the dead and was now busier than ever before. Shortly after his return to the chambers at 221b Baker Street, he was confronted with several cases, including one that put us in grave danger and nearly cost us both our lives.

Just a few weeks had passed since my return to our shared lodgings. I had sold my private practice and now once more enjoyed Holmes's company. His manner hadn't changed at all, even though his absence and his travels under the alias of the Norwegian explorer Sigerson had surely changed him as a person. In some respects he appeared to be more patient, while in other situations he simply couldn't hold his temper. Of course the same was true of me as well. I had lost my beloved wife Mary and my life without her and my good friend had taken its toll on me. Still, it was with the greatest pleasure that I was once again able to participate in his adventures, and the following affair was very much an adventure.

It was a mild summer's day and my friend was in a good mood. "We should indeed, my dear Watson," he said while folding the newspaper which he had just finished reading.

"Should indeed what?" I asked astounded. After Holmes's long absence, I had forgotten just how remarkable were his powers of deduction.

"Ah, this is quite elementary. You were looking out of the window for a while, enjoying the sun and its warmth. After you checked the clock you looked for your umbrella. Yes, Doctor, we should use the remaining two hours until our client appears and take a walk through the park. Bringing the umbrella would be wise, as some dark clouds are slowly approaching. We should move out immediately!"

Before I could even react, our plans were interrupted by someone aggressively knocking on the front door. Our landlady, Mrs. Hudson, rushed to open it and we heard a loud voice arguing with her. Only moments later the door to our sitting room flew open and a man, perhaps in his mid-twenties, stood there with a fearful expression on his face. "Help *mij*! Help *mij, alstublieft*!" he shouted. The poor man was shaking all over. I took a few steps towards him and tried to calm him down. "Please, sir, have a seat. I'll get you something to drink, and then you can explain to us what help you need."

A few moments later our guest was able to talk. "Please excuse my sudden intrusion, but I fear that my life is being threatened. My name is Marten Hendricus de Koning. I was born in Heeg in the province Friesland, which lies in the Netherlands. I currently reside in Franeker, Friesland, with my wife Geertje and our little daughter, Ijbeltje. It has always been my dream to become a steamboat captain one day. Currently I am working on the Dutch steamship *Friesland* under Captain Lambertus Visser. We are transporting all kinds of goods throughout the Netherlands, as well as to Great Britain."

Mijnheer de Koning was a man of medium size. His hands indicated that he spent a lot of time outside, just what one would expect from a man working on a steamship. He had a clean-shaven face and dark hair. I could barely make out a Dutch accent, which indicated that our guest had travelled to Britain on a regular basis.

Holmes had been listening carefully to what our client had to say. While Mijnheer de Koning was taking a deep breath he asked him, "Now that you have seemingly recovered, please tell us what has happened that made you panic in such a way."

Our visitor nodded and continued. "I am just a regular working man who tries to earn an honest living. There are times when I am away from home for several weeks and have no opportunity to see my lovely wife and daughter. I think my captain will tell you that I am an honest man and never get into any trouble. That is, until recently."

He looked out of the window as if unsure as to how to continue. "Somehow things changed for me, and I cannot tell why. Just three weeks ago, I had the strange feeling of being followed. I had been in the local pub, like I do once in a while, and was on my way home. The street was deserted, but still I heard steps in the dark. When I turned around, nobody was there. Without incident I got home, and for the next few days I did not give it any thought. But only three nights later, when I was on my way home from the pub, I once again heard steps behind me. This time I glimpsed a shadow.

"Mr. Holmes, I am not a fearful person, but at this point I was feeling a little scared and I started to hasten. Suddenly I made out the sound of two pairs of shoes following me. In desperation I started to run and reached the door of my house, opened it, and slammed it shut behind me. I leaned against the wall while I regained my breath."

Holmes, who had been listening with his eyes closed, now opened them and asked our guest, "Mijnheer de Koning, during the two nights in the pub, did you notice any strangers there? People who may have watched you? No? Pray, continue!" He again closed his eyes and Mijnheer de Koning resumed his narrative.

"As I did not want to scare my family, I kept all of this to myself. As a matter of fact, nothing else of importance happened after that night. Last week I returned to work on the *Friesland*. The destination of the ship was London and we arrived here yesterday. All of the crew, together with the captain, went to The Blind Beggar, a pub in Whitechapel. We had a good time, as we always do, playing cards and other games. It must have been around four o'clock in the morning when we were heading back to our steamship.

"Suddenly, a group of maybe fifteen men attacked us and a violent fight ensued. At some point I was grabbed and pulled into an alley. I shouted for help, but nobody heard me."

Our client took a deep breath, before continuing. I could see the horror in his eyes. "'What do you want from me?' I screamed in despair. One of my attackers responded. 'That is not for us to tell. We will take you to our leader. That's all you need to know!' In a desperate move I was able to free myself and push my opponents against each other. I ran like I've never run before. I didn't look back."

Again, he paused, taking the cup of coffee I had offered him.

"What happened then?" I asked. "How did you end up here? Why didn't you go to the police?" Holmes still had his eyes closed, but I could sense that his mind was working.

Mijnheer de Koning continued. "I have been in London several times now and gotten to know some people. One of them gave me shelter for the rest of the night. He also was the one who recommended you, Mr. Holmes. The police wouldn't take my case seriously. They would simply state that this was a common bar fight. Mr. Holmes, please help me! I don't even know who has any interest in me or why. Even on my way to Baker Street, I again felt that I was being followed, which is why I arrived in the state you find me in."

Holmes kept his eyes closed. "Mijnheer de Koning, you mentioned 'other games' that you were playing. To what other games are you referring?"

Our visitor seemed to be uneasy with this question but after a while offered an answer. "Well, Mr. Holmes, as it seems, my brain works a little differently to the brains of other people. I am able to memorize all kinds of information and calculate with quite large numbers purely mentally. So sometimes people challenge me by giving me two numbers which I have to multiply or shuffle a deck of playing cards which I have to memorize."

Holmes raised his eyebrows. "That sounds impressive. Do you make any money with these kinds of performances?"

Mijnheer de Koning shook his head. "No, Mr. Holmes, I just do it to entertain."

My friend smiled. "I see. Do you have any debts? Is it possible that someone wants to collect money from you?" Again, our guest responded in the negative.

"I am proud to say that while I am not a rich man, I never had any debts. My father taught me the value of independence, and I have succeeded in following his advice."

Holmes, nodding slightly, added, "I have one final question for you. Is there anyone among the crew who might mean you harm? Have there been any disputes between you and another crew member, for instance?"

Our client thought for a while. "I know that I sometimes have a temper, but I would not have thought that a reason for someone to hold a grudge against me. We are all like a big family. This is very important when one is working on a ship. Your life may depend on it."

A brief silence followed. Suddenly my friend rose and looked from the window of our sitting room. "As it appears, you are right about being followed. There is a suspicious looking fellow watching the entrance of our house from across the street." I joined him, getting a good look at the fellow without being observed. "We have to make sure that he doesn't see you when you leave. We will provide a cover for you. Fortunately I have stored lots of disguises, so this shouldn't be a problem. Mijnheer de Koning, I need you to give me the location of the *Friesland*, as well as the name and address of the friend with whom you stayed last night. Are all crew members living on the steamboat during your stay in London?"

"Yes, all the time."

"Good. I will have to make some enquiries and we shall meet again here in twenty-four hours. Please stay with your friend. You're safe there, aren't you? Dr. Watson will accompany you and make sure that no one is following you – if that's all right with you."

I nodded. "Is there anything else I can do?"

"Please meet me back here in Baker Street tonight at eight o'clock. The two of you should leave the building through the back door. Do not take a cab. And take your service revolver with you. Something evil is afoot!"

De Koning gave us the location of the ship and told Holmes how to find his friend. Then, after Holmes had made our guest unrecognizable, Mijnheer de Koning and I left. I was confident that we weren't being followed. Now and then I cautiously looked around but saw nothing out of the ordinary. So it was an uneventful walk of about three miles and we arrived unharmed at his friend's home. After saying goodbye, I made my way back to Baker Street, enjoying the warm sun. But, as is the usual, Holmes was right – after a short while it started to rain. As I had forgotten to take my umbrella with me, I hastened to the nearest café.

While looking for somewhere to rest myself, I took off my wet jacket. In that same moment I noticed a sinister-looking person outside the establishment. It was the same stranger who had been standing on the other side of Baker Street, watching our entrance. He must have followed us after all! My heart skipped a beat and the hairs on my neck stood on end. Mijnheer de Koning was in great danger and I had to warn him, if it wasn't already too late!

I ran to the exit, and in my haste I collided with another customer who shouted at me. "Watch out! You've hurt me! Wait – you'll pay for this!" I murmured an excuse and continued to the door, but the firm grip of the man kept me from making another step. Then, in a low voice, I heard, "Stay here, Watson, and sit down. We need to talk."

I have mentioned before that Sherlock Holmes could have been one of the most feared criminal masterminds of all time if he had chosen to do so. On the other hand, his talent for the big stage was in no way inferior to that. The world had lost a great actor when my friend decided to follow a career as the first consulting detective. Holmes had once more managed to hide in plain sight, even from me.

"What are you doing here?" I asked in puzzlement. "We need to hurry!" I cried. "Mijnheer de Koning is in great danger. We must have been followed!"

Holmes tried to calm me down. "Hush, Watson! There is no time for explanations now. Be assured, Mijnheer de Koning is taken care of. I need you to stay here while I go back on the street to investigate this matter further. Just take your time and be back in Baker Street at eight p.m. For now, you need to trust me."

Before I could say another word, my friend disappeared. As my readers may know, I was used to Holmes's behavior. Still, in situations like this, I felt a little bit sidelined, simply sitting and doing nothing. "All in good time, Watson," as Holmes would say.

I had read every article in the newspaper, had drunk too much coffee, and had eaten a delicious apple pie, when I finally made my way back home. Several hours had passed and my mystery pursuant was still waiting outside of the café. I did as Holmes had ordered and walked down the street, never turning around, even though I was aware that I was being followed.

I reached our house in Baker Street shortly before eight and walked up the steps to our chambers after asking Mrs. Hudson for some sandwiches and a pot of tea. Entering our sitting room, I was heartily greeted by Holmes. "Watson, old friend, I am glad to see you! You are right on time. Please, have a seat."

After I had made myself comfortable, I looked at him in anticipation. "Now would be a good time to bring me into the light."

My friend settled into his armchair and nodded. "I know I owe you an explanation. You have every right to look at me that way. A lot of things happened today and I'll fill you in as much as possible. Let me assure you that you have been of invaluable help.

"When you left with our client earlier, I was aware that our little distraction wouldn't be successful. But I needed to find out how many people might be involved. Shortly after your departure, I followed you in my disguise, but not before I ordered young Wiggins and his Baker Street Irregulars to get to Mijnheer de Koning's friend ahead of you and warn him about the impending danger. Right after you left them, the Irregulars took our client to a hiding place of their own. You know that I can always count on those boys. They know the streets of London better than anyone. He will be safe there.

"After our little incident in the café, I went to see Captain Visser on the *Friesland.* He accepted my invitation to visit us at nine o'clock this evening. It's for the better that we question him here, away from eavesdroppers. I hope we can shed some light onto this matter.

"When I got back home, I sent some cables to my contacts on the Continent, as well as to my brother Mycroft. We should have answers within the hour. As it seems we are dealing with a force that possibly equals the evil of Professor Moriarty. It might even endanger the peace in Europe."

I looked at Holmes with horror. This came as a shock to me. I had developed my own theories about this case – But this? Before I was able to respond, Holmes received a telegram, which he tore open impatiently. It was from Mycroft Holmes, who worked for the government, but in what capacity was unclear to me. It must have been something of importance, though. My friend told me that in some cases, Mycroft did not just work for the government – he *was* the government.

Holmes read:

> *You were correct about Mijnheer de Koning. Problem is of national interest. The Prime Minister asks for your involvement. Ensure the help of Mijnheer de Koning and decrypt the following encryption:*

5187768865916059H96754548184685115976369F2217314
12686017532511019871

Hurry.
M.H.

I must admit, I was more confused than before. "For goodness sake, Holmes, what is this all about?"

Before I could get an answer, Mrs. Hudson led our guest, Captain Lambertus Visser, into our sitting room.

"Good evening, gentlemen!" the captain said. "Mr. Holmes, Dr. Watson, how can I be of service?"

He eased himself into the armchair that I offered. My friend came right to the point. "Captain Visser, thank you for coming. It is crucial that you answer my questions as accurately as possible. The life of many people may depend on it."

Our guest was aware of the situation and kept himself together. "I will do my very best, sir."

Holmes nodded. "Very well. I take it that you are aware of the special skills of Mijnheer de Koning. How well is this known to other people?"

The captain scratched his head. "Well, Marten has never made a secret of his abilities. Anyone could know about this. He often challenges people to give him a problem containing numbers for him to solve."

Showing him Mycroft's message, my friend asked, "Captain, have you ever seen him solving a riddle like this?"

Captain Visser seemed surprised. "Why, yes! It must have happened about three weeks ago, when one of my crew members challenged him with something quite similar. I remember that Marten was somewhat frustrated, as he was able to see a pattern in it, but was unable to make any sense of it."

"Interesting," Holmes mused. "What is the name of the crew member? It's imperative that I also speak with him immediately!"

"It was Johan de Boer, my first mate. I've told my crew to stay on the ship, so we should be able to meet him there right now."

"Very well, Captain, we should waste no time. I would like to ask my colleague, Dr. Watson, to accompany you to your ship. I have to make some arrangements first, but will follow you both as soon as possible."

When we were about to leave, Holmes took me aside. "Watson, you must not – under any circumstances! – allow anyone to leave the ship. And take your service revolver with you. I fear for the worst!"

Not knowing what would await us, I rode with the captain to his ship. Night had fallen. The moon was just visible through the clouds. While the

411

temperatures were still relatively high, I felt a chill down my back. It was situations like this one that made me immensely nervous. I held tightly to my weapon, hoping that there would be no need to make any use of it. While I did everything to hold myself together, I asked the captain about his first mate. The special interest that Holmes had in him made me suspicious. "Captain Visser, what can you tell me about Johan de Boer? What kind of man is he?"

"Well, Dr. Watson, he is a giant of a man, nearly six-and-a-half feet tall, and very muscular. I have never met a stronger man in my life. As first mate I trust him with my life. In all the years that we have worked together, he has never let me down."

"Do you think he came up with the riddle all by himself?"

"That I cannot say. Johan always amazes me with his skills. I would not be surprised if he indeed had developed it himself. But he is not a man of many words. Why do you ask?"

"Just curious."

That statement wasn't true, of course. I had developed my own theory by using Holmes's methods, but I didn't know whom I could trust in this affair. Thus, I kept my true intentions to myself. The captain had said nothing to alleviate my suspicions.

After nearly half-an-hour we reached the *Friesland*. Hoping that Holmes wouldn't be far behind, we entered the vessel. The Captain led me to his cabin and asked me to wait while he went looking for his first mate. The cabin was a small room with a bed, a table, and some chairs – surprisingly basic for a captain's quarters.

It took just a few minutes for the sailors to join us. The first mate of the ship was a giant indeed. I felt like a small child when I shook his hand. He gave me the impression that I wouldn't like him if he was angry. Nevertheless, I tried to start a conversation with him.

"Good evening, sir, and thank you for coming. I am Dr. Watson. We should wait for Sherlock Holmes, as he would like to ask you some questions. It should only take a few minutes. How are you, sir?"

Johan de Boer looked at me sternly, but didn't say a word. He clearly did not like to wait and obviously didn't want to talk more than was absolutely necessary. I tried to examine him without him becoming suspicious. Clearly he wasn't the most pleasant man I had met. Still, could he be the villain in this case? The prolonged silence was awkward, and I was relieved when my friend finally arrived.

"You must be Mijnheer de Boer. It is a pleasure to meet you."

Still the mood of the giant did not improve. The first mate simply grunted.

"I'm sorry to disturb you at this late hour," Holmes began. "It is of the utmost importance that you answer my questions as accurately as possible. Now, Captain Visser informed me that three weeks ago you were the one to present a number-related problem to your fellow crew member. Regarding the riddle you gave to Mijnheer de Koning: Did you develop it yourself, or did somebody give it to you?"

"Neither. I simply found it in my jacket when I left the ship the night before we all met in the pub back home. Don't know how it got there. Would that be all? Are we finished here?"

"Not at all. Get yourself together – this is important" Holmes was beginning to lose his patience. "This matters to all of you. You are all in danger. Think again. Who might have put it into your pocket? Was there any stranger on the ship that day? Think, man, think!"

"I don't know anything! I just want to be left alone!" With this he left. His heavy footsteps could be heard for some time afterwards. The captain looked puzzled.

Holmes sat there in deep thought. I knew this wasn't the way that he had hoped things would develop. Eventually he rose, rushed outside the cabin, and came back moments later, accompanied by Mijnheer de Koning.

"Holmes, how on earth did he get here? Surely it's much too dangerous for him to be on the ship!"

"Don't worry, Watson. Like I said earlier, Wiggins and the Irregulars know every corner of this city, and they were able to lead him here without being seen. I need Mijnheer de Koning's aid with this matter, as mentioned in Mycroft's message. Only our combined skills will solve this riddle."

While our client had taken a seat, Holmes presented Mycroft's message to him. "Mijnheer de Koning, is this the same combination of digits as the one that was presented to you back in Franeker?"

After taking a closer look at it, the Dutchman shook his head. "No, this one is different. The other one went this way – " He wrote down the following:

3631458667E98596879844531441548723285093060 67R22
10381294012469459

How a man was able to recall such a long string of characters, I will never understand. After the writing was finished, my friend looked at it and his face lit up. "I'm quite experienced when it comes to encryptions. Now that we are in possession of two different examples of these, our chances of finding a solution are much improved. Mijnheer de Koning, you had some ideas about the first one. Please share them with us."

413

"Well, as I know quite a lot about numbers, I immediately recognized some patterns. It starts with *363*, which is three times the square of eleven, followed by *1458*, which is two times the cube of 9. After that there is *667*, which is *23* times *29*. Both are prime numbers, which means they only have themselves and *1* as divisor. The following *E* is something I cannot make anything of."

"I see," Holmes mused. "As a matter of fact, this makes things a little bit clearer!"

"How so, Holmes?" I responded.

"If I am not mistaken, this is the first key to the encryption. Everything that follows is written in this key. Mijnheer de Koning, please take another look at the digits following the letter. Are you able to discover three squares, followed by two cubes and then the product of two primes?"

For a while our client was working on the string of numbers. Then his face brightened. "Why, yes!" he cried. "These numbers are larger than the others before, but this pattern continues indeed! Look:

"*98596*, *879844*, and *531441* are the squares of *314*, *938*, and *729*. *531441* is the cube of *81* as well. Then, *54872* and *328509* are the cubes of *38* and *69*. Finally, *306067* is the product of the two prime numbers *421* and *727*."

My friend looked at him appreciatively. "Mijnheer de Koning, your skills concerning numbers are indeed extraordinary. I haven't seen anything like it."

My head was spinning. "Holmes, how is this helping us?"

"Yes, Mr. Sherlock Holmes, how is this helping us, indeed?" a voice came from outside the cabin. It clearly had a German accent. A man holding a gun entered from out of the darkness. I reached for my pocket but was interrupted by the armed stranger. "I wouldn't do that if I were you, Dr. Watson. Put it to the ground and push it over to me. Thank you!" I did as I was told.

"Who are you and what do you want?" I cried angrily.

"I think I can shed some light on this for you, Watson," my friend interjected. "That is, if Herr Friedrich von Hasberg doesn't mind me doing so."

Our uninvited guest visibly winced, realizing that he had been exposed, but quickly regained his composure. "By all means," came the response in a clearly sarcastic tone. "If the great Sherlock Holmes gives me the honor to introduce me, who am I to argue with that?"

My friend seemed unimpressed. "Herr von Hasberg is part of a European-wide group of spies who offer their services to the highest bidders. These may be private persons, companies, and even governments. I have followed the development of this organization for some time now.

They are very dangerous and a threat to the peace of our country – and indeed to the whole continent. My contacts all over Europe keep me informed on a regular basis. The head of this group is known as *Der Fuchs* – *The Fox*. While his real name is unknown, every source confirms that he is a brilliant mastermind who never gets his hands dirty, but leaves this kind of work to people like Friedrich von Hasberg or his nephew who, I am afraid, is a member of your crew, Captain Visser."

The captain, who hadn't spoken for quite a while, barked, "What are you talking about? What member?"

"That would be me," another voice came from the dark.

"Cornelis Jansen?" cried the captain. "Is that you? What is the purpose of this? Have you lost your mind?"

"Not at, all, Captain. My mind has never been any clearer than it is right now."

Sherlock Holmes resumed. "These two intercepted a secret message sent between two European royal houses. The key to this message lies in the code that was given to Mijnheer de Koning. The British Secret Service found another key and a race for the decryption began. If one could decipher either of the codes, it would be very likely that the keys to future messages could be decoded as well. This kind of encryption is new and may be the future of secret communications. Neither party made much headway, however.

"Then the skills of Mijnheer de Koning came to light. If I'm not mistaken, Mijnheer Jansen here received a message from his uncle in order to pass the riddle to our client. He was the one who slipped the encryption into the pocket of your first mate, Captain, in order to test him. While Mijnheer de Koning wasn't able to crack the code at first sight, it was obvious that he could shed more light onto the business than anybody else before. It was then that a plan to abduct him was hatched.

"Fortunately this attempt ended in failure. The *Friesland* went to London, and the skills of one Sherlock Holmes were already known on the Continent. What better way to solve the encryption than to have two experts work on it? The second attempted abduction was meant to lead Mijnheer de Koning to the steps of 221b Baker Street, and it worked out just fine. We've been watched ever since he stepped into our chambers. Did I miss something, Herr von Hasberg?"

"Oh, you have explained everything quite accurately, Mr. Holmes," the German responded. "But, enough talking. I need the solution of the encryption and I need it now. Our clients are not known for their patience."

"I'm sorry to disappoint you, Herr von Hasberg," Holmes replied. "This encryption is the most advanced that I've ever seen. It could take weeks, even months, to decrypt it. Right now, I'm afraid, I can give you nothing."

The face of the German turned red, but he maintained his composure. With a grin, he turned to Holmes. "Then you are of no further use for me. My superior will be quite upset and, I must add, I'm very disappointed by the exaggeration of your skills in Dr. Watson's narratives. You are neither help nor threat to us. The worries of *Der Fuchs* were completely unnecessary."

I was outraged by such rudeness. Unable to hold myself back, I was about to give him a piece of my mind when my friend intervened. "He is right, Watson. This is far beyond anything that I can solve. Please, sit down." Shaking my head, I took a seat again. Why would Holmes say something like this? If not him, then who would be able to solve this?

My inner rage was stopped abruptly. The events that followed will forever remain blurry in my mind. Friedrich von Hasberg sent Cornelis Jansen to the cargo hold to fetch some ropes. They then tied us to our chairs. The German spy looked satisfied and sent his accomplice away once more. Jansen came back, carrying two gas cylinders.

"I fear that this will be the end of our business relationship, Mr. Holmes. And by the way, this will be your end as well. Even though this may be a failure for us, our organization will look into a bright future. Good-bye, gentlemen!"

With this, the two men opened the cylinders, shut the door to the captain's chamber, and sealed it. The gas spread quickly into the air. I desperately tried to loosen the ties that secured me to the chair. However, my efforts were in vain. I looked around and saw the other men also trying to break free. While my senses started to fade, I could see Holmes struggling with his ropes. My hopes vanished. Even if Holmes were successful, how could he ever open the door in time? The room had not a single window, and the door appeared to be made of solid steel. And yet, against the odds, my friend somehow set himself free and rushed to the door. Pounding upon it, he cried for help. Mijnheer de Koning was already unconscious. The last thing that I saw was Holmes trying to work on the door lock. As I was losing consciousness, I could hear whistles blowing and people shouting. Then everything went dark.

"Watson, wake up! Watson!" My head hurt, and when I opened my eyes, I saw the worried face of my friend leaning over me. "Good old chap, you are alive!" he exclaimed. "When I awoke, I feared for the worst. What a relief!"

I found myself lying on the floor outside of the captain's cabin. The sound of voices all around me made my head hurt even more. While I tried

416

to get my senses back in order, I looked around me. "Holmes, what happened? Were you able to open the door?"

"You need to rest, my friend. We barely survived this assault on our lives. I'll tell you all you need to know." The detective sat down next to me and crossed his legs.

"The only reason we are still alive is that Johan de Boer is a far better person than he likes to admit. While all of the other crew members were held hostage in one of the cargo holds, he was the one who kept his head together and sneaked past all of the guards in order to get to this room. He was able to smell the gas from the outside and did the one thing that could save us. Using only a sledgehammer and his brute strength, he smashed the door down. We owe him our lives.

"Only moments later Scotland Yard arrived. I had alerted Inspector Lestrade before I got here and he came to arrest all of the criminal elements that had this ship under their thumb."

"Did they catch all of those culprits?" I enquired.

"All but one."

"Who escaped? Cornelis Jansen?"

"No, he was caught and will most probably be locked away for a very long time. By some miracle, and to my great discomfort, it was Herr von Hasbergen who escaped. Every inch of this ship was searched, but he was nowhere to be found." With this he hit the ground with his fist. "I will get him! One day he will have to answer for what he has done!"

"What do you mean by that?" I asked. While I let my eyes wander through the room again I discovered a blanket which obviously covered a body. "Wait a minute, Holmes! Who is lying there?"

"I am deeply sorry to inform you that not all of us made it out alive. Our client, Mijnheer de Koning, suffocated from the gas. We couldn't save him." He took a deep breath. "This is my fault. I wasn't able to protect him. He came for my help and I failed him."

I knew that there was nothing I could say that would ease his mind. He had done everything in his powers to guard his client. But this adversary, this new enemy, had indeed have proven to be not only a match for his skills and abilities, but also ruthless. This fact wouldn't allow him to rest until he had brought to justice the people behind this – specifically Herr von Hasberg, as well as the head of the criminal organization, *Der Fuchs*. I hoped this would happen sooner rather than later. How little I knew then.

Epilogue

On the evening of the fourteenth of December, 1906, I arrived at my friend's cottage in the Sussex Downs, to which he had retired about three years earlier. While he had taken up beekeeping as his primary activity, the cold weather always gave him an opportunity to write some of his monographs. This particular night I found him busy scribbling. He didn't even look up when he addressed me.

"Watson, old chap, it is wonderful to see you. You must have lost almost a pound since the last time we met."

I looked down at my body and wondered how he might have deduced that. Still focused, Holmes gestured me to sit down. There was a letter lying on the armchair he had pointed me to.

"Please, read it, Watson. This will delight you."

Doing as I was told, I opened the letter. It read like this:

Dear Mr. Holmes,

I trust you are in good health. With so many years having passed I thought it appropriate that I told you how my life has evolved since the dramatic events twelve years ago. When you and your brother, the well-respected Mr. Mycroft Holmes, strongly recommended that I change my name and begin a new life at another place, everything fell apart for me at first. My lovely daughter had died during my absence. It was hard to see my wife in such great pain. When after a short while our first son, Hendricus, was born, things seemed to improve. Four more children followed, of which to our great grief two more died at a very early age. But now as I write this letter we are expecting one more child.

Living under a new name was not an easy adjustment. Your brother provided us with the necessary documents and some money, but leaving behind all of my friends, growing a beard to hide my face from the ones I knew, and of course to the perpetrators of the affair on the Friesland, *was quite difficult. But in the end, it all worked out. We live a safe life, and I am proud to tell you that I have become the captain of the steamboat* Anna. *I now see a bright future for me and my family. All thanks to you and your brother.*

I lowered the letter and looked at my friend. "This is from the man that saved our lives, isn't it? I never heard of him again. What was his name? The giant Dutchman?"

"You mean Johan de Boer?"

"That would be him, yes."

"Think again, Watson. Why would he have to change his name? Just because he had saved us from certain death?"

"Well, if you put it that way, it does sound unreasonable. But by whom was this letter written then?"

"I think if you finish it, all will be revealed. Let me assure you, old chap, that I am sorry about what you are about to find out. It was necessary, however."

I looked at Holmes with a questioning face but decided to simply continue my reading.

> *Mr. Holmes, I would never have been safe because of my skills, were it not for your brilliant idea to let the world think that I am dead. Please give my apologies to your dear friend and colleague Dr. Watson, whom we also left in the dark. You assured me that it would be for the better and I trust you with this. Still I feel a little bit uncomfortable about it.*
>
> *Not using my arithmetical skills in public was hard for me at first, but after a while I found out that I could use them for all kinds of calculations and I was able to create ships by planning them completely in my head. I have started to write down everything I know about mental calculations. Maybe one day one of my descendants will have better use of these skills.*
>
> *I will always be in your debt.*
>
> *Yours sincerely*
> *Gerrit-Reint van Koningsveld*
> *Leeuwarden/Friesland*

I could not believe what I just read. "Holmes! All this time, our client whom I thought to be dead, was alive? Why on earth didn't you tell me?"

"My dear Watson, please forgive me! As I mentioned before, this was absolutely necessary. When I woke up on the *Friesland*, it was clear to me that Herr von Hasberg had acted carelessly. His task was to decrypt the code in order to have the key for all messages that would be sent between the European royal houses and their secret services. This would have given them the advantage in any negotiations that were to come.

"You remember that I was able to convince him that I couldn't solve this riddle by myself. If he thought Mijnheer de Koning to be dead, there would be no further danger to him. But if he knew he was still alive, Herr von Hasberg eventually would have gotten back to our client and maybe even blackmailed him or threatened his life. So in that moment I decided to declare him dead. Mycroft made sure that he was brought back to the Netherlands discreetly. It was for the better that you didn't know he was alive. You are far more convincing that way."

While I wasn't entirely happy with this explanation, I nodded in agreement. Holmes was absolutely right, of course.

"You know that I did eventually crack the code. Fortunately, *Der Fuchs* did not, or the fate of Europe would have been totally different. Still, he and his organization haven't left us in peace for more than a decade now."

"Holmes, you never shared the secret of the code with me. I think that now is the time that you enlighten me! My readers will want to know!"

"Oh, Watson, why is it that you always want to keep your readers from thinking for themselves? Why is it that you always present the complete solution to them? That way they will never learn! Let them use their brains for once. Who knows, maybe this way another Mijnheer de Koning will come to the surface after the danger has passed.

"One day you may write down all of these adventures regarding the organization, but for now, everything that has happened must be kept a secret. The situation on the Continent is very unstable. We will have our hands full to prevent a war that will affect the whole world. I have been informed that a certain German named von Bork has entered the field. He belonged to *Der Fuchs* but now works for the Kaiser. I'm curious when our paths will cross in the future. It is only a matter time!"

Our months of partnership had not been so uneventful as he had stated, for I find, on looking over my notes, that this period includes the case of the papers of ex-President Murillo, and also the shocking affair of the Dutch steamship Friesland, *which so nearly cost us both our lives . . . .*

– Dr. John H. Watson
"The Adventure of the Norwood Builder"

420

The Forgetful Detective
by Marcia Wilson

It is an interesting fact that if a troubled man is offered tea or a drink, he begins to think his medical visit is now a social call, and thus grows more open to sharing the information that is necessary to his treatment. This was my course of action when, on a miserably chill day in 1894, Lestrade came calling. Holmes was consulting upstairs in our rooms, but Mrs. Hudson had loaned me her kitchen and breakfast room to see a few patients while she was away on a much-deserved rest. Soon the inspector and I were ensconced in the old breakfast-nook, wrapping our wind-blued hands against my ancient samovar.

"Can you tell me anything about head-wounds?" he blurted without warning, and I felt he had been holding this question long enough that the words had simply escaped him at their first chance. As he heard himself, his sallow face coloured and he even clapped his hand over his mouth. Rarely have I seen him in a state of such contrition, and it was always when he realised some sort of mistake on his part.

"I fear I know more about head-wounds than many," I soothed him with a self-depreciating laugh and poured the tea. "Personal experience as well as that of a medical man. Being a callow youth with more impulse than common sense didn't spare me from gravity, nor any other Nature's Laws, and when I took the Queen's Shilling, that led to an inestimable education in how a man can wreck harm both intentional and unintentional."

"And then you moved to Baker Street," he added with a flash of mischief.

"And then I moved to Baker Street. Perhaps I should say I do not regret the wisdom gained in my injuries, but I do regret the *price* of wisdom. It never seems to come cheap."

"No." He stared. "No, you're right." That seemed to marginally calm his spirits.

"I've been lucky, Doctor," he said at last. "Damned lucky. Being injured is part of the job, and you don't accept the post if you can't deliver the mail, as my old sergeant would say. Broken bones happen as often as rainclouds, and the scrapes and bruises become our new skin. I think the new coppers are as blue under their coats more often than not. But some injuries . . . they're harder to put aside."

"If you are concerned about the nature of an injury to yourself or someone else, I can assure you of my confidence as a physician."

"No doubt to you there, sir!" He almost laughed. "Well, let's see if I can stop skipping about and get to the point: I've had some hard knocks to my skull, and I have reason to believe it is affecting my work."

This simple statement took considerable effort to get out, for few things are as horrifying to a proud workman than his loss of faculties. I did not insult him with bland reassurance. "Are you referring to an injury that I treated you for in the past?" I guessed.

"I think I may have been knocked about today. Or yesterday. Somewhere around that time."

I did not like this at all. "I am not a specialist in brain trauma,"

"But you take it seriously!" Lestrade clutched at my wrist. "Look, you know old Dr. Roanoke down at the station. He's always spoken well of you and he says a surgeon who never went to war isn't a real surgeon, and so he couldn't say he was ever better than you in experience.

"Have you been to his private office? He has framed up on his wall the first page of your *A Study in Scarlet*." At my surprise he grinned, temporarily forgetting his troubles. "Yes! And he has underlined in red crayon '*subclavian artery*' with '*Learn the Words*' writ in the margin." I confessed I knew not what to make of it. "Well, I'm sure I know nothing about it," Lestrade said with a wink, "but base rumour has it he's been approached to write of his own exploits and it seems things went far enough when a relative of his who owns a publishing company – of which I know nothing about – complained that his writings were 'too educated' and 'would be above the heads of the reading public'.

"These same publishers, so I hear from rumour (and Gregson gossiping like a girl) makes plenty of money in sensationalist novels, where the hero or heroine manages to dramatically escape and bring the villains to justice even after suffering most terrible wounds. A bullet to the shoulder is Dr. Roanoke's bugbear, and he has been known to write with a blood-red pen at novelists and *their* agents and publishers, denouncing how they earn their gains at the expense of public gull, thus undermining the public's safety by spreading false information. Or so I'm told. I'm sure I know nothing about it."

"That quarrel is true," I laughed. "My agent oft-mourns the bridge kept between the facts of the writer's hand, and the brain of the reader who follows. I shall do my best to honour Dr. Roanoke's faith and, if you have time for an examination, we may satisfy us both."

Lestrade thought this a fine idea and submitted to an examination and questioning. There were no wounds, marks, scratches, loss of hair, nor discolouration of skin, scalp, tongue, gums, nails, or lips, nor any anomalous signs to indicate an outside agency such as poison, disease, or assault. Internal agencies such as disease, conditions, syndromes, or infection came to nil. His temperature was perfect. I outruled stroke, heart congestion, diabetes, and metal-poisoning. I disliked the sound of his lungs and his colouring, but only a transfer far from the smoke of London would cure that. His neurology was good. He tested as normal in everything but his scalp exam. There was a fresh bruise, no older than four-and-twenty hours at most, and a walnut-sized purpling at the back of the skull just below the arch of the lambdoid suture that could possibly be a concussion. If the corresponding region of the brain was injured, it would be very lightly, as Lestrade was displaying none but one of the symptoms of disruption: The gaps in his memory.

"There is only one way in which I can be sure the skull is not cracked," I warned. "You will at least take a common anodyne."

Lestrade went pale but he was an old hand at seeing field-injuries and nodded. "I know." He took a dose of salicylate powder straight from the envelope and chased it down with the rest of his tea and a grimace. "How long?"

"A quarter-hour." I wrote down the time in the record. "As we wait, we may as well continue."

Together we pieced together his actions of the day, with my cross-referencing events in his medical files. I was fortunate to be on friendly terms with Dr. Roanoke. The old fellow had insisted we trade copies of our patients' files when we worked together, and Lestrade is one of the policemen who owns the dubious honour of having two hard-nosed old surgeons keeping him healthy.

Lestrade's root memory (for he held on to it with the ferocity of a ship down to its last anchor), was of coming in to work as usual and putting up a file of a recently closed case – the infamous Silk Poisoner of Hyde. As he was closing his cabinet, Tim the Messenger-boy put his head in the doorway saying, "Go ahead sir – you've been approved!" He dipped in, placed a message on Lestrade's desk, and was just as fast gone.

But Lestrade could not recall that message. He didn't know its content, but he felt that it meant something – now it was a blank slate. He had no memory of it except plucking it up and reading the date scrawled on the envelope of the message was inexplicably off by an entire day.

Perhaps, he thought, he was getting over-worked. It was time he found a solid point and went from there. Policemen, he admitted most begrudgingly, are often checking and re-checking their memories in cases simply because of the sheer overwhelming number that they saw. It wasn't uncommon for a PC, bleary from a fourteen-hour day on foot and short of food and sleep, to arrive in court to give testimony to a criminal he didn't

423

remember arresting only a few days before. Notes were the lifeblood of the copper. He could pass them to trusted colleagues or hold them for future cases – (Coppers, especially old coppers, did not believe a case was over until it was "tied up with hemp".) – copy them for the court, or even (not usually permissible) sell them to a writer, but above all he must have them. He, for one, was grateful for the required literacy tests that made this paper-map of London.

Bearing the weight of all this responsibility, Lestrade returned to his desk and pulled up the calendar to find his dread confirmed: This was the fourth, not the third. He had come into office on one of his rare days off, and his wife would be most concerned at his unexplained absence!

Strokes could cause memory-loss, he knew. Or blood-vessels behaving out of true, side-effects from poison, noxious chemicals – a policeman saw or heard of everything possible. He ought to seek medical help – but first, assure his wife. All he need do was pull a blank page out of his note-book, draft a quiet message to his wife, and write the address on the back so (God Forbid!) he would know what to do if he lost his memory again on the way to the telegraph office.

With a sick feeling, he realized the inside pocket kept for his notebook was empty. In disbelief he stuck his fingers inside it and pulled out a handful of curly yellow bone splinters!

Lestrade admitted if he had been fully in his right mind, he would have been in a complete panic at this point. His entire world was growing less and less familiar, and yet he was not panicking – he was compelled to carry on. He would get to the telegraph office, send that note, and get medical help. Over and over he hammered this intention into his brain as he walked the short distance to the office in question.

The wire-operator took his message and sent it out, giving him odd looks as he did so. Like many men, Lestrade had a side pocket for a few loose coins to lure the pickpocket away from his more valuable wallet kept inside his coat. He pulled out the money from his coin-pocket to pay the operator and, as was his usual wont, pulled out his wallet to file the wire's receipt.

Only then did he realise the extent of his trouble. Inside his wallet were two identical receipts. Now he surrendered to a degree of panic. There was a grease pencil on the writing-desk for the customers. In a fever he pulled up his sleeve and wrote on his starched cuff: *Ask Dr. Watson – Why Memory Gone?* And yanked the sleeve down, turning straight toward Baker Street. He almost stopped back at the Yard to lock up his office but wondered if doing that had caused him to forget his errands the last two times.

Re-living what would be a hellish day for any man, Lestrade held himself still when he finished, awaiting my diagnosis, ignoring the ripples in his teacup.

"Lestrade, these are all causes for concern, but it is too early to plan for unproved emergencies. Now, I believe it is time."

Brain injuries were hostile to most forms of sedatives, and it was just as well that he had the infamous stoicism to pain known to the civilian soldier. I did not shave the scalp. It is a poor doctor who does not know his patient's wife. Mrs. Lestrade was an excellent field-nurse trained in the rough mills of Lancashire, and her temper was well matched to her husband's. She would take upon herself any prevention of infection. As I was only his doctor, I felt it best to stay out of her way.

I cut in a triangle and pulled back the scalp. To my relief, there was no sign of a fracture on the exposed bone. I dressed the wound with oil and stitched it shut, holding everything in place with a roll of lint.

"There is no fracture. Fortunately, your symptoms are consistent with a specific type of amnesia I encountered on the battlefield. Based on your testimony, I expect you to recover from this injury. Keep making extensive notes. This is not the amnesia of sensationalist novels, where the protagonist wakes up with a miraculous lack of memory only to just as miraculously regain it! This is an amnesia of a lesser degree. I say this because its characteristic is in the struggle of the brain to develop and maintain *new* memories after an injury."

"I've never heard of such a thing! I know that when one of us has a good knock on the head, we all try to keep an eye on 'em. Back in the old days our teachers thought if you didn't vomit or go blind following a blow you'd be perfectly fine, but they don't teach the new coppers that anymore – thank heavens. I've seen too many of us after a brawl in the tavern go to the station looking perfectly fine but dead as could be in the morning. The poachers taught us to wear hard-crowned hats. That's spared quite a few of us a cab to the nearest hospital . . . or the graveyard."

"Your memory is traditionally excellent," I assured him. "Your verbal description of Joseph Stangerson's murder room was so precise that I felt as though I was there."

"That was then. This is now," he said wearily. "Now I rely on my notes more and that is a trial, I can tell you, as I have always trusted this," Lestrade reached up and tapped his temple. "I thought we had a nice arrangement, my brain and I," he said with a dark humour. "I gave it one job, and it was to give me back what I put there." Without warning, his sallow face turned an alarming pale. "And what if this isn't from one too many knocks? What if this is something more serious? I'm not a green goose anymore – haven't been for decades! This could be senility!"

"That is a prospect for the bravest of men. Your courage commends you."

"This isn't courage, Doctor. This is whistling past the graveyard."

Something about our conversation felt odd, but I couldn't at the moment place it. "Are you concerned for your work?"

Lestrade made a scoffing sound. "I don't think a single policeman doesn't worry about that every day of his life! Leastaway, I've never met one who didn't!" His calm destroyed, the little man slapped his hand into his knee. "It feels as though I'm writing the words on my own tombstone."

Again, I felt an odd thrill of a something out-of-place. Such feelings are often a form of the rare intuition in men, where a thing that is out of place draws attention to a graver matter – such as an innocuous-looking wet patch on a dry road revealing itself to be an underground spring destroying the cobbles. Lestrade was speaking in ways I didn't normally associate with him, and I considered this an important clue. We both lapsed into thought together, as I mentally reviewed what I had studied (academically and in-person) for brain trauma.

By now my position should be clear. Lestrade had come to me as a physician trusted with an intimate knowledge of the risks he faced. At best his fears would be addressed and dismissed. If he went to a doctor with an open tie to Scotland Yard, he risked being reported as incompetent and summarily retired or placed on leave with a pittance as difficult for a family man to survive on as I had my inconsequential wound pension. While I knew as well as any physician that putting him on a regimen without stimulation would worsen the problem, the Home Office had yet to recognise and adopt these measures. It was courageous for him to come to me at all.

I am no candle to Sherlock Holmes, but I am an investigative physician. I decided that the strange ivory sherds in Lestrade's pocket could bear a closer examination, and perhaps add valuable information on his missing hours.

I lit my best lamps, directed the mirrors to my microscope, and examined the yellowed twigs from his pocket. What I saw was this:

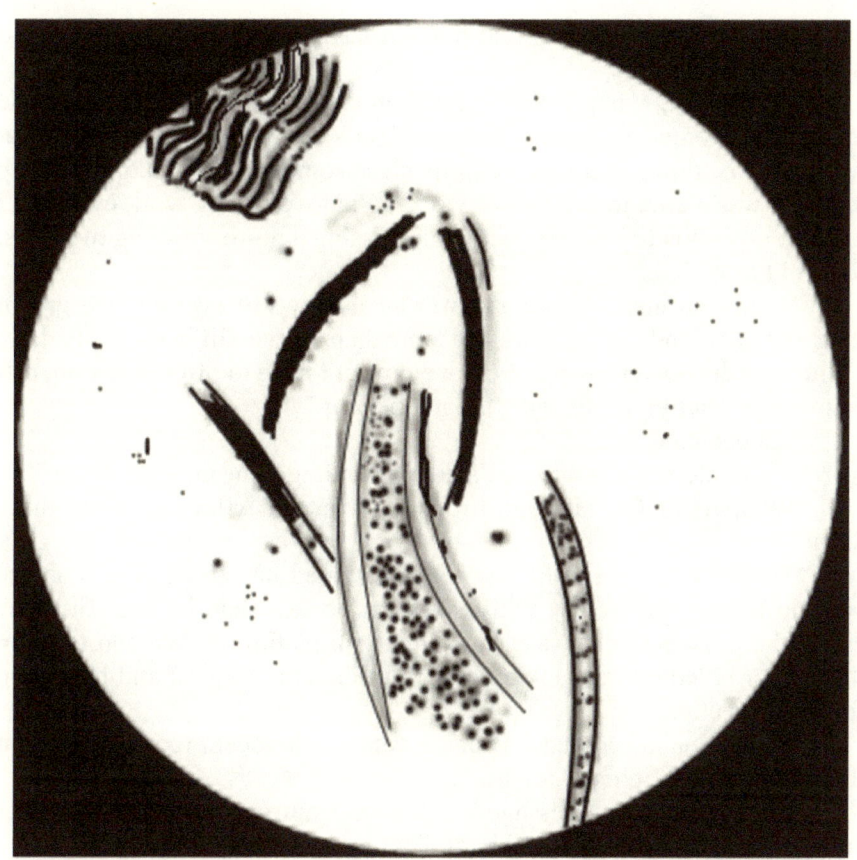

"I'm positive these are shards of a boar's tusk. The curve implies the lower 'whetter' or 'cutter' tusk, not the upper tusk."

Lestrade's reaction was to stare at me as though it were *my* brains under court examination. "I've seen plenty of ivory and bone-stuffs when we nicked someone's hoard, but boar tusk! What would I be doing with that in my pocket?"

"I cannot say, but I *have* seen this before. Here, look for yourself. Young students are schooled to examine the bones of different animals in order to appreciate the design.

"This is a low-quality ivory typical of the boar's tusk. Not many beasts generate such a generous ratio of dental pulp against the enamel and dentin. The pitted structures you see here is the pulp in the centre."

"I'm impressed, Dr. Watson."

"Ah, but you see, there was once hope of taking pig-tusks and fashioning artificial teeth for human mouths! It was sensibly ended when the experiments proved the tusks, for all their fierceness, are too brittle for

427

our use. They yellow to this odd tint and lastly, they shatter or splinter if not kept with caution."

"And again, what would I be doing with any of that?" Lestrade reasonably wanted to know. "If it was only my missing notebook, that would be one thing. But to have in its place something I wouldn't pick up unless it was a clue in my line of work? What would my work even be? I have no notebook to help me recall this missing day – or missing two days, for all I know!"

"I have an idea," I said at last. The shadows of evening had grown long into dark, and my lamp was no more than an eye-slit in the sooty dark. "You have the power to approve or veto what I have to offer. After all, this is my case – but you, Lestrade, are my patient."

"I understand."

"We could request Holmes's help in finding your missing notes."

"What! Holmes? He's up to his browline in Affairs of State these days!"

"The very few times he has been pressured into those case, I assure you, no bribery or flattery will make him do less than he sees fit. If he cannot help, he will not waste our time with platitudes. We can tell him this." I scribbled out a quick note that outlined my request and held it up for his inspection.

He read it and blinked. "That's a very . . . innocent request. My first thought was you ciphered a wire."

"My sending any message to Holmes from my 'practice' is cipher enough. It isn't at all my usual habit."

Lestrade nodded. "Take up the note," he said quietly, and he might have been requesting the reading of his own Will and Testament.

I also sent a reassuring message to Mrs. Lestrade explaining that her husband was delayed while I determined his health. She responded with a more detailed explanation of Lestrade's injuries: He had returned from work the night before, wearing 'a purple dove's egg' on the back of his head, but seemed otherwise fine. He had chatted to her and the childer as normal, and everyone had been looking forward to the luxury of a quiet day at home. It had been to everyone's surprise that he had risen at his usual hour and donned his work-suit, not the clothes he kept at home for home affairs.

Mrs. Lestrade had asked where he thought he was going, and his calm answer, "To work," had simply led her to assume there had been some matter unattended. He never spoke out of turn regarding his cases, for they were usually sensitive or gruesome or both.

"Now that I think of it," the woman wrote, *"as he left he paused by the door and put a Sheepsnose instead of an Old Maid in his pocket."*

My expression must have been confused enough for Lestrade to take pity on me, for he explained, "I usually keep something in my pocket in case there's no time to eat a real meal – or bribe an informant. We ah, alternate the apples we eat to keep them from spoiling and to keep the young ones from being too greedy with a favorite. This month we're eating Sheepsnoses and Old Maids. Sheepsnoses are large but not quite as good to eat out of hand as the Old Maid in Winter – that's what her family calls the Knobbed Russett. The ugliest apple you ever saw in your life. Good eating out of hand, though." His face twisted ruefully. "I thought it was yesterday and picked up yesterday's Sheepsnose. No wonder I was still convinced it was yesterday, if I had yesterday's tea in my coat."

As we waited for Holmes to conclude his matters upstairs, Lestrade and I crafted a plan: He would provide an un-explained presence, allowing me to explain to Holmes that I had a patient in some distress regarding a missing item coupled with the inability to say where it had been lost. In this way confidence could in no way be compromised with his work at the Yard.

Sherlock Holmes shall forever astonish men in the matters of his brain and thought processes, but I like to think I know how to pique his interests. We heard the steps creak as his client departed. Then, with the door barely shut, his "Upstairs, gentlemen!" rang down the well. Considering the speed in which he responded to my note, he must have raced the page boy to the Grand Trunk. We gathered by the grate just as the grocers delivered a cold supper for three.

He listened to my proposal and agreed easily to the circumstances.

"I have no cases at the moment," he announced, to the great relief of Lestrade. We knew that Holmes absolutely refused to work on more than one case at a time – contaminating, he claimed, his memory and soiling his thought-processes. [1]

We sat down to supper. The side-board groaned under cold meat, cheese, fruit, and bread, for I reasoned that between Lestrade's injury (amnesiacs often forget to eat) and Holmes's forgetfulness while he was on a case, it would do no harm to combine our meal with business.

Holmes finished his plate and poured a final glass of water. "The matter is simple, but few simple matters are courteous enough to be easily solved," he announced. "Well! I should be happy to accept this puzzle. The restrictions provide a challenge, and I can never resist that! But first I require you, Watson, as the physician attending, tell me everything you can about this form of amnesia, and then if you would read aloud to me your notes so I do not receive any unnecessary datum like names! What I

429

will need at that point are the details as you wrote them down and also still fresh in your mind."

I dutifully did as he directed and, after my lengthy description of the amnesia diagnosis was given, I produced my files and read aloud everything but Lestrade's name. Holmes listened with his eyes closed, occasionally sipping from his cigarette. Several times he opened his eyes and asked me to re-read a point or two, or repeat what I had said about the amnesia, but I admit I didn't know how they were any more noteworthy than the rest. It was difficult for Lestrade to listen to what was already a painful time in his life, and he did his best not to fidget in his chair like an impatient child.

When I finished, Holmes remained silent for nearly a full minute.

Without warning, he opened his eyes and fixed them upon us. "Watson, you say this form of amnesia is common even if it is usually overlooked?"

"Common? I should call it Legion! It is not exclusive of the battlefield – rather a condition impossible to overlook due to its prevalence. Brain-injuries from blows, fevers, or even close-proximity to very loud noises (such as cannon-fire, or train-wreck), and a few other examples could manifest in the soldier. Those that were in the habit of keeping a diary suffered much less than those who did not. It is a chancy thing to depend on one's fellows to remind one what they must do when there is war! [2]

"I personally suffered it when I was discharged. It was almost a year before I could stop relying on my personal notes to keep to my agendas, and by then the habit was so entrenched that to this day, I feel quite empty without writing-tools in my pocket."

"Events can be shoved away to make room for more events – the trick is to keep the ones you need and let the rest go off to that attic in the brain," Holmes mused. He lapsed in silence again, and just as suddenly, appeared to wake from a long sleep. "Inspector, if I may ask you a few pertinent questions regarding what you know of Dr. Watson's case?"

It was convoluted, but Lestrade understood. "If I can," he responded cautiously.

"Speaking in the most generalized of terms, do you remember where you conducted your last business for Scotland Yard?"

Lestrade caught himself in the act of reaching for the side-pocket where his notebook no longer rested, and winced. "I was in Finchley. Bram's Station."

"Lestrade, as I am not your physician, I am taking a dreadful liberty, but I request you spend the night here under Watson's vigilant eye. You have given me a fine skein of threads. Now all I need do is decide which hand I shall place them in for the untangling." With an odd smile on his thin face, my friend rose. "This is a most welcome respite from the tiresome cabbages and kings of my current calendar, old friend, but I shall not delay in finding answers. Watson, there is no knowing when I shall return. There is no knowing when I shall return. Lestrade, my first act will be to personally reassure your doting wife that you will return before too much time has passed."

We did as directed, but Lestrade found himself in no mood for a strange bed, and dozed in the upright chair by the fire. I spent the time quietly, muddling my way through my collection of medical tomes that might give me some insight on the rarely understood amnesia that Lestrade was now suffering. It did occur to me that I had been remiss in not studying it myself, but I had been a shattered man in all ways upon my return from my service. For all I know, I had studied it and swiftly left it forgotten. I hadn't been well enough to hold a pen, much less have cause to write more than a few lines upon paper.

I was frustrated. My references were considered up to date and respectable, but the vague, clipped notes left me with no sense of accomplishment. If I had been reading up the topic, it was no wonder I carried no memory of it.

Deep into the night, Holmes turned the key in the door and stepped through, holding before him a large fishing creel full of food. He was typical of his usual nights in London seeking clues: Dripping with the black London dew, smeared at the sides and shoulders from leaning on crumbling wall-brick, red-cheeked against the cold and in fine spirits. I opened my mouth to greet, but he pressed his finger to his lips, and I stopped. He gently lowered the basket to the table and crept to the door where Lestrade had hung his hat and duster, his shoes resting beneath, collar, cuffs and tie neatly placed to the side.

Holmes slipped his fingers over and into the detective's pockets. In the space of a minute he had everything completely examined, even the shoes. A moment of satisfaction gleamed on his face but it was gone as fast as it had appeared.

"Mrs. Lestrade sends her regards," he announced, and her husband sat upright, wide-eyed and fully awake. "And what appears to be a kedgeree pasty . . . she did mutter that it was a crime against flavour, but for some reason the mere sight of me caused her to extrapolate that all three of us need a proper feed."

"That sounds like her." Lestrade smiled wryly. "Did you find anything?"

"All in good time. I believe we should have a very early breakfast and wash-up before we visit the boreal parish of Finchley."

431

"At this hour? What could we hope to find?" I protested.

"Why, Watson, shall I speculate without data? What can we not hope to find, you may as well ask! Crime keeps no clock coincidental to our own!"

Holmes purchased a newspaper from a boy and read it with his pocket-lamp as the cabbie complained loudly about his three-quarters-of-an-hour fare. Lestrade's temper emerged and he shouted back up that we weren't likely to change our mind as it was still better than two hours on foot.

"He was probably hoping we'd feel guilty enough to pay him extra."

"I'm feeling a lot of things, Doctor, but I can't say I'm feeling guilty."

Holmes lit a cigarette. "We shall be there soon enough, and time on hoof beats time on foot. Gentlemen, if I may trouble you to humour me when we part ways with our charming driver: I request that you play specific roles. Lestrade, as far as anyone is concerned, you are accompanying me to ensure I am not violating the law. Watson, you shall stand as witness for us both." To this we agreed. When it comes to his cases, no power can make Sherlock Holmes reveal his facts ahead of their time.

We left our cab for a London coated in heavy yellow fog trapped in the atmospheric pressures. In the light of day Finchley is a pleasing borough. Here in the swirling degrees of darkness I felt as lost as a wayward soul in the Greek Underworld. The blue of the policeman's lamp showed us close to the station against the Great North Road, but the fog's texture made it seem far away.

Holmes did not go to the blue lamp but crossed the street from it and stopped before a plain grey wall of plank behind an ancient iron gate – the low sort with arrows to dissuade wandering livestock from the days when Finchley saw many beasts come to the stockyards for sale or slaughter. Lestrade and I hurried to catch up, but he was merely studying the writing painted upon the boards.

"'*The Asphodel Meadows*' – and lo, how it fits the advertisement of Homer's *Odyssey* – dark, gloomy, mirthless." Holmes held up his pocket-lamp and by degrees, the humble wooden sign of a rude cemetery was revealed.

The Asphodel Meadows
Place of Rest
"Lo, I Remember Beyond the Tomb"

432

It was scabious from too many coats of paint on spoiling wood, and clearly more than one hand had been assigned the task to lengthen its life with another sticking-plaster of paint. Its presence was hardly in order with the house-proud folk of North London, but it was good company with the residents fallen from their rude prosperity into a level just above destitution. When I first came to London, I was all too aware that a further slide down in fortune would send me to such a place. I snorted at my new maudlin streak.

"Penny for your thoughts?" Lestrade asked of me quizzically.

"I was thinking of the juxtaposition in naming a realm for the dead after a sweet-smelling flower."

He soon caught my meaning. "Ah. Because the grave smells sweet?"

"Infamously so." It was something the three of us, irrespective of our different professions, knew from personal experience.

Holmes brazenly unclipped the old hasp-and-tongue holding the gate and it swung open, protesting with squeaks and much shedding of rust. He ushered us inside and turned to close the gate after us.

"Who goes there?" Squeaked a thready, high-pitched voice. Before we could reply a brief flare followed a match-scratch, like some Jack-o'-lantern hobbling through a tormentuous swamp-path, the dirty yellow gleam struggled from a point made far from the foggy mire of tombstones to challenge us. "Show yourselves at once!" demanded the voice. "I say, we've got enough trouble over here without letting it in for free! Speak up!"

"Hello the light!" Holmes called. "We apologise for losing our way. Our cab-driver was not so reliable as advertised."

"Eh? Well, I suppose that's likely." By degrees, a hunched-over little gnome of a man became solid. He was half-dressed for bed. A tobacco-smoke-stained nightcap hung crookedly over one ear, and his white muslin night-shirt, yellowed about the collar and sleeves, flopped over un-braced trousers of a rusty, musty wool made black with frequent applications of the weakest of dyes. His shoes were still on his feet but battered into shapeless slippers, and the stockings were mis-matched. Cataracts had made milk-glass of his light blue eyes, and his mouth fixed open in the fashion of a purse-seine, puckered and round to breathe. The badly-broken nose spread over the side of his face explained his difficulty in drawing a normal breath. Holmes has often accused me of writing fancifully, but this poor church sexton was a pitiful sight.

"Eh, I've no place for you at this hour, gentlemen, unless you prefer the company of my clients. My congregation. They're all in their homes tonight. Long-homes." He cackled without warning, and Lestrade jumped in response. "They never mind." He was finally close enough to stop, and a clouded eye fixed uncertainly on Holmes, myself, and finally the little professional with much head-cocking, wheezing, and neck-twisting. He reminded me of a confused chicken. "Here . . . do I know you, sir?

"Do you?" Lestrade countered, falling back on the trusty policeman's defence against a question as another question returned.

"I do beg your pardon," Holmes stepped forward with a smile. "As you can see, we are lost. I should not hope to trouble you for a place to rest inside your chapel – "

"I should hope not! It's only a few hours until dawn. You can wait like the rest of us!"

" – but perhaps there is a bench?" A coin dandled between Holmes's gloved finger-tips.

"Hmm! Well!" The Sexton drew himself back importantly. "Yes, there be a bench or two 'gainst the mere-trees. They'll keep the wet off. You realise I am placing my trust in your honest predicament, gentlemen?"

A second coin chimed softly against the first. "Naturally we could not beg charity," Holmes assured with a great deal more sobriety than I felt the occasion warranted. Behind him, Lestrade was making a great show of staring down as he fiddled with his glove-buttons, hoping to hide his face until he regained some control.

"Naturally," the Sexton clucked.

"I should hope that a donation to this fine resting-place would not be out of place."

"You think proper – 'tis a cold time of year and extra work goes into the upkeep. Why, the upheaval and the moles alone, howking up the coffins – "

"We are most grateful." Holmes swept the money into the wrinkled yellow paw, smiled beautifully, and we walked in the direction of the Sexton's knobby weathervane of a finger.

Before long the three of us were quietly perched on a large stone bench. It was very cold, just on the edge of freezing wet, as were the very airs about us, and condensation dripped dirty pearls from the yew-needles and arils. Behind us the occasional flutter of sound from the Great North Road whispered through the gaps in the living trees. The police station could have been in another world, so remote a gleam was the blue flame. We could hear the occasional bang of the front door open and shut, and bursts of conversation, soon swallowed in the fog.

As we watched, the Sexton's lantern bobbed up and down across the shrouded grave-field like a lost spirit. Scraps of his self-amused muttering and gasping floated with the fog, unfathomable to translate.

"He looks like one of the graves howked him right up," Lestrade muttered darkly, which was not dissimilar to my own thoughts. "Good thing you gave him two coins, Mr. Holmes. He can put them on his eyes when he goes back to bed."

Holmes sniffed. "This is an excellent moment to tell you, Lestrade, that your wife forewarned me about your irritability around poorly kept graveyards."

"Too right I'm irritable. This – "

A heavy wooden *clang* – the chapel's door, I imagined, for I could not see it – snuffed out the lantern-light, leaving us in the darkness with Holmes's pitifully smaller pocket-lamp. The billowing fogs had become a curtain, the humble belfry-room lit by the Sexton's lantern a single, glaring orange eye. The tombstones were now poorly angled blackened lumps in a shifting field. Even if the road was less than three yards' behind us, I felt purely isolated in that lonely garden of death.

I felt the typical man's instinct to fill up a large silence with my own chatter. "Why 'poorly kept', Lestrade?"

I could hear him turn his head to stare at me in the obfuscation. "Would *you* like to stay in a place like this?"

"What, do you mean my mortal remains?"

"I didn't mean your living ones. I bet you've got a much better neighborhood picked out than this."

"As a matter of fact, I do."

"Good." Lestrade shuddered. "That Sexton made me feel as though I'm not the only one with their brains light on the scales."

"What a pity," Holmes drawled, "that transcription is impossible for now. I shall have to rely on my memory to record this *comedie*. But who would purchase it?"

"This isn't my idea of comedy, Mr. Holmes," Lestrade hissed softly as another late-night cab splashed past us. "My head's addled, but I'm quite certain Halloween's long in the future."

"Not long enough," I heard Holmes say under his breath. The association that holiday had with superstition, the antithesis of logic and common sense, never failed to spark his acidic temper.

"Ha! Hello!" Holmes hopped up, for the single window had winked out. "Our friend is abed and we may he sleep sound! Gentlemen, it is time for a little cleverness."

With no more warning, Holmes unleashed himself and dashed into the knee-deep fogs. Lestrade and I had to struggle to follow, for though I was the swifter, my night-vision was poor, and Lestrade's policeman's instincts were loathe to leave my side if he could still see Holmes. Later, he admitted that his instincts were always to stick by the doctor when they were on a night-job.

Like a hound on the scent, Holmes darted in straight lines, occasionally looking to the weary chapel for orientation, but fixing his attention to the ground at his feet. Twice he paused, but resumed the hunt just as we were about to catch up with him. Whatever he was seeking, he knew what it was.

He stopped for the third time and knelt on the freezing grass before a very old stone. "Hah!" He muttered in triumph. "And there it is!"

"What – " Lestrade and I finally caught up. "What is it, Holmes?"

"A moment. Can you make out the lettering?"

We were in the oldest quarter of the graveyard, and like many of its neighbors, this stone was well-clad in moss. Holmes rested his lamp before the face to make out words nearly dissolved by time:

In Memory of
Hyacint Lebron
Lost at Sea
Jn 9 1700 – F 21 1742
"Each Man His Own Sexton"

Before the stone was a shovel-hammered plateau of ubiquitous grave-earth, studded with the marly clay and sea-fossil pebbles so common to the area.

"That is peculiar," I muttered. "The grave is fresh but the stone is positively ancient."

"Yes, isn't it?" Holmes chuckled merrily. "And what a charming face." The moss had partially – but not completely – covered the roughly cut winged skull and scythe. "Do not move, gentlemen." He crawled about the stone – never across it – running his gloves through the freezing wet grass. After almost a minute he gave a cry and jumped up, a small leather book in his grip.

"Here!" Lestrade gasped and clutched it in his hands. "You knew my notes were here?"

"A reasonable assumption. Now. I ask that you both stay here. I shall return – if all goes well – very soon and with some help."

"Help?" Lestrade cried at his melting shadow. "Help with what?" I was tempted to laugh, having been the recipient of Holmes's queer humours more than once – and seemingly abandoned more than I care to recall.

"There's a reason why the Yard consults with that man," I heard Lestrade say under his breath. "No one else can do what he does. That's possibly just as well."

"I'm confident we'll have an answer before long," I assured him. "Are you well enough to stand?"

"I'll make a chair of the grass if I have to. I'm not about to risk walking away from the one spot where I know he'll return."

It must have been akin to torture, being returned to his precious notes but not having a light to read them by. Fortunately for us both (for the cold fog was actively freezing now), we had less than a quarter-hour standing in the icy fields. A pin-point of elfin light gleamed through the iron gate and, with a rusty clink and clank, they parted. Holmes whistled. I was familiar with his bird-calls by now – and we stamped our freezing feet as three shapes drew near.

A bobbing light was coming down our path, but it was neither a Sexton's poor lantern nor an aimless ghost: It was the familiar sweeping bull's-eye of the policemen.

"Hello, gennulmen!" rumbled a giant's voice, and from behind the closing light a large constable rolled up, barrel-chested and bewhiskered. Hiked across his broad shoulder was a large digging-shovel and at his side strode a slightly smaller plainclothes detective wrapped up against the clammy cold. Holmes, himself a tall man, appeared shrunk in comparison.

"Ill-met by lamplight, Lestrade," said the plainclothes detective. "Alluz glad to see you. How's the head?" His dark eyes were sharp but warm, and his thick blond beard was ageing white as the night froze it. He gave Lestrade a friendly nod and then tapped his brim to me as the constable held back. "Doctor, I am Inspector George G. Bishop, CID, Finchley Branch. This little fellow here is PC U'ren.

Lestrade was shaking hands with his fellows. "Double-duty again, U'ren?"

"He's a charming fellow, Sexton Helmut Smith – or what parts of him that's here," U'ren grinned. Even his voice was larger than life – it rolled like a church-bell. "Half-deaf, half-blind, and three-quarters daft. We've been keepin' an eye on him a long time."

"Well, to be truthful," Bishop sighed, "We've been watching *him* only about seventy years or so – that's when he started walking. His father, and his father and his father before, adds up to a lot of watching. You'll find if you come here, there's generations of coppers, thief-takers, and ministers handing down the duty to watching generations of Great North Road Smiths."

"And you've not found anything on him?" Lestrade blinked.

"Oh, we've found plenty on his family – a nicer, more charming bucket of vipers you'll never meet. Thank goodness you're not likely to 'em . . . not unless you 'ave a medium to go with your shovel." The policeman looked meaningfully about the graves. "If something's sellable, they'll put it to the test. And they don't ask questions on where the goods came from. Generations of that lot – really a rare breed when you think of it. They're one of the few naturally-born criminals here instead of the Highwaymen that came up from the South." Mr. Bishop tutted sadly for the frailties of man. "They broke his nose when he was a tot and probably a lot of his common sense too. His engine stops more than it starts. But I do go on. How can we help you gentlemen?"

Holmes had been shifting impatiently through the small speech. "If I may trouble you gentlemen, I believe a case involving the Smiths is about to draw close."

PC U'ren cleared his throat. "I'm pleased to help. The more the merrier, I say, when you need to be certain all is proper and according to procedure."

"There you are. Would you be so kind, Constable?"

Without another word the gigantic man moved as silently as a ghost to the front of the gravestone. "Ready when you are, Mr. Holmes."

"Very good, Constable." Holmes knelt upon the freezing grass and with his walking-stick raised high, brought it down hard into the disturbed earth. It was a stupefying action, yet when nothing happened he pulled back and repeated his actions, twice, thrice, a fourth time.

There was no warning – the metal ferrule of Holmes's stick went down and through. A dull drum of its metal striking hollow wood was just barely audible. He removed the stick and began clawing the soil away from the small black hole.

"Oh, no," Lestrade whispered to me with a frown. "There shouldn't be anything there, if he was lost at sea . . . ."

I was the only one who heard him. U'ren had endured enough of a civilian doing his job, and he knelt, large hands pushing aside pawsful of dirt and calcified shells. When there was room, he added the shovel to the work. Before long a thin board coffin lid, raw and new, emerged. It was three feet down – far too shallow for a proper grave. A rough iron ring was bolted on its top, making it look more like a door than the hinge of a grave.

"Well. That is the question," Mr. Bishop quoted dryly. "Mr. Holmes, if you wouldn't mind stepping back please?" The inspector bent and grabbed the iron ring and with a grunt, heaved. The wood was far too thin and light to be a genuine coffin-lid, and it cracked under his pull.

PC U'ren, the least talkative of the two, stepped back with a Cymric oath on his lips at what the lantern exposed.

It was a skeleton, pitted with age and decay and sadly jumbled, still clad in the earth of a buttery yellow loam alien to the marly clay of the graveyard. Originally it had been hastily stuffed into a badly-laced oilskin, decayed and cracked open, its contents spilt in all directions. The lips of the bag pressed against the skull, propping over the gaping jaws. Curlicues of yellow boar-tusk mingled with the chalky human bones, but I barely noticed these, for I had seen the teeth poking out of the upper and lower jaws of the dead man.

He had extra teeth – Everywhere there ought to be one canine, he wore two. An extra tooth or two was not an unknown phenomenon and not even all that rare, especially among men, but I had never seen a specimen with so many extra canines. They were crooked and slanting outward and must have caused him considerable pain in life, but from the tangled-up snarl of muddy purplish red trapezohedral beads about the remnants of his collar-bones, he had been wealthy enough to survive the obstacles.

PC U'ren had stopped swearing. Mr. Bishop whistled softly, long and low. "Something rich and strange. Is that what – or who – I think this is, Lestrade? Mr. Holmes? Anyone?"

"I believe his credentials speak for himself." Holmes knelt at the lip of the false grave and fished about before pulling up a rough bead. Close to his pocket-lamp it gleamed sullenly under yellow dust. "A solid garnet, perfect honeycomb. Watson, as a medical man, can you verify the teeth are unique?"

"They are," I vouched. "There is only one man in all of history recorded to have eight canines in his jaws."

"There you have it," Holmes's grey eyes glittered and he observed the dull beauty of the gem in his fingers with a cold, intellectual detachment. "The Boar King of poor Denis Addleton's British Barrow, rudely stolen from his tomb, murdering Addleton in the process, and held for ransom on December 21st, 1724. What a pity the kidnappers had been so reliant on their loathsome master, the criminal Jonathan Wilde for support.

"1724 was a most unfortunate year for Wilde, as you may recall his own cleverness came to an end, and he was caught up in a chain of ever-enlarging scandals until his hanging at Tyburn in May of 1725."

"Not that it did any good to the Addletons." Lestrade had taken up one of the beads and was frowning at it with a strange perplexity, I thought he looked as though he disapproved of the thing. "The looters were the Smiths? You said they were one of the few native highwaymen here. The Great North Road was what – two days' ride?"

439

"I suspect they were not the actual thieves," Holmes replied. "As you said – Highwaymen. They robbed the robbers on their way to Wilde, doubtless leaving them dead in the fashion of their trade and only too late did they realise what they had on their hands – a treasure of bones, ivory, and garnets so priceless and well known none would dare buy them on pain of hanging. The very person to fence the treasure to was Wilde – whose men they had killed! What to do? Move it to safe-keeping and hope the world forgot about it.

"But the world never did. And one day the hated police built their new station within shouting-distance of the cache."

"God bless." PC U'ren shook his head back and forth. "My Tad told me the Smiths were all sour about it, yes, but everyone thought it was because their favorite pub was on the other side of the church-yard!"

"How did Helmut Smith become the Sexton of this chapel, Inspector?" I asked of Mr. Bishop.

The big man pursed up his lips inside his yellow beard. "The way I heard it, Helmut was too meek and weak to be of use to his family – they were all brutes – but he couldn't stand up to them. They would have killed him easy as breathing. The old sexton was retiring, and he put in a good word for the boy – boy at the time, I mean to say. He's been here ever since, and he's outlived every last one of his nasty kinfolks. But honestly, Mr. Holmes, even when he was young, there was something not quite right with his brains. I suppose they trusted him with the grave-spot and told him to keep an eye on it, make sure no one bumbled into it."

"Ah, well," Holmes burst into one of his rare smiles. "If I may suggest, Mr. Bishop, a careful look be given to the rest of the graveyard? It is quite possible the family has more than one cache hiding amongst these good folk!"

And while levity was hardly appropriate for a graveyard, the expressions the three officers wore was cause for amusement.

"An ordinary enough case in method, but extraordinary for results. That is an excellent reason to accept any case if it has the slightest ring of the *outré* – and this one did."

Sherlock Holmes was holding audience in the Station House as he, Lestrade, and myself took a brief respite from the flurry of reports and questions, spiced with the endless cups of tea and sandwiches the police were so anxious to share. Lestrade was the first one to finish his interrogation and was pragmatically seizing a nap by the grate. He was as deeply asleep as a beggar on the corner, and his mates from Finchley were amusing themselves by sneaking up and dropping small coins and religious tracts into his upturned hat in his lap. I dreaded his waking.

"It is a dangerous thing to rely on half-formed facts," Holmes commented. "My first maneuver was to re-trace what I could of Lestrade's days. That led to his wife, who was able to supply much material in way of his in-home hours.

"Tracing his steps as a policemen took a little more thought, but it shall be a day far in the future when I trade in all the favours the Yard owes to me, and it took merely a handful of them to learn Lestrade had been working on a case in the Finchley parish. I lost a few hours on more than a few box-canyons, but that is the punishment one may accept for assumptions. Lestrade had not been on a case at all, but he was helping *close* a case by secret delivery to the police-station a file of confidential documents!

"It was a beautiful little knot of camaraderie, policeman protecting policemen, as they had the mistaken idea I was acting the Pinkerton. Eventually I was able to persuade them that I had no one's head for my pike, and they were much more charming.

"Lestrade had been under orders to deliver sensitive papers to Inspector Charles Munro and, while in the station, suffered a blow to the back of the head by a man resisting his right to lawful criminal procedure. Neither the man, a common thief gone violent, nor Lestrade had anything to do with each other save for that accidental encounter. It was a stroke of bad luck, but everyone, Lestrade included, thought all was well.

"As the official story had him anywhere but at this station, it is no wonder his peers were under a fog. Silences, happily, are golden, and it was but a small bit of work to extrapolate around the data for the missing piece of the puzzle. It was fortunate for me that one of the men present was PC Rhys U'ren, a self-avowed 'gentleman of the beat' who can brag of being an old friend of Lestrade. U'ren gave up most of the details I was missing. He was a gold nugget unexpectedly found in the oatmeal, which goes to show that while logic and cunning solves many a case, it is a foolish logician who cannot concede the worth of serendipity.

"Duty finished, Lestrade had left the Finchley Station planning to return to the Yard and then home. He was nursing his headache and waiting for a cab outside the Asphodels when he was alerted to the sound of crying children. Being a father as well as a policeman, his instincts were to run to the sound of trouble, and there he came upon a governess with her young charges, who had until now not known the dire consequences of not listening to their governess.

"But I get ahead of myself. The governess was a thoroughly charming spinster, Miss Garnette Bennett – or so she was to U'ren. One cannot say the same for her charges: A rascally set of identical twins as ever an adult has had the poor fortune to mentor, Charles and Edward Driff! Miss

441

Bennett was charged to take them to their tailor's for the last fittings of their Christmas Suits, and had been unable to resist the temptation to pay her respects to the grave of her brother, Gaye Bennett, on the way home. She had warned the twins not to run over the graves as it was 'naughty' and 'disrespectful', but they had not listened. Never lie to children when the truth is bound to do the trick, Watson! Charles Driff did not know the dangers of causing an old grave's collapse and he did as he pleased. His foot went through the brittle shell of an empty grave – our Mr. Hyacinth.

"Lestrade carefully freed the frightened child's leg but, in the struggle, the boy dropped his brother's bilbo. Lestrade now had to recover the toy by sticking his hand into a dark coffin or face the much-less-pleasant prospect of Charles and Edward's healthy howls against his headache.

"Lestrade had no hopes of victory, as his arm was hardly long enough to reach the required six-foot depth of a grave! Yet he had to appear as though he was doing *something*. His mind was on his headache and keeping up the appearances of the thing. The child would remember only that a policeman hadn't tried his best. Pride has manipulated many men, as we well know!

"As you recall, Watson, Mr. Lebron's stone clearly reads '*Lost at Sea*', so Lestrade was expecting anything but the rattle of bones and coffin-plank under his groping fingers! It did not take him long to realize the difference between a child's wooden toy and a rib cage, and it was all he could do to recover the bilbo and keep composed. The grave was ridiculously close to the surface but, when there is no body to fret over, mock-burials are dug no deeper than the job needs.

"Toy retrieved, Lestrade endured the gratitude of the governess, the children, and loud crowd of well-wishers attracted by the twins' foghorn-quality vocal cords. Watson, I have many regrets in my life, but as of now my greatest one is not being present to witness Lestrade's effort to pretend all was well through a splitting head as he tried to think of his next course of action. It must have been worthy of high theatre." Holmes stopped his narrative to fill up his pipe, laughing the entire time at the imagined drama.

"One of the last to join the crowd was PC U'ren! With one of those secret signs the policemen keep amongst their little Freemasonry, U'ren dispersed the crowd and stood watch as Lestrade explained what had happened and sought out our friend the noble Sexton.

"Helmut was as hard of hearing then as he is now and insisted Lestrade must be wrong! Lestrade had little choice but to march the old fellow to the scene, and before U'ren's witness, plumbed the coffin again by lying on the earth, pushing his arm through the hole drilled by the unlucky Charles, and pulling up a clutched handful of bone.

"Helmut did not know what to make this, and after much head-scratching suggested someone was in there. 'Good heavens, really,' countered Lestrade with what U'ren says was a face cut of bedrock. After some thought, the Sexton decided he should re-cover the grave, and as he scuttled off get his spade, Lestrade had a hasty word with U'ren.

"Everything about the Sexton felt suspicious, but this was a church-yard and required some delicacy. Policemen are schooled to be hard-headedly ignorant of superstition, but the possibility that they could be accused of molesting a grave was severe, possibly a permanent score against their records. What could they do? Lestrade wasn't even supposed to be in Finchley. His records at the Yard insisted he was still in his office, doing paperwork. There was also the matter of the bone-fragments. The yellowed curls were clearly some sort of ivory, possibly an important clue. As they talked it out, they picked over the fragments of human bone, which was much paler and porous compared to the ivory. U'ren says it was at this point Lestrade was getting his attention by repeating himself, and paused to write everything down in his notebook, but he didn't think too much of it. He was writing everything down too.

"They returned the bone-fragments to the grave, and with no time to lose! Helmut had found his shovel and was anxious to work. The police were quick to back away and leave him to it.

"Their plan was for Lestrade to stick to his original schedule, with a quiet word to his superiors who knew the real reason for his presence in Finchley. U'ren would do the same. The ivory, the strangest of clues, was kept by Lestrade. He made his way back, although I'm sure I don't know how he managed it, sent a request from his station, went home, carried on as usual, went to sleep, and woke up the next morning thinking it was still his last day of the week.

"It was the timing of his odd comments about graves and graveyards that took my attention, Watson. You had assured me that a man under this amnesia will, under moments of clarity, continue to function, but their minds will jettison all but the details it deems important.

"You and I have known Lestrade a long time, and it is not like him at all to comment on graves and graveyards. He avoids such language with the fervor of a cat walking around a muddy puddle. Lestrade renders to Cesar with a religious fervor. Work takes up his attention. Ergo, I entertained the possibility that his brain was revolving around a lost bit of data, and that it was related to graveyards."

"That is reasonable as you put it." I clapped.

"This is all quite wonderful, Holmes," Mr. Bishop exclaimed, "But tell me, why is it that Lestrade never remembered this? I thought his amnesia recalls only the events that are the most urgent to him."

Sherlock Holmes laughed. Lestrade jerked awake and instinctively reached for his hat. He stared at what was now inside it.

"Believe the word of the married man," I chuckled as Lestrade glared at suddenly-retreating constables in the station. "The brain would not in this case forget the most urgent item on the mind – and not unlike myself in similar affairs, Lestrade's brain was focused solely in survival – he had to be home before his wife worried for him!"

Thus, the reader knows how Sherlock Holmes discovered the lost contents of the British Barrow. The flurry of news that followed was annoying to a man who had so recently come out of hiding, and his valued privacy was threatened. I prescribed a few days at the seaside and we narrowly avoided the journalists at the station. Soon we settled into a cozy little cottage in a quiet salt cove. It was time well spent in fishing and exploring the shingle. Through all of this Holmes never said a word about the case, but I could tell he was still thinking it over. Like a composer doubting his performance the night before, he was playing the steps of the case in his mind.

"They should have left my name out of it," he complained as our holiday drew to a close.

"The Boar King is a matter of British pride, Holmes. No other relics have been found in our country with such riches."

"Pah. King? There's no proof! He was at best a wealthy man and the public decided that meant royalty. His gold fripperies were stripped centuries ago – the garnets left behind from haste." Holmes prepared his evening pipe and lounged back on the lawn-chair, smoking in silence for some time. "Not that a gem is useful when you think of it. It has no edibility, cannot be drunk, give wisdom, extend life or health. A primitive mind would think the worst after a look at those teeth." He blew six smoke-rings as the sea-winds lulled. "I received a letter from the Addletons this morning."

"Oh? I hope they are in good health."

"I have no idea. What I do know is they wish me to help them out with a little problem involving the barrow."

"Not more murder and bones, I hope!"

"No, nothing so redundant."

"Redundant!"

"They wish me to help them find a lost map. Without, it they cannot hope to drain the spring that is flooding the barrow. It was the *draining* of said spring that allowed the thieves to rob the barrow in the first place. If it is matter of simple deduction there should be little trouble . . . I have no hope of adding civil engineering to my already-handsome list of skills."

444

When I look at the three massive manuscript volumes which contain our work for the year 1894 I confess that it is very difficult for me, out of such a wealth of material, to select the cases which are most interesting in themselves and at the same time most conducive to a display of those peculiar powers for which my friend was famous. As I turn over the pages I . . . find an account of the Addleton tragedy and the singular contents of the ancient British barrow . . . .

– Dr. John H. Watson
"The Adventure of the Golden Pince-Nez"

NOTES

1 – "I had waited patiently for the opportunity for I was aware that he would never permit cases to overlap, and that his clear and logical mind would not be drawn from its present work to dwell upon memories of the past." – *The Hound of the Baskervilles*

2 – We now know this is *anterograde amnesia*.

The Smith-Mortimer Succession
by Tim Gambrell

It may be considered a facile observation, but I have always found that ill news impacts upon me more deeply during periods of inclement weather. One needs the warmth and reassurance of the sun to instill a sense of hope. We could certainly have done with some sunshine on the day in question. The November frost had bitten so deeply that I had to scrape the sheen off the inside of the windows when I rose. I wouldn't relinquish my day coat, even when seated in the face of a roaring hearth.

I opened *The Times*, but it offered me little of any comfort or interest. I must have drifted into a stupor, because the next thing I knew the newspaper was whipped from my fingers, causing me to awaken with a start. My good friend Sherlock Holmes stood before me, an intense look on his face. There was no point in me remonstrating with him when he was concentrating like that. His entire being was focussed on the bottom of the front page. I tried, without success, to recall the subject of the articles there.

After a few moments, Holmes glanced at me over the top of the folded broadsheet and spoke as if we were mid-conversation.

"I must express my surprise that you did not consider the article regarding the bludgeoned coach driver to be worthy of comment."

I had a vague recollection of the story. The regular London-to-Luton coach, which calls at some of the villages along the way not yet covered by the railway network. Something about a crash and death by misadventure, was it? I freely admitted that I was struggling to stay awake. Holmes began to prowl the sitting room, adamant that the only misadventure was in the writing of the article.

"A mess, that's what it is, Watson, a mess." He smacked the newspaper against the back of the *chaise-longue* as he passed. "An apparently empty coach falls foul of the road. The horses live, yet the driver dies from a head wound. Papers which the driver was carrying are missing. Pah! How this is considered death by misadventure is beyond my reason."

"What papers?" I asked, easing myself out of the chair to pour a coffee from the still-warm pot. "Could it not have been an opportunist thief, after the event?"

"Perhaps, but we're talking about the London-to-Luton stagecoach route, and this is hardly the time of Dick Turpin! I believe a bracing morning's walk to Camden is in order."

I downed my coffee and reached for more. "In this cold? To what end?"

"The offices of the coach company. If we can find out what the papers were, even in general terms, I think that would satisfy me as to whether this was a premeditated hold-up or your opportunist thief."

I must admit, I felt strongly that this was one of Holmes's whims, and that he only needed to satisfy himself that he could work out more about the case from a half-hearted newspaper article than the local police seemed to be able to from studying all the evidence. Some little time later we returned to Baker Street, chilled to the bone despite our heavy overcoats, and not a great deal the wiser. The offices of the coach company had refused to reveal to us the nature of the stolen paperwork. They had referred us to a Reverend Hume, from whom, they said, they received the private charter. But they could provide no address or details for the Reverend, only his name.

Holmes was undeterred. "I shall summon my Irregulars, Watson. I have every faith in them being able to trace a Reverend by that name, and the correct one, to boot."

I hastened up the stairs behind my friend, my lungs slowly adjusting to the much warmer climate inside. Mrs. Hudson appeared behind me and called to Holmes, but he was too focussed on his next action to pay us any heed. By the time Mrs. Hudson and I joined him in our rooms, he was pouring three brandies. Nearby him stood a meek-looking parson.

Mrs. Hudson gave a harried sigh.

"It's all right, Mrs. Hudson," Holmes said. "You may leave us with our unexpected guest."

"Very good, Mr. Holmes," she replied, breathlessly, as she hurried out again.

Holmes handed the man a brandy and he spoke. "Reverend Hume, Rector of the parish of St Mary, Kilburn, at your service, gentlemen."

We sat, and I could only marvel at the level of serendipity that seemed to fill our lives from time to time.

"I take it your visit has something to do with the death of the coach driver on the Luton service?" Holmes asked.

Reverend Hume was a thin and pasty-skinned individual, with strands of thinning steel-grey hair slicked across his otherwise-bald pate. His aquiline nose and redundant chin, above a black cassock, gave him somewhat the profile of a tall penguin. He leaned back in his chair and raised his brows.

"My, my, Mr. Holmes, but how could you possibly know that?"

I reassured him that we had just come from the coach company's offices, having taken an interest in the matter upon reading that morning's *Times*. The Reverend was clearly relieved by this – and touched. I sensed he was a genuine and empathetic individual, a true Christian soul, perfectly suited to his role.

"The floor is yours, Reverend," continued Holmes, magnanimously. "You have saved us the considerable trouble of tracking you down. Now, please do tell us what service we can provide for you in return."

The Reverend spent a moment rubbing his palms together – clearly a habit or affectation. Then he commenced his story.

"You may, perhaps, have heard of the recent death of Sir Philip Smith-Mortimer, the naturalist?"

I knew the name. Holmes, as expected, was fully versed in the details.

"A tragic case," Holmes said. "Hunting accident, as I recall. Shot himself. And, having devoted his life to his studies and never taken a wife, he died without issue – much to the good fortune of the Baronet's industrialist cousin. Up north, I should think."

That's where I knew the name from! I recalled some disputes towards the end of the previous year over the poor pay and working conditions in their manufactories.

"Died without *acknowledged* issue," replied the Reverend, "which leads me to the purpose of my visit."

A glance passed between us and I saw Holmes's eyes flash with interest.

"One of my flock, a Mrs. Gladys Shields . . . ." The Reverend stumbled on his words, here, as if unsure of how to tell us what he wanted to say. "Some years ago, she chanced upon an encounter with the Baronet. She informed me of her sin at the time and, alas, the meeting resulted in a child – something which had escaped the lady in her marriage. But she made certain that the birth certificate recorded Sir Philip as the father."

Here the Reverend paused again, this time to sip at his brandy.

"Mrs. Shields never informed him?" asked Holmes.

"She did, Mr. Holmes, by letter, but no response was received. Alas, the gentry are wont to have their pleasures where they feel obliged. As the Baronet is now lying in state, before his burial, and as it was noted in the press that he died without issue, Mrs. Shields has felt emboldened to embrace her shame and attempt to secure for her son, Geoffrey, that which is surely his inheritance by right."

"And you are assisting her in this?" I enquired.

The Reverend smiled. "I will do what I can, Doctor, yes, for one of my most dear parishioners who has lived a life of hardship and suffering, yet still proven herself to be meek and charitable. I drafted a letter, to accompany the birth certificate, by way of an introduction – or character witness, if you will. Mrs. Shields and I agreed it was best to send these papers on to Mowltenbury Manor, Sir Philip's country seat, in advance, before we attended in person."

"I can see the sense in that," said Holmes, "without anyone of similar social standing to support your claim. It was this, I assume, that the coach driver was couriering when he was attacked on the road."

The Reverend nodded. "Alas, so."

"An obvious first question: Who else knew of this situation?"

"No one, sir."

"Not even Mr. Shields?"

"Dead these past five years, and ignorant of his son's true father to the last."

Holmes lit a pipe and began to pace. I noticed how the carpet was wearing thin along his favoured route.

"Assuming that your account is thorough, Reverend, the only other lead would appear to be the letter Mrs. Shields wrote some years hence. How old is the boy?"

"Two-and-twenty come the spring, sir. It was in late Seventy-Three, when the child was some months old, that the letter was sent. The lady didn't keep a copy for fear of it being discovered by her husband. Mr. Shields was, I regret to advise, a brutal and dishonest man."

A thought occurred to me. "Was it not something of a risk, then, for the lady to have recorded Sir Philip as father on the birth certificate?"

"Indeed, it was, Watson. Indeed, it was!"

The Reverend looked as though he'd been caught out. He took a short shuddering breath and sucked his teeth before speaking again.

"Forgive me, gentlemen, but in that instant, I am guilty of a minor deception, for which I can only pray forgiveness. I have some skill in calligraphy. To avoid unnecessary pain for Mrs. Shields, I fabricated a birth certificate for her son, naming Mr. Shields as the father. It would never pass muster in the real world – nor was it ever designed to. But for the eyes of her husband, it had all the authenticity required." He paused to rub the side of his beak-like nose. "The real document was safely concealed and known only to me, the lady, and eventually her son, when he came of age."

"I assume, Reverend, you wish for our assistance in securing the lad, Geoffrey, his right of succession?"

"Indeed, Mr. Holmes."

"And to establish the murderer of the coach driver."

"That would, no doubt, bring some relief to his widow and young family, of course."

"Do you know who represents the Smith-Mortimer estate?"

"I don't, no." He looked suddenly troubled. "It hadn't occurred to me that Geoffrey might need to apply to the family solicitor, rather than directed to the house itself."

"It will, I'm sure, do no harm to approach both ways, so you may leave that with us. Just to be clear, are we acting on your behalf, or that of Mrs. Shields?"

"She knows of our meeting but is happy to allow me to direct proceedings."

Holmes chewed his bottom lip in momentary thought.

"A problem, Mr. Holmes?"

"Indeed, not," he replied, brightening. "Now, Reverend, do not let us detain you from your parishioners any further. I believe we have enough to be getting on with for the time being, and it is a fair journey back to Kilburn. We shall notify you of our progress in due course."

The Reverend paid his respects and left.

Holmes's eyes glinted once again as he turned to me.

"There is plenty to ponder on with this problem, I perceive," he said, with playful alliteration. "But our first step will be to find that coach, in whatever condition it now remains."

The remains of the coach had been transferred to a compound just north of Hampstead, so we had a lengthy cab ride. Once we'd arrived, the driver was happy to wait, knowing he'd be well rewarded for the return too. Predictably, Holmes whiled away the journey there by quizzing me regarding the Reverend Hume.

"I saw a genuine, caring pastor," I told him. "A man who was going out of his way to assist those he could."

"As did I, Watson, as did I. I also saw the younger son of a middle-class family."

"The cloth is not an irregular calling for an educated younger son, especially if there is no family business for them to move into. No doubt his mention of a skill in calligraphy gave that away."

"That, and his good quality shoes which had been re-soled at least three times, as far as I could count, and the frayed seams of his tailored trousers."

"I noted that his hands had never done an honest day's labour," I added, with a smile.

"What made you, then, of him rubbing his palms before speaking?"

"A habitual nervous gesture," I replied.

Holmes snapped his fingers in my face. "Precisely. A *habitual. Nervous. Gesture.*" He punctuated each word with a wag of his index finger. "I am suspicious of someone who has been a practising parson for upwards of twenty years and still exhibits nervous tendencies when speaking to people."

"We were strangers."

"Did he reveal any other expressions of nervousness?"

I recalled that he stumbled over his words at times. Holmes agreed.

"And again," he continued, "this is someone who should be used to speaking with all manner of persons in his day-to-day life."

"You believe, then, that he was not as he seemed?"

I watched Holmes chewing over his response for a few moments. "Not exactly. More that he was putting on an act. Giving us a performance."

I couldn't help but raise my hands in despair. "If you suspect him of deception, why in Heaven's name are we off on this goose chase?"

My friend gave a sharp bark of a laugh. "You mistake me, Watson. I don't believe the deception was undertaken with malicious intent. I believe that the Reverend chose his method as a way of engendering our sympathy for his undertaking, so that we would be more likely to accept the case."

"So he didn't trust his case to be sufficiently engaging or persuasive."

"Or, perhaps, he lacked faith in his ability to portray the detail without some *dressing.*"

I will admit that this hadn't occurred to me, but once Holmes had pointed it out, it did make a certain amount of sense. It wouldn't be the first time that potential clients have felt the need to dress up their scenario for the great consulting detective, fearing that he wouldn't be interested without some heightened sense of personal suffering or damage.

"We are all flawed, Holmes," I told him. "Even the meekest of us."

Holmes sat in brooding silence the rest of the way.

When we arrived at the compound, the police were about to release the splintered wreck of the coach back to the coach company. After some brief negotiations, and a little bribery, we were permitted a short time to examine the remains. It was surprising to know that the horses had survived without injury, while the coach itself had suffered so much damage, until we were advised by the police that little care was taken in getting the coach to the compound in one piece.

Holmes gave full vent to his frustrations, at which point the duty police officer felt it best to leave us to it. Regardless of the subsequent damage done, Holmes still chose to pore over the wreckage. Eventually, however, the Coach company's breaker ran out of patience and began to remove any fixtures and fittings that the company could use for spares and repairs. The rest would be burned where it lay and Holmes was told, under no uncertain circumstances, that he was welcome to burn with it if he didn't remove himself forthwith.

I noticed a sly grin on my friend's face as the cab driver began the return journey to Baker Street. In response to my raised eyebrows, he produced a strip of paper from his inside jacket pocket.

"You found something?"

"Caught in the springs under the driver's seat."

He passed it to me. Not paper. Velum. The bottom edge was ragged, as if torn. Clearly from an official document, though. The top edges of some of the header lettering were visible. No details were contained, but there was enough to show that it was clearly part of a birth certificate.

When we reached 221b Baker Street, a familiar face awaited us.

"Athelney Jones!" Holmes swept forward and clasped the man's hand, taking him, and me, somewhat by surprise. "We recognised the brown Derby and the muddy boot prints in the hallway, didn't we, Watson?"

"Gentlemen," the Welshman replied, standing and offering his hand to me.

"Can I get you a brandy? Oh!" Holmes pointed to the glass in the inspector's hand and continued. "I see you've already had one."

"Well, yes," the poor man fumbled about. "Wasn't sure how long you were going to be. And it is a bitter day out there."

"Indeed, indeed. So, to what do we owe this pleasure?" Holmes enquired, maintaining his uncharacteristic ebullience.

"I had a call advising that you'd been poking around the broken carriage from the Luton Road."

"Ah, yes. Death by misadventure, I understand from the newspaper report?"

"Indeed. Careless driving, Mr. Holmes. Poor blighter got what he deserved."

"Our client is quite concerned about the whole matter."

"Client?"

"Oh yes." Holmes looked grave. "We have a client. He chartered the coach privately."

"I see. Lose something, did he?"

"Papers, Mr. Jones, that's all. Just papers."

"Pertaining to what, Mr. Holmes?"

453

Holmes looked sharply at the detective. "The Smith-Mortimer succession."

"Crumbs." Jones licked his lips and tugged at his shirt collar. "Well, just so you gentlemen know, we've been over the whole lot with a fine-tooth comb and I'm afraid it couldn't tell us anything."

"I see," said Holmes. "So you deliberately left this scrap of birth certificate behind, did you?" He produced the torn end and Jones shot forward to snatch it.

"No, we didn't, Mr. Holmes. Thank you *most* definitely. I reckon, if we can match this up with the rest of the birth certificate – "

"You'll have your murderer, no doubt," Holmes finished.

The detective looked Holmes square in the face. "To be frank with you, Mr. Holmes, death by misadventure was something of a misnomer. It feels more like murder, to me, but so far I've drawn a blank."

"Mr. Jones, there is hope for you yet!"

"Thank you," he said, accepting the back-handed compliment with a smile. "Where were you thinking of looking next?"

I couldn't suppress my laughter at this and instead had to hide it with a cough. Athelney Jones had never been good at subtly soliciting Holmes's assistance.

"I think a trip to Abbots Langley is in order," Holmes replied. "Let's see what's going on at Mowltenbury Manor, shall we?"

The following morning found Holmes, Jones, and me *en route* to the Hertfordshire village of Abbots Langley, where sat Mowltenbury Manor. Although the railway network covered much of Hertfordshire, many of these smaller villages were still only accessible by the main coach routes out of London. Indeed, the London-to-Luton service made a selling point of this, as reflected by the fact that the coach was almost full for much of the journey. I could only rue the fact that the quality of the roads did not mirror the convenience of the service.

As for Athelney Jones, he never seemed to change. He talked for virtually the entire journey, even when other passengers openly glared at him. Occasionally, Holmes indulged him by quietly and briefly explaining the reasoning behind a few of our old cases. He tried our patience, and yet, despite being a blustering braggart, with little social grace, I couldn't help but feel sorry for the man. Professionally he was clearly out of his depth a lot of the time and achieved results through sheer good fortune, simply arresting everyone until he found who he should be looking for. I considered him quite pathetic in many ways. Holmes's attention was elsewhere for much of the time, except when plucked at by our detective companion. He stared through the window with a frown of concentration etched onto his features, and I knew he'd be mulling over the points of some case or other.

Inspector Jones had sent a wire ahead and had been promised the services of two local constables. Upon our arrival in the village, with no welcoming constables to be found, the detective wandered off in search of the local police station. Holmes held up a cautionary hand to me and angled his beaky features into the air. A beatific smile washed over him.

"You hear that, Watson?"

I listened for a moment. Bird song. "A chaffinch?" I ventured.

"And no trace of Athelney Jones!" He gave me a broad grin and we headed off towards Mowltenbury Manor.

The manor was, I have to say, a rather vulgar-looking mock-Tudor house set in several acres of flat, unappealing land. Part of the estate was farmed (by locals, I was later informed), and the remainder showed signs of having been designed for sport or pleasure at some point in its past. It was clearly left wanting these days, although the overgrowth may have been down to Sir Philip being a naturalist and encouraging habitats for the purpose of study. I was, however, very much aware that my opinions were being coloured by my enjoyment of the coach journey.

The staff were liveried in mourning. I felt very much that we were being assessed on the doorstep by the butler. He was a stern-looking fellow, probably in his late fifties, with an aloof bearing. Like the best of his kind, he gave the impression of being as one with the building in which he served, like a natural defence born of the very fabric of the house. He stood before us and prevented our entering.

We explained that we had travelled from London to pay our respects to Sir Philip, lying in state, and further that we brought some news pertaining to the late Baronet's estate.

"You'll be wanting Sir Roger, I presume?"

"Sir Roger?" I enquired, edging forward.

"Sir Roger Smith-Mortimer," the man replied, his tone laced with scathing judgment. "Sir Philip's industrialist cousin from the north. He arrived yesterday, apparently to take charge of the estate. Even though nothing has been settled yet. We've already been informed we're to be sold off as *investment capital*."

"I say!"

"All very troubling, I'm sure," snapped Holmes, "but for goodness" sake let us enter and get comfortable, man."

The butler finally stood to one side, as if hinged, like a door.

"I am Hammond, sirs. The butler." He took our hats and coats while we set our bags down to one side. Ahead of us lay a grand staircase which led to a mezzanine before bisecting and rising to either side of the first-floor landing. I may not have been that impressed with the exterior, but the interior was very fine in my humble view.

"If you'd care to proceed through to the library, I will inform Sir Roger of your arrival." He indicated where we should go, and then headed away up the stairs.

A middle-aged man was comforting a woman of similar years in the library as we entered. They turned to look in surprise, the woman hastily wiping away the last few tears.

"We're sorry to interrupt," I said. "I am Doctor Watson, and this is Sherlock Holmes. We've just travelled up from London."

The man introduced himself as Wickham, the groundskeeper. I resisted the urge to comment on them. The lady was the housekeeper and his wife. They were clearly in mourning for Sir Philip, although it was Sir Roger that was the cause of the tears.

"Sirs, do forgive me," Mrs. Wickham cried. "But to be turned out of service, at our age, and in such a way – " She couldn't continue and rushed out.

"Trying times, gentlemen," grumbled Mr. Wickham. "I should get back to my duties."

"Aye, so you might," burst a loud, brash, northern accent behind us. "I've never paid for idleness before now and I'm not about to start."

We turned to find Roger Smith-Mortimer – now modelling himself *Sir* Roger Smith-Mortimer, on account of his perceived succession. He was dressed in a loose-fitting mourning suit. I was aware that Wickham had left the room. Sir Roger closed the door behind him and bid us be seated before pouring us each a drink and joining us.

"Your good health, gentlemen," he said, before downing the measure in one gulp.

It was a very fine single malt. For my part, I wished to savour it.

"I'm Roger Smith-Mortimer, or Sir Roger, as I should now remember."

"Sherlock Holmes, Doctor Watson," Holmes introduced us, briefly. "You're an industrialist, I understand?"

"I have several large matchmaking factories up in Leeds, yes."

I reached into my pocket and produced a book of Mortimer's matches with a triumphant grin.

"There we are," said Sir Roger, smiling in return. "A man of discerning taste."

It occurred to me that his northern drawl seemed oddly out of place in a library. I distracted myself by using the matches to light my own cigarette, Holmes's pipe, and Sir Roger's cigar. We sat there, puffing away for a short while, filling the room with a combination of tobacco aromas, before Sir Roger spoke again.

"So, gentlemen, to business. I understand from Hammond that you've travelled here with news pertaining to my deceased cousin's estate?"

"This is true," Holmes said.

"But you're private investigators, aren't you? I am aware that you have some notoriety."

Holmes flicked the edge of his tongue around his lips – a sign that he was unimpressed.

"I'm a consulting detective, Sir Roger. And Doctor Watson, here, is my voice of reason."

"Then I must assume that something is wrong. Otherwise why would you be here?"

"We understand that your cousin left no will."

"That's right. That's why I'm here. Next in line, you see."

"Is the family solicitor currently present? We were led to believe that would be the case," Holmes lied.

"Indeed not, Mr. Holmes. Nathaniel Forbes, of Forbes, Forbes, and Mealing, is due to arrive the day after tomorrow to establish everything in my name."

"I see. Then it is perhaps to their offices in Charing Cross that we need to apply," Holmes said, with some regret. He was playing Sir Roger, and it worked.

"Wait, hang on. If this is something about the succession, then I need to know."

Holmes sucked his teeth thoughtfully before speaking again. "All right, but it must go no further. We've been approached regarding a young gentleman who, it is purported, is the son of Sir Philip from a private tryst with the boy's mother some two-and-twenty years back."

Sir Roger could have reacted to this in several ways, but I admit I did not expect him to burst out laughing as he did.

"Philip? A son? Well, I'll be . . . I didn't think he'd know one end of a woman from t'other."

Holmes ignored the vulgarity. "Be that as it may, Sir Roger, if the claim is sound, he will be the first in line."

Sir Roger's expression grew terse and he stood. "Fine. Produce this bastard offspring then. But until I'm told otherwise, I shall be pressing forward with my plans for this place." He prodded the air with a petulant finger. "I hate all this frippery and indulgence. I'm going to take the money back up to Leeds and Manchester so I can expand my industries. Decadence. Bone-idleness." He almost walked into Hammond as the butler entered. "Get out of my way!" the industrialist barked, swiping a hand in Hammond's direction but clearly not intending to strike him. He stormed past and out of the library.

It was clear from the expression on Hammond's face that he had a deep dislike of Sir Roger. The Wickhams entered also, through the door by which they'd previously left.

"Everything all right, sirs? We heard shouting."

I stood. "Fine, no need to worry. Sir Roger is under some strain following the sudden death of his cousin, that's all."

"We had hoped you'd brought news of another heir – one that might maintain our positions here, truth be told," said the housekeeper.

I was certain that they'd all been listening at their various doors throughout our interview with Sir Roger.

"Was Sir Philip the sort of man who would go to London and have illicit encounters?" I asked.

"Heavens, no, sir. Anyone would tell you," said the groundskeeper. "He was a solitary, God-fearing gentleman. He enjoyed his studies and kept his own company for much of the time. When he travelled to London to speak or present his findings, he always rushed back afterwards and would tell us how much he hated the hustle and bustle of the big city."

"Although," added the housekeeper, butting in, "if he did dabble a bit, years ago, we're very inclined to welcome the poor unfortunate you spoke of – if it keeps us our positions." She nodded her affirmation and looked to the other two for support. Mr. Wickham rolled his eyes and looked to the floor. Hammond pursed his lips and changed the subject.

"Would you care to pay your respects to Sir Philip now, gentlemen?"

The room was lit by a few solemn candles. The open coffin lay on a trestle in the centre of the room. Sir Philip's corpse had been laid over with a shroud, embroidered with the Smith-Mortimer coat of arms.

"You will understand the reason for the shroud, sirs, I'm sure, sirs," said Hammond.

I advised him that we didn't know anything regarding the Baronet's death, beyond the little that was mentioned in the press.

"I assume, then, that Sir Philip doesn't look as . . . noble as he might, in death?" said Holmes. "Hence the need for a shroud."

Hammond nodded.

"Is there anyone in the household who can tell us about the accident in any detail?" I asked.

"That would be me," said Hammond. "Sir Philip was out grousing. One of his few active pursuits these days."

The butler paused, affected by the memory, and uttered an apology. We bid him take his time and continue.

"Sir Philip had become a little clumsy with his hands – due, no doubt, to his years of close, dextrous study of nature. He was wont to drop his gun, for example, while reloading. Particularly if on the move. That day, he was out, alone, with his fowling piece. I can only assume that he must have fumbled it somehow. From the manner of his death, and the position when I discovered him, it looked like the gun had landed between his feet, square on the end of the hilt, and fired. Perhaps it was faulty or needed cleaning. Either way, it had shot the Baronet up through his own chin and very nearly blown his whole head off."

"Tragic," I muttered.

"Extraordinary," Holmes exclaimed.

The butler nodded. "Indeed, sirs. The local police and coroner thought the same. But I could only say what I found."

"There were no witnesses?"

"He would often go out alone. He'd purport to be grousing, but he'd also be studying and observing at the same time. He was disinclined to company as it made him feel obliged, he said, to perform either one or the other, and not both simultaneously, as he preferred to do. I noticed that he hadn't returned for lunch. When he didn't appear for dinner, either, Wickham and I went searching for him in the dark. I had the misfortune, as you might say, of finding him."

"I can understand the need for the shroud," I said.

Holmes nodded his agreement and turned to Hammond. "Perhaps we may be permitted a few minutes alone, to pay our respects?"

The butler inclined his head and silently left us.

Holmes glanced at me. "I'm intrigued, Watson," he said, very quietly. We were both aware that Hammond, or another of the household, would probably be listening at the door to monitor us.

I nodded. "The manner of death. I can't imagine how improbable it would be for someone to shoot themselves like that."

Holmes bent over, looking at his own feet. With his hand he drew a rough line upwards from where a dropped gun might supposedly land. It seemed almost impossible to hit his own chin unless he was looking straight ahead.

He tutted. "We'd better examine the evidence – if they've left us much to see, after cleaning him up."

"Do you mean – "

"Why not? You're a doctor, after all. Professional curiosity, second opinion – call it what you will."

Checking that we remained unobserved, I pulled back the shroud to reveal the head and torso. Some cleaning and tidying of the corpse had obviously been undertaken, but what was clear to us both immediately was that the greater damage was to the chin and lower jaw – or would have been, if there'd been anything more than ragged remains left. The wound to the top of the head was mild by comparison. I quickly replaced the shroud and breathed out very slowly.

Holmes looked at me darkly. "Some great wickedness is afoot in all of this."

We were prevented from further discussion by the arrival of Inspector Jones.

"Ah, the butler said you'd be in here. This has already been an effort and no mistake," the inspector announced, brashly, as he joined us. "I eventually located my two constables in the public house. Somewhat the worst for wear, to boot."

"I suspect the local coroner was there as well," I quipped, without humour. "He'd need to have been drunk to have claimed this as accidental."

"Another murder?" Jones's eyes lit up with unhealthy zest.

Without forewarning, I showed him Sir Philip's head under the shroud. The poor man had to turn away quickly.

Holmes grinned, cruelly. "Still squeamish, Inspector, even after all these years?"

Jones took a few moments to compose himself, patting his ample stomach, puffing out his cheeks, and rubbing his face with his pudgy hands.

"Do you agree?" Holmes continued. "Entry wound clearly in the top of the skull, exiting through the lower jaw?"

"I don't think anything could be plainer, Mr. Holmes," the inspector agreed. "Leave this to me, gentlemen. Murder is my speciality. I'll start by rounding everyone up." And with that, he rushed off.

It was habitual for us, by now, to pause a few moments after Athelney Jones had left a room. He seemed to leave something of a vacuum in his flustered wake, and one had to wait for the atmosphere to normalize, or risk being drawn out after him.

"Have we just blown everything wide open?" I asked, tentatively.

Holmes looked pensive. "I think, on this occasion, our colleague's blunderbuss methods may help to light a few paths. And while he's putting the cat among the pigeons with the household, I'd like to cast my eye over the murder site."

Hammond was nowhere to be found, but we encountered Mr. Wickham ushering some of the staff to the drawing room, where Jones awaited them all. We could hear the inspector arguing with Mrs.

Wickham, who was protesting at his abrupt *London* manner in a house of mourning.

Mr. Wickham rolled his eyes at us. "Trouble is, she's as stubborn as any inspector."

Holmes asked him to direct us to where Hammond had found Sir Philip. He looked at us archly.

"Why'd you want to go looking around there? Police have been all over it already."

"I daresay," replied Holmes. "But I prefer to trust to my own methods."

"Not much light left in the day."

"Which is why we want to get there with all haste, Mr. Wickham. So, the directions, if you please?"

"All right, I was only saying, that's all." He then described to us the area, at the front of the house and across to the left, partly concealed behind some fruit bushes he'd been cultivating over the past few years. We thanked him and took our leave as he found himself obliged to join the rest of the household.

As we left by the front door, the two local constables were escorting Sir Roger down the stairs, his northern bluster in full flow. No doubt he and Athelney Jones would get on like chalk and cheese.

It was only a matter of a few minutes" walk before we reached the murder site. It was obscured from the manor house by a row of dense yew trees which lined the gravel forecourt. Wickham's fruit bushes partially obstructed the view of the driveway.

"All in all, a well-concealed spot. Ripe for a good murder," Holmes said, with sepulchral wit.

As Wickham had hinted, the afternoon was pressing on, but the light was still plenty good enough for us to find tell-tale blood spatters on the long grass. Thankfully, these had lingered despite the light rain which had fallen since Sir Philip's death. Much of the unkempt grass had been trampled when the body was collected and the area cleared. Despite this, Holmes pored over the ground, immediately around the greatest concentration of blood spatters, confident that this was most likely the murder spot.

"I hope you're not looking for the poor man's teeth," I grumbled, putting on my gloves against the chill.

Holmes responded indistinctly, stepping forward in a crouched posture and parting the grasses like a myopic naturalist seeking a slow worm. He carried on in this vein for some time before uttering a triumphant "A-ha!" and holding something aloft which glinted in the now failing daylight.

461

I peered at it in his gloved palm. A tie clip.

Holmes ran a finger along the face. "Inscribed *Smith-Mortimer*."

"The Baronet's?"

He shook his head. "I would expect it to be caked in gore if it was. This is clean. Besides, his corpse is wearing one. I noticed it earlier."

"The murderer's, then?"

"I think it more likely, although again we must be cautious. It may have fallen from one of the staff when they collected his body. I assume you noticed that Hammond wore one of these?"

I hadn't, and Holmes knew I hadn't. I gave him a look that told him just that.

"But not Mr. Wickham," he continued. "As groundsman, he'd spend most of his time in workman's clothes anyway."

"Is there a manufacturer's mark?" I asked.

He turned the clip over. There was a small engraving. He produced a magnifying glass from somewhere within his ulster.

"Made in Sheffield. No mark. Evidently polished steel."

"Sheffield isn't far from Leeds," I pointed out.

"It's also the centre of the British steel industry. If the Baronet was going to provide them as part of his livery, they would certainly come marked thus."

"So, where do we go next?"

Holmes paused and held out a hand, gesturing behind me, past the fruit bushes, towards the far end of the driveway. A figure, distant and indistinct in the falling dusk, was walking away from the house, at pace, towards the gated main entrance by which we had entered some hours before.

"We go after that person there," Holmes confirmed. "But stealthily. He mustn't know we're trailing him. What an intriguing time for anyone to be leaving the house."

We closed in on the figure from our perpendicular approach. We were aiming for the perimeter stone wall, which would provide cover the closer we got. A few times we found ourselves hunkering down in the overgrown grass, lest we stepped into the man's peripheral vision, although there was no indication that he felt he might be overlooked. The figure was clearly a man. As we reached the safety of the shadow of the wall, another figure stepped into view from behind our nearside gatepost, with his back to us, much to our good fortune.

We paused, cautious of approaching too near and risking drawing attention to ourselves. Our footsteps through the long grass were not as stealthy as we wished them to be. The two shadowy figures greeted each other familiarly with a firm hand clasp. They spoke quickly and quietly and, although we could hear their hushed tones, we couldn't discern any of the words. Their tryst complete, the figures nodded to each other, turned about, and parted.

"They've turned the other way," grumbled Holmes into my ear. "Damn! I wanted to get a good look at both of them."

I glanced at Holmes, and he indicated that I should trail the figure back to the manor house. He would follow the other out beyond the gate. With a nod of affirmation, we parted.

I allowed the unknown figure a good thirty yards lead or more before I set off in pursuit. I walked casually, not to say brazenly, so as not to appear suspicious should the figure turn around. But he was either confident of his solitude or as equally set as I upon brazening it out. As he passed the tree line, I lost sight of him in the dark and I realised I'd made an error of judgment. I hastened forward but alas, by the time I breached the tree line myself and entered the forecourt, my quarry was nowhere to be seen. I had no idea whether he'd walked in through the front door or crept away around either side of the house.

I cursed my carelessness and saw little option for myself other than entering via the front door. I hoped Holmes was having better fortune with his hunt. On the steps outside the front door I found the two local constables, wrapped in their greatcoats, dozing. I coughed loudly as I mounted and they jumped to attention. I knew there was no point in asking them about the figure who'd entered the forecourt before me.

The door was opened, with an apology, by Mrs. Wickham, the housekeeper. It was immediately obvious why she had taken on such duties. A furious row was underway between Sir Roger Smith-Mortimer, Hammond the butler, and Inspector Jones. Sir Roger was wearing his coat and boots – which caught my attention straight away. They paused momentarily, with a glance in my direction, as I entered and removed my hat, coat, and gloves. Then they were back at it. Sir Roger waved an arm, gesturing at everybody.

"You lot, you'll get what you deserve and no mistake. There's not one amongst this house I'd give a job to in one of my factories – servants and policemen alike. Work-shy, opinionated layabouts!" He turned an accusing finger at Hammond. "And you? You've only been here two years – you've no history here at all. The old man must have been going soft in the head to make an ex-postmaster a butler."

"Oh, sir!" protested the Wickhams, in simultaneous shock.

"Hear that? Quick enough to defend him and happy enough normally to complain about his morose attitude."

463

"Sir Roger," said Jones, puffing himself up. "I hardly think offending the household is going to help anyone right now. Particularly when you're *all* under suspicion of possible double-murder."

"Balderdash, sir! *Balderdash!*" he yelled into the inspector's ruddy face. "I've had enough of servants who think they are above themselves." He gestured at Hammond. "Welsh idiots with madcap ideas about my poor cousin's death and – " Looking at me. " – busybodies trying to claim my rightful inheritance for some jumped-up bastard from the gutters of London. I am leaving this house, now. You shall hear from me again only through my solicitor."

Jones moved to stand squarely in his way.

Sir Roger could barely contain his rage. "You will step aside, sir."

"I don't know what type of police officer you're used to dealing with, Sir Roger, but you don't get past Athelney Jones that easily when there's a murder under investigation – "

"I've already told you what I think of – "

"*Either* of the murders." Jones stressed, his face set. "Sir."

"Oh yes, the poor coachman?" Sir Roger rolled his eyes sarcastically. "Why in the Lord's name would I want to do away with a coachman, I ask you?"

"Because of what he carried."

Sir Roger bared his teeth. "Get out of my way, you jumped-up nobody!"

"Sir Roger, if you leave this house, I have two constables waiting, poised to arrest anybody who sets foot outside."

I couldn't resist a wry smile at this.

"You are more than welcome to spend the night in a police cell rather than here in the comfort of the manor house, should that be your desire, but those are your options." It was now his turn to take in the whole assembled household in the hallway. "The same applies to all of you. Understand?"

There was a moment of silence, broken by a disgruntled "Hmph" from Sir Roger.

"I don't approve of your tone, Inspector, but have it your way. I shall remain in my quarters until you have relinquished this ridiculous quest and left us all in peace. Hammond, serve me all my meals and refreshments upstairs from now on." He glared at the butler. "And in silence. I have less desire to hear more of your bleating moans than I do of this Welsh – " Whatever epithet he planned to use died on Sir Roger's lips, which was probably all the better for him. He stormed away up the stairs instead.

Sir Roger left rather a lull in his wake. Mr. Wickham held his wife in comfort and Hammond, somewhat red in the cheeks, remained stock-still except for his eyes, which had followed the industrialist's retreat. His mouth was firmly set in disapproval, but I must say, this appeared to be the norm for him (and many other butlers I've encountered over the years!)

Jones was the first to swing back into action. One of his strengths was his stubbornness, and although this was often a cause for much frustration on the part of Sherlock Holmes, today it stood the inspector in good stead. The haranguing he received from Sir Roger was as much water off the back of a duck.

"Mrs. Wickham," he said, rubbing his pudgy palms down his waistcoat. "I'll see your kitchen staff now, if you please. One by one. In the drawing room, since Sir Roger has retired. And a bit of that cold meat pie I saw in the kitchen, if it's not too much trouble."

He walked away, leaving the housekeeper to compose herself and hurriedly follow. Taking this as a cue, the remaining staff quickly returned to their business, also.

Hammond looked at me, as if taking me in properly for the first time.

"It is unfortunate, Doctor Watson, that you and Mr. Holmes, and the inspector, have to witness the tantrums and behaviours of our new master." As he said this he looked around. "Where is Mr. Holmes?"

"He's taken a constitutional," I replied. "It helps him think."

"I see. Would you care to take some afternoon refreshment in the library?"

As we hadn't had lunch, I gladly accepted the offer.

I was casually flicking through a rather splendid copy of Henry Walter Bates' *The Naturalist on the River Amazons* when Hammond returned with some items of late afternoon tea. I could tell immediately that this was all a pretence for a private conversation, and I indicated that he should speak freely.

"I've no wish to burden you with our troubles, Doctor Watson, but you seem a learned and reasonable man, and these qualities have been somewhat lacking in this house of late."

"I can see that all is not as it should be here, indeed."

"Sir Roger is totally set upon his intent. I know I am speaking out of turn, but it is grossly unfair that generations of loyal local service will be cast aside for nought if Sir Roger is allowed to sell the estate to finance his failing industries."

My surprise must have been evident on my face.

"You were not aware of this, Doctor?"

"Indeed, I wasn't," I confirmed. "I know nothing of Sir Roger beyond what has been reported in the press. I might ask how you became aware of this, though? Sir Roger told us he simply wished to reinvest the capital to expand his empire, not bail himself out. That paints a very different picture."

"I have overheard Sir Roger on the telephone in the hallway from time to time. He is usually very discreet in his conversations, but there are times, as I'm sure you can appreciate, where his temper gets the better of him – particularly when discussing money. But also, Sir Philip confided in me last year, when the press reported some troubles with his cousin's factories. His cousin had written to him, requesting that the Baronet invest in the family business up there, since the troubles had near enough broken Roger. Sir Philip declined. He was not fond of industry, being a naturalist and a Romantic at heart. I believe he made his feelings clear in the reply. I cannot but think this was a sour point which has now set Sir Roger upon a course of revenge."

"Thank you," I replied, my mind spinning around various possibilities. I hoped I could retain the salient points to pass onto Holmes upon his return. He'd been gone a goodly while now, and I had a momentary distraction wondering if he was all right. Hammond's tie clip glinted against the electric light above, and it seemed to me that now was as good an opportunity as any to enquire as to their origin.

"They were a gift to Sir Philip from his cousin, sir. He sent them with the letter pleading for financial assistance last year. Sir Philip took a shine to them and insisted that he and I wear one each. Wickham has one too, for his formal livery. Although, now I think of it, I haven't noticed him wearing it. Perhaps he forgot?"

"Perhaps he did," I replied. "He's had a lot on his mind, after all."

"Sir Roger," said Hammond, returning to his original point, "is not interested in living here and maintaining the estate. He told us as much, almost as soon as he arrived. He wants to do what he knows best. Industry. That's the future, as far as he's concerned."

As Hammond was being so candid, I felt it only right to try to press him on other matters if I could.

"And why are you here, Hammond? As Sir Roger rather publicly informed us earlier, you were a postmaster. Why are you now a butler?"

"I was indeed a postmaster, sir. At Leavesden, one of the nearby villages."

I recalled that Leavesden was the coach stop prior to Abbots Langley.

"I come from a line of shopkeepers. I had a wife and family. My brother felt the Lord's call and became the local parish minister, All Saints and St. Hilda. Then there was an accident. Don't ask me to repeat the

466

details. They were all taken from me. The community lost a devoted minister, and I lost everything. I found I couldn't go on. I was trapped in a life that had revolved around my family, and without them there it brought me nothing but pain."

My heart filled for a moment as I thought upon Mary, and my own happiness, taken from me so tragically.

Hammond continued. "I had to walk away, try to find a new calling, build a new life. When the position came up here, it seemed a good opportunity to start over."

"And now you find yourself faced with the prospect of having to go through it all again."

"That's right, Doctor Watson. Is it any wonder we're all so against Sir Roger's plans? Take the Wickhams: They grew up here, fell in love, and married here. This estate has been their lives. All our lives."

Hammond moved out from behind the chair opposite me. My eyes drifted to the floor, moved, as I was, by his plea. I couldn't help noticing a smear of mud along the sides of his otherwise immaculate shoes, which distracted me.

When I didn't reply, the butler muttered an apology.

"I'm sorry," I said, shaking off the distraction. "Thank you for being so open with me. Alas, we came here upon a different potential injustice. We will have to see if resolving one can resolve both."

"Indeed, sir." He checked his fob watch. "I should be about my duties. Please, Doctor Watson, feel free to remain here and peruse the books. I will call you when dinner is served."

I glanced down at the table where I'd left Henry Walter Bates and heard the door close as Hammond left the room. I pushed the book away. Beyond a casual interest, I had no particular care for Bates or any of the hundreds of other collections, almanacs, and gazetteers lining the shelves all around me. What I really needed was for Holmes to return so I could report my findings. I tutted and stood impatiently.

"Oh, Holmes, where are you?"

"Right here, my good fellow."

"Holmes?"

A pair of floor-length curtains parted, and a familiar head poked through.

"What the devil – ?" I beamed at him and he at me.

"French windows, Watson. Unlocked. I entered via them, just before Hammond showed you in. I was going to make my presence known immediately, but then you appeared to be doing such a fine job on your own. And the butler was being incredibly candid, so I opted to remain where I was, in silence, and listen in. I was able to observe, unseen, at times, when the curve of the curtain allowed. Did you notice the muddy smears along the sides of his patent leather shoes?"

"I did, as a matter of fact."

"He's clearly been outside."

"When I got back, though, Sir Roger was wearing his hat and coat."

"Was he your man, then?"

I looked a little sheepish. "I miscalculated the distance at the tree line and lost him before I could see him properly."

Holmes drew his lips back over his teeth.

"Did you fair better?"

"Possibly. It was a young man – I was able to tell that much. But I couldn't get enough of a view to be sure to recognise him again. I trailed him some little way out of the village to where he'd left a pony and trap. As with you and the masking tree line, the lad had mounted and moved off before I could get close enough to speak with him. I tried calling, but he didn't look back. I was going to feign being lost, but I have a suspicion that he may have realised by then that he was being followed."

Somewhat grateful that I hadn't solely let the side down, we then chewed over what we'd both learned from Hammond, plus what I'd witnessed from Sir Roger in the hallway earlier.

"Of course, as far as I can tell, none of this helps us with the murder of the coachman at all," I said, by way of a frustrated conclusion.

Holmes tapped his fingertips against his pursed lips thoughtfully. Before he could speak, Hammond returned. After first expressing some surprise at the presence of Holmes, he asked if we required rooms for the night. We confirmed that we would appreciate that very much. Holmes excused his presence, advising that he'd entered via the unlocked French windows, and that he'd subsequently bolted them shut. Hammond expressed his thanks and advised us that dinner was served, if we wished to eat. We did, and so we followed him out.

Inspector Jones was waiting expectantly in the dining room. Sir Roger, we were advised, would not be joining us – to no one's surprise. As we were each seated, I observed Holmes subtly indicate to Hammond the mud on his shoes.

"I can only apologise, sir," he said. "That will be from earlier, when I had to show the inspector, here, around the outside of the house."

"Most useful it was, too," confirmed Jones.

"I was immediately summoned by Sir Roger upon my return, and it subsequently slipped my mind."

Holmes brushed the matter aside. Hammond acknowledged the gesture before turning to the inspector.

"Mr. Jones, on Sir Roger's instruction, we have offered rooms for the night to Doctor Watson and Mr. Holmes, here."

"Oh, thank you," Jones replied, in the manner of one who assumes the same courtesy was intended for him, too. He was mistaken.

"Unfortunately, those were our only two available rooms."

The inspector gave an experienced chuckle. "I don't mind not having a room to myself. I'll sleep anywhere."

Hammond clearly attempted to belie his discomfort with a nod and a half-hearted smile.

"Hopefully there will be somewhere in the village that you can stay." He swiftly turned and left.

Athelney Jones sat there, gaping like a fish for a minute or so until the starter was served. I couldn't help but feel sorry for the disillusioned fellow. One glance at Holmes, though, and I knew I shouldn't offer to share my room. Perhaps he had a use for the inspector whilst he wasn't under this roof.

"You'll be all right, I'm sure," I said, as encouragingly as I could.

He gave me a resilient nod. "One of the constables will put me up."

A pause. The aroma of the soup was exquisite, and I was desperate to tuck in, but the inspector showed no such interest.

"Shall we?" I asked, indicating the soup, not wanting to appear ill-mannered.

"Indeed," agreed Holmes, clearly also unwilling to wait any longer. The soup was an excellent mutton-and-winter vegetable, seasoned to perfection. The inspector, though, remained lost in his own thoughts.

"That butler." Jones shook his head. "No wonder Sir Roger gets annoyed with him. His attitude. It's all wrong."

"I hardly think Hammond will have taken the decision on whether or not to offer us accommodation, Inspector. That will have come from Sir Roger, I'm sure."

"It's not just that, Doctor Watson. I can see the contempt in his eyes when he addresses me."

Holmes indicated with his spoon. "Whatever you do, Inspector, don't let the soup go to waste."

He grabbed a spoon with his pudgy fingers (the wrong one, I noted) and gave his starter a slow stir, but he remained distracted.

"Only been here two years at most, according to the Wickhams. Yet he treats the place like his own. Did before the old man died, so they said. Even more so, now. And he still has a family over at Leavesden. As far as they know, anyway. Don't think he sees them, though."

I shook my head. "Hammond spoke with me very candidly, earlier, Inspector. I fear he's been mis-represented. He told me his family died in an accident some years back."

Jones pursed his lips and gave a disapproving tut. "Countryside. Always full of gossip."

I thought that seemed pretty rich, considering he'd brought it up in the first place. But it was sufficient to break his ponderous spell, and the inspector finally committed to a spoonful of soup. His eyes lit up immediately.

"Oh, my, Mr. Holmes! You were right, it is good, isn't it?"

He proceeded to consume the starter like a man possessed. That was one thing that could be said about Athelney Jones: He did everything wholeheartedly. Shortly after, the main course was served – an equally delightful breast of fowl in a rich wine sauce. This time the inspector didn't hold back, but opted, instead, to chatter throughout.

"Of course, you know why Sir Roger isn't eating with us, I'm sure."

"Yes," I replied. "He dislikes us all, and the staff. He publicly said as much earlier."

Jones shook his head determinedly. His jowls wobbled against his clenched jaws.

"He did it, that's why. He must have. It's the obvious answer. Killed his cousin and arranged for the coach accident to make sure the young pretender from London lost his claim."

"But my dear Inspector," countered Holmes. "Sir Roger was still up in Leeds when all this happened."

"*Says* he was, Mr. Holmes. *Says* he was. Come on, I'm sure you've said to me often enough that it's insufficient to merely trust the word of anyone in an investigation."

I saw the edges of Holmes mouth curl into a smile to have such a thing thrown at him like that, and by Athelney Jones of all people. The inspector continued.

"And even if he was, he could have an agent, either in Abbot's Langley or here in the household. Someone who could have actioned his plans. Almost certainly the person we'd least expect, too."

I cast my mind momentarily to the tie clip and Mr. Wickham. I wondered just how near to the truth Jones may have stumbled.

"As it seems, I'll be there already. I plan to extend my investigations into the village tomorrow. Ruffle a few feathers, see if anything gets uncovered. What do you think, Mr. Holmes?"

"I think that's a capital plan," Holmes confirmed.

Jones almost glowed at this. Experience may not have tempered the inspector's unsubtle methods, but it had, at least, developed a level of respect for Sherlock Holmes. This tended to express itself unwittingly from time to time when Holmes granted Jones his approval in some way.

After the main course, the inspector grabbed his bag and left, conscious that he still needed to arrange accommodation with his two constables, wherever they'd got to.

Holmes and I were about to head to the drawing room for a smoke and a brandy when the dining room door burst open and Sir Roger appeared. He stopped short at the sight of us.

"I was under the impression that all of today's unwelcome visitors had now left."

"I take it, then, Sir Roger, that it was not at your request that Doctor Watson and I be given rooms here for the night?"

"Hammond." The industrialist uttered the name as if it were a curse word. "Not that imbecile of a police inspector, as well, I hope?"

"He is making his own arrangements." Holmes responded with a level tone, showing that (on this occasion, at least) he was not prepared to countenance such a disrespectful attitude.

As if on cue, Athelney Jones's voice could then be heard outside in the grounds. He was complaining about the cold and arguing with the local constables as to which of them should put him up. Neither were apparently keen.

Sir Roger looked at us again. "At least you two are gentlemen, as far as I'm aware."

"Indeed," Holmes responded, brightly. "And we have just enjoyed a simply wonderful dinner, for which your staff must be truly praised. Watson and I were just about to head to the drawing room for a pipe and a brandy."

"Oh, were you now? Making yourselves at home and no mistake."

Holmes ignored the jibe. "Perhaps you'd care to join us, Sir Roger?"

Seemingly, Sir Roger's planned retort died on his lips and his brow relaxed

"Why not," he said, with something like resignation.

We sat in the comfort of the drawing room, the three of us, each warming a brandy glass. A log fire roared nearby. Sir Roger smoked another of his cigars, Holmes his pipe, and I, as usual, favoured my cigarettes from Bradley's.

"We are thankful for your hospitality, Sir Roger," I said, "A warm fire and an exceptional cognac. Who could wish for anything else on such a chilly evening?"

"Aye, there is that," he replied. "You'll be returning to London tomorrow, no doubt?"

471

I hid my smile at his lack of subtlety behind my glass.

"Tell me," began Holmes, ignoring the question. "If the succession remains with you, why won't you just move in and take over the estate?"

Sir Roger gestured around the finely furnished room, with its portraits and classical ornaments.

"All this fancy frippery – it's not for me. I can't abide indolence. I'm a practical man, Mr. Holmes. I'm a doer, not a studier or a society man. What do I want with books and art and *specimens*?"

"Such things won't satisfy your creditors?"

Sir Roger sucked his teeth and looked long and hard at Holmes, clearly measuring up his response. Holmes was being deliberately provocative, of that much I was sure. When Sir Roger eventually spoke, I was surprised that he kept his tone, and his temper, in check.

"I had no idea my financial standing was common knowledge."

"It isn't, Sir Roger, I can assure you. I am simply more thorough in my methods than most."

The industrialist peered into his glass. "It's true, circumstances last year have left me in some difficulties. Thankfully, a few well-placed payments have meant the press haven't delved too deeply with their reporting." He raised a finger. "But, Mr. Holmes, *I'm* a self-made man, despite the fancy surname. None of this family money – " He gestured at the room around him. " – ever came our way, up north, until now. That's why it's only Mortimer on the matches." He drained the last of his cognac.

Holmes asked, "Do you have one of the family name tie clips that you sent Sir Philip last year?"

"Yes, I do, as a matter of fact. I don't have it with me, though. They're something of a whimsical affectation, really. I didn't realise Sir Philip had issued them to the staff until I got here."

"He wore one himself, too. Still does, in fact – we saw it when we paid our respects."

"Is that so? It must have been added since, then. When I arrived and looked him over there was nothing."

Holmes looked at me. "That may, then, account for the one we found at the murder scene."

"You found a tie clip in the long grass?"

"Yes," replied Holmes. "So, we're checking on everyone who ought to have one, in case that helps identify the murderer. But you left yours in Leeds, you say."

Sir Roger scowled. "I did. I thought the inspector was investigating the so-called murder?"

Holmes savoured a long sip of his cognac. He sat and looked directly at Sir Roger, who met his gaze firmly. If Holmes was going to reply, he missed his chance.

"Think what you might," said Sir Roger, standing. "But I didn't do over my cousin for the inheritance. If what you report is true, and there's a child with a prior claim, and that means I'm bankrupted. Well, you just wait and see if I don't bounce back through my own hard effort. But you'd better be sure about that boy you represent, gentlemen, because if there's one thing they say about Roger Smith-Mortimer it's that I'm tenacious. I'll fight this succession all the way if I have to. Goodnight, gentlemen."

And with that, he stubbed out his cigar and left.

"That could have gone better," I said, after a moment's pause.

"It could have gone a lot worse," Holmes replied. "I was being deliberately provocative, after all. People tend to say careless things when they're worked up."

"Indeed, but that was the calmest I've seen Sir Roger since we first arrived here."

Holmes poured us both another cognac. It was indeed very fine.

"What are your thoughts on all this, then?" I asked as he seated himself again.

Holmes sniffed, then batted the question back to me. I pondered on it for a few moments before responding.

"On the one hand, Sir Roger has to be a suspect, since he stands to gain so much – although he clearly has no fondness for the estate and his only interest is financial. But there's no indication he knew anything about Geoffrey Shields before we arrived, so he wouldn't have known about the coach. Unless Athelney Jones is correct and he has a local accomplice – and we saw a figure, possibly Sir Roger, speaking with a lad at the gates of the grounds."

"Agreed."

"On the other hand," I continued, "there's the Wickhams, Hammond, and the other household staff, who all seem to have adored the old Baronet. And one of them could possibly have known of young Geoffrey. But why would any of them want to kill Sir Philip and then scupper the coach bringing Geoffrey's proof of birth? It makes no sense to me – they'd stand to lose everything and gain nothing."

"Fine logic, my friend." Holmes puffed on his pipe and stared past the end of his nose. "It's clear that the motive rests most strongly with Sir Roger at present. However, I'm starting to wonder if we're approaching this in the wrong way. There have been two murders. We've immediately fallen into the assumption that they're linked and were therefore perpetrated by the same person. But we could be looking at two *murderers*, as well. The only thing of which we can be sure is that there is still too much that we don't yet know."

There was a knock at the door and Hammond entered.

"Sorry to disturb you, gentlemen, but Sir Roger has returned to his room, and we are, habitually, a house that retires early in order to rise early."

"No apology necessary, Hammond," burst Holmes. "That is a fine code of conduct you adhere to. Watson and I are done. We've had a very long and active day, after all."

The butler inclined his head. "Then I will show you to your rooms."

"One quick question before we retire, if I may?"

"Certainly, Mr. Holmes."

"Can you find out for me, please, when the first London train leaves Watford tomorrow morning?"

"Train, sir?" Hammond gave a frown. "I thought you came up by the coach?"

"We did, but it played havoc with Doctor Watson's war wound, so I'd like to try a cab to Watford and a train from there."

I patted my leg for emphasis, although I was unaware what Holmes was up to.

"Indeed, sir," the butler replied. "The trains are very regular, but it will take some time to travel from here to Watford. If you wanted to be in London early tomorrow, it would have been best to travel to Watford this evening and take lodgings there overnight."

"I see. Never mind. There are no stables here at the manor, I perceive?"

"No, sir. The Baronet rarely travelled while I was in his service. I believe prior to Sir Philip there was always a coach and four in residence here."

If that was the case, I asked how Sir Philip was provided with for travel.

"There are a few people with horses and carts in the village, Doctor Watson. One or other were always happy to give of their time when the Baronet was required to travel."

"Splendid," said Holmes. "Have one of them ready to pick us up at nine o'clock tomorrow, bound for Watford."

"Thank you, sir."

"Oh, and Hammond?"

"Sir?"

"Is there a Post Office in Abbots Langley?"

"There is, sir, yes."

"Excellent. I need to send a telegram to Mrs. Shields, in London, to let her know that Watson and I will be calling on her at her convenience after our return. I appreciate the hour, but have you a lad who can run that to the village for me this evening?"

"No, sir, but I shall see to it myself, personally."

Holmes thanked him for the courtesy, and we retired to our rooms where, no doubt, Holmes furnished Hammond with the telegram and, I suspect, something for his service.

I spent a pleasant night in a modest room, and I was grateful for the solitude. Until I was shown the room, I hadn't realised quite how exhausted the day had left me. Hammond nudged a little heat from the remaining embers in the fireplace, but the room was already plenty warm enough and I quickly surrendered myself to the lure of the pillows and blankets.

The household was indeed up and about early the following day. I awoke, refreshed, to a pleasantly chilly morning. Hammond passed me on the landing and advised that Sir Roger wouldn't be joining Holmes and me for breakfast or seeing us again before we left. The butler had been instructed to use that very wording. Holmes, on the other hand, had been up since dawn and was awaiting me in the dining room, after having spent the morning, thus far, conversing familiarly with most of the household staff.

I had no doubt that this was a further instance of Holmes gathering information and seeking the links that drew events together. As I entered the dining room I was met with a blast of chilly air. Holmes looked my way with an acknowledgement before returning to speak to Mr. Wickham, through the side window. He'd raised the sash fully open for the purpose.

"And you say you've mislaid your tie clip?"

"Indeed, sir. Searched high and low for it, I have. Mrs. Wickham, too. I can't think where it's gone. Worst thing is, I should have been wearing it all this time in memory of Sir Philip. He used to chuckle when he saw Hammond and me wearing ours, and then he'd hold up his and tell us we was all brothers."

"Do you have any idea when you last saw it, or wore it?"

"That I do, Mr. Holmes. Day before Sir Philip had his accident."

"Could you have lost it around the grounds, somewhere?"

"It's possible, I suppose. To be honest, if Sir Roger gets his way, I can't see me ever needing – or wanting – to wear it again, anyway. Perhaps it's best that it remains lost."

"Very likely. Thank you for your time, Mr. Wickham. Now, I fear Doctor Watson may be frosting over before he's had his kippers, so I shall leave you to your duties and return to the breakfast table."

"Good day to you, sirs," Wickham saluted, and Holmes lowered the sash.

He turned to me with a grin. "A most profitable overnight stay, Watson. We have definitely stumbled upon a tangled web of intrigue here. But never mind that now. Do have a kipper, and I recommend the kedgeree also."

I took his recommendation and was grateful for it.

"Hammond informed me that you've been interrogating the staff," I said, as I wiped the corners of my mouth.

"That's true – although they wouldn't have known it from my *modus operandi*, and I doubt Hammond did, either, unless I've underestimated his perspicacity somewhat."

I smiled broadly. "Indeed, the phrase he used was *conversing familiarly*. From that, I knew what you were really up to. Anything to share?"

"Only that I obtained the recipe for the mutton-and-vegetable soup, to pass on to Mrs. Hudson."

I laughed and asked him if there was anything pertaining to the murders to share. "Or is it all caught up with this *tangled web* you mentioned?"

He looked at me apologetically. "There is much for me to ponder on, and one or two plans to set in motion. I can't risk revealing any more at present."

A horse and cart appeared for us at nine o'clock, as Holmes had requested. It bore Inspector Jones and his two constables, who claimed the walk from the village was not their preferred way to start the day. As I loaded our bags onto the cart, I saw Holmes take Jones to one side and speak with him in private for a few minutes. *More laying of plans*, I thought, unless the inspector had some information from the village for him.

Had it been the summer, a long trip to Watford on an open cart like this would have been a fine way to spend a morning. As it was, Holmes and I were both wrapped up as if about to embark on an Arctic voyage. Hammond was nowhere to be seen as we mounted and left. The Wickhams were there to wave us off and wish us a safe journey. I saw Sir Roger watching us from an upstairs window. I wondered how soon we would see him again, and in what fashion.

As we left the grounds, Holmes called on the driver to first take us to the local Post Office.

"I thought Hammond had taken care of your telegram?" I asked.

"I want to get confirmation of receipt," he replied, pulling his scarf down from his face in order to be heard. "All that Hammond could confirm, this morning, was that he was present as it was sent."

Thankfully, it was only a short detour, and Holmes was in and out again in just a few minutes. As we set off again, Holmes called forward to the driver once more.

"Do you go via Leavesden, my man?"

"I do indeed, sir. Follow the Luton stagecoach road as much as possible. Best condition, in these parts."

Holmes sat back and I asked him if he'd got what he wanted at the Post Office. He looked at me with one of his sly grins.

"Oh yes, my friend. I got *exactly* what I wanted." Then he pulled his scarf up about his ears once again and hunkered down inside his ulster to keep warm.

We stayed that way until Leavesden, when Holmes suddenly shot forward from his seat and called on the driver to stop.

"Heavens, sir. Whatever is it?" the driver asked.

"We're getting off here, instead," Holmes said, grabbing his bag and dismounting.

"Holmes?" I asked, somewhat flummoxed.

"Yes, we've changed our minds about the journey, and we'll take the stagecoach instead." He pointed across the village square. "I believe that's the first one of the day, loading at this very moment."

Holmes took off for the London coach, where two people were at this moment boarding. Then he hurried back across to us.

"Space for two more, the driver says. We're in luck, Watson."

"What about me?" bleated our driver. "I set aside a morning's work to take you two to Watford."

Holmes reached inside his ulster and produced two sovereigns. "Will this cover your loss?

The driver's eyes nearly left his skull. "Nicely, sir, and with thanks aplenty on top."

"Then have it and go with our best wishes – and don't drink it all at once. Come, Watson, the rest of our journey awaits."

We hurried across the green to where the Luton to London coach was waiting. At least, as a carriage, it was enclosed and ought to be considerably warmer than the cart we'd been riding on.

"Bags under the seat inside, if you please," called down the driver.

"Righto," I replied. Holmes opened the rear side door.

"No more, please, driver," called an urgent female voice from inside.

"Nay, madam," the driver called back. "Easily squeeze these two in next to you and the young gentleman at the back."

We stepped up inside and the two people who'd presumably just boarded, a lady and a younger man, if the skin around the eyes was anything to go by, shifted along the bench seat to leave just enough room for Holmes and me. Four other travellers, two women, a child of perhaps around ten years old, and an elderly man, were seated opposite. There were a further eight travellers in the forward compartment, too. We greeted our fellows politely. It being such a cold day, everyone was wrapped up with hats and mufflers. The lady and young man sharing our seat kept their scarves about their faces the whole time. Any talk was, therefore, rather muted, and everyone tended to keep themselves to themselves.

The journey was agonising at times, at least until the number of passengers thinned and we could sit more comfortably. Despite regular stops and several changes of passengers, Holmes and I were never left alone in the coach. I was desperate to ask him why we had changed our plans so suddenly, but it would never do to speak of such things in front of others.

Finally, as we approached London, Holmes and I had the rear to ourselves. The lady and younger gentleman who had also boarded in Leavesden were the only other passengers and they had moved forward into the front compartment several stops earlier. The luxury of having more space was offset by us being exposed much more to the cold draughts which whistled in around the ill-fitting carriage doors. I endeavoured to strike up a conversation, but Holmes remained guarded – cautious, it seemed, of the other two passengers.

We finally alighted at the Camden terminus, whereupon I looked forward to a bracing walk back to Baker Street to stretch my legs and warm me, followed by a well-needed late lunch. I expressed our thanks to the driver and wished our two fellow travellers a fond farewell, for which I received a cursory gesture only. However, Holmes was adamant that we needed to keep moving and immediately hailed a cab to take us to the parish of St Mary, Kilburn.

The further journey may not have been my preference, but at long last I could ask Holmes why he had changed our travel plans so suddenly that morning.

"You must bear with me on that, Watson," he replied. "I have set a number of wheels in motion, some of which you will more ably assist if you don't already know what I know."

This was nothing new to me, of course, so there was little point in me pressing him further. It wasn't an issue of trust. If anything, it showed that

Holmes could rely on my natural reactions when he needed to. And I was always happy that my assistance was required in at least some respect.

"You're moving closer to a resolution, then, I perceive?"

"Very much so. In fact, I strongly suspect we will tighten the noose around this whole puzzling case today."

I was relieved about this. I didn't care for the prospect of many more coach trips to-and-from Abbots Langley.

"There is one thing," Holmes said, after a while. "I shan't be revealing to the Reverend, or to Mrs. Shields and young Geoffrey, that we have already been up to Abbots Langley. As far as they're concerned, we are only now giving them our full attention."

I nodded my understanding.

"The rest, as I've said, will unfold," he continued. "Now, do you know much regarding the etymology of names?"

It wasn't uncommon for Holmes to ask sudden, seemingly random questions of me like this. I puffed my cheeks and blew out a breath.

"I know a little, but doubtless not much more than most educated men. My name, Watson, for example. It comes from 'Son of Watt'. Hardly takes a genius to come to that conclusion. I couldn't guess at yours, though, for example."

He nodded. "Holmes is geographical – or perhaps I should say topographical in origin. In northern Middle English, a *holm* was an island."

"Ha! Your ancestors were island dwellers, then?"

"Something like that, it seems, yes."

"Am I to assume that this holds any specific relevance to the Smith-Mortimer case?"

"Unless I am barking up completely the wrong tree, I believe it does, yes. There was at least one useful volume in the library at Mowltenbury Manor, you'll be pleased to learn."

Soon after, we arrived at the parish of St Mary, Kilburn. The cab dropped us off at the Rectory and, as ever, Holmes was generous with his fare. The driver offered to wait, but, instead, Holmes tipped him twice as much again and asked the man to return our travel bags to Mrs. Hudson at Baker Street, Unsurprisingly, he willingly agreed.

"Shouldn't we have sent on ahead to let the Reverend know that we planned to call?" I asked.

Holmes brushed my concerns aside and rang the bell. An elderly housekeeper answered. She regretted to inform us that the Reverend was out visiting his parishioners.

"Never mind, my good woman," Holmes replied. "Perhaps, instead, you could direct us to the abode of Mrs. Shields?"

She did, and a short walk later found us at Rose Cottage. It was a small, detached house with low-ceilings – likely one of the older buildings still standing in the parish. Homely, yet clearly in need of some work. I raised my cane to knock at the door, but Holmes reached in ahead of me and pushed. The door swung open, off the latch. I turned to him with a concerned frown. He indicated that I should enter.

"Hello?" I called as we stepped in. "Anyone home?"

There was the sound of movement inside. I glanced at Holmes – had we chanced upon an interloper?

The inner door opened to reveal the Reverend Hume. He looked relieved to see us and welcomed us through into the small living area beyond.

"You fair made me jump when you called out like that, Doctor Watson, I must say."

I apologised to him.

He rubbed his palms together, as he had done in Baker Street, and tentatively asked if we had any progress to report.

Holmes answered immediately. "Not yet, Reverend, no. We had some outstanding business to close off first, but the purpose of our visit today is to inform you – and the Shields – that Watson and I are now fully dedicated to your case and seeing justice done to Geoffrey and his mother."

"And the matter of the coach driver?"

Holmes gave the Reverend a broad smile. "In the hands of Scotland Yard's finest. We've been asked not to trouble ourselves further on that matter."

"Hopefully justice will be served," he replied.

Holmes, as was his wont, had set immediately to studying the room, peering into nooks and crannies.

The Reverend was somewhat flustered by this, most likely as he was an intruder there himself – albeit a welcome one, considering his position.

"I . . . er . . . I'm not sure we should – *erm* . . . I've not long been here myself, gentlemen. Geoffrey and Gladys must be about some business. I assume it was them you wished to see?"

"It was, indeed, Reverend," Holmes confirmed. "I'm sure they won't mind us waiting."

"May I suggest that, instead, we return to the Rectory? I've been out around the parish all morning and I hadn't realised how the time had escaped me. Perhaps you'd care to join me in some refreshment if you haven't already luncheoned? We can return here later."

I eagerly confirmed that we had neither eaten nor drunk anything since breakfast and I, for one, was quite famished. The Reverend gathered some papers from the table and led the way out. I followed eagerly. Holmes came after, looking for all the world like a disappointed bloodhound.

The Reverend Hume introduced us to his housekeeper, Mrs. Endicott, who quickly prepared some simple refreshment for the three of us. I knew that Holmes didn't rely on such things, but I felt myself to be much more alert without a gaping chasm for a stomach. As we ate, the Reverend informed us that, since he'd been to speak with us a few days earlier, a discovery had been made. Mrs. Shields hadn't sent the correct birth certificate with the fatal coach after all.

"I say, that's a turn up!" I burst.

"Isn't it just?" the Reverend replied. "When you found me, I'd popped around to inform Gladys and Geoffrey that I've written another plaintive letter, along the same lines, to accompany the birth certificate. From what Gladys – Mrs. Shields – said, the coach driver was a hasty fellow, eager to get there and back before sundown on these short winter days. He caused the poor lady to rush. In so doing, she accidentally sent the forged birth certificate I'd made up to reassure her husband, years ago."

"Then we should be thankful, at least, that it didn't arrive as planned. Otherwise it would have caused considerable embarrassment."

"My thoughts exactly, Doctor Watson," said the Reverend. "I also thought that we should try presenting it in person this time. Clearly some villain knows our plans and should they endeavour to interfere with its passage again, then a number of us in the coach will provide more protection."

"A solid suggestion, Reverend, indeed," agreed Holmes. "It does seem that someone is aware of your moves and options. For our part, we've been advised that the Smith-Mortimer family solicitor, Nathaniel Forbes, is due at Mowltenbury Manor tomorrow."

"I see. That is troubling. A shame you weren't able to take any positive action before now, Mr. Holmes. We might already have seen this off. Our aim was to ensure the household was fully accepting of young Geoffrey before we established proceedings with the solicitor. We're ordinary people, small fry, and if the matter is challenged, Mrs. Shields has nothing in the way of financial backing." The Reverend rose and began to pace, worrying himself about the palms, as he did so. "I wonder, then, if the Baronet's industrialist cousin has already arrived there from the north, to lay claim to the estate?"

481

"It seems likely that he will have done, yes," said Holmes. He held up the newspaper that lay on the dining table. "Your local paper is fascinating, Reverend. Do you mind awfully if I take some cuttings?"

"I've finished reading it, so please proceed. Is there something that's taken your fancy?"

"A few minor curios, nothing more," he replied, taking out his penknife and very carefully scoring around one column.

"I must speak with the Shields," said the Reverend. "We should look to try to head up towards Abbots Langley today. Perhaps by train to Watford, then seek a hostel there overnight. We should be able to get to Mowltenbury Manor early tomorrow morning before Mr. Forbes arrives." He paused and turned to us on the sudden. "Gentlemen, could I prevail upon you to accompany us?"

"By train?" I asked. "Willingly."

Before we could reply further, there was an insistent banging at the front door and shortly afterwards, Gladys and Geoffrey Shields entered, somewhat out of breath. They appeared relieved to see the Reverend, then a little shocked at finding him with company. As they were introduced, I immediately stood. Holmes was rather lost in his eccentricities at first, and only peered at the new arrivals through one of the narrow holes he'd cut in the newspaper.

"These gentlemen come with grave news, I'm afraid," said the Reverend, indicating Holmes and me. "We need to look at travelling up to the estate with all haste, to stake Geoffrey's claim. Mr. Holmes and Doctor Watson will accompany us."

I saw a look of mild panic pass between mother and son.

"Don't fret," I said. "We will do all we can to help."

"How soon can you be ready to leave?" the Reverend asked of the lady.

"We will need to grab some things, that's all," Mrs. Shields replied.

"Fine," said the Reverend. "You return home and gather your bags. I shall call on Mr. Trumbull and I'll see you back here shortly."

"Don't forget to wrap up warm," warned Holmes, placing the newspaper back on the table and pocketing his cuttings. "It's bitter cold weather for travelling."

With a nod, Geoffrey and Gladys Shields left. The Reverend turned to us.

"Mr. Trumbull is our local cab driver. Please wait here, gentlemen. I shall seek his assistance and return for you both. I'll be but a few minutes, hopefully."

He left us, calling to Mrs. Endicott on his way out and asking her to pack an overnight bag for him, urgently. Holmes held up a cautionary hand until he was sure that both were out of earshot, then he peered into an adjacent room.

"The Reverend's study. Keep watch!" he hissed at me, before disappearing inside. I could hear him rifling around in the Reverend's bureau, frantically opening and closing drawers. He gave a small cry of delight. There then followed a tearing sound.

"Holmes," I whispered. "What the deuce – ?"

He returned, a triumphant glint in his eye and a folded sheet of paper in his hand, which he concealed in his breast pocket.

"By Jove, Watson, we're galloping apace now. The end is very much in sight!"

"Anything but another coach journey to Abbot's Langley!" I said, as we heard the front door open once again.

We were hastily ushered outside the Rectory and the cab arrived shortly after, pulled by an old grey mare who, we were assured, had plenty of life left in her. Mrs. Shields and her son hurried along to join us, with their bags but only a light jacket on each.

"Heavens, Mrs. Shields," said Holmes. "Have you both nothing warmer? I fear you will freeze. Is there not even a scarf to protect your face and neck?"

Mrs. Shields replied that this was all they had, being a poor family.

As we set off, Holmes called up to the cabby and told him to go via Baker Street. To the concerned faces inside, he said this was so we could grab our own bags, since we hadn't come prepared for an overnight stay. This detail seemed to have escaped the Reverend's notice up to now.

"You must all come in when we get there," Holmes said. "Our housekeeper, Mrs. Hudson, is about your size, Mrs. Shields. She will have a warm coat you could borrow. And I'm sure that between Watson and me, we can furnish something for young Geoffrey to use to fend off the chills."

I nodded my agreement. Geoffrey was more Holmes's height, but stockier like me.

"Perhaps on the way, Mrs. Shields, you can tell us your story? It may be useful to have all the details to hand."

The lady blushed. "Oh, Mr. Holmes, what a thing to ask. How could you expect me to discuss such matters in front of poor young Geoffrey here?"

"As you wish, madam," he replied. "But if Geoffrey is of the Smith-Mortimer line, he's going to need to account for his origins himself, at some point, I'm sure."

"Perhaps when we're on the train would be the best time for such a discussion?" suggested the Reverend. "Mr. Holmes and Mrs. Shields can take a compartment on their own while they discuss the details."

Mrs. Shields cast a sidelong glance at the Reverend. "Thank you for the suggestion," she said.

Conversation was patchy all the way to Baker Street. Neither Mrs. Shields nor Geoffrey appeared willing to speak much. At one point, the Reverend leaned in close to me.

"I think they are both a little overawed by your presence," he whispered. "They had anticipated that only I would be liaising with you,"

Holmes, by contrast, was in a garrulous mood. When he failed to get responses from the Shields, he instead drew my attention to sights of interest through the cab windows. When we finally pulled up outside 221b Baker Street, he was the first to jump out and hold the door to encourage the rest of us to disembark. Mrs. Shields resisted at first.

"'Tis not for the likes of us to enter such houses, Mr. Holmes," she complained. "I'll take any hand-me-downs – I'm not proud. Just bring 'em with you when you come back."

But Holmes wouldn't hear anything of it. Eventually, Mrs. Shields was prised from the cab. Holmes tipped the driver for his pains while they sorted their affairs inside.

My friend led the way up the stairs. As the other host, I brought up the rear. When we arrived on our landing, the Reverend Hume, Mrs. Gladys Shields, and Geoffrey were hastily ushered into our rooms and as I closed the door behind, I learned the reason why.

"You received my wire then, Inspector?" said Holmes to Lestrade, who was standing by the window, opposite.

"I'm sorry, who's this?" asked the Reverend.

Mrs. Shields and Geoffrey stood stock still in the centre of the room. Four constables revealed themselves, peeling away from the shadowy walls to the sides.

"I did, Mr. Holmes, thank you," replied Lestrade. "Got here about half-an-hour ago. Wasn't sure how long you'd be."

"Well-timed for sure," Holmes said. "It was a nauseatingly long journey back from Abbots Langley."

Again, the Reverend tried to gain some information. "Sorry, Mr. Holmes, did you say Abbots Langley? Have you been there, then? Are these policemen here to escort us back up there?"

Holmes walked over to stand with Lestrade. I remained by the door. And one of the constables joined me.

"These policemen, Reverend, are here to arrest Gladys and Geoffrey for murder and attempted fraud."

"What?" The Reverend was aghast.

"We've been tricked!" Gladys yelled. "You've got a nerve, Mr. Holmes, luring us in here like that! What right have you got to make such accusations at poor people?"

"No right, Mrs. Shields," he replied. "Simply proof." He called over to me. "You recall, Watson, that we changed our travel plans suddenly this morning, and took the coach as it loaded at Leavesden."

"Yes, indeed. I was both flummoxed and somewhat put out by the change, I must say."

"You'll recall, also, that two other travellers boarded at Leavesden? Very heavily wrapped against the cold. They tried to stop us boarding but the driver insisted."

Again, I agreed.

"Those same two travellers are here with us now – Gladys and Geoffrey. They couldn't wear their heavy winter coats and scarves when we left Kilburn because they knew we would recognise them from the stagecoach straight away."

"What were they doing in Leavesden?" I asked.

"My dear friend, they have a dwelling there. Young Geoffrey, here, we spotted late yesterday afternoon at the gates, speaking with his father."

"Sir Roger?"

Holmes shook his head. "Hammond – the butler. The Wickhams were right – he did still have a family there. They've been living a double life between Leavesden and Kilburn this past two years, since Hammond took the position of butler. It was all part of their grand plan to lay false claim to the inheritance."

I placed my hand to my temple. "I see. Forgive me. I find that this is all very . . . sudden."

Holmes looked at the middle-aged Mrs. Shields – or Mrs. Hammond as it now seemed she was.

"Would you care to explain, madam?" he asked.

She spoke not, but instead began to tear at the envelope she was holding. Two constables leapt forward and quickly wrested in from her grasp before she could get too far. Lestrade took the torn pieces and placed them on the side table.

Holmes picked up the story instead. "I was very much in the dark on this whole business until last night. I'd been pondering every aspect of it. I had the feeling that all it needed was one clue, one spark to light up the whole case, and then everything would slot into place. That came last night, but it was actually Inspector Jones, at dinner, who planted the seed."

He glanced at Lestrade. "Although whatever you do, don't tell him that! He suggested that maybe Sir Roger had an accomplice, either in the household or nearby. I'd been certain of Sir Roger's innocence from the start – he was too obvious a choice. So I considered the possibility that someone else in the house was working with an accomplice – which could also explain the meeting we witnessed at the gates, Watson.

"I needed, first, to discount Mrs. Shields, here, and Geoffrey. As it happens, I stumbled upon the truth straight away. When I asked Hammond to arrange for my telegram to be sent to Kilburn, for Mrs. Shields, he was eager to deal with the matter himself because he knew that she was at home in Leavesden, with Geoffrey. He had the Abbots Langley Post Office send it there, as well as to Kilburn. I became suspicious of Hammond because I noticed how very late it was that he returned to the manor house last night. I was still up, thinking, of course. He didn't see me in the dark, but I saw him. It was near midnight and I knew he'd been doing more than I'd asked of him.

"He added a note of his own to my telegram, asking Geoffrey to head out and meet him, as the hour was already too late for him to walk all the way to Leavesden and back. I found this out this morning when I stopped off at the Abbots Langley Post Office and sent Inspector Lestrade, here, a wire asking him to meet us here with four officers at mid-afternoon. The post-mistress unwittingly showed me where my telegram was sent, and I could also see what Hammond had sent immediately afterwards.

"It stood to reason, then, that his wife and son would attempt to get back to London as early as they could in order to be at home when we called, as I'd suggested we would in my telegram. The first coach of the day seemed the likely candidate, and we were fortunate enough to get spaces on it too, despite Gladys' demands to the contrary. At the Camden terminus, when we jumped into a cab, I imagine, they assumed that we were heading here to Baker Street. So, they walked home to Kilburn. Their surprise was certainly evident when they arrived at the Rectory to find us there. I recognised them from their eyes and the shape of their brows, which was all we could see of them on the coach."

I realised, then, that this was why Holmes only looked at them through the gap he'd cut in the Reverend's newspaper.

"Am I correct so far, Mrs. Hammond?" he asked.

She cast her glance to the floor.

"If they hadn't been so hot and flustered after their walk and decided to leave their coats and bags at Rose Cottage first, you would have recognised them immediately, too, Watson. Had that been the case, I fear this might have been a far less tidy conclusion, and Inspector Lestrade's time may have been wasted here."

I still needed to get a few facts straight. "Are you suggesting that one of these two killed Sir Philip Smith-Mortimer?"

"Oh no, my friend. That was definitely the butler. Had to have been. And that was his tie clip we found in the grass. He then stole Mr. Wickham's to replace it, which was why Wickham couldn't find his when he needed it."

"But what about what Sir Roger told us about the clip not being on Sir Philip's corpse at first?"

"Remember what I said to you about the likely state of Sir Philip's tie clip? It wasn't on the corpse at first because it had to be thoroughly cleaned. Then it was put back where it belonged. If Wickham was of a more questionable character, he'd have replaced his missing one with Sir Philip's when his wife scrubbed it clean."

This seemed reasonable. "What about Hammond, though? If he's guilty of murder, he's still at large at the manor."

"Not if Jones has done as I asked, he isn't."

I remembered Holmes taking the inspector aside as we were leaving the manor house, that morning.

"I had a wire through before we left Scotland Yard," said Lestrade. "Inspector Jones has indeed taken Mr. Hammond into custody as you suggested."

Mrs. Shields gave a moan and sank into a chair at this news. Geoffrey placed a hand on her shoulder.

Leaving the door guarded by the constable, I approached Holmes and Lestrade. I was still trying to make something of the patchwork myself.

"So Hammond killed Sir Philip, with a plan to try to pass his own son off as the illegitimate heir to the Smith-Mortimer estate."

"Indeed, Watson. Then, when Geoffrey here was in place, he would invite Mrs. *Shields* to live at the manor house with him. Naturally, she would fall madly in love with her charming butler. Hammond could feign a marriage, and suddenly he's been elevated to stepfather of the heir, ready for a life of wealthy indolence."

The Reverend spoke for the first time in a while. "But, Mr. Holmes, what about the dead coach driver?"

Holmes's face turned deadly serious, and his tone dropped as he responded.

"I don't know what aspect of this is the more sickening or evil, Reverend. Whether it's shooting an innocent, kindly and well-loved old man through the head simply because they wanted to try to get his title and money, or whether it's arranging for the death of an innocent coach driver, simply as an act of window-dressing to try to ensure *my* services. And that is the only justification I can arrive at for the act – to somehow make the claim appear more legitimate, by having someone trying to conceal it, in the hope that it both reinforced the claim and brought me on side."

He turned his withering gaze onto Gladys, as she sat silently weeping.

"You were clearly unaware of my methods, Mrs. Hammond. I spend as much time considering the apparent victim and their surroundings as I do the apparent perpetrator."

"And very thorough you are, too, Mr. Holmes," said Lestrade. "Their guilt manifests itself perfectly in their grim acceptance of your logic, but we'll get a full confession back at the station."

"One moment, Inspector, before you go. Geoffrey?"

The young man looked away from his mother.

"Please let us see what you've got in your jacket pocket, there."

Geoffrey looked down. We could all see the edge of a folded sheet of paper. He removed it and opened it out, looking confused. It was actually velum and roughly the top quarter was missing, having been torn off. He shrieked and dropped it.

"No!" he yelled.

"What have you done, you stupid boy?" spat his mother, through angry tears. "What did you – ?" She stopped, biting back her words.

There was a pause. Holmes collected the fallen velum and finished the sentence for the lady.

"'*What did you give your father?*' I think you were about to say, madam. He gave him the original, don't worry, and it was planted within Sir Roger's things, last night, as arranged, in an attempt to frame him for the murder of the coachman. Only I saw Hammond return late, and I observed what he was up to. I made sure the truth was known where necessary before we left this morning." He waved the sheet. "This was a little forgery, a little deception on my part. I slipped it into young Geoffrey's pocket in the cab on the way here. And it served its purpose admirably in revealing who really killed the coachman."

Geoffrey clenched his fists, but before he could act two of the constables had grabbed him and held him firm. He didn't struggle.

Holmes continued in a very matter-of-fact way. "Correct me if I'm wrong, Geoffrey, but although the company understood the coach to be carrying no passengers, you persuaded the driver to let you come along when he called for the papers. Then, at the agreed point along a quiet stretch of the route – a route you knew very well – you asked the driver to stop. And you beat him to death."

Geoffrey said nothing but gave the merest hint of a nod of acquiescence.

"Good Lord," I breathed.

"That's why the horses were all fine, but the driver was dead," Holmes continued. "He's a strong-looking young man. Strong enough, I'll wager, to work a stagecoach over onto its side. And the torn top section from the forged birth certificate he'll have skewered on the springs under the driver's seat, as we then found it." He paused, then nodded at Lestrade. "Thank you, Inspector."

"You can take these two away, now, lads," said Lestrade.

"There's a cab already waiting down there for you to use," Holmes informed them.

Gladys and Geoffrey were handcuffed and escorted out by three of the constables. The fourth constable remained in front of the door. There was clearly more to be done.

"Well, gentlemen," said the Reverend, with a long exhalation. I noticed, once again, that he was rubbing his palms. "I am shocked and distressed by all this. I took them for genuine parishioners with a true grievance. But now all of that is done, I think I ought to be getting back to my duties."

There was something edgier about him now, more desperate. He made to leave, but the constable stood resolute. He turned back to the room with a nervous laugh.

"What is this?"

Holmes still held the folded sheet of torn velum. He also picked up the documents which Gladys had tried to rip up earlier.

"Where did you get that piece you used to trick Geoffrey, Holmes?" I asked.

"The best forgers, Watson, will practice regularly. Some will destroy their unwanted work. Some will keep it just in case. The Reverend, here, falls into the latter category, it seems. I found this blank birth certificate in his bureau."

"I don't know what you're suggesting here, Mr. Holmes," the Reverend said, his voice quivering with nerves. "There's nothing like that in my bureau."

Holmes smiled. "Quite possibly – now. This was the only one I found. And you said yourself, only two days ago, here, in this very room, that your calligraphy skills allowed you to forge a birth certificate to fool Mrs. Shields' ogre of a husband, twenty-two years ago. But that story holds no truth, as we have seen. Except in one way, it does. The birth certificate you forged wasn't to fool some imaginary husband. It was *this* one."

He held up the document Mrs. Shields had torn in two.

"Designed to fool the world and defraud the Smith-Mortimer family of their rightful succession. And it's an excellent job, I grant you. As is this blank one also, which makes it so much more of a shame, therefore, that those skills couldn't be put to better, more Christian use. You, Reverend, are as equally complicit in all this as the two who have just left – you and your brother up in Abbots Langley."

The Reverend staggered, thoroughly shocked, and only kept himself upright with the back of a chair. Frankly, I was shocked, too.

"How do you know they're brothers? The other's a Hammond. He's a Hume."

"Etymology of names, my dear Son of Watt, as we discussed in the cab to Kilburn. I said one of the reference books in the manor house library was useful to me. 'Hammond' means 'Home Protector'."

I was about to question the relevance of this when the realisation hit me. This wasn't the Reverend Hume – it was the Reverend *Home*, as in Lord Dunglass, Charles Douglas-Home! The names were pronounced the same way.

"Perfidies of the English language, eh, my friend? I saw the name written on the ledger at the coach company's office. But, of course, standing behind me you only heard it spoken."

I looked at the Reverend again, as if seeking reassurance. His chin had sunk completely into his chest, his face an angular mask of guilt.

Holmes continued. "The Baronet's butler, then, has been looking out for his younger brother here, who took the pseudonym when he came into the diocese about two years ago."

"Then – "

"Yes. This is the former minister of All Saints and St. Hilda, Leavesden, previously reported dead. Easier for him to take on a new identity than the butler, who was already known at the manor. And they made it a sort of joke, hidden behind a quirk of pronunciation. They opted for a similar pun with their other false creation, as well. Protector: *Shields*."

The Reverend raised his head, his bitter mouth twisting to form a curse, but the words died on his lips.

"You, Mr. *Hammond* are the very worst kind of villain. Not content with perpetrating your crimes, you lusted after the satisfaction of trying to make me accessory to them. You dangled your very guilt before our eyes, smug in the misguided assurance that we would be looking elsewhere for the crime and thus leave you untouched." He turned to me. "I should have trusted my initial instincts. Do you remember, Watson?"

I did. "You felt he was putting on an act, giving us a performance."

"But benign, which is why I brushed it aside. Curse my sluggish brain. You, Reverend, are guilty of fraud, and accessory to murder. But more than that. You are a man of the cloth. Communities build themselves around you. They look to you for guidance. They trust you to be a beacon for what is right and wrong in the world. And yet, here you are, selfishly trying to raise your own family to the level of gentry by the most evil, foul and unholy means. You are a disgrace, sir. *A disgrace!*"

With a sudden flash of speed, the Reverend made a desperate bid to escape. Caught unawares, the constable guarding the door was felled by a deft knee to the stomach. But he dropped where he stood, obstructing the door. Thin and wiry, the Reverend was just squeezing through the available gap when I reached him. I was incensed by what I'd heard, and what I'd witnessed. I grabbed his arm and yanked him back into the room, before felling him with single punch. He crashed to the floor, spilling the contents of a large plant pot over the hearth rug as he did so. I had put all my anger into that punch. That we – that *I* – could be so taken in! That a genuine man of the cloth could stoop so low to put personal and financial gain over duty and moral rectitude.

Holmes and Lestrade congratulated me, but the whole affair left me feeling sickened. The constable was helped by a constitutional tot of brandy, of which Lestrade also felt the need, I observed. The Reverend was cuffed in his sluggish state and escorted away to join the others back at the station.

I took a walk by myself a short while after, leaving Holmes to assist Mrs. Hudson in clearing away the mess from the overturned plant pot. Although the waning afternoon was bitter cold, I needed the fresh air to help me think, to enable me to put everything properly into perspective.

I felt foolish for having been gulled by the Reverend and his cunning brother up at the manor house. But I knew it was natural to trust the Reverend. Ministers have a special, palliative place in our lives. A caring, supporting position in our society. Wicked schemers, such as Hammond, only serve to cause malcontent and distrust of the clergy through their activities. I also felt incredibly sorry for the Wickhams and the other household staff up at Mowltenbury Manor. Sir Roger would, now, rightly succeed and that would bring terrible upheaval and uncertainty to all their lives. Unless someone purchased the estate from Sir Roger wholesale and opted to keep everyone on – which was always a faint possibility. Time would tell.

When I returned to Baker Street, I found that Holmes had company. Or, more correctly, Holmes was just finishing a private interview, since the gentleman in question was just leaving. He wished me well as he passed me on the landing.

Holmes welcomed me warmly. "My dear Watson, I trust you are feeling less anxious after your exercise?"

I told him that I was, before enquiring after the gentleman who'd just left. Did he have another case already?

"Oh, no, no," Holmes replied, pouring me a drink to match the one he already held. "That was one Nathaniel Forbes, of Forbes, Forbes, and Mealing. When we stopped at the Abbots Langley Post Office this morning, as well as alerting Lestrade, I sent a wire to the Smith-Mortimer family solicitors, in Charing Cross. I asked if they'd do me the courtesy of calling here late this afternoon before they headed up to Mowltenbury Manor. I've just explained what we've been about for the last two days. Poor Mr. Forbes has already had several angry telephone calls today from Sir Roger, once he realised Hammond had tried to frame him for murder."

"It's a shame he's already gone," I said, with regret. "I would like to have asked him if he could do anything to protect the livelihood of the household staff at the manor."

"Then let me set your mind at rest." Holmes seated himself and indicated that I should do the same. "Although Sir Philip didn't leave a will, the Mowltenbury Manor estate is protected by a long-established affidavit. Unless the family becomes insolvent, the estate cannot be sold. If the incumbent chooses not to live there, that's up to them, but they must maintain the estate as part of the family heritage. Doubtless Sir Roger didn't know this as, by his own admission, his branch of the family has never had much to do with Sir Philip's. So you see? It should all work out well for the household, after all."

"Not necessarily," I countered. "Sir Roger's creditors, remember? Hammond may have lied to us about a lot of things, but we had Sir Roger's own word to back that up. If things are as bad as he hinted, then the estate may well have to be sold off."

Holmes shook his head. "Mr. Forbes was very clear on that matter, too. Sir Roger owns his factories. The land they're on, the bricks that built them. He would be forced to sell them first, and anything else that's specifically his before he'd be allowed to touch Mowltenbury Manor in that way. And even then, there would be grounds for other family members to object. No, my friend, Sir Philip wasn't as careless in not leaving a will as we thought. The family have done plenty to protect their country seat from unscrupulous heirs. Sir Roger hasn't so much inherited a fortune as a custodial management role."

I couldn't help the broad grin spreading across my face. "I don't envy Mr. Forbes his interview with Sir Roger, then."

Holmes gave a chuckle. "I prepared him as best I could."

"And knowing the Baronet, I suspect he'll disappear back up north to sort out his factories and leave the Wickhams to maintain the manor."

"That seems a likely outcome, I agree."

"Just a shame it's come about through the brutal murder of two people, one so innocent and well-liked."

Holmes brow darkened. "I cannot disagree. The fact that there was no motive of revenge behind it – nothing tangible beyond the simple fact of a wicked family seeing an opportunity to take advantage of a pleasant, well-meaning old man with no close family or heir. It will stick with me, I'm sure, as one of the most heinous and diabolical of all my cases."

It was, indeed, one that we rarely spoke of again.

When I look at the three massive manuscript volumes which contain our work for the year 1894 I confess that it is very difficult for me, out of such a wealth of material, to select the cases which are most interesting in themselves and at the same time most conducive to a display of those peculiar powers for which my friend was famous. As I turn over the pages I see my notes upon the . . . famous Smith-Mortimer succession case . . . .

– Dr. John H. Watson
"The Adventure of the Golden Pince-Nez"

The Repulsive Matter of the Bloodless Banker
by Will Murray

Many callers turn up unexpectedly at 221b Baker Street in London, where my good friend Sherlock Holmes holds forth as the city's sole consulting detective engaged in a private practice. Often they are anxious. Some are literally breathless. No matter the hour, Holmes sees them without delay.

Other, more polite souls write in advance to formally request an appointment.

Colin Crosby was one of the latter individuals – or should I say in this instance, one of the unfortunates. But I get ahead of my tale.

His letter arrived by post in the mid-afternoon mail of December 8, 1894. Billy the page boy brought it up. Holmes slit the envelope at one end. Out slid a folded piece of bond paper. Holmes read this in silence. He was between pipes, so he wasn't smoking. Setting the letter on his lap, Holmes looked up and asked, "Are you familiar with the name Colin Crosby?"

"A banker, if I'm not mistaken. Affiliated with Drummonds Bank. Has he written you?"

Carefully folding the sheet and restoring it to its envelope, Holmes nodded. "Crosby begs to come round next Thursday for a consultation. He didn't go into the matter of concern. Only that he requests my ear."

"You will write him back, of course."

"Of course. The matter doesn't appear to be urgent. I'll do it tonight."

Holmes did exactly that, and the postman took his reply away during his final round of the day.

I thought no more of it until I returned home one evening to find Holmes deep in his briar and pondering so heavily that his brow seemed to be weighed down by his thoughts. I could tell from his expression that he had seized upon a problem.

"What is the matter?" I asked.

"I have a return letter from banker Crosby. The fellow has had second thoughts. He will not be coming around Thursday next after all."

"Obviously the matter was a small moment," I pointed out. "Why do you wear such a perplexed expression?"

"A man of Crosby's standing doesn't normally consult someone such as myself on minor matters. I wondered if perhaps he had tripped over some evidence of embezzlement, and wished for a discrete investigation rather than summoning Scotland Yard."

"If so, perhaps the matter has been settled internally."

Holmes frowned. "Banks and bankers do prefer discretion. But I don't fear for my reputation in that regard. It is only that my imagination had begun to enlarge upon his request for an appointment."

"In what way?"

"The trend of my thoughts now inclines towards a personal matter. Something where a different kind of sort of discretion is required."

"Have you seen any evidence of this conjecture?" I asked, taking my seat on the other side of the fireplace.

"No, not quite. The wording of his original letter prompted my thinking, but only because of the absence of certain language. Also, the letter was on private stationary. If this was a bank matter, he might have written in his official capacity."

"Not if discretion was paramount in his mind."

"True, true, Watson. I imagine we will never know the truth of it."

"Unless he changes his mind once again," suggested I.

"Men like Colin Crosby rarely do. I think we have heard the last of him. Too bad, for times are slim in the matter of mysteries to seize upon and unravel."

Shrugging, I reached for *The London Times* and fell to perusing the front page. In my mind I was certain that another client would show up at 221b Baker Street before long. One often does. The droughts Holmes experienced between cases seemed to drag interminably in his mind, but I always thought they passed rapidly.

Hardly a week had gone by before more was heard of the fellow.

The morning papers carried an account of the finding of the body of banker Colin Crosby in his bed. The man lived alone, for he was a bachelor.

Sherlock Holmes arose late that morning, owing to his having been immersed in some experimental endeavor the previous evening, so it fell me to break the news to him.

"Striking tidings, Holmes. Do sit down and have some eggs."

Dropping into the chair opposite, he asked, "What news? Tell me. I've been steeped in common chemicals half the night and crave something refreshing to stir my brain cells."

"According to the paper, Colin Crosby was found deceased in his Covent Garden townhouse."

A lively sparkle came into my friend's keen grey eyes. Life returned to his ascetic features. "If you're done with that," he said, extending one hand, "I wish to peruse it."

I was happy to turn the newspaper over to him. As I did so, I continued speaking. "The account says nothing about cause of death, only that his passing was mysterious."

Holmes began reading avidly, his eyes never still. "Only thirty-six," he murmured. "A young man yet. Found dead in bed, I see."

"If it were murder, I am certain the newspapers would say so."

"They could hardly avoid it," agreed Holmes.

Laying aside the newspaper, Holmes cast his vision upward towards the ceiling, and I could tell that the machinery of his great brain was lurching into a higher, more profound gear.

"Watson," he murmured, "I think it suspicious that Mr. Crosby perished only a week after begging off his appointment with me. I think I shall go have a talk with Lestrade. I'm most curious to know what befell the poor fellow, striking him down in the prime of life."

"Men like Colin Crosby are prone to stresses and strains that others do not experience," I pointed out. "He isn't too young to have had a heart attack."

"No, nor is apoplexy entirely to be ruled out – although I think the latter possibility less likely."

"I quite concur, speaking medically."

"If the matter were a suicide, given Crosby's prominence, it might be suppressed. But such suppression, however, is usually of short duration. Inevitably, truth will out."

Holmes took his breakfast in silence. but I knew that he was keen to speak with Lestrade.

Having a full calendar of activities that day, I couldn't accompany him. It was of no moment, however, for I missed little of significance. I was to have the full story from him soon enough, at any rate.

When I returned to Baker Street that evening, Holmes was seated by an active fire and puffing furiously on his favorite briar. The aroma of black shag tobacco filled the room.

"Good evening," I said by way of greeting. "You have eaten?"

Holmes shook his head distractedly. I saw that the original letter from banker Crosby and its mate lay upon his lap. He had obviously been rereading both messages.

"Good, then we shall dine together."

"I seem to have misplaced my appetite," returned Holmes coolly.

"I would offer to help you locate it," I rejoined, taking my own seat, "but I scarcely know where to look. Unless you lost it at Lestrade's office."

"You might say that," murmured Holmes. "For I've been engrossed in other concerns since I left Scotland Yard."

"I see," said I. "As ever, I'm keen to hear all about it."

"That is the distressing aspect of the matter," replied Holmes thoughtfully. "There is little to tell, but what there is to tell is exceedingly thought-provoking."

"Has a definite cause of death been established?"

"The answer to that is yes, but also no."

"My word, Holmes! That *is* intriguing. Tell me more."

"While the cause of Colin Crosby's death remains to be established, the condition of his corpse is suggestive in the extreme."

I set a cigarette alight and began smoking, knowing that Holmes would release his thoughts in a measured way, and at his own pace. His brain was quite active, even though his pose was languid, his gaze distant yet penetrating withal.

"You see, Watson, when Colin Crosby was discovered by his housekeeper, lying in bed as if he had fallen asleep, he was uncomfortably thin and his hollowed face possessed a corpsey pallor that was a shade beyond remarkable."

"He must have died in his sleep, poor chap," I suggested, "and lay undiscovered long enough to have acquired a significant pallor."

"Actually, the body was still warm, according to Lestrade, but only slightly. Crosby couldn't have been dead much more than an hour, and conceivably half of that span, asserted the corner who oversaw the removal of the body to the morgue, Mr. Crosby appeared to have had the greater quantity of his life's blood removed from his veins and arteries."

"By what means?" I ejaculated.

"That is the portion of the story that vexes me. The body was stripped at the scene and no wound or puncture was found, nor was there any external blood soaking his sheets. Yet there he lay, as if visited by some blood-lusting phantasm of the evening."

"I can see why you are so engrossed in the problem," I allowed. "I've never heard of such a thing."

"Nor have I," admitted Holmes. "I only wish that I had been present at the scene of death, for I would like to have gone over it in detail."

"I, for one, wish that Mr. Crosby had paid you a visit. Perhaps that would have enlightened us, even after the fact."

"Indeed," muttered Holmes darkly.

"Is this the end of it?" I wondered. "Do you intend to pursue the matter further?"

"Come now, Watson! For how many years have we been in association? You know me better than that. I'm like a dog with a bone in its mouth who can smell the marrow, but must grind away before I can taste its sweetness. I wouldn't lay the strange death of Colin Crosby aside for the Crown Jewels. For your information, I've managed to obtain an invitation to Mr. Crosby's autopsy, which is scheduled for later this evening. I'm hoping that you might attend, purely as my advisor. I imagine it might spoil your supper plans, so that is up to you entirely."

"Spoil my supper plans!" I exclaimed. "Good heavens, this will wreck my appetite beyond repair."

"I take it that you are declining the invitation?"

I gave this some thought before replying.

"I have attended autopsies before, as you know," I said slowly.

"Which is why your company would be invaluable."

"I have the stomach for it. My only concern is for my supper."

"I will treat you to the best supper available, Watson. The only question is whether you would take it tonight, or put it off for a more congenial evening."

"What time is the autopsy?"

"Eight o'clock sharp."

"I'll accompany you," I said with a trace of reluctance that no doubt Holmes detected in my voice. "I'll steel myself, and I'm sure we'll get through it all right."

For reasons having to do with the peculiar and unsavory nature of what I'm about to reveal, I was to regret those words.

Ten minutes short of eight o'clock, a hansom cab deposited Holmes and myself at the mortuary, where we alighted.

A Doctor Weir solemnly received us, and we were soon solemnly arrayed around the gleaming porcelain autopsy table.

Colin Crosby lay tented under a sheet, and from the way it draped his still form, I concluded that he had been a rather slight man.

When the sheet was pulled away, I gave a start.

A practiced eye told me that in life, Colin Crosby had been a healthy man weighing perhaps ten stone and standing just short of six feet tall. But the flesh on his bones possessed a wasted look, and his pallor was beyond anything I had seen in a corpse so fresh.

I said nothing. Dr. Weir took up his scalpel and commenced his sombre work, the details of which I need not closely describe.

The scalp was laid bare and the skull bones removed, exposing the brain, into which was carefully examined after removal.

Nothing remarkable was discovered among its inert convolutions.

498

Then came the time to slit the thorax and peel back the skin so that the viscera and abdominal organs could be examined and then extracted. This was done in a methodical manner, during which interval Holmes and I watched closely but carried on no conversation. None was necessary. It was all routine – all except for the condition of the corpse.

The dead do not bleed for the most part, and this corpse gave up no sanguinary clues, for it could not. The veins and arteries were long flat voids.

I couldn't see how this condition was accomplished, but I didn't remark upon it.

During the course of the autopsy, Holmes moved about the room, studying the procedure from various angles, thereby giving the body of Colin Crosby careful examination.

At one point he stopped, bending down to look at the man's shrunken right shoulder with his pocket glass. Dr. Weir paid him little heed, being engrossed in his grisly work.

"A moment, Dr. Weir," Holmes said abruptly.

The mortician looked up. "Yes?"

"Have you examined this man's armpits?"

"I have not. Why do you ask?"

"I believe I spy a red extrusion of some sort. Come over here and take a look."

Setting down his scalpel, Dr. Weir stepped over to Holmes's side of the autopsy table and peered narrowly through the offered glass.

"A cyst, perhaps," he suggested.

"You might verify that," suggested Holmes.

Dr. Weir reached down and took hold of the arm and brought it up and over, exposing the man's armpit to the light.

The gas light showed a terrible sight. It wrenched an oath from Dr. Weir's lips, but Holmes merely brought his glass more closely to the object of concern.

It was a short scarlet thing perhaps the size of a grown man's thumb – and there was no question that it glistened with life!

"What is that horrid thing?" gasped Dr. Weir.

Holmes picked up a pair of tweezers, grasping the thing gingerly. It squirmed under the cold pinch of the steel tongs. He pulled it away with some slight difficulty and then held it up to the light, revealing a tiny round sucker fringed with horrid teeth.

It was then that Holmes vouchsafed a quite strange thing.

"If I am not very much mistaken," he said, "this is a species of red herring."

"Herring!" exploded Dr. Weir. "It is no such thing!"

Smiling thinly, Holmes dropped the sluggish creature into a dish meant for receiving smaller organs and said, "I was merely expressing a conjecture. This unsavory abomination is clearly an example of *Hirudo medicinalis* – once commonly used as a medicinal leech."

"Yes, yes, I see that now. I also observe that it has been feeding."

I stepped closer to see for myself the size of the leech, after which I said to both men, "I cannot see how this creature, no matter how prodigious its appetite, could have drawn every drop of the blood from this poor man's body."

"It plainly did not!" snapped Holmes. "That is why I dubbed it a red herring. You are familiar with the term, no doubt."

Dr. Weir said, "Yes, yes. Kippered herring are used to train foxhounds for the hunt, who are sometimes prone to following the wrong scent if it is stronger than fox. What do you mean by using such a term, Mr. Holmes?"

"I mean that whoever planted this hungry leech under Colin Crosby's armpit meant that it be eventually found so that a false theory as to his death might be contemplated."

"No one could possibly believe that such a comparatively small creature could have drained a full-grown man of his blood supply."

"The murderer wouldn't necessarily know that," stated Holmes quietly.

"Murderer? Why, what do you mean?"

A trifle brusquely, Holmes returned, "What do you imagine I could mean, Doctor? I mean that Crosby was murdered in some yet-to-be understood fashion, the blood taken entirely out of his body by surreptitious means that would appear to defy logic and smack of the supernatural."

"Other than the sucker mark under the right armpit, I have discovered no wounds. How would you account for that?"

"As yet," admitted Holmes frankly, "I cannot. But that doesn't mean that an explanation cannot be discovered. I'm not a man to gravitate towards supernatural theories. There is an explanation for this. It is up to us to discover it. Carry on, Dr. Weir. Perhaps we'll uncover it before the night is through."

Frowning, the nonplussed mortician returned to his unpleasant work, and one by one the major organs of Colin Crosby were laid on the table, weighed, and examined for morbidities.

It was during the portion of the autopsy where the man's bowels were removed and bisected that a gasp of horror was wrenched from my lips, as well as those of Dr. Weir.

Apparently unmoved, Holmes leaned in and once again the pocket glass lifted in his hand.

For out of the burst bowels squirmed a great length of living muscle, livid and unpleasant to behold.

Entirely taken aback, Dr. Weir goggled at the elongated thing squirming on the stainless steel table. He gasped out, "Good God in heaven! That is the largest tapeworm I have ever beheld in my entire life!"

Having rid himself of that observation, Weir took up a scalpel and savagely slashed the flattish thing in twain, producing copious amounts of blood. It continued to squirm for some minutes, one portion tumbling onto the floor. The doctor's foot came down hard, crushing the life out of it, producing even more flowing blood.

After a few more minutes elapsed, the writhing tapeworm squirmed no more.

Holmes studied the portion sprawled upon the autopsy table. After a time, he straightened up and pocketed his glass.

"This worm," he announced solemnly, "I am confident to say, is one that is presently unknown to science."

Neither Dr. Weir nor I could muster a response to that flat assertion. Holmes said it was true. I had no reason to doubt it. But what that meant was beyond me.

"This, Dr. Weir," he said, "constitutes further proof that Colin Crosby was murdered, for here is the instrument of his destruction. A tapeworm that feeds upon the blood, and not the fleshy parts."

Gathering his wits, Dr. Weir protested weakly. "But Mr. Holmes, tapeworms are often harbored by human hosts, and entirely unsuspected by them."

"If it were not for the fact this worm is of a species hitherto unidentified, and that the red leech was planted under the victim's armpit, I might be inclined to agree with you. But I called the creature a red herring for good reason. I deem it unlikely that banker Crosby was leeching himself and happened also to silently harbor a blood-sucking worm in his intestinal tract. Ergo, my verdict is murder most foul. And I must further assert that this is the most foul form of murder I have ever encountered in my career to date. We must inform Inspector Lestrade of our findings at once."

Dr. Weir took slight umbrage of this, saying, "You may inform him of your rather fantastic theory. I'll inform him of the cold facts of my autopsy. Now if you are satisfied with what you have witnessed, kindly leave me to complete my duty undisturbed."

"I am pleased to do," returned Holmes. "For I have seen all that I need to see. Good evening to you, Dr. Weir."

With that, we went out into the bitter night.

As I bundled up, I asked my friend, "You are, as always, supremely certain of your own opinion."

This was not a criticism, nor did Holmes take it as such.

"That unfortunate man was murdered, as surely as the new moon will be soon upon us. Come, let us hurry to Scotland Yard. I hope to catch Lestrade whilst still in his office."

A hansom cab conveyed us to the gates of Scotland Yard and we were soon bracing the inspector in his gaslit office. After Holmes had conveyed the gruesome results of the autopsy, Lestrade turned to me and asked, "Doctor, what opinion do you hold in this matter?"

"The tapeworm in question was the largest I have ever seen in my life. I cannot imagine but that it had been swallowed whilst quite small and persisted for some weeks before achieving the size it had reached, apparently by feeding off poor Crosby's lifeblood."

Lestrade nodded gravely. Turning his gaze back to Holmes, he stated, "And you call it murder."

"Murder most foul, and committed by an intimate. What I cannot yet conceive is where the entomologist fits into this thin web of horror."

Lestrade blinked furiously. "Entomologist? Please explain yourself."

"I hold that only an entomologist could have introduced that unclassified tapeworm into poor Crosby's system. Of course, the learned fellow could be an accomplice. And if an accomplice, he may or may not be a knowing accomplice, one who has participated in murder with malice aforethought."

"Please explain your reasoning, for it eludes me."

"Had this tapeworm been a common one, I would be at a loss to proceed," explained Holmes. "Of course, had it been a common tapeworm, death wouldn't have resulted from its ingestion. But no matter. Someone possessing a tapeworm hitherto unclassified and having the guile to apply an ordinary leech to Crosby's corpse must possess the specialized knowledge of an entomologist. Once we identify this person, we'll have found the author of the crime – or his accomplice."

"I quite follow your reasoning," allowed Lestrade. "And I'm candidly open to following where your theories lead us. Now as to Crosby himself, my detectives have established that he has been absent from work for nearly two weeks. An illness, it is said."

"An illness whose source would have gone to the grave with the victim had an autopsy not been performed," Holmes declared.

"You believe the tapeworm had been feeding for at least that length of time?" asked Lestrade.

"At the very least," replied Holmes, "but likely longer. For it to have grown to that immense size, it would necessarily have had to have dwelt within Colin Crosby's viscera for considerably longer than two weeks. More than one month, I should judge. If we're pursuing the matter from the standpoint of when the tapeworm larva was originally ingested, we must go back approximately six weeks. Furthermore, Crosby would likely have been unwittingly fed the tapeworm through an ordinary meal. Therefore, we're looking for an intimate, someone who would dine with him and not be suspected of harboring malice. I cannot otherwise imagine how he would have acquired such a novel parasite."

"Crosby had few intimates," Lestrade stated. "He was a man of work. It drove him. He was unmarried, and therefore dedicated to his profession."

"He could hardly have been without friends," countered Holmes. "Locate them and you'll have a starting point."

"I'll have his fellow workers and staff questioned, as well as the woman who kept his flat for him."

"I should like to speak with the latter. She's more likely to have knowledge of his personal life."

"You may do so, Mr. Holmes, but in the company of one of my detectives, if not myself. I intend to have a word with her tomorrow. Shall we say nine o'clock in the morning?"

"Nine o'clock it will be," said Holmes.

"Good. Come round at nine, and we'll visit her together."

With that established, Holmes and I went back out into the cold winter night.

"I congratulate you," I said as we sought a cab. "You appear to have traveled far in a comparatively short time – at least as far as your theories are concerned."

"The trail has barely begun, Watson," Holmes retorted. "Have you any idea how many entomologists are currently cataloging and classifying insects in London in this present year?"

"I do not."

"Including the amateur category of entomologist, I would say that there are dozens of them. We'll be doing well to winnow out those who aren't involved."

"I would hope that would be most of them."

Frowning, Holmes took out his pipe and lit it. "All but one, all but one. But *which* one?"

The next morning at nine, we rendezvoused with Inspector Lestrade and were soon hurtling along in a four-wheeler to Covent Garden.

As we pulled up, Lestrade finished his explanations.

"Miss Morgan kept house for Crosby. She has been asked to help pack up his things, which the family has requested, for they dwell in distant Yorkshire."

"She is trusted then?" asked Holmes.

"Implicitly so," Lestrade stated as we alighted and sent the carriage on its way.

Going to the front door, we stood waiting as Lestrade knocked in his strenuous manner. Before long a woman of perhaps thirty poked her head out and said, "It's well that you gentlemen have come, for I've found something strange in Mr. Crosby's papers."

The housekeeper threw the door open and we entered.

"This is Mr. Sherlock Holmes, and his associate, Dr. Watson," said Inspector Lestrade by way of introduction.

"Holmes the specialist?"

"I am he," declared Holmes.

"There is no other," said I gallantly.

Miss Morgan made a little curtsy and said, "Pleased to meet you gentlemen all. Now come this way."

Passing through the hall, we entered the dining room. Miss Morgan had made a pile of papers on the dining room table. They stood about in neat bundles held together by ribbons.

"I have been sorting this correspondence," she explained, "and there's a letter addressed to Mr. Holmes. I've read it, but can make nothing of it."

"If it is agreeable to Inspector Lestrade," said Holmes, "I would like to see that letter.

Lestrade nodded his head silently. The letter was produced and Holmes read it rapidly.

"Remarkable," he said. "Not illuminating, but nevertheless remarkable."

With that, he handed the note over to Lestrade. Reading it over, the inspector's face gathered darkly. "According to this, Crosby said that he feared for his life, and he wrote that he preferred to go into the details in person, but that his concern was that he wasn't certain which party he should fear. Only that they were *two* of them."

"Are there no details at all?" I asked.

"None," replied Lestrade, handing the letter to me. "He plainly had suspicions about two individuals, but there was no clarity to the suspicions, only vagueness. Probably this is why he set aside the letter instead of posting it."

I protested, "It's unusual for one man to fear two enemies at the same time."

"Perhaps not for a banker of Crosby's stature," suggested Lestrade.

"I've never believed that Crosby's worries were professional in nature," Holmes said. "They were most likely personal, and so it's highly probable that the two unnamed individuals were connected in some way."

"What leads you to that conclusion, Mr. Holmes?" demanded Lestrade, his voice a trifle perplexed.

"If they were professional concerns," stated Holmes simply, "I would think he would have taken them to the head of his bank. Instead, he wrote to me."

Turning to Miss Morgan, Lestrade invited, "Tell us about Mr. Crosby's friends."

"He had few, and in recent weeks, he wasn't social at all. He didn't feel well. Something concerned him, but I never pried. Nor did he ever confide in me. But it seemed to me that he had fallen away from social contacts."

"Had Crosby been seeing anyone romantically?"

"Yes, there was a woman several weeks ago. He saw her quite often, but then he appeared to stop. I'm quite sure I don't know her full name. Only that he referred to her as 'Miss Sanders'."

"Common enough," mused Lestrade. "Have you her description?"

"I'm certain I never laid eyes on the woman – only that I heard him speak of her. I believe that he was quite fond of her, but that was three or four weeks ago."

"Have you anything to add to that?" pressed Lestrade.

"Only that there was a falling out with a man named Persano around the same time. It was quite serious, I believe. I wasn't privy to the details, but the friendship had turned quite sour. There was bad blood between them towards the last. "

Holmes remarked, "Perhaps there is correspondence that would shed light on this issue."

Miss Morgan said, "You gentlemen are welcome to go through these letters, I'm certain, for I have no objection."

"Let us do that, Lestrade," suggested Holmes. "Perhaps we will uncover a clue or two."

Each man took a sheaf of papers, sat down, and went through them in silence. I remained out of it, not possessing the perspicacity to be of service.

It wasn't long before Holmes stood up in an attitude of triumph and shouted "A-ha! I have something, Lestrade. Kindly peruse this missive."

The inspector took the offered sheet and read quickly. "Reading between the lines, there are threats implied," he declared.

Holmes replied, "Note that the letter is addressed to someone by the initials *I. P.* No doubt that is Mr. Persano."

"Conceivably," allowed Lestrade. "But I glean nothing more about him."

Holmes and Lestrade fell to reading further correspondence. This time, it was Lestrade who gave out a small cry of discovery. "Here is another addressed to someone named '*Isadora*'. Would that be the woman?"

Holmes pointed out that Isadora was a name that has been applied to both men and women. "Therefore," he added, "we may either looking for Isadora Persano, or possibly Isadora Sanders."

"Isadora Persano!" I exclaimed. "There is a journalist by that name – a journalist who is also something of a duelist."

"I've never heard the name," said Holmes. "Is he well-known?"

"Only moderately so. I believe he writes for *The Strand*. Perhaps we should drop 'round and speak to the editor, whom I know well."

Turning to Miss Morgan, Lestrade said, "Pray continue with your sorting and cataloging. If you come across anything else of interest, let Scotland Yard know. We may return at any time to continue our perusal of these letters, but for now I think we shall follow this trail."

After Miss Morgan let us out, I said, "The offices of *The Strand* can be reached through a brisk walk. I suggest we not waste time seeking a cab."

Holmes nodded. His pipe was alight once more.

We walked along in silence, at last coming to Southampton Street, and the building housing *The Strand's* editorial offices. We went up to the topmost floor and made ourselves known. I, of course, knew the editor very well, having sold him many narratives of my friend's intriguing cases. The genial fellow greeted us warmly. After he had showered effusive praise upon an abashed Sherlock Holmes, he was only too glad to help us.

"Yes, I know Isadora Persano. He would sell us a line or two now and again. He was nothing special in that department. He was the type I would call a scribbler. Often unreliable. Since he became interested in exhibition dueling, I've seen little of him."

"Have you his most recent address on hand?" asked Lestrade.

"A moment, please." Standing up, the editor went over to an oak cabinet containing his files and came back with an address, which he copied for us. It was in Chelsea.

"When did you last hear of Persano?" asked Holmes, glancing up from the address.

"Three weeks. Perhaps it was four. As I said before, he wrote for us rather infrequently. He was a middling sort of writer, but useful in his way. I would have used him more often had he been more reliable."

"Thank you," said Lestrade. "Good day to you, sir."

"Good day to you all. Wonderful to meet you at last, Mr. Holmes. It is an honor. And Watson – I trust I will see another manuscript from you ere long."

I promised to do so, and we were soon back in the bustle of Charing Cross's ever-busy streets.

It was necessary to take a four-wheeler to Chelsea, and soon we were knocking on Persano's door in a genteel rooming house.

No response was aroused by our knocking. We sought out the landlady, who was quite to the point.

"I haven't seen him in two weeks. If I had, I would have evicted him. He is one month behind in his rent."

"Who would you know anyone who knows him? That is to say, who are his friends?"

"Layabouts. Scroungers. Scalawags. Drunkards. I know none of them by name. Plus Mr. Persano was quite the carouser. I'm sorry I ever laid eyes on him. Should you happen upon him, tell him to come and get his things. They'll be on the pavement by evening."

Without another word, the landlady turned her bent back on us and returned to her business.

"Most peculiar," said Inspector Lestrade. "Now we have a missing man – a missing man who is connected to another poor fellow who is deceased."

"And neither of them entomologists," murmured Holmes. "I believe that we have waded into deep waters – quite deep waters indeed."

"They are too deep for me to fathom," admitted Lestrade.

"If you don't mind," said Holmes, "I would like to return to further inspect Mr. Crosby's voluminous correspondence. I suspect there are additional clues yet to be unearthed, if I apply the requisite patience."

"I wouldn't deny you the pleasure," returned Lestrade. "Now good day."

Holmes and I found a cab and were soon wheeling back to Covent Garden.

"Watson, I don't think I shall require your good company for the next several hours, for whatever can be gleaned from banker Crosby's correspondence must be sifted by one set of eyes attached to one brain. It promises to be a tedious business, but it must be done."

"If you don't think I can be helpful to you," I replied, "I'll leave you to your winnowing."

507

Holmes alighted at the Covent Garden townhouse, and I continued on to Baker Street. I didn't hear from him until late that evening.

Upon his return, Holmes went immediately to claim his armchair by the fireplace and began loading his long-stemmed cherry-wood pipe with black shag.

"Well, good evening," I greeted. Taking the opposite chair, I inquired, "What progress have you made? For I know you as I know the lines of my palm. I have every confidence that you have made progress by now."

"Progress, yes, but a solution as yet eludes me."

Holmes's brow appeared troubled as he loaded his pipe and set it to light. Soon he was puffing away most industriously.

"Mr. Crosby was the most fastidious man," he mused aloud. "I imagine most bankers are. He had a helpful habit of saving letters that he choose not to mail. Perhaps he intended to use them as scrap. Possibly he was an inveterate packrat. I'm inclined toward the latter theory. Be that as it might, I've spent the better part of the day reading his unsent correspondence, as well as those letters he received in the course of the last few months."

"What did these letters tell you?"

"Given the fact that only the letters never posted survived in his possession, I find that I'm in possession of a great puzzle whose most significant pieces aren't all at my disposal. But the letters that he saved were quite illuminating."

From a pocket of his coat, he removed an envelope and handed it to me. "Of the letters received, this one appears to be the most significant."

I looked at the envelope. It was addressed to Colin Crosby, but there was no return address. Undoing the flap, I pulled out a folded note. This I unfolded carefully.

My dear Crosby,

Since we cannot come to a common understanding over our recent disagreement, I feel that we must meet on the field of honor. Would that not settle matters with finality? Only one of us may win the day.

Write back your consent and we will set the time and place. I await your prompt response, sir.

Yours more sincerely,

I. Persano

"My word!" I exclaimed, "Persano appears to have challenged Colin Crosby to a duel."

"That is as plain as the ink upon the paper you hold in your hands," said Holmes. "But over what slight remains to be discovered."

"This letter is dated approximately two weeks ago," I pointed out. "Had there been a duel, might Persano have fallen before Crosby's bullet?"

"You are assuming a duel with pistols, Watson."

"Given the recent vogue for exhibition dueling with pistols, I believe I stand on firm ground in that regard."

"I don't entirely disagree, but I will point out that we lack sufficient facts to establish the nature of the duel – assuming that such a contest took place."

"Mr. Persano has been missing for approximately that length of time," I pointed out.

"The man's absence might point in the direction of an undiscovered body, but until such a body turns up, it is rank speculation that the duel took place."

"I'm inclined to believe that it did. The available facts seem to suggest it."

Holmes waved his pipe about, producing vague clouds. "Dark clouds suggest rain, but rain doesn't always fall. But I will admit that we cannot yet state whether or not a duel took place. Only that it's possible that one did. But how does that explain the horrible tapeworm in banker Crosby's gut?"

"That baffles me," I admitted.

Holmes descended into silence and resumed puffing away madly. I knew all the outward symptoms of his moods. He was terribly vexed. The problem that he had seized upon had, in turn, taken firm hold of his imagination. Wheels were turning in his keen brain the way tumblers turn in a lock until they fall into place.

Holmes was attempting to manipulate the mechanism of the problem in an effort to coax the tumblers into their proper positions, thereby unlocking a solution. What he lacked was key facts. That was what vexed him.

"Do you imagine that Persano is dead?" I ventured to ask.

"What I imagine doesn't matter," snapped Holmes. "I must have reliable data to arrive at conclusions. Finding Persano, alive or dead, might uncover some aspects of the mystery, but I fear that it wouldn't reveal all. Particularly if the fellow is deceased."

An hour passed and Holmes appeared to have gotten nowhere with his thinking. "Perhaps," he said suddenly, "I have been barking up the wrong tree."

"What tree is that?"

"Kindly hand me down my index. The volume labeled '*T* .'"

Arising from my chair, I pull down the heavy thing. In this tome, Holmes had inscribed such facts and pasted clippings as he found interesting. It was a veritable repository of handy data, if inclined toward miscellany.

"It is a faint hope, given the number of entomologists presently pursuing their work," he said, "but perhaps I might narrow the field to one or two likely fellows."

Holmes applied himself to a thorough perusal of the book. He took no notes, but from time to time, his eyes took on a knowing gleam. By some means known only to him, he was weeding out the unlikely candidates, and presumably by a process of elimination, reducing the number of interesting parties to a manageable number.

"I have my man!" he suddenly exclaimed.

"I don't doubt it," I replied. "But however did you discover him?"

Closing the book and setting it aside, Holmes stood up and said briskly, "There's no time to discuss the matter. I must see Lestrade. Come with me if you wish, but I will not delay."

I flew to my hat and coat. Before many minutes had passed we were hailing down a passing four-wheeler and climbing aboard.

About him, Holmes had an aura that was almost electric. I had seen him go from torpid lethargy to frenetic action in the same manner many times before. Turning over a problem in his mind, he lounged supine, but once discovering an important clue, or grasping salient facts leading to a reliable conclusion, he sprang into action like a much younger man.

Inspector Lestrade was leaving the building for the evening when we pulled up. We were fortunate that we intercepted him before he was gone.

"Lestrade!" shouted Holmes, stepping to the curb. "I have news!"

Lestrade turned. Recognizing Holmes, he released his cab with a curt wave of dismissal.

"What have you found, Mr. Holmes?" he asked once we had joined him.

"I have the name of the woman with whom Colin Crosby was smitten. I believe that she will have much to tell us."

"You do, do you? What causes you to conclude that?"

"For one thing, her last name, which is Sanders. And for another, the occupation of her husband."

Lestrade's eyebrows shot up.

"You intrigue me, Holmes. Let us not delay by engaging in idle chit-chat."

And very quickly we were on our way. Our destination was Kensington, for Holmes gave the driver an address in that quarter.

"How go your own inquiries, Lestrade?" asked Holmes.

"I've talked with certain parties at Drummonds Bank. All spoke highly of Crosby. He had fallen ill some weeks back and had left his office early. I'm told that he was quite pale of complexion. His return has been expected on a nearly daily basis, yet the illness lingered. A physician had seen him, and prescribed iron pills for anemia, but they did no good."

"Any irregularities in the bank's books?"

"None has been discovered."

"I thought not. We can safely rule out that line of inquiry. This affair revolves around the fellow's personal life."

"Agreed," said Lestrade. "Now, pray tell me, Mr. Holmes. Where are we bound at this late hour?"

"To pay a call upon James Spencer, otherwise Lord Dunston."

I was aghast to hear that name. Lord Dunston was a man above reproach.

Lestrade was no less puzzled than I, for his voice had a noticeable quaver in it when he asked, "What is our interest in Lord Dunston?"

"First and foremost, the man is a helminthologist."

"I confess to being unfamiliar with the term," Lestrade stated.

"A helminthologist," said Holmes patiently, "is an entomologist who specializes in the study of worms – specifically ones of the parasitic variety, such as tapeworms and leeches."

"I see," said Lestrade deliberately. "I imagine few such men can be discovered in London."

"Or in the world, I suppose," remarked Holmes. "I was drawn to the man's name due to his verminous interests. When I learned that he had spent some time in Egypt, my ears perked up, as it were."

"Go on," said Lestrade as we rattled along. "I must know as much as you do ere we arrive. This is a delicate matter, as you are aware."

"More delicate than you can imagine," said Holmes. "The worm found in the intestinal tract of the late Colin Crosby isn't yet known to the world – or at least the world of natural science. But I'll wager it's something like the Guinea Worm of Africa in that it's a pest of tropical climates. I imagine that this unknown worm was brought to England by a party interested in studying it. Therefore, an entomologist. More specifically, a helminthologist, one who studies parasitic worms."

"I see, I see," murmured Lestrade. "Do you imagine that Lord Dunston was responsible for Crosby's unpleasant demise?"

511

"If not directly," said Holmes, "at least indirectly. But we will see what Lord Dunston has to say about it. Halloa! I see we have arrived."

Lestrade looked over, slightly startled. "Already? I would like to know more before we enter."

"As would I," replied Holmes. "But as matters stand, we must feel our way forward with care, for we wade through very turbid waters indeed. Let me suggest that we are merely consulting Lord Dunston in his capacity as a helminthologist. We shall accuse him of nothing."

"I'm satisfied with that," said Lestrade, disembarking. "Well, here we go. Let us all be on our best behaviors. Lord Dunston isn't a man to be trifled with."

As we rang the doorbell of Holmwood, the Dunston manor, we composed ourselves and donned our most grave expressions. A dour-faced butler opened the door and inquired after our business.

"Good evening. I am Inspector Lestrade of Scotland Yard. My associates are Sherlock Holmes and Dr. Watson, whose names might or might not be familiar to Lord Dunston. We are here on official business."

The butler let us in. We were escorted into a sumptuous drawing room. Lord Dunston shortly put in appearance.

He struck me at first glance as a rather Jupiterian figure. I judged him to be a year or two beyond the age of fifty, quite portly, bespectacled, and rather fussy in his mannerisms. His hands were never still.

Upon entering the room, Lord Dunston offered an agreeable enough smile, saying, "I'm pleased to make all of your acquaintances. But you must forgive me, as I cannot imagine why you are calling at such an hour."

Lestrade spoke first. "Kindly forgive us, my Lord. Mr. Holmes informs me that you are a helminthologist of some note. We are interested in your professional opinion."

Lord Dunston's subdued expression brightened and he waved us to comfortable chairs whilst he dismissed the butler.

"I'm pleased to be of service to Scotland Yard. Tell me, how may I assist?"

"If I may," inserted Holmes. "I have some knowledge in this area. Lord Dunston, you have been to Egypt in recent years."

The portly fellow all but shot out of his chair with excitement.

"Can you tell that just by glancing at me? By studying my attire? My mannerisms? I have read about your remarkable mental powers, Mr. Holmes. I beg of you tell me how you arrived at that startling deduction."

Holmes suppressed an amused smile. "By having read about you in the newspapers, your Grace."

Lord Dunston's glee dwindled. "Oh. Is it only that?"

512

The man settled back into his damask chair and, with a broad wave of one hand, invited Holmes to continue.

"You are familiar with the African Guinea Worm, no doubt. It has the unpleasant habit of borrowing under the skin of a human host."

"Yes, a persistent nematode of the genus *Dracunculus*. I have one in my collection. Alas, it is struggling in England's cooler climate."

"Tell me, Lord Dunston, have you ever heard of a tapeworm which feeds upon the blood of its host? I don't refer to the common blood fluke, but to a flatworm of the *Eucestoda* subclass."

I noticed that Lord Dunston turned a stark shade paler.

He hesitated before speaking. "I don't know how to respond to that, Mr. Holmes. Is this a deduction? A guess? Are you psychic?"

"It isn't a guess, nor am I psychic, to the best of my knowledge," replied Holmes smoothly. "I asked merely if you are familiar with such a creature."

"Then I must turn the tables upon you, my dear fellow. How is it you know of this parasite?"

"I would rather you respond to my question before I reply to yours," returned Holmes coolly. "If you aren't averse to doing so," he added.

"Averse, no. I hesitate because you were describing a flatworm I discovered in Cairo during my last trip to Egypt. I'm studying this species intently. I've been writing up my observations in the hope of publishing my findings. And further – that the worm might be named by myself, who is his discoverer. Unless – "

Lestrade asked quickly, "Unless? Please finish your thought, your Grace."

Composing himself, Lord Dunston said, "Unless I'm not, in fact, the discoverer of this worm. Oh, I hope I haven't been beaten out of the honor. You see, I've contributed little of significance to the study of worms. This would make my name in the field. Tell me, have I delayed too long in writing up my paper?"

"You may be assured that you have not," replied Holmes generously. "The worm in question remains obscure, if not unknown."

Lord Dunston clapped his pudgy hands together with barely restrained glee.

"Oh, I am so pleased to learn this. I had hoped to announce my discovery before this, but my uncle recently passed away, and I've been away in Kent, dealing with legal issues relating to his estate. In fact, I returned only yesterday, much to my wife's surprise."

Holmes said, "Yes, I recall reading about that. You stand come into quite a sum beyond your current station in life."

Lord Dunston waved away the suggestion, saying only, "A pile of gold on top of another pile of gold is still a pile of gold, only larger. At the moment, I'm more interested learning how you know of my worm. As far as I know, I am in possession of the only specimens outside of Egypt."

"Before I explain," said Holmes deferentially, "pray tell me: With whom else have you shared this knowledge?"

"Why, no one. I've been guarding it both zealously and jealously. As I said before, had it not been for my uncle's untimely passing, I would have long before this presented my paper to the *Proceedings of the Royal Society.*"

"I see," said Holmes. "That is unfortunate."

"Why is that, sir?"

"Because a living example of this worm was discovered in the gut of a man who died of severe blood loss only a few days ago. This leads us to wonder, if you are the only one in possession of scientific specimens, how the worm got into his body."

Lord Dunston gripped the right arm rest of his chair, first loosely and then with increasing tension. I noticed that his colorless eyes had become slightly glassy. From his expression, I imagine confusion with vying with suspicion in his mind.

"Who was the unfortunate fellow?"

"A banker named Colin Crosby," stated Inspector Lestrade. "Is that name familiar to you, Lord Dunston?"

"It is not. I've never heard of the fellow. Nor can I imagine how the unfortunate man came to ingest the larvae of *Draculunus egyptus,* as I propose to name the species."

Holmes said, "We suspect he consumed it unwittingly."

"That hardly illuminates the conundrum," said Lord Dunston, his voice was becoming agitated. Gaining control of himself, he added, "Until you gentleman called upon me, I had been absolutely certain that the only specimens of *Draculunus egyptus* outside of Egypt thrive in this house."

"This is awkward, Lord Dunston," said Inspector Lestrade. "We are inclined in the belief that Colin Crosby was fed the larva of the vampire worm in a meal, for the man had enemies."

"I trust you don't count me among them, for I don't know the fellow at all. His name means nothing to me. Nothing, I tell you."

"You must remain calm, Lord Dunston," said Holmes agreeably. "We're accusing you of nothing. We are only trying to understand how the tapeworm came to be in Colin Crosby's system."

"Well, I cannot imagine how," Lord Dunston exclaimed haplessly. "It is beyond me."

"Are you certain you told no one else?"

"I wouldn't want word to get out prematurely. It is of great moment to me."

"Not even your wife?" pressed Holmes.

"Well, of course my wife knows about *Draculunus egyptus*. I share all my research with her. She is, after all, my beloved spouse. But I swore her to secrecy."

Inspector Lestrade said gently, "Women have been known to betray confidences, often without meaning to. Perhaps we should speak with her."

Hesitation was written upon Lord Dunston's heavy features, but at last he rang the bell and the butler appeared.

"Please summon Lady Dunston. Inform her that we have illustrious guests."

When Lady Dunston arrived, I was struck by a mild shock. I expected a dowager, but instead I beheld a beauteous young woman easily twenty-five years Lord Dunston's junior with a crown of chestnut curls framing her oval features.

We all stood up at her entrance. Lord Dunston made proper introductions.

Whilst Lestrade was introduced, I noticed one corner of her red mouth quirk noticeably, but she mastered her expression quickly. When Holmes's name was spoken, it was if all the color had drained out of her body and flowed into the hardwood floor.

"I am undone!" she said breathily. With that, she fainted.

"Set her on the couch," said Holmes, "for we have struck a nerve."

The butler assisted Holmes and Lestrade. Lady Dunston was laid out on the couch, and smelling salts were produced. They had no immediate effect.

While I ministered to the poor woman, Holmes pressed Lord Dunston with further questions.

"Do you know a journalist named Isadora Persano?"

"I do not. The name means nothing to me. Why do you ask?"

"Isadora Persano was apparently an enemy of Colin Crosby, and he is missing."

His face reddening with frustration, Lord Dunston said, "I know nothing of him either! What does this have to do with me?"

"I'm inclined to believe very little," said Holmes. "But I can see that your wife may have known them both. When she recovers, with your forgiveness, we must ply her with necessary questions."

"I won't stand for it! Look at her! Why this uproar? What have you gentlemen dragged into my house? What has caused Evelyn to lose her senses as she has?"

"I must inform you now, Lord Dunston," Lestrade said firmly, "that I am conducting an investigation into a murder, and I cannot leave this house until I have receive satisfactory answers to official questions."

"But I have answered truthfully in every regard," snapped Lord Dunston.

"I was referring to your wife, your Grace." Turning to me, Lestrade asked, "Dr. Watson, how are you coming along?"

"I believe she is rousing from her fainting spell," I told him.

"Allow me, Inspector," said Holmes, looming over the woman.

"Lady Dunston, as you heard, I am Sherlock Holmes, and while I do not purport to know all, I believe that I have assembled in my mind many of the facts of your recent nefarious activities."

Lady Dunston batted her eyes, and said weakly, "I suppose you seek the remains of Isadora Persano."

"He is dead?"

"By now, he surely is."

"What is this!" cried Lord Dunston. The man was all but beside himself.

Ignoring the outburst, Holmes asked the woman, "Where can the body be found?"

"In the potting shed. You will find it in the north corner of the root cellar of this house."

All eyes went to Lord Dunston. His lips moved, but no words came forth. He was literally speechless. Every effort to form audible syllables appeared to fail.

"I have your wife's confession," said Lestrade gravely. "Now I am asking for your permission to search your cellar."

Stumbling over to his armchair, Lord Dunston collapsed into it. Waving his hand weakly, he mumbled, "If you must, you must . . . ."

The butler took us down into the commodious root cellar, and we picked our way to the north corner. It was in this very cellar that Lord Dunston kept his menagerie, if that is the proper word. There were worms squirming in great earth-filled clay tubs and bins. The noisome smell was something beyond unpleasant.

We went to the north corner, which was walled-off, the rude door padlocked. Sherlock Holmes handed the lantern to the nervous butler whilst he picked the lock with a steel tool he invariably carried. It soon surrendered to his expertise, and the door was thrown open. We all four leaned in to peer into the darkened cubicle. There we saw something that filled us with cold horror.

We expected to find a cold corpse. Instead, we discovered a man huddled in one corner, his back to the musty wall, clutching his stomach and staring at an open matchbox in the center of the earthen floor – a matchbox that contained a smaller specimen of the blood-drinking worm that had devoured Colin Crosby. Near it was an empty bowl.

"Are you Isadora Persano?" asked Holmes.

The man looked up. His face was a twisted caricature of humanity under an unkempt shock of hair. His eyes were alive, but I knew that his mind was gone.

"I had to eat what was in the bowl. I had no choice. There was no other food! I ate the horrible, wretched meal, and now it is inside me gnawing, gnawing . . . ."

Raising his filthy hands, Isadora Persano gave out a terrible shriek.

Stepping in, Holmes kicked the matchbox with its blood-red worm into a corner. Taking firm hold of the man, he dragged him out of his confinement.

"This man must go to a hospital at once. He may be saved. But if he is, I'm afraid it will be the asylum for him thereafter, for his mind has snapped. She shut him into this cubicle with the only meal infested with the larvae of the terrible worm. No doubt he held out as long as he could. No doubt also, she told him what his fate would be. How she accomplished this – well, she will have to tell us all. She will have no choice in the matter, either."

We all trudged upstairs to break the terrible news to Lord Dunston whilst Inspector Lestrade summoned a constable.

On the morning of the next day, after a fitful night sleep in which inchoate nightmares rose up from time to time, I joined Holmes and Lestrade in the latter's office.

Holmes gravely recounted his understanding of the case, which was now concluded with the arrest of Lady Dunston and the hospitalization of poor Isadora Persano.

"If I know women of Lady Dunston's stripe," Holmes were saying, "she will make a full confession in time. I'm afraid that her future is distressingly dark. But here is how I conceive events have run.

"You have all noted the marked difference in age between Lord Dunston and his wife. I imagine she became fatigued listening to his obsessions with unusual worms. They have been married some seven years, and she felt herself yet young whilst he crept steadily through middle age.

"Thinking to divorce him, she began casting about for a suitable future husband. Whether she encountered the banker Crosby first or the dashing duelist Persano is of no importance. She began to weave her wiles about them both, and in the course of events, one found out about the other.

Conceivably, she threw over Persano in favor of the banker. Bad blood resulted. Persano thought he could do away with his rival by means of an illegal duel, but Crosby was too wise to agree to such a meeting.

"All of these events appear to have taken place approximately six weeks ago. It was after that time that Lord Dunston's uncle died unexpectedly and he found himself immersed in legal issues – issues which will inevitably result in his inheritance being magnified considerably.

"All at once, Lady Dunston found her husband immensely more attractive than previously. Gold has that peculiar allure. With a swiftness typical of her sex, she abruptly reversed course, deciding to remain Lady Dunston until the inheritance was properly settled. Unfortunately for her, she was inconvenienced by not one, but two ardent suitors. Their hot pursuit threatened to reveal her indiscretions to Lord Dunston, and she knew she must take strong action or become divorced and penniless. I think we will discover that she goaded Isadora Persano into challenging Colin Crosby into a duel, thinking that one man would fall, leaving her with only one inconvenient suitor. But Crosby failed to take the bait. So she had to resort to other means to dispose of him. It would seem that she had aroused their passions so fiercely that neither man would easily withdraw from the rivalry."

"I imagine she arranged for a farewell meal for Crosby, contriving to insert one or more larvae into his meal, which he innocently consumed. After that, she counted on nature to taking her course. After waiting a suitable period of time, she paid Crosby a last visit, finding him in dire straits. By some artful means, she fixed the leech to his weakened body, and let nature bring about its grisly climax. Perhaps he agreed to her applying the leech, thinking she meant him well.

"That accomplished, during her husband's absence she lured Isadora Persano to her home and invited him into the root cellar, where she locked him away with the bowl containing a meagre meal contaminated with juvenile parasites.

"From what Persano revealed, she must have taunted him, informing him of what the meal contained, and telling him what his fate would be if he consumed it. She knew the man would either starve to death or succumb to hunger and eat that terrible last meal. She hadn't counted on was his ability to hold out as long as he did. Otherwise she would have removed Persano's remains before her husband's return. Nor did she imagine that the tapeworm would be discovered during Crosby's autopsy, thereby arousing suspicion. Finally, I have no doubt but that having twice perpetrated cold-blooded murder, Lady Dunston would have eventually gotten around to feeding her unsuspecting husband a cold dish of his own discovery, thereby freeing herself for all time of his tiresome company."

Lestrade wore a grey face when he said, "A terrible tale, Mr. Holmes. A ghastly chain of events. I have only to thank you for your insight. Otherwise these crimes would never have come to light."

Holmes noted with equal gravity. "It was a beastly foul scheme," he remarked. "All but incredible that it was hatched in the mind of a beautiful young woman. Yet the facts remain to stun our gentlemanly senses. Lady Dunston may well escape the gallows, but it wouldn't surprise me if she wound up in the same madhouse to which Isadora Persano has been consigned, now that the doctors have purged the odious worm from his body."

When I look at the three massive manuscript volumes which contain our work for the year 1894 I confess that it is very difficult for me, out of such a wealth of material, to select the cases which are most interesting in themselves and at the same time most conducive to a display of those peculiar powers for which my friend was famous. As I turn over the pages I see my notes upon the repulsive story of the red leech and the terrible death of Crosby the banker . . . .

– Dr. John H. Watson
"The Adventure of the Golden Pince-Nez

Somewhere in the vaults of the bank of Cox and Co., at Charing Cross, there is a travel-worn and battered tin dispatch-box with my name, John H. Watson, MD, Late Indian Army, *painted upon the lid. It is crammed with papers, nearly all of which are records of cases to illustrate the curious problems which Mr. Sherlock Holmes had at various times to examine. Some, and not the least interesting, were complete failures, and as such will hardly bear narrating, since no final explanation is forthcoming. A problem without a solution may interest the student, but can hardly fail to annoy the casual reader. Among these unfinished tales is that of . . . Isadora Persano, the well-known journalist and duellist, who was found stark staring mad with a matchbox in front of him which contained a remarkable worm, said to be unknown to science . . . .*

– Dr. John H. Watson
"The Problem of Thor Bridge"

Appendix:
The Untold Cases

The following has been assembled from several sources, including lists compiled by Phil Jones and Randall Stock, as well as some internet resources and my own research. I cannot promise that it's complete – some Untold Cases may be missing – after all, there's a great deal of Sherlockian Scholarship that involves interpretation and rationalizing – and there are some listed here that certain readers may believe shouldn't be listed at all.

As a fanatical supporter and collector of pastiches since I was a ten-year-old boy in 1975, reading Nicholas Meyer's *The Seven-Per-Cent Solution* and *The West End Horror* before I'd even read all of The Canon, I can attest that serious and legitimate versions of all of these Untold Cases exist out there – some of them occurring with much greater frequency than others – and I hope to collect, read, and chronologicize them all.

There's so much more to The Adventures of Sherlock Holmes than the pitifully few sixty stories that were fixed up by the First Literary Agent. I highly recommend that you find and read all of the rest of them as well, including those relating these Untold Cases. You won't regret it.

David Marcum

A Study in Scarlet

- Mr. Lestrade . . . got himself in a fog recently over a forgery case
- A young girl called, fashionably dressed
- A gray-headed, seedy visitor, looking like a Jew pedlar who appeared to be very much excited
- A slipshod elderly woman
- An old, white-haired gentleman had an interview
- A railway porter in his velveteen uniform

The Sign of Four

- The consultation last week by Francois le Villard
- The most winning woman Holmes ever knew was hanged for poisoning three little children for their insurance money

- The most repellent man of Holmes's acquaintance was a philanthropist who has spent nearly a quarter of a million upon the London poor
- Holmes once enabled Mrs. Cecil Forrester to unravel a little domestic complication. She was much impressed by his kindness and skill
- Holmes lectured the police on causes and inferences and effects in the Bishopgate jewel case

The Adventures of Sherlock Holmes

"A Scandal in Bohemia"
- The summons to Odessa in the case of the Trepoff murder
- The singular tragedy of the Atkinson brothers at Trincomalee
- The mission which Holmes had accomplished so delicately and successfully for the reigning family of Holland. (He also received a remarkably brilliant ring)
- The Darlington substitution scandal, and . . .
- The Arnsworth castle business. (When a woman thinks that her house is on fire, her instinct is at once to rush to the thing which she values most. It is a perfectly overpowering impulse, and Holmes has more than once taken advantage of it

"The Red-Headed League"
- The previous skirmishes with John Clay

"A Case of Identity"
- The Dundas separation case, where Holmes was engaged in clearing up some small points in connection with it. The husband was a teetotaler, there was no other woman, and the conduct complained of was that he had drifted into the habit of winding up every meal by taking out his false teeth and hurling them at his wife, which is not an action likely to occur to the imagination of the average story-teller.
- The rather intricate matter from Marseilles
- Mrs. Etherege, whose husband Holmes found so easy when the police and everyone had given him up for dead

"The Boscombe Valley Mystery"
    NONE LISTED

"The Five Orange Pips"
- The adventure of the Paradol Chamber
- The Amateur Mendicant Society, who held a luxurious club in the lower vault of a furniture warehouse
- The facts connected with the disappearance of the British barque *Sophy Anderson*
- The singular adventures of the Grice-Patersons in the island of Uffa
- The Camberwell poisoning case, in which, as may be remembered, Holmes was able, by winding up the dead man's watch, to prove that it had been wound up two hours before, and that therefore the deceased had gone to bed within that time – a deduction which was of the greatest importance in clearing up the case
- Holmes saved Major Prendergast in the Tankerville Club scandal. He was wrongfully accused of cheating at cards
- Holmes has been beaten four times – three times by men and once by a woman

"The Man with the Twisted Lip"
- The rascally Lascar who runs The Bar of Gold in Upper Swandam Lane has sworn to have vengeance upon Holmes

"The Adventure of the Blue Carbuncle"
NONE LISTED

"The Adventure of the Speckled Band"
- Mrs. Farintosh and an opal tiara. (It was before Watson's time)

"The Adventure of the Engineer's Thumb"
- Colonel Warburton's madness

"The Adventure of the Noble Bachelor"
- The letter from a fishmonger
- The letter a tide-waiter
- The service for Lord Backwater
- The little problem of the Grosvenor Square furniture van
- The service for the King of Scandinavia

"The Adventure of the Beryl Coronet"

NONE LISTED

"The Adventure of the Copper Beeches"
  NONE LISTED

The Memoirs of Sherlock Holmes

"Silver Blaze"
  NONE LISTED

"The Cardboard Box"
- Aldridge, who helped in the bogus laundry affair

"The Yellow Face"
- The (First) Adventure of the Second Stain was a failure which present[s] the strongest features of interest

'The Stockbroker's Clerk"
  NONE LISTED

"The "Gloria Scott"
  NONE LISTED

"The Musgrave Ritual"
- The Tarleton murders
- The case of Vamberry, the wine merchant
- The adventure of the old Russian woman
- The singular affair of the aluminum crutch
- A full account of Ricoletti of the club foot and his abominable wife
- The two cases before the Musgrave Ritual from Holmes's fellow students

"The Reigate Squires"
- The whole question of the Netherland-Sumatra Company and of the colossal schemes of Baron Maupertuis

The Crooked Man"
  NONE LISTED

The Resident Patient"

- [Catalepsy] is a very easy complaint to imitate. Holmes has done it himself.

"The Greek Interpreter"
- Mycroft expected to see Holmes round last week to consult me over that Manor House case. It was Adams, of course
- Some of Holmes's most interesting cases have come to him through Mycroft

"The Naval Treaty"
- The (Second) adventure of the Second Stain, which dealt with interest of such importance and implicated so many of the first families in the kingdom that for many years it would be impossible to make it public. No case, however, in which Holmes was engaged had ever illustrated the value of his analytical methods so clearly or had impressed those who were associated with him so deeply. Watson still retained an almost verbatim report of the interview in which Holmes demonstrated the true facts of the case to Monsieur Dubugue of the Paris police, and Fritz von Waldbaum, the well-known specialist of Dantzig, both of whom had wasted their energies upon what proved to be side-issues. The new century will have come, however, before the story could be safely told.
- The Adventure of the Tired Captain
- A very commonplace little murder. If it [this paper] turns red, it means a man's life . . . .

"The Final Problem"
- The engagement for the French Government upon a matter of supreme importance
- The assistance to the Royal Family of Scandinavia

The Return of Sherlock Holmes

"The Adventure of the Empty House"
- Holmes traveled for two years in Tibet (as) a Norwegian named Sigerson, amusing himself by visiting Lhassa [*sic*] and spending some days with the head Llama [*sic*]
- Holmes traveled in Persia
- . . . looked in at Mecca . . .

527

- . . . and paid a short but interesting visit to the Khalifa at Khartoum
- Returning to France, Holmes spent some months in a research into the coal-tar derivatives, which he conducted in a laboratory at Montpelier [*sic*], in the South of France
- Mathews, who knocked out Holmes's left canine in the waiting room at Charing Cross
- The death of Mrs. Stewart, of Lauder, in 1887
- Morgan the poisoner
- Merridew of abominable memory
- The Molesey Mystery (Inspector Lestrade's Case. He handled it fairly well.)

"The Adventure of the Norwood Builder"
- The case of the papers of ex-President Murillo
- The shocking affair of the Dutch steamship, *Friesland*, which so nearly cost both Holmes and Watson their lives
- That terrible murderer, Bert Stevens, who wanted Holmes and Watson to get him off in '87

"The Adventure of the Dancing Men"
NONE LISTED

"The Adventure of the Solitary Cyclist"
- The peculiar persecution of John Vincent Harden, the well-known tobacco millionaire
- It was near Farnham that Holmes and Watson took Archie Stamford, the forger

"The Adventure of the Priory School"
- Holmes was retained in the case of the Ferrers Documents
- The Abergavenny murder, which is coming up for trial

"The Adventure of Black Peter"
- The sudden death of Cardinal Tosca – an inquiry which was carried out by him at the express desire of His Holiness the Pope
- The arrest of Wilson, the notorious canary-trainer, which removed a plague-spot from the East-End of London.

"The Adventure of Charles Augustus Milverton"

"The Adventure of the Six Napoleons"
- The dreadful business of the Abernetty family, which was first brought to Holmes's attention by the depth which the parsley had sunk into the butter upon a hot day
- The Conk-Singleton forgery case
- Holmes was consulted upon the case of the disappearance of the black pearl of the Borgias, but was unable to throw any light upon it

"The Adventure of the Three Students"
- Some laborious researches in Early English charters

"The Adventure of the Golden Pince-Nez"
- The repulsive story of the red leech
- . . . and the terrible death of Crosby, the banker
- The Addleton tragedy
- . . . and the singular contents of the ancient British barrow
- The famous Smith-Mortimer succession case
- The tracking and arrest of Huret, the boulevard assassin

"The Adventure of the Missing Three-Quarter"
- Henry Staunton, whom Holmes helped to hang
- Arthur H. Staunton, the rising young forger

"The Adventure of the Abbey Grange"
- Hopkins called Holmes in seven times, and on each occasion his summons was entirely justified

"The Adventure of the Second Stain"
- The woman at Margate. No powder on her nose – that proved to be the correct solution. How can one build on such a quicksand? A woman's most trivial action may mean volumes, or their most extraordinary conduct may depend upon a hairpin or a curling-tong

The Hound of the Baskervilles

- That little affair of the Vatican cameos, in which Holmes obliged the Pope

- The little case in which Holmes had the good fortune to help Messenger Manager Wilson
- One of the most revered names in England is being besmirched by a blackmailer, and only Holmes can stop a disastrous scandal
- The atrocious conduct of Colonel Upwood in connection with the famous card scandal at the Nonpareil Club
- Holmes defended the unfortunate Mme. Montpensier from the charge of murder that hung over her in connection with the death of her stepdaughter Mlle. Carere, the young lady who, as it will be remembered, was found six months later alive and married in New York

The Valley of Fear

- Twice already Holmes had helped Inspector Macdonald

His Last Bow

"The Adventure of Wisteria Lodge"
- The locking-up Colonel Carruthers

"The Adventure of the Red Circle"
- The affair last year for Mr. Fairdale Hobbs
- The Long Island cave mystery

"The Adventure of the Bruce-Partington Plans"
- Brooks . . .
- . . . or Woodhouse, or any of the fifty men who have good reason for taking Holmes's life

"The Adventure of the Dying Detective"
   NONE LISTED

"The Disappearance of Lady Frances Carfax"
- Holmes cannot possibly leave London while old Abrahams is in such mortal terror of his life

"The Adventure of the Devil's Foot"

- Holmes's dramatic introduction to Dr. Moore Agar, of Harley Street

"His Last Bow"
- Holmes started his pilgrimage at Chicago . . .
- . . . graduated in an Irish secret society at Buffalo
- . . . gave serious trouble to the constabulary at Skibbareen
- Holmes saves Count Von und Zu Grafenstein from murder by the Nihilist Klopman

The Case-Book of Sherlock Holmes

"The Adventure of the Illustrious Client"
- Negotiations with Sir George Lewis over the Hammerford Will case

"The Adventure of the Blanched Soldier"
- The Abbey School in which the Duke of Greyminster was so deeply involved
- The commission from the Sultan of Turkey which required immediate action
- The professional service for Sir James Saunders

"The Adventure of the Mazarin Stone"
- Old Baron Dowson said the night before he was hanged that in Holmes's case what the law had gained the stage had lost
- The death of old Mrs. Harold, who left Count Sylvius the Blymer estate
- The compete life history of Miss Minnie Warrender
- The robbery in the train de-luxe to the Riviera on February 13, 1892

"The Adventure of the Three Gables"
- The killing of young Perkins outside the Holborn Bar
- Mortimer Maberly, was one of Holmes's early clients

"The Adventure of the Sussex Vampire"
- *Matilda Briggs*, a ship which is associated with the giant rat of Sumatra, a story for which the world is not yet prepared
- Victor Lynch, the forger
- Venomous lizard, or Gila. Remarkable case, that!

- Vittoria the circus belle
- Vanderbilt and the Yeggman
- Vigor, the Hammersmith wonder

"The Adventure of the Three Garridebs"
- Holmes refused a knighthood for services which may, someday, be described

"The Problem of Thor Bridge"
- Mr. James Phillimore who, stepping back into his own house to get his umbrella, was never more seen in this world
- The cutter *Alicia*, which sailed one spring morning into a patch of mist from where she never again emerged, nor was anything further ever heard of herself and her crew.
- Isadora Persano, the well-known journalist and duelist who was found stark staring mad with a match box in front of him which contained a remarkable worm said to be unknown to science

"The Adventure of the Creeping Man"
NONE LISTED

"The Adventure of the Lion's Mane"
NONE LISTED

"The Adventure of the Veiled Lodger"
- The whole story concerning the politician, the lighthouse, and the trained cormorant

"The Adventure of Shoscombe Old Place"
- Holmes ran down that coiner by the zinc and copper filings in the seam of his cuff
- The St. Pancras case, where a cap was found beside the dead policeman. Merivale of the Yard, asked Holmes to look into it

"The Adventure of the Retired Colourman"
- The case of the two Coptic Patriarchs

About the Contributors

The following contributors appear in this volume:
The MX Book of New Sherlock Holmes Stories
Part XXIII – Some More Untold Cases (1888-1894)

Hugh Ashton was born in the U.K., and moved to Japan in 1988, where he remained until 2016, living with his wife Yoshiko in the historic city of Kamakura, a little to the south of Yokohama. He and Yoshiko have now moved to Lichfield, a small cathedral city in the Midlands of the U.K., the birthplace of Samuel Johnson, and one-time home of Erasmus Darwin. In the past, he has worked in the technology and financial services industries, which have provided him with material for some of his books set in the 21st century. He currently works as a writer: Novelist, freelance editor, and copywriter, (his work for large Japanese corporations has appeared in international business journals), and journalist, as well as producing industry reports on various aspects of the financial services industry. However, his lifelong interest in Sherlock Holmes has developed into an acclaimed series of adventures featuring the world's most famous detective, written in the style of the originals. In addition to these, he has also published historical and alternate historical novels, short stories, and thrillers. Together with artist Andy Boerger, he has produced the *Sherlock Ferret* series of stories for children, featuring the world's cutest detective.

Brian Belanger is a publisher and editor, but is best known for his freelance illustration and cover design work. His distinctive style can be seen on several MX Publishing covers, including *Silent Meridian* by Elizabeth Crowen, *Sherlock Holmes and the Menacing Melbournian* by Allan Mitchell, *Sherlock Holmes and A Quantity of Debt* by David Marcum, *Welcome to Undershaw* by Luke Benjamen Kuhns, and many more. Brian is the co-founder of Belanger Books LLC, where he illustrates the popular *MacDougall Twins with Sherlock Holmes* young reader series (#1 bestsellers on Amazon.com UK). A prolific creator, he also designs t-shirts, mugs, stickers, and other merchandise on his personal art site: *www.redbubble.com/people/zhahadun*.

Leverett Butts teaches composition and literature at the University of North Georgia. His poetry and fiction have appeared in *Eclectic* and *The Georgia State University Review*. He is the recipient of several fiction prizes offered by the University of West Georgia and TAG Publishing. His first collection of short fiction, *Emily's Stitches: The Confessions of Thomas Calloway and Other Stories*, was nominated for the 2013 Georgia Author of the Year Award in Short Fiction. The collection of the first two volumes of his *Guns of the Waste Land* was nominated in 2016, and the third volume of the series won honorable mention in the 2018 Georgia Independent Author of the Year Award in historical fiction. He recently completed the fourth and final volume, *Desinence*. He lives in Carrollton, Georgia, with his wife, son, their Jack Russell terrier, and an antisocial cat.

Mike Chinn lives in Birmingham UK with his wife Caroline and their guinea pigs. He has published over sixty short stories, some of which have found their way into two collections: *Give Me These Moments Back* (The Alchemy Press, 2015) and *Radix Omnium Malum* (Parallel Universe Publications, 2017). He has edited three volumes of *The Alchemy Press Book of Pulp Heroes* (2012, 2013 and 2014) and *Swords Against the Millenium* (2000) for The Alchemy Press. The first publication of his Damian Paladin collection, *The Paladin Mandates* (The Alchemy Press, 1998), was short-listed for the British Fantasy Award in

1999, and a second Paladin collection, *Walkers in Shadow*, was published by Pro Se Publications in 2017 (who are due to republish an expanded and revised edition of *The Paladin Mandates* in 2020). He sent Sherlock Holmes to the Moon in *Vallis Timoris* (Fringeworks, 2015), and in 2018 Pro Se published his first Western: *Revenge is a Cold Pistol.*

Barry Clay is a graduate of Shippensburg University with a BA in English. He's dug ditches, stocked grocery shelves, tutored for room and board, cleaned restrooms, mopped floors, taught cartooning, worked in a bank, asked if you'd like fries with that (and cooked the fries to boot), ordered carpet for cars, and worked commission sales at Sears. Currently, he is a thirty-two year veteran of the Federal employee workforce. He has been writing all his life in different genres, and he has written thirteen books ranging from Christian theology, anthologies, speculative fiction, horror, science fiction, and humor. His Sherlockian volumes include *The Darkened Village* and *The Leveson-Gower Theft.* He volunteers as conductor of a local student orchestra and has been commissioned to write music. His first two musicals were locally produced. He is the husband of one wife, father of four children, and "Opa" to one granddaughter. He is honored to have been asked to contribute to this collection.

Sir Arthur Conan Doyle (1859-1930) *Holmes Chronicler Emeritus.* If not for him, this anthology would not exist. Author, physician, patriot, sportsman, spiritualist, husband and father, and advocate for the oppressed. He is remembered and honored for the purposes of this collection by being the man who introduced Sherlock Holmes to the world. Through fifty-six Holmes short stories, four novels, and additional Apocryphal entries, Doyle revolutionized mystery stories and also greatly influenced and improved police forensic methods and techniques for the betterment of all. *Steel True Blade Straight.*

Steve Emecz's main field is technology, in which he has been working for about twenty years. Steve is a regular trade show speaker on the subject of eCommerce, and his tech career has taken him to more than fifty countries – so he's no stranger to planes and airports. He wrote two novels (one a bestseller) in the 1990's, and a screenplay in 2001. Shortly after, he set up MX Publishing, specialising in NLP books. In 2008, MX published its first Sherlock Holmes book, and MX has gone on to become the largest specialist Holmes publisher in the world. MX is a social enterprise and supports three main causes. The first is Happy Life, a children's rescue project in Nairobi, Kenya, where he and his wife, Sharon, spend every Christmas at the rescue centre in Kasarani. In 2014, they wrote a short book about the project, *The Happy Life Story.* The second is the Stepping Stones School, of which Steve is a patron. Stepping Stones is located at Undershaw, Sir Arthur Conan Doyle's former home. Steve has been a mentor for the World Food Programme for the last several years, supporting their innovation bootcamps and giving 1-2-1 mentoring to several projects.

Matthew J. Elliott is the author of *Big Trouble in Mother Russia* (2016), the official sequel to the cult movie *Big Trouble in Little China, Lost in Time and Space: An Unofficial Guide to the Uncharted Journeys of Doctor Who* (2014), *Sherlock Holmes on the Air* (2012), *Sherlock Holmes in Pursuit* (2013), *The Immortals: An Unauthorized Guide to* Sherlock *and* Elementary (2013), and *The Throne Eternal* (2014). His articles, fiction, and reviews have appeared in the magazines *Scarlet Street, Total DVD, SHERLOCK,* and *Sherlock Holmes Mystery Magazine,* and the collections *The Game's Afoot, Curious Incidents 2, Gaslight Grimoire, The Mammoth Book of Best British Crime 8,* and *The MX Book of New Sherlock Holmes Stories – Part III: 1896-1929.* He has scripted over 260 radio plays, including episodes of *Doctor Who*, *The Further Adventures of Sherlock Holmes*, *The Twilight Zone*, *The New Adventures of Mickey Spillane's Mike Hammer*, *Fangoria's Dreadtime Stories*, and award-winning adaptations of *The Hound of the Baskervilles* and *The War of the Worlds*. He is the only radio dramatist to adapt all sixty original stories from The Canon for the series *The Classic Adventures of Sherlock Holmes*. Matthew is a writer and performer on *RiffTrax.com*, the online comedy experience from the creators of cult sci-fi TV series *Mystery Science Theater 3000* (*MST3K* to the initiated). He's also written a few comic books.

Mark A. Gagen BSI is co-founder of Wessex Press, sponsor of the popular *From Gillette to Brett* conferences, and publisher of *The Sherlock Holmes Reference Library* and many other fine Sherlockian titles. A life-long Holmes enthusiast, he is a member of *The Baker Street Irregulars* and *The Illustrious Clients of Indianapolis*. A graphic artist by profession, his work is often seen on the covers of *The Baker Street Journal* and various BSI books.

Tim Gambrell lives in Exeter, Devon, with his wife, two young sons, three cats, and now only four chickens. He has previously contributed stories to *The MX Book of New Sherlock Holmes Stories*, and also to *Sherlock Holmes and Dr Watson: The Early Adventures* and *Sherlock Holmes and The Occult Detectives*, also from Belanger Books. Outside of the world of Holmes, Tim has written extensively for Doctor Who spin-off ranges. His books include two linked novels from Candy Jar Books: *Lethbridge-Stewart: The Laughing Gnome – Lucy Wilson & The Bledoe Cadets*, and *The Lucy Wilson Mysteries: The Brigadier and The Bledoe Cadets* (both 2019), and *Lethbridge-Stewart: Bloodlines – An Ordinary Man* (Candy Jar, 2020, written with Andy Frankham-Allen). He's also written a novella, *The Way of The Bry'hunee* (2019) for the Erimem range from Thebes Publishing. Tim's short fiction includes stories in *Lethbridge-Stewart: The HAVOC Files 3* (Candy Jar, 2017, revised edition 2020), *Bernice Summerfield: True Stories* (Big Finish, 2017) and *Relics . . . An Anthology* (Red Ted Books, 2018), plus a number of charity anthologies.

Paul D. Gilbert was born in 1954 and has lived in and around London all of his life. His wife Jackie is a Holmes expert who keeps him on the straight and narrow! He has two sons, one of whom now lives in Spain. His interests include literature, ancient history, all religions, most sports, and movies. He is currently employed full-time as a funeral director. His books so far include *The Lost Files of Sherlock Holmes* (2007), *The Chronicles of Sherlock Holmes* (2008), *Sherlock Holmes and the Giant Rat of Sumatra* (2010), *The Annals of Sherlock Holmes* (2012), *Sherlock Holmes and the Unholy Trinity* (2015), *Sherlock Holmes: The Four Handed Game* (2017), and *The Illumination of Sherlock Holmes* (2019).

John Atkinson Grimshaw (1836-1893) was born in Leeds, England. His amazing paintings, usually featuring twilight or night scenes illuminated by gas-lamps or moonlight, are easily recognizable, and are often used on the covers of books about The Great Detective to set the mood, as shadowy figures move in the distance through misty mysterious settings and over rain-slicked streets.

Arthur Hall was born in Aston, Birmingham, UK, in 1944. He discovered his interest in writing during his schooldays, along with a love of fictional adventure and suspense. His first novel, *Sole Contact*, was an espionage story about an ultra-secret government department known as "Sector Three", and was followed, to date, by three sequels. Other works include five Sherlock Holmes novels, *The Demon of the Dusk*, *The One Hundred Percent Society*, *The Secret Assassin*, *The Phantom Killer*, and *In Pursuit of the Dead*, as

535

well as a collection of short stories, and a modern detective novel. He lives in the West Midlands, United Kingdom.

Paul Hiscock is an author of crime, fantasy, and science fiction tales. His short stories have appeared in several anthologies and include a seventeenth century whodunnit, a science fiction western, and a steampunk Sherlock Holmes story. Paul lives with his family in Kent, England, and spends his days chasing a toddler with more energy than the Duracell Bunny. He mainly does his writing in coffee shops with members of the local NaNoWriMo group, or in the middle of the night when his family has gone to sleep. Consequently, his stories tend to be fuelled by large amounts of black coffee. You can find out more about his writing at *www.detectivesanddragons.uk.*

In the year 1998 **Craig Janacek** took his degree of Doctor of Medicine at Vanderbilt University, and proceeded to Stanford to go through the training prescribed for pediatricians in practice. Having completed his studies there, he was duly attached to the University of California, San Francisco as Associate Professor. The author of over seventy medical monographs upon a variety of obscure lesions, his travel-worn and battered tin dispatch-box is crammed with papers, nearly all of which are records of his fictional works. To date, these have been published solely in electronic format, including two non-Holmes novels (*The Oxford Deception* and *The Anger of Achilles Peterson*), the trio of holiday adventures collected as *The Midwinter Mysteries of Sherlock Holmes*, the Holmes story collections *The First of Criminals, The Assassination of Sherlock Holmes, The Treasury of Sherlock Holmes, Light in the Darkness, The Gathering Gloom, The Travels of Sherlock Holmes*, and the Watsonian novels *The Isle of Devils* and *The Gate of Gold*. Craig Janacek is a *nom de plume.*

Steven Philip Jones has written over sixty graphic novels and comic books including the horror series *Lovecraftian, Curious Cases of Sherlock Holmes*, the original series *Nightlinger, Street Heroes 2005*, adaptations of *Dracula*, several H. P. Lovecraft stories, and the 1985 film *Re-animator*. Steven is also the author of several novels and nonfiction books including *The Clive Cussler Adventures: A Critical Review, Comics Writing: Communicating With Comic Book , King of Harlem, Bushwackers, The House With the Witch's Hat, Talisman: The Knightmare Knife*, and *Henrietta Hex: Shadows From the Past.* Steven's other writing credits include a number of scripts for radio dramas that have been broadcast internationally. A graduate of the University of Iowa, Steven has a Bachelor of Arts in Journalism and Religion, and was accepted into Iowa's Writer's Workshop – M.F.A. program.

Roger Johnson BSI, ASH is a retired librarian, now working as a volunteer assistant at the Essex Police Museum. In his spare time, he is commissioning editor of *The Sherlock Holmes Journal*, an occasional lecturer, and a frequent contributor to *The Writings about the Writings*. His sole work of Holmesian pastiche was published in 1997 in Mike Ashley's anthology *The Mammoth Book of New Sherlock Holmes Adventures*, and he has the greatest respect for the many authors who have contributed new tales to the present mighty trilogy. Like his wife, Jean Upton, he is a member of both *The Baker Street Irregulars* and *The Adventuresses of Sherlock Holmes.*

David Marcum plays *The Game* with deadly seriousness. He first discovered Sherlock Holmes in 1975 at the age of ten, and since that time, he has collected, read, and chronologicized literally thousands of traditional Holmes pastiches in the form of novels, short stories, radio and television episodes, movies and scripts, comics, fan-fiction, and unpublished manuscripts. He is the author of over sixty Sherlockian pastiches, some published in anthologies and magazines such as *The Strand*, and others collected in his own books, *The Papers of Sherlock Holmes*, *Sherlock Holmes and A Quantity of Debt*, and *Sherlock Holmes – Tangled Skeins*. He has edited fifty books, including several dozen traditional Sherlockian anthologies, such as the ongoing series *The MX Book of New Sherlock Holmes Stories*, which he created in 2015. This collection is now up to 24 volumes, with more in preparation. He was responsible for bringing back August Derleth's Solar Pons for a new generation, first with his collection of authorized Pons stories, *The Papers of Solar Pons*, and then by editing the reissued authorized versions of the original Pons books, and then volumes of new Pons adventures. He is now doing the same for the adventures of Dr. Thorndyke. He has contributed numerous essays to various publications, and is a member of a number of Sherlockian groups and Scions. He is a licensed Civil Engineer, living in Tennessee with his wife and son. His irregular Sherlockian blog, *A Seventeen Step Program*, addresses various topics related to his favorite book friends (as his son used to call them when he was small), and can be found at *http://17stepprogram.blogspot.com/* Since the age of nineteen, he has worn a deerstalker as his regular-and-only hat. In 2013, he and his deerstalker were finally able make his first trip-of-a-lifetime Holmes Pilgrimage to England, with return Pilgrimages in 2015 and 2016, where you may have spotted him. If you ever run into him and his deerstalker out and about, feel free to say hello!

Will Murray has been writing about popular culture since 1973, principally on the subjects of comic books, pulp magazine heroes, and film. As a fiction writer, he's the author of over 70 novels featuring characters as diverse as Nick Fury and Remo Williams. With the late Steve Ditko, he created the Unbeatable Squirrel Girl for Marvel Comics. Murray has written numerous short stories, many on Lovecraftian themes. Currently, he writes The Wild Adventures of Doc Savage for Altus Press. His acclaimed Doc Savage novel, *Skull Island*, pits the pioneer superhero against the legendary King Kong. This was followed by *King Kong vs. Tarzan* and two Doc Savage novels guest-starring The Shadow. *Tarzan, Conqueror of Mars*, a crossover with John Carter of Mars, was just published. *www.adventuresinbronze.com* is his website.

Sidney Paget (1860-1908), a few of whose illustrations are used within this anthology, was born in London, and like his two older brothers, became a famed illustrator and painter. He completed over three-hundred-and-fifty drawings for the Sherlock Holmes stories that were first published in *The Strand* magazine, defining Holmes's image forever after in the public mind.

Otto Penzler, proprietor of The Mysterious Bookshop in New York City, founded The Mysterious Press in 1975, and publishes e-books through *MysteriousPress.com*. Penzler has won two Edgar Awards, *The Mystery Writers of America*'s Ellery Queen Award, and The Raven. He has been given Lifetime Achievement awards by Noircon and *The Strand Magazine*. He founded two new publishing companies in 2018, Penzler Publishers, reissuing American Mystery Classics in hardcover and trade paperback, and Scarlet, which publishes original psychological suspense novels. He has edited more than sixty anthologies.

Tracy J. Revels, a Sherlockian from the age of eleven, is a professor of history at Wofford College in Spartanburg, South Carolina. She is a member of *The Survivors of the Gloria Scott* and *The Studious Scarlets Society*, and is a past recipient of the Beacon Society Award. Almost every semester, she teaches a class that covers The Canon, either to college

537

students or to senior citizens. She is also the author of three supernatural Sherlockian pastiches with MX (*Shadowfall*, *Shadowblood*, and *Shadowwraith*), and a regular contributor to her scion's newsletter. She also has some notoriety as an author of very silly skits: For proof, see "The Adventure of the Adversarial Adventuress" and "Occupy Baker Street" on YouTube. When not studying Sherlock, she can be found researching the history of her native state, and has written books on Florida in the Civil War and on the development of Florida's tourism industry.

Jane Rubino is the author of *A Jersey Shore* mystery series, featuring a Jane Austen-loving amateur sleuth and a Sherlock Holmes-quoting detective, *Knight Errant, Lady Vernon and Her Daughter,* (a novel-length adaptation of Jane Austen's novella *Lady Susan,* co-authored with her daughter Caitlen Rubino-Bradway, *What Would Austen Do?,* also co-authored with her daughter, a short story in the anthology *Jane Austen Made Me Do It, The Rucastles' Pawn, The Copper Beeches from Violet Turner's POV,* and, of course, there's the Sherlockian novel in the drawer – who doesn't have one? Jane lives on a barrier island at the New Jersey shore.

Jacqueline Silver is the newly-appointed Headteacher of Stepping Stones School. She has developed her career from her early days as an accomplished Drama teacher and has a strong background in school leadership. She has always had a passion for creating nurturing and positive school environments for mixed ability children. Her recent career history has seen her spearhead pastoral care provision at a number of schools where she has also been resolute in her vision for safeguarding, particularly of the most vulnerable children in our society. Since her recent appointment as Headteacher of Stepping Stones School, she can realise her prime personal focus for improving the employability of young people with learning needs. Quality of life, independence, and positive engagement with society are linchpins of Jacqueline's vision for the future. Stepping Stones will flourish under her leadership.

Shane Simmons is the author of the occult detective novels *Necropolis* and *Epitaph,* and the crime collection *Raw and Other Stories.* An award-winning screenwriter and graphic novelist, his work has appeared in international film festivals, museums, and lectures about design and structure. He was born in Lachine, a suburb of Montreal best known for being massacred in 1689 and having a joke name. Visit Shane's homepage at *eyestrainproductions.com* for more.

Dacre Stoker is the great-grand-nephew of Bram Stoker, and the international best-selling co-author of *Dracula the Un-Dead* (Dutton, 2009), and *Dracul* (Putnam 2018). Dacre is also the co-editor (with Elizabeth Miller) of *The Lost Journal of Bram Stoker: The Dublin Years* (Robson Press, 2012). A native of Montreal, Canada, Dacre taught Physical Education and Sciences for twenty-two years, in both Canada and the U.S. He has participated in the sport of Modern Pentathlon as an athlete and a coach at the international and Olympic levels for Canada for twelve years. He currently lives in Aiken, SC, and together with his wife Jenne, they manage The Bram Stoker Estate.

Jan van Koningsveld was born in Emden, Germany, having both the German and the Dutch citizenship. He has been a fan of Sherlock Holmes and Dr. Watson since 1982, when a TV series starring Geoffrey Whitehead and Donald Pickering was aired in Germany. The first Holmes story that he read was *A Study in Scarlet.* In his study, he has a library containing more than 1,000 books regarding Sherlock Holmes, and he is a collector of different versions of *The Hound of the Baskervilles* in different languages. He is married and father of three children, works as an account and instructor, and is the author of the books *The Mental Calculator's Handbook* (with Dr. Robert Fountain) and *Become a Human Calendar in just 7 Days*. He is the organizer of multiple events regarding Mental Calculation (such as the World Championships for students), and also a tutor for workshops, all non-profit. HE is the creator and maintainer of the Pi World Ranking List (since 2001) *www-pi-world-ranking-list.com* and the holder of more than twenty world records in Mental Calculation, a 4-time World Cup winner, and a 2-time Memoriad winner. He is a consultant for German TV shows regarding math, and has made several appearances on German and Dutch TV shows. His German website is: *www.janvankoningsveld.com*

Margaret Walsh was born Auckland, New Zealand and now lives in Melbourne, Australia. She is the author of *Sherlock Holmes and the Molly-Boy Murders*, *Sherlock Holmes and the Case of the Perplexed Politician*, and *Sherlock Holmes and the Case of the London Dock Deaths*, all published by MX Publishing. Margaret has been a devotee of Sherlock Holmes since childhood and has had several Holmesian related essays printed in anthologies, and is a member of the online society *Doyle's Rotary Coffin*. She has an ongoing love affair with the city of London. When she's not working or planning trips to London. Margaret can be found frequenting the many and varied bookshops of Melbourne.

I.A. Watson is a novelist and jobbing writer from Yorkshire who cut his teeth on writing Sherlock Holmes stories and has even won an award for one. His works include *Holmes and Houdini*, *Labours of Hercules*, *St. George and the Dragon* Volumes 1 and 2, *Women of Myth*, and the non-fiction essay book *Where Stories Dwell*. He pens short detective stories as a means of avoiding writing things that pay better. A full list of his many works published works appears at:
http://www.chillwater.org.uk/writing/iawatsonhome.htm

Marcia Wilson is a freelance researcher and illustrator who likes to work in a style compatible for the color blind and visually impaired. She is Canon-centric, and her first MX offering, *You Buy Bones*, uses the point-of-view of Scotland Yard to show the unique talents of Dr. Watson. This continued with the publication of *Test of the Professionals: The Adventure of the Flying Blue Pidgeon* and *The Peaceful Night Poisonings*. She can be contacted at: *gravelgirty.deviantart.com*

The MX Book of New Sherlock Holmes Stories

Part XXII – Some More Untold Cases (1877-1887)
and
Part XXIV – Some More Untold Cases (1895-1903)

Ian Ableson is an ecologist by training and a writer by choice. When not reading or writing, he can reliably be found scowling at a clipboard while ankle-deep in a marsh somewhere in Michigan. His love for the stories of Arthur Conan Doyle started when his grandfather gave him a copy of *The Original Illustrated Sherlock Holmes* when he was in high school, and he's proud to have been able to contribute to the continuation of the tales of Sherlock Holmes and Dr. Watson.

Derrick Belanger is an educator and also the author of the #1 bestselling book in its category, *Sherlock Holmes: The Adventure of the Peculiar Provenance*, which was in the top 200 bestselling books on Amazon. He also is the author of *The MacDougall Twins with Sherlock Holmes* books, and he edited the Sir Arthur Conan Doyle horror anthology *A Study in Terror: Sir Arthur Conan Doyle's Revolutionary Stories of Fear and the Supernatural*. Mr. Belanger co-owns the publishing company Belanger Books, which has released numerous Sherlock Holmes anthologies including *Beyond Watson, Holmes Away From Home: Adventures from the Great Hiatus, Sherlock Holmes: Before Baker Street, Sherlock Holmes: Adventures in the Realms of H.G. Wells, Sherlock Holmes and the Occult Detectives, Sherlock Holmes and the Great Detectives*, and *Beyond the Adventures of Sherlock Holmes*. Derrick resides in Colorado and continues compiling unpublished works by Dr. John H. Watson.

S.F. Bennett has, at various times, been an actor, a lecturer, a journalist, a historian, an author and a potter. Whilst some of those things still apply, she has always been an avid collector, concentrating mainly on ephemera and other related items concerning Sherlock Holmes and British science-fiction of the 1970's. To date, she has written articles on aspects of The Canon for *The Baker Street Journal, The Sherlock Holmes Journal*, and *The Torr*, the journal of *The Sherlock Holmes Society of the West Country*. When not collecting, she can be found writing science-fiction and mystery stories, and has contributed to several anthologies of new Sherlock Holmes pastiches. Her first novel was *The Secret Diary of Mycroft Holmes: The Thoughts and Reminiscences of Sherlock Holmes's Elder Brother, 1880-1888* (2017). She is also the author of *A Study in Postcards: Sherlock Holmes in the Golden Age of the Picture Postcard* (*Sherlock Holmes Society of London*, 2019).

Bob Bishop is the author of over twenty stage plays, musicals, and pantomimes, several written in collaboration with Norfolk composer Bob McNeil Watson. Many of these theatrical works were first performed by the fringe theatre company of which he was principal director, The Fossick Valley Fumblers, at the Edinburgh Festival Fringe between 1982 and 2000. Amongst these works were four Sherlock Holmes plays, inspired by the playwright's lifelong affection for the works of Sir Arthur Conan Doyle. Bob's other works include the comic novel, *A Tickle Amongst the Cornstalks*, an anthology of short stories, *Shadows on the Blind*, and a number of Sherlock Holmes pastiche novellas. He currently lives with his wife and three poodles in North Norfolk.

Thomas A. Burns, Jr. is the author of the *Natalie McMasters Mysteries*. He was born and grew up in New Jersey, attended Xavier High School in Manhattan, earned B.S degrees in Zoology and Microbiology at Michigan State University, and a M.S. in Microbiology at North Carolina State University. He currently resides in Wendell, North Carolina. As a kid, Tom started reading mysteries with The Hardy Boys, Ken Holt, and Rick Brant, and graduated to the classic stories by authors such as A. Conan Doyle, Dorothy Sayers, John Dickson Carr, Erle Stanley Gardner, and Rex Stout, to name a few. Tom has written fiction as a hobby all of his life, starting with The Man from U.N.C.L.E. stories in marble-backed copybooks in grade school. He built a career as technical, science, and medical writer and editor for nearly thirty years in industry and government. Now that he's truly on his own as a novelist, he's excited to publish his own mystery series, as well as to contribute stories about his second-most-favorite detective, Sherlock Holmes, to *The MX Book of New Sherlock Holmes Stories*.

Chris Chan is a writer, educator, and historian. He works as a researcher and "International Goodwill Ambassador" for Agatha Christie Ltd. His true crime articles, reviews, and short fiction have appeared (or will soon appear) in *The Strand*, *The Wisconsin Magazine of History*, *Mystery Weekly*, *Gilbert!*, *Nerd HQ*, Akashic Books' *Mondays are Murder* web series, *The Baker Street Journal*, and *Sherlock Holmes Mystery Magazine*. His latest book is *Sherlock and Irene: The Secret Truth Behind "A Scandal in Bohemia"*

Leslie Charteris was born in Singapore on May 12th, 1907. With his mother and brother, he moved to England in 1919 and attended Rossall School in Lancashire before moving on to Cambridge University to study law. His studies there came to a halt when a publisher accepted his first novel. His third one, entitled *Meet the Tiger*, was written when he was twenty years old and published in September 1928. It introduced the world to Simon Templar, *aka* The Saint. He continued to write about The Saint until 1983 when the last book, *Salvage for The Saint*, was published. The books, which have been translated into over thirty languages, number nearly a hundred and have sold over forty-million copies around the world. They've inspired, to date, fifteen feature films, three television series, ten radio series, and a comic strip that was written by Charteris and syndicated around the world for over a decade. He enjoyed travelling, but settled for long periods in Hollywood, Florida, and finally in Surrey, England. He was awarded the Cartier Diamond Dagger by the *Crime Writers' Association* in 1992, in recognition of a lifetime of achievement. He died the following year.

Craig Stephen Copland confesses that he discovered Sherlock Holmes when, sometime in the muddled early 1960's, he pinched his older brother's copy of the immortal stories and was forever afterward thoroughly hooked. He is very grateful to his high school English teachers in Toronto who inculcated in him a love of literature and writing, and even inspired him to be an English major at the University of Toronto. There he was blessed to sit at the feet of both Northrup Frye and Marshall McLuhan, and other great literary professors, who led him to believe that he was called to be a high school English teacher. It was his good fortune to come to his pecuniary senses, abandon that goal, and pursue a varied professional career that took him to over one-hundred countries and endless adventures. He considers himself to have been and to continue to be one of the luckiest men on God's good earth. A few years back he took a step in the direction of Sherlockian studies and joined the *Sherlock Holmes Society of Canada* – also known as *The Toronto Bootmakers*. In May of 2014, this esteemed group of scholars announced a contest for the writing of a new Sherlock Holmes mystery. Although he had never tried his hand at fiction before, Craig entered and was pleasantly surprised to be selected as one of the winners.

Having enjoyed the experience, he decided to write more of the same, and is now on a mission to write a new Sherlock Holmes mystery that is related to and inspired by each of the sixty stories in the original Canon. He currently lives and writes in Toronto and Dubai, and looks forward to finally settling down when he turns ninety.

John William Davis is a retired US Army counterintelligence officer, civil servant, and linguist. He was commissioned from Washington University in St. Louis as an artillery officer in the 101st Air Assault Division. Thereafter, he went into counterintelligence and served some thirty-seven years. A linguist, Mr. Davis learned foreign languages in each country he served. After the Cold War and its bitter aftermath, he wrote *Rainy Street Stories, Reflections on Secret Wars, Terrorism, and Espionage*. He wanted to write about not only true events themselves, but also the moral and ethical aspects of the secret world. With the publication of *Around the Corner*, Davis expanded his reflections on conflicted human nature to our present day traumas of fear, and causes for hope. A dedicated Sherlockian, he's contributed to telling the story of the Great Detective in retirement.

Harry DeMaio is a *nom de plume* of Harry B. DeMaio, successful author of several books on Information Security and Business Networks, as well as the thirteen-volume *Casebooks of Octavius Bear*. He is also a published author for Belanger Books, the Dear Holmes series, and the MX Sherlock Holmes anthologies edited by David Marcum. A retired business executive, former consultant, information security specialist, pilot, disk jockey, and graduate school adjunct professor, he whiles away his time traveling and writing preposterous books, articles, and stories. He has appeared on many radio and TV shows and is an accomplished, frequent public speaker. Former New York City natives, he and his extremely patient and helpful wife, Virginia, and their late, lamented Bichon Frisé, Woof, live in Cincinnati (and several other parallel universes.) They have two sons living in Scottsdale, Arizona and Cortlandt Manor, New York, both of whom are quite successful and quite normal, thus putting the lie to the theory that insanity is hereditary. His e-mail is *hdemaio@zoomtown.com* and you can also find him on Facebook. His books are available on Amazon, Barnes and Noble, directly from MX Publishing and at other fine bookstores. His website is *www.octaviusbearslair.com*

Ian Dickerson was just nine years old when he discovered The Saint. Shortly after that, he discovered Sherlock Holmes. The Saint won, for a while anyway. He struck up a friendship with The Saint's creator, Leslie Charteris, and his family. With their permission, he spent six weeks studying the Leslie Charteris collection at Boston University and went on to write, direct, and produce documentaries on the making of *The Saint* and *Return of The Saint,* which have been released on DVD. He oversaw the recent reprints of almost fifty of the original Saint books in both the US and UK, and was a co-producer on the 2017 TV movie of *The Saint*. When he discovered that Charteris had written Sherlock Holmes stories as well – well, there was the excuse he needed to revisit The Canon. He's consequently written and edited three books on Holmes' radio adventures. For the sake of what little sanity he has, Ian has also written about a wide range of subjects, none of which come with a halo, including talking mashed potatoes, Lord Grade, and satellite links. Ian lives in Hampshire with his wife and two children. And an awful lot of books by Leslie Charteris. Not quite so many by Conan Doyle, though.

Jayantika Ganguly BSI is the General Secretary and Editor of the *Sherlock Holmes Society of India*, a member of the *Sherlock Holmes Society of London*, and the *Czech Sherlock Holmes Society*. She is the author of *The Holmes Sutra* (MX 2014). She is a corporate lawyer working with one of the Big Six law firms.

Dick Gillman is an English writer and acrylic artist living in Brittany, France with his wife Alex, Truffle, their Black Labrador, and Jean-Claude, their Breton cat. During his retirement from teaching, he has written over twenty Sherlock Holmes short stories which are published as both e-books and paperbacks. His initial contribution to the superb MX Sherlock Holmes collection, published in October 2015, was entitled "The Man on Westminster Bridge" and had the privilege of being chosen as the anchor story in *The MX Book of New Sherlock Holmes Stories – Part II (1890-1895)*.

John Linwood Grant is a writer and editor who lives in Yorkshire with a pack of lurchers and a beard. He may also have a family. He focuses particularly on dark Victorian and Edwardian fiction, such as his recent novella *A Study in Grey*, which also features Holmes. Current projects include his *Tales of the Last Edwardian* series, about psychic and psychiatric mysteries, and curating a collection of new stories based on the darker side of the British Empire. He has been published in a number of anthologies and magazines, with stories range from madness in early Virginia to questions about the monsters we ourselves might be. He is also co-editor of *Occult Detective Quarterly*. His website *greydogtales.com* explores weird fiction, especially period ones, weird art, and even weirder lurchers.

Denis Green was born in London, England in April 1905. He grew up mostly in London's Savoy Theatre where his father, Richard Green, was a principal in many Gilbert and Sullivan productions, A Flying Officer with RAF until 1924, he then spent four years managing a tea estate in North India before making his stage debut in *Hamlet* with Leslie Howard in 1928. He made his first visit to America in 1931 and established a respectable stage career before appearing in films – including minor roles in the first two Rathbone and Bruce Holmes films – and developing a career in front of and behind the microphone during the golden age of radio. Green and Leslie Charteris met in 1938 and struck up a lifelong friendship. Always busy, be it on stage, radio, film or television, Green passed away at the age of fifty in New York.

Arthur Hall *also has two stories in Part XXIV*

Paula Hammond has written over sixty fiction and non-fiction books, as well as short stories, comics, poetry, and scripts for educational DVD's. When not glued to the keyboard, she can usually be found prowling round second-hand books shops or hunkered down in a hide, soaking up the joys of the natural world.

Stephen Herczeg is an IT Geek, writer, actor, and film-maker based in Canberra Australia. He has been writing for over twenty years and has completed a couple of dodgy novels, sixteen feature-length screenplays, and numerous short stories and scripts. Stephen was very successful in 2017's International Horror Hotel screenplay competition, with his scripts *TITAN* winning the Sci-Fi category and *Dark are the Woods* placing second in the horror category. His work has featured in *Sproutlings – A Compendium of Little Fictions* from Hunter Anthologies, the *Hells Bells* Christmas horror anthology published by the Australasian Horror Writers Association, and the *Below the Stairs, Trickster's Treats, Shades of Santa, Behind the Mask*, and *Beyond the Infinite* anthologies from OzHorror.Con, *The Body Horror Book, Anemone Enemy*, and *Petrified Punks* from Oscillate Wildly Press, and *Sherlock Holmes In the Realms of H.G. Wells* and *Sherlock Holmes: Adventures Beyond the Canon* from Belanger Books.

Christopher James was born in 1975 in Paisley, Scotland. Educated at Newcastle and UEA, he was a winner of the UK's National Poetry Competition in 2008. He has written three full length Sherlock Holmes novels, *The Adventure of the Ruby* Elephant, *The Jeweller of Florence*, and *The Adventure of the Beer Barons*, all published by MX.

Susan Knight's newest novel from MX publishing, *Mrs. Hudson Goes to Ireland*, is a follow-up to her well-received collection of stories, *Mrs. Hudson Investigates* of 2019. She is the author of two other non-Sherlockian story collections, as well as three novels, a book of non-fiction, and several plays, and has won several prizes for her writing. She lives in Dublin where she teaches Creative Writing. Her next Mrs. Hudson novel is already a gleam in her eye.

John Lawrence served for thirty-eight years as a staff member in the U.S. House of Representatives, the last eight as Chief of Staff to Speaker Nancy Pelosi (2005-2013). He has been a Visiting Professor at the University of California's Washington Center since 2013. He is the author of *The Class of '74: Congress After Watergate and the Roots of Partisanship* (2018), and has a Ph.D. in history from the University of California (Berkeley).

David Marcum *also has stories in Parts XXII and XXIV*

Stephen Mason has been the Third Mate (President) of *The Crew of the Barque* Lone Star scion society in Dallas/Fort Worth for over seven years. He is also the Chair of the Communications Committee for *The Beacon Society*, a national educational scion society. With Joe Fay and Rusty Mason, he produces the *Baker Street Elementary* comic strip each week, the first adventures of Sherlock Holmes and John Watson.

Mark Mower is a member of the *Crime Writers' Association, The Sherlock Holmes Society of London*, and *The Solar Pons Society of London*. He writes true crime stories and fictional mysteries. His volumes of Holmes pastiches include *A Farewell to Baker Street, Sherlock Holmes: The Baker Street Case-Files*, and *Baker Street Legacy* (all published by MX Publishing) and he has contributed multiple stories to the ongoing *The MX Book of New Sherlock Holmes Stories*. He has also had stories in two anthologies by Belanger Books: *Holmes Away From Home: Adventures from the Great Hiatus – Volume II – 1893-1894* (2016) and *Sherlock Holmes: Before Baker Street* (2017). More are bound to follow. Mark's non-fiction works include *Bloody British History: Norwich* (The History Press, 2014), *Suffolk Murders* (The History Press, 2011) and *Zeppelin Over Suffolk* (Pen & Sword Books, 2008).

This work represents **Richard Paolinelli**'s fifth published Sherlock Holmes pastiche. He began his writing journey as a freelance writer in 1984 and gained his first fiction credit serving as the lead writer for the first two issues of the Elite Comics sci-fi/fantasy series, *Seadragon*. Following a twenty-year newspaper writing career, he returned to his fiction writing roots and has since published several novels, two non-fiction sports books, and has appeared in several anthologies. His novel, *Escaping Infinity*, was a 2017 Dragon Award Finalist for Best Sci-Fi novel. He also writes weekly short fiction on his website, *www.richardpaolinelli.com*.

Gayle Lange Puhl has been a Sherlockian since Christmas of 1965. She has had articles published in *The Devon County Chronicle, The Baker Street Journal*, and *The Serpentine Muse*, plus her local newspaper. She has created Sherlockian jewelry, a 2006 calendar entitled "If Watson Wrote For TV", and has painted a limited series of Holmes-related nesting dolls. She co-founded the scion *Friends of the Great Grimpen Mire* and the Janesville, Wisconsin-based *The Original Tree Worshipers*. In January 2016, she was awarded the "Outstanding Creative Writer" award by the Janesville Art Alliance for her first book *Sherlock Holmes and the Folk Tale Mysteries*. She is semi-retired and lives in Evansville, Wisconsin. Ms. Puhl has one daughter, Gayla, and four grandchildren.

Tracy J. Revels *also has stories in Parts XXII and XXIV*

Roger Riccard of Los Angeles, California, U.S.A., is a descendant of the Roses of Kilravock in Highland Scotland. He is the author of two previous Sherlock Holmes novels, *The Case of the Poisoned Lilly* and *The Case of the Twain Papers*, a series of short stories in two volumes, *Sherlock Holmes: Adventures for the Twelve Days of Christmas* and *Further Adventures for the Twelve Days of Christmas*, and the new series *A Sherlock Holmes Alphabet of Cases,* all of which are published by Baker Street Studios. He has another novel and a non-fiction Holmes reference work in various stages of completion. He became a Sherlock Holmes enthusiast as a teenager (many, many years ago), and, like all fans of The Great Detective, yearned for more stories after reading The Canon over and over. It was the Granada Television performances of Jeremy Brett and Edward Hardwicke, and the encouragement of his wife, Rosilyn, that at last inspired him to write his own Holmes adventures, using the Granada actor portrayals as his guide. He has been called "The best pastiche writer since Val Andrews" by the *Sherlockian E-Times.*

Geri Schear is a novelist and short story writer. Her work has been published in literary journals in the U.S. and Ireland. Her first novel, *A Biased Judgement: The Diaries of Sherlock Holmes 1897* was released to critical acclaim in 2014. The sequel, *Sherlock Holmes and the Other Woman* was published in 2015, and *Return to Reichenbach* in 2016. She lives in Kells, Ireland.

Brenda Seabrooke's stories have been published in a number of reviews, journals, and anthologies. She has received grants from the National Endowment for the Arts and Emerson College's Robbie Macauley Award. She is the author of twenty-three books for young readers including *Scones and Bones on Baker Street: Sherlock's (maybe!) Dog and the Dirt Dilemma*, and *The Rascal in the Castle: Sherlock's (possible!) Dog and the Queen's Revenge*. Brenda states: "*It was fun to write from Dr. Watson's point of view and not have to worry about fleas, smelly pits, ralphing, or scratching at inopportune times.*"

Award-winning author **Dr. Liese Sherwood-Fabre** doesn't remember a time she didn't know of Sherlock Holmes – be it the old Basel Rathbone movies, Tom and Jerry in deerstalker hats, or the original Conan Doyle tales. During her thirty-plus years as a federal employee, Dr. Sherwood-Fabre worked and lived in various countries, including Mexico and Russia, finding inspiration for stories based on events taking place around her. She garnered a prestigious Pushcart nomination for a short story inspired by her experiences in Mexico, and having lived through the tumultuous years of Russia's budding democracy, her first published novel, *Saving Hope*, centered around an unemployed Russian microbiologist who must choose between saving her daughter's life or working with a former KGB agent to stop the sale of bioweapons to Iran. After returning to the United States, Dr. Sherwood-Fabre revived her early interest in Sherlock Holmes and the Victorian period. For the past six years, she has shared her knowledge with other Sherlockians by contributing regularly to several society newsletters, as well as the prestigious *Baker Street Journal* and *Canadian Holmes* publications. Besides her own recently launch series *The*

Early Case Files of Sherlock Holmes, she has contributed to Sherlockian anthologies through *Mocha Memoirs* and *The Crew of the Barque Lone Star* scion – and now MX Publishing. Visit her Website *www.liesesherwoodfabre.com* for more about her publications and to sign up for her newsletter.

Denis O. Smith's first published story of Sherlock Holmes and Doctor Watson, "The Adventure of The Purple Hand", appeared in 1982. Since then, numerous other such accounts have been published in magazines and anthologies both in the U.K. and the U.S. In the 1990's, four volumes of his stories were published under the general title of *The Chronicles of Sherlock Holmes*, and, more recently his stories have been collected as *The Lost Chronicles of Sherlock Holmes* (2014), *The Lost Chronicles of Sherlock Holmes Volume II* (2016), *The Further Chronicles of Sherlock Holmes* (201). He also wrote a Holmes novel, *The Riddle of Foxwood Grange* (2017). Born in Yorkshire, in the north of England, Denis Smith has lived and worked in various parts of the country, including London, and has now been resident in Norfolk for many years. His interests range widely, but apart from his dedication to the career of Sherlock Holmes, he has a passion for historical mysteries of all kinds, the railways of Britain and the history of London.

Robert V. Stapleton was born and brought up in Leeds, Yorkshire, England, and studied at Durham University. After working in various parts of the country as an Anglican parish priest, he is now retired and lives with his wife in North Yorkshire. As a member of his local writing group, he now has time to develop his other life as a writer of adventure stories. He has recently had a number of short stories published, and he is hoping to have a couple of completed novels published at some time in the future.

Joseph W. Svec III is retired from Oceanography, Satellite Test Engineering, and college teaching. He has lived on a forty-foot cruising sailboat, on a ranch in the Sierra Nevada Foothills, in a country rose-garden cottage, and currently lives in the shadow of a castle with his childhood sweetheart and several long coated German shepherds. He enjoys writing, gardening, creating dioramas, world travel, and enjoying time with his sweetheart.

Tim Symonds was born in London. He grew up in Somerset, Dorset, and Guernsey. After several years in East and Central Africa, he settled in California and graduated Phi Beta Kappa in Political Science from UCLA. He is a Fellow of the *Royal Geographical Society*. He writes his novels in the woods and hidden valleys surrounding his home in the High Weald of East Sussex. Dr. Watson knew the untamed region well. In "The Adventure of Black Peter", Watson wrote, *"the Weald was once part of that great forest which for so long held the Saxon invaders at bay."* Tim's novels are published by MX Publishing. His novels include *Sherlock Holmes and the Nine Dragon Sigil. Sherlock Holmes and The Sword of Osman, Sherlock Holmes and the Mystery of Einstein's Daughter, Sherlock Holmes and the Dead Boer at Scotney Castle*, and *Sherlock Holmes and the Case of The Bulgarian Codex*. His collection of Holmes short stories is called *A Most Diabolical Plot*.

Kevin P. Thornton is a seven-time Arthur Ellis Award Nominee. He is a former director of the local Heritage Society and Library, and he has been a soldier in Africa, a contractor for the Canadian Military in Afghanistan, a newspaper and magazine columnist, a Director of both the *Crime Writers of Canada* and the *Writers' Guild of Alberta*, a founding member of *Northword Literary Magazine*, and is either a current or former member of *The Mystery Writers of America, The Crime Writers Association, The Calgary Crime Writers, The International Thriller Writers, The International Association of Crime Writers, The Keys* – a Catholic Writers group founded by Monsignor Knox and G.K. Chesterton – as well as, somewhat inexplicably, *The Mesdames of Mayhem* and *Sisters in Crime*. If you ask, he will join. Born in Kenya, Kevin has lived or worked in South Africa, Dubai, England, Afghanistan, New Zealand, Ontario, and now Northern Alberta. He lives on his wits and his wit, and is doing better than expected. He is not one to willingly split infinitives, and while never pedantic, is on occasion known to be ever so slightly punctilious.

William Todd has been a Holmes fan his entire life, and credits *The Hound of the Baskervilles* as the impetus for his love of both reading and writing. He began to delve into fan fiction a few years ago when he decided to take a break from writing his usual Victorian/Gothic horror stories. He was surprised how well-received they were, and has tried to put out a couple of Holmes stories a year since then. When not writing, Mr. Todd is a pathology supervisor at a local hospital in Northwestern Pennsylvania. He is the husband of a terrific lady and father to two great kids, one with special needs, so the benefactor of these anthologies is close to his heart.

D.J. Tyrer is the person behind Atlantean Publishing, was placed second in the Writing Magazine "Local Reporter" competition, and has been widely published in anthologies and magazines around the world, such as *Disturbance* (Laurel Highlands), *Mysteries of Suspense* (Zimbell House), *History and Mystery, Oh My!* (Mystery & Horror LLC), and *Love 'Em, Shoot 'Em* (Wolfsinger), and issues of *Awesome Tales*, and in addition, has a novella available in paperback and on the Kindle, *The Yellow House* (Dunhams Manor) and a comic horror e-novelette, *A Trip to the Middle of the World*, available from Alban Lake through Infinite Realms Bookstore.
His website is: *https://djtyrer.blogspot.co.uk/*
The Atlantean Publishing website is at *https://atlanteanpublishing.wordpress.com/*

Marcia Wilson *also has a story in Part XXIV*

The MX Book of New Sherlock Holmes Stories
Edited by David Marcum
(MX Publishing, 2015-)

"This is the finest volume of Sherlockian fiction I have ever read, and I have read, literally, thousands." – Philip K. Jones

"Beyond Impressive . . . This is a splendid venture for a great cause!
– Roger Johnson, Editor, *The Sherlock Holmes Journal,*
The Sherlock Holmes Society of London

In Preparation
Part XXV – 2021 Annual

. . . and more to come!

The MX Book of New Sherlock Holmes Stories
Edited by David Marcum
(MX Publishing, 2015-   )

Publishers Weekly <u>says</u>:

Part VI: *The traditional pastiche is alive and well . . . .*

Part VII: *Sherlockians eager for faithful-to-the-canon plots
and characters will be delighted.*

Part VIII: *The imagination of the contributors in coming up with variations on the
volume's theme is matched by their ingenious resolutions.*

Part IX: *The 18 stories . . . will satisfy fans of Conan Doyle's originals. Sherlockians will
rejoice that more volumes are on the way.*

Part X: *. . . new Sherlock Holmes adventures of consistently high quality.*

Part XI: *. . . an essential volume for Sherlock Holmes fans.*

Part XII: *. . . continues to amaze with the number of high-quality pastiches . . .*

Part XIII: *. . . Amazingly, Marcum has found 22 superb pastiches . . . This is more catnip
for fans of stories faithful to Conan Doyle's original*

Part XIV: *. . . this standout anthology of 21 short stories written in the spirit of Conan
Doyle's originals.*

Part XV: *Stories pitting Sherlock Holmes against seemingly supernatural phenomena
highlight Marcum's 15th anthology of superior short pastiches.*

Part XVI: *Marcum has once again done fans of Conan Doyle's originals a service.*

Part XVII: *This is yet another impressive array of new but traditional Holmes stories.*

Part XVIII: *Sherlockians will again be grateful to Marcum and MX for high-quality new
Holmes tales.*

Part XIX: *Inventive plots and intriguing explorations of aspects of Dr. Watson's life and
beliefs lift the 24 pastiches in Marcum's impressive 19th Sherlock Holmes anthology*

Part XX: *Marcum's reserve of high-quality new Holmes exploits seems endless.*

Part XXI: *This is another must-have for Sherlockians.*

The MX Book of New Sherlock Holmes Stories

Edited by David Marcum

(MX Publishing, 2015-   )

MX Publishing

MX Publishing is the world's largest specialist Sherlock Holmes publisher, with several hundred titles and over a hundred authors creating the latest in Sherlock Holmes fiction and non-fiction.

From traditional short stories and novels to travel guides and quiz books, MX Publishing caters to all Holmes fans.

The collection includes leading titles such as *Benedict Cumberbatch In Transition* and *The Norwood Author*, which won the 2011 *Tony Howlett Award* (Sherlock Holmes Book of the Year).

MX Publishing also has one of the largest communities of Holmes fans on *Facebook*, with regular contributions from dozens of authors.

www.mxpublishing.co.uk (UK) and *www.mxpublishing.com* (USA)